READER'S DIGEST

CONDENSED BOOKS

FIRST EDITION

THE READER'S DIGEST ASSOCIATION LIMITED
25 Berkeley Square, London W1X 6AB

**THE READER'S DIGEST ASSOCIATION
SOUTH AFRICA (PTY) LTD**
Nedbank Centre, Strand Street, Cape Town

Printed in Great Britain by Petty & Sons Ltd, Leeds

Original cover design by Jeffrey Matthews F.S.I.A.D.

For information as to ownership
of copyright in the material in this book see last page

ISBN 0 276 00012 9

Reader's Digest
CONDENSED BOOKS

THE MAN FROM ST. PETERSBURG
Ken Follett

FEVER
Robin Cook

FLASH
Joyce Stranger

COLD IS THE SEA
Edward L. Beach

COLLECTOR'S LIBRARY
EDITION

In this Volume:

The Man from St.Petersburg

by Ken Follett (p. 11)

It is summer, 1914. Summoned by Churchill from his country estate, Lord Walden is given the important task of arranging an alliance with Russia through Prince Aleksey Orlov, the nephew of Walden's adored wife Lydia. But stalking the streets of London is a fearless Russian anarchist who will go to any lengths to sabotage the vital negotiations. His secret mission will shatter the Waldens' peaceful lives for ever . . . . The author of *Storm Island* has written another crackling story of romantic suspense.

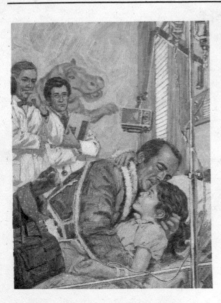

FEVER

by Robin Cook (p. 167)

Thirteen-year-old Michelle's favourite retreat had always been her playhouse down by the stream: as a child she had spent her happiest hours playing there. And now she had a terrible fever. Was it coincidence that upstream a factory was illegally discharging toxic waste into the river? Michelle's father, research doctor Charles Martel, thinks not. Desperately worried about his daughter's serious illness, enraged by bureaucratic red tape and lack of interest, he starts his own investigations. But he faces opposition from more than one quarter . . . .

Flash

by Joyce Stranger (p. 303)

Only eleven years old, Geordie had lost both his parents in a car accident and had come to live with his elderly grandmother in Scotland. Life was strange and lonely; until Flash was born. The tiny sheepdog puppy became Geordie's best friend and constant companion. And when a cruel blow of fate separated the two, Geordie vowed that somehow he would find his faithful pet.

COLD IS THE SEA

by Edward L. Beach (p. 381)

The US Navy's latest nuclear submarine *Cushing* hovers under the frozen surface of the Arctic ocean, carrying out a top-secret mission. As it waits, motionless and vulnerable, a threatening presence looms out of the inky blackness. For the command at home a frightening question arises: are hostile forces lurking in those icy waters? And as the tension mounts the submariners' wives watch and wait. Captain Beach, himself a veteran of the submarine service and the author of *Run Silent, Run Deep*, has created a heart-stopping story in this exciting drama of modern warfare.

THE MAN FROM
ST. PETERSBURG
Ken Follett

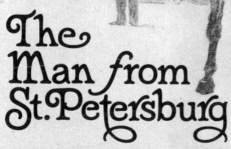

The Man from St. Petersburg

A CONDENSATION OF THE BOOK BY
Ken Follett

ILLUSTRATED BY CECIL VIEWEG
PUBLISHED BY HAMISH HAMILTON

In May 1914 a Russian prince arrives in London, apparently to visit his uncle and aunt, the Earl and Countess of Walden. Only a few know Prince Orlov's real purpose: to work out a treaty of Anglo-Russian alliance, of the highest importance to Britain in the face of impending war with Germany . . . .

While the men negotiate, Lydia Walden prepares for her daughter Charlotte's presentation at court. Secure in their ordered existence, they little realize that beyond the safety of the Walden mansion lurks an anarchist sworn to murder the prince—a fanatic whose secret knowledge may destroy the Waldens' private world even as he threatens to tip the balance of international power.

Once again Ken Follett has created the heady mixture of suspense and romance that readers of *Storm Island* and *The Key to Rebecca* have come to expect.

Chapter One

It was a slow Sunday afternoon, the kind Walden loved. He stood at an open window and looked across the park. The broad, level lawn was dotted with mature trees: a Scots pine, a pair of mighty oaks, several chestnuts and a willow like a head of girlish curls. The sun was high and the trees cast dark, cool shadows. The birds were silent, but a hum of contented bees came from the flowering creeper beside the window. The house was still, too. Most of the servants had the afternoon off. The only weekend guests were Walden's brother, George, George's wife, Clarissa, and their children. George had gone for a walk, Clarissa was lying down, and the children were out of sight. Walden was comfortable; in an hour or two he would put on his white tie and tails for dinner, but in the meantime he was at ease in a tweed suit and a soft-collared shirt. Now, he thought, if only Lydia will play the piano tonight, it will have been a perfect day.

He turned to his wife. "Will you play, after dinner?"

Lydia smiled. "If you like."

Walden heard a noise and turned back to the window. At the far end of the drive, a quarter of a mile away, a motorcar appeared. It moved up the drive, turned into the gravel forecourt and came to a noisy halt opposite the south door. The driver got out, wearing helmet, goggles and heavy motoring coat, and opened the door for the passenger. A short man in a black coat and a black felt hat stepped down from the car. Walden recognized him, and his heart sank; the peaceful summer afternoon was over.

"It's Winston Churchill," he said.

Lydia said, "How embarrassing."

The man just refused to be snubbed. On Thursday he had sent a note, which Walden had ignored. On Friday he had called on Walden at his London house and had been told that the earl was not at home. Now, on a Sunday, he had driven all the way to Walden's country house in Norfolk.

Churchill would be turned away again. The Liberal government in which he was a Cabinet minister was engaged in a vicious attack on the very foundations of English society: they advocated taxing landed property, undermining the House of Lords, trying to give Ireland away to the Catholics, emasculating the Royal Navy and yielding to the demands of trade unions and socialists. Walden would not shake hands with such people.

The door opened, and Pritchard came into the room. He was a tall, black-haired cockney, who had run away to sea as a boy and had jumped ship in East Africa. Walden, there on safari, had hired him to supervise the native porters, and they had been together ever since. Now Pritchard was Walden's majordomo, and as much of a friend as a servant could be.

"The first lord of the admiralty is here, my lord," he said.

"I'm not at home," Walden said.

Pritchard looked uncomfortable; he was not used to throwing out Cabinet ministers. "Mr. Churchill said you'd say not at 'ome, my lord, and 'e said to give you this letter." He proffered an envelope on a tray.

Walden did *not* like to be pushed. He said crossly, "Give it back to him." Then he stopped and looked at the handwriting on the envelope. There was something familiar about the large, sloping letters.

"Oh, dear," he said. He took the envelope, opened it and drew out a single sheet of heavy white paper, folded once. At the top was the royal crest, printed in red. Walden read:

Buckingham Palace
May 1st, 1914

My dear Walden,
    You will see young Winston.

George R.I

"It's from the King," Walden said to Lydia.

He was so embarrassed that he flushed. It was *frightfully* bad form to drag the King into something like this. Walden felt like a schoolboy who is told to stop quarrelling and get on with his work. He sighed. Churchill had defeated him.

"Ask Mr. Churchill to come in," he said to Pritchard.

He handed the letter to Lydia. "This is becoming awfully boring," she said.

She was not bored at all, Walden thought; in fact, she probably was finding it exciting. She said that because it was the kind of thing an English countess would say, and since she was Russian by birth, she liked to say typically English things.

Pritchard returned and said, "Mr. Winston Churchill."

Churchill was forty, exactly ten years younger than Walden. He was a short, slender man who dressed in a way Walden thought was a shade too elegant to be quite gentlemanly. His hair was receding, leaving two curls at the temples that, together with his short nose and the sardonic twinkle in his eye, gave him a mischievous look.

Churchill shook hands, and said, "Good afternoon, Lord Walden." He bowed to Lydia. "Lady Walden, how do you do."

Lydia offered him tea, and they sat down, but Walden would not make small talk; he was impatient to know what all the fuss was about.

Churchill began. "First of all, my apologies for imposing myself on you. I should not have done so, other than for the most compelling reasons."

Walden nodded. He was not going to say it was perfectly all right. "You'd better tell me what they are."

Churchill said, "German companies have been calling in foreign debts on a vast scale, collecting cash and buying gold. A few more weeks of this and Germany will have got in everything owing to her from other countries, while leaving her debts to them outstanding—and her gold reserves will be higher than they have ever been before."

"They are preparing for war."

"In this and other ways. They have raised a levy of one billion marks, over and above normal taxation, to improve an army that is already the strongest in Europe—"

"Yes, indeed," Walden interrupted. He did not want Churchill

13

making speeches. "We Conservatives have been worried about German militarism for some time. Now, at the eleventh hour, you're telling me that we were right."

Churchill was unperturbed. "Germany will attack France, almost certainly. The question is, will we come to the aid of France?"

"No," Walden said in surprise. "The foreign secretary has assured us that we have no obligations to France."

"Sir Edward is mistaken," Churchill said. "We could not possibly stand aside and watch France defeated by Germany."

Walden was shocked. The Liberals had convinced everyone, himself included, that they would not lead England into war; and now one of their top ministers was saying the opposite. The duplicity of the politicians was infuriating, but that thought was overtaken by another, and he said, "But can we win?"

Churchill looked grave. "I think not."

Walden stared at him. "Dear God, what have you people done?"

Churchill became defensive. "Our policy has been to avoid war, and you can't do that and arm yourself to the teeth at the same time."

"But you have failed to avoid war."

Churchill looked belligerent for a moment, then swallowed his pride. "Yes."

"So what will happen?"

"If England and France together cannot defeat Germany, then we must have another country on our side—Russia. If Germany is divided, fighting on two fronts, we can win. The Russian army is incompetent and corrupt, of course, but it will at least draw off part of Germany's strength."

Walden was highly intrigued by what Churchill was saying. "Russia already has an alliance with France," he said.

"It's not enough," Churchill said. "Russia is obliged to fight if France is the victim of aggression. It is left to Russia to decide whether France is the victim or the aggressor in a particular case. When war breaks out, both sides always claim to be the victim. Therefore the alliance obliges Russia to do no more than fight if she wants to. We need Russia to be freshly and firmly committed to our side."

"I can't imagine you chaps joining hands with the Czar."

"You misjudge us. To save England, we'll deal with the devil."

14

"Your supporters won't like it."

"They won't know."

"What have you in mind? A secret treaty? Or an unwritten under-standing?"

"Both."

Walden looked at Churchill through narrowed eyes. So the Liberals want a secret deal with the Czar, he thought, despite the hatred which the English people have for the brutal Russian regime—but why tell me? They want to rope me in somehow, that much is clear. For what purpose? So that if it all goes wrong, they will have a Conservative on whom to put the blame? "Go on," he said.

"I have initiated naval talks with the Russians, and now a young Russian admiral is coming to London. His name is Prince Aleksey Andreyevich Orlov."

Lydia said, "Aleks!"

Churchill looked at her. "I believe he is related to you, Lady Walden."

"Yes," Lydia said, and for some reason Walden could not even guess at, she looked uneasy. "He is the son of my elder sister. I didn't know he had become an admiral. Aleks is young to have so much authority."

"He's thirty," Churchill said to Lydia. His expression seemed to say: The world belongs to young men like me and Aleksey Orlov. And Walden recalled that Churchill, at forty, was very young to be in charge of the entire Royal Navy.

"In addition," Churchill went on, "through his late father, Orlov is nephew to the Czar, and he is one of the few people other than Rasputin whom the Czar likes and trusts. If anyone in the Russian naval establishment can swing the Czar onto our side, Orlov can."

"And my part in all this?" Walden asked.

"I want you to represent England in these talks, and I want you to bring me Russia on a plate."

This young demagogue can never resist the temptation to be melodramatic, Walden thought. "You want Aleks and me to negotiate an Anglo-Russian military alliance?"

"Yes."

Walden saw immediately how difficult, challenging and reward-ing the task would be, but he concealed his excitement.

15

Churchill was saying, "You know the Czar personally. You know Russia and speak Russian fluently. You're Orlov's uncle by marriage. In a nutshell, you were the Czar's choice. It seems you are the only Englishman in whom he has any faith. Anyway, he sent a telegram to his cousin, His Majesty King George the Fifth, insisting that Orlov deal with you."

Churchill paused, and Walden said, "How would all this be kept secret?"

"It will seem like a social visit. If you agree, Orlov will stay with you for the London season. You will introduce him to society. Am I right in thinking that your daughter, Charlotte, is due to come out this year?" He looked at Lydia.

"That's right," she said.

"So you'll be going about a good deal, anyway. Since Orlov is a bachelor and obviously very eligible, we can noise it abroad that he's looking for an English wife. He may even find one."

"Good idea." Walden was enjoying himself. In the past, under the Conservatives, he had acted as a semi-official diplomat. Now he had a chance to play a role in international politics again. The Russians were not easy to deal with, but Aleks would be manageable. When Walden married Lydia, Aleks had been at the wedding, a young boy in a sailor-suit. Later he had spent a couple of years at Oxford and had visited Walden Hall in the vacations. The boy's father was dead, so Walden had given him rather more time than he might normally have spent with an adolescent, and was delightfully rewarded by a friendship with a lively young mind. It was a splendid foundation for a negotiation.

Churchill said, "May I take it, then, that you'll do it?"

"Of course," said Walden.

LYDIA STOOD UP. "No, don't get up," she said as the men rose with her. "I'll leave you to talk politics. Will you stay for dinner, Mr. Churchill?"

"I've an engagement in town, unfortunately."

"Then I shall say goodbye." She shook his hand.

She went out of the Octagon, which was where they always had tea, and walked across the great hall, through the passage, and into the flower room. At the same time, one of the gardeners came in through the garden door with an armful of tulips—pink and

16

yellow—for the dinner table. He touched his cap and laid the flowers on a marble table, then went out. Lydia sat down and breathed the cool, scented air. This was a good room in which to recover from shocks, and the talk of St. Petersburg had unnerved her. She remembered Aleksey Andreyevich as a shy, pretty little boy at her wedding; and she remembered *that* as the unhappiest day of her life.

It was perverse of her, she thought, to make the flower room her sanctuary. This house had rooms for almost every purpose; her own suite had a bedroom, a dressing room and a sitting room. And yet, when she wanted to be at peace, she would come here and sit on a hard chair and look at the crude stone sink and the cast-iron legs of the marble table.

So Aleks would be her guest in London for the season. They would talk of home, and the snow and the ballet; and seeing Aleks would make her think of another young Russian, the man she had not married.

It was nineteen years since she had seen that man, but still the mere mention of St. Petersburg could bring him to mind and make her skin crawl beneath the watered silk of her tea gown. He had been nineteen, a year older than she, a hungry student with long black hair, the face of a wolf and the eyes of a spaniel. He was thin, and his skin was white; and he had clever, clever hands. She blushed now at the thought of her body betraying her, maddening her with pleasure. I was wicked, she thought, and I am wicked still, for I should like to do it again.

She thought guiltily of Lord Walden—Stephen, her husband. She had not loved him when they married, but she loved him now. He was strong and warmhearted, and he adored her. He was happy, she thought, only because he had never known that love could be wild and hungry.

I no longer crave that kind of love, she told herself. I have learned to live without it, and over the years it has become easier. And so it should!

Some of her friends were still tempted, and they yielded, too. Lydia knew that at some country-house parties there was . . . well, adultery. People said all this immorality was the fault of the late King Edward VII, but Lydia did not believe them. He had stayed at Walden Hall twice, and he had behaved impeccably both times.

She wondered whether the new King would ever visit them. It was a great strain to have a monarch to stay, but such a thrill to make the house look its very best and to buy twelve new dresses just for one weekend.

She thought about her present houseguests—the family of Stephen's younger brother, George. His daughter, Belinda, was eighteen, the same age as her own daughter, Charlotte. Both girls would be coming out this season. Belinda's mother had died some years ago, and George had married Clarissa, much younger than he, and quite vivacious. She had given him twin sons, one of whom would inherit Walden Hall when Stephen died, unless Lydia were to give birth to a boy late in life. I could, she thought; I feel as if I could, but it just doesn't happen.

It was almost time to be getting ready for dinner. She sighed; now she would have to be laced into a corset and have her fair hair piled high on her head. It was said that some of the young women were giving up corsets altogether. That was all right if you had the figure, but she was small in all the wrong places.

She got up and went outside. A gardener was standing by a rose tree, talking to one of the maids—Annie, a pretty, voluptuous, empty-headed girl with a wide, generous smile. She stood with her hands in the pockets of her apron, turning her round face up to the sun and laughing. Lydia said sharply, "Annie! Where are the young ladies? It's time they were changing for dinner."

Annie's smile disappeared and she dropped a curtsy. "I can't find them, m'lady."

The gardener moved off sheepishly.

"You don't seem to be looking for them," Lydia said. "Off you go."

"Very good, m'lady." Annie ran towards the back of the house. Lydia sighed; the girls would not be there, but she could not be bothered to call Annie back.

Lydia strolled across the lawn, pushing St. Petersburg out of her mind. The rhododendron and azalea bushes on the west side of the park were now in full, glorious bloom. We must get somebody to paint a picture of the house, she thought.

She looked back at Walden Hall. The grey stone of the south front looked beautiful and dignified in the afternoon sunshine. In the centre was the pillared portico of the main entrance. The farther, east wing contained the drawing room and various dining rooms

18

and, behind them, a straggle of kitchens, pantries and laundries running higgledy-piggledy to the distant stables. Nearer to her, on the west side, were the Octagon and at the corner the library; then, along the west wing, the gun room, her flower room and the garage. On the second floor, the family bedrooms were mostly on the south side, the main guest rooms on the west side, and the servants' rooms over the kitchens to the northeast. Above the second floor was an irrational collection of towers, turrets and attics. The whole façade was a riot of ornamental stonework in the best Victorian rococo manner, with flowers and sculpted dragons, lions and cherubs. Lydia loved the place.

She saw Charlotte and Belinda emerge from the shrubbery across the lawn. Annie had not found them, of course. They both wore wide-brimmed hats and summer frocks with schoolgirls' black stockings and low black shoes. Charlotte was occasionally permitted to put up her hair and to dress for dinner, but most of the time Lydia treated her like the child she was, for it was bad for children to grow up too fast. The two cousins were deep in conversation, and Lydia wondered what they were talking about. What was on my mind when I was eighteen? she asked herself; and then she remembered a young man with clever hands, and she thought, Please, God, let me keep my secrets.

"WILL WE *feel* grown-up after we've come out?" Belinda said.

Charlotte had thought about this. "I shan't. I don't see how a lot of parties and balls can make a person feel grown-up."

"We'll have to have corsets."

Charlotte giggled. "I tried mine on last week."

"How did you look?"

"Awful." Charlotte gestured with her hands to indicate an enormous bust. They both collapsed laughing.

"It will be fun, though," said Belinda.

"The season? Yes," Charlotte said doubtfully. "But what's the point of it all?"

"To meet the right sort of young man, of course."

"To look for husbands, you mean."

They reached the great oaks in the middle of the lawn, and Belinda sat down on the seat beneath one of them. "You think coming out is all very silly, don't you?" she said.

19

Charlotte sat beside her and looked across the carpet of turf to the long south front of Walden Hall, its tall Gothic windows glinting in the afternoon sun. She said, "What's silly is being treated like a child still. I hate having supper with Marya; she's quite ignorant, or pretends to be. When I get bored Marya suggests we play cards. I don't want to *play* anything; I've been playing all my life." She sighed. Talking about it had made her angrier. She looked at Belinda's calm, freckled face with its halo of red curls. Charlotte's own face was oval, with a rather distinctive straight nose and a strong chin, and her hair was thick and dark. Happy-go-lucky Belinda, she thought; these things really don't bother her; *she* never gets intense about anything.

They were silent for a while. Sometimes Charlotte wished she were passive like Belinda. Life would be simpler—but then again, it would be awfully dull. She said, "I asked Marya what I'm supposed to *do* after I get married and do you know what she said?" She imitated her governess's throaty Russian accent. "Do? Why, my child, you will do *nothing.*"

"Oh, that's silly, too," Belinda said.

"Is it? What do my mother and yours do?"

"They're Good Society. They have parties and stay at country houses and go to the opera and—"

"That's what I mean. Nothing."

"They have babies—"

"Now that's another thing. They make such a *secret* about having babies. Don't you think they might tell us something about how it happens? They're very keen for us to know all about Mozart and Shakespeare and Leonardo da Vinci."

Belinda looked uncomfortable but very interested. I wonder how much she knows, Charlotte thought. She said, "Do you realize they grow inside you?"

Belinda nodded, then blurted out, "But how does it start?"

"Oh, it just happens, I think, when you get to about twenty. That's probably why you have to be a debutante—to make sure you get a husband before you start having babies." It maddened Charlotte that there was no way to find out these things, no one to ask. . . . Suddenly she was struck by an idea. "There's a locked cupboard in the library. I bet there are books about this sort of thing in there. Let's look! I know where the key is."

Belinda hesitated. "There'll be a row."

"I don't care if there is." Charlotte turned and walked towards the house, and in a moment Belinda ran up beside her. They went through the pillared portico and into the great hall. Turning left, they passed the Octagon and entered the library.

This was Charlotte's favourite room. Being on a corner of the house it was very bright. In winter there was a fire all day, and there were games and jigsaw puzzles as well as two or three thousand books. Charlotte would often find Papa here, reading at the Victorian pedestal desk; but he—unlike Marya—never interfered with her choice of books.

The room was empty now. Charlotte went straight to the desk, opened a small drawer in one of the pedestals and took out a key with which she unlocked a wall cupboard.

Inside were twenty or thirty books and a pile of old magazines. Hastily she picked out two books without looking at the titles. She closed and locked the cupboard and replaced the key in the desk drawer. "There!" she said triumphantly.

"Where can we go to look at them?" Belinda hissed.

"Remember the hideaway?"

"Oh! Yes!"

They went to the door. Suddenly they heard a voice in the hall, calling, "Lady Charlotte . . . Lady Charlotte!"

"It's Annie; she's looking for us," Charlotte said. "We'll go out the other way, quickly." She crossed the library and was about to go through the far door into the gun room, but there was someone there. She listened for a moment.

"It's my papa," Belinda whispered, looking scared. "He's been out with the dogs."

Fortunately a pair of french windows led from the library onto the west terrace. The girls crept out and closed the doors quietly behind them. The sun cast long shadows across the lawns.

"Now what do we do?" Belinda said.

"Over the roofs. Follow me!" Charlotte stuffed the books into the bodice of her dress and ran around the back of the house and through the kitchen garden to the stables. In a corner of the stable yard was a low iron bunker used to store logs. From there she climbed, by a series of easy steps, to the slate roof of the wash-house. She looked behind; Belinda was following.

Lying face down on the slates, Charlotte crawled up the roof until it ended against a wall.

Belinda caught up with her and said, "Isn't this dangerous?"

"I've been doing it since I was nine years old."

In a gable above them was the window of an attic bedroom shared by two parlourmaids. Charlotte stood upright and peeped into the room. No one was there. She pulled herself onto the window ledge and stood up.

She leaned to the left, got an arm and a leg over the edge of the roof, which sloped down beside the window, and hauled herself onto the slates. She turned back and helped Belinda up.

They lay there a moment, catching their breath. From this point it was possible to reach any part of the roofs by using the footways and ladders provided for the workmen who came every spring to clean gutters and replace broken tiles. Charlotte remembered being told that Walden Hall had four acres of roof.

Charlotte got up. "Come on, the rest is easy," she said. There was a ladder to the next roof, then a board footway, then a short flight of wooden steps leading to a small, square door. She unlatched the door and crawled through, and she was in the hideaway.

It was a low, windowless room with a door at one end, which led into a closet off the nursery. Charlotte had discovered the hideaway when she was eight or nine, and had used it occasionally in her lifelong effort to escape supervision. There were cushions on the floor, candles in jars and a box of matches.

Belinda crawled in, and Charlotte lighted the candles. She took the two books from her bodice and looked at the titles. One was called *Household Medicine* and the other *The Romance of Lust*. The medical book seemed more promising. She sat on a cushion and opened it. Belinda sat beside her, looking guilty.

Charlotte leafed through the pages. The book seemed explicit and detailed on rheumatism, broken bones and measles, but when it arrived at childbirth it suddenly became impenetrably vague. This chapter had evidently been written for people who already knew a lot about the subject.

"This book's no good," Charlotte said. She opened the other at random and read aloud a lurid description of the sex act.

The two girls stared at each other. "So *that's* how it happens!" Belinda gasped.

Chapter Two

Feliks Kschessinsky sat in a cold railway carriage. It was dark outside, and he could see his own reflection in the window: a tall man with a neat moustache, wearing a black coat and a bowler hat. He might have been the travelling representative of a Swiss watch manufacturer, except that to anyone who looked closely, the coat was cheap, his suitcase was cardboard and the face was not that of a man who sold watches.

The train moved off, and soon Feliks was watching the sun rise over the orchards and hopfields of Kent. He never ceased to be astonished, like any Russian peasant, at how *pretty* Europe was. Watching the English farms come to life in the early morning, he recalled dawn in his home village: a grey, boiling sky and a bitter wind; a frozen swampy field with puddles of ice and tufts of coarse grass rimed with frost; himself in a worn canvas smock, his feet numb in felt shoes and clogs; his father striding along beside him, wearing the threadbare robes of a country priest. His father had loved the Russian people, because he thought God loved them. It had always been obvious to Feliks that God hated the people, for He treated them so cruelly.

Their discussions had been the start of a long journey that had taken Feliks from Christianity through socialism to anarchist terror, from Tambov province through St. Petersburg and Siberia to Geneva. And in Geneva he had made the decision which brought him to England. He recalled the meeting.

HE HAD BEEN to Krakow, to negotiate with the Polish Jews who smuggled the magazine *Mutiny* across the border into Russia. He had arrived in Geneva after dark, and had gone straight to Ulrich's tiny back-street printing shop. The editorial committee was in session: four men and two women, gathered around a candle in the rear of the shop, breathing the smells of newsprint and oiled machinery, planning the Russian revolution.

Ulrich brought Feliks up to date. He had seen Josef, their spy in the Russian secret police. Josef's news had been sensational. "The Czar wants a military alliance with England," Ulrich told Feliks. "He is sending Prince Orlov to London to negotiate."

Feliks took off his hat and sat down.

"The point being," Ulrich went on, "that England could then have a war with Germany and make the Russians fight it."

Feliks nodded.

One of the women said, "And it won't be the princes and counts who get killed—it will be the ordinary Russian people."

She was right, Feliks thought. The war would be fought by the peasants. Prince Orlov would take them and march them in front of cannon to be shot to pieces or maimed for ever, for the very best reasons of international diplomacy. It was things such as this that made Feliks an anarchist.

"What is to be done?" said Ulrich.

They began to discuss how the story should be handled in *Mutiny*. Feliks listened. Editorial matters interested him little. He distributed the magazine and wrote articles about how to make bombs, and he was deeply discontented. Russia was in turmoil. A million workers were on strike. Czar Nicholas II was the most incompetent ruler a degenerate aristocracy could produce. The country was a powder barrel waiting for a spark, and Feliks wanted to be that spark. But it would be fatal for him to go back. The secret police knew the exiled revolutionaries better than they knew those still at home.

He looked around at this group of anarchists. They were sincere and hardworking, and Feliks knew the importance of their smuggled periodicals to the desperate people inside Russia. Yet economic tracts were no protection against police bullets, and fiery magazine articles would not burn palaces.

"It's not enough to spread the news," Yevno, a philosophy student, said excitedly. "We must put a stop to this! Orlov is a traitor, betraying the people, and he should be assassinated."

"Would that stop the negotiation?"

"It probably would," said Pyotr, who was a dispossessed count. "Especially if the assassin were an anarchist. Remember, England gives political asylum to anarchists, and this infuriates the Czar. Now, if one of his princes were killed in England by one of our comrades, the Czar might be angry enough to call off the talks."

Yevno said, "What a story we would have then! We could say that Orlov had been assassinated for treason against Russia."

"Every newspaper would carry *that* report," Ulrich mused.

"Think of the effect it would have at home. If the Russian peasants learned that the Czar was planning to make them fight a major European war, the rivers would run red with blood. . . ."

Ulrich said, "I think you're in dreamland, Yevno. I know the London comrades—they've never assassinated anyone. I don't see how it can be done."

"I do," Feliks said. They all looked at him, the shadows on their faces shifting in the flickering candlelight. "I know how it can be done. I'll go to London. I'll kill Orlov."

The room was suddenly quiet. They stared at him in surprise, all except Ulrich, who smiled knowingly, almost as if he had planned that it would turn out this way.

LONDON WAS unbelievably rich. Feliks had seen extravagant wealth in Russia and much prosperity in Europe, but not on this scale. Here *nobody* was in rags. Feliks saw carters, street vendors, sweepers, labourers and delivery boys—all sporting factory-made clothes without holes or patches. All the children wore boots. Every woman had a hat decorated with ribbons, feathers, flowers or fruit. The streets were teeming. He saw more motorcars in the first five minutes than he had in his whole life.

But when he went into the East End, towards the address Ulrich had given him, his initial impression of great wealth was modified. He saw crumbling tenements, squalid courtyards and stinking alleys where ragged human wrecks picked over piles of garbage.

He made his way to 165 Jubilee Street. On the outside was a notice that said the Workers' Friend Club and Institute was open to all working men regardless of politics.

Feliks went in. In the lobby, notices on the walls advertised lessons in English, a trip to Epping Forest, a lecture on *Hamlet*. Feliks stepped into the large clubroom. There was a stage at one end and a bar at the other. On stage, a group rehearsed a play. Perhaps this was what anarchists did in England, Feliks thought. He went over to the bar. There was no sign of alcoholic drink, but on the counter he saw—oh, joy!—a samovar.

A WEEK LATER, on the day that Prince Orlov was to arrive in London, Feliks had lunch at a French restaurant in Soho. He arrived early and picked a table near the door. He ate onion soup

26

and fillet steak, and drank half a bottle of red wine. He ordered in French. The waiters were deferential. When he finished, it was the height of the lunch-hour rush. At a moment when the three waiters were in the kitchen, he got up, went to the door, took his coat and hat and left without paying.

He had quickly learned how to live in this town on almost no money. For breakfast he would buy sweet tea and a slab of bread from a street stall for twopence, but that was the only food he paid for. At lunchtime he stole fruit or vegetables. In the evening he would go to a charity soup-kitchen and get a bowl of broth and unlimited bread in return for listening to an incomprehensible sermon and singing a hymn. He had five pounds in cash, but it was for emergencies.

Feliks was living in a five-storey tenement building in Stepney Green, where lived half the leading anarchists in London. He paid no rent, but each day he stole something—sausages, oranges—and brought it home for the communal larder.

He told the other anarchists he was there to study at the British Museum and finish his book about natural anarchism in primitive communities. They believed him. They were friendly, dedicated and harmless; they sincerely believed the revolution could be brought about by education and trade unionism.

Nevertheless, among such groups there were generally a few violent men. When Feliks needed them he would seek them out. Meanwhile, he worried about how he would kill Orlov, and for distraction he worked on his English. During the long train journey across Europe, he had studied a textbook for Russian children and an English translation of his favourite novel, *The Captain's Daughter*, by Pushkin. Now he read *The Times* every morning, and in the afternoons he walked, striking up conversations with people in the streets. The printed words in books began to mesh with the sounds all around him, and before long he could say anything he needed to.

After leaving the French restaurant he walked north, across Oxford Street, and all the way through Regent's Park to the middle-class suburb to its north. He wandered down the tree-lined streets, looking into the small gardens of the neat brick houses, searching for a bicycle to steal. It was the perfect vehicle for shadowing someone, for it was manoeuvrable and inconspicuous, and in city traffic it was

27

fast enough to keep up with a motorcar or a carriage. Sadly, the citizens of this part of London kept their bicycles locked away, and Feliks was beginning to toy with alternative strategies when at last he saw what he needed.

A man of about thirty came out of one of the gardens, wheeling a bicycle. He wore a straw hat, and a striped blazer bulged over his paunch. He leaned his cycle against the garden wall and bent down to put on his trouser clips.

The man saw Feliks approaching, looked up and muttered, "Good afternoon."

Feliks knocked him onto his back, then fell on him, dropping one knee into the middle button of the striped blazer. The man was winded, helpless, gasping for air. Feliks climbed on the bicycle and rode away rapidly.

A man who has no fear can do anything he wants, Feliks thought.

HE SAT ON A BENCH in Liverpool Street Station, the bicycle leaning against the wall beside him. He wondered if Orlov would come on the train Josef had specified. Feliks was confident he would recognize him if he did, for Russians of his type did not travel unobtrusively, secret mission or no.

A few minutes before the train was due, a closed carriage drawn by four magnificent horses clattered straight up onto the platform. There was a coachman in front and a liveried footman hanging on behind. The stationmaster, in a frock coat and top hat, opened the carriage door for the passenger to step down.

A railwayman walked back past Feliks's bench, and Feliks grabbed his sleeve. "Please, sir," he said, putting on a naïve, wide-eyed expression. "Is that the King of England?"

The railwayman grinned. "No, mate, it's only the Earl of Walden." He walked on.

So Josef's information had been accurate. Walden was tall, about Feliks's height, and about fifty. He wore a light grey morning coat and a top hat of the same colour, and he had a spade-shaped beard patterned after that of the late King Edward VII. He stood on the platform, leaning on a cane, while the coachman, the footman and the stationmaster bustled about him like bees around their queen. He paid no attention. He is used to this, Feliks thought; all his life he has been the important man in the crowd.

28

The train appeared, smoke billowing from the funnel of the engine. I could kill Orlov now, Feliks thought, but he had already decided not to do the deed today. He was there to observe and plan, not to act.

The train halted with a great sigh of steam. Feliks stood up and moved a little closer to the platform. Towards the far end of the train was what appeared to be a private coach, differentiated from the rest by the colours of its bright new paintwork. It came to a stop precisely opposite Walden's carriage. The stationmaster stepped forward eagerly and opened a door.

For a moment everyone waited; then Orlov was there. He paused in the doorway for a second, and Feliks's eye photographed him. He was a small man, wearing an expensive-looking Russian coat with a fur collar, and a black top hat. His face was pink and youthful, almost boyish, with a small moustache and no beard. He smiled hesitantly. He looked vulnerable. So much evil is done by people with innocent faces, Feliks thought.

Orlov stepped off the train. He and Walden embraced, Russian fashion, but quickly; then they got into the coach.

The footman and two porters loaded luggage onto the carriage, which then turned and pulled away. Feliks mounted his bicycle and followed them. In the tumult of the London traffic it was not difficult for him to keep pace. He trailed them along the Strand and across St. James's Park. On the far side of the park the coach turned abruptly into a walled forecourt.

Feliks jumped off his bicycle and wheeled it along the grass at the edge of the park until he stood across the road from the gateway. He could see the coach drawn up at the imposing entrance to a large house. Beyond the coach he saw two top hats, one black and one grey, disappear into the building. Then the door closed, and he could see no more.

LYDIA STUDIED her daughter critically. Charlotte stood before a large pier-glass, trying on the gown she would wear to be presented at court. Madame Bourdon, the dressmaker, fussed about her, adjusting a flounce here and a ruffle there.

Charlotte looked both beautiful and innocent—just the effect called for in a debutante. The dress, of white embroidered tulle, went almost to the floor. The train was four yards of cloth of silver

29

lined with pale pink chiffon and caught at the end by a huge white-and-silver bow. Charlotte's dark hair was piled high and fastened with a diamond tiara that had belonged to the previous Lady Walden, Stephen's mother. In her hair she wore the regulation two white plumes of a debutante.

Lydia said, "It's very lovely, Madame Bourdon."

"Thank you, my lady."

Charlotte said, "It's terribly uncomfortable."

Lydia sighed. "I wish you wouldn't be so frivolous."

When Charlotte knelt to pick up her train, Lydia said, "You don't have to kneel to do it. Look, I'll show you. Turn to the left." Charlotte did so, and the train draped down her left side. "Gather it with your left arm, then make another quarter turn to the left." Now the train stretched out along the floor in front of her. "Walk forward, using your right hand to loop the train over your left arm as you go."

"It works." Charlotte smiled. When she smiled you could feel the glow. She used to be like this all the time, Lydia thought. When she was little, I always knew what was going on in her mind. Growing up is learning to deceive.

Charlotte's governess, Marya, came into the room. She was an efficient woman in an iron-grey dress, the only servant Lydia had brought from St. Petersburg so many years ago. She said, "Prince Orlov has arrived, my lady. Why, Charlotte, you look magnificent!"

Lydia said, "Come down as soon as you've changed, Charlotte." Charlotte immediately began to unfasten the shoulder straps that held her train. Lydia went out.

She found Stephen in the drawing room, sipping sherry. He touched her bare arm and said, "I love to see you in summer dresses."

She smiled. "Thank you." He looked rather fine himself, she thought, in his grey coat and silvery tie. *We might have been so happy, you and I.* . . . Suddenly she wanted to kiss his cheek, but there was a footman at the sideboard, pouring sherry. She sat down and accepted a glass from him. "How is Aleks?"

"Much the same as always," Stephen replied. "You'll see, he'll be down in a minute. What about Charlotte's dress?"

"The gown is lovely. It's her attitude that disturbs me. I should hate her to become *cynical*."

Stephen refused to worry. "Wait until some handsome guards officer pays attention to her—she'll soon change."

The remark irritated Lydia, implying as it did that Charlotte was no different from any other eighteen-year-old girl. But Lydia knew that Charlotte had in her make-up a streak of something wild and un-English, which had to be suppressed.

Irrationally, Lydia felt hostile towards Aleks on account of Charlotte. It was not his fault, but he represented the St. Petersburg factor, the danger of the past. She shifted restlessly in her chair, and Stephen's shrewd eye caught it. He said, "You can't possibly be nervous about meeting little Aleks."

She shrugged. "Russians are so unpredictable." The door opened. Be calm, Lydia told herself.

Aleks came in. "Aunt Lydia!" he said, and bowed over her hand.

"How do you do, Aleksey Andreyevich," she said formally. Then her tone softened. "Why, you still look eighteen!"

"I wish I were," he said, and his eyes twinkled.

She asked him about his trip. As he replied, she found herself wondering why he was still unmarried. His title alone was enough to knock many girls off their feet.

"Your sister sends her love," Aleks was saying, "and asks for your prayers." He frowned. "St. Petersburg is very unsettled now; it's not the town you knew. There are strikes and riots. The Czar is no longer believed to be holy."

"What is to be done?" Stephen asked.

Aleks sighed. "Russia must join the twentieth century. We need efficient farms, more factories, trade unions, freedom of speech. Either we, the nobility, must do it, or the people will destroy us and do it themselves." He accepted a glass of sherry from the footman.

Lydia thought he sounded very radical. How things must have changed at home, that a prince could talk like this!

Stephen said, "There is a third possibility, you know; a way in which the aristocracy and the people might yet be united."

Aleks smiled, as if he knew what was coming. "And that is?"

"A war."

As Aleks nodded gravely, Charlotte came in, and Lydia stared at her in surprise. She was wearing a frock Lydia had never seen, of cream lace lined with chocolate-brown silk. Lydia would never have chosen it—it was rather *striking*—but there was no denying that

Charlotte looked ravishing. When did she start buying clothes without taking me along? Lydia wondered.

Stephen stood up—a clearly involuntary acknowledgment of his daughter's grown-up status. The effect on Aleks was even greater. He sprang to his feet, spilled his sherry and blushed crimson. He transferred his dripping glass from his right hand to his left, so that he was unable to shake hands with either, and he stood there looking helpless. Lydia was about to make some inane remark when Charlotte took over.

She pulled the silk handkerchief from Aleks's breast pocket and wiped his right hand with it, saying, "How do you do, Aleksey Andreyevich," in Russian. She shook his now dry right hand, took the glass from his left hand, wiped the glass, wiped the left hand, gave him back the glass, stuffed the handkerchief back into his pocket and made him sit down. She sat beside him and said, "Now that you've finished throwing the sherry around, tell me about Diaghilev. Have you met him?"

Aleks smiled. "Yes, he's an interesting man."

As Aleks talked, Lydia marvelled. Charlotte had dealt beautifully with the awkward moment. Where had she learned such poise?

Lydia caught her husband's eye. He was smiling from ear to ear in a glow of fatherly pride.

FELIKS SAT ON a bench in St. James's Park, in a position from which he could see the graceful white façade of Walden's town house, rising over the forecourt wall like a noble head above a starched collar. He thought, They believe they are safe in there.

Middle-class London swarmed about him, the clerks and shop-keepers walking homeward, the top-hatted gentlemen on their way to and from the clubs of St. James's.

Until today the killing of Orlov had been planned in the abstract, Feliks reflected—a matter of international politics. Now suddenly, it was flesh and blood—a real man, of a certain size and shape; a youthful face with a small moustache, a face that must be smashed by a bullet; a short body in a heavy coat, which must be turned into blood and rags by a bomb. Feliks felt completely capable of doing it. More than that, he was eager. There were problems—they would be solved; it would take nerve—he had plenty.

He visualized Orlov and Walden inside that beautiful house, in their fine clothes, surrounded by quiet servants. Soon they would have dinner at a long table, set with crisp linen and silver cutlery. They would consume a tenth of the food provided and send the rest back to the kitchen. Meanwhile, the people who were to fight the war they contrived went hungry in Russian hovels. What a joy it will be to kill Orlov, he thought; what sweet revenge. When I have done that, I can die satisfied. He shivered.

He got up from the bench and walked across the grass towards the house. He sat on the ground with his back to a tree. He would have to observe this house for a day or two and find out what kind of life Orlov would lead in London. He wanted to be able to predict his movements so that he could lie in wait for him. And he had yet to choose a weapon; that would depend upon the detailed circumstances of the killing.

THAT NIGHT, in Lydia's room, Walden lay in the dark with her head on his shoulder, remembering St. Petersburg in 1895.

He was always travelling in those days—America, Africa, Arabia—mainly because England was not big enough for him and his father both. He found St. Petersburg society gay but prim. Languages came easily to him, but Russian was the most difficult he had ever encountered, and he enjoyed the challenge.

As the heir to an earldom, Stephen was expected to pay a courtesy call on the British ambassador; and it was at a reception in the British embassy that he first met Lydia.

He had already heard her spoken of as a paragon of virtue and a great beauty. She *was* beautiful, with her pale skin, pale blonde hair, and a white gown. She was also modest and scrupulously polite. There seemed to be nothing to her, and Stephen detached himself from her company quite quickly.

But later he found himself seated next to her at dinner. He said something about the government of Russia, and she replied with the usual reactionary platitudes. He spoke about big-game hunting in Africa, and she was interested until he mentioned the naked Pygmies, at which point she blushed and turned away to talk with the man on her other side. Stephen told himself that she was the kind of girl one married, and he was not planning to marry. Still, she left him with the nagging feeling that there was more to her than met the eye.

He had seen her once more that evening, when he lost his way in the labyrinthine embassy and wandered into the music room. She was there alone, sitting at the piano, filling the room with wild, passionate music. The pale, untouchable beauty was gone; her eyes flashed, her head tossed, her body trembled with emotion, and she seemed altogether a different woman.

He never forgot that music. Later he discovered that it had been Tchaikovsky's Piano Concerto in B Flat Minor, and he went to hear it played at every opportunity, although he never told Lydia why.

When he left the embassy, he went back to his hotel to change his clothes, for he had an appointment to play cards at midnight; but he did not keep that rendezvous. Pritchard, his manservant, was tying Stephen's tie when the British ambassador knocked on the door of the suite. His Excellency looked disturbed.

"Bad news, I'm afraid," said the ambassador. "You'd better sit down. Cable from England. It's your father."

The old tyrant was dead of a heart attack at sixty-five.

"Well, I'm damned," Stephen said. "So soon."

"My deepest sympathy," the ambassador said.

"It was very good of you to come personally."

"Not at all. Anything I can do."

"You're very kind."

The ambassador shook his hand and left. Stephen stared into space, thinking about the old man. He had been immensely tall, with a will of iron and a sour disposition. His sarcasm could have brought tears to your eyes.

Pritchard brought a bottle of whisky on a tray and said, "This is a sad day, my lord."

That "my lord" startled him, but now, of course, Stephen was the Earl of Walden. Along with the title, he now possessed several thousands of acres in the south of England, a big chunk of Scotland, six racehorses, Walden Hall, a villa in Monte Carlo, a hunting lodge in Scotland and a seat in the House of Lords.

He would have to live at Walden Hall, for the earl always lived there. He would put in electric light, he decided. He would sell some of the farms and invest in London property and North American railways. He would make his maiden speech in the House of Lords. He would have to appear at court in the season, and give shooting parties and hunt balls. . . .

34

He needed a wife. Someone must be hostess at all those parties; someone must reply to invitations, discuss menus with cooks, and sit at the foot of the long table in the dining room of Walden Hall. There must be a Countess of Walden. There must also be an heir.

"I need a wife, Pritchard."

"Yes, my lord. Our bachelor days are over."

The next day Walden saw Lydia's father and formally asked permission to call on her.

Twenty years later he found it difficult to imagine how he could have been so wickedly irresponsible. He had asked himself only whether she was good countess material; he had never wondered whether he could make her happy. He had assumed that the hidden passion released when she played the piano would be released for him, and he had been wrong.

He called on her every day for two weeks—there was no possibility of getting home in time for his father's funeral—and then he proposed, not to her but to her father, who saw the match in the same practical terms as Walden. Walden explained that he wanted to marry immediately, although he was in mourning, because he had to get home and manage the estate. Lydia's father understood perfectly. They were married eight weeks later. What an arrogant young fool I was, he thought.

The moon came out from behind a cloud, and he looked down at Lydia's sleeping face. I didn't foresee that I would fall helplessly in love with you, he thought. I asked only that we should like each other, and that's been enough for you but not for me.

WALDEN SURVEYED the breakfast table. There were pots of coffee, China tea and Indian tea; jugs of cream, milk and cordial; a big bowl of hot porridge; plates of scones and toast; and little pots of marmalade, honey and jam. On the sideboard was a row of silver dishes, each warmed by its own spirit lamp, containing scrambled eggs, sausages, bacon, kidneys and haddock. The fruit bowl was piled with nectarines and oranges.

This ought to put Aleks in a good mood, he thought.

He helped himself to eggs and kidneys and sat down. The Russians would have their price, he thought; they would want something in return for their promise of military help. He was worried about what the price might be. He would have to

35

manipulate Aleks. He felt uncomfortable. It might have been easier to negotiate in a tough way with someone about whom one did not care personally.

Aleks came in, looking bright-eyed and well-scrubbed. "Sleep well?" Walden asked him.

"Wonderfully well." Aleks took a nectarine and began to eat it with a knife and fork.

"Is that all you're having?" Walden said. "You used to love an English breakfast."

"I'm not a growing boy any more, Uncle Stephen."

I might do well to remember that, Walden thought.

After breakfast they went into the morning room. "Our new five-year plan for the army and navy is about to be announced," Aleks said. "It's a massive programme. The budget is seven and a half billion roubles."

At ten roubles to the pound, Walden calculated, that made seven hundred and fifty million pounds. He said, "The first thing you should do is increase the size of the guns on your dreadnoughts. Churchill has gone over to fifteen-inch guns for ours."

"And he's right. Our commanders know that, but our politicians don't. You know Russia, Uncle: new ideas are viewed with the utmost distrust. Innovation takes for ever."

"What is your priority?" Walden asked.

"A hundred million roubles will be spent immediately on the Black Sea fleet."

"I should have thought the North Sea more important."

Aleks hesitated. "The great weakness of the Russian navy," he said, "is that we have no warm-water port."

We're getting to the heart of the matter, Walden thought. But he continued to fence. "What about Odessa?"

"It's on the Black Sea coast. While the Turks hold Constantinople and Gallipoli, they control the passage between the Black Sea and the Mediterranean; so the Black Sea might as well be an inland lake. But Russian control of the Balkans would help us."

"No doubt; although it's not on the cards, as far as I can see."

"Would you like to give the matter some thought?"

Walden opened his mouth to speak, then closed it abruptly. This is it, he thought; this is their price. But we can't give Russia the Balkans, for heaven's sake!

Walden frowned as if puzzled and said, "If Britain had control of the Balkans, we could give them to you. But we can't give you what we haven't got, so I'm not sure how we can help there."

Aleks's reply was quick. "You might acknowledge the Balkans as a Russian sphere of influence."

Ah, that's not so bad, Walden thought. That we *might* be able to manage. He needed time to reflect. For Britain to do as Russia wanted would mean a significant shift in international alignments, and such shifts, like movements of the earth's crust, caused earthquakes in unexpected places.

"You may like to talk with Churchill before we go any further," Aleks said with a little smile.

You know damn well I will, Walden thought. How well Aleks had handled the whole thing! First he had scared Walden with a completely outrageous demand; then, when he put forward his real demand, Walden had been so relieved that he welcomed it. He smiled. "I'm proud of you, my boy," he said.

THAT MORNING FELIKS figured out when, where and how he was going to kill Prince Orlov.

The plan began to take shape while he read *The Times* in the library of the Workers' Friend Club in Jubilee Street. His imagination was sparked by a paragraph in the Court Circular column:

> Prince Aleksey Andreyevich Orlov arrived from St. Petersburg yesterday. He is to be the guest of the Earl and Countess of Walden for the London Season. Prince Orlov will be presented to Their Majesties the King and Queen at the Court on Thursday, June 4th.

Now he knew for certain that Orlov would be at a certain place at a certain time. The next problem was how to get sufficiently close to Orlov to kill him, but this question also was answered by *The Times*. On the same page as the Court Circular column, although in a less prominent position, he read:

> ### THE KING'S COURT
> #### ARRANGEMENTS FOR CARRIAGES
> In order to facilitate the arrangements for calling the carriages of the company at Their Majesties' Courts at Buckingham Palace, we are requested to state that the coachman of each carriage returning to

take up passengers is required to give the constable stationed on the left of the gateway the name of the lady or gentleman to whom the carriage belongs.

It is necessary that a footman should accompany each carriage, as no provision can be made for calling the carriages beyond giving the names to the footmen waiting at the door, with whom it rests to bring the carriage. The doors will be open for the reception of the company at 8.30 o'clock.

Feliks read this several times; there was something about the prose style of *The Times* that made it extremely difficult to comprehend. It seemed to mean that as people left the palace their footmen were sent running to fetch their carriages. There must be a way, he thought, that I can contrive to be in or on the Walden carriage when it returns to the palace to pick them up.

One major difficulty remained. He had decided that a gun would be his weapon, but he had no gun. He could have got one easily in Geneva, but might have been refused entry into England if his baggage had been searched.

In London, he was most reluctant to make open inquiries; his only hope was the anarchists at the Jubilee Street club. His best prospect there, he decided, was a young man named Nathan Sabelinsky, whom he had also seen around the bookmakers off the Commercial Road.

Feliks left the club library and went downstairs to look for him. There was no sign of him, so he went back to Stepney Green to pack his razor, his clean underwear and his spare shirt in his cardboard suitcase. Since he had determined that his contact for the gun would be Nathan, he thought it prudent to sever his ties with Jubilee Street and move to another part of London, to avoid the risk of being traced. He strapped the suitcase to the bicycle rack and rode to central London, then north to Camden Town. Here he found a street of once grand houses, and in one of them he rented a dingy room in the basement from an Irishwoman called Bridget Callahan. He paid her ten shillings in advance for two weeks' rent.

By midday he was back in Stepney Green, outside Nathan Sabelinsky's small terraced house. The front door was wide open. Feliks walked in.

The noise and the smell hit him like a blow. There, in a sweatshop

38

about twelve feet square, some fifteen or twenty people were working furiously at tailoring. Men were using machines, women were sewing by hand and children were pressing finished garments. The machines clattered, and the workers jabbered incessantly. Nobody looked up at Feliks.

He spoke to a girl with a baby at her breast, hand-sewing buttons on a jacket. "Is Nathan here?" he said.

"Upstairs," she said without pausing in her work.

Feliks went up and found Nathan in a back room, sitting on the edge of a bed. "I need to talk to you," he said.

"So talk."

"Come outside."

Nathan put on his coat and they went out into the sunshine, standing close to the open window of the sweatshop, their conversation masked by the noise within.

"My father's trade," said Nathan. "He'll pay a girl fivepence for machining a pair of trousers—an hour's work for her. He'll pay another threepence to the girls who cut, press and sew on buttons. Then he will take the trousers to a West End tailor and get paid ninepence. Profit, one penny—enough to buy one slice of bread. If he asks the West End tailor for tenpence, he'll be thrown out of the shop. I won't live like that."

"Is that why you're an anarchist?"

"Those people make the most beautiful clothes in the world, but did you see how *they* are dressed?"

"And how will things be changed? By violence?"

"I think so."

"I was sure you felt that way. Nathan, I need a gun."

Nathan laughed nervously. "What for?"

"Why do anarchists want guns?"

After a moment Nathan said, "Go to the Frying Pan pub at the corner of Brick Lane and Thrawl Street. See Garfield the Dwarf."

"Thank you!" said Feliks. He shook Nathan's hand.

Nathan watched him climb on his bicycle. "Maybe you'll tell me about it, afterwards."

Feliks smiled. "You'll read about it in the papers." He waved a hand and rode off. He cycled along Whitechapel High Street, then turned into Osborn Street. This was the most run-down part of London he had yet seen. The streets were narrow and very dirty, the people wretched. Crowds gathered around street stalls and prostitutes worked every corner.

Feliks left his bicycle outside the door of the Frying Pan. Inside was a crowded room, with a bar at the far end. Feliks went to the bar and asked for a glass of ale and a cold sausage.

He looked around and spotted Garfield the Dwarf standing on a chair. He was about four feet tall, with a large head and a middle-aged face, and a very big black dog sitting on the floor beside him. The dwarf was drinking what looked like gin, and talking to two large, tough-looking men holding quart pots of ale. Perhaps they were bodyguards. The barman handed Feliks his ale and his sausage. "And a glass of the best gin, too," Feliks said.

When the gin came, he paid and walked over to the dwarf's group, which was standing near a small window that looked onto the street. Feliks stood between them and the door and addressed the dwarf, offering the glass of gin. "May I speak to you about business?"

Garfield took the glass, drained it and said, "No."

Feliks sipped his ale. Then he said, "I heard about you at the Jubilee Street club. I wish to buy a gun."

Garfield looked him up and down. "What kind of gun would you want, if I had any?"

"A revolver. A good one."

"I haven't got one. If I had, I wouldn't sell it. And if I sold it, I'd have to ask five pounds."

"I was told a pound at the most."

"You was told wrong."

Feliks reflected. The dwarf had decided that, as a foreigner, he could be rooked. All right, he thought, we'll play it your way. "I can't afford more than two pounds."

"I couldn't come down below four."

"Would that include a box of ammunition?"

"All right, four pounds, including a box of ammunition."

"Agreed," Feliks said. He noticed one of the bodyguards smothering a grin. After paying for the drinks and the sausage, Feliks had only three pounds fifteen shillings left.

Garfield nodded at one of his companions. The man went behind the bar and out through the back door. A minute or two later he came back, carrying what looked like a bundle of rags. He glanced at Garfield, who nodded. The man handed the bundle to Feliks.

Feliks unfolded the rags and found a revolver and a small box. He took the gun from its wrappings and examined it. It was clean and oiled, and the action worked smoothly. He then opened the box of cartridges and loaded the chambers with swift, practised movements.

"Put the bloody thing away," the dwarf hissed. "Give me the money quick and get out of here. You're mad."

A bubble of tension rose in Feliks's throat. He took a step back and pointed the gun at the dwarf. "Shall I test it?" Feliks said.

The two bodyguards stepped sideways in opposite directions, so that Feliks could not cover them both with the one gun. Their next move would be to jump him. The pub was suddenly silent. Feliks realized he could not get to the door before one of the bodyguards reached him. The big dog growled, sensing the tension in the air.

Feliks smiled and shot the dog.

The bang of the gun was deafening in the little room. Nobody moved. The dog slumped to the floor. The dwarf's bodyguards were frozen where they stood.

Feliks took another step back, reached behind him and found the door. He opened it, still pointing the gun at Garfield, and stepped out.

He slammed the door, stuffed the gun into his coat pocket and jumped on his bicycle. He pushed off and began to pedal. Half a minute later he was lost in the warrens of Whitechapel.

He thought, Six bullets left.

Chapter Three

Charlotte was ready. To complement her gown she wore a single blush rose in her corsage and carried a spray of the same flowers. Her diamond tiara and the two white plumes were fixed firmly in her upswept hair. Everything was fine.

Lydia came into the bedroom. She held her daughter at arm's length. "My dear, you're beautiful," she said, and kissed her. When Charlotte drew away, she was surprised to see tears in her mother's eyes.

"You're beautiful too, Mama," she said.

Lydia's gown was of ivory charmeuse, with a train of old ivory brocade lined with purple chiffon. Being a married lady, she wore three feathers in her hair. "Are you ready?" she said.

"I've been ready for ages," Charlotte said.

Marya opened the door. Charlotte stood aside to let her mother go first, but Mama said, "No, dear—it's your night."

They walked along the corridor in procession, Marya bringing up the rear. When Charlotte reached the top of the grand staircase, she heard a burst of applause.

The whole household was gathered at the foot of the stairs: butler, housekeeper, cook, footmen, maids, grooms and boys—all looking up at her with pride and delight. In the centre of the throng was her father, looking magnificent in a black velvet tailcoat, breeches and silk stockings, with a sword at his hip and a cocked hat in his hand.

Charlotte walked slowly down the stairs. "Papa."

Walden kissed her and said, "My little girl."

Aleks bowed to her, resplendent in the uniform of an admiral in the Russian navy. What a handsome man he is, she thought.

Two footmen opened the front door. The coach was waiting outside. William, the coachman, and Charles, the footman, wearing the blue-and-pink Walden livery, stood at attention on either side of the door. Walden handed Charlotte into the coach and the other three got in. Pritchard brought a hamper and put it on the floor of the coach before closing the door.

The coach pulled away. Charlotte looked at the hamper. "A picnic?" she said. "But we're only going half a mile!"

"Wait till you see the queue," Walden said. "It will take us almost an hour to get there."

Sure enough, the carriage stopped at the Admiralty end of The Mall, half a mile from Buckingham Palace. Walden opened the hamper and took out a bottle of champagne. The basket also contained chicken sandwiches, hothouse peaches and a cake.

Charlotte sipped champagne, but she could not eat anything. She looked out of the window. Throngs of idlers were watching the procession of the mighty. She saw a tall man with a thin, handsome face leaning on a bicycle and staring at their coach. Something about his look made her shiver and turn away, but by the time the coach had passed through the palace gates she was beginning to feel her normal self—sceptical and irreverent.

42

The coach stopped at the grand entrance, and the door was opened. Charlotte gathered up her train, stepped down from the coach and walked into the palace.

The great red-carpeted hall was a blaze of light and colour, of white-gowned women, and men in glittering uniforms. The diamonds flashed, the swords clanked and the plumes bobbed.

Charlotte and Lydia left their wraps in the cloakroom and then, escorted by Walden and Aleks, walked slowly through the hall and up the grand staircase, between the Yeomen of the Guard with their halberds. From there they went through the picture gallery and into the first of three state drawing rooms with enormous chandeliers and mirror-bright parquet floors. Here people stood around in groups, chatting and admiring one another's clothes. Charlotte saw her cousin Belinda with Uncle George and Aunt Clarissa. The two families greeted each other.

Papa took out his watch. "We must take our places in the Throne Room; we'll leave you to look after Charlotte, if we may, Clarissa." Papa, Mama and Aleks left.

Belinda said to Charlotte, "Your dress is gorgeous."

"It's awfully uncomfortable."

"I *knew* you were going to say that!"

Silence descended suddenly. The crowd fell back towards the sides of the room. Charlotte looked round and saw the King and Queen enter the drawing room, followed by their pages, several members of the royal family and the Indian bodyguard. There was a great sigh of rustling silk as every woman in the room sank to the floor in a curtsy.

IN THE THRONE ROOM, the orchestra in the Minstrels' Gallery struck up "God Save the King". Lydia looked towards the huge doorway guarded by gilt giants. Two attendants walked in backwards, one carrying a gold stick and one a silver. The King and Queen entered at a stately pace, smiling faintly. They mounted the dais, turned and stood in front of the twin thrones. The rest of their entourage took their places nearby, remaining standing.

Queen Mary wore a gown of gold brocade and a crown of emeralds. She's no beauty, Lydia thought, but they say he adores her.

The presentations began with the diplomats. One by one the

44

wives of ambassadors came forward, curtsied to the King, to the Queen, then backed away. The ambassadors followed, dressed in a variety of gaudy uniforms, all but the United States ambassador, who wore ordinary black evening clothes.

When that ritual ended, the King and Queen sat down, and the presentation of the debutantes began. Each girl paused just outside the Throne Room while an attendant took her train from her arm and spread it behind her. Then she began the endless walk along the red carpet to the thrones, with all eyes on her. If a girl could look graceful and unselfconscious there, she could do it anywhere.

As the debutante approached the dais she handed her invitation card to the lord chamberlain, who read out her name. She curtsied to the King, then to the Queen. Few girls curtsied elegantly, Lydia thought. Then the debutante walked on, careful not to turn her back on the thrones until she was safely hidden in the watching crowd.

Suddenly Charlotte was at the entrance, and the attendant was laying down her train; then she was walking along the red carpet, head held high, looking perfectly serene and confident. Lydia thought, This is the moment I have lived for.

The girl ahead of Charlotte curtsied—and then the unthinkable happened. Instead of getting up from her curtsy, the debutante looked at the King, stretched out her arms in a gesture of supplication and cried in a loud voice, "Your Majesty, for God's sake, stop torturing women!"

Lydia thought, A suffragette! Her eyes flashed to her daughter. Charlotte was standing dead still, halfway to the dais, staring at the tableau with an expression of horror on her ashen face.

The shocked silence in the Throne Room lasted only a second. Two gentlemen-in-waiting sprang forward, took the girl firmly by either arm and marched her away.

The Queen was blushing crimson. The King managed to look as if nothing had happened. Now all eyes were on Charlotte. A little colour was coming back into her cheeks. Lydia could see that she was taking a deep breath.

Then she walked forward. Lydia could not breathe. Charlotte handed her card to the lord chamberlain, who said, "Presentation of Lady Charlotte Walden." Charlotte stood before the King.

She curtsied perfectly. She curtsied again to the Queen. She half turned and walked away.

45

Lydia let out her breath in a long sigh. The woman standing next to her whispered, "She handled that very well."

"She's my daughter," Lydia said with a smile.

WALDEN WAS SECRETLY amused by the suffragette. Spirited girl! he thought. Of course, if Charlotte had done such a thing, he would have been horrified, but as it was someone else's daughter, he regarded the incident as a welcome break in the interminable ceremony. Charlotte had carried on, unruffled; he would have expected no less of her.

Finally the last debutante curtsied and moved on, and the King and Queen stood up. The orchestra played the national anthem again; the King bowed, and the Queen curtsied. The King took the Queen by the hand. The pages picked up her train. The attendants went out backwards. The royal couple left, followed by the rest of the company in order of precedence.

They divided to go into three supper rooms: one for the royal family and their close friends, one for the diplomatic corps and one for the rest. Walden was a friend, but not an intimate friend, of the King's; he went with the general assembly. Aleks went with the diplomats.

In the supper room, Walden met his family again. Lydia was glowing. Walden said, "Congratulations, Charlotte."

Lydia said, "Who was that awful girl?"

"I heard she's the daughter of an architect," Walden replied.

"But why does she think the King tortures women?" asked Charlotte.

"She was talking about the suffragettes. But let's not go into all that tonight; this is a grand occasion for us. Let's have supper."

There was a long buffet table loaded with flowers and hot and cold food. Servants in the scarlet-and-gold royal livery waited to offer the guests lobster, filleted trout, quail, York ham, plovers' eggs and a host of pastries and desserts. Walden took a loaded plate and sat down to eat with his brother, George.

Sooner or later, Walden thought, Charlotte would have to learn about the suffragettes, their hunger strikes, and the consequent force-feeding; but the subject was indelicate, to say the least, and the longer she remained in ignorance the better. At her age, life should be all parties and frocks, gossip and flirtation.

Walden saw Churchill pushing through the crowd towards them. He had written to Churchill about his talk with Aleks, and he was impatient to discuss the next step, but not *here*. He looked away, hoping Churchill would take the hint. He should have known better; a moment later Churchill was bending over Walden's chair. "Can we have a few words together?"

Walden threw his brother a resigned look and got up.

"Let's walk in the picture gallery," Churchill said.

Walden followed him out, and the two men walked side by side through the long gallery. Churchill said, "We can't acknowledge the Balkans as a Russian sphere of influence."

"I was afraid you'd say that."

"What do they want the Balkans *for?*"

"They want passage through to the Mediterranean."

"That would be to our advantage, if they were our allies."

"Exactly."

They reached the end of the gallery and stopped. Churchill said, "Is there a way we can give them passage to the Mediterranean without redrawing the map of the Balkan Peninsula?"

"I've been thinking about that."

Churchill smiled. "And you've got a counter-proposal?"

"Suppose that whole passage between the Black Sea and the Mediterranean could be declared an international waterway, with free passage to ships of all nations guaranteed jointly by Russia and England. If they have that, they won't need the Balkans."

Churchill started walking again, slow and thoughtful. Eventually he said, "That passage *ought* to be made international in any event. What you're suggesting is that we offer, as if it were a concession, something we want anyway."

"Yes."

Churchill looked up and grinned suddenly. "When it comes to Machiavellian manoeuvring, there's no one to beat the English aristocracy. All right. Go ahead and propose it to Orlov."

"You don't want to put it to the Cabinet?"

"Not at this stage. Only when the deal is fully elaborated."

"Very well." Walden wondered just how much the Cabinet knew about what Churchill and he were up to. He said, "I'll put the proposal to Orlov tomorrow morning."

Churchill seemed disposed to argue, but he restrained himself and said, "I don't suppose Germany will declare war tonight. Very well." He looked at his watch. "I'm going to leave. Keep me fully informed."

"Of course. Goodbye."

Churchill went down the staircase, and Walden went back into the supper room. The party was breaking up, so he collected his family and took them downstairs. They met Aleks in the great hall, and Walden summoned his carriage.

All in all, he thought, it had been a rather successful evening.

THE MALL REMINDED FELIKS of streets in the Old Equerries Quarter of Moscow. It was a wide, straight avenue that ran from Trafalgar Square to Buckingham Palace. On one side was a series of grand houses, including St. James's Palace. On the other side was St. James's Park. The carriages and motorcars of the great were lined up along The Mall for half its length. Chauffeurs and coachmen leaned against their vehicles, yawning, waiting to be summoned to the palace to collect their masters and mistresses.

The Waldens' carriage waited on the park side of The Mall. Their stout and greying coachman stood beside the horses, reading a newspaper by the light of a carriage lamp. A few yards away, in the darkness of the park, Feliks stood watching him.

Feliks was desperate. His plan was in ruins. He had not understood the difference between the English words "coachman" and "footman" and consequently he had misunderstood the notice in *The Times* about summoning carriages. He had thought that the driver of the coach would wait at the palace gate until his master emerged, then would come running to fetch the coach. At that point, Feliks had planned, he would overpower the coachman, take his livery, and drive the coach to the palace himself.

It was not until he had seen the Walden coach driving to the palace with the footman at the back that he realized his error. What happened in fact was that the coachman stayed with the vehicle and the footman waited at the palace gate. When the coach was wanted, the footman would come running. That meant Feliks had to overpower two people, not one. He had worried at the problem ever since, while he watched the coachman chatting with his colleagues, who called him William.

It might have been sensible to abandon the plan and kill Orlov another day. But Feliks hated that idea. He wanted to kill Orlov now. He had been anticipating the bang of the gun, the way the prince would fall; he had pictured the newspaper headlines and then the final wave of revolution sweeping through Russia. I can't postpone this any longer, he thought.

In his mind he ran over the probable sequence of events. Walden and Orlov would come to the palace door. The doorman would alert Walden's footman, who would run from the palace to the carriage—a distance of about a quarter of a mile. The footman would arrive at the parking place to find that the carriage was no longer there. He would search for a while, finally admit defeat and return to the palace to report that he could not find the coach. By that time Feliks would be driving the coach and its passengers through the park.

It was risky, but there was no more time for reflection. The first two or three footmen were already running down The Mall. William put on his top hat in readiness.

Feliks emerged from the bushes and walked a little way towards him, calling, "Hey! Hey, William!" The coachman looked towards him, frowning, and Feliks beckoned urgently. "Come here, quick!"

William folded his newspaper, hesitated, then walked slowly towards Feliks. "What?" he said, mystified, as he drew level.

"This." Feliks showed him the gun. "If you make a noise, I'll shoot you."

William was terrified.

"Walk on," Feliks said. William walked into the bushes and Feliks followed him. When they were about fifty yards from The Mall, Feliks said, "Stop."

William stopped and turned round.

Feliks said, "Take off your clothes."

"What? You're mad," William whispered.

"You're right—I'm mad! Take off your clothes!"

Feliks cocked the gun and William began to undress.

Feliks could hear the increasing activity in The Mall. Any minute now the footman might come running for the Walden coach. "Faster!" he said.

At last William stood naked, shivering with fear. "Lie on the ground, face down," said Feliks. The man did so.

Feliks put down the gun. Hurriedly he took off his coat and hat and put on the livery coat and the top hat which William had dropped on the ground. When he was sitting up on the coach no one would notice his trousers and boots.

He put the gun into the pocket of his own coat and folded the coat over his arm. He picked up the rest of William's clothes.

William tried to look round. ·

"Don't move!" Feliks said sharply as he walked away.

He pushed William's clothes under a bush, then emerged into the lights of The Mall.

This was where things might go wrong. If one of William's friends should look closely at his face, the game would be up. He climbed rapidly onto the coach, put his own coat on the seat beside him, released the brake and flicked the reins. The coach pulled out into the road.

I've got this far, he thought; I'll get Orlov!

As he drove down The Mall he watched the pavements, looking anxiously for a running footman in the blue-and-pink livery. The worst possible mischance would be for the Walden footman to see him now, recognize the colours and jump onto the back of the coach. There was no sign of him.

At the palace end of the avenue, Feliks spotted an empty space on the right, the side of the road farther from the park. The footman would come along the opposite pavement and would not see the coach. He pulled into the space and set the brake.

He climbed down from the seat and stood behind the horses, watching for the footman. He wondered whether he would get out of this alive.

In his original plan there had been a good chance that Walden would get into the carriage without so much as a glance at the coachman, but now he would surely notice that his footman was missing. The palace doorman would have to open the coach door and pull down the steps.

Would Walden stop and speak to the coachman before getting in? What will I do then? Feliks thought.

I'll shoot Orlov at the palace door and take the consequences.

He saw the footman running along the far side of The Mall. Feliks jumped back onto the coach and drove into the courtyard of Buckingham Palace.

There was a queue. Ahead of him, the beautiful women and the well-fed men climbed into their carriages and cars. And somewhere in The Mall, the Walden footman was running about, hunting for his coach. How long before he returned?

The line moved, and a servant approached Feliks. "The Earl of Walden," Feliks said. The servant went inside and the line moved forward; now there was only a motorcar in front of him. Pray God it doesn't stall, he thought. The chauffeur held the doors for an elderly couple. The car pulled away.

Feliks moved the coach to the entrance, halting it a little too far forward, beyond the wash of light from inside, with his back to the palace doors. He waited, not daring to look round.

He heard a young girl say, in Russian, "And how many ladies proposed marriage to you this evening, Cousin Aleks?"

A drop of sweat ran down into Feliks's eye, and he wiped it away with the back of his hand.

A man said, "Where the devil is my footman?"

Feliks got his hand on the butt of the revolver in the coat beside him. A palace servant opened the door of the coach. The vehicle rocked slightly as someone got in.

"I say, William, where's Charles?"

Feliks tensed. The girl's voice said, "Come on, Papa," from inside the carriage.

"William's getting deaf in his old age. . . ." Walden's words were muffled as he got into the coach. The door slammed.

Feliks breathed out and drove off. Orlov was in his power, caught behind him like an animal in a trap. He felt a surge of elation.

He drove into the park. Shifting the reins from hand to hand, he struggled to get into his topcoat, standing up and shrugging the coat up over his shoulders. He felt in the pocket and touched the gun. He sat down again and wound a scarf round his neck.

Feliks was ready. Now he had to choose his moment.

He had bicycled along this road the night before and found a place where a streetlamp would illuminate his victim and where there was a thick shrubbery nearby for his getaway afterwards.

He saw the spot now, at a bend in the road. He made the horses trot a little faster. From inside the coach he heard the girl laugh.

He came to the bend. His nerves were as taut as piano wire.

Now.

He dropped the reins and heaved on the brake. The horses staggered, and the carriage shuddered and jerked to a halt.

From inside the coach he heard a woman cry and a man shout. Something about the woman's voice bothered him, but there was no time to wonder why. He jumped down, pulled the scarf up over his mouth and nose, took the gun from his pocket and cocked it.

Full of strength and rage, he flung open the coach door.

A woman cried out again, and time stood still.

Feliks knew the voice. The sound hit him like a mighty blow. The shock paralysed him.

He was supposed to locate Orlov, point the gun at him, pull the trigger, then turn and run into the bushes. . . .

Instead, he looked for the source of the cry, the gun pointing nowhere, and saw her face. It was as if he had last seen it only yesterday, instead of nineteen years ago. Her eyes were wide with panic, and her small red mouth was open.

Lydia. My Lydia—here in *this carriage* . . .

As he stood at the door of the coach staring at her, he was dimly aware that Walden was moving close to him; then he saw that Walden had drawn a sword! And the blade was glinting in the lamplight as it swept down. Feliks moved too slowly and too late; the sword bit into his right hand, and he dropped the gun. It went off with a bang as it hit the road.

The explosion broke the spell.

Walden drew back the sword and thrust at Feliks's heart. Feliks moved sideways and the point of the sword went into his shoulder. He felt a rush of warm blood inside his shirt.

He stared down at the road, looking for the gun, but he could not see it. He realized he was unarmed and helpless. He had failed utterly, and all because of the voice of a woman from the past. Full of despair, he turned and ran away.

Walden roared, "Damned villain!"

Feliks's wound hurt at every step. He heard someone running behind him, the footsteps too light to be Walden's; Orlov was chasing him. Orlov is chasing *me*, he thought, and I am running away!

He darted off the road and into the bushes. He heard Walden shout, "Aleks, come back, he's got a gun!" They don't know I dropped it, Feliks thought. He ran a little way farther, then stopped to listen. He could hear nothing. Orlov had given up.

He leaned against a tree, exhausted. When he had caught his

breath, he took off his topcoat and the livery coat and gingerly touched his wounds. They hurt like the devil. His shoulder bled slowly and throbbed. His hand had been sliced in the fleshy part between thumb and forefinger, and it bled fast.

With difficulty he drew on the topcoat again. He left the livery coat lying on the ground. Wearily he headed towards The Mall.

Chapter Four

Lydia. It was the second time in his life that she had caused a catastrophe. The first time, in 1895, in St. Petersburg . . .

No. He would not allow himself to think about her, not yet. He needed his wits about him now.

He found his bicycle where he had left it, under the branches of a big tree. He wheeled it across the grass to the edge of the park and into the road. Everyone was busy; nobody looked at him. Keeping his right hand in his coat pocket, he pushed off and began to pedal, steering with his left hand.

There were bobbies all round the palace. If Walden mobilized them quickly, they could cordon off the park and the roads around it. Feliks looked ahead, towards Admiralty Arch. There was no sign of a roadblock. He began to get the knack of riding one-handed. He increased his speed, and soon he was riding through the arch and into Trafalgar Square.

Too slow, Walden, you've lost me, he thought with satisfaction. From Trafalgar Square he rode up St. Martin's Lane, then crossed into Bloomsbury. He had just a mile or two more to go, but pushing the pedals had become an enormous effort.

Outside Euston Station he suddenly felt dizzy. A streetlight blinded him. The front wheel hit the kerb. He fell.

Feliks lay on the ground, dazed and weak. He opened his eyes and saw a policeman approaching. He struggled to his knees, and the policeman took his right arm and hauled him to his feet. Feliks managed to keep his bleeding right hand in his pocket.

The policeman sniffed audibly, but his attitude became more genial when he discovered that Feliks did not smell of drink. "Would you like a cab?"

"No, thank you. I have only a little way to go."

The policeman picked up the bicycle. "I should wheel it home if I were you."

Feliks took the bicycle from him. "I will do that." With an effort he produced a smile. Pushing the bicycle with his left hand, he walked away.

He made himself keep on walking, although he desperately needed to lie down. The next alley, he thought. But when he came to an alley, he thought, Not this one, but the next. And in that way he got home to Bridget's house in Camden Town.

To get to his room he had to go down a flight of stone steps to the basement area. He leaned the bicycle against the wrought-iron railings while he opened the little gate. He then made the mistake of trying to wheel the bicycle down the steps. It slid out of his grasp and fell with a loud clatter. A moment later his landlady appeared at the street door in a shawl. "What the devil is it?" Bridget called.

Feliks sat on the steps and made no reply. Bridget came down and helped him to his feet. "You've had a few too many drinks," she said. "Give us your key."

Feliks gave it to her and she opened the door. They went in, and she lighted the lamp.

"Let's have your coat off," she said.

He let her remove his coat, and she saw the bloodstains. "You look as if you have been fightin' and lost!"

"I have," said Feliks. He went and lay on the bed. He passed out, but an agonizing pain brought him round. He opened his eyes to see Bridget bathing his wounds with something that stung like fire. "This hand should be stitched," she said.

"Tomorrow," Feliks breathed.

She made him drink from a cup. It was warm water with gin in it. She said, "I haven't any brandy." He lay back and let her bandage him. "I could fetch the doctor, but I couldn't be payin' him."

"Tomorrow."

"I'll look at you first thing in the morning."

"Thank you."

She left, and at last Feliks allowed himself to remember. . . .

It has happened in the long run of ages that everything which permits men to increase their production, or even to continue it, has been appropriated by the few. The coalpits, which represent the

54

labour of generations, belong again to the few. . . . The railways belong to a few shareholders, who may not even know where is situated the railway which brings them a yearly income larger than that of a mediæval king. And if the children of those people who died by the thousand digging the tunnels should gather and go—a ragged and starving crowd—to ask bread or work from the shareholders, they would be met with bayonets and bullets.

Feliks looked up from Kropotkin's pamphlet. The bookshop was empty. The bookseller was an old revolutionary, who made his money selling novels to wealthy women and kept a hoard of subversive literature in the back of the shop. Feliks spent a lot of time in here among the shelves.

He was nineteen. He was about to be thrown out of the prestigious Spiritual Academy for truancy, long hair and associating with nihilists. He was hungry and broke, and soon he would be homeless, and life was wonderful. He cared about nothing but ideas, and he was learning new things every day about poetry, history, psychology and, most of all, politics.

The anarchist slogans had sounded ridiculous when he had first heard them: Property is theft; Government is tyranny; Anarchy is justice. It was astonishing how, when he had really thought about them, they came to seem not only true but obvious. Kropotkin's point about the evil of property laws, for example, was undeniable. No laws were required to prevent theft in Feliks's home village; if one peasant stole another's horse, then the whole village would see the culprit in possession of the animal and make him give it back.

Feliks was vaguely aware that a customer had come into the shop and was standing close to him, but he was concentrating on Kropotkin.

No more laws! No more judges! Liberty, equality and practical human sympathy are the only effective barriers we can oppose to the anti-social instincts of certain among us.

The customer dropped a book, and Feliks lost his train of thought. He saw the book lying on the floor beside the customer's long skirt and automatically bent down to pick it up for her. As he handed it to her he saw her face. He gasped.

"Why, you're an angel!" he said with perfect candour.

She was blonde and petite, and she wore a pale grey fur the colour of her eyes, and everything about her was pale and light and fair. He had never seen a more beautiful woman. She stared back at him and blushed, but she did not turn away.

After a moment he looked at her book. It was *Anna Karenina*. "Sentimental rubbish," he said, and his words broke the spell. She took the book and turned away. He saw then that there was a maid with her, for she gave the book to the maid and left the shop. The maid paid for the book. Looking through the window, Feliks saw the woman get into a carriage.

He found out from the bookseller that she was the daughter of Count Shatov. Her name was Lydia. He learned where the count lived, and the next day he hung around outside the house in the hope of seeing her. She went out twice in her carriage, and the last time her carriage passed she looked directly at him.

The next day he went to the bookshop and read for hours without understanding a word. Every time a carriage passed he looked out of the window. Whenever a customer came into the shop his heart missed a beat.

She came in at the end of the afternoon.

This time she left the maid outside. She murmured a greeting to the bookseller and came to the back of the shop, where Feliks stood. They stared at one another. He meant to speak to her, but instead he threw his arms round her and kissed her. She kissed him back, hungrily, digging her fingers into his back.

It was always like that with them when they met they threw themselves at one another like animals about to fight.

They met twice more in the bookshop and once, after dark, in the garden of the Shatov house. After that time she gave him money so that he could rent a room of his own, and she came to see him almost every day for six astonishing weeks.

The last time was in the early evening. He was sitting wrapped in a blanket against the cold, reading Proudhon's *What Is Property?* by candlelight. He heard her footstep on the stairs and she rushed in, wearing an old brown cloak with a hood. She kissed him and threw off the cloak. Under it she was wearing a white evening gown. "Unfasten me quickly," she said breathlessly. "I'm on my way to a reception at the British embassy; I only have an hour."

56

In his haste he ripped one of the hooks out of the material. "Damn, I've torn it."

"Never mind!" She stepped out of the dress and flung herself into his arms.

Later, Lydia was in a reflective mood. She ran a finger along the line of his nose. "You have the face of a prince."

"But I'm a peasant."

She giggled. "I'm such an actor. Everyone in St. Petersburg thinks I'm so *good*. I'm held up as an example to younger girls, just like Anna Karenina. If my father knew I was here, like this, he'd die of rage."

Feliks looked at her. "What are we going to do, Lydia?"

"When?"

"In the long term."

"We're going to be lovers until I come of age, and then we'll be married."

He stared at her. "Do you mean that?"

"Of *course*. Isn't that what you want?"

"Oh yes," he breathed. "That's what I want."

She stroked his hair. "Then that's what we'll do."

"Tell me how you manage to get away to come here."

"I tell lies and I bribe servants," she said. "Tonight, for example, I left home at six o'clock and I'll get to the embassy at a quarter past seven. The carriage is in the park; the coachman thinks I'm taking a walk with my maid. The maid is outside this house, dreaming about how she will spend the ten roubles I shall give her for keeping her mouth shut."

"It's ten to seven," Feliks said.

"Oh, Feliks . . ."

That night Feliks was asleep, dreaming, when they burst into his room, carrying lamps. He woke instantly and jumped out of bed, thinking at first it was a student prank. Then one of them punched his face and kicked him in the stomach, and he knew they were the secret police.

He assumed they were arresting him on account of Lydia, and he was terrified for her. Would she be publicly disgraced?

He was marched out of the building and thrown into a four-wheeled cab. They drove across the Chain Bridge and then followed the canals, as if avoiding the main streets. When they went over the

Palace Bridge he realized he was being taken to the notorious Fortress of St. Peter and St. Paul, and his heart sank.

The carriage entered a darkened arched passage, and stopped at a gate. Feliks was taken into a large, damp room, where the prison governor sat at a table. He said, "You are charged with being an anarchist. Do you admit it?"

Feliks was elated. So this had nothing to do with Lydia! "Admit it?" he said. "I boast of it."

He was stripped and given a green flannel dressing gown, a pair of thick woollen stockings, and yellow felt slippers, much too big. Then an armed guard took him to a cell containing a bed, a table, a stool and a washstand. Feliks sat on the bed.

He thought proudly, This is where Peter I had his own son tortured and killed. This is where Catherine II buried her enemies alive. Dostoevsky was once imprisoned here. Feliks was both elated to be in such heroic company and terrified at the thought that he might be here for ever.

The key turned in the lock. A little bald man with spectacles came in, carrying a pen, a bottle of ink and some paper. He set them down on the table and said, "Write the names of all the subversives you know."

Feliks sat down and wrote: "Karl Marx, Friedrich Engels, Pëtr Kropotkin, Jesus Christ—"

The bald man snatched away the paper. He went to the door of the cell and knocked. Two hefty guards came in. They strapped Feliks to the table and took off his slippers and stockings. They began to lash the soles of his feet with whips.

The torture went on all night. Each time he passed out they revived him. It was not until dawn that he passed out for the last time and was left alone.

When he came round, he was lying on the bed. There were bandages on his feet. He was in agony. He wanted to kill himself, but he was too weak to move. A doctor came to see him. Feliks tried to pump him for information. Had there been any messages? Had anyone tried to visit? The doctor just changed the dressings and went away.

Eight weeks later, when he could walk almost normally, they released him without explanation. He went to his lodging. He hoped to find a message from Lydia there, but there was nothing.

He went to the bookshop. The old bookseller said, "I've got a message for you. It was brought yesterday by *her* maid."

Feliks tore open the envelope with trembling fingers. It was written, not by Lydia, but by the maid. It read, "I have been Let Go and have no job it is all your fault She is wed and gone to England yesterday now you know the wages of Sin."

He looked up at the bookseller with tears of anguish in his eyes. "Is that all?" he cried.

He learned no more for nineteen years.

AT THE WALDEN HOUSE, Charlotte sat in the kitchen with the servants. She had had no time to be frightened. At first, when the coach stopped so abruptly in the park, she had been merely puzzled; and after that her concern had been to stop Mama from screaming. When they got home, she had found herself a little shaky, but now, looking back, she found the whole thing rather exciting, and the servants felt the same way.

William, the coachman, had recovered rapidly from the indignity of having been stripped stark naked. He described several times the wild look in his assailant's eyes.

Charles, the footman, said, "Imagine how I felt when I come running through the park, and I find the carriage, and my lady having hysterics, and my lord with blood on his sword!"

Mrs. Mitchell, the housekeeper, said, "And after all that, nothing stolen."

"A lewnatic," said Charles. "An ingenious lewnatic."

There was general agreement.

The cook poured the tea and served Charlotte first. "How is my lady now?" she asked.

"Oh, she's all right," Charlotte said. "She went to bed and took a dose of laudanum. She must be asleep by now."

The cook sighed heavily. "Robbers in the park and suffragettes at court—I don't know what we're coming to."

Charlotte said, "What did the suffragette mean about the King torturing women?" She looked at Pritchard, the majordomo, who was sometimes willing to explain things to her.

"She was talking about force-feeding," Pritchard said. "Apparently it's painful."

"Force-feeding?"

"When they won't eat, they're fed by force."

"Why should they refuse to eat?" Charlotte asked.

"It's a protest," said Pritchard. "Makes difficulties for the prison authorities."

Charlotte was astonished. "Why are they in prison?"

"For breaking windows, making bombs, disturbing the peace."

"But what do they want?"

There was a silence as the servants realized that Charlotte had no idea what a suffragette was.

Finally Pritchard said, "They want votes for women."

"Oh," said Charlotte, and thought, Did I know that women couldn't vote?

"I think this discussion has gone quite far enough," Mrs. Mitchell said firmly. "You'll be in trouble, Mr. Pritchard, for putting wrong ideas into my lady's head."

There was a ring, and they all looked at the bell board. "Front door!" said Pritchard. He went out, pulling on his coat.

Charlotte drank her tea. The suffragettes were rather frightening, she decided; but all the same she wanted to know more.

Pritchard came back. "Plate of sandwiches, please, Cook," he said. "Charles, take a fresh soda siphon to the drawing room." He began to arrange plates and napkins on a tray.

"Well, come on," Charlotte said. "Who is it?"

"A gentleman from Scotland Yard," said Pritchard.

BASIL THOMSON was a bullet-headed man with receding light-coloured hair, a heavy moustache and a penetrating gaze. He had been educated at Eton and Oxford and had gravitated towards police work, specializing in the mixed criminal-anarchist milieu of London's East End. This expertise had got him the top job in the Special Branch, the political police force.

Walden sat him down and began to recount the evening's events. As he spoke he kept an eye on Aleks. He was superficially calm, but his face was pale, and he sipped steadily at a glass of brandy and soda. Walden concluded, "Lady Walden screamed, and that seemed to disconcert the fellow. Anyway, he hesitated, and I poked him with my sword."

"Did you do him much damage?"

"I doubt it. I couldn't get a swing, and of course the sword isn't particularly sharp. I blooded him, though. I wish I had chopped off his damned head."

The butler came in, and conversation stopped while he served sandwiches and drinks. Walden said, "You'd better stay up, Pritchard, but you can send everyone else to bed."

"Very good, my lord."

When Pritchard had gone, Walden said, "It is possible that this was just a robbery. However, a robber would hardly have made such an elaborate plan. I am perfectly certain that it was an attempt on Aleks's life."

Thomson looked at Aleks. "I'm afraid I agree. Have you any idea how he knew where to find you?"

Aleks shrugged. "My movements haven't been secret."

"That must change." Thomson turned to Walden. "I wonder whether the villain knew what you have told me about the reason for Prince Orlov's visit. *Would* this be an effective way to sabotage your talks?"

"Very effective indeed," Walden said. The thought made him go cold. "If the Czar's nephew were to be assassinated in London—especially if it were by an expatriate Russian revolutionary—the Czar would turn against us. You know how the Russians already feel about us having their subversives here—our open-door policy has caused friction at the diplomatic level for years. Something like this could destroy Anglo-Russian relations. There would be no question of an alliance then."

Thomson nodded. "I was afraid of that. I'll set my department to work immediately." He turned to Aleks. "As for you, Prince Orlov, I propose you move out of this house tomorrow. We'll take the top floor of one of the hotels for you, and give you a bodyguard. You'll have to discontinue social engagements, of course."

"Of course."

Thomson stood up. "It's very late. I'll set all this in motion."

Walden rang for Pritchard, who saw Thomson out, and Aleks went off to bed. Walden then went upstairs.

He was not sleepy. As he undressed he let himself relax and feel all the conflicting emotions he had so far held at bay. He got into bed and lay awake, reliving the moment when the carriage door flew open and the man stood there with the gun; and now he was frightened, not for himself or Aleks, but for Lydia and Charlotte.

The thought that they might have been killed made him tremble in his bed. He got up and went to Lydia's room. She was in a deep sleep, lying on her back, her hair a blonde skein across the pillow. Lydia, he thought, I could not live without you.

Chapter Five

Charlotte looked forward with mixed feelings to Belinda's coming-out ball. She had been to country balls and she liked to dance, but she hated the cattlemarket business of sitting out with the wall-flowers and waiting for a boy to ask her to dance. She wondered whether this might be handled in a more civilized way tonight.

They got to Uncle George and Aunt Clarissa's Mayfair house half an hour before midnight. Charlotte was unprepared for what she saw when she went in: the whole side garden had been turned into a Roman atrium. The lawns and the flower beds had been covered over with a hardwood dance floor stained in black and white squares to look like marble tiles. A colonnade of white pillars linked with chains of laurel bordered the floor. In the middle of the floor a fountain splashed in a marble basin, the streams of water lighted by coloured spotlights. On the balcony of a bedroom a band played. A huge canvas roof, painted sky-blue, covered the whole area.

"It's a miracle!" Charlotte said. She studied the guests and realized she knew nobody. Who will dance with me, she wondered, after Papa and Uncle George? However, Aunt Clarissa's younger brother Jonathan waltzed with her, then introduced her to three of his Oxford friends, each of whom danced with her. She found their conversation monotonous: they said the floor was good, and the band was good; then they ran out of steam. Charlotte tried asking, "Do you believe that women should have the vote?" The replies she got were, "Certainly not," "No opinion," and "You're not one of *them*, are you?"

The last of her partners, a rather sleek young man whose name was Freddie, took her into the house for supper.

The rooms were festooned with flowers and bright with electric light. For supper there was hot and cold soup, lobster, quail, strawberries, ice cream and hothouse peaches. "Always the same old food," Freddie said. "They all use the same caterer."

After supper Charlotte and Freddie got into conversation with Belinda's and Freddie's friends. They talked about a new play, called *Pygmalion*, which was said to be absolutely hilarious but quite vulgar. They discussed jazz music; Freddie disliked it. They all drank coffee and Belinda smoked a cigarette. Charlotte began to enjoy herself.

It was Charlotte's mother who came along and broke up the party. "Your father and I are leaving," she said. "Shall we send the coach back for you?"

Charlotte realized she was tired. "No, I'll come," she said. "What time is it?"

"Four o'clock."

As they walked to the door Lydia said, "Did you have a lovely evening?"

"Yes, thank you, Mama."

Walden had called the carriage, and as they drove away from the bright lights of the party he held Lydia's hand. They seemed happy. Charlotte felt excluded, and she looked out of the window. In the dawn light, as the carriage rounded Hyde Park Corner, Charlotte saw something odd. "What's that?" she said.

Lydia looked out. "What's what, dear?"

"On the pavement. Looks like people. What are they doing?"

"Sleeping."

Charlotte was horrified. There were eight or ten of them, bundled in newspapers, some of the bundles small enough to be children. "Why do they sleep there?"

"I don't know, dear," said Lydia.

Walden said, "Because they've nowhere else to sleep, of course."

"I didn't know there was anyone that poor," said Charlotte. "How dreadful. We should do something for them."

"We?" asked her father. "Why should *we*?"

"Because the strong should take care of the weak. I've heard you say that to Mr. Samson." Samson was the bailiff at Walden Hall, and he was always trying to save money on repairs to tenanted cottages.

"We already take care of rather a lot of people," said Walden. "The servants, the tenants who farm our land, the workers in the companies we invest in—"

"But those poor people are sleeping on the *street*," Charlotte interrupted. "What will they do in winter?"

Lydia said sharply, "Charlotte, those people on the pavement are idlers, criminals, drunkards and ne'er-do-wells."

"Even the children?"

"Don't be impertinent. You still have a great deal to learn."

"I'm just beginning to realize how much," Charlotte said.

As the carriage turned into the courtyard of their house, Charlotte glimpsed a street sleeper beside the gate. She decided she would take a closer look.

The coach stopped beside the front door. Charles handed Lydia down, then Charlotte. Charlotte ran across the courtyard and into the street. She heard her father say, "What the devil . . . ?"

The sleeper was a woman. She lay slumped on the pavement with her shoulders against the courtyard wall. She wore a man's boots, a dirty blue coat and a very large, once-fashionable hat with a bunch of grubby artificial flowers on its brim. Her face was turned towards Charlotte, and there was something familiar about it. Charlotte cried, "Annie!" The sleeper opened her eyes.

Charlotte stared at her in horror. Just two months ago Annie had been a housemaid at Walden Hall, a pretty girl in a crisp, clean uniform. "Annie, what happened to you?"

Annie scrambled to her feet and bobbed a pathetic curtsy. "Oh, Lady Charlotte, I was hoping I would see you, you was always good to me, I've nowhere to turn—"

"But how did you get like this?"

"I was let go, m'lady, without a character, when they found out I was expecting the baby; I know I done wrong—"

"But you're not married!"

"But I was courting Jimmy, the gardener."

Charlotte recalled the book she had looked at with Belinda. Obviously it was possible for girls to have babies without being married. "Where is the baby?"

"I lost it."

"You *lost* it?"

"I mean, it came too early, m'lady, it was born dead."

"How horrible," Charlotte whispered. "And why isn't Jimmy with you?"

"He run away to sea. He *did* love me, but he was frightened to wed, he was only seventeen. . . ." Annie began to cry.

Papa called, "Charlotte, come in this instant."

She turned to him. He was standing at the gate in his evening clothes, with his silk hat in his hand, and suddenly she saw him as Annie must have seen him—a smug, cruel man. She said, "This is one of the servants you care for so well."

Papa looked at the girl. "Annie! What is the meaning of this?"

Annie said, "Jimmy run away, m'lord, so I couldn't wed, and I couldn't get another position because you never gave me a character, and I was ashamed to go home, so I come to London."

"You came to London to beg," Papa said harshly.

"Papa!" Charlotte cried. She put her arm round Annie. "She needs a bath and a hot breakfast."

"All right," Papa said. "Take her into the kitchen. The parlour-maids will be up by now. Tell them to take care of her. Then come and see me in the drawing room."

They went in. Charlotte took Annie downstairs and asked for food and clothing for her. Now there will be trouble, she thought, as she went back upstairs and marched into the drawing room.

Papa stood beside the fireplace holding a glass. Mama sat at the piano, playing minor chords with a pained expression on her face. She had drawn back the curtains, and the room looked odd with the cold early light on the edges of things.

"Now then, Charlotte," Papa began. "You don't understand what kind of woman Annie is. She did something very wrong which I cannot explain to you—"

"I know what she did," Charlotte said, sitting down.

Lydia gasped, and Walden said, "I don't believe you have any idea what you're talking about."

"And if I haven't, whose fault is it?" Charlotte burst out. "How did I reach the age of eighteen without learning where babies come from . . . or that some people are so poor they sleep in the street, or that maids who are expecting babies get dismissed without a character reference? Don't tell me I don't understand these things and I have a lot to learn! I've spent all my life learning and now I discover most of it was lies! How dare you! How dare you!" She burst into tears.

Papa sat beside her and took her hand. "I'm sorry you feel like that," he said. "If we did not tell you just how cruel and coarse the world is, it was only because we wanted you to enjoy your childhood for as long as possible. Perhaps we made a mistake."

Mama snapped, "We wanted to keep you out of the trouble that Annie got into!"

"I wouldn't put it quite like that," Papa said mildly. "We did what we did for your own good. And we have never lied to you."

Charlotte's rage evaporated. She felt like a child again. She wanted to put her head on Papa's shoulder, but her pride would not let her.

"Shall we all forgive each other and be pals again?" Papa said.

Charlotte said, "But what is to be done about Annie?"

"I will give her money for decent lodgings, and see that she gets a factory job," Papa said.

Charlotte sighed. Papa patted her hand. "She will be very grateful," he said. "I suggest you go and tell her the arrangement and then go to bed. I'll see to all the details."

"Very well," she said wearily. She wanted to tell Papa that she loved him, but the words would not come. She got up and left the room.

THE NEXT DAY FELIKS WAS awakened at noon by Bridget. She stood by the bed with a large cup in her hand. Feliks sat up and took the cup. The drink was wonderful. It seemed to consist of hot milk, sugar, melted butter and lumps of bread.

Bridget went away and came back again with another Irish-woman, who was a nurse. The woman stitched his hand and put a dressing on the puncture wound in his shoulder. She charged him a shilling and said, "You won't die. If you'd had yourself seen to straightaway, you wouldn't have bled so much. As it is, you'll feel weak for days."

When she had gone, Bridget talked to him. She was a heavy, good-natured woman in her late fifties. Her husband, Sean, had got into trouble in Ireland, and they had fled to London, where he died of the booze, she explained. There was a vein of bitterness in her, which showed in an occasional sarcastically humorous remark, usually at the expense of the English. Feliks went to sleep while she was talking. She woke him in the evening to give him hot soup.

On the following day his physical wounds began visibly to heal, but all the despair and self-reproach that he had felt in the park as he ran away now came back to him. Running away! How could it have happened?

67

Lydia. She was now Lady Walden. He had known that she had married and had gone to England. Obviously her husband was likely to be both an aristocrat and a man with a strong interest in Russia. Equally obviously, the person who negotiated with Orlov had to be a member of the Establishment and an expert on Russian affairs. I couldn't have guessed it would turn out to be the same man, Feliks thought, but I should have realized the possibility. The coincidence was not as remarkable as it had seemed, but it was no less shattering.

Feliks could not imagine a greater happiness than that which he had had with Lydia—nor a disappointment more appalling than that which followed. After she had left he had begun to tramp the Russian countryside, dressed as a monk, preaching the anarchist gospel. He told the peasants that the land was theirs because they tilled it; that nobody had a right to govern them except themselves; and because self-government was no government it was called anarchy. He was a wonderful preacher and he made many friends, but he never fell in love again.

His preaching phase had ended in 1899, during a strike, when he was arrested as an agitator and sent to Siberia. Working in a chain gang, using wooden tools to dig gold in a mine, labouring on when the man chained to his side had fallen dead, seeing boys and women flogged, he came to know bitterness, despair and finally hatred. In Siberia he learned the facts of life: steal or starve, hide or be beaten, fight or die. There he acquired cunning and ruthlessness.

He escaped, and returned to civilization as a full-blooded revolutionary. He went to St. Petersburg, where he founded an anarchist group, The Unauthorized, and planned the successful assassination of the Grand Duke Sergey. That year there were killings, mutinies, strikes and riots throughout the land, which collectively became known as the Revolution of 1905.

Then came the repression—more fierce, more efficient and a great deal more bloodthirsty than anything the revolutionaries had ever done. The secret police came in the middle of the night to the homes of The Unauthorized, and they were all arrested except Feliks, who killed one policeman and maimed another and escaped to Switzerland.

In all those years, and even in the quiet years in Switzerland that followed, he had never loved anyone. Many women sensed his violent nature and shied away from him, but those who did find him attractive found him extremely so. Looking back, he could see his life since Lydia as a slow slide into anaesthesia. He had survived by becoming less and less sensitive. He no longer cared even for himself; this, he had decided, was the basis for his lack of fear.

His love was not for people as individuals; it was for *the* people. Nor did he hate anybody in particular—just all princes, all landlords, all capitalists and all generals.

This was the Feliks that had formed over the years, as his mature personality emerged from the fluidity of youth. What had been so devastating about Lydia's scream, he thought, was that it had reminded him that there might have been a different Feliks, a warm and loving man, a man capable of jealousy, greed, vanity and fear. Would I rather be that man? he asked himself. That man would long to stare into her wide grey eyes and stroke her fine blonde hair, to see her collapse into helpless giggles as she tried to learn how to whistle. That man would be *playful*.

He would also be *concerned*. He would wonder whether Lydia was happy. He might be reluctant to kill her nephew in case she were fond of the boy. That man would make a poor revolutionary.

No, he thought as he went to sleep that night, I would not want to be that man. He is not even dangerous.

ON THE THIRD DAY he went out. Bridget gave him a shirt and a coat that had belonged to her husband. Feliks's own trousers and boots were still wearable.

It was a glorious, sunny day. He felt peculiarly happy, walking through the streets of London in the summer weather. I've nothing to be happy about, he thought; my clever, well-organized, daring assassination plan was a fiasco!

He made his way to St. James's Park and took up his familiar station opposite the Walden house. The trouble was, the intended victim was now on his guard: it would be difficult indeed to kill Orlov, because he would be taking precautions. But Feliks would find out what those precautions were.

The carriage went out and returned several times, but there was no sign of Orlov. It rather looked as if he had moved out.

I'll find him then, he thought. On his way back to Camden Town he bought a newspaper. When he arrived home, Bridget offered him tea, so he read the paper in her parlour. There was nothing about Orlov in the Court Circular or the Social Notes.

Bridget saw what he was reading. "Interesting material, for a fellow such as yourself," she said sarcastically.

Feliks smiled and said nothing.

Bridget said, "I know what you are, you know," she said. "You're an anarchist."

Feliks was very still.

"Who are you going to kill?" she said. "I hope it's the bloody King." She drank tea noisily. "Well, don't stare at me like that. You needn't worry, I won't tell on you. My husband did for a few of the English in his time."

Feliks was nonplussed. She had guessed—and she approved! He stood up. "You're a good woman," he said.

"If I was twenty years younger, I'd kiss you. Get away before I forget myself."

"Thank you for the tea," Feliks said. He went out.

He spent the rest of the evening sitting in the drab basement room, staring at the wall, thinking. Of course Orlov was lying low, but where? He might even be out of London, at a house in the country. But suppose he were still living in Walden's house and had simply decided not to go out? Feliks saw no way to check all the possibilities, and meanwhile the negotiations would be progressing and war drawing nearer.

He went to sleep gnawing at the problem and woke up in the morning with the solution. He would ask Lydia.

He polished his boots, washed his hair and shaved. He borrowed from Bridget a white cotton scarf that, worn around his throat, concealed the fact that he had neither collar nor tie. He put on his bowler hat and looked at himself in the mirror. He looked dangerously respectable. He left the house.

He had no idea how Lydia would react to him. He was quite sure that she had not recognized him on the night of the fiasco; his face had been covered, and her scream had been a reaction to the sight of a man with a gun. Assuming he could get in to see her, what would she do? Would she throw him out? He wanted her to be shocked and dazed and still in love with him, so that he would be able to make her tell him a secret; but she might be totally indifferent.

At ten o'clock he arrived at the park and waited until the carriage appeared at the gate with Walden inside, and as soon as it had passed, Feliks walked over and went through the gateway and across the courtyard. He climbed the steps to the porch and pulled the bell at the front door.

Perhaps she will call the police, he thought.

A moment later a servant opened the door. Feliks stepped inside. "Good morning," he said.

"Good morning, sir."

So I *do* look respectable, Feliks thought. "I should like to see the Countess of Walden," he said. "It is a matter of great urgency. My name is Konstantin Dmitrich Levin. I am sure she will remember me from St. Petersburg."

"If you will be so good as to wait here, sir, I'll see if the countess is in."

Feliks nodded, and the servant went away.

Chapter Six

The Queen Anne bureau bookcase was one of Lydia's favourite pieces of furniture in the London house. Two hundred years old, it was of black lacquer decorated in gold with Chinese pagodas, willow trees and flowers. The flap front folded down to form a writing table. There were large drawers in the bombé base, and the top was a bookcase with a mirrored door, showing a cloudy, distorted reflection of the room behind her.

On the writing table was an unfinished letter to her sister, Tatyana, Aleks's mother, in St. Petersburg. She had written, in Russian, "I don't know what to think about Charlotte," and then she had stopped. She sat looking into the mirror, musing about the incident with Annie. We're not harsh, Lydia thought; as employers we're relatively generous. Yet Charlotte reacted as if Annie's plight were our fault. I don't know where she gets her ideas. I dedicated my life to bringing her up to be pure and decent, not like me. *Don't even think that—*

Pritchard came in. "A Mr. Konstantin Dmitrich Levin to see you, my lady."

Lydia frowned. "I don't think I know him."

"The gentleman seemed to think you would remember him from St. Petersburg." Pritchard looked dubious.

Lydia hesitated. The name was distinctly familiar, and from time to time Russians whom she hardly knew would call on her in London. "All right," she said. "Show him in."

Pritchard went out. Lydia inked her pen and wrote: "What can one do when the child is eighteen years old and has a will of her own? Stephen says I worry too much. I wish—"

The door opened, and Pritchard said, "Mr. Konstantin Dmitrich Levin."

Lydia spoke over her shoulder in English. "I'll be with you in a moment, Mr. Levin." She heard the butler close the door as she put down her pen and turned round.

He spoke to her in Russian. "How are you, Lydia?"

It was as if something cold and heavy descended over her heart, and she could not breathe. Feliks stood in front of her: tall and thin as ever, in a shabby coat with a scarf, holding a foolish English hat in his left hand. He was as familiar as if she had seen him yesterday.

He said, "I'm sorry to shock you."

Lydia could not speak. She struggled with a storm of mixed emotions: shock, fear, affection and dread. She stared at him.

He was studying her, too. "You look like a girl," he said wonderingly.

She tore her eyes away from him. Dread became her dominant feeling. With an effort, she said, "Go away."

"I expected that you would be afraid to admit to yourself that you are happy to see me."

He had always been able to see into her soul with those soft sad eyes. What was the use of pretending?

He drew up a chair and sat close to her. She jerked back convulsively. He said, "I won't hurt you—"

"Hurt me?" Lydia gave a laugh that sounded unexpectedly brittle. "You'll ruin my life!"

"You ruined mine," he replied; then he frowned as if he had surprised himself.

"Oh, Feliks, I didn't mean to."

He was suddenly tense. "What happened?"

She hesitated. All these years she had been longing to explain to him. She began, "That night you tore my gown . . ."

72

"WHAT ARE YOU GOING to do about this tear in your gown?" Feliks had asked.

"The maid will put a stitch in it before I arrive at the embassy," Lydia replied.

He helped her into the brown cloak. "You'll come tomorrow?"

"Yes."

At the door she kissed him and said, "Thank you."

"I love you dearly," he said.

She went down the stairs and out into the street. Her maid was waiting on the corner. Together they walked to the park, where the carriage was waiting. In the coach, the maid hastily repaired the back of Lydia's gown and Lydia changed the old brown cloak for a fur wrap. She gave the maid ten roubles for her silence. Then they were at the British embassy.

Lydia composed herself and entered the hall, looking young and a little nervous. She met her cousin, Kiril, who was nominally her escort. He worked for the foreign minister, and because his wife was dead and Lydia's parents did not enjoy going out, Kiril and Lydia were often invited together. Lydia always told him not to trouble to call for her. This was how she managed to meet Feliks clandestinely.

"You're late," Kiril said.

"I'm sorry," she replied insincerely.

Kiril took her into the salon. They were greeted by the ambassador and his wife, and then introduced to Lord Highcombe, elder son of the Earl of Walden. He was a tall, handsome man of about thirty, in well-cut but rather sober clothes. He looked very English, with his short, light-brown hair and blue eyes. He had a smiling, open face, and Lydia found him mildly attractive. "He seems rather pleasant," Lydia said to Kiril as they moved on. "Why is he here?"

"In St. Petersburg? Well, the story is that he has a very rich and domineering father, with whom he doesn't see eye to eye; so he's partying his way around the world while he waits for the old man to die."

Lydia did not expect to speak to Lord Highcombe again, but the ambassador's wife had seated them side by side at dinner. They conversed enough to satisfy the dictates of etiquette, but clearly neither of them was keen to go further.

73

After dinner she played the ambassador's wonderful grand piano for a while; then Kiril took her home. She went straight to bed, to dream of Feliks.

The next morning after breakfast a servant summoned her to her father's study. The count was a small, thin, exasperated man of fifty-five. When Lydia came in, he was standing in front of a writing table, his hands behind his back, his face twisted with fury. Lydia's maid stood near the door with tears on her cheeks.

There was no preamble. Her father began by shouting, "You have been seeing a boy secretly!"

Lydia folded her arms to stop herself shaking. "How did you find out?" she said, with an accusing look at the maid.

Her father made a disgusted noise. "Don't look at *her*," he said. "The coachman told me of your extraordinary long walks in the park. Yesterday I had you followed." His voice rose again. "How *could* you act like that—like a peasant girl?"

How much did he know? Not everything, surely! "I'm in love," Lydia said.

"In love!" he roared. Lydia thought he was about to strike her. He knew everything. It was total catastrophe.

Lydia whispered, "What are you going to do?"

"You'll be confined to your room for now. As soon as I can arrange it, you'll enter a convent."

Lydia stared at him in horror. It was a sentence of death. She ran from the room.

Never to see Feliks again—the thought was utterly unbearable. Tears rolled down her face as she ran to her bedroom. She could not possibly suffer this punishment. I shall die, she thought, I shall die.

Rather than leave Feliks for ever she would leave her family. As soon as this idea occurred to her, she knew it was the only thing to do—and it must be now, before her father had her locked into her room. She took some jewellery, put on her coat and left the house by the servants' door.

She hurried through the streets, and suddenly the whole affair did not seem so disastrous. She and Feliks could leave the city, even go abroad. Feliks was educated, so he could at least be a clerk, possibly better. She might take in sewing. They would rent a small house and furnish it cheaply. They would have children—strong boys and pretty girls.

She reached his house and climbed the stairs. As she took out her key, she saw that the door to his apartment hung open, askew on its hinges. She called, "Feliks, it's me— Oh!"

She stopped in the doorway. The whole place was in a mess, as if it had been burgled, or there had been a fight. Feliks was not there. She walked around the small apartment, feeling dazed. All his books were gone. The mattress had been slashed.

Lydia wandered into the hall. The occupant of the next apartment stood in his doorway. "What happened?" she said.

"He was arrested last night," the man replied.

She felt faint. Arrested! Why? It was too much to bear, that this should have happened on the very day that—"Father," Lydia whispered. "Father did this."

"You look ill," the neighbour said. "Would you like to come in and sit down for a moment?"

She pulled herself together and, without answering, made her way down the stairs and out into the street.

She walked slowly, going nowhere, wondering what to do. Somehow she had to get Feliks out of jail. She had no idea how to go about it. Should she appeal to the minister of the interior? To the Czar? She fought back the tears. She was so ignorant of the world of police and jails.

There was only one thing to do. She must go and plead with her father for Feliks's release. Wearily she turned and headed for home.

Her anger towards her father grew with every step she took. He was supposed to care for her and ensure her happiness—and what did he do? Tried to ruin her life. She arrived home in a rage. She walked into his study without knocking. "You've had him arrested," she accused.

"Yes," her father said. His mood had altered. His mask of fury had gone, to be replaced by a thoughtful, calculating look.

Lydia said, "You must have him released immediately."

"They are torturing him at the moment."

"No," Lydia whispered. "Oh, no."

"They are flogging the soles of his feet"—Lydia screamed, and her father raised his voice—"with thin, flexible canes—"

Lydia went berserk and rushed at her father, screaming, "I hate you, I hate you, I hate you!" He caught her wrist and pushed her into a chair. She burst into hysterical tears.

After a few minutes her father began to speak again, calmly, as if nothing had happened. "I could have it stopped immediately," he said. "I can have the boy released whenever I choose."

"Oh, please," Lydia sobbed. "I'll do anything you say."

"Will you?" he said.

She looked up at him through her tears. An access of hope calmed her. Did he mean it? Would he release Feliks? "Anything," she said. "Anything."

"I had a visitor while you were out," he said. "The Earl of Walden. He was Lord Highcombe when you met him, but his father has just died, so now he's the earl. He asked permission to call on you."

Lydia stared at her father uncomprehendingly. She could not understand why her father was suddenly rambling on about the Englishman. She said, "Don't torture me. Tell me what I must do to make you release Feliks."

"Marry Lord Walden," her father said abruptly.

She stared at him, dumbstruck. It sounded insane.

He continued. "Walden will want to marry quickly. You would go to England with him, and this appalling affair could be forgotten. It's the ideal solution."

"And Feliks?" Lydia breathed.

"The torture would stop today. The boy would be released the moment you leave for England. You would never see him again."

"No," Lydia whispered. "Oh, no."

They were married eight weeks later.

FELIKS SAID SOFTLY, "So, you never betrayed me, after all."

The things they had to say were so many and so weighty that they sat in silence. Lydia thought, Thank God, he has not guessed the rest of it. She wanted him to leave, and with equal desperation she wanted him to stay. Eventually she said, "What made you come here?"

"Oh . . ." Feliks seemed momentarily confused by the question. "I need to see Orlov."

"Aleks? Why?"

"There's an anarchist sailor in jail; I have to persuade Orlov to release him. You know how things are in Russia; there's no justice, only influence."

76

"Aleks isn't here any more. Someone tried to rob us in our carriage, and he got frightened."

"Where can I find him?" Feliks seemed suddenly tense.

"The Savoy Hotel, but I doubt if he'll see you. You're still . . . political?"

"It's my life."

"Most young men lose interest as they grow older."

He smiled ruefully. "Most young men get married and have a family." He reached out and took her hand.

She snatched it back and stood up. "Don't touch me," she said.

He looked at her in surprise.

"I've learned my lesson, even if you haven't," she said. "I was brought up to believe that lust is evil, and destroys. And look what happened—I ruined myself and I ruined you. Lust *does* destroy, and I will never forget it." She took a deep breath. "I want you to go away now, and never come back."

He looked at her in silence for a long moment; then he stood up. "Very well," he said.

Lydia thought her heart would break.

He took a step towards her. She stood still, knowing she should move away from him, unable to do so. He put his hands on her shoulders and looked into her eyes, and then it was too late. He drew her to him and kissed her, folding her into his arms. It was just as before; she was melting. She pushed her body against his. She searched for his hands to hold them tightly in her own—

He gave a shout of pain.

They broke apart. She stared at him, nonplussed.

He held his right hand to his mouth. She saw that he had a nasty wound, and she had made it bleed. She moved to take his hand, to say she was sorry, but a change had come over him; the spell was broken. He turned and strode to the door. Horrified, she watched him go out.

She fell into a chair, shaking uncontrollably. Her emotions whirled and boiled for minutes, and she could not think straight. Eventually they settled, leaving one predominant feeling: relief that she had not yielded to the temptation to tell him the secret lodged deep within her.

Like a piece of shrapnel in a healed-over wound, it would stay there until the day she died.

FELIKS STOPPED IN THE HALL to put on his hat. He looked at himself in the mirror, and his face twisted into a grin of savage triumph. He composed his features and went out into the midday sunshine.

She was so gullible. She had believed his half-baked story about an anarchist sailor and had told him, without a second's hesitation, where to find Orlov. He was exultant that she was still in his power. She married Walden for my sake, he thought, and now I have made her betray her husband.

Nevertheless, the interview had had its moment of danger for him. As she was telling her story he had watched her face, and a dreadful grief had welled up within him; but the dangerous moment had passed. I'm not really vulnerable to sentiment, he told himself: I lied to her, kissed her and ran away; I *used* her.

Fate is on my side today. It's a good day for a dangerous task.

He needed a new weapon. For an assassination in a hotel room a bomb would be best, because wherever it landed it would kill everyone in the room. If Walden should happen to be with Orlov, so much the better, Feliks thought.

He went to a chemist's shop and bought two bottles of a common acid in concentrated form. He took them home and put them on the floor of the basement room.

He went out again, and bought another bottle of the same acid in a different shop. The chemist asked him what he was going to use it for. "Cleaning," he said.

In a third chemist's he obtained a different acid and a glass rod a foot long. Finally he bought a pint of pure glycerine.

He went up to Bridget's kitchen and borrowed her mixing bowl.

"Would you be baking a cake?" she asked him.

He said, "Yes."

"Don't blow us all up, then."

"I won't."

Nevertheless, she took the precaution of spending the afternoon with a neighbour.

Feliks went back downstairs, took off his jacket and rolled up his sleeves. He put the mixing bowl in the washbasin.

The first part of the job was not very dangerous. He mixed the two kinds of acid together in the bowl, waited for it to cool, then rebottled the mixture. He washed the bowl, dried it, put it back into the washbasin and poured the glycerine into it.

The basin was fitted with a rubber plug on a chain. He wedged the plug into the drain hole sideways, so that it was partly blocked. He turned on the tap. When the water level reached almost to the rim of the bowl, he adjusted the tap so that the water was flowing out as fast as it was flowing in.

Gingerly he began to add the mixed acids to the glycerine, stirring gently but constantly with the glass rod.

Occasionally a wisp of reddish-brown smoke came off the bowl, a sign that the chemical reaction was beginning to get out of control; then Feliks would stop adding acid, but carry on stirring, until the flow of water through the washbasin cooled the bowl and moderated the reaction. When the fumes were gone he waited a minute or two, then carried on mixing.

When he had finished he had a bowl of nitroglycerine, an explosive liquid twenty times as powerful as gunpowder. It could be set off by a lighted match or even the warmth from a nearby fire. A bottle of nitroglycerine could explode if just dropped on the floor.

With the utmost care, Feliks dipped a clean brown bottle into the bowl and let it fill with the explosive. When it was full he closed the bottle, making sure there was no nitroglycerine caught between the neck of the bottle and the glass stopper. There was some liquid left in the bowl. Of course it could not be poured down the sink.

Feliks went over to his bed and picked up the pillow. He tore a small hole in it and pulled out some of the stuffing, which he put into the bowl, to absorb the liquid. He added more stuffing until all the liquid was soaked up; then he rolled it into a ball and wrapped it in newspaper. It was now much more stable, like dynamite—in fact, dynamite was what it was.

He washed and dried the mixing bowl again. He plugged the sink, filled it with water and gently placed the bottle of nitroglycerine in the water, to keep it cool. Then he went off to reconnoitre the Savoy Hotel.

Chapter Seven

After he had changed for dinner, Walden sat in the drawing room sipping sherry, waiting for his wife and his daughter to come down. They were to dine out.

Negotiations with the Russians were going slowly. Walden had put to Aleks the counter-proposal: an international waterway from the Black Sea to the Mediterranean. Aleks had said flatly that this was not good enough, for in wartime—when the passage would become vital—neither Britain nor Russia could prevent the Turks from closing the channel. Russia wanted not only the right of passage but also the power to enforce that right.

While Walden and Aleks argued about how Russia might be given that power, Germany's gold reserves reached a record high, as a result of the financial manoeuvres that had prompted Churchill's visit to Walden Hall in May. Germany would never be better prepared for war; every day that passed made an Anglo-Russian alliance more indispensable. But Aleks had true nerve: he would make no concessions in haste.

And as Walden learned more about Germany—its industry, its army, its natural resources—he realized that it had every chance of replacing Britain as the most powerful nation in the world. Personally, he did not much mind whether Britain was first, second or ninth, so long as she was free. She was not going to be spoiled by square-headed Prussian invaders if he could help it.

However, he was not sure he *could* help it. How far did he really understand modern England, with its anarchists and suffragettes, ruled by young Liberal firebrands like Churchill and Lloyd George, swayed by even more disruptive forces such as the burgeoning Labour Party? Walden's kind of people still ruled, but sometimes he had a feeling that it was all slipping out of control.

Charlotte came in, reminding him that politics was not the only area of life in which he seemed to be losing his grip. Walden said, "We must go soon."

"I'll stay at home, if I may," she said. "I've a slight headache."

"You look a little pale. Have a small glass of sherry; it'll give you an appetite."

"All right."

She sat down and he poured the drink for her. As he gave it to her he said, "Annie has a job and a home now."

"I'm glad," she replied coldly.

He took a deep breath. "I was at fault in that affair."

"Oh!" Charlotte said, astonished.

"Of course, I didn't know that her . . . young man had run off and

80

she was ashamed to go to her mother," he went on. "But I should have inquired."

Charlotte said nothing, but she came over and sat beside him on the sofa and took his hand. He was touched.

He said, "I often wonder whether we've protected you too much. There are people who say that children ought not to be protected from, well, what might be called the facts of life; but those people are few, and they tend to be a very coarse type."

They were quiet for a while. As usual, Lydia was taking for ever to dress for dinner. There was more that Walden wanted to say to Charlotte, but he was not sure he had the courage.

Lydia would be ready in a moment. It was now or never. So he cleared his throat. "You'll marry a good man, and learn about all sorts of things that are perhaps a little worrying to you now. But there is one thing you need to know in advance. Your mother should tell you, really, but somehow I think she may not."

He lit a cigar, just to have something to do with his hands.

"You said you know what Annie and the gardener did. Well, they aren't married, so it was wrong. But when you are married, it's a very fine thing to do indeed." He felt his face redden. "It's very good just physically, you know," he plunged on. "However, the main thing, the thing I'm sure you don't realize, is how wonderful the whole thing is spiritually. Somehow it seems to express all the affection and tenderness and respect and . . . well, just the love there is between a man and his wife. You don't necessarily understand that when you're young, and some unfortunate people never discover that side of it at all. But if you're expecting it, and you choose a good, kind man for your husband, it's sure to happen. So that's why I've told you. Have I embarrassed you terribly?"

To his surprise she turned her head and kissed his cheek. "Yes, but not as much as you've embarrassed yourself," she said.

That made him laugh.

Pritchard came in. "The carriage is ready, my lord, and my lady is waiting in the hall."

Walden stood up. "Not a word to Mama, now," he murmured.

"I'm beginning to see why everybody says you're such a good man," Charlotte said. "Enjoy your evening."

"Goodbye," he said. As he went out to join his wife he thought, Sometimes I get it right, anyway.

81

AFTER THAT, CHARLOTTE almost changed her mind about going to the suffragette meeting. She had been in a rebellious mood, following the Annie incident, when she saw the poster stuck to the window of a shop in Bond Street. The headline VOTES FOR WOMEN had caught her eye; then she had noticed that the hall in which the meeting was to be held was not far from her house. There and then she had decided to go to the meeting.

Her talk with Papa had been a revelation. She was no longer raging at him for allowing her to grow up in ignorance. But nothing altered the fact that she could not trust her parents to tell her the whole truth about things, especially about things like the women's suffrage movement. So, when the servants were having their supper, she put on a hat and coat and went out.

It was a warm evening. She walked quickly towards Knightsbridge. She felt a peculiar sense of freedom. Nobody knows where I am, she thought.

As she approached the hall she noticed more and more women heading the same way, singly or in groups. Outside the hall there were hundreds, many in the suffragette colours of purple, green and white. Some were handing out leaflets or selling a newspaper called *Votes For Women*. There were several policemen about, wearing expressions of amused contempt.

Charlotte joined the queue to get in and took her seat in the hall, quite close to the front. The place was almost full of women, with just a scattering of men. The women were mostly middle-class; as far as Charlotte could see, there were no working-class women in the audience. Up on the platform was a lectern draped with a "Votes for Women" banner.

The audience applauded as five women walked to their seats on the platform. They were all impeccably dressed in rather less-than-fashionable clothes. Were these the people who broke windows, made bombs and disturbed the peace? They looked too respectable.

The speeches began. They were about organization, finance, amendments and by-elections. Charlotte was disappointed; she was learning nothing. After almost an hour she was ready to leave. Then two women appeared at the side of the stage. One was an athletic-looking girl in a motoring coat. Walking with her, and leaning on her for support, was a small woman in a green spring coat and a large hat. It was Emmeline Pankhurst, the celebrated movement leader. The women on the platform stood up. The audience began to applaud; there were shouts and cheers, and in seconds a thousand women were on their feet.

Mrs. Pankhurst walked slowly to the lectern. She was a handsome woman, with dark, deep-set eyes and a strong chin. The effects of her repeated imprisonments and hunger strikes showed in the flesh-lessness of her face and hands and her yellow skin. She raised her hands for quiet, and began to speak, her voice strong and clear.

"In 1894 I was elected to the Manchester Board of Guardians, in charge of the workhouse. The first time I went into that place I was horrified to see little girls of seven and eight years old on their knees, scrubbing the cold stones of the long corridors. These little girls were clad, summer and winter, in thin, short-sleeved cotton frocks. At night they wore nothing at all, nightdresses being considered too good for paupers. The fact that bronchitis was epidemic among them had not suggested to the guardians any change in the fashion of the clothes. I need hardly add that, until I arrived, all the guardians were men.

"I found that there were pregnant women in that workhouse, scrubbing floors, doing the hardest kind of work. Many of them were unmarried women, very, very young, mere girls. When they had their babies they had to make a choice of staying in the workhouse and earning their living by scrubbing and other work, in which case their babies were put in a boarding home; or of leaving with a newborn baby, without money, without anywhere to go. What became of those girls, and what became of their hapless infants?"

Charlotte was stunned. Could all this be true?

Mrs. Pankhurst's voice rose a fraction. "Under the law, a man who ruins a girl pays a lump sum of twenty pounds if the baby is placed in a boarding home. The home is immune from inspection as long as it takes in only one child at a time. Of course the babies die with hideous promptness. Then the baby farmers are free to solicit another victim. For years women have tried to get this aspect of the Poor Law changed, to make it impossible for any scoundrel to escape future liability for his child because he has paid down the lump sum. But we have always failed"—here her voice became a passionate cry—"because the only ones who really care about this are mere women!"

83

The audience burst into applause. Charlotte turned to the woman next to her and said, "Is this *true?*"

But Mrs. Pankhurst was speaking again. "In 1899 I was appointed to the office of registrar of births and deaths in Manchester. Even after my experience on the Board of Guardians I was shocked when little girls of thirteen came to register the births of their babies, illegitimate, of course. The age of consent is sixteen years, but a man can claim that he thought the girl was older. During my term of office a very young mother of an illegitimate child exposed her baby, and it died. The girl was tried for murder and sentenced to death. The father of the baby received no punishment at all.

"Many times in those days I asked myself what was to be done. I hoped that through the Labour Party might come a demand for women's enfranchisement that the politicians could not ignore. It did not.

"Finally, with the absolute conviction that no other course was open to us, we lighted the torch of militancy. Our years of work and sacrifice had taught us that the government would not yield to right and justice, only to expediency. Our task was to show the government that it was expedient to yield to women's just demands. In order to do that we had to make English life insecure and unsafe; we had to hurt business, destroy valuable property, upset the whole orderly conduct of society, even prostrate ourselves at the foot of the throne! We have to do this until the people of England come to the point of saying to the government, 'Stop this, in the only way it can be stopped, by giving the women of England representation.' Then we should extinguish our torch.

"Over one thousand of our women have gone to prison in the course of this agitation, have come out of prison injured in health, weakened in body but not in spirit. They are women who seriously believe that these horrible evils will never be removed until women get the vote. There is only one way to put a stop to this agitation. It is not by deporting us—"

"No!" someone shouted.

"It is not by locking us up in jail!"

The whole crowd shouted, "No!"

"It is by doing us justice!"

"Yes!"

Charlotte found herself shouting with the rest.

DURING THE DAY a dreadful suspicion had dawned on Lydia. After lunch she had gone to her room to lie down. She had been unable to think about anything but Feliks. She was still vulnerable to his magnetism; it was foolish to pretend otherwise. But she was no longer a helpless girl, and she was determined that she would not let Feliks wreck the placid life she had so carefully made for herself.

He had given Pritchard a false name. Clearly he had been afraid that she would not let him in. She realized why Konstantin Dmitrich Levin had seemed familiar: it was the name of a character in *Anna Karenina*, the book she had been buying when she first met Feliks. He was sly, to remind her of all that.

Suddenly Lydia began to wonder if Feliks had told her the truth about his reason for being in London. After all, he was still an anarchist. In 1895 he had been determinedly non-violent, but he might have changed.

If Stephen knew that I had told an anarchist where to find Aleks . . .

She had worried about it all through tea and dinner; nevertheless, it was not until the end of the evening, when she sat in her bedroom brushing her hair, that it occurred to her to connect Feliks and his cut hand with the madman in the park. The thought was so frightening that she dropped her gold-backed hairbrush onto the dressing table.

What if Feliks had come to London to kill Aleks?

She stared at herself in the mirror. The woman she saw there had grey eyes, blonde hair, a pretty face and the brain of a sparrow.

Could it be true? Could Feliks have deceived her so? Yes—because he had spent nineteen years imagining that she had betrayed him. She had to warn Stephen. She put on a cashmere robe over her silk nightgown and went through to his bedroom.

Stephen was sitting at the window, in pyjamas and a dressing gown, with a small glass of brandy in one hand and a cigar in the other. He stood up with a welcoming smile and embraced her.

She said, "I want to talk to you."

He released her. "At this time of night?"

"I think I may have done something awfully silly."

He sat down, and Lydia said, "A man called this morning. He said he had known me in St. Petersburg, and I thought I vaguely recalled him. . . ."

"What was his name?"

"Levin. He said he wanted to see Prince Orlov."

Stephen was suddenly very attentive. "Why?"

"Something to do with a sailor who had been unjustly imprisoned. This . . . Levin . . . wanted to make a personal plea for the man's release."

"What did you say?"

"I told him he'd gone to the Savoy Hotel."

"Damn," Stephen cursed, then apologized. "Pardon me."

"Afterwards it occurred to me that Levin might have been up to no good. He had a cut hand—and I remembered the madman in the park. . . . I've done something dreadful, haven't I?"

"It's not your fault. I should have told you that we suspected a plot against Aleks, but I didn't want to frighten you." He stood up. "I'll go and rouse Pritchard. He can drive me to the hotel."

Lydia said, "I'm so sorry."

"It may be for the best," Stephen said.

She looked at him in surprise. "Why?"

"Because, when he comes to the Savoy to assassinate Aleks, I shall catch him."

And then Lydia knew that before this was over, one of the two men she loved would surely kill the other.

FELIKS GENTLY LIFTED the bottle of nitroglycerine out of the washbasin. His pillow was on the mattress, and he enlarged the hole he had torn in it until it was about six inches long. He put the bottle into the pillow and arranged the stuffing all around it, like a cocoon. He picked up the pillow and, cradling it, placed it in his open suitcase. He closed the case and breathed more easily.

He put on his coat, his scarf and his respectable hat. Carefully he picked up the cardboard suitcase and went out.

The journey into the West End was a nightmare. Every time his foot hit the pavement he imagined the shock wave that must travel up his body and down his arm to the bomb in his case. Crossing Euston Road was a dance with death. He stood at the kerb for five minutes, waiting for a good-sized gap in the traffic, and then he almost ran across.

In Tottenham Court Road he went into a stationer's shop. An assistant in a morning coat said, "Can I help you, sir?"

"I need an envelope, please."

The assistant raised his eyebrows. "Just the one, sir?"

"Yes. White, and a sheet of paper."

"One sheet of paper, sir."

In Leicester Square he went into a bank, sat down at one of the writing tables and relaxed for a moment. Then he took a pen and wrote on the front of his envelope: "Prince A.A. Orlov, The Savoy Hotel, Strand, London W."

He folded the blank sheet of paper and slipped it inside the envelope, so it would not seem empty. He sealed it shut, then picked up the suitcase and left the bank.

He passed Charing Cross Station and walked east along the Embankment. Near Waterloo Bridge a group of urchins played, throwing stones at the seagulls on the river. Feliks spoke to the most intelligent-looking boy. "Do you want a penny?"

"Yes, guv!"

"Do you know where the Savoy Hotel is?"

"Too right!"

Feliks assumed this meant the same as "Yes." He handed the boy the envelope and a penny. "Count to a hundred slowly, then deliver this letter to the hotel. Do you understand?"

"Yes, guv!"

At the steps to the bridge, Feliks went into a newsagent's, where he bought *The Times*. When he left he turned off the Strand and went into the Savoy Hotel. In the lobby, he sat down and placed the suitcase on the floor between his feet. He could see both doors and the hall porter's desk. The lobby was crowded; it was just before ten o'clock. This is when the ruling class has breakfast, Feliks thought.

He examined the other people in the lobby over the top of *The Times*. There were two men who might be detectives. Feliks wondered whether they would impede his escape.

Through the glass door he saw the urchin coming up to the hotel entrance. Feliks could see the envelope in his hand; he held it by one corner, almost distastefully, as if it were dirty and he were clean. He approached the door but was stopped by a doorman in a top hat. There was some discussion; then the boy went away. The doorman came into the lobby with the envelope and handed it to the hall porter. The porter looked at it, picked up a pencil, scribbled something—a room number?—and summoned a pageboy.

It was working!

Feliks stood up, gently lifted his case and headed for the stairs. The pageboy passed him on the first landing and went on up. Felix allowed him to get one flight of stairs ahead, then quickened his step to keep him in view.

On the fourth floor, the boy walked along the corridor. Feliks stopped and watched.

The boy knocked on a door. It was opened. A hand came out, took the envelope and gave the boy a tip. He said, "Thank you very much indeed, sir." The door closed.

Feliks started to walk along the corridor.

The boy saw his case and reached for it, saying, "Can I help you with that, sir?"

"No!" Feliks said sharply, and the boy passed on.

Feliks walked to the door of Orlov's room and put the suitcase down on the carpet outside. He opened the case, reached inside the pillow and carefully withdrew the brown bottle.

He straightened up slowly; then he knocked on the door.

Chapter Eight

Walden looked at the envelope. He would have liked to know what was inside, but Aleks had moved out of the hotel and it was, after all, his mail.

Basil Thomson had no such scruples. He ripped the envelope open and took out a single sheet of paper. "Blank!" he said.

There was a knock at the door.

They all moved quickly. Thomson's two detectives moved to either side of the room and drew their guns. Walden stood behind a sofa, out of the line of fire, and Thomson stood in the middle of the room.

The knock came again.

Thomson called, "Come in. It's open."

The door opened, and there he stood—a tall man with a gaunt white face. In his left hand he held a brown bottle. His eyes swept the room, and he understood in a flash that this was a trap.

He lifted the bottle and said, "Nitro!"

"Don't shoot!" Thomson barked at the detectives.

Walden was sick with fear. He knew what nitroglycerine was; that if the bottle fell, they would all die.

There was a long moment of silence. Nobody moved.

Thomson broke the silence. "Give yourself up," he said. "Put the bottle on the floor. Stop being a fool."

The killer stood motionless, bottle raised high. He's looking at me, Walden realized. The man spoke to Walden in Russian: "You're not as stupid as you look." Then he was gone.

Walden made for the door. The other three were ahead of him. Out in the corridor, the detectives knelt on the floor, aiming their guns. Walden saw the killer running away, holding the bottle as steady as possible while he ran.

Walden thought, Could it kill us at this distance? Probably not. Thomson was thinking the same. He said, "Shoot!" Two guns crashed.

The killer stopped and turned. Was he hit?

He swung his arm and hurled the bottle at them. Thomson and the detectives threw themselves flat. The bottle turned over in the air as it flew at them. It was going to hit the floor five feet away from Walden. He ran *towards* the flying bottle.

It descended in a flat arc. He reached for it with both hands. He caught it, and like a goalkeeper catching a soccer ball, he cushioned it against his body and spun around in the direction of travel of the bottle; then he lost his balance and fell to his knees, still holding the bottle, and thinking, I'm going to die.

Nothing happened.

The others stared at him, on his knees, cradling the bottle in his arms like a newborn baby.

One of the detectives fainted.

FELIKS STARED IN AMAZEMENT at Walden for a split second longer; then he turned and raced down the stairs.

Walden was amazing. What a nerve, to catch that bottle!

He heard a distant shout. "Go after him!"

It's happening again, he thought; I'm running away again. What is the matter with me?

The stairs were endless. One pursuer was one or two flights behind him. He reached the foot of the staircase. He composed himself and walked into the lobby.

Out of the corner of his eye he spotted the two men he had identified as possible detectives. They were deep in conversation, looking worried; they must have heard distant gunfire.

He walked slowly across the lobby, fiercely resisting the urge to break into a run. He reached the door and went out.

"Cab, sir?" said the doorman.

Feliks jumped into a waiting cab and it pulled away.

As it turned into the Strand he looked back at the hotel. One of Thomson's detectives burst out of the door, followed by the two from the lobby. They spoke to the doorman, then drew their guns and ran after Feliks's cab.

The traffic was heavy. The cab stopped in the Strand. Feliks jumped out, dodged through the traffic to the far side of the road and ran north.

He looked back over his shoulder. They were still after him.

Feliks ran faster. His heart pounded and his breath came in ragged gasps. He turned a corner and found himself in the fruit and vegetable market of Covent Garden.

The cobbled streets were jammed with motor lorries and horse-drawn wagons. Everywhere there were porters carrying wooden trays on their heads or pushing handcarts.

Feliks plunged into the heart of the market. He hid behind a stack of empty crates and peered through the slats. After a moment he saw his pursuers. They stood still, looking around. There was some conversation; then they split up to search.

Feliks moved round the crates and found himself alone in a little backwater, concealed by the boxes all round him. It's Walden who's the danger, he thought. Twice now he's got in the way. Who would have thought an aristocrat with grey hair would have so much spunk? Feliks looked out. He could not see any of the detectives, so he walked out of the market and made his way back to the Strand.

He began to feel safe.

I ALMOST DIED, Walden kept thinking; I almost died.

He sat in the Savoy Hotel suite while Thomson gathered his team of detectives. Walden was fascinated to see a police manhunt swing into operation. Somebody gave him a glass of brandy and soda, and that was when he noticed that his hands were shaking. He could not put out of his mind the image of that bottle of nitroglycerine.

90

He tried to concentrate on Thomson, who was talking. "This man has slipped through our fingers. It is not going to happen again. We know something about him now, and we're going to find out a great deal more." He went on to assign his men to various lines of investigation: trying to pick up the lead to the killer among the Russians and anarchists of the East End, finding who had sold him the envelope, the bottle and the chemical ingredients of the bomb.

Walden was impressed. He had not realized that the killer had left behind so many clues. He began to feel better.

Thomson addressed a young man in a felt hat and soft collar. "Taylor, yours is the most important job. Lady Walden has had a good, long look at the killer. You'll come with us to see her ladyship, and with her help and ours you'll draw a picture of the fellow. I want the picture printed tonight and distributed to every police station in London by midday tomorrow."

Surely, Walden thought, the man cannot escape us now.

FELIKS LOOKED IN THE MIRROR. He had had his hair cut very short, like a Prussian's, and he had plucked his eyebrows until they were thin lines. He would stop shaving immediately. He had bought a pair of secondhand spectacles with wire rims. The lenses were small, so he could look over the top of them. He had changed his bowler hat and black coat for a sailor's blue pea-jacket and a tweed cap with a peak. To a passerby's casual glance he was a completely different man.

He knew he had to leave Bridget's house. He had bought all his chemicals within a mile or two of here, and when the police learned that, they would begin a house-to-house search. Sooner or later they would end up in this street. He gathered up his razor, his spare underwear, his homemade dynamite and his Pushkin novel, and tied them all up in his clean shirt. Then he went to Bridget's parlour.

"What have you done to yourself?" she said. "You used to be a handsome man."

"I must leave," he said. "If the police come, you don't have to lie to them."

"I'll say I threw you out because I suspected you were an anarchist."

"Goodbye, Bridget." Feliks kissed her cheek and went out.

"Good luck, boy," she called after him.

He took the bicycle, and for the third time since he had arrived in London, he went looking for lodgings.

He rode through North London and the City, then crossed the river at London Bridge. On the far side, he headed southeast, and in the region of the Old Kent Road he found the kind of slum where he could get cheap accommodation and no questions asked. He took a room on the fourth floor of a tenement owned, the caretaker told him, by the Church of England.

The room was grim. The one window was covered with a sheet of newspaper, the paint was peeling and the mattress stank. There was no running water in the building, and Feliks had to pay four weeks rent in advance.

He said, "Where can I keep my bicycle?"

"I'd bring it up here if I were you, or it'll get nicked. If you want to decorate, I can get you half-price paint."

"I'll let you know." The room was the least of his problems.

Tomorrow he had to start looking for Orlov again.

"STEPHEN! THANK HEAVEN, you're all right!" said Lydia.

He put his arm round her. "Of course I'm all right."

"What happened?"

"I'm afraid we didn't catch our man."

Lydia almost fainted with relief. Ever since Stephen had said "I shall catch him," she had been terrified twice over; terrified that Feliks would kill Stephen, and terrified that if not, she would be responsible for putting Feliks in jail for the second time in her life. She knew what he had gone through the first time, and the thought sickened her.

"You know Basil Thomson, I think," Stephen said, "and this is Mr. Taylor, the police artist. We're all going to help him draw the face of the killer."

Lydia's heart sank.

They sat down, and the artist got out his sketchbook. Over and over again he drew that face. At first she tried to make the artist get it wrong, by saying "Not quite" when something was exactly right and "That's it" when something was awry; but Stephen and Thomson had both seen Feliks clearly, if briefly, and they corrected her. They ended up with a very good likeness.

After that her nerves were so bad that she took a dose of laudanum and went to sleep. She dreamed that she was going to St. Petersburg to meet Feliks.

FELIKS WOKE UP angry with himself. The killing of Orlov was not a superhuman task. The man might be guarded, but Feliks was intelligent and determined. He could find a way.

So he got up, washed at the standpipe in the courtyard, had tea and bread at a street stall and cycled to St. James's Park. The first thing he saw was a uniformed policeman pacing up and down outside the Walden house. That meant he could not take up his usual position for observing; he had to retreat farther into the park.

At about midday a motorcar emerged from the house. He had not seen the car go in, so presumably it was Walden's.

Feliks cut across the grass to intercept the car, and it was a few yards ahead of him when he reached the road. He kept up with it easily around Trafalgar Square, and as it headed north up Charing Cross Road. At the end of Tottenham Court Road, the car turned east, and he risked going close enough to see inside. In the back was a man with grey hair and a beard—Walden!

I'll kill him too, Feliks thought. At the junction with King's Cross Road, the car turned north. The traffic was fairly heavy, and he was able to keep pace, although he was tiring. He began to hope that Walden was going to see Orlov. A house in North London, discreet and suburban, might be a good hiding place. His excitement mounted. He might be able to kill them both. After half a mile or so the traffic began to thin out. The car picked up speed and pulled remorselessly away from Feliks. When it was a quarter of a mile ahead and still accelerating, he gave up.

He coasted to a halt and sat bent over the handlebars, waiting to recover his strength. Walden was plainly going out of town. Orlov could be anywhere north of London within half a day's journey by fast motorcar. Feliks was utterly defeated—again.

For want of a better idea, he turned round and headed back towards St. James's Park.

THE DAY AFTER the suffragette meeting Charlotte was still tingling from Mrs. Pankhurst's speech. She saw all the women around her— servants, shop assistants, nurses in the park, even Mama—in a new light. She felt she was beginning to understand how the world worked and she wanted to find out things for herself, so that she could be sure of the truth.

In the morning she went shopping with a footman, and while he waited with the carriage at the main entrance to Liberty's, in Regent Street, she slipped out of a side entrance and walked until she found a woman selling the suffragette newspaper *Votes For Women*. It cost a penny. Then she returned to the carriage.

She read the paper in her room after lunch. She learned that the incident at the palace during her debut had not been the first demonstration before the King and Queen. Last December three suffragettes in beautiful evening gowns had barricaded themselves inside a box at Covent Garden Theatre, where the King and Queen were present with a large entourage. At the end of the first act, one of the suffragettes stood up and began to harangue the King through a megaphone. It took the police half an hour to break down the door and get the women out of the box. Then forty more suffragettes in the front rows of the balcony stood up, threw down showers of pamphlets and walked out en masse.

After this incident the King had refused to give an audience to Mrs. Pankhurst. Arguing that all subjects had a right to petition the King about their grievances, the suffragettes announced that a deputation of women would march to the palace.

Charlotte realized that the march was to take place today—this afternoon—now. She wanted to be there. It was no good understanding what was wrong if one did nothing about it.

Papa had gone off with Pritchard in the motorcar. Mama was lying down after lunch, as usual. There was nobody to stop her.

She put on her most unprepossessing hat and coat; then she went quietly down the stairs and out of the house.

FELIKS WALKED ABOUT the park, keeping the house always in view, racking his brains.

Somehow he had to find out where Walden was going in the motorcar. Could he try Lydia again? She would hardly tell him Orlov's hiding place, now that she no doubt knew why he wanted to know. Could he hide in Walden's motorcar? Could the chauffeur be bribed? Made drunk? Kidnapped?

Feliks's mind was elaborating these possibilities when he saw the girl come out of the house. She might be a servant, but she had come out of the main entrance. She could be Lydia's daughter and might know where Orlov was. He decided to follow her.

She walked towards Trafalgar Square. Leaving his bicycle in the bushes, Feliks went after her and got a closer look. He recalled that there had been a girl in the coach on the night he had first tried to kill Orlov. He was quite sure he had never looked closely at her, yet he had a strong sense of déjà vu as he watched her walk, straight-backed and with a determined, quick pace, through the streets. Occasionally he saw her face in profile when she turned to cross a road. Did she remind him of the young Lydia? Not at all, he realized; Lydia had always looked small and frail, and her features were all delicate. This girl had a strong-looking, angular face. It reminded Feliks of a painting by an Italian artist that he had seen in a Geneva gallery. After a moment the painter's name came back to him: Modigliani.

He got closer to her, and a minute later he saw her full-face. His heart skipped a beat, and he thought, She's just beautiful.

Where was she going? To meet a boyfriend, perhaps.

He heard a distant noise. He followed the girl round a corner. Suddenly he was in a street full of women, many wearing the suffragette colours of green, white and purple and carrying banners. Somewhere a band played marching tunes.

The girl joined the demonstration and began to march.

Feliks thought, Wonderful!

The route was lined with policemen facing the marchers, so Feliks could dodge along the pavement behind them, keeping the girl in sight. He had been in need of a piece of luck, and he had been given one.

One way or another, Feliks thought, I'll get what I want from her.

CHARLOTTE WAS THRILLED. The march was orderly, with female stewards keeping the women in line. Most of the marchers were well-dressed, respectable-looking types. The band played a jaunty two-step. There were even a few men. Charlotte no longer felt like a misfit with heretical views. Why, she thought, all these thousands of women think and feel as I do!

The march crossed Trafalgar Square and entered The Mall. Suddenly there were many more policemen, watching the women.

There were also many spectators, mostly male, along the sides of the road. They shouted and whistled derisively.

Charlotte noticed that many women carried a staff with a silver arrow at the top. She asked another marcher what it meant.

"The arrows on prison clothing," the woman replied. "All the women who carry that have been to jail."

"To jail!" Charlotte was taken aback. As she looked round she saw hundreds of silver arrows, and for the first time it occurred to her that she herself might end the day in prison. The thought made her feel weak. Then she squared her shoulders and marched in time to the band.

Buckingham Palace loomed up at the end of The Mall. A line of policemen, many on horseback, stretched before it. Charlotte was near the head of the procession; she wondered what the leaders intended to happen when they reached the line.

And then they were at the palace gates.

Last time I was here, Charlotte thought, I had an invitation.

The head of the procession came up against the line of policemen. For a moment there was deadlock. The people behind pressed forward. Suddenly Charlotte saw Mrs. Pankhurst. She wore a jacket and skirt of purple velvet, a high-necked white blouse and a green waistcoat. She had detached herself from the march and had managed to reach the far gate of the palace courtyard. She was such a brave little figure, marching with her head held high to the King's gate!

She was stopped by a police inspector, a burly man at least a foot taller than she. There was a brief exchange of words; then, to Charlotte's horror, the policeman grabbed Mrs. Pankhurst, lifted her off her feet and carried her away.

Charlotte was enraged, and so was every other woman in sight. The marchers pressed fiercely against the police line. The horses shifted, their ironshod hooves clattering threateningly on the pavement. Several women struggled with policemen and were thrown to the ground. A group of men in straw boaters waded into the crowd, pushing and punching the women, and Charlotte screamed, terrified. Suddenly a team of suffragettes wielding Indian clubs counter-attacked, and straw boaters flew everywhere. There were no longer any spectators; everyone was in the melee. Charlotte was pushed from behind and fell down, bruising her

knees. Someone trod on her hand. She tried to get up and was knocked down again. She realized she might be trampled by a horse and die. Desperately she hauled herself to her feet. The fighting was becoming vicious. She began to feel angry as well as scared. The men, police and civilians alike, punched and kicked women with relish. Charlotte thought hysterically, Why do they *grin* so? Suddenly she was confronted by a well-dressed man in his middle twenties. He punched her in the stomach with his fist. The shock was bad and the pain was worse, but what made her panic was that she could not breathe. She stood, bending forward, with her mouth open, sure she was going to die. She was vaguely aware of a tall man pushing past her, dividing the crowd as if it were a field of wheat. He grabbed the lapel of the young man and hit him on the chin, knocking him off his feet.

At last Charlotte was able to breathe, and she sucked in air with a great heave. The tall man put his arm firmly around her shoulders and said in her ear, "This way." She realized that she was being rescued.

The tall man propelled her towards the edge of the crowd. Suddenly they were out of it. Charlotte began to cry, but the man made her keep walking. "Let's get right away," he said. He spoke with a foreign accent. Charlotte followed him.

After a while he stopped outside a Lyons Corner House and said, "Would you like a cup of tea?"

She nodded, and they went in. He led her to a chair, then sat opposite her. She looked at him for the first time. With his long face and curved nose, he looked somehow rapacious. But then she saw that there was nothing but compassion in his eyes.

She took a deep breath and said, "How can I ever thank you?"

He ignored the question. "Would you like something to eat?"

"Just tea." She had recognized his accent, and she began to speak in Russian. "Where are you from?"

He looked pleased that she could speak his language. "I was born in Tambov province. You speak Russian very well."

"My mother is Russian, and my governess."

A waitress came, and he said, "Two teas, please, love."

Charlotte thought, He is learning English from cockneys. She said, "I don't know your name. I'm Charlotte Walden."

"Feliks Kschessinsky. You were brave, to join that march."

She shook her head. "Bravery had nothing to do with it. I simply didn't know it would be like that."

"What did you expect?"

"On the march? I don't know. . . . Why do those men *enjoy* attacking women?"

"That is an interesting question." He was suddenly animated. "You see, we put women on a pedestal and pretend they are pure in mind and helpless in body. So, in polite society at least, men must tell themselves that they feel no hostility towards women, ever. Now, here come some women—the suffragettes—who plainly are not helpless and need not be worshipped. What is more, they break the law. They deny the myths that men have made themselves believe, and so they can be assaulted with impunity, and the men give expression to all that repressed anger. That is a great release of tension, and they enjoy it."

Charlotte looked at him in amazement. It was fantastic—a complete explanation, just like that, off the top of his head! I like this man, she thought.

She said, "What do you do for a living?"

He became guarded. "Unemployed philosopher."

The tea restored Charlotte somewhat. She was intrigued by this tall Russian, and she wanted to draw him out. She said, "You seem to think that all this—putting women on a pedestal, worshipping them—is just as bad for men as it is for women."

"I'm sure of it."

"Why?"

He hesitated. "Men and women are happy when they love. Love and worship are not the same thing. When we worship a woman we cannot love her."

"I never thought of that," Charlotte said wonderingly.

He said, "I think you have been put on a pedestal yourself."

"You can't imagine how awful it is," she said fiercely. "To have been kept so ignorant!" She wanted to take him home, so that he could explain things to her day and night. She said, "How did things get like this—all this pretending?"

"I'm sure it has to do with power. Men have power over women, and rich men have power over poor men. A great many fantasies are required to legitimize this system—fantasies about monarchy, capitalism, breeding and sex. Without these fantasies someone would lose his power. And men will not give up power, unless it is taken from them by violence."

"Are you a revolutionary?"

He said in English, "I'll give you three guesses."

Charlotte laughed. She tipped back her head and chuckled richly, deep in her throat.

It was the laugh that did it.

Feliks was transported back in time twenty-five years, to a three-room hut in which a boy and a girl sat opposite one another at a crude table. On the fire was a pot containing a cabbage, a small piece of bacon fat and a great deal of water. Soon the father would be home for his supper. Thirteen-year-old Feliks had just told his eighteen-year-old sister, Natasha, a joke, and she threw back her head and laughed.

Feliks stared at Charlotte. She looked exactly like Natasha. He said, "How old are you?"

"Eighteen."

There occurred to Feliks a thought so astonishing, so incredible and so devastating that his heart stood still.

He swallowed, and said, "When is your birthday?"

"The second of January."

He gasped. She had been born exactly seven months after the wedding of Lydia and Walden; nine months after the last occasion on which Feliks had made love to Lydia.

And now Feliks knew the truth.

Charlotte was his daughter.

"WHAT IS IT?" Charlotte said to Feliks. "You look as if you'd seen a ghost."

"You reminded me of someone. Tell me all about yourself."

She frowned at him. He seemed to have a lump in his throat. She said, "You've got a cold coming."

"I never catch colds. Did you have a happy childhood?"

"You wouldn't ask that if you knew my governess. Her name is Marya and she's a Russian dragon: 'Little ladies *always* have clean hands.' She's still around—she's my chaperone now."

"Still, you had good food, and clothes, and you were never cold, and there was a doctor when you were sick."

"Is that supposed to make you happy?"

"I would have settled for it. What's your father like?"

For a complete stranger, Feliks was remarkably interested in her, Charlotte thought. "I think Papa is probably a terribly. *good* man. . . ."

"But?"

"He often treats me as a child." The intensity of Feliks's gaze was beginning to make her uncomfortable. "Papa is a very lovable man. Why are you so interested?"

He gave a twisted smile. "I've been fighting the ruling class all my life, but I rarely get the chance to talk to one of them."

Charlotte said, "I'm not a member of the ruling class, any more than one of my father's dogs is."

He smiled. "And what are you going to do with your life?"

"What a question! I suppose I shall have to marry."

"Why?"

"Well, Walden Hall won't come to me when Papa dies, you know. It goes with the title—and I can't be the Earl of Walden. It will be left to Peter, the elder of my twin cousins."

"I see."

"And I couldn't earn my own living."

"Of course you could."

"What could I do?"

Feliks shrugged. "Raise horses. Be a shopkeeper. Join the civil service. Become a professor of mathematics. Write a play."

"You talk as if I might do anything I put my mind to."

"I believe you could. But I have one quite serious idea. Your Russian is perfect. You could translate novels into English."

"Do you really think I could?"

"I've no doubt whatsoever."

Charlotte bit her lip. "Why is it that you have such faith in me and my parents haven't?"

He thought for a minute, then smiled. "If I had brought you up, you would complain that you were forced to do serious work all the time and were never allowed to go dancing."

"You've no children?"

He looked away. "I never married."

Charlotte was fascinated. "Did you want to?"

"Yes. But the girl married someone else."

"What was her name?" Charlotte could not resist asking.

101

"Lydia."

"That's my mother's name. Lydia Shatova. You must have heard of Count Shatov, if you know St. Petersburg."

"Yes, I have. Do you carry a watch?"

"What? No."

"Nor do I." He looked around and saw a clock on the wall.

Charlotte followed his glance. "Heavens, it's five o'clock! I intended to get home for tea." She stood up.

"Will you be in trouble?" he said, getting up.

"I expect so."

He went to the counter to pay, and then came and held the door for her. "I'll walk part of the way with you."

Feliks took her arm as they walked along the street. The sun was still strong. Charlotte said, "I love June."

"The weather in England is wonderful."

"Do you think so? You've never been to the south of France, then. We've a villa in Monte Carlo." She was struck by a thought. "I hope you don't think I'm boasting."

"Certainly not." He smiled. "You must realize that I think great wealth is something to be ashamed of, not proud of."

"Do you despise me, then?"

"No, but the wealth isn't yours."

"You're the most interesting person I've ever met," Charlotte said. "May I see you again?"

"Yes," he said.

"You *are* catching a cold," she said. "Your eyes are streaming."

"You must be right." He wiped his eyes. "Shall we meet at that café?"

"It's not very attractive, is it?" she said. "I know! We'll go to the National Gallery. Then, if I see somebody I know, we can pretend we aren't together."

"All right."

"Good! How about the day after tomorrow, at two o'clock?"

"Fine."

It occurred to her that she might not be able to get away. "If something goes wrong, can I send you a note?"

"Well . . . er . . . I move about a lot. . . ." He was struck by a thought. "But you can always leave a message with Mrs. Bridget Callahan at number nineteen Cork Street, in Camden Town."

102

She repeated the address. "I'll write that down as soon as I get home." She hesitated. "You must leave me here. I hope you won't be offended, but it really would be best if no one saw me with you." She held out her hand. "Goodbye."

"Goodbye." He shook her hand firmly.

She turned and walked away. There would be trouble when she got home, she thought, but somehow she did not care. She had found a true friend. She was very happy.

WALDEN ARRIVED AT Walden Hall suffering from nervous indigestion. He had rushed away from London as soon as the police artist had finished drawing the face of the assassin, and now he was fiercely impatient to get down to business with Aleks. He guessed that Aleks had a counter-proposal and hoped it was something he could present to Churchill as a triumph.

When he walked into the Octagon, Aleks got up eagerly and said, "What happened?"

"The man came, but we failed to catch him," Walden said.

Aleks looked away. "He came to kill me. . . ."

Walden felt a surge of pity for him. He was young, he had a huge responsibility, he was in a foreign country and a killer was stalking him. But there was no point in letting him brood. Walden put on a breezy tone of voice. "We have the man's description now. Thomson will catch him in a day or so. And you're safe here—he can't possibly find out where you are."

"We thought I was safe at the hotel—but he found me."

"That can't happen again." This was a bad start to a negotiating session, Walden reflected. "Have you had tea?"

"I'm not hungry."

"Let's go for a walk; it will give you an appetite for dinner."

"All right." Walden got a shotgun—for rabbits, he said—and they walked down to the Home Farm. One of the two bodyguards provided by Basil Thomson followed behind them.

Aleks admired the sturdy brick cottages of the tenants, the tall white-painted barns and the magnificent shire horses.

"I don't make any money out of the Home Farm, of course," Walden said. "All the profit is spent on new stock, or drainage, or buildings, or fencing . . . . but it sets a standard for the tenanted farms; and it will be worth a lot more when I die than it was when I

103

inherited it. It's a good method, even though I have to give something away."

Aleks smiled. "Which brings us back to the Balkans."

Thank heavens—at last, Walden thought.

"Shall I sum up?" Aleks went on, as he and Walden started back towards the house.

"By all means," Walden replied.

"There is an area of about ten thousand square miles, from Constantinople to Adrianople—it amounts to half of Thrace—which is at present part of Turkey. Its coastline guards the whole of the passage between the Black Sea and the Mediterranean." He paused. "Give us that, and we're on your side."

Walden concealed his excitement. Here was a real basis for bargaining. He said, "But it isn't ours to give away. Besides, I wonder how the Thracians would feel about it."

"They would rather belong to Russia than to Turkey."

"I expect they'd like to be independent."

Aleks gave a boyish smile. "Neither you nor I—nor, indeed, either of our governments—is in the least concerned about what the inhabitants of Thrace might prefer."

"Quite," Walden said. He was forced to agree. Aleks's combination of boyish charm and thoroughly grown-up brains kept putting him off-balance.

They walked up the hill that led to the back of Walden Hall and went into the house. Walden rang for a footman. "I'll telegraph Churchill, making an appointment for tomorrow at noon."

"Good," Aleks said. "Time is running short."

CHARLOTTE GOT A DEFINITE reaction from the footman who opened the door to her. "Oh! Thank goodness you're home, Lady Charlotte!" he said. "Lady Walden has been worried. She asked that you should be sent to her as soon as you arrived."

"I'll just go and tidy myself up," Charlotte said. She went up to her room and washed her face and unpinned her hair. She went behind a screen, took off her dress and slipped into a robe. She heard her bedroom door open.

"Charlotte!" It was Mama's voice.

Charlotte came from behind the screen, thinking, Oh, dear, she's going to be hysterical.

104

"We've been frantic with worry!" Lydia said.

"Well, here I am, safe and sound, so you can stop worrying."

Lydia reddened. "You impudent child!" she shrilled. She stepped forward and slapped Charlotte's face.

Charlotte fell back onto the bed. She was stunned, not by the blow but by the idea of it. Her mother had never struck her before. She said, "I shall never forgive you for that."

"That you should speak of forgiving *me!*" In her frantic rage Lydia was speaking Russian. "And how soon should I forgive you for joining a mob outside Buckingham Palace?"

Charlotte gasped. "How did you know?"

"Marya saw you marching along The Mall with those . . . those suffragettes. I feel so *ashamed*. God knows who else saw you. If the King finds out, we shall be banished from the court."

"I see." Charlotte was still smarting from the slap. "So you weren't worried about my safety, just the family reputation." Lydia looked hurt, and Charlotte went on, "Don't you think women should have the vote?"

"Certainly not, and you shouldn't think so, either."

"But I do," Charlotte said. "There it is."

"You know nothing; you're still a child."

"We always come back to that, don't we? I'm a child. Well, you know perfectly well that I'm nothing of the kind. You would be quite happy to see me married by Christmas. And some girls are mothers by the age of thirteen, married or not."

Mama was shocked. "Who tells you such things?"

"Certainly not Marya. She never told me anything important. Nor did you."

Mama said plaintively, "I only want you to be happy!"

"No, you don't," Charlotte said stubbornly. "You want me to be like you."

"No, no, no!" Mama cried. "I don't want you to be like me! I don't!" She burst into tears and ran from the room.

Charlotte stared after her, mystified and ashamed.

FELIKS COULD NOT STOP crying. His heart was breaking.

People stared at him as he walked through the park to retrieve his bicycle. He shook with uncontrollable sobs, and the tears poured down his face. He was helpless with grief, weeping not for what he

105

had found, but for what he had lost. For eighteen years he had been a father without knowing it.

He found the bicycle where he had left it beneath a bush and sat down on the grass beside it. This beautiful, brave, inquisitive, admirable young woman, he thought, and I'm her father.

What was it she had said? *You're the most interesting person I've ever met. May I see you again?* He had been preparing to say goodbye to her for ever. When he knew that he would not have to, his self-control had begun to disintegrate.

I'm becoming maudlin, he thought. I must pull myself together.

He stood and picked up the bicycle. It was suppertime, but he knew he would not be able to eat. He mounted the bicycle and made his way back to the tenement, where he carried the machine up the stairs to his room on the top floor. He took off his hat and coat and lay on the bed.

He would see her again in two days. They would look at paintings together. He cast his mind back to the moment when she came out of the house.

He had seen her from a distance, never dreaming . . . What was I thinking of at that moment? he wondered.

And then he remembered.

I was wondering whether she might know where Orlov is. In all probability she *does* know where he is; if not, she could find out. I might use her to help me kill him. Am I capable of that?

No, I am not. I will not do it. No, no, no!

What is happening to me?

WALDEN SAW CHURCHILL at the Admiralty at noon. The first lord was impressed. "Thrace," he said. "Surely we can give them half of Thrace. Who cares if they have the whole of it!"

"That's what I thought," Walden said. He was pleased with Churchill's reaction. "Now, will your colleagues agree?"

"I believe they will," Churchill said thoughtfully. "I'll see Grey after lunch and Asquith this evening."

"And the Cabinet?"

"Tomorrow morning." Churchill stood up. "Have they caught that damned anarchist yet?"

"I'm having lunch with Basil Thomson of the Special Branch—I'll find out then."

"Keep me informed."

"Naturally."

Walden was in a buoyant mood as he walked from the Admiralty to his club in Pall Mall. Just inside the door he handed his hat and gloves to a servant. The weather had been remarkably fine for months Walden reflected, as he went up to the dining room. When it broke, there would probably be storms. We shall have thunder in August, he thought.

Thomson was waiting. They shook hands, and Walden sat down. A waiter brought the menu. They ordered, and Walden chose a bottle of hock.

"Well?" said Walden. "Have you caught him?"

"All but," Thomson said.

That meant no. Walden's heart sank. "I wonder if you realize how important this is?" he said. "My negotiations with Prince Orlov are almost complete. If he were to be assassinated, the whole thing would fall through—with serious consequences for the security of this country."

"I do realize, my lord," said Thomson. "Let me tell you what progress we've made. Our man is Feliks Kschessinsky. He is thirty-eight, the son of a country priest, and he comes from Tambov province. St. Petersburg has a thick file on him; he's been arrested three times." Thomson went on to trace Feliks's movements until his disappearance from Bridget Callahan's.

The soup came, and the two men ate in silence. Walden liked this club for its relaxed atmosphere. The chairs were old and comfortable, the waiters were old and slow, the wallpaper was faded and the paintwork was dull.

As the poached salmon arrived, Walden said, "Do you think Mrs. Callahan knows where our man went?"

"If she does, she won't say. The point is, Feliks may return to her place. I'm having it watched. One of my men has rented his old room in the basement."

A waiter served them a slice of mutton from the joint. Walden said, "What's your next move?"

"The picture of Feliks Kschessinsky is pinned up in every police station in London. He's bound to be spotted by an observant bobby sooner or later. And in addition, my men are visiting cheap hotels and lodging houses, showing the picture."

It was all too vague, Walden felt. Feliks was *loose*, and he would not feel safe until the fellow was locked up.

Thomson said, "Feliks is clever, and formidably determined. We have hidden Orlov away, but by contrast you are still walking about London as large as life."

"Why should I not?"

"If I were Feliks, I would attempt to kidnap and torture you until you told me where Orlov was. I want you to travel by motorcar—your Lanchester will do—and I want you to have a bodyguard."

Walden shook his head. "I've got my man Pritchard. He would risk his life for me."

"Can he shoot?"

"Very well."

"Then let him carry a pistol."

"All right," Walden assented.

To finish the meal, Walden had a peach and Thomson a pear. Afterwards, they left the club and took a cab to Walden's house; then Thomson went on in the cab to Scotland Yard.

Walden entered the house, feeling the need to talk. He looked at his watch: Lydia would have had her siesta by now and would be ready to have tea. He went through to her room.

She was sitting at her mirror in a robe. He put his hands on her shoulders, looking at her reflection, then bent to kiss the top of her head. "Feliks Kschessinsky."

"*What?*" She seemed frightened.

"That's the name of our assassin. Do you recognize it?"

"No."

"I thought it seemed to mean something to you."

Walden went to the window and looked out over the park. The paths were crowded with perambulators, and every bench was occupied. He said, "Thomson believes that when Feliks realizes Aleks is hidden away, he will try to kidnap me."

Lydia got up from her chair and came to him. She put her arms round his waist and looked up at him, and to his surprise he saw that her grey eyes were full of tears. He could feel the warmth of her body through the robe. He wanted to make love to her, right now.

He kissed her, and she pressed her body against his. He could not remember her being like this ever before. He went to the door, thinking to lock it.

108

Someone knocked.

"Damn!" Walden said quietly.

Lydia dabbed at her eyes with a handkerchief.

Pritchard came in. "Excuse me, my lord. An urgent telephone communication from Mr. Basil Thomson. They have tracked the man Feliks to his lodging. If you want to be in at the kill, Mr. Thomson will pick you up here in three minutes."

"Get my hat and coat," Walden told him.

Chapter Nine

Every time Feliks considered exactly how he would bamboozle Charlotte into telling him the whereabouts of Orlov, he seemed to run up against a brick wall in his mind; his imagination recoiled at each visualized scene.

Yet, when he thought about what was at stake, he found his feelings ridiculous. He had a chance to save millions of lives and possibly spark off the Russian revolution—and he was worried about deceiving an upper-class girl! It was not as if he intended to do her any harm—just use her, deceive her and betray her trust, his own daughter, whom he had only just met . . .

To occupy his hands he fashioned his homemade dynamite into a primitive bomb. He packed the nitroglycerine-soaked cotton into a cracked china vase. He stuffed half a dozen matches into the cotton, upright, so that only their bright red heads showed. It was difficult to get the matches to stand upright, because his hands were unsteady.

My hands never shake. What is happening to me?

He twisted a piece of newspaper into a taper and stuck one end into the middle of the match heads, then tied the heads together. He longed to see Charlotte again.

He heard shuffling footsteps on the landing outside; there was a knock at the door.

"Come in," he called carelessly.

The caretaker came in, coughing. "Morning."

"Good morning, Mr. Price." *What did the old fool want now?*

"What's that?" said Price, nodding at the bomb on the table

"Homemade candle," Feliks said. "What do you want?"

"I wondered if you needed a spare pair of sheets. I can get them at a very low price—"

"No, thank you," Feliks said. "Goodbye."

"Goodbye, then." Price went out.

I should have hidden that bomb, thought Feliks. What is happening to me?

"YES, HE'S IN THERE," Price said to Basil Thomson.

Tension knotted in Walden's stomach.

They sat in the back of a police car parked round the corner from Canada Buildings, where Feliks was. With them were an Inspector Sutton, from the Special Branch, and a uniformed superintendent from the nearest police station.

Thomson said, "Mr. Price identified Feliks from our artist's drawing. Well done, Price."

"Thank you, sir."

The police superintendent unfolded a plan. "Canada Buildings consists of three four-storey tenements around a courtyard. Feliks is on the top floor of Toronto House. Behind Toronto House is the yard of a builder's supply store. On your left is Vancouver House, and the third building is Montreal House, which backs onto the railway line."

Thomson directed the superintendent to dispose his men in order to block all possible routes of escape. "Finally," he said, "let's have a nice show of strength there in the courtyard. Does that meet with your approval, Superintendent?"

"More than adequate, I'd say, sir."

He doesn't know the man we're dealing with, Walden thought.

Thomson said, "You and Inspector Sutton here can make the arrest. Got your gun, Sutton?"

Sutton pulled aside his coat to show a small revolver. Walden had thought that no British policeman ever carried a firearm, but obviously the Special Branch was different.

Thomson said, "Let's go."

FELIKS REALIZED he was hungry. He had not eaten for more than twenty-four hours. Money was getting to be a problem. Surely the caretaker knows I've no money, he thought. He was an optimist to think I could afford a pair of sheets! Suddenly Price's reason for coming to Feliks's room seemed suspect. Feliks stood up and went to the window.

He stared down in horror; the courtyard was alive with blue-uniformed policemen. His instincts screamed, Run! Run! Run!

Where? They had blocked all exits from the courtyard. Then he remembered the back windows.

He ran from his room and along the landing to the back of the tenement. From a window there, he peered down into the builder's yard and saw five or six policemen taking up positions among stacks of planking. No exit that way.

That left only the roof.

He ran back to his room and looked out. Two men—one in uniform and one in plain clothes—were walking towards Feliks's stairway. He picked up his bomb and the box of matches and ran down to the landing below. There was a cupboard beneath the stairs, and Feliks opened it and placed the bomb inside. He lighted the fuse and closed the door. He turned round. He could run up the stairs before the fuse burned down. . . .

A baby girl was crawling up the stairs. *Damn.*

He picked her up and dashed through an open door into a room where a woman sat on a dirty bed. Feliks thrust the baby into her arms and yelled, "Stay here! Don't move!"

He ran out. The two men were one floor down. Feliks raced up the stairs to his landing. They heard him, and one shouted, "Hey, you!" They broke into a run.

Feliks dashed into his room, picked up the chair, carried it out to the landing and positioned it directly under the trapdoor leading to the loft. As the two men reached the stairs to the top floor he pushed open the trapdoor.

The uniformed policeman shouted, "You're under arrest!"

The plain-clothes man raised a gun and pointed it at Feliks.

The bomb went off.

There was a big, dull thud and the staircase broke up into matchwood, the two men were flung backwards and the flying debris burst into flames. Feliks hauled himself up into the loft. .

WALDEN HEARD THE EXPLOSION and thought, It's going wrong again. Shards of glass crashed to the ground. He and Thomson ran across the courtyard.

Thomson picked two policemen at random and ordered, "Come with me." He turned to Walden. "You stay here."

Walden backed across the courtyard, looking up at the broken windows of Toronto House.

Where is Feliks?

The residents were coming to their doors and windows to see what was going on, and the courtyard began to fill with people. A woman ran out of Toronto House, screaming, "Fire!"

Thomson and a policeman came out carrying Inspector Sutton. He was unconscious, his pistol still in his hand.

Some slates fell from the roof, and Walden looked up. There was a hole in the roof, and Feliks was climbing up through it.

"There he is!" Walden yelled.

They all watched, helpless, as Feliks crawled onto the roof.

Walden knelt over the unconscious body of Sutton and prised the pistol from his fingers. He looked up again. Feliks was kneeling on the ridge of the roof. Walden lifted the gun and sighted along the barrel. Feliks looked at him. Their eyes met.

A shot rang out. Feliks felt nothing. He began to run.

It was like running along a tightrope. He had to hold out his arms for balance and place his feet squarely on the narrow ridge. He avoided thinking of the fifty-foot drop to the courtyard.

There was another shot. The end of the roof loomed up. He could see the down-sloping roof of Montreal House ahead. He had no idea how wide the gap was between the two buildings. He slowed down, hesitating; then Walden fired again.

Feliks ran full tilt towards the end of the ridge.

He jumped. He flew through the air. He caught a glimpse of policemen staring up at him, open-mouthed, then he hit the roof of Montreal House, landing hard on his hands and knees.

The impact winded him. He slid backwards down the roof until his feet hit the gutter and he stopped.

He was frightened. His mind protested, But I'm never frightened! He scrambled to the roof-peak and down the other side.

Montreal House backed on to the railway. There were no policemen on the lines or the embankment. They didn't anticipate this, Feliks thought exultantly; they thought I was trapped in the courtyard; it never occurred to them that I might be able to escape over the rooftops.

He peered down at the wall of the building. There were no drainpipes; the gutters emptied through spouts from the roof. But the top-floor windows had wide ledges.

Feliks positioned himself over a window, gripped the gutter with both hands, and eased himself over the edge until his feet found the window ledge.

He took his right hand from the gutter and got his fingers into a shallow groove in the brickwork round the window, then let go of the gutter with his other hand.

He kicked the window in and dropped into the room. He rushed out through the doorway and down the stairs.

He reached the last landing and stopped at the top of the stairs, breathing hard. A blue uniform appeared at the front entrance. Feliks spun round and raced to the back of the landing. He lifted the window. It stuck. He gave a mighty heave and threw it open. He heard boots running up the stairs. He clambered over the window-sill, hung by his hands for a moment, then dropped.

He landed in the long grass of the railway embankment. To his right, two policemen were jumping over the fence of the builder's yard.

Feliks ran up the embankment. There were four or five pairs of railway lines. In the distance, a train was approaching fast on what seemed to be the furthermost track. He broke into a run, to cross in front of the train.

The two policemen from the builder's yard chased him, and a shot rang out. He began to duck and zigzag. The train sounded very loud. He heard its whistle. There was another shot. He stumbled and fell onto the last railway line. There was a terrific thunder in his ears as the locomotive bore down on him. He jerked convulsively, catapulting himself off the line onto the gravel on the far side. The train roared past. He caught a split-second glimpse of the engine driver's face, white and scared.

He stood up and ran down the embankment.

WALDEN STOOD WITH Basil Thomson, waiting for the train to pass. It seemed to take for ever.

When it had gone, there was no sign of Feliks.

"The bastard's got away," a policeman said.

Walden turned and walked back to the car.

FELIKS DROPPED OVER a wall and found himself in a poor street of small terraced houses.

He kept running until he reached a busy shopping thoroughfare. There, on impulse, he jumped onto an omnibus.

He had escaped, but he was terribly worried. He remembered the thought in his mind as he slid down the roof: I don't want to die. In Siberia he had lost the ability to feel fear. Now it had come back. For the first time in years he wanted to stay alive. I have become human again, he thought.

It was a disaster. It would slow him down, cramp his style, interfere with his work. I'm afraid, he thought. I want to live.

I want to see Charlotte again.

THE FIRST TRAM of the day woke Feliks. He opened his eyes and watched it go by, striking bright blue sparks from the overhead cable. He lay on the pavement under Waterloo Bridge, his body wrapped in a blanket of newspapers. He got up, aching after a night in the cold street, and walked out into the sunshine. Today he was to meet Charlotte, and she would be smelling of perfume and dressed in silk. No doubt he looked and smelled like a tramp. He went looking for a municipal bathhouse.

He found one, with a notice on the door announcing that it would open at nine o'clock. Feliks thought it typical of a capitalist government to build a bathhouse for working men, then open it only when everyone was at work.

He found a tea stall near Waterloo Station and had breakfast. He was tempted by the fried-egg sandwiches, but he could not afford one. He had his usual bread and tea and saved the money for *The Times*. He went to sit on a bench outside the bathhouse and read the paper while he waited for the place to open.

The news shocked him to the core.

AUSTRIAN HEIR AND HIS WIFE MURDERED
SHOT IN BOSNIAN TOWN
A STUDENT'S POLITICAL CRIME

The Austro-Hungarian Heir-Presumptive, the Archduke Francis Ferdinand, and his wife, the Duchess of Hohenberg, were assassinated yesterday morning at Serajevo [sic], the capital of Bosnia.

114

The assassin is described as a high school student, who fired bullets at his victims with fatal effect . . . as they were returning from a reception at the Town Hall. . . .

Felix was stunned. He was delighted that another aristocratic parasite had been destroyed, but what occupied his mind most was what must surely follow. The Austrians, with the Germans backing them, would take their revenge on Serbia. The Russians would protest. Would the Russians mobilize their army? France was bound to them by treaty; if they were confident of British support as well, they probably would. Russian mobilization would mean German mobilization; and once the Germans had mobilized, no one could stop their generals from going to war.

There was no real reason for Russia to go to war, Feliks thought angrily. The same applied to England. It was France and Germany that were belligerent: since 1871 the French had wanted to win back their lost territories of Alsace and Lorraine.

What might stop Russia from going to war? A quarrel with her allies. What would cause a quarrel? The killing of Orlov.

If the assassination in Sarajevo could start a war, another assassination in London could stop a war.

And Charlotte could help him find Orlov. Feliks knew now that he *would* use her. His whole life seemed to lead up to the murder of Orlov. There was a momentum in his progress towards that goal, and he could not be deflected, even by the knowledge that his life had been founded on a mistake. Poor Charlotte.

The bathhouse doors opened, and Feliks went in to wash.

CHARLOTTE HAD IT ALL PLANNED. Lunch was at one o'clock, and by two thirty Mama would be in her room, lying down. Charlotte would be able to sneak out of the house in time to meet Feliks at three. She would spend an hour with him. By four thirty she would be at home, washed and changed and demurely ready to pour tea and receive callers with Mama.

It was not to be. Late that morning Lydia said, "Oh, I forgot to tell you—we're lunching with the Duchess of Middlesex."

"Oh, dear," Charlotte said. "I really don't feel like a luncheon party."

"Don't be silly, you'll have a lovely time."

116

Charlotte tried again. "I'm sorry, Mama, but I don't want to go."

"You're coming, and no nonsense," Mama said. "I want the Duchess to get to know you; she is most useful. And the Marquess of Chalfont will be there. He's charming, don't you think?"

"Who is the Marquess of Chalfont?"

"You know, Freddie. You met him at Belinda's party."

"Oh, him. Charming? I haven't noticed."

Luncheon parties generally started at one thirty and went on till past three. I might be home by three thirty, so I could get to the National Gallery by four, Charlotte thought; but by then he will have given up and left. I could send a note to that address in Camden Town, but he wouldn't get it before three o'clock.

Mama was saying, "I fancy you may have bewitched him."

"Who?"

"*Freddie*. Charlotte, you really must pay a little attention to a young man when he pays attention to you."

So that was why she was so keen on this lunch party. "Oh, Mama, don't be silly."

"All right, I won't tease. Go and change. Put on that cream dress with the brown lace; it suits your colouring."

Charlotte gave in. She got dressed, and in due course they went to the Duchess's house in Grosvenor Square.

The lunch was a ladies' party. The only men present, apart from Freddie, were a nephew of the Duchess and a Conservative member of Parliament. Of course it was difficult for the Duchess of Middlesex to have interesting parties, because so many people were banned from her table: all Liberals, all Jews, anybody in trade, anybody who was on the stage, and all divorcées. It made for a dull circle of friends.

The Duchess's favourite topic was the question of what was ruining the country. Today, however, the ruin of England took second place to the Archduke's death. The Duchess had a theory about the bomb-thrower at Sarajevo. Her doctor had explained that all suffragettes had a nervous ailment known as hysteria. In her view, the revolutionaries suffered from the male equivalent of this disease.

Charlotte, who had read *The Times* from cover to cover that morning, said, "On the other hand, perhaps the Serbs simply don't want to be ruled by Austria." Lydia gave her a black look, and everyone else ignored what she had said.

Freddie was sitting next to her. He said in a low voice, "I say, anyone would think you approved of shooting archdukes."

"I think if the Austrians tried to take over England, you would shoot archdukes, wouldn't you?"

"You're priceless," Freddie said.

Charlotte turned away from him. By this time she felt as if she were in jail. A carriage clock on the mantel struck three. Feliks was now waiting for her on the steps of the National Gallery. She had to get out of the Duchess's house.

Mr. Shakespeare, the Conservative MP, said, "I must get back to the House." His wife stood up to go. Charlotte saw a way out and, pleading a headache, she arranged with the Shakespeares to accompany them.

Mama was talking to the Duchess. Charlotte interrupted them and repeated the headache story. "I know Mama would like to stay a little longer, so I'm going with the Shakespeares. Thank you for a lovely lunch, your grace."

The Duchess nodded regally.

I managed that rather well, Charlotte thought, as she walked out into the hall and down the stairs.

She gave her address to the Shakespeares' coachman, and at three twenty she was standing outside her home, watching the coach drive off, after having been advised by Mrs. Shakespeare to take a spoonful of laudanum for the headache. Instead, she headed for Trafalgar Square.

She arrived just after three thirty and ran up the steps of the National Gallery. She could not see Feliks. Then he emerged from behind one of the massive pillars.

"I'm sorry to have made you wait about," she said as she shook his hand. "I got involved in a dreadful luncheon party."

"It doesn't matter, now that you're here."

They went inside. Charlotte loved the cool, hushed museum, with its glass domes and marble pillars, and the paintings shouting out colour and beauty and passion.

He turned his sad dark eyes on her. "There's going to be a war." He seemed actually moved by the possibility.

Charlotte said, "Why are you so concerned? Shall you have to fight?"

"I'm too old. But I think of all the millions of innocent Russian

118

boys who will be crippled or blinded or killed in a cause they don't understand and wouldn't care about if they did."

Charlotte said, "I never looked at it that way."

"The Earl of Walden never looked at it that way, either. That's why he is making it happen."

Charlotte frowned, puzzled. "What do you mean?"

"That's why Prince Orlov is here."

Her puzzlement deepened. "How do you know about Aleks?"

"I know more about it than you do. Walden and Orlov are negotiating a treaty, the effect of which will be to drag Russia into the war on the British side. I'm afraid Walden doesn't care how many Russian peasants die, so long as England dominates Europe."

Yes, of course, Papa would see it in those terms, she thought. "It's awful," she said. "Why don't you *tell* people?"

"Who would listen? We need a dramatic way of bringing the thing to their notice."

"Such as?"

Feliks looked at her. "Such as kidnapping Prince Orlov."

The idea was so outrageous that she laughed, then stopped abruptly. "You don't mean that," she said incredulously.

"I'll explain it to you." He led her to a seat. "The Czar already distrusts the English, because they let political refugees like me come to England. If one of us were to kidnap his favourite nephew, there would be a real quarrel, and then they could not be sure of each other's help in a war. Do you see?"

Charlotte watched his face as he talked. He was quiet, reasonable, and everything he said made sense, but it seemed to be about a different world, not the world she lived in.

"I do see," she said. "But you can't kidnap Aleks; he's such a nice man."

"That *nice man* will lead a million other nice men to their deaths if he's allowed to. Half the misery in the world is caused by nice men like Orlov, who think they have the right to organize wars."

She was struck by a frightening thought. "You've already tried once to kidnap him."

He nodded. "In the park. You were in the carriage. It went wrong."

"Oh, my word." She felt sickened and depressed.

He took her hand. "You know I'm right, don't you?"

119

It seemed to her that he *was* right. His world was the real world; she was the one who lived in a fairy tale, where debutantes in white were presented to the King and Queen.

"I know you're right," she said to Feliks.

"That's very important," he said. "You hold the key to the whole thing. I need your help. You see, I can't find Orlov."

She felt miserable and trapped. She wanted to help Feliks, but Aleks was her cousin. How could she betray him?

"I don't know where Aleks is," she said evasively.

"But you could find out. Will you?"

"I don't know."

He looked crestfallen. "I wish I didn't have to ask you."

She squeezed his hand. "I'll think about it."

He opened his mouth, but she put a finger to his lips to silence him. "You'll have to be satisfied with that," she said.

AT SEVEN THIRTY WALDEN went out in his Lanchester, wearing evening dress and a silk hat. Pritchard was in the driver's seat, with a revolver holstered beneath his jacket. They drove to the back entrance of Number 10 Downing Street. Now Walden was to hear whether or not the Cabinet had approved the deal he had worked out with Aleks.

He was shown into the small dining room. Churchill was already there with Lord Asquith, the prime minister.

Asquith said, "I'm afraid the Cabinet would not approve your proposal."

Walden's heart sank. "Why not?"

"The opposition came mainly from Lloyd George."

Walden looked at Churchill and raised his eyebrows.

Churchill nodded. "L.G. says we're passing the Balkans around like a box of chocolates: help yourself—Thrace, Bosnia, Bulgaria, Serbia. Small countries have their rights, he says. That's what comes of having a Welshman in the Cabinet."

They sat down to dinner. At the end of the first course, Asquith said, "We must have this treaty, you know. There will be a war between France and Germany sooner or later; and if the Russians stay out of it, Germany will conquer Europe."

Walden asked, "What must be done to make Lloyd George change his mind?"

120

The butler served a quail to each man and poured claret. Churchill said, "We must come up with a modified proposal which will meet L.G.'s objection."

Churchill's casual tone infuriated Walden. "You know perfectly well it's not that simple," he snapped. "I've spent the past month beating the Russians down."

"Still, the murder of Francis Ferdinand changes the complexion of things," Asquith said. "Now that Austria is getting aggressive in the Balkans again, the Russians need more than ever that toehold in the area which, in principle, we're trying to give them."

Walden set aside his disappointment and thought constructively. After a moment he said, "What about Constantinople?"

"What do you mean?"

"Suppose we offered Constantinople to the Russians. Would Lloyd George object to that?"

Asquith put down his knife and fork. "Well. Now that he has made his principled stand, he may be keen to show how reasonable he can be when offered a compromise. I think he may agree to it. Will it be enough for the Russians?"

Walden was not sure, but impulsively he said, "If you can sell it to Lloyd George, I can sell it to Orlov."

"Splendid!" said Asquith. "Now, what about the anarchist?"

Walden's optimism was punctured. "They're doing everything possible to protect Aleks, but it's still damned worrying."

"I thought Basil Thomson was a good man."

"Excellent," Walden said. "But I'm afraid Feliks might be even better."

Churchill said, "I don't think we should let the fellow *frighten* us—"

"I *am* frightened, gentlemen," Walden interrupted. "Three times Feliks has slipped through our grasp; the last time we had thirty policemen to arrest him. I don't see how he can get at Aleks now, but that doesn't mean that *he* can't see a way. And we know what will happen if Aleks is killed: our alliance with Russia will fall through. Feliks is the most dangerous man in England."

Asquith nodded, his expression sombre. "If you're less than perfectly satisfied with the protection Orlov is getting, please contact me directly."

Walden refused the cigar which the butler offered. "Life must go

121

on," he said, "and I must go to a reception at Mrs. Glenville's."

He finished his wine and stood up. The butler brought his hat and gloves, and he took his leave.

At home, Walden went upstairs to wash his hands. On the landing he met Charlotte. "Is Mama getting ready?" he asked.

"Yes, she'll be a few minutes. How goes your politicking?"

"Slowly. But don't you worry your pretty little head—"

"I shan't worry. But where on earth have you hidden Aleks?"

He hesitated. There was no harm in her knowing; yet once she knew, she would be capable of accidentally letting the secret out. Better for her to be left in the dark. He said, "If anyone asks you, say you don't know." He smiled and went on up to his room.

THERE WERE TIMES when the charm of English life wore thin for Lydia. Usually she enjoyed cocktail receptions. Several hundred people would gather at someone's home to do nothing whatsoever. You shook hands with the hostess, took a glass of champagne and wandered round some great house chatting to your friends. But today she was too worried—about Stephen, about Feliks and about Charlotte—to enjoy socializing.

She ascended the broad staircase, with Stephen on one side and Charlotte on the other. Her diamond necklace was admired by Mrs. Grenville. They moved on. Stephen peeled off to talk to one of his cronies in the House of Lords.

Charlotte said, "By the way, Mama, where has Aleks gone?"

"I don't know, dear," Lydia said absently. "Ask your father. Good evening, Freddie." She moved on, leaving Charlotte with Freddie Chalfont, and in a room where a string quartet played inaudibly she met her sister-in-law, Clarissa. They talked about their daughters, and Lydia was secretly comforted to learn that Clarissa was terribly worried about Belinda. "She goes to the most dreadful places to listen to jazz music, and last week she went to a boxing match!"

"What about her chaperone?"

Clarissa sighed. "I've said she can go out without a chaperone if she's with girls we know. Now I realize that was a mistake."

Lydia said, "Charlotte is frightfully disobedient. Once she sneaked out and went to a suffragette meeting."

"We must marry them off quickly, before they come to any harm," said Clarissa.

122

"Yes, absolutely!" Lydia moved on, feeling better.

The Duchess of Middlesex was in the next room. Lydia approached her, and the Duchess said, "I gather Charlotte is quite recovered from her headache."

"Yes, indeed; it's kind of you to inquire."

"Oh, I wasn't inquiring," the Duchess said. "My nephew saw her in the National Gallery at four o'clock."

The National Gallery! She had sneaked out again! But Lydia was not going to let on to the Duchess. "She has always been fond of art," she improvised.

"She was with a man," the Duchess said. "Who is he?"

"Just one of their set," Lydia said desperately.

"Oh, no," said the Duchess with a malicious smile. "He was about forty, and wearing a tweed cap."

"A tweed cap!" Lydia was being humiliated, and she knew it.

The Duchess went on, "In my day the chaperone system was found effective in preventing this sort of thing."

Lydia was suddenly very angry at the pleasure the Duchess was taking in this catastrophe. "That was a hundred years ago," she snapped. She walked away. A tweed cap! Forty years old! Oh, Charlotte, Charlotte, what are you doing to yourself?

CHARLOTTE WAS CHATTING with Belinda when Mama walked past and said, "We're leaving, Charlotte."

Belinda said, "She looks cross."

Charlotte shrugged. "Nothing unusual in that. I'd better go."

Charlotte went down the stairs and got her wrap from the cloakroom. She felt as if two people were inhabiting her skin: one who smiled and talked to Belinda about girlish matters, one who thought about kidnapping and treachery and asked sly questions in an innocent tone. She went outside and said to the footman, "The Earl of Walden's car."

A couple of minutes later the Lanchester pulled up at the kerb. Pritchard got out and held the door for Charlotte.

She said, "Pritchard, where is Prince Orlov?"

"It's supposed to be a secret, m'lady. I'd rather you asked your papa."

It was no good. She gave up, and said, "You'd better go into the hall and tell them I'm waiting in the car."

123

"Very good, m'lady."

Charlotte sat back on the leather seat. She had asked the three people who might have known where Aleks was, and none of them would tell her. She had not decided whether to help Feliks. Now, perhaps, she would not have to make that decision. She had arranged to meet him the day after tomorrow. Would he despise her for turning up empty-handed? No, he was not like that. She could not wait to see him again.

Walden and Lydia got into the car, and Pritchard drove off. Lydia looked at Charlotte. "What were you doing in the National Gallery this afternoon?"

Charlotte's hands started to shake, and she held them together in her lap. "I was looking at pictures."

"You were with a man."

Walden said, "Oh, no. Charlotte, what *is* all this?"

"Just somebody I met—you wouldn't approve of him."

"Of course we wouldn't!" said Lydia. "He wears a tweed cap!"

"A tweed cap! Who the devil is he?" Walden demanded.

"He's a terribly *interesting* man, and he understands things. There's no romance. You've nothing to fear."

"Nothing to fear?" Lydia said with a brittle laugh. "That evil old Duchess knows all about it, and she'll tell everyone."

"How could you do this?" Walden said disgustedly. "This episode is a social catastrophe for all of us."

"We'd better put her in a convent!" Lydia said hysterically.

"I'm sure that won't be necessary," replied Walden. "However, she can't stay in London, after this."

The car pulled into their courtyard, and they went into the house. Walden said, "Come into the drawing room."

He made a brandy and soda and sipped it. "Think again, Charlotte," he said. "Will you tell us who this man is?"

She wanted to say, He's an anarchist, who is trying to prevent you starting a war! But she merely shook her head.

"Then you must see," he said, almost gently, "that we can't possibly trust you." He turned to Lydia. "She'll just have to go to the country for a month, to keep her out of trouble. I'm driving down to Norfolk in the morning, to see Aleks. I'll take her with me."

Charlotte was stunned. *Aleks is at Walden Hall. I never even thought of that!*

Now I know!

"She'd better go up and pack," Mama said.

Charlotte stood up and went out, keeping her face down so that they should not see the light of triumph in her eyes.

Chapter Ten

At a quarter to three Feliks was in the lobby of the National Gallery. He was nervous and restless, sick of waiting and hiding. He had slept rough again for the past two nights, once in Hyde Park and once under the arches at Charing Cross. During the day he had hidden in alleys, coming out only to get food.

He watched the clock on the wall. At half past three Charlotte still had not come. He wished she would. . . . He wished a lot of things. He wished he had not deceived her. He wished he could find Orlov without her help. He wished he had married Lydia and known Charlotte as a baby.

It was four thirty. The museum seemed to be emptying out. Feliks wondered what to do next. He went outside and down the steps. There was no sign of her. She was not going to come.

Face it, he thought. She has decided to have nothing more to do with you, and quite sensibly. But she might have sent a note. . . . She had Bridget's address. She *would* have sent a note.

Feliks headed north, imagining: "Dear Mr. Kschessinsky, I regret I am unable to keep our appointment today. Yours sincerely, Lady Charlotte Walden." No, it would surely not be like that. "Dear Feliks, Prince Orlov is staying at the home of the Russian naval attaché, 25A Wilton Place, second floor, left front bedroom. Your affectionate friend, Charlotte." That was more like it. "Dear Father, Yes— I have learned the truth. But my 'papa' has locked me in my room. Please come and rescue me. Your loving daughter, Charlotte Kschessinsky." Don't be a damned fool.

He reached Cork Street. There were no policemen guarding the house. It looked safe, so he went up and knocked on Bridget's door. As he waited, he looked down at the window of his old basement room, and saw that there were new curtains. The door opened.

Bridget looked at him and smiled widely. "If it isn't my favourite international terrorist," she said. "Come in, come in."

She led him into her parlour. "Do you want some tea? It's hot."
"Yes, please." He sat down. "Did the police trouble you?"
"Yes, a superintendent. You must be a big cheese."
"What did you tell him?"
She looked contemptuous. "He got nothing out of me. Did you want your room back? I've let it, but I'll chuck the fellow out; he's got side-whiskers, and I never could abide side-whiskers."
"No, I don't want my room. Have you got a letter for me?"
"I suppose that's what you came for." She went to the mantelpiece and took a letter from behind the clock.
Feliks saw the crest on the envelope. He ripped it open. Inside were two pages covered with neat, stylish handwriting.

Walden Hall
July 1st

Dear Feliks,

By the time you get this you will have waited in vain for me at our rendezvous. I am most awfully sorry to let you down. Unfortunately I was seen with you on Monday and it is assumed I have a clandestine lover!!!

If she's in trouble she seems cheerful enough about it, Feliks thought.

I have been banished to the country for the rest of the season. However, it is a blessing in disguise. Nobody would tell me where Aleks was, but now I know because he is here!!!

Feliks was filled with savage triumph.

Take a train from Liverpool Street Station to Waldenhall Halt. That is our village. The house is three miles out of the village on the north road. However, don't come to the house of course!!! On the left-hand side of the road you will see a wood. I always ride there, along the bridle path, before breakfast between 7 and 8 o'clock. I will look out for you each day until you come.

I am doing this because you are the only person I ever met who talks sense to me.

Yours most affectionately,
Charlotte

126

Feliks sat back in his seat and closed his eyes. He was so proud of her, and so ashamed of himself, that he felt close to tears. He pulled himself together and tore the envelope in half and dropped it in the wastepaper basket. He was about to rip up the letter, but he thought, This may be all I'll have to remember her by. He folded the two sheets and put them in his coat pocket.

He stood up. "I've got a train to catch."

"Have you money for your fare?" Bridget put her hand into the pocket of her apron and took out a sovereign. "Here. You can buy a cup of tea as well."

Feliks took the coin and kissed her goodbye. "You have been kind to me."

"It's not for you, it's for my husband Sean, God rest his merry soul. Good luck to you, boy."

Feliks went out.

WALDEN WAS IN AN OPTIMISTIC mood as he entered the Admiralty. He had done what he had promised: he had sold Constantinople to Aleks, and the previous afternoon Aleks had sent a message to the Czar. Walden was confident that the Czar would follow the advice of his favourite nephew. But he was not so sure that Lloyd George would bend to the will of Asquith.

He was shown into the office of the first lord of the admiralty. Churchill jumped up and came round his desk to shake hands. "We sold it to Lloyd George," he said triumphantly.

"That's marvellous!" Walden said. "And I sold it to Orlov!"

"I knew you would. Sit down."

Walden sat on a leather chair and glanced round the room, at the charts on the walls and the naval memorabilia on the desk. "We should hear from St. Petersburg at any moment," he said. "The Russian embassy will send a note directly to you."

"The sooner the better," Churchill said. "According to our intelligence, Count Hoyos went to Berlin to ask the Kaiser whether Germany would support Austria in a war against Serbia. Our intelligence also says the answer is yes."

"Can nothing be done to make peace?"

"Everything is being done," Churchill said. "Sir Edward Grey is working night and day; the King is firing off telegrams to his cousins Kaiser 'Willy' and Czar 'Nicky'. It'll do no good."

There was a knock, and a male secretary came in with a piece of paper.

"A message from the Russian ambassador, sir," he said.

Walden tensed. Churchill glanced at the paper, then looked up. "They've accepted."

Walden beamed. "Bloody good show!"

The secretary went out. Churchill said, "I'll have the treaty drafted overnight and bring it down to Walden Hall tomorrow to be signed. It will have to be ratified by the Czar and Asquith, of course, but that's a formality."

The secretary knocked and came in again. "Mr. Basil Thomson is here, sir."

"Show him in."

Thomson came in and spoke without preamble. "We've picked up the trail of our anarchist again."

"Good!" said Walden.

Thomson sat down. "You'll remember that I put a man in his old basement room in Cork Street, in case he returned."

"I remember," Walden said.

"He did go back there. When he left, my man followed him."

"Where did he go?"

"To Liverpool Street Station." Thomson paused. "And he bought a ticket to Waldenhall Halt."

Walden went cold. His first thought was for Charlotte. She was vulnerable there; the bodyguards were concentrating on Aleks, and she had nobody to protect her but the servants. How could I have been so stupid? he thought.

He was nearly as worried for Aleks, who thought he was safe in Walden's home—and now Feliks was on his way there to kill him.

"Why the devil haven't you stopped him?" he burst out.

Thomson said mildly, "I don't think it's a good idea for one man alone to tackle our friend Feliks, do you? My chappie has instructions to follow him and report."

"It's not enough."

Churchill interrupted. "At least we know where the fellow is. With all the resources of His Majesty's Government at our disposal, we shall catch him. What do you propose, Thomson?"

"I've spoken by telephone with the chief constable of the county, sir. He will have a large detachment of men waiting at Waldenhall

128

Halt to arrest Feliks as he gets off the train. Meanwhile, my man will stick to him like glue."

"That won't do," Walden said. "Stop the train and arrest him before he gets anywhere near my home."

"Too dangerous," Thomson said. "Much better to let him go on thinking he's safe, then catch him unawares."

Churchill said, "I agree."

"It's not your home!" Walden said.

"We must leave this to the professionals," Churchill said.

Walden stood up. "I shall motor to Walden Hall immediately. Will you come, Thomson?"

"Not tonight. I'm going to arrest the Callahan woman. Once we've caught Feliks, she may be our chief prosecution witness. I'll come down tomorrow to interrogate Feliks."

"I don't know how you can be so confident," Walden said angrily.

"We'll catch him this time," said Thomson.

THE TRAIN STEAMED into the falling evening. Feliks watched the sun setting over the English wheat fields. He was alone in the carriage but for a young man reading the *Pall Mall Gazette*. Feliks's mood was almost gay. Tomorrow he would see Charlotte. How fine she would look on a horse, with the wind streaming through her hair. She was on *his* side now. Except—

Except that he had told her he was only going to kidnap Orlov. When he recalled this, he wanted to squirm in his seat. What is to be done? he wondered. I must prepare her for the truth.

The train slowed down and entered a little country station. From the map he had looked at before boarding, he recalled that Waldenhall Halt was the fourth station after this one.

The train pulled out again. His travelling companion finished his paper and put it down on the seat beside him. Feliks asked to borrow it, and he glanced at the headlines. His companion stared out of the window. He had the kind of facial hair that had been fashionable in Russia when Feliks was a boy. What was the English word? . . . Side-whiskers.

Side-whiskers. *Did you want your room back? I've let it, but I'll chuck the fellow out; he's got side-whiskers. . . .*

And now Feliks recalled that this man had been behind him in the queue at the ticket office. He felt a stab of fear.

129

He held the newspaper in front of his face and made himself think calmly and clearly. The police had placed a detective in the room Feliks had vacated. The detective had followed Feliks to the station. He had heard him ask for Waldenhall Halt and bought himself a ticket to the same destination. Then he had boarded the train along with Feliks.

No, not quite. Feliks had sat in the train for several minutes before it pulled out. The man with the side-whiskers had jumped aboard at the last minute. In those few minutes he had probably telephoned to report. Feliks imagined the conversation: "I'm at Liverpool Street Station. The anarchist bought a ticket to Waldenhall Halt. Shall I have the train delayed while you get a team down here?"

"No. Our man might get suspicious and bolt. Stay with him. . . ."

And what, Feliks wondered, would they do next? They could either take him off the train somewhere along the route, or wait to catch him at Waldenhall.

He had to get off the train, fast. But what about the detective? He must be left behind, unable to give the alarm, so that Feliks would have time to get clear.

The train began to slow down; a few houses could be seen alongside the track. The brakes squealed, and a station slid into view. The platform appeared empty. The locomotive shuddered to a halt with a hiss of steam.

People began to get off. A handful of passengers walked past Feliks's window, heading for the exit.

The police trap could be at the next station. I must get off now. The engine whistle blew. Feliks stood up.

The detective looked startled.

Feliks said, "Is there a lavatory on the train?"

"Er . . . sure to be," the detective said.

Feliks stepped out of the compartment and ran to the end of the carriage. The train chuffed and jerked forward. He went into the lavatory and came out again. The detective had poked his head out of the compartment. Feliks went to the carriage door. The detective came running.

Feliks turned back and punched him full in the face. A woman screamed. Feliks got the detective by the coat and dragged him into the lavatory. The man struggled and threw a wild punch, which

130

caught Feliks in the ribs and made him gasp. He got the detective's head in his hands and banged it against the edge of the washbasin again and again. The man went limp. The train picked up speed. Feliks dropped him and stepped out into the corridor. He went to the carriage door, opened it and jumped. The door banged shut behind him. He landed running. He stumbled and regained his balance. The train moved on.

Feliks looked around. He was alone. He walked briskly away from the station.

On the outskirts of the town, Feliks climbed over a gate and went into a wheat field, where he lay down to wait for nightfall.

THE BIG LANCHESTER roared up the drive to Walden Hall. A policeman stood at the door and another was patrolling the terrace. Pritchard brought the car to a halt. He opened the door, and Walden got out and went into the house.

He found Aleks and Sir Arthur Langley in the drawing room, leaning on the mantelpiece with brandy glasses in their hands. Both wore evening dress. Sir Arthur was the chief constable of the county and an old school friend of Walden's.

Walden shook Langley's hand. "Did you catch the anarchist?"

"I'm afraid he slipped through our fingers—"

"Damnation!" Walden exclaimed. "I was afraid of that." He shook hands with Aleks. "I don't know what to say to you, dear boy. You must think we're a lot of fools." He turned back to Sir Arthur. "What happened, anyway?"

"Feliks hopped off the train at Tingley."

"Where was Thomson's precious detective?"

"In the lavatory with a broken head."

"Marvellous," Walden said bitterly. He slumped into a chair. "He's on his way here, do you realize that?"

"Yes, of course," said Sir Arthur in a soothing tone.

"Tell me what is being done."

"I've got five patrols covering the roads between here and Tingley, and I've brought a constable and a sergeant to guard the house."

"I saw them outside."

"They'll be relieved every eight hours, day and night. The Prince already has two bodyguards from the Special Branch, and Thomson

131

is sending four more tonight. They'll take twelve-hour shifts, so he'll always have three men with him. My men aren't armed, but Thomson's are. My recommendation is that until Feliks is caught, Prince Orlov should remain in his room."

Aleks said, "I will do that." He was pale but calm.

He's very brave, Walden thought. He said, "I don't think a few bodyguards is enough. We need an army."

"We'll have one by tomorrow," Sir Arthur replied. "We're mustering a hundred and fifty men from all over the county."

"Where is Charlotte?" Walden said suddenly.

Aleks answered, "She went to bed."

"She mustn't leave the house while all this is going on," Sir Arthur said. "Um, there is something else, Stephen." He seemed embarrassed. "I mean, the question of just what made Feliks suddenly catch a train to Waldenhall Halt."

In all the panic Walden had not even considered that. "Yes. How in heaven's name did he find out?"

"As I understand it, only two groups of people knew where Prince Orlov had gone. One is the embassy staff, of course. The other group is your people here."

"A traitor among my servants?" Walden said, appalled.

"Yes," said Sir Arthur hesitantly. "Or among the family."

LYDIA HAD DINNER GUESTS at the London house, but she was so distracted that her conversation was barely polite, let alone sparkling. Her mind was full of nightmares. Feliks being arrested, Stephen being shot. Charlotte's disgrace and exile to the country.

Fortunately her friends did not linger after dinner; they were all going on somewhere else. As soon as the last one had left, Lydia went into the hall and picked up the telephone. Walden Hall was not yet on the telephone, so she called Basil Thomson at Scotland Yard. Thomson was still at his desk, working late.

"Lady Walden, how are you?" he said.

Lydia said, "What is the news?"

"Bad, I'm afraid. Our friend Feliks has slipped through our fingers again."

Relief washed over her. "Thank . . . thank you," she said.

"I don't think you need to worry too much," Thomson went on. "Prince Orlov is well guarded now."

Lydia blushed with shame: she had momentarily forgotten to worry about Aleks and Stephen. "I'll try not to worry," she said. "Goodnight."

She put down the telephone and went upstairs. Feliks is so *clever*, she thought. How on earth did he find out where Aleks is hiding? We wouldn't even tell Charlotte!

Lydia went cold. Charlotte? She cried, "Oh, no!"

He was about forty, and wearing a tweed cap.

A horrible sense of inevitability possessed her. She buried her face in her hands, trying to think. Charlotte met a man in the National Gallery. That evening, she asked me where Aleks was. I didn't tell her. Perhaps she asked Stephen, too; he wouldn't have told her. Then she was sent home, to Walden Hall, and of course she discovered that Aleks was there. Two days later Feliks went to Waldenhall Halt.

Feliks was the man in the tweed cap. Charlotte had met her father. It was horrible, horrible.

She must be conspiring with him still.

I must warn Stephen. She rang for her maid. When she came, Lydia said, "Start packing. I shall leave first thing in the morning for Walden Hall."

AFTER DARK FELIKS headed across the fields. It was a warm, humid night, and very dark; heavy cloud hid the stars and the moon. He had to walk slowly, for he was almost blind. He found his way to the railway line and turned north.

Walking along the tracks, he passed through dark stations, their names stamped on sheet-metal signs. When he reached Waldenhall Halt, he recalled Charlotte's directions: *The house is three miles out of the village on the north road.* The railway line was running roughly north-northeast. He followed it another mile or so, then decided to find the road. He moved off the railway line to the left, stumbled across a short stretch of rough ground, then came up against a flimsy wire fence.

He waited for a moment. There was no darkness like a dark night in the country. He heard a movement close to him, and out of the corner of his eye he saw something white. He bent down and fumbled until he found a small stone, then threw it at the white thing. There was a whinny, and a horse cantered away.

133

Feliks listened. He heard nothing, so he stooped and clambered through the fence. Walking forward slowly he came up against another wire fence. He climbed through it and bumped into a wooden building. Immediately there was a tremendous noise of chickens clucking. A dog started to bark. A light came on in the window of a house. Feliks threw himself flat and lay still. The light showed him a small farmyard. He had bumped into the henhouse. Beyond the farmhouse he could see the road he was looking for. The chickens quietened, the dog gave a last howl and the light went out. Feliks walked to the road.

It was a dirt road bordered by a dry ditch. Beyond the ditch there seemed to be woodland. Feliks remembered: *On the left-hand side of the road you will see a wood.* He was almost there.

He walked along the road, his hearing strained for any sound. After more than a mile he sensed a wall on his left. A little farther on the wall was broken by a gate, and he saw a light.

He leaned on the iron bars of the gate and peered through. There seemed to be a long drive. At its far end he could see, dimly illuminated by a pair of flickering lamps, the pillared portico of a vast house. As he watched, a tall figure walked across the front of the house—a sentry.

In that house, he thought, is Prince Orlov.

Chapter Eleven

Charlotte woke at six o'clock. Her first thought was for Feliks. Today he would surely be waiting for her in the wood. She jumped out of bed, washed in cold water and dressed quickly in a long skirt, riding boots and a jacket.

She went downstairs. She saw nobody. She went out of the front door and almost bumped into a large uniformed policeman.

"Heavens!" she exclaimed. "Who are you?"

"Constable Stevenson, m'lady."

"What are you doing here?"

"Guarding the house, m'lady."

"Oh, I see. How reassuring. How many of you are there?"

"Two outside and four inside. But there'll be a lot more later. I hear there'll be a hundred and fifty men here by nine."

134

"Why?"

"Big search party, m'lady. We'll get this anarchist chappie—"

"How splendid!"

She walked away, round the east wing of the house to the stables. She went inside and found her mare, Spats, so called because of the white patches on her forelegs. She stroked her nose for a minute and gave her an apple. Then she saddled her, led her out of the stable and mounted.

She rode away from the back of the house and round the park in a wide circle, staying out of sight of the policeman. She galloped across the west paddock and jumped the low fence into the wood. She walked Spats through the trees until she came to the bridle path, then let her trot.

She thought, What can Feliks do against a hundred and fifty men? His plan was impossible now; Aleks was too well guarded. At least she could warn him off.

She reached the end of the wood without seeing him. She dismounted and walked back, leading Spats. She stopped in a glade to watch a squirrel. Suddenly she felt she was being watched. She turned, and there he was, looking at her with a peculiarly sad expression.

He said, "Hello, Charlotte."

She went to him and took both his hands. His beard was unkempt, his clothes were covered with bits of greenery and he looked dreadfully tired.

"Listen," she said. "You must go away. If you leave now, you can escape." She explained what he was up against.

He smiled. "And if I escape, what will I do with the rest of my life? No, I want to kidnap Orlov."

"But I won't help you commit suicide!"

"Let's sit down," he said. "I have something to tell you."

She sat on the grass. Feliks sat in front of her and crossed his legs like a cossack. Dappled sunlight played across his weary face. He spoke rather formally. "I told you I was in love, once, with a woman called Lydia; and you said, 'That's my mother's name.' Do you remember?"

"I remember everything you've ever said to me." She wondered what this was all about.

"It *was* your mother."

She stared at him. "You were in love with Mama?"

"More than that. We were lovers. She used to come to my apartment, alone. Do you understand what I mean?"

Charlotte blushed with embarrassment. "Yes, I do."

"Her father, your grandfather, found out. The old count had me arrested; then he forced your mother to marry Walden. You were born seven months after the wedding."

Charlotte's heart was pounding. "What do you mean?"

"You look *exactly* like my sister, Natasha."

Charlotte's heart seemed to rise into her throat and she could hardly speak. "You think you might be my father?"

"I'm sure of it."

"Oh, God." Charlotte put her hands to her face and stared into space, seeing nothing. She thought of Papa, but he was not her papa; she thought of Mama having a lover; she thought of Feliks, her friend and suddenly her father. . . .

She understood, now, the odd, painful way he had looked at her sometimes. She said, "What are we going to do?"

Feliks took her hand and stroked it. He said, "I suppose all the love and concern that a man normally gives to his wife and children went, in my case, into politics. I have to try to get Orlov, even if it's impossible; the way a man would have to try to save his child from drowning, even if he could not swim." He took a deep breath. "Could you get me inside the house and hide me?"

She thought for a moment. "Yes," she said.

He mounted the horse behind her, and Charlotte urged it into a trot. She followed the bridle path for a while, then turned off and headed through the wood. Feliks realized she was circling round the house to approach from the north side.

She was an astonishing child. She had such strength of character. She had listened to him turn her world upside down, and she had shown emotion but no hysteria—she did not get that kind of equanimity from her mother.

They went into a little lane that led to an orchard. Looking between the tops of the trees, Feliks could see the roofs of Walden Hall. The orchard ended at a wall, and they followed it round a corner. "What's behind the wall?" Feliks asked.

"Kitchen garden. Better not talk now."

They stopped at the next corner and dismounted. Feliks could see some low buildings and a yard. "The stables," Charlotte murmured. "Wait till I give you a signal. Then follow me as fast as you can."

"Where are we going?"

"Over the roofs."

Feliks watched her cross to the stables and look inside. Then he heard her say, "Oh, hello, Peter."

A boy of about twelve years said, "Good morning, m'lady."

Feliks thought, How will she get rid of him?

Charlotte said, "Where's Daniel?"

"Having his breakfast, m'lady."

"Go and fetch him, will you, and tell him to come and unsaddle Spats."

"I can do it, m'lady."

"No, I want Daniel," she said imperiously. "Off you go."

The boy ran off. Marvellous, Feliks thought. Charlotte turned towards him and beckoned. He ran to her.

She jumped onto the low iron bunker, leading him up to the roofs and over them by the same route she and Belinda had travelled in May.

"There are four acres of roof," Charlotte told him.

It was quite a sight. On all sides were roofs of every material, size and pitch. Ladders and strips of decking were provided, so that people could move around without treading on the slates and tiles. "I've never seen such a big house," Feliks said.

Charlotte led him up a ladder, then along a board footway leading to a small door set in a wall. She opened the door and crawled through.

Gratefully Feliks followed her into the welcoming darkness.

LYDIA BORROWED A MOTORCAR and driver from her brother-in-law, George, and, having lain awake all night, left London very early. The car entered the drive at Walden Hall at nine o'clock, and she was astonished to see, in front of the house and spreading over the park, hundreds of policemen, dozens of vehicles and scores of dogs.

A trestle table had been set up on the south terrace, and behind it sat Stephen with Sir Arthur Langley, giving instructions to half a dozen police officers. Stephen looked up, saw Lydia and left the group to speak to her.

"Good morning, my dear, this is a pleasant surprise. Still, I wish you had stayed in town for your safety."

"I should have spent every minute worrying." Lydia studied her husband's face and saw signs of tiredness and tension. A guilty impulse made her reach up and touch his cheek. "Don't wear yourself out," she said.

A whistle blew. The policemen hastily formed themselves into six groups. There were a lot of shouted orders; then the first group went south, towards the wood. Two more headed west, into the paddock. The other three groups went down the drive towards the road.

In the house, Lydia met Charlotte on the stairs. Charlotte was surprised. "Hello, Mama," she said. "I didn't know you were coming down. How did you get here?"

"I borrowed Uncle George's car." Lydia saw that Charlotte was making small talk and thinking of something else.

"You must have started very early," Charlotte said.

"Yes." She's very bright-eyed, thought Lydia. Why should she look like that, when hundreds of policemen are combing the county for Feliks? Why is she not anxious, as I am? It must be that for some reason she thinks he is safe.

Charlotte said, "Tell me something, Mama. How long does it take for a baby to grow and be born?"

Lydia's mouth fell open and the blood drained from her face. She stared at Charlotte, thinking, She knows! She knows!

Charlotte nodded, looking faintly sad. "Never mind. You've answered my question." She went on down the stairs.

Lydia held on to the banister, feeling faint. Feliks had told Charlotte; it was just too cruel. The hall spun around her and she heard a maid's voice say, "Are you all right, my lady?"

"A little tired after the journey," she said. "Take my arm."

The maid took her arm, and they walked up to her room. Lydia sat down. "Leave me now," she said. "Unpack later."

The maid went out. Lydia thought about Charlotte's bright mood. She recognized it. It was the mood you were in when you had spent time with Feliks. You felt that life was endlessly fascinating, that there were important things to be done, that the world was full of colour and passion and change. Charlotte had seen Feliks, and she believed him to be safe.

138

Lydia thought, What am I going to do?

She spent time washing her face and changing her dress, taking the opportunity to calm herself. Then she went out. On the way downstairs she met a maid with a tray laden with sliced ham, bread and butter, milk, coffee and grapes. "Who is that for?" she asked.

"For Lady Charlotte, m'lady," said the maid.

Had Charlotte not even lost her appetite? Lydia went into the Octagon and sent for the cook, to discuss menus. She learned that Basil Thomson would be arriving for lunch, and Mr. Churchill for dinner.

She sent the cook away and moved around the room, looking at the little bronzes, the glass ornaments, the writing table. She had a headache. Her nerves were very bad. Had Charlotte found Feliks a hiding place?

She left the room and went along to the library with the idea of getting a book to take her mind off everything. When she walked in she saw that Stephen was there, at his desk. He looked up at her, smiled in a welcoming way and went on writing.

Lydia wandered along the bookshelves. She took a book at random and sat down with it open on her lap. Stephen said, "That's an unusual choice for you." She looked at the book she was holding. It was Thomas Hardy's *Wessex Poems*.

They had often sat like this, she and Stephen, when they first came to Walden Hall. She recalled nostalgically how she would sit and read while he worked. He had been less tranquil in those days, she remembered; it was after the birth of Charlotte that everything seemed to settle down. The servants adored the baby and loved Lydia for producing her. Lydia got used to English ways and was well liked by London society. There had been eighteen years of tranquillity.

Lydia sighed. Those years were coming to an end.

She looked down at the open page and read:

> She would have given a world to breathe "yes" truly,
> So much his life seemed hanging on her mind,
> And hence she lied, her heart persuaded throughly
> 'Twas worth her soul to be a moment kind.

Is that me? she wondered. Did I give my soul when I married Stephen in order to save Feliks from prison? Ever since then I've

139

been playing a part, pretending I'm not wanton and sinful. But I am! And if I had been just a little wanton, perhaps Stephen would have come to my bed more often, and we might have had a son. She sighed again.

"A penny for your thoughts," Stephen said.

"I was thinking what a shame it is that we never had a son."

He said, "It's not too late. Do let's keep trying."

She got up from her chair and went over to stand beside her husband. "Yes," she said. "Let's keep trying." She bent down and kissed his forehead. "I *do* love you," she said.

He smiled. "I know you do."

Suddenly she could stand it no longer. She said, "I must go and change for lunch before Basil Thomson arrives." She went upstairs to her bedroom. She had to talk to Charlotte. Without having a clear idea of what she would say, she headed for her daughter's room on the next floor.

Her footsteps made no noise on the carpet. She reached the top of the staircase and looked along the corridor. She saw Charlotte disappearing into the old nursery. She was about to call out, then stopped herself. What had Charlotte been carrying? It had looked like a plate of sandwiches and a glass of milk.

Puzzled, Lydia went to Charlotte's bedroom. There, on the table, was the tray Lydia had seen the maid carrying. All the ham and bread had gone. Why would Charlotte order a tray of food, then make sandwiches and take them to the nursery?

Lydia went along the corridor and into the nursery. There was the old rocking horse, his ears making twin peaks in the dust sheet. Through an open door she could see the schoolroom, with maps and childish drawings on the wall. Another door led to the bedroom; that too was empty but for shrouds. Will all this ever be used again? Lydia wondered. Will we have a nanny, and tiny, tiny clothes?

But where was Charlotte? The closet door was open. Suddenly Lydia remembered. Of course! Charlotte's hideaway! The little room she thought no one else knew of. One of the few indulgent decisions Lydia had made was to allow Charlotte her hideaway, and to forbid Marya to "discover" it; for she knew how important it was to have a place of one's own. So Charlotte still used that little room! Then she heard a voice—a man's voice—speaking in Russian, in low tones; a voice like a caress, a voice that sent a shudder through her.

140

Feliks was in there.

Lydia thought she would faint. Feliks! Within touching distance! Hidden in Walden Hall, while the police searched the county for him! Hidden by Charlotte.

She was shaking. I must get away, she thought. I don't know what to do.

Her head ached horribly. She needed a dose of laudanum. She tiptoed out of the nursery and almost ran along the corridor and down the stairs to her room. The laudanum was on the dresser. She opened the bottle. She could not hold the spoon steady, so she took a gulp. After a few moments she began to feel calmer, a mild contentment coming over her.

Nothing would really matter now, for a while.

FELIKS PACED THE TINY ROOM like a caged tiger, bending his head to avoid the ceiling, listening to Charlotte.

"Aleks's door is always locked," she said. "There are two armed guards inside and one outside. The inside ones won't unlock the door unless their colleague outside tells them to."

"One outside and two inside." Feliks scratched his head and cursed in Russian. Here I am, right in the house, with an accomplice in the household, and still it isn't easy. "Could you draw a plan of the house?" he asked.

Charlotte made a face. "I can try."

She found a piece of paper and a pencil among her childhood treasures and knelt at a little table.

Feliks ate another sandwich and drank the rest of the milk. As he ate he watched her draw, frowning and biting the end of her pencil. He found the sight of her like this very touching. So she must have sat, he thought, for years in the schoolroom.

She handed him her sketches, and he became businesslike again. He studied them. "Where are the guns kept?" he said.

"In the gun room." She pointed it out on the plan. "You really did have an affair with Mama."

"Yes."

"I find it so hard to believe that she would do such a thing."

"She was very wild then. She still is, but she pretends otherwise."

Charlotte became pensive. "What will you do when you have Aleks?"

141

He looked away so she would not see the guilt in his eyes. "That depends on how and when I kidnap him, but most likely I'll keep him tied up right here. You'll have to send a coded telegram to my friends in Geneva, and when the news has achieved what we want, we'll let Orlov go."

"And then?"

"They will look for me in London, so I'll go north and lose myself. After a few weeks I'll make my way back to Switzerland, then eventually to St. Petersburg—that's the place to be, that's where the revolution will start."

"So I'll never see you again."

You won't want to, he thought. He said, "Why not? If there is such a thing as fate, it seems determined to bring us together."

"That's true," she said with a brittle smile, and he saw that she did not believe it, either. She got to her feet. "Now I must get you some water to wash in."

LUNCHEON WAS DREARY, Walden thought. Lydia was in a daze, and Charlotte was uncharacteristically silent. Thomson was taciturn. Sir Arthur Langley attempted to be convivial, but nobody responded. Walden himself was obsessed by the puzzle of how Feliks had found out that Aleks was at Walden Hall.

After lunch Sir Arthur went back to the Octagon, where he had set up his headquarters. Walden and Thomson took their cigars out onto the terrace. From the drawing room came the crashing opening chords of the Tchaikovsky piano concerto. Lydia was playing.

Thomson said, "I didn't want to say this in front of Lady Walden, but we have a clue to the identity of the traitor."

Walden went cold.

Thomson went on, "Last night I interviewed Bridget Callahan, the Cork Street landlady. I got nothing out of her, but I left my men to search her house. This morning they showed me what they had found." He took from his pocket an envelope that had been torn in half, and handed the two pieces to Walden. He saw with a shock that the envelope bore the Walden crest.

Thomson said, "Do you recognize the handwriting?"

Walden turned the pieces over and looked at the address. He said, "Oh, dear God, not Charlotte."

142

Thomson was silent.

"She led him here," Walden said. "My own daughter." He stared at the envelope, willing it to disappear.

"Look at the postmark," Thomson said. "She wrote it as soon as she arrived here. It was mailed from the village."

"Feliks was the man in the tweed cap," Walden said. "It all fits." He felt hopelessly sad, as if someone dear to him had died. "What a damnable life this is, Thomson."

"I'll have to interview her," Thomson said.

"So will I."

They put out their cigars and went inside.

In the hall, Walden stopped a maid. "Tell Lady Charlotte I wish to speak to her in her room immediately."

"Very good, m'lord."

Thomson and Walden waited. Walden looked round at the marble floor, the carved staircase. A footman crossed the hall and picked up the letters for posting from the hall table, just as he must have the day Charlotte's treacherous letter to Feliks was written. The maid came down the stairs.

"Lady Charlotte is ready to see you, m'lord."

Walden and Thomson went up.

Charlotte's room was at the front of the house, looking over the park. It was sunny and light, with pretty fabrics.

"You look rather fierce, Papa," Charlotte said.

"I've reason to be," Walden replied.

Thomson said, "Lady Charlotte, where is Feliks?"

Charlotte turned white. "I've no idea, of course."

"Lady Charlotte, I'm a policeman, and I can prove that you have committed conspiracy to murder. Now my concern, and your father's, is to let this go no further; and, in particular, to ensure that you will not have to go to jail."

Walden stared at Thomson. Jail! But he realized with a sense of overwhelming dread that he was right.

Thomson went on, "As long as we can prevent the murder, we feel we can cover up your participation. But if the assassin succeeds, I will have to bring you to trial, and then the charge will be accessory to murder. In theory, you could be hanged."

"No!" Walden shouted. He buried his face in his hands.

Thomson said, "You must save yourself that agony—and not only

144

yourself, but your parents. You must do everything in your power to help us find Feliks and save Prince Orlov."

Charlotte stood behind a chair, gripping its back with both hands. Finally she spoke. "I have nothing to tell you."

Walden groaned aloud. She seemed a stranger.

"Have you warned Feliks of our security precautions here?" Thomson asked her.

She looked blank. Walden noticed a change of tone in Thomson's voice. He seemed angry now.

"You may think that your father can save you from justice," Thomson said. "But if Orlov dies, I swear to you that I will bring you to trial for murder. Now think about that!"

Thomson left the room.

CHARLOTTE WAS DISMAYED to see him go. Alone with Walden, she was afraid she would break down.

"I'll save you if I can," Walden said sadly.

Charlotte swallowed thickly and looked away. I wish he'd be angry, she thought; I could cope with that.

Walden looked out of the window. "I can't understand how this has happened," he said. "Can you explain it to me, please?"

"Yes, I can," she said. She was eager to make him understand. "I don't want you to succeed in causing Russia to go to war, sending millions of their innocent peasants to be wounded and killed."

He looked surprised. "Is *that* why you've done these awful things?" he said. "Is that what Feliks is in this for?"

Perhaps he *will* understand, she thought joyfully. "Yes," she said. She went on. "Feliks also wants a revolution in Russia, and he believes it will begin when his people learn that the Czar, through Aleks, has been trying to drag them into war."

"But if there's to be a war, wouldn't you be *glad* to have the whole Russian nation on our side?"

"Of course, especially if the Russian nation had chosen to help us. But they won't choose, will they, Papa? You and Aleks will choose. You should be working to prevent war, not to win it."

"Charlotte, I promise you that the arithmetic of human suffering is not as straightforward as Feliks has led you to believe. Feliks wants to *kill* your cousin. Does that make no difference?"

145

"He's going to kidnap Aleks, not kill him."

Papa shook his head. "Charlotte, he's tried twice to kill Aleks and once to kill me. He's not a kidnapper, he's a murderer."

"I don't believe you."

"But why not?" he said plaintively.

"Did you tell me the truth about suffragism? Did you tell me the truth about Annie? Did you tell me that in democratic Britain most people still can't vote? Did you tell me about sex?"

"No, I didn't." To her horror, Charlotte saw that his cheeks were wet with tears. "It may be that everything I ever did, as a father, was mistaken. I didn't know the world would change the way it has. I had no idea of what a woman's role would be in the world of 1914. And now I'm paying the price. But it's not your politics that are making me cry. It's the betrayal. I mean, I shall fight tooth and nail to keep you out of the courts, even if you do succeed in helping Feliks, because you're my daughter. For me, you come above all principles, all politics, everything. That's how it is in families. What hurts me so much is that you will not do the same for me. Will you?"

She wanted desperately to say yes.

"Will you be loyal to me, for all that I may be in the wrong, just because I am your father?"

But you're not, she thought. She bowed her head; she could not look at him.

They sat in silence for a minute. Then Walden blew his nose. He got up and went to the door. He took the key out of the lock and went outside. He closed the door behind him. Charlotte heard him turn the key, locking her in.

She burst into tears.

WINSTON CHURCHILL BROUGHT the treaty that evening. He and Aleks signed it, but there was no rejoicing at dinner, for everyone knew that if Aleks were assassinated, the Czar would refuse to ratify the deal. Churchill said that the sooner Aleks was off English soil the better. Thomson said he would devise a secure route and Aleks could leave tomorrow. Everyone went to bed early, for there was nothing else to do.

Lydia knew she would not sleep. She had spent the afternoon in a drugged haze, trying to forget that Feliks was there, in her house. Aleks would leave tomorrow; if only he could be kept safe for a few more hours. She wondered whether there might be some way she could make Feliks lie low for another day. Should she go to him and tell him a lie? Tell him that he would have his opportunity to kill Aleks tomorrow night? He would never believe her. The scheme was hopeless. But once she had conceived the idea of going to see Feliks, she could not get it out of her mind. She thought, Out of this door, along the passage, up the stairs, along another passage, through the nursery, and there . . .

She closed her eyes tightly and pulled the sheet up over her head. Her nerves were bad again and she felt another headache coming on. It was a very warm night.

Feliks's presence in the nursery was like a bright light shining in her eyes, keeping her awake. She threw off the sheet, got up and went to the window. She opened it wider. What was he doing up there? Was he making a bomb? Sharpening a knife? Or trying to find a way to get past Aleks's bodyguards?

There's nothing I can do, she thought; nothing. Her headache was now so bad she thought her skull would split. She went to the dresser and took a gulp from the bottle of laudanum.

Then she went up to the nursery.

Chapter Twelve

Something had gone wrong. Feliks had not seen Charlotte since midday, when she had brought him a basin, a jug of water, a towel and a cake of soap. There must have been some kind of trouble to keep her away; but she had not given him away, evidently, for here he was in the little hideaway.

Anyway, he did not need her any more.

He knew where Orlov was and he knew where the guns were. He could not get into Orlov's room, so he would have to make Orlov come out. He knew how to do that.

He had not used the soap and water immediately, but now he felt very hot and sticky, so he took the water into the nursery. There he took off his clothes and washed by the light of a single candle. A pleasant feeling of anticipation filled him. I shall win tonight, he thought savagely, no matter how many I have to kill. He rubbed himself all over roughly with the towel.

Then he heard Lydia say, "Why, you've grown a beard."

He spun round and stared into the darkness, stupefied.

She came forward into the circle of candlelight. Her blonde hair was unpinned and hung around her shoulders. She wore a long, pale nightdress with a fitted bodice and a high waist.

They stood looking at one another, and the candlelight glinted off the tears on her cheeks. She realized she was crying, and she could not understand why. She stepped forward and kissed him, and he said, "I have always loved you, all these years."

It was then that she lost control.

SHE HAD FAINTED, and Feliks laid her gently on the floor. Her face in the candlelight was peaceful, all the tension gone. He knew she had been half asleep, probably drugged.

He quickly put on his clothes, then picked up the candle and looked at her. He wanted to touch her once more, to kiss her. He hardened his heart. Never again, he thought reluctantly. He turned and went through the door.

He walked softly along the carpeted corridor and down the stairs. His candle made moving shadows in the doorways. I may die tonight, but not before I have killed Orlov, he thought.

He stepped off the last flight of stairs onto a marble floor, and his boot made a loud noise. He froze and listened. There was no sound from the rest of the house. He took off his boots and went on in his bare feet.

Holding the candle close to the paper, he consulted the plan Charlotte had drawn for him. Then he turned to his right and padded along the corridor.

He went through the library into the gun room.

He closed the door softly and looked around. A hideous head seemed to leap at him, and he grunted with fear before he realized it was a tiger's head, a trophy, mounted on the wall.

Feliks put the candle down on a table. The guns were racked along one wall, secured by a chain through their trigger guards. He looked along the chain. It was padlocked to a bracket screwed into the wooden end of the rack.

He knew he had to have a gun. He looked again at Charlotte's plan. Next to the gun room was the flower room. He picked up his candle and went through the communicating doorway. He found himself in a small room with a marble table and a stone sink, over which hung a few tools: shears, a small hoe, a knife. He took the knife and returned to the gun room. He used the blade to undo the screws and unchain the guns.

There were three cupboards in the room. One held bottles of brandy and whisky; another held sporting magazines. The third was locked: that must be where the ammunition was kept.

Feliks broke the lock with the garden knife.

Of the three types of gun available—Winchester, shotgun or elephant gun—he preferred the Winchester. However, he found no cartridges for it. All the ammunition consisted of number six shot, so he had to be content with a shotgun. To be sure of killing his man he would have to-fire at close range—no more than twenty yards, to be absolutely certain. And he would have only two shots before reloading.

He loaded the gun.

AND NOW, LYDIA THOUGHT, I shall have to kill myself.

She saw no other possibility. All her years of self-discipline had come to nothing, just because Feliks had returned. She could not live with the knowledge of what she was. She wanted to die, now.

She considered how it might be done. An overdose of laudanum? She was not sure she had enough. Then she thought of the lake. Yes, that was the answer.

She left the nursery and walked along the corridor. She saw a light under Charlotte's door and hesitated. The key was in the lock on the outside. She unlocked the door and went in.

Charlotte sat in a chair by the window, fully dressed but apparently asleep. She had unpinned her hair. Lydia closed the door and went over to her. Charlotte opened her eyes.

"What's happened?" she said.

"Nothing," Lydia said. She sat down. "You must hate me. I understand. I hate myself."

"I don't hate you, Mama. I've felt dreadfully angry with you, but I've never hated you."

"But you think I'm a hypocrite."

"Not even that. I'm beginning to understand why you're so fiercely respectable, why you were so determined that I should never know anything about sex . . . you wanted to save me from

149

what happened to you. I think I've judged you harshly, when I had no right to judge you at all."

"Do you know that I love you?"

"Yes . . . and I love you, Mama."

Lydia was dazed. After all that had happened—Charlotte still loved her. She felt suffused with a kind of tranquil joy.

Charlotte yawned. "I think I'll sleep now." She stood up.

Lydia kissed her cheek, then embraced her.

Charlotte said, "I still love Feliks, you know; that hasn't changed."

"I understand," said Lydia. "I do, too."

"Goodnight, Mama."

"Goodnight."

Lydia went out quickly and closed the door behind her. She hesitated again, then decided to save Charlotte the anxiety of decision. She turned the key in the lock.

She went down the stairs, feeling glad she had talked to Charlotte. Perhaps, she thought, this family could be mended, after all. She went into her room.

"Where have you been?" said Stephen.

ALL FELIKS HAD TO DO now was get Orlov out of his room. He knew how to do that. He was going to burn the house down.

Carrying the gun in one hand, the candle in the other, he walked—still barefoot—through the west wing and across the hall into the drawing room. He passed through two dining rooms and a serving room and entered the kitchens, looking for the way out. He found a door and quietly opened it.

In front of him was a small cobbled courtyard. On its far side, if Charlotte's plan was right, there was a garage—and probably a petrol tank.

He crossed the yard. The garage had once been a barn, he guessed, and the front of it was open. He could vaguely make out the great round headlights of two large cars. Where was the fuel tank? He stepped forward, and something hit his forehead. It was a length of flexible pipe with a nozzle at the end. It made sense: they put the cars in the barn and the fuel tank in the hayloft and filled up through the pipe.

Good! he thought.

Now he needed a container—a two-gallon can would be ideal. He walked around the cars. There were no cans.

He recalled the plan again. He was close to the kitchen garden. There might be a watering can in that region. He was about to go and look when he heard a sniff. He froze.

A policeman went by, the light from his oil lamp meandering around the courtyard. Did I shut the kitchen door? Feliks thought in panic. The lamp shone on the door; it looked shut.

The policeman went on, and after a minute Feliks went in the same direction, looking for the kitchen garden.

He found no cans there, but he stumbled over a coil of garden hose. He estimated its length at about a hundred feet. It gave him a wicked idea.

First he needed to know how frequently the policeman patrolled. He began counting while he carried the garden hose back to the garage and concealed it behind the motorcars.

He had reached nine hundred and two when the policeman came round again. He had about fifteen minutes.

He attached one end of the hose to the nozzle of the fuel pipe, then walked out into the courtyard, paying out the hose as he went. He paused in the kitchen to find a sharp meat skewer and to relight his candle. Then he went through the house, laying the hose in the kitchen, the dining rooms, then across the passageway to the west wing, and on into the library. The hose was heavy, and it was difficult to do the job silently. He listened all the while for footsteps. Would someone come down to get a book from the library, or a glass of brandy from the drawing room, or a sandwich from the kitchen?

If that were to happen, he thought, the game would be up.

Just a few more minutes—just a few more minutes!

He had been worried about whether the hose would be long enough, but it just reached through the library door. He walked back, following the hose, making holes in it every few yards with the point of the meat skewer, except where it crossed the hall.

He went out through the kitchen door and over to the garage. He held his shotgun two-handed, like a club.

He seemed to wait an age.

At last he heard footsteps. The policeman stopped with a grunt of surprise, shining his lamp on the hose.

Feliks hit him with the gun. The policeman staggered, and Feliks hit him again with all his might.

The policeman fell down and was still.

Feliks turned to the fuel pipe and opened the tap.

"BEFORE WE MARRIED," Lydia said impulsively, "I had a lover."

"Good Lord!" said Stephen.

"My father found out about it. He had my lover jailed and tortured. He said that if I would agree to marry you, the torture would stop immediately; and that as soon as you and I had left for England, my lover would be released from jail."

She watched Stephen's face. He was horrified. He said, "Your father was wicked."

"I was wicked to marry without love."

Now Stephen looked pained. "For that matter, I wasn't in love with you when I proposed; I needed a wife to be Countess of Walden. It was later that I fell in love with you. I'd say I forgive you, but there's nothing to forgive."

Could it be this easy? she thought. Might he forgive me everything and go on loving me? She found herself plunging on. "There's more to be told," she said, "and it's worse."

His expression was painfully anxious. "You'd better tell me."

"I was . . . I was already with child when I married you."

Stephen paled. "Charlotte!"

Lydia nodded silently, finished finally with all that lying.

"She . . . she's not mine?"

"No." Now I have hurt you, she thought. She said, "Oh, Stephen, I am so dreadfully sorry."

He stared at her. "Not mine," he said stupidly. "Not mine."

She remembered him looking at Charlotte and murmuring, *"Bone of my bones, and flesh of my flesh"*; it was the only verse of the Bible she had ever heard him quote.

His face was grey and drawn. He looked suddenly older. He said, "Why are you telling me this now?"

I can't, she thought. I've hurt him so much already. But she blurted, "Because Charlotte has met her real father, and she knows everything."

Stephen looked up at her, his face frighteningly expressionless. "And the father is Feliks, of course."

152

She gasped, and he nodded, as if her reaction was all the confirmation he needed. He said, "Do you know where Feliks is?"

She made no reply. If I tell, she thought, it will be like killing Feliks. If I don't tell, it will be like killing Stephen.

"You do know," he said. "Will you tell me?"

She looked into his eyes.

Stephen said, "Choose."

Lydia felt as if she were falling headlong into a pit. She said, "He's in the house."

"Good God! Where?"

It was done. "He's been hiding in a room off the nursery," she said.

His expression was no longer wooden. His cheeks coloured and his eyes blazed with fury. He turned and ran from the room.

FELIKS RAN THROUGH the flower room and through the gun room, carrying his candle and the shotgun. He could smell the sweet, slightly nauseating vapour of petrol. Through the door to the library he saw petrol gushing out of the end of the pipe and running over the floor. Feliks went in and pulled handfuls of books off the shelves and threw them into the spreading puddle. Then he went back and, standing in the gun room doorway, threw his candle into the puddle.

There was a noise like a huge gust of wind, and the library caught fire. Books and fuel burned fiercely. In a moment the curtains were ablaze; then the seats and the panelling caught.

Feliks went from the gun room into the flower room. He unbolted the door to the garden, opened it and stepped out.

He walked directly west, away from the house, for two hundred paces; then he took a wide circle south and east until he was directly opposite the main entrance to the house, across the darkened lawn. Between Feliks and the house, about fifty yards from the portico, was a big chestnut tree. Feliks went up behind the tree and leaned against it, with the shotgun in his hands.

He thought, Any minute now, any minute now.

WALDEN RAN ALONG the corridor, knocked on the door of Thomson's room and went in.

"What is it?" Thomson's voice said from the bed.

153

Walden turned on the light. "Feliks is in the house."

"Good grief!" Thomson leaped out of bed. "Do we know where?"

"In the nursery. Have you got your revolver?"

"No, but I've got three men with Orlov. I'll take two of them and then capture Feliks."

"I'm coming with you."

The two men went to Aleks's room. The bodyguard outside stood up and Thomson asked him to tell his colleagues inside to open the door.

The door opened, and Thomson said, "Feliks is in the house. Barrett and Anderson, come with me and his lordship. Bishop, stay inside the room. Check that your pistols are loaded, please, all of you."

Walden led the way along the corridor and up the back stairs to the nursery suite. His heart was pounding, and he felt the curious mixture of fear and eagerness that had always come over him when he got a big lion in the sights of his rifle.

Barrett and Anderson drew their pistols.

Walden and Thomson stood on either side of the door, out of the line of fire.

Barrett flung open the door and threw the light switch.

The nursery was empty and bright. There was a bowl of dirty water on the floor, and next to it a crumpled towel.

Walden pointed to the cupboard door. "Through there is a little attic."

Barrett opened the cupboard. They all tensed. Barrett went though with his gun in his hand.

He came back a moment later. "He *was* there."

Walden said, "We must search the house. Come *on.*"

They followed him out of the nursery and along the corridor to the staircase. As they went down the stairs Walden smelled smoke. "What's that?" he said.

Thomson sniffed.

The smell became more powerful, and now Walden could hear a noise like wind in the trees. "My house is on fire!" he shouted. He raced down the stairs.

The hall was full of smoke. Walden ran across the hall and pushed open a door. Heat hit him like a blow and he staggered back. The room was an inferno. He looked along to the west wing and saw that the library was on fire, too. He turned. Thomson was behind him, with Anderson and Barrett. Thomson was cool and collected. He began to give orders.

"Anderson, go and wake up those two bobbies outside. Send one to find a garden hose and a tap. Send the other running to the village for a fire engine. Then run up the back stairs and through the servants' quarters, waking everyone. Tell them to get out the quickest way they can and gather on the front lawn. Barrett, go and wake up Mr. Churchill and make sure he gets out. I'll fetch Orlov. Walden, you get Lady Walden and Charlotte."

Walden ran upstairs and into Lydia's room. She was sitting on the chaise-longue, her eyes red with weeping. "The house is on fire," Walden said breathlessly. "Go out quickly, onto the front lawn. I'll get Charlotte." Then he thought of something—the dinner bell. "No," he said. "You get Charlotte. I'll ring the bell."

He raced down the stairs again. In the hall was a long silk rope which would ring bells all over the house to alert guests and servants that a meal was about to be served. Walden pulled on the rope, and heard faintly the response of the bells from various parts of the house. He kept on pulling the rope.

FELIKS WATCHED ANXIOUSLY. The blaze was spreading too quickly. Already large areas of the second floor were burning; he could see the glow in the windows. He thought, Come out, you fools. He did not want the wrong people to die—

Just then the front door opened, and someone rushed out in a cloud of smoke. It's happening, Feliks thought. He hefted the shotgun and peered through the darkness but he could not see the face of the newcomer. The man shouted something, and a policeman on the portico ran off. I've got to be able to see their faces, Feliks thought; I'll have to get nearer. He moved across the lawn. Within the house, bells began to ring.

Now they will come, thought Feliks.

LYDIA RAN ALONG the smoke-filled corridor. How could this happen so *quickly?* In her room she had smelled nothing, but now there were flames flickering underneath the doors she passed. She reached Charlotte's room and turned the handle of the door. Of course, it was locked. She turned the key. She tried again to open the door. It would not move. She turned the handle and threw her weight against the door. Something was wrong; the door was jammed. Lydia began to scream and scream—

"Mama!" Charlotte's voice came from within the room. "Open the door!"

"I can't, I can't, I can't—"

"It's locked!" Charlotte said.

"I've unlocked it and it won't open and the house is on fire. Help, oh help—"

The door shook and the handle rattled as Charlotte tried to open it from the inside.

"Mama, stop screaming, and listen. The fire has shifted the floor, and the door is wedged in its frame. Go and fetch help!"

"I can't leave you—"

"Mama! Go and get help or I'll burn to death!"

Lydia turned and ran, choking, towards the staircase.

WALDEN WAS STILL ringing the bell. Through the smoke he saw Aleks and Thomson coming down the stairs. Churchill and Lydia and Charlotte should be here too, he thought; then he realized that they might use any one of several staircases; the only place to check was out on the front lawn, where everyone had been told to gather. He followed Aleks out of the house.

IT WAS A VERY SWEET moment for Feliks.

He lifted the gun and walked towards the house.

Orlov and another man walked towards him. They had not yet seen him. As they came closer, Walden appeared behind them.

Like rats in a trap, Feliks thought triumphantly.

Orlov was twenty yards away.

This is it, Feliks thought. He put the stock of the gun to his shoulder, aimed carefully at Orlov's chest and—just as Orlov opened his mouth to speak—pulled the trigger.

A large black hole appeared in Orlov's nightshirt as an ounce of number six shot tore into his body. The other two men heard the bang and stared at Feliks in astonishment. Blood gushed from Orlov's chest, and he fell backwards.

I did it, Feliks thought exultantly; I killed him.

He pointed the gun at Walden, "Don't move!" he yelled.

Walden and the other man stood motionless.

They all heard a scream, and saw Lydia come running out of the house with her hair on fire.

Feliks hesitated for a split second, then he dashed towards her. Walden did the same.

As he ran, Feliks dropped the gun and tore off his coat. He reached Lydia a moment before Walden. He wrapped the coat around her head, smothering the flames.

She pulled the coat off her head and yelled at them, "Charlotte is trapped in her room!"

Walden turned and ran towards the house.

Feliks ran with him.

CHARLOTTE'S CARPET was smouldering.

She put her fist to her mouth to keep from screaming.

She went to the window, opened it and looked out. Smoke and flames poured out of the windows below her. The wall of the house was faced with smooth stone; there was no way to climb down. I'll jump; it will be better than burning, she thought. The idea terrified her.

She ran to the door and shook the handle impotently. "Somebody, help, quickly!" she screamed.

Flames rose from the carpet, and a hole appeared in the centre of the floor.

She ran round the edge of the room to be near the window, ready to jump.

THE HALL WAS FULL OF SMOKE. Feliks stayed close behind Walden, thinking, Not Charlotte, I won't let Charlotte die.

They ran up the staircase. The whole second floor was ablaze. Walden dashed through a wall of flame and Feliks followed him, up to the third floor. They stopped outside Charlotte's door. Walden was seized by a fit of coughing. Helpless, he pointed at a door. Feliks rattled the handle and pushed the door with his shoulder. It would not move. He shouted, "Run at the door!" He and Walden, still coughing, threw themselves at the door together.

The wood split, but the door stayed shut.

Walden shouted, "Again!" Again they ran at the door.

It cracked a little more.

From the other side, they heard Charlotte scream.

Walden gave a roar of anger. He looked about him desperately. He picked up a heavy oak chair and smashed it against the door. The wood began to splinter, and Feliks put his hands into the crack and tore at the splintered wood. Walden swung the chair again. The chair broke, but there was now a hole in the door big enough for Feliks—but not for Walden—to crawl through.

Feliks dragged himself through the hole and fell into the bedroom. The floor was on fire, and he could not see Charlotte.

"Charlotte!" he shouted at the top of his voice.

"Here!" Her voice came from the far side of the room.

Feliks ran round the edge of the room, where there was less fire. Charlotte was sitting on the sill of the open window, breathing in ragged gulps. He picked her up and threw her over his shoulder. He ran back round the edge of the room to the door.

Walden reached through the hole to take Charlotte from Feliks. Her eyes were wide with terror. Feliks's face and hands were burned black, and his trousers were on fire. Behind him the floor began to collapse. Flames licked around Charlotte's nightdress, and she screamed. Walden said, "All right, Papa's got you." Suddenly he was taking her entire weight. As he drew her through the hole she fainted and went limp. He pulled her out, and just then the bedroom floor fell in. Walden saw Feliks's face as he dropped into the inferno.

Walden whispered, "May God have mercy on your soul."

Then he ran downstairs, carrying Charlotte.

LYDIA, HELD IN AN IRON grip by Thomson, stood staring at the door, willing the two men to appear with Charlotte.

A figure appeared. It was Stephen, carrying Charlotte.

Thomson let Lydia go. She ran to them. Stephen laid Charlotte gently on the grass. Lydia stared at him in panic.

"She's not dead," Stephen said. "Just fainted."

Lydia fell to the grass and cradled Charlotte's head in her lap. "Oh, my baby," she said.

She looked at Stephen. His trousers had burned, and his skin was black and blistered. But he was alive.

He took her hand. "He saved her," he said. "He passed her to me. Then the floor fell in. He's dead."

158

Lydia's eyes filled with tears. Stephen saw, and squeezed her hand. He said, "I saw his face as he fell. I don't think I'll ever forget it. His eyes were open, and he was conscious, but he wasn't frightened. In fact, he looked . . . satisfied."

The tears streamed down Lydia's face.

Churchill said, "Get rid of Orlov's body."

Poor Aleks, Lydia thought, and she cried for him, too.

Thomson said incredulously, "What?"

Churchill said, "Hide his body, bury it, throw it into the fire, I don't care what you do. I just want you to get rid of that body."

Lydia stared at him aghast, and through a film of tears she saw him take a sheaf of papers from the pocket of his dressing gown.

"The agreement is signed," Churchill said. "The Czar will be told that Orlov died by accident, in the fire that burned down Walden Hall. Orlov was not murdered, do you understand?" He looked around at them, with his aggressive, pudgy face set in a fierce scowl. "There was never anybody called Feliks."

Stephen stood up and went over to where Aleks's body lay. Someone had covered his face. Lydia heard Stephen say, "Aleks, my boy . . . what am I going to say to your mother?"

Lydia looked at the fire, burning all those years of history, consuming the past. Stephen came over and stood beside her. He whispered, "There was never anybody called Feliks."

She looked up at him. Behind him, the sky in the east was pearly grey. Soon the sun would rise, and it would be a new day.

Epilogue

On August 4, 1914, Germany invaded Belgium. Within days the German army was sweeping through France. Towards the end of August, when it seemed that Paris might fall, vital German troops were withdrawn from France to defend Germany against a Russian invasion from the east; and Paris did not fall.

In 1915 the Russians were officially given control of Constantinople and the Bosphorus.

Many of the young men Charlotte had danced with at Belinda's ball were killed in France. Freddie Chalfont died at Ypres. Charlotte trained as a nurse and went to the front.

In 1916 Lydia gave birth to a boy. The delivery was expected to be difficult because of her age, but there were no problems. They called the boy Aleks.

Charlotte caught pneumonia in 1917 and was sent home. During her convalescence she translated *The Captain's Daughter*, by Pushkin, into English. After the war women got the vote. Lloyd George became prime minister. Basil Thomson got a knighthood.

Charlotte married a young officer she had nursed in France. The war had made him a pacifist and a socialist, and he was one of the first Labour members of Parliament. Charlotte became the leading English translator of nineteenth-century Russian fiction. In 1931 the two of them went to Moscow and came home declaring that the USSR was a workers' paradise. They changed their minds at the time of the Nazi-Soviet pact. Charlotte's husband was a junior minister in the Labour government of 1945.

Charlotte is still alive. She lives in a cottage on what used to be the Home Farm. The cottage was built by her father for his bailiff, and it is a spacious, sturdy house full of comfortable furniture and bright fabrics. Walden Hall was rebuilt by Lutyens and is now owned by the son of Aleks Walden.

Charlotte is sometimes a little confused about the recent past, but she remembers the summer of 1914 as if it were yesterday. She's not all memories, though. She denounces the Communist Party of the Soviet Union for giving socialism a bad name, and Margaret Thatcher for giving feminism a bad name. If you tell her that Mrs. Thatcher is no feminist, she will say that Leonid Brezhnev is no socialist.

She doesn't translate any more, of course, but she is reading *The Gulag Archipelago* in the original Russian. As she can read for only half an hour in the morning and half an hour in the afternoon, she calculates that she will be ninety-nine by the time she gets to the end, but she's determined to finish the book.

Somehow I think she'll make it.

Ken Follett

A few years ago professors of philosophy at London University were predicting a brilliant future for one of their students, a young Welshman. The perspicacious dons have not been disappointed, but it may sometimes startle them to see the name of the promising young philosopher at the top of the bestseller lists. Ken Follett turned to journalism after graduation, working as a newspaper reporter in Cardiff. He then became an editor in a London publishing house and began to write fiction. He wrote several novels and children's books, constantly sharpening his skills until, in 1978, he published *Storm Island*. This instant bestseller, now filmed as *The Eye of the Needle*, was followed by more—*Triple*, *The Key to Rebecca*, and now *The Man from St. Petersburg*.

Has Ken Follett discovered a magic formula? More likely his success is due to a lively imagination and a capacity for hard work. He devoted nine months to planning the structure of *The Man from St. Petersburg* before he began any writing. Then, when he had completed the first draft, he changed his mind about the ending and completely rewrote the last third of the book.

Ken Follett has achieved success at an enviable time of life—he is thirty-three—and has the energy and enthusiasm to enjoy it thoroughly. He and his wife, Mary, who were married in their late teens, spend winters in the Caribbean, summers in the south of France, and will fly almost anywhere for a good rock concert. Some of their friends are musicians, and Ken likes to compose lyrics for their songs. He also plays the banjo and the guitar, and an evening at his home is more than likely to be a musical one. The Folletts have a thirteen-year-old son and an eight-year-old daughter, with whom they recently moved into a newly-converted house in Surrey.

FEVER
Robin Cook

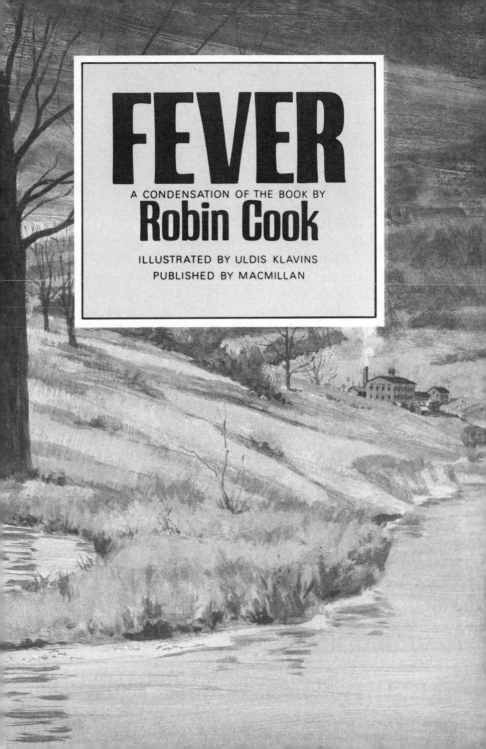

FEVER

A CONDENSATION OF THE BOOK BY
Robin Cook

ILLUSTRATED BY ULDIS KLAVINS
PUBLISHED BY MACMILLAN

Brilliant cancer research doctor Charles Martel is certain he is on the brink of a major medical discovery when two cruel blows suddenly disrupt his life. His young daughter, Michelle, is stricken with leukaemia, and the powerful research institute where he works forces him to drop his project and take up another. Any man might crack under such stress, and Cathryn Martel watches helplessly as her husband's behaviour grows more and more bizarre. Suspecting the cause of his daughter's illness, and desperate to save her from treatment he considers misguided, Charles finally takes a step that could ruin all their lives. Is he a madman or a hero? In the dramatic days that follow, his family and colleagues watch and wonder.

Prologue

THE poisonous molecules of benzene arrived in the bone marrow in a crescendo. The foreign chemical surged with the blood and was carried between the narrow spicules of supporting bone into the farthest reaches of the delicate tissue. It was like a horde of barbarians descending on Rome. The result was equally disastrous. The complicated nature of the marrow, the body's chief producer of blood cells, succumbed to the invaders.

Within minutes the poisonous molecules had reached the very heart of the marrow, the primitive, finely structured stem cells. These were the actively dividing units, serving as the source of the circulating blood cells. Here was played out the incredible mystery of life, an organization more fantastic than the wildest scientific dream. The benzene molecules indiscriminately penetrated these busily reproducing cells, interrupting the orderly replication of the DNA molecules, the basis of heredity. Most of these cells either halted their life processes in a sudden agonal heave or, having been released from the mysterious central control, tumbled off in frenzied undirected activity.

After the benzene molecules had been washed away by repeated surges of clean blood, the marrow could have recovered except for a single stem cell. This cell had been busy for years turning out white blood cells whose function, ironically enough, was to help the body fight against foreign invaders. When the benzene penetrated this cell's nucleus, it damaged a very specific part of the DNA, destroying its fine balance between repro-

167

duction and maturation. The cell instantly divided, and the resulting daughter cells had the same defect. No longer did they listen to the mysterious central control and mature into normal white blood cells. Instead they responded to an unfettered urge to reproduce their altered selves, and they absorbed nutrients at an alarmingly selfish rate. They had become parasites within their own house.

After only twenty divisions there were over one million of these lawless cells. By thirty divisions there were over one billion; they then began to break free from the mass. First a trickle of sick cells entered the circulation, then a steady stream, finally a flood. These cells charged out into the body eager to establish fertile colonies.

It was the beginning of an aggressive, acute myeloblastic leukemia in the body of a twelve-year-old girl, starting on December 28. Her name was Michelle Martel, and she had no idea what was wrong except for a single symptom: she had a *fever!*

Chapter 1

A COLD January sun tentatively fingered its way over the frigid landscape of Shaftesbury, New Hampshire. Reluctantly the shadows began to pale as the winter sky slowly lightened, revealing featureless gray clouds. It was going to snow.

The red brick buildings of old Shaftesbury huddled along the Pawtomack River, which sprang from the snow-laden White Mountains in the north and ran to the sea in the southeast. As the river coursed past the town, its flow was interrupted by a crumbling dam and a large waterwheel that no longer turned. Lining the riverbanks were block after block of empty factories, reminders of a time when New England mills were the center of the country's textile industry. The last brick mill building, at the extreme southern end of town, was occupied by a company called Recycle, Ltd., a rubber, plastic, and vinyl recycling plant. A wisp of acrid black smoke rose from its smokestack and a foul, choking odor of burned rubber and plastic hung over the area.

South of the town the river ran through rolling hills, interspersed with snow-covered meadows and bordered by fieldstone fences. Six miles below the town the river took a lazy curve to form an idyllic peninsula. In the center was a shallow pond connected to the river by an inlet. Behind the pond rose a hill capped by a white frame Victorian farmhouse with gabled roofs and gingerbread trim. A long, winding driveway bordered with oaks and sugar maples led down to Interstate 301 heading south toward Massachusetts. Twenty-five yards from the house was a weather-beaten barn.

Built on piles at the edge of the pond was a miniature copy of the main house; it was a shed turned playhouse.

The effect was that of a beautiful New England landscape in a calendar scene, except for a slight macabre detail: there were no fish in the pond and no vegetation within six feet of it.

Inside the picturesque white house, the pale morning light diffused through lace curtains and gently nudged Charles Martel from a satisfying sleep. He rolled over onto his left side, enjoying a sense of order and security. This was a feeling that Charles had never expected to experience again after his first wife, Elizabeth, had been diagnosed as having lymphoma. She had died nine years ago, leaving him with three children to raise.

For a time life had been something to endure, but the awful wound had slowly healed. And then, to Charles's surprise, even the void had been filled. Two years ago he had remarried, but he was still afraid to acknowledge his newly regained contentment. Cathryn, his new wife, was a joyous and giving person. Charles had fallen in love with her the day they met and had married her five months later.

As the darkness receded, Charles could see the placid profile of his sleeping wife. She looked much younger than her thirty-two years, a fact that initially had emphasized the difference in their ages. Charles was forty-five. Resting on his elbow, he stared at Cathryn's delicate features and shoulder-length brown hair. Her face, lit by the early morning light, seemed radiant to Charles, and watching her he felt a stirring deep within him.

He looked over at the clock; another twenty minutes before the alarm. Thankfully he lowered himself back under the down coverlet and nestled against his wife, marveling at his sense of well-being. He even looked forward to his days at the institute. Work was progressing at an ever increasing pace. He felt a twinge of excitement. What if he, Charles Martel, made the first real step in unraveling the mystery of cancer? Charles knew it was possible, and the irony was that he was not a formally trained research scientist. He'd been an internist specializing in allergy when Elizabeth had become ill. After she died he gave up his lucrative practice to become a researcher at the Weinburger Research Institute.

Cathryn turned over and found herself in an enveloping hug. She looked at Charles and smiled. "What's going on in that mind of yours?" she asked.

"I've just been watching you."

"Wonderful! I'm sure I look my best."

"You look devastating," teased Charles, pushing her thick hair back from her forehead.

As the first snowflakes settled on the gabled roofs, they embraced each other with a depth of passion and tenderness that never failed to overwhelm Charles. Then the alarm went off. The day began.

MICHELLE could hear Cathryn calling from far away, interrupting her dream. She tried to ignore the call, but it came again. She felt a hand on her shoulder and turned over to look up into Cathryn's smiling face.

"Time to get up," her stepmother said brightly.

Michelle took a deep breath and nodded her head. She'd had a bad night, full of disturbing dreams that left her soaked with perspiration. Several times she'd thought about going in to Charles. She would have if her father had been alone.

"My goodness, you look flushed," said Cathryn. She touched Michelle's forehead. It felt hot. "Do you feel sick?"

"No," said Michelle. She didn't want to be sick again. She did not want to stay home from school. She wanted to get up and make the orange juice, which had always been her job.

"I think you have a fever again," said Cathryn. She went into the adjoining bathroom and reappeared with a thermometer. She placed it under Michelle's tongue. "I'll be back after I get the boys up."

The door closed and Michelle quickly pulled the thermometer from her mouth. The mercury had already risen to 99. She had a fever and she knew it. Her legs ached and there was a tenderness in the pit of her stomach. She put the thermometer back into her mouth. From where she lay she could look out the window and see her playhouse, which Charles had made out of an ice shed. She longed for spring and the lazy days that she spent in that fantasy house. Just she and her father.

WHEN the door opened, Jean Paul, age fifteen, was already awake, propped up in bed with his physics book. Behind his head the small clock radio played soft rock 'n' roll.

"You've got twenty minutes," Cathryn said cheerfully.

"Thanks, Mom," said Jean Paul with a smile.

Cathryn paused, looking down at the boy, and her heart melted. She felt like swooping him into her arms, but she resisted the temptation. She'd learned that all the Martels were somewhat chary about physical contact, a fact that had been a little hard for her to deal with. Cathryn came from Boston's Italian North End, where touching and hugging was a constant.

"See you at breakfast," she said.

Jean Paul knew that Cathryn loved to hear him call her Mom, and he gladly obliged. It was a low price to pay for the warmth and attention that she showered on him. After the marriage she had legally adopted the three children. Jean Paul loved Cathryn as much as his real mother; at least what he could remember of her. He'd been six when she died.

CHUCK's eyes blinked open at Cathryn's touch, but he pretended sleep, keeping his head under his pillow. Chuck was eighteen years old and in his first year at Northeastern University. He wasn't doing too well and he dreaded his upcoming semester finals. They were going to be a disaster.

"Fifteen minutes," said Cathryn. She lifted the pillow and tousled his long hair. "Your father wants to get to the lab early."

"Hell," said Chuck. "I'm not getting up."

"Oh, yes, you are," said Cathryn as she yanked the covers back. "And I told you to watch your language."

She walked out and Chuck leaped up. He saw her go into Michelle's room before he slammed the door. Just because his father liked to get to his lab before eight, Chuck had to get up at the crack of dawn like some farmer. The big-deal scientist!

Chuck rubbed his face and noticed the open book at his bedside. *Crime and Punishment.* He'd spent most of the previous evening reading it, though he should have studied chemistry. What would Charles say if he flunked it? Chemistry had been Charles's major.

"I don't want to be a doctor anyway," snapped Chuck as he stood up and pulled on his dirty Levi's. In the bathroom, he decided not to shave. He thought maybe he'd grow a beard.

CLAD in a terry-cloth robe, Charles lathered his chin. He was trying to chart his schedule for the day. He wanted to start work with the new HR7 strain of mice, which carried hereditary mammary cancer. He hoped to make the animals "allergic" to their own tumors, a goal that he felt he was nearing.

Cathryn was in the shower. She pulled the curtain open a bit and called to Charles. "I think I've got to take Michelle to see a real doctor," she said, before disappearing back behind the curtain.

Charles paused in his shaving, trying not to be annoyed by her sarcastic reference to a "real" doctor. "Michelle still feeling lousy?" he asked.

"I shouldn't have to tell you. I thought that a doctor could at least guarantee good medical attention for his family."

With exasperation Charles reached out and drew back the edge of the shower curtain. "Cathryn, I'm a cancer researcher, not a pediatrician. The flu has been going around and Michelle has a touch of it. People feel lousy for a week and then it's over."

Cathryn turned to face him. "The point is, she's been feeling lousy for four weeks."

"Four weeks?" he asked. Time had a way of dissolving in the face of his work.

"Four weeks," repeated Cathryn. "She has a fever again today. I think I'd better take her to Pediatric Hospital to see Dr. Wiley. Then I can visit the Schonhauser boy."

"All right, I'll take a look at Michelle," said Charles, turning back to the sink. "What's wrong with Tad?" The Schonhausers were neighbors, and Tad and Michelle were in the same class.

Cathryn stepped out of the shower. "Elastic anemia or something," she said, toweling herself off.

172

"Aplastic anemia? That's awful."

"What is it?" Cathryn experienced a reflex jolt of panic.

"It's a rare disease where the bone marrow stops producing blood cells. It's often fatal."

Cathryn's arms hung limply at her sides. She could feel a mixture of sympathy and fear. "Is it catching?"

"No. It's usually associated with some drug or chemical. It's either a poisoning or an allergic reaction. Although most of the time the actual cause is never found. That poor kid."

"And to think I haven't even called Marge," said Cathryn. She tried to imagine the emotional strain Tad's mother was under and decided she'd better start making lists of things to do. There was no excuse for such thoughtlessness.

CHARLES knocked lightly on Michelle's door, then he quietly opened it. Michelle was lying in bed, facing away from him. Abruptly she turned over and their eyes met. A line of tears ran down her flushed cheeks. Charles's heart melted.

Sitting on the edge of her bed, he bent down and kissed her warm forehead. He could tell she had a fever. Straightening up, Charles looked at his little girl. He could so easily see Elizabeth in Michelle's face. There was the same thick, wavy hair, high cheekbones, and full lips, the same flawless olive skin. Charles thought her the most beautiful twelve-year-old in the world. With the back of his hand he wiped the wetness from her cheeks.

"I'm sorry, Daddy," said Michelle through her tears.

"What do you mean, sorry?" asked Charles softly.

"I'm sorry I'm sick again. I don't like to be a bother."

Charles hugged her. "You're not a bother. I don't want to even hear you say such a thing." He pulled away to examine her. "Tell me how you feel."

"I just feel a little weak, that's all."

"Sore throat?"

"A little. Not much. Cathryn said I couldn't go to school."

"Let me see your tongue." Michelle stuck out her tongue and watched her father's eyes for the slightest sign of concern. Charles felt under the angle of her jaw and she pulled her tongue back in. "Tender?" asked Charles as his fingers felt some small lymph nodes.

"No," said Michelle.

Charles percussed Michelle's back, somewhat clumsily but well enough to be convinced that her lungs were clear. Then he had her lie back on her bed, and he drew her nightgown up to palpate her abdomen. "Try to relax. If I hurt you, just say so."

Michelle attempted to remain still, but she squirmed beneath Charles's cold hand. Then it hurt.

"Where?" asked Charles. Michelle pointed, and Charles determined that her abdomen was tender at the midline. Putting his fingers just beneath the right ribs, he asked her to breathe in. When she did, he could feel the blunt edge of her liver pass under his fingers. She said that hurt a little. Then, with his left hand under her for support, he felt for her spleen. To his surprise he had no trouble palpating it. He'd always had trouble with that maneuver when he was in practice, and he wondered if it wasn't enlarged.

Straightening up again, Charles surveyed his daughter. She had minor aches and pains, a few slightly enlarged lymph nodes, and a fever. That could be just about any minor viral illness. But four weeks! Cathryn was right. She should be seen by a "real" doctor. He said, "Cathryn is going to take you to Pediatric Hospital today to see Dr. Wiley."

"I want you to take me."

"I can't, dear. I've got to go to the lab. Why don't you get dressed and come down for some breakfast?"

When Charles left the room, Michelle's tears welled up anew. She wanted her father to love her more than anything else in the world, and she knew that he became impatient when any of the kids got sick. She struggled up to a sitting position and braced herself against a wave of dizziness.

"CHUCK, you look like a pig," said Charles with disgust.

Chuck ignored his father. He got out some cold cereal, poured milk over it, then sat down to eat. He was wearing a stained sweater filled with holes, plus dirty jeans with frayed bottoms. His hair was uncombed and he obviously hadn't shaved.

"Do you really have to be so sloppy?" continued Charles. "I thought the hippie look was passé now."

"You're right. Hippie is out," said Jean Paul, coming into the

174

kitchen and pouring himself a glass of the orange juice Cathryn had made. "Punk is in now."

Ignoring Jean Paul, Chuck looked into his father's face. "I'm not a doctor," he said. "I don't have to adhere to a dress code."

Charles stared at his son, marveling at how much arrogance the boy could manufacture with so little basis. He was intelligent enough but hopelessly lazy. His performance in high school had been such that Charles's alma mater, Harvard, had rejected him, and Charles had a feeling that he wasn't doing well at Northeastern. Charles wondered where he, as a father, had gone wrong. He glanced at his other son: neat, easygoing, studious. It was hard to believe that both boys had sprung from the same genetic pool and grown up together.

"I hope," said Charles evenly to Chuck, "your appearance and your grades have nothing in common. I trust you are doing all right at college. We haven't heard much about that."

"I'm doing all right," said Chuck.

Cathryn reached over and put her hand on Charles's arm. "If I'm going into Boston, I'll need some extra cash," she said, hoping to change the subject. "And speaking of money, the oil people called and said our account isn't settled."

"Remind me tonight," said Charles quickly. He didn't want to discuss money.

"Also my semester tuition is way overdue," said Chuck. "I got a note saying I won't get my credits till it's paid."

"But the money was taken out of the account," said Cathryn.

"I used the money in the lab," explained Charles.

"What?" Cathryn was aghast.

"We'll get it back. I needed a new strain of mice and there was no more grant money until March."

"That's just wonderful," said Cathryn. "And how are we to eat from now until March after Chuck's bill is paid?"

"For Pete's sake! I'll take care of it," said Charles.

Michelle stepped into the kitchen, dressed in a pink monogrammed sweater over a white cotton turtleneck. She went to the counter and poured herself some orange juice.

"Well, well," said Jean Paul. "If it isn't the little princess playing sick to stay home from school."

"Don't tease your sister," commanded Charles.

175

Suddenly Michelle sneezed violently and a surge of blood gushed from her nose. "Dad!" she cried as the blood splattered to the floor.

In unison Charles and Cathryn jumped up. Cathryn snatched a dish towel while Charles picked Michelle up and carried her into the living room.

The two boys looked at the small pool of blood. "Ugh," said Chuck. "I wouldn't be a doctor for a million dollars. I can't stand blood." He got up and threw the remains of his cereal down the disposal. Then, skirting the blood on the floor, he headed up to his room.

Jean Paul finished his cereal and put his dish in the sink. Then he wiped up Michelle's blood with a paper towel.

"Good grief," said Charles as he went outside through the kitchen door. The northeast wind brought the stench of burned rubber from the recycling plant. "What a stink."

He tucked his chin into his sheepskin jacket to keep out the blowing snow and trudged toward the barn. Chuck and Jean Paul followed. There was about an inch of new snow.

The boys were bickering about something, but Charles ignored them. It was too cold to pause. The little gusts of wind felt abrasive and the smell was awful. It hadn't always been that way. The recycling plant had opened in 1971, a year after he and Elizabeth had bought the house. The move had really been Elizabeth's idea. She wanted her children to grow up in clear, crisp country air. What an irony, thought Charles, as he unlocked the barn.

"Dad," said Jean Paul, staring down at the pond. "How come the water never freezes around Michelle's playhouse?"

Charles looked out over the pond. "I don't know. I never thought about it. Must be something to do with the current from the river. The inlet isn't frozen either."

"Ugh," said Chuck, pointing beyond the playhouse. There on the edge of the pond was a dead mallard. "I guess that duck couldn't stand the smell either."

"That's strange," said Charles. "We haven't seen ducks here for years. When we first moved in, I used to hunt them, but then they disappeared."

"There's another one," cried Jean Paul. "But he's not dead. It's flopping around. Come on, let's go help it."

Jean Paul took off over the crusted snow. Neither Charles nor Chuck shared Jean Paul's enthusiasm, but they followed just the same. When they reached him, he was bending over the poor creature, who was in the throes of a seizure.

"What's wrong with him, Dad?" asked Jean Paul.

"I have no idea. I never studied avian medicine."

"Can I put it in the barn for the day?" pleaded Jean Paul.

"All right," said Charles, "but don't touch it. I'm not sure if psittacosis is carried by ducks. Get a box or something."

Jean Paul took off like a rabbit, and came back a few minutes later with a large cardboard box. He'd cut open an old pillow and filled the box with the feathers. Using the collapsed pillow as a rag, he picked up the duck and put it into the box. As he explained to Charles, the feathers would both keep the duck warm and protect it from injury if it had another seizure. Charles nodded approval and Jean Paul brought the box into the barn.

They all climbed into the five-year-old red, rusted Pinto. Charles backed out of the barn, slid down the drive, and turned north on Interstate 301, heading toward Shaftesbury. The boys turned on the radio and began to argue over the station.

"All right! No music." Charles switched off the radio. "A little quiet contemplation is a good way to begin the day."

The brothers looked at each other and rolled their eyes.

Their route took them along the Pawtomack River as it snaked its way through the countryside. The closer they got to Shaftesbury, the more intense the stench became from Recycle, Ltd. The first view of the town was the factory's smokestack, spewing its black plume into the air.

Jean Paul got out at the regional high school at the northern end of town. A group of his friends were waiting, and they entered the school together. Jean Paul was on the junior varsity basketball team and they practiced before class. Charles watched his younger son disappear, then drove on.

The trip to Boston was made largely in silence. Chuck got out of the car at the Northeastern campus and, after a perfunctory good-by, walked away in the wet snow. Charles watched him go. He looked like some late 1960s caricature, out of place among his

178

peers. Charles sighed, put the car in gear, and headed toward Cambridge. Soon his spirits began to rise. It was infinitely easier to deal with the complications of intracellular life than the uncertainties of child rearing. At Memorial Drive, he turned into the parking area of the Weinburger Research Institute.

As he got out of his car, he noticed an unusual number of cars there for that time of the morning; even the director's blue Mercedes was in its spot. Charles stood for a moment, puzzled, then started toward the institute, a modern, four-story brick and glass structure.

The receptionist saw him through the mirrored glass and pressed a button, sliding open the thick glass door. Charles started across the carpeted reception area. In the waiting room a small crowd of people were milling about excitedly. "Dr. Martel!" a man called.

Surprised to hear his name, Charles stepped into the room and was instantly engulfed by people all talking at the same time. The man who had called to Charles held out a microphone.

"I'm from the *Globe,*" he shouted. "Is it true you're going to take over the study?"

"I don't give interviews," replied Charles, pushing his way back to the hall.

"What is going on?" he muttered to himself as he hurried toward his lab. He hated the media. Elizabeth's illness had for some reason attracted the attention of the press, and their private tragedy had been publicized for people to read while having their morning coffee. He entered the lab and slammed the door.

Ellen Sheldon, Charles's laboratory assistant for the last six years, jumped. "If I slammed the door like that, I'd never hear the end of it," she said. Ellen was a darkly attractive woman of thirty, and when he'd hired her, Charles had received jealous kidding from his colleagues. But as far as he was concerned, her most important attributes were her intellect, her eagerness, and her superb MIT training.

"I'm sorry if I scared you," he said, hanging up his jacket. "But there's a bunch of reporters out there, and you know how I feel about reporters." He walked over to his desk. "What are they all doing here anyway? Did our fearless leader Morrison make some scientific breakthrough in his bathtub last night?"

"Be a little more generous," said Ellen. "Actually it concerns Dr. Brighton. The episode involving him was leaked to *The New York Times*."

Charles shook his head. "I thought that after that rave review in *Time* magazine a month ago Brighton would have been satisfied. What did he do now?"

"Don't tell me you haven't heard," said Ellen incredulously. "It's been the in-house gossip for a week."

"Ellen, I come here to work. You of all people should know that."

"Well, the news is bad," she said. "The head of the animal department reported to the director that Dr. Thomas Brighton had been sneaking into the lab to substitute healthy mice for his own cancer-carrying animals."

"Wonderful," said Charles with contempt. "Obviously the idea was to make his drug appear miraculously effective."

"Exactly. Which is interesting because it's his drug, Canceran, that has gotten him all the recent publicity. I feel sorry for him. This will have a terrible effect on his career."

"Am I hearing right?" asked Charles. "You feel sorry for that conniving little creep? I hope they throw him right out of medicine. That guy is supposed to be a medical doctor. Cheating on research is as bad as cheating on patient care. No, it's worse! In research you can end up hurting many more people."

"I wouldn't be so quick to judge. Maybe he was under a lot of pressure because of all the publicity."

"Don't give me that bull," said Charles.

"Okay, I won't. But a little human generosity would do you good, Charles Martel. You don't care at all about other people's feelings." Ellen's voice trembled with emotion.

A strained silence fell over the lab. Ellen ostensibly went back to her work. Charles opened a lab book, but he could not concentrate. He hadn't meant to sound so angry, and obviously he had offended Ellen. He wondered if her remark had anything to do with the brief affair they'd had just before he'd met Cathryn. It had been more the result of propinquity than romance, and it had lasted only a month. Then Cathryn had arrived at the institute as temporary summer help. Afterward he and Ellen had never discussed the affair.

"I'm sorry if I sounded angry," he said. "I didn't mean to."

"And I'm sorry I said what I did," she replied. "Oh, I just remembered, Dr. Morrison called. He wants to see you as soon as possible."

"He can wait," said Charles. "Let's get things going here."

Chapter 2

CATHRYN was irritated at Charles. In light of Michelle's nosebleed, he could have altered his schedule and taken her to Pediatric Hospital himself. After all, he was the doctor, and Cathryn, who had suffered through a complicated appendectomy as a child, hated and feared hospitals.

Deciding there was some safety in numbers, Cathryn sat down to call Marge Schonhauser to see if she wanted a ride into Boston. The phone was answered by Nancy, the Schonhausers' eighteen-year-old daughter.

"My mother's already at the hospital," Nancy said.

"Well, I thought I'd try," said Cathryn. "How's Tad doing?"

"He's awfully sick, Mrs. Martel. He had to have a marrow transplant. They tested all us kids and Lisa was the only one who matched. He's living in a tent to protect him from germs."

"I'm terribly sorry to hear that," said Cathryn. A marrow transplant sounded serious. She said good-by to Nancy and hung up the phone. For a moment she sat thinking. Tad's illness made her own fears about Michelle seem petty. Taking a deep breath, Cathryn went into the living room.

Michelle was propped up on the couch, watching the *Today* show. After some orange juice and a rest, she felt considerably better, but she was still upset. She was certain that her father was disappointed in her.

"I called Dr. Wiley's office," said Cathryn as brightly as she could, "and the nurse said we should come as soon as possible. So let's get the show on the road."

"Cathryn, I feel much better," said Michelle, forcing a smile. "I think I can go to school." She swung her legs to the floor and stood up. Her smile wavered through a flurry of weakness.

Cathryn looked at her adopted daughter with affection. Perhaps Michelle was afraid of the hospital, too. She walked over and put her arms around the child, hugging her close. "You don't have to be afraid, Michelle."

"I'm not afraid," she said, resisting Cathryn's embrace. "I just want to go to school."

Cathryn released her hold and examined the defiant face in front of her. In so many ways Michelle remained a mystery. She was such a precise, serious little girl who seemed mature for her age, but for some reason she always kept Cathryn at arm's length.

"I tell you what we'll do. We'll take your temperature again. If you still have a fever, we go. If you don't, then we won't."

Michelle's temperature was 100.8.

An hour and a half later Cathryn pulled the old station wagon into the garage at Pediatric Hospital and took a ticket from the machine. It had been an uneventful ride. Michelle had hardly spoken. To Cathryn she seemed exhausted.

When they had found a parking space, Michelle said suddenly, "I don't feel good, Cathryn. I feel really bad. I think you are going to have to help me out of the car."

Cathryn put her arms around the child, and this time she didn't resist. "I'll be glad to help you, Michelle. I'll help you whenever you need me. I promise."

Cathryn felt warm tears touch her arm. She had the feeling that she'd finally crossed some undefined threshold. It had taken two and a half years of patience, but it had paid off.

In the hospital, Michelle was so weak that Cathryn requested a wheelchair. She pushed the child down to Dr. Wiley's offices. There were already five patients in the waiting room. To Michelle's disgust, none was over two years of age. She glimpsed the examining rooms through an open door and whispered, "You don't think I'll get a shot, do you?"

"I have no idea," said Cathryn. "But afterward, if you feel up to it, we can do something fun. Whatever you like."

"Could we go visit my father?" Michelle's eyes brightened.

"Sure," said Cathryn. She parked Michelle next to an empty seat, then sat down herself. A mother and a whimpering five-year-old boy emerged from the examining room. One of the mothers with a tiny baby got up and went in.

"I'm going to see if I can use the nurse's phone," said Cathryn.

"I want to find out where Tad is. You're okay, aren't you?"

"I'm okay," said Michelle. "In fact, I feel better again."

"Good," said Cathryn as she got up.

Michelle watched Cathryn's long brown hair bounce on her shoulders as she walked over to the phone. Remembering hearing her father say how much he liked it, Michelle wished hers were the same color.

WITH a sigh Charles climbed the fire stairs to the second floor on his way to see Dr. Peter Morrison, the department head. Once Morrison had been a good researcher. Now his life was dominated by his ambition to become director of the institute. All he did was push paper, go to meetings, and attend benefits.

Charles had no idea why Morrison had summoned him, but he guessed it was going to be another pep talk to get him to publish a paper. Although research careers often were measured by the number of articles a doctor published, Charles had never been inclined to rush into print. Even so, he had won the respect of his colleagues by his dogged dedication and brilliance. It was only the administration that complained.

The administration area on the second floor was a world apart from the utilitarian labs on the ground floor. Its opulent decor seemed better suited to a successful law office than to a nonprofit medical organization. Charles was about to enter Morrison's office when he noticed that all the secretaries were watching him. There was a feeling of suppressed excitement in the air.

As Charles entered, Morrison stood up and came around his broad mahogany desk. He wore a freshly pressed pin-striped suit, white shirt, and silk tie; his hand-sewn loafers were professionally shined. As usual, Charles was wearing a blue oxford shirt, open at the collar, with his tie loosened. His trousers were baggy khakis and his shoes, scuffed cordovans.

"Welcome," said Morrison. With a sweep of his hand he motioned Charles to a leather couch. "Have you seen *The New York Times* today?"

Charles said no.

Morrison picked up the paper from his desk, then walked over and handed it to Charles, directing his attention to a headline on the front page: SCANDAL AT THE WEINBURGER RESEARCH INSTI-

TUTE. Charles read the first paragraph, which confirmed what Ellen had already told him. That was enough.

"Terrible, eh?" intoned Morrison, again seating himself behind his desk.

Charles nodded half-felt agreement. In truth he hoped that the incident would take some of the emphasis away from chemotherapeutic agents like Canceran. He felt that the answer to cancer lay in immunology, not chemotherapy.

"We're going to have to let Dr. Brighton go," said Morrison.

Charles nodded as Morrison launched into his explanation of Brighton's behavior. Finally Charles said, "This is all very interesting, but I have an important experiment in progress downstairs. Is there something specific you wanted to tell me?"

"Of course," said Morrison. He brought the tips of his fingers together, forming a steeple. "The board of directors of the institute had an emergency meeting last night. We fear that if we don't act quickly, the real victim of the Brighton affair could be the new and promising drug Canceran. I assume you can understand this concern?"

"Yes," said Charles, but on the horizon of his mind a black cloud began to form.

"It was decided that the only way to salvage the project was to appoint our most prestigious scientist to complete the tests. And I'm happy to say, Charles Martel, that you were chosen."

Charles closed his eyes for a moment and tried to contain himself. "Well," he began in as steady a voice as he could manage, "please convey my thanks to the board of directors, but unfortunately I'm not in a position to take over the Canceran project. You see, my own work is progressing extremely well. The board will have to find someone else."

"I hope you're joking," said Morrison.

"Not at all. With the progress I'm making, there is no way I can leave my current work."

"But the institute needs your services now. As soon as you finish the Canceran project, you can go back to your own work."

Charles felt a sense of desperation. "I'll tell you why I can't take over the Canceran project," he said. "I don't believe in it!"

"What the hell does that mean?" Morrison's patience was wearing thin.

184

"It means that cellular poisons like Canceran are not the ultimate answer to cancer. The presumption is that they kill cancer cells faster than they kill normal cells, so that after the malignancy is stopped, the patient will still have enough normal cells to live. But that's only an interim approach. To cure cancer we need a better understanding of the cellular processes, particularly the chemical communication between cells."

Charles stood up and began to pace the room. "Why does a liver cell only do what a liver cell does? Or a heart cell, or a brain cell? The answer is chemical communication. But cancer cells are not responsive to this communication. They have broken free, gone back to a more primitive stage. A real cure for cancer can come only from the study of this communication: immunology."

Morrison cleared his throat. "Very interesting," he said. "Unfortunately the immunological approach has been worked on for more than a decade but has contributed very little to the prolongation of the cancer victim's life—"

"That's the point," interrupted Charles. "Immunology will give a cure, not just palliation."

"There is very little money available for immunology at the present time," said Morrison. "However, the Canceran project carries huge grants from the National Cancer Institute and the American Cancer Society. The Weinburger needs that money."

Charles slumped back onto the couch. The institute's bureaucracy seemed to surround him like a giant octopus.

Morrison removed his glasses and placed them on his blotter. "You are a superb scientist, Charles, and that's why we need you at this moment. But you're also a maverick. You have enemies here, and I have had to defend you in the past. But at the meeting last night, when I mentioned that you might refuse to take over the Canceran project, it was decided that if you did, your position here would be terminated."

Terminated! The word echoed painfully in Charles's mind. He tried to collect his thoughts.

"Dr. Morrison," Charles said, "I believe I am truly close to understanding cancer and possibly to finding a cure."

Morrison studied the other man's face, trying to garner a hint as to his sincerity. He knew that Charles was a brilliant worker, but a loner. He suspected that his idea of "truly close" might well constitute ten years.

"A cure for cancer," he said. "Wouldn't that be nice. We'd all be very proud. But it will have to wait until the Canceran study is done. Lesley Pharmaceuticals, who hold the patent, are eager to get production rolling. Now, Dr. Martel, if you'll excuse me, I have work to do. The Canceran lab books are available to you. Good luck."

Charles stumbled out of the office in a daze, crushed at the prospect of being forced away from his own research at such a critical time. He descended the fire stairs, his mind reeling. Reaching the first floor, he walked toward his lab. He needed some time to think.

IT WAS their turn. A nurse called out Michelle's name and held the door open. Michelle left the wheelchair and gripped her stepmother's hand as they entered the inner office. Cathryn wasn't sure which one of them was more tense.

Dr. Wiley looked up from a chart and peered at them over half-glasses. He was in his late fifties and exuded that comfortably paternal air that people traditionally associate with doctors. He had closely cropped graying hair and a bushy gray mustache.

"My, my," he said. "Miss Martel, you have become a lady. You look beautiful—a little pale, but beautiful. Please, sit down."

Dr. Wiley motioned Michelle and Cathryn to the chairs facing his desk. As a consummate clinician, he had started the examination the moment Michelle had entered his office. Besides her pallor, he'd noticed the girl's tentative gait, her slumped posture, the glazed look in her blue eyes. Spreading open her chart, which he'd reviewed earlier, he picked up a pen. "Now then, what seems to be the trouble?"

Cathryn described Michelle's illness, saying that it had started gradually with fever and general malaise. They'd thought she'd had the flu, but it would not go away.

"Very well," said Dr. Wiley. "Now I'd like some time alone with Michelle. If you don't mind, Mrs. Martel."

Cathryn gave Michelle's shoulder a little squeeze. At the door she paused. "How long will you be? Do I have time to visit a patient?"

186

"I think so," said Dr. Wiley. "We'll be about thirty minutes."

"I'll be back before that, Michelle," said Cathryn. Michelle waved and the door closed.

Armed with directions from the nurse, Cathryn retraced her steps to the main lobby, then took the elevator to the fifth floor.

She hurried past the intensive care unit and down a narrow hallway to the isolation unit. All the doors to the rooms were closed and there were no patients to be seen. Cathryn approached the nurses' station. A clerk looked up and cheerfully asked if he could help her.

"I'm looking for the Schonhauser boy," said Cathryn.

"Five twenty-one," said the clerk, pointing.

Cathryn thanked him and walked over to the closed door. "Just go right in," called the clerk. "But don't forget your gown and mask."

Cathryn opened the door and found herself in a small anteroom with shelves for linen and other supplies, and a large laundry hamper. Beyond the hamper was another closed door, containing a small glass window. She searched through the shelves until she found a mask and a gown. She put them on, feeling ridiculous, and opened the inner door.

The first thing she saw was a plastic tent surrounding a bed. Through it she could make out Tad Schonhauser's form. In the fluorescent light the boy was a pale, slightly greenish color. There was a low hiss of oxygen. Marge Schonhauser sat reading by the window.

"Marge," whispered Cathryn. "It's me. Cathryn."

The masked and gowned woman looked up. "For goodness sake," she said. She got up and led Cathryn back to the anteroom, where they both pulled off their masks. "Thank you for coming," Marge said. "I really appreciate it."

"How is he?"

"Very bad. He had two marrow transplants from Lisa, but they haven't worked."

"I spoke to Nancy this morning," said Cathryn. "I had no idea Tad was this sick."

"I'd never even heard of aplastic anemia," said Marge.

Then she burst into tears, and Cathryn found herself weeping in sympathy. At last Marge controlled herself enough to speak again. "The doctors told me this morning that Tad might be terminal. They're trying to prepare me. I don't want him to suffer, but I don't want him to die."

Cathryn was stunned. Terminal? Die? These were words that referred to old people, not to a young boy who so recently was in her kitchen bursting with life and energy.

"I just can't help but ask why," sobbed Marge. "They say the good Lord has His reasons, but I'd like to know why. He's such a good boy. It seems so unfair."

Marshaling her strength, Cathryn began to talk about God and death in a way that surprised her. It just came out. Yet she must have made sense because Marge calmed down and even managed a weak smile.

"I've got to go," said Cathryn finally. "But I'll call tonight, I promise." Marge kissed her before going back in to her son.

"It doesn't seem to me that we have a whole lot of choice," said Ellen. She was sitting on a laboratory stool, looking at Charles, who was slumped in his chair before his desk.

She reached out and put her hand on his arm. "It will be all right. We'll just have to slow down a little."

"This Canceran nonsense is going to take some time," he said. "Six months to a year, and that's only if everything goes very smoothly."

"Why not do Canceran and our own work?" said Ellen. "We can work nights. I'd be willing to do it for you."

Charles stood up. "I've got a better idea. I'm going to go over Morrison's head to the director and explain that it's infinitely more important for us to stay with our own work."

"I can't imagine it will help," cautioned Ellen. "Dr. Ibanez is not going to reverse the board of directors' decision."

"I think it's worth a try. I'll show him what we've been doing." Charles got the main protocol book and the most recent data books from his desk. Then, rehearsing what he would say, he left the lab and headed back up the stairs.

The row of administrative secretaries warily monitored his progress down the hall. The entire group already knew that he had been ordered to take over the Canceran study and that he wasn't happy with the idea. Charles approached Dr. Carlos

188

Ibanez's secretary, Miss Veronica Evans. "I'd like to see the director," he said in a no-nonsense voice.

Miss Evans got up reluctantly and disappeared within the director's office. When she returned, she held the door open and motioned Charles inside.

In the large corner office, Dr. Ibanez was seated at an antique Spanish desk, and he gestured with his long, thin cigar for Charles to take a chair. The director was a small man in his early sixties, with a perpetually tanned face framed by silver hair and a silver goatee. His voice was surprisingly robust. "Hello, Charles. Tell me, what do you think about the Brighton affair? There are two people I'd like to strangle. The person from here who leaked the story and the reporter who wrote it. The press has a habit of blowing things out of proportion, and this is a good example."

"It seems to me," said Charles, "that you're blaming the wrong people. After all, this is a moral issue, not just an inconvenience."

Dr. Ibanez eyed Charles across the expanse of his desk. "Dr. Brighton should not have done what he did, but the moral issue does not bother me as much as the potential damage to the institute and to the drug, Canceran."

Charles was astounded that he and Ibanez could view the event from such fundamentally different perspectives. He was about to unleash a diatribe on the difference between right and wrong when there was a knock on the door and Jules Bellman, the institute's public relations man, came in. He looked like a puppy with his tail between his legs. "I didn't know about the *Times* story until this morning," he squeaked. "I don't know how it happened, but it didn't come from anyone in my office."

Ibanez glowered. "Well, I want the leak found. Meanwhile, I want you to schedule a press conference. Acknowledge that errors were found in the Canceran experimental protocol, but don't admit to any fraud. Just say that Dr. Brighton has been granted a leave of absence. Emphasize that the Weinburger Institute still has full confidence in Canceran. And the way to show this is by announcing that we are putting our most renowned scientist on the project, Dr. Charles Martel."

"Dr. Ibanez," began Charles, "I—"

189

"Just a minute, Charles," interrupted Ibanez. "Let me finish with Jules here. Now, Jules, I want you to make Charles sound like Louis Pasteur reincarnated, understand?"

"I've got it," said Bellman excitedly. "Dr. Martel, can you tell me your latest publications?"

"Damn it!" shouted Charles, slamming his lab books down on Ibanez's desk. "This is a ridiculous conversation. You know I haven't published anything recently."

"Charles, calm down," said Dr. Ibanez. "Actually it's probably better you haven't published. Right now, interest in immunological cancer research has slackened. It wouldn't be good to admit you've been working exclusively in this area; the press might suggest you were unqualified to take over Canceran."

"Give me strength," groaned Charles through clenched teeth. He stared at Ibanez, breathing heavily. "That's why I came up here in the first place: to tell you that I don't feel capable of taking on the Canceran project."

"Nonsense," said Ibanez. "You're more than capable."

"I'm not talking about my intellectual capabilities," snapped Charles. "I'm talking about my lack of interest. I don't believe in Canceran and the approach to cancer it represents. A real cure can only come through the study of immunology."

"Dr. Martel," said Dr. Ibanez, "the fact is that while there is plenty of funding for chemotherapy research, there is very little for immunological studies."

"That's because chemotherapy agents like Canceran can be patented, whereas immunological processes, for the most part, cannot be," said Charles.

"It seems to me," said Ibanez, "that the expression 'Don't bite the hand that feeds you' applies here. The cancer community has supported you, Dr. Martel. But right now we are in the midst of a crisis. If we lose the grant for Canceran, the whole institute is in financial jeopardy."

"But I'm at a critical point in my own research," Charles said. "I have made an astounding breakthrough. It's right here." He tapped one of his lab books. "I can take a cancer cell, any cancer cell, and isolate the chemical difference between that cell and a normal cell from the same individual."

"In what animals?" asked Dr. Ibanez.

190

"Mice, rats, and monkeys," said Charles.

"What about humans?"

"I haven't tried it yet, but I'm sure it will work."

"Can this chemical difference stimulate the production of an antibody—is it antigenic?"

"It should be. Unfortunately I have not yet been able to sensitize a cancerous animal. There seems to be some kind of blocking mechanism, or what I call a blocking factor. And that's where I am in my work, trying to isolate this factor. Once I do, I intend to make an antibody to it, and that should permit the animal to respond immunologically to its tumor."

"I must admit it sounds interesting and I can assure you the Weinburger will support you, as it has in the past. But it sounds as if you have a long way to go, and first you are going to have to help the institute. You must take over the Canceran project immediately. If you refuse, you will have to take your research elsewhere. I want no more discussion. The issue is closed."

For a moment Charles sat there, his face reflecting his inner uncertainty. The suggestion of being fired was far more terrifying coming from Ibanez than from Morrison.

"You're not the most popular man on the staff," added Ibanez gently, "but you can change that now by pitching in. I want you to tell me, Dr. Martel: Are you with us?"

Charles nodded his head without looking up. Then he gathered up his lab books and left without uttering another word.

After the door closed, Bellman looked at Ibanez. "What a strange reaction. You sure he's the best man to take over Canceran?"

"He's the only man. No one else is available who has his professional reputation. All he has to do is finish the study."

"But if he screws up somehow . . ."

"Don't even suggest it," said Ibanez. "If he mishandles Canceran at this point, we'll all be looking for a job."

For the second time that day, Charles slammed the door to his lab, rattling the glassware on the shelves. Ellen deftly caught a pipette she'd knocked off the counter when she spun around.

"If you say I told you so, I'll scream," said Charles, flinging himself onto his metal swivel chair.

191

"Dr. Ibanez wouldn't listen?" asked Ellen guardedly.

"He listened. He just wouldn't buy, and I caved in."

"I don't think you had any choice," said Ellen. "So don't be so hard on yourself. Anyway, what's the schedule?"

"We finish the Canceran study, and we start right away. In fact, why don't you go get the Canceran lab books? I don't want to talk to anyone for a while."

"All right," said Ellen softly. She was relieved to have an errand to take her out of the lab for a few minutes.

After Ellen left, it was quiet except for the low hum of the refrigerator compressors and the tick of the automatic radioactivity counter. These were familiar sounds and they had a soothing effect on Charles. Maybe, he thought, the Canceran affair wouldn't be too bad. Suddenly the phone rang. He picked it up.

"Hello," said the caller. "This is Mrs. Crane from the bursar's office at Northeastern University."

"Yes," said Charles.

"Sorry to bother you, but the $1650 semester tuition for your son is way overdue. Can we expect the money soon?"

"Of course," said Charles. "I'll have a check on its way. I'm sorry for the oversight."

Charles hung up. He knew that he'd have to get a loan, and he decided to go immediately to the bank. He felt that he could use some fresh air and a little time away from the Morrisons and Ibanezes of the world.

FLIPPING the pages of a magazine, Cathryn wrestled with a sense of foreboding. Michelle had been in the examining area for over an hour. Something must be wrong!

She began to fidget, crossing and uncrossing her legs, checking her watch repeatedly. Finally she stood up and walked over to the nurse. "Excuse me," she said. "My little girl, Michelle Martel. Do you have any idea how much longer she'll be?"

"I'm sure she'll be out shortly," said the nurse politely.

"Does he frequently take over an hour?"

"Certainly," said the nurse. "He takes whatever time he needs. He never rushes. He's that kind of a doctor."

Cathryn returned to her seat and picked up another magazine. She glanced at the advertisements showing smiling, happy peo-

192

ple. Then she tried to decide what to fix for dinner but never completed the thought. Her fears mounted.

Finally the door opened and Dr. Wiley leaned into the room. "Mrs. Martel, can I speak to you for a moment?"

Cathryn got up and hurried after him, closing the door behind her. "Is everything all right?" she asked. She tried to sound normal, but her voice was too high.

"Everything is under control. But we need your permission for a test." He handed a form to Cathryn. She took it, her hand quivering.

"Where is Michelle?" Her eyes scanned the form.

"She's in one of the examining rooms. You can see her right after we do the bone marrow aspiration."

"Bone marrow?" Cathryn's head shot up. "Does Michelle have aplastic anemia?"

"Absolutely not." Dr. Wiley was perplexed at her response. "What made you ask that?"

"Just a few minutes ago I visited our neighbor's child, who has aplastic anemia. When you said bone marrow . . ."

"I understand," said Dr. Wiley. "Don't worry. I can assure you that aplastic anemia is not a possibility here. Let me explain the test. Bone marrow aspiration is done with a needle similar to the one we use for drawing blood. We use a little local anesthesia so it's practically painless. It's truly a simple procedure."

Cathryn managed a smile and said they could go ahead with the test. She signed the form, then allowed herself to be escorted back to the waiting room.

MICHELLE lay very still on the examining table. Even with her head propped up on the pillow, her view was mostly ceiling with frosted glass over fluorescent lighting. She had on a nightie of sorts, but it was open in the back, and she could feel her skin on the paper that covered the table. A white sheet was spread over her. She wanted her clothes and to go home. She'd been stuck with needles three times. Once in each arm and once in a finger. Each time she'd asked if it were the last, but no one would say.

There was a scraping sound, and the door to the examining room opened. It was the fat nurse, and she was pulling something into the room. Michelle heard the sound of metal jangling against metal. Once clear of the door, the nurse swung around, pushing a small table on wheels, covered with a blue towel.

"What's that?" Michelle asked anxiously.

"Some things for the doctor, sweetheart," said Miss Hammersmith, as if she were talking about treats. Her name tag was pinned high on her shoulder like a battle ribbon.

"Is it going to hurt?" asked Michelle.

"Sweetheart, why do you ask that kind of question? We're trying to help you." Miss Hammersmith sounded offended.

"Ah, my favorite patient," said Dr. Wiley, opening the door with his shoulder. He kept his hands away from his body because they were wet. Most alarming to Michelle, he was wearing a surgical mask.

"What are you going to do?" she asked.

"Well, I'm afraid I've got good and bad news," said Dr. Wiley, drying his hands on a sterile towel. "I'm afraid you have to have one more little needle stick, but the good news is that it will be the last for a while." He pulled on a pair of rubber gloves from a package Miss Hammersmith held open for him.

"I don't want any more needles," said Michelle, her eyes filling with tears. "I just want to go home."

"Now, now," soothed Miss Hammersmith.

Michelle tried to sit up, but she was restrained by a cinch about her waist. "I want my father," she managed.

"Michelle!" said Dr. Wiley sharply, then his voice softened. "I know this is hard for you, but it will be over in a minute if you help us." He gestured to Miss Hammersmith. "Maybe Mrs. Levy could come in here for a moment and give us a hand."

Miss Hammersmith lumbered out of the room.

"Okay, Michelle, just relax for a moment," said Dr. Wiley. "I'm sure your dad will be real proud of you when I tell him how brave you were. This will only take a moment. I promise."

Michelle lay back and closed her eyes, feeling the tears run down the side of her face. The door opened again and Miss Hammersmith came in, followed by two other nurses.

"Come on, sweetheart," cajoled Miss Hammersmith, coming up alongside Michelle. One nurse went around to the opposite side while the other went to the foot of the table. Miss Hammer-

194

smith pulled the sheet down over Michelle's legs and drew up her nightie.

Michelle watched while the nurse whisked the towel from the table with the wheels. Dr. Wiley busied himself with the instruments on it, his back to her. When he turned, he held a wet piece of cotton. "I'm just going to clean your skin a little," he explained as he began scrubbing Michelle's hipbone.

This was a new experience, not like the previous needles. "Where are you going to stick me?" Michelle shouted, trying again to sit up. As soon as she moved, she felt strong arms grip her and force her back onto the table. "No!" she cried in panic.

"Easy now," said Dr. Wiley as he positioned a drape with a hole in the center over Michelle's hipbone. Then he turned again to the small wheeled table. When he reappeared in Michelle's view, he was holding a huge syringe with three stainless steel finger rings.

"No!" cried Michelle again, and with all her might she tried to break from the grasp of the nurses. Instantly she felt Miss Hammersmith's arm across her chest. Then she felt the needle pierce her skin over her hipbone.

CHARLES took a bite of his pastrami sandwich, the only good thing put out by the institute cafeteria. Ellen had brought it back to the lab, since Charles did not want to see anyone. Except for his brief foray to the bank, he'd stayed at his desk, poring over the Canceran experimental protocol. He'd been through all the lab books and had begun to feel that completing the study would not be as difficult as he had initially imagined; maybe they could get it done in six months. He picked up his pencil. "Here's the way we'll handle this," he said to Ellen. "We'll start out the mice with a dose of Canceran equal to one sixteenth of the LD50."

Charles reminded Ellen that LD50 is the dose of a drug that causes death in fifty percent of the animals in a test. With his pencil he began to make a flow diagram of the project, explaining each step as he wrote. It was half an hour before he was done.

"Whew," sighed Ellen as she stretched her arms. "I guess I didn't know what was involved."

"Did you mean what you said about working nights?" asked Charles. In his mind he tried to estimate the feasibility of continuing work on the blocking factor while they labored with Canceran. It would be slow and they'd have to put in long hours; but if they could isolate even a single protein that functioned as a blocking agent in a single animal, they'd have a basis for persuading the institute to back his study.

"Look," said Ellen. "I know how much your research means to you, and if you're willing to work nights, so am I."

"You understand that I have no idea whether I can get Morrison to pay you overtime?" he said.

"I don't—" began Ellen, but the phone interrupted her. She answered it, then handed it to Charles. "It's your wife."

Of all times for Cathryn to be calling, he thought. "What is it?" he asked impatiently.

"I want you to come over here to Dr. Wiley's office," said Cathryn in a stiffly controlled voice.

"What's going on?"

"I don't want to discuss it over the phone."

"Cathryn, I can't leave now."

"I'll be waiting for you," said Cathryn. Then she hung up.

"Damn!" shouted Charles as he slammed down the receiver. But the thought of Michelle planted a seed of concern in his mind. Vividly he remembered her nosebleed. "I've got to drive over to Pediatric Hospital," he said to Ellen. "It won't take very long. Meanwhile, why don't you prepare the dilution of Canceran and have the mice brought up here? We'll inject the first batch as soon as I return."

Ellen watched the door close behind Charles, feeling an absurd mixture of disappointment and anger. She had allowed the idea of working together at night to excite her. But she knew deep down that it would not lead to anything.

She went over to the counter where the sterile bottles of Canceran had been left. It was a white powder, like confectioner's sugar, waiting to be reconstituted with sterile water. As she was working out the dilution, Dr. Morrison came into the lab.

"Dr. Martel isn't here," said Ellen.

"I know," said Morrison. "I saw him leave the building. I wasn't looking for him. I wanted to talk to you for a moment." He produced a slim gold cigarette case, snapped it open, and extended it toward Ellen. When she shook her head, Morrison withdrew a cigarette and with a gold lighter made an elaborate ritual of lighting it. "I suppose you know that Charles has been selected to continue the Canceran study?"

Ellen nodded. "Dr. Martel has already started on it," she said.

"Good, good," said Morrison. "I want him to concentrate on it exclusively." He hesitated. "I don't know exactly how to put this," he went on. "But I was wondering if you would do me and the institute a big favor. I'm concerned about Charles's emotional stability. I'd like you to report any abnormal behavior on his part in relation to the Canceran project. I know this is an awkward request, but the entire board of directors will be grateful for your cooperation."

"All right," said Ellen quickly, not sure how she really felt about it. At the same time she thought of all the effort she had put forth for Charles, and how he hadn't appreciated it. "I'll do it provided that anything I say remains anonymous."

"Absolutely," agreed Morrison. "That goes without saying. And, of course, you will report to me directly." At the door he paused. "It's been nice talking with you, Miss Sheldon. Maybe we can have dinner sometime."

"Maybe," said Ellen.

Chapter 3

DR. WILEY'S nurse led Charles into a large paneled office. Bookshelves filled with medical periodicals and textbooks lined one wall. In the center of the room was a round oak table surrounded by half a dozen captain's chairs. One of them scraped back as Cathryn stood up.

She ran to Charles and threw her arms around his neck. "Cathryn," he said, "what's the matter?"

"It's my fault," she said. As soon as she spoke she started to cry. "I should have brought Michelle in sooner. I know I should have." Charles helped her to a chair and sat down beside her.

"Cathryn, you must tell me what is going on."

His wife looked up, her blue eyes awash with tears, but before she could speak, Dr. Wiley stepped into the room.

Charles stood up, searching the man's face for a clue to what was happening. He had known Jordan Wiley for almost twenty

197

years and had always been impressed with his knowledge, intelligence, and empathy.

"It's good to see you again," Dr. Wiley said, grasping Charles's hand. "I'm sorry it's under such trying circumstances."

"Perhaps you could tell me what these trying circumstances are," said Charles, annoyance camouflaging his fear.

"You haven't been told?" Dr. Wiley glanced at Cathryn, who shook her head; then he scrutinized Charles's face. "It's about Michelle. I'm sorry to say that she has leukemia."

Charles's mouth slowly dropped open. He didn't move a muscle; he didn't even breathe. Dr. Wiley's news had released a flood of memories. Over and over Charles heard, "I'm sorry to inform you, Dr. Martel, but your wife, Elizabeth, has an aggressive lymphoma. . . . I'm awfully sorry to report that your wife is not responding to treatment. . . . Dr. Martel, I'm sorry to say that your wife has entered a terminal leukemic crisis. . . ."

"No! It's not true. It's impossible!" he shouted.

Dr. Wiley reached out and placed a sympathetic arm on Charles's shoulder. "Charles—" he began.

With a lightning movement Charles knocked Dr. Wiley's hand away. "Don't you dare patronize me!"

Dr. Wiley stepped back in surprise. He spoke gently but firmly. "Charles, I know this is difficult for you, but you have to get control of yourself. Michelle needs you."

Charles struggled to anchor his thoughts. "What kind of leukemia?" He spoke slowly, with great effort. "Lymphocytic?"

"No," said Dr. Wiley. "Unfortunately it's acute myeloblastic. There are circulating leukemic cells. Her white count is over fifty thousand."

A deathly silence descended over the room.

Charles began to pace, moving with quick steps. "A diagnosis of leukemia isn't certain until a bone marrow is done," he said abruptly.

"It's been done," said Dr. Wiley.

"I didn't give permission," snapped Charles.

"I did," said Cathryn, her voice hesitant.

Ignoring her, Charles continued to glower at Dr. Wiley. "I want to see the smears myself."

"As you wish." Dr. Wiley led Charles and Cathryn down the

hall to a small clinical lab. "Over here," he said, and motioned to a shrouded microscope. He plucked off the plastic cover, revealing a binocular Zeiss. Charles sat down, adjusted the eyepieces, and snapped on the light. Dr. Wiley opened a nearby drawer and pulled out a cardboard slide holder. Gently he lifted one of the slides out and extended it toward Charles.

Charles took the slide between his thumb and first finger. His hand trembled as he placed the slide on the mechanical stage and put a drop of oil on the cover glass. Watching from the side, he lowered the oil emersion lens until it just touched the slide.

Taking a deep breath, Charles put his eyes to the oculars and tensely began to raise the barrel of the scope. All at once a multitude of pale blue cells leaped out of the blur, and the blood began to pound in his temples. Instead of the usual population of cells in all stages of maturation, Michelle's marrow had been all but replaced by large, undifferentiated cells with correspondingly large, irregular nuclei, containing multiple nucleoli.

"I think you'll agree it's conclusive," said Dr. Wiley gently.

Charles leaped to his feet, knocking his stool over with a crash. "Why?" he screamed at Dr. Wiley, as if the pediatrician were part of an encircling conspiracy. He grabbed the man's shirt and shook him violently.

Cathryn threw her arms around her husband. "Charles, stop!" she shouted. "It's not Dr. Wiley's fault."

As if waking from a dream, Charles let go of Wiley. Embarrassed, he bent down and righted the stool, then stood up. "Where is Michelle?" he asked.

"She's been admitted to the hospital," said Dr. Wiley. "She's on Anderson six, a floor with a wonderful group of nurses."

"I want to see her," said Charles, his voice weak.

"I'm sure you do. But we should discuss her care first. We have here at Pediatric one of the world's authorities on childhood leukemia, Dr. Stephen Keitzman. He's a pediatric oncologist, and with Cathryn's permission I've already contacted him. He agreed to meet with us as soon as you arrived."

AT FIRST Cathryn wasn't sure about Dr. Stephen Keitzman. He was a small young man with a large head, dark curly hair, and rimless glasses. His manner was abrupt, his gestures nervous, and he had a slight facial tic. But he spoke with an authority that gave Cathryn confidence.

Certain that she would forget what was being told to them, she pulled out a small note pad and ball-point pen. It confused her that Charles didn't seem to be listening. Instead he was staring out the window, seemingly watching the flurries of snow. He was acting strangely—angry one minute, detached the next.

"In other words," summed up Dr. Keitzman, "the diagnosis of acute myeloblastic leukemia is established beyond any doubt."

Swinging his head around, Charles surveyed the room. He knew he had a precarious hold on his emotions. He felt he'd spent the whole morning watching people undermine his security, destroy his family, rob him of his newly found happiness. Rationally he knew there was a big difference between Morrison and Ibanez on the one hand and Wiley and Keitzman on the other, but at the moment they all triggered the same unreasoning fury.

"In order to allay the inevitable sense of guilt," Keitzman was saying, "I want to emphasize that the cause of leukemia like Michelle's is unknown. Parents should not try to blame specific events for initiating the disease. The goal will be to treat the condition and bring about a remission. I'm pleased to be able to report that we have had very favorable results with acute myeloblastic leukemia. We are able to engineer a remission in about eighty percent of cases."

Charles spoke up. "That's wonderful, but can you tell us how long the remission lasts in Michelle's form of the disease?" It was as if Charles had to goad Keitzman into revealing the worst news at once.

Keitzman cleared his throat. "Dr. Martel, I am aware that you know more about your daughter's disease than most parents would. But even if you are already familiar with these facts, perhaps they are helpful to Mrs. Martel."

"Why don't you answer my question?" said Charles.

Dr. Keitzman looked at Cathryn's frightened face. He glanced at Dr. Wiley for support, but Wiley had his head down. Keitzman said in a low voice, "The probability of a five-year survival is not high in acute myeloblastic leukemia."

"To be more exact," said Charles, jumping to his feet, "the

median survival in acute myeloblastic leukemia if a remission is obtained is only one to two years. And in Michelle's case, with circulating leukemic cells, her chances of a remission are less than twenty percent." He abruptly walked to the window. "Why don't you tell Mrs. Martel what the survival time of the non-responder is . . . the patients who don't have a remission?"

"I'm not sure what good this—" began Dr. Keitzman.

Charles whirled around. "What good? I'll tell you what good it is. The worst thing about disease is the uncertainty. Humans are capable of adapting to anything as long as they know. It's the hopeless floundering that drives people crazy."

Charles stormed over to Cathryn as he spoke. He grabbed her pad and threw it into the wastebasket. "We don't need notes on this! I know all too well about leukemia." He turned to Dr. Keitzman, his face flushed. "Come on, Keitzman, tell us about the survival time of nonresponders."

Keitzman sat stiffly in his chair, his hands gripping the edge of the desk. "It's not good," he said. "Weeks, months at most."

Charles didn't answer. Having successfully backed Dr. Keitzman into a corner, he was suddenly adrift. Slowly he sank down into his chair.

"I think we should discuss therapy," offered Dr. Wiley.

"I agree," said Dr. Keitzman. "In fact, I'd like to start treatment immediately. But, of course, we are going to need consent because of the nature of the drugs."

"The side effects are pretty rough." Charles was speaking more calmly now, but he remembered the suffering Elizabeth had endured, the violent nausea, the terrible weakness. "When the chances of a remission—let alone a cure—are less than twenty percent, I don't know if it's worth subjecting a child to the additional pain."

Dr. Keitzman stood up and pushed back his chair. "I believe in treating all cases aggressively. Every patient deserves a chance at life, whatever the odds. Chemotherapy is a truly remarkable weapon against cancer. But you are entitled to your opinion. Perhaps you would prefer to find another oncologist."

"No! We need you," cried Cathryn, terrified at the prospect of being abandoned by Dr. Keitzman. "Charles, please. We can't fight this alone."

"I think you should cooperate," urged Dr. Wiley.

Charles sagged under the pressure. He knew he could not care for Michelle, even though he was convinced the prescribed treatment was wrong. "All right," he said softly.

Dr. Keitzman sat down again and rearranged some papers on his desk. "Very well," he said at length. "Our protocol for myeloblastic leukemia involves these drugs: daunorubicin, Thioguanine, and Cytarabine. After our workup we'll start with daunorubicin, given intravenously by rapid infusion."

As Dr. Keitzman outlined the treatment schedule, Charles recalled the potential side effects of daunorubicin. Michelle's fever was probably caused by an infection due to her body's depressed ability to fight bacteria, and the daunorubicin would make that worse. And besides causing her to be essentially defenseless to infection, the drug would devastate her digestive system and possibly affect her heart.

He squirmed in his seat as Keitzman spoke. "I believe it is important to tailor the psychological approach to the patient. I tend to work by age: under five, school age, and adolescents. In the school-age group the fear of separation from parents and the pain of hospital procedures are the major concerns of the child. We try to relieve these anxieties by telling the patient only what he specifically asks to know."

"I think Michelle is going to feel the separation aspect a lot," said Cathryn.

"With adolescents," Dr. Keitzman went on, "treatment approaches that of an adult. Psychological support is geared toward eliminating confusion and uncertainty without destroying denial, if that is part of the patient's defense mechanism. In Michelle's situation, the problem falls between the school age and the adolescent. I'm not sure what is the best way to handle it."

"Are you talking about whether Michelle should be told she has leukemia?" asked Cathryn.

"That's part of it," agreed Dr. Keitzman. "But no decision has to be made now. For the time being, Michelle can be told that we are trying to figure out what's wrong with her. Before we go to see her—does Michelle have any siblings?"

"Yes," said Cathryn. "Two brothers."

"Good," said Dr. Keitzman. "They should be blood-typed to

202

see if they match Michelle's HLA and ABO loci. We'll probably need platelets, granulocytes, and maybe even marrow."

Cathryn had no idea what Dr. Keitzman was talking about, but she assumed Charles did. The only problem was that Charles seemed to be having more trouble than she was with the news.

Going up in the elevator, Charles fought to control himself. On the one hand, he could not wait to see his daughter, to hold her and protect her; on the other, he dreaded seeing her because he knew too much. She would see the truth in his face.

The elevator stopped. Dr. Wiley led them down a pale blue hall with pictures of animals on the walls. It was busy with nurses, parents, and pajama-clad children.

Michelle had a single room, painted the same shade of pastel blue as the hallway. On the wall beside the door to the lavatory was a dancing hippopotamus. There were windows on two sides of the room. Next to the bed was a steel pole supporting a small plastic bag as well as an IV bottle. The plastic tubing snaked down and entered Michelle's arm. She turned from looking out the window when she heard the group enter.

"Hello, peanuts," said Dr. Wiley. "Look who I brought."

At the first glimpse of his daughter, Charles's dread vanished in a wave of affection and concern. He rushed to her and scooped her up in his arms. She responded by throwing her free arm around his neck.

Cathryn stepped around the bed to the opposite side. She saw that Charles was struggling to hold back tears. After a minute, he lowered Michelle's head to the pillow and smoothed out her hair to form a fan about her pale face. Michelle reached for Cathryn's hand and grasped it tightly.

"How do you feel?" asked Charles.

"I feel fine now," said Michelle, obviously overjoyed to see her parents. But then her face clouded. "Is it true, Daddy?"

Charles's heart leaped in his chest. He glanced at Dr. Keitzman in alarm.

"Is what true?" asked Dr. Wiley casually.

"Daddy?" pleaded Michelle. "Is it true I have to stay here overnight?"

Charles smiled with relief. "Just for a few nights," he said. "We need to make some tests to see what's causing your fever."

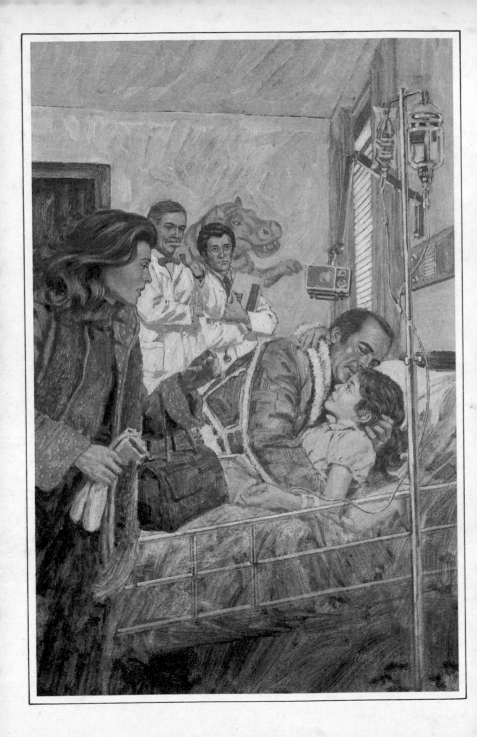

"I don't want any more tests," said Michelle, her eyes widening in fright. She'd had enough pain.

"The doctors will only do the tests they absolutely need," said Cathryn gently. "You're going to have to be a big girl."

Charles was struck by how tiny and vulnerable Michelle looked in the hospital bed. Somewhere in her bone marrow a group of her own cells was waging war against her body. And there was nothing he could do to help her . . . absolutely nothing.

"Well, I've got to be going," said Dr. Keitzman as he moved to the door. "I'm available anytime you'd like to speak to me."

Cathryn acknowledged the offer with a smile, but Charles didn't look up from Michelle.

Dr. Wiley followed Dr. Keitzman into the hall, and together they walked toward the nurses' station.

"I think Charles Martel is going to make this a very difficult case," said Keitzman. "Did you hear what he said about withholding chemotherapy? You'd think he would know about the advances we've made with it."

"He knows," said Wiley. "He's just angry. He went through all this when his wife died. Still, he scared me for a moment. I thought he'd totally lost control."

When the two men reached the nurses' station, they stopped and leaned against the counter. "Are you thinking what I am?" asked Dr. Keitzman.

"Probably. I'm wondering just how stable Charles Martel is."

"Maybe we should talk to his wife for a moment," Keitzman suggested. "What do you think?"

"Let's try." Wiley saw the charge nurse in the corridor. "Miss Shannon! Could you come here for a moment?"

The nurse came over to the two doctors. Dr. Wiley explained that they wanted to speak to Mrs. Martel without her husband and asked her if she would try to engineer it.

As they watched Miss Shannon walk briskly down the hall, Dr. Keitzman said, "It goes without saying that the child is desperately ill. Martel is right about one thing. Her chance of a remission is very slim."

"At times like these I don't envy you your specialty."

They fell silent as Miss Shannon appeared with Cathryn. "What's wrong?" Cathryn asked as she came up to them.

"It's about your husband," began Dr. Keitzman cautiously.

"We're concerned that he may interfere in Michelle's treatment," Dr. Wiley explained. "It's hard for him. First, he knows too much about the disease himself. Then, he has watched someone he loved die despite chemotherapy."

"Perhaps you could give us some idea of his emotional state," said Dr. Keitzman. "We'd like to know what to expect."

"I think he will be fine," assured Cathryn. "He had a lot of trouble adjusting when his first wife died, but he never interfered with her treatment."

"But what about the kind of emotional outburst he had today?" asked Keitzman.

"He does have a temper," said Cathryn, "but he usually keeps it under control."

"Well, that's encouraging. Maybe it's not going to be so difficult after all. Thank you, Mrs. Martel. You've been most helpful." Turning to Dr. Wiley, he said, "I've got to get things rolling. I'll speak to you later." He moved off at a run.

"Cathryn, you couldn't get a better oncologist," said Dr. Wiley, "but we're going to count on your strength."

"My strength?" questioned Cathryn, aghast. "Hospitals and medical problems aren't my strong points."

At that moment she caught sight of Charles emerging from Michelle's room and ran to meet him. They stood for a moment in a silent embrace. When they came back to Dr. Wiley, Charles seemed more in control. "Michelle's a good kid," he said. "I asked her if she minded if I went back to the lab. She said no, as long as you stayed here, Cathryn. I hope you understand. I feel such a terrible powerlessness. I've got to keep busy."

"I understand," said Cathryn. "I'll be happy to stay. I'll call my mother. She'll take care of things for me at home."

Charles spoke to Dr. Wiley. "May I have a sample of Michelle's blood?" he asked.

"Why, yes. Come to the lab," said Wiley. Charles's question unnerved him.

"Fine. Let's go." Charles started toward the elevator.

Confused, Dr. Wiley hurried after him, nodding a quick good-by to Cathryn. Charles had apparently gone off on a new tangent. His daughter's blood? Well, he was a physician.

206

CLUTCHING THE FLASK OF Michelle's blood, Charles hurried through the foyer of the Weinburger Institute and down the corridor to his lab. Ignoring Ellen, he went over to the apparatus they used to separate the cellular components of blood and began the complicated process of priming the unit.

Wiping her hands, Ellen came around the end of the workbench. "I finished injecting the first batch of mice with Canceran," she said.

"Wonderful," replied Charles without interest. Carefully he introduced a portion of Michelle's blood into the machine.

"What are you doing?" Ellen followed all his movements.

"Michelle has myeloblastic leukemia," said Charles. He spoke as evenly as if he were giving the weather report.

"Oh, no!" gasped Ellen. "Charles, I'm so sorry."

"I have a sample of her blood. I'm going to see if our method of isolating a cancer antigen works on her leukemic cells. It makes me feel I'm doing something to help her. I've decided we'll continue our own work while we work on Canceran."

"Charles, Morrison came by while you were out. He emphasized that he wants you to work exclusively on Canceran."

"Morrison doesn't have to know what we're doing."

"I really don't think it's advisable to go against the administration on this. Particularly when the reason is personal."

For a moment Charles froze, then he slammed his open palm against the slate counter top. "That's enough!" he yelled. "I've had enough of people telling me what to do. If you don't want to work with me, then just get out of here!"

Ellen watched incredulously as Charles turned back to his work, running a nervous hand through his hair. In a moment he said, "Don't just stand there; get me the radioactive-labeled nucleotides."

Ellen walked over to the radioactive-storage area. As she opened the lock, she noticed that her hands were trembling. Obviously Charles was just barely in control of himself. She put the chemicals on the counter and thought about what she was going to say to Dr. Morrison.

"Thank you," Charles said simply, as if nothing had happened. "While I was driving over here, I had an inspiration. The biggest hurdle in our work has been this blocking factor and our inability to elicit an antibody response to the cancer antigen in the cancerous animal. Well, why not inject the cancer antigen into a related, noncancerous animal, where we can be absolutely certain of an antibody response?"

Ellen scrutinized Charles's face. In seconds he'd metamorphosed from an infuriated child to a dedicated researcher. Without waiting for an answer, he went on. "As soon as the noncancerous animal is immune to the cancer antigen, we'll isolate the responsible T-lymphocytes, purify the transfer factor protein, and transfer sensitivity to the cancerous animal. It's so fundamentally simple, I can't believe we didn't think of it before. Well . . . what's your impression?"

Ellen shrugged. The transfer factor did not work well in the animal systems they were using; in fact, it worked best with humans. But technical questions were not foremost in her mind.

"Call the animal room," said Charles. "Tell them we want a fresh batch of control mice. We'll inject them with the mammary tumor antigen. God, I wish there were more than twenty-four hours in a day."

"Pass the fettucine, please," said Jean Paul, breaking the silence that had descended over the dinner table. No one had spoken since he had announced that the duck he'd put in the barn that morning was "deader than a doorknob."

Gina Lorenzo, Cathryn's mother, passed him the bowl and gestured toward Cathryn's untouched plate. "You need some nourishment."

Forcing a smile, Cathryn shook her head no.

"You don't like my fettucine?" asked Gina.

"It's wonderful," said Cathryn. "I'm just not hungry."

"You gotta eat," said Gina. "You too, Charles."

Dutifully Charles took a bite of the fettucine. The reality of the day's disasters had hit him with renewed force, once he'd left the lab to pick up Chuck and drive home. When Charles had told his son that Michelle had leukemia, Chuck's response had been a simple "Oh!" Then he'd asked if he might catch it.

Charles had marveled at the depths of his older son's selfishness. At least Jean Paul had reacted appropriately. He'd cried and then asked if he could go and see Michelle.

Charles looked at Cathryn, who kept her head down as she pushed her food around her plate. He was thankful that he had said nothing to her about the troubles at the institute. She had enough to worry about.

"Have another pork chop, Charles," said Gina.

He tried to say no, but she quickly plopped one onto his plate. He looked away, trying to stay calm. He found Gina difficult even under the best of circumstances.

"How do they know Michelle has leukemia?" asked Jean Paul, and everyone turned to Charles.

"They looked at her blood, then examined her bone marrow."

"Bone marrow?" questioned Chuck with disgust. "How do they get bone marrow to look at?"

Charles eyed his son. "They get bone marrow by ramming a large-bore needle into the breastbone or the hipbone, then sucking the marrow out."

"Ugh," said Chuck. "Nobody is ever going to do a bone marrow on me!"

"I'm not so sure," said Charles. "Michelle's doctor wants you boys to go in to be blood-typed. There's a chance one of you may match Michelle and can be a donor for platelets, granulocytes, or even a marrow transplant."

"Not me!" said Chuck, putting down his fork. "No way."

Charles placed his elbows on the table and leaned toward Chuck. "I'm not asking you. I'm telling you that you're going to be tissue-typed. Do you understand me?"

"Why me?" yelled Chuck. "You're the father. Why can't you be the donor, or aren't big-deal doctors allowed to donate marrow?"

Charles leaped to his feet in blind fury. "Your selfishness is only rivaled by your ignorance. You're supposed to have had biology. The father only donates half of the chromosomes to the child. There is no way I could match Michelle. I wish I could change places with her."

"I'll bet," muttered Chuck.

Charles started around the table, but Cathryn leaped up and caught him. "Charles, please," she said, bursting into tears.

Gina was crossing herself. "Charles! Don't tempt the Lord!"

Charles mouthed some inaudible words, then spun on his heels, wrenched open the door, and stormed out into the night.

He had no goal other than to escape the infuriating atmosphere in the kitchen. Crunching through the crusted snow, he ran down toward the pond. An arctic front had moved in. Charles felt a raw chill, especially since he'd not taken the time to get his jacket. Without a conscious decision, he veered toward Michelle's playhouse, noting that the change in the wind had eliminated the smell from the chemical factory.

After stamping the snow from his feet, Charles bent his head and entered the miniature house. The interior was only ten feet long, and a central partition divided it in two: one half was the living room, the other the kitchen, with a small table and sink. The playhouse had running water (in the summer) and an electric hot plate. From about age six to nine Michelle had made tea here for Charles on Sunday summer afternoons.

Leaning forward, Charles gazed out the front window at the sky. It had become a clear, star-studded night, and he could see forever, out into distant galaxies. The sight was beautiful but lifeless, and all at once Charles felt an overwhelming sense of futility and loneliness. His eyes filled with tears. What was he going to do about Michelle? If the chance of a remission faded, could he stand to watch her suffer with the treatment?

He glanced down at the silver-blue snowscape and patch of water in front of him. Guessing that the temperature was close to zero, Charles began to wonder about the open water. His explanation to Jean Paul that morning had been that the current prevented it from icing over. But that was when the temperature hovered near the freezing mark. Now it was some thirty degrees colder. Suddenly he was aware of a sweet aromatic smell. It was vaguely familiar. He'd smelled it before, but where?

Sniffing around, Charles found that the odor was strongest near the floor. He tried again to place the smell. Suddenly it came to him: it was an organic solvent such as benzene, toluene, or xylene. But what was it doing in the playhouse?

Braving the cold wind, Charles went outside. The odor was diminished because of the wind, but bending down, he determined that it was coming from the area around and under the playhouse. At the edge of the pond, he followed the open water to the point where it merged with the inlet from the river. There he crouched down and scooped up some water. The odor was stronger. Breaking into a jog, Charles followed the inlet to the juncture with the Pawtomack River. It, too, was unfrozen, and here the odor was even more intense. Shaking from the cold, he stared upstream. Recycle, Ltd., the plastic and rubber recycling plant, was up there. Charles knew from college chemistry that benzene was used as a solvent for both plastics and rubber.

Benzene!

A powerful thought gripped his mind: benzene causes leukemia; in fact, it causes myeloblastic leukemia! His eyes followed the trail of the unfrozen, open water. It led directly to Michelle's playhouse.

Like a crazed man, Charles sprinted for the house and thundered up the back steps. Cathryn, already taut as a bowstring, shrieked as he hurled himself into the kitchen.

"I want a container," he gasped, ignoring her reaction.

"A container?" asked Cathryn. "What kind of a container?"

"Glass," said Charles. "Glass with a tight top."

"What for?" she asked. It seemed like an absurd request.

"For pond water." Charles went to the refrigerator and pulled out a jar of apple juice. Without a moment's hesitation he dumped the contents down the sink and rinsed the jar thoroughly. He yanked his sheepskin jacket off its hook and went out the door again. Cathryn stared after him. Was Charles having a nervous breakdown? It was a terrifying thought.

Charles rushed down to the pond, gingerly approached the water's edge, and filled the jar. He screwed the cap on tightly before running back to the house.

Although his sudden return surprised Cathryn, it had nowhere near the effect of his previous entrance.

"Charles, tell me what you are doing," she said.

"There's benzene in the pond," he hissed. He put the jar of pond water in the refrigerator. "And you can smell it in Michelle's playhouse."

He whirled back to the door and Cathryn ran after him, managing to get hold of his jacket. "Charles, where are you going? What's the matter with you?"

Charles wrenched free. "I'm going to Recycle, Limited. That's where the benzene is coming from. I'm sure of it."

Chapter 4

CHARLES pulled the red Pinto off Main Street and stopped in front of the gate in the heavy wire mesh fence surrounding Recycle, Ltd. The gate was unlocked and opened easily. He stepped back into his car and drove through to the factory's parking area.

The night shift couldn't have been too large, because there were only half a dozen or so cars parked near the entrance to the old brick mill building. As soon as Charles got out of his car, he was enveloped by the same stench that had assaulted his house that morning. Above the entrance was a sign: UNAUTHORIZED ENTRY FORBIDDEN. Charles tried the door. It was unlocked. Inside, the odor was far worse. Choking on the heavy, chemical-laden air, he found himself in a small office of sorts with a heavy door at one end. He pushed, and it opened on a huge, two-story-high room, dominated by a row of gigantic ovens. Metal ladders and catwalks ascended and crisscrossed in bewildering confusion. Noisy conveyor belts brought in piles of plastic and vinyl debris mixed with other trash. A pair of sweating men in sleeveless undershirts were sorting through it.

"Is there a manager here?" yelled Charles, trying to be heard over the din.

One of the men looked up for an instant, indicated that he couldn't hear, then went back to his sorting. At the end of the conveyor belt was a large hopper, which, when full, would rise up, position itself over an available oven, and dump in its load of plastic scrap. Charles saw a man on a catwalk slit open two bags of chemicals and pour them into the oven. Then he closed the hatch and activated the steam, sending a fresh mixture of smoke, odor, and noise into the room.

Charles skirted the conveyor belts and passed the automated machinery that brought tires in to be melted down. At the end of the room he came to a large wire cage secured with a stout padlock. It was a storeroom with shelves of spare parts, tools, and containers of industrial chemicals. Through the wire mesh Charles scanned the labels on the containers. He found what he was looking for directly in front of him. There were two steel drums labeled BENZENE. There were also the familiar skull-and-crossbones decals warning that the contents were poisonous.

A hand gripped Charles's shoulder and he spun about, flattening himself against the wire mesh.

"What can I do for you?" a huge man yelled. He was a full head taller than Charles, and his perspiring face was so pudgy that his eyes were mere slits. His undershirt was stretched over a beer belly of awesome dimensions and his forearms were tattooed with hula dancers. "You checking our chemicals?"

Charles nodded.

"I think we need more carbon black," the man yelled.

Charles realized that the man thought he belonged there.

"What about the benzene?" yelled Charles.

"We got plenty. Benzene comes in hundred-gallon drums."

"What do you do with it after you use it?"

"You mean the spent benzene? C'mere. I'll show you."

He led Charles across the main room, between two of the ovens. They ducked under an overhang and entered a hallway that led to a lunchroom. Between a soda dispenser and a cigarette machine was a window. The man took Charles over to it and pointed outside. "See those tanks out there?"

Charles peered out. Fifty feet away and quite close to the riverbank were two cylindrical tanks. Even with the bright moon he couldn't see any details. "Does any of the benzene go into the river?" he asked.

"Most of it is trucked away by a disposal company. But when the tanks get too full, we drain them into the river; it's no problem. We do it at night and it washes out to the ocean. To tell the truth"—the man leaned close—"I think the disposal company dumps it into the river, too. And they charge a fortune."

Charles felt his jaw tighten. He could see Michelle in the hospital bed with the IV running into her arm.

"Where's your supervisor?" he snapped.

"You mean Nat Archer," said the worker. "He's in his office."

"Show me where it is."

Back in the main room, the man indicated a door at the end of a metal catwalk one flight up. "Up there," he yelled above the din.

The office was like a soundproofed crow's nest with windows that looked out on the whole operation. As Charles came through the door, Nat Archer stood up, smiling in obvious puzzlement.

Charles suddenly realized he knew the man. He was the father of Steve Archer, a close friend of Jean Paul's.

"Charles Martel!" said Nat. "Good to see you."

Taken off-balance, Charles stammered that he wasn't making a social call. "I want to know who owns Recycle, Limited."

Nat sounded wary. "Breur Chemical of New Jersey is the parent company. Why do you ask?"

"Who's the manager here?"

"Harold Dawson out on Covered Bridge Road. Charles, I think you should tell me what this is all about."

"My daughter was diagnosed as having leukemia today."

"I'm sorry to hear that," said Nat, confusion mixing with sympathy.

"I'll bet you are," said Charles. "You people have been dumping benzene into the river. Benzene causes leukemia."

"What are you talking about? We haven't been dumping benzene. The stuff gets hauled away."

"Don't give me any bull," snapped Charles. "That big guy downstairs with the tattoos told me you dumped benzene."

Nat Archer picked up his phone. He told Wally Crabb to get up to his office on the double, and hung up. Then he turned back to Charles. "Man, you gotta have your head examined."

Wally Crabb came through the door as if he expected a fire. He skidded to a halt.

"Wally, this man says you told him we dumped benzene in the river."

"Hell, no!" said Wally, out of breath. "I told him the benzene is taken away by the Draper Brothers Disposal."

"You're a liar!" shouted Charles.

"Nobody calls me a liar," growled Wally, starting for Charles.

"Ease off!" yelled Nat, pulling Wally back and grasping Charles's arm. He started walking Charles to the door.

"Get your hands off me," Charles shouted. He jerked free and shoved Nat away. Nat recovered his balance and thrust Charles back against the wall of the small office.

"Let me give you some advice," said Nat. "Don't cause trouble around here. You're trespassing, and if you ever come back, you'll be sorry. Now get out before we throw you out."

Charles turned and thundered down the metal stairs. He

214

strode through the main room and the office and burst outside, thankful for the cold and relatively clean air of the parking lot. In the car, he gunned the engine mercilessly before shooting out through the gate.

The farther he got from Recycle, Ltd., the less fear he felt and the more anger. As he drove, he vowed he'd destroy the factory for Michelle's sake, no matter what it took. He pulled into his driveway and skidded to a stop by the back porch.

He sat for a moment, gripping the steering wheel. The reckless drive had calmed his emotions and given him a chance to think. Perhaps it had been stupid to charge up to Recycle, Ltd., like that. As a scientist he knew that the mere presence of benzene in the pond did not constitute proof that it had caused Michelle's leukemia. No one had yet proved that benzene caused leukemia in humans, only in animals.

Slowly he got out of the car. He was startled when Cathryn met him in the doorway, her face awash with tears.

"What's wrong?" asked Charles, frightened. His first reaction was that something had happened to Michelle.

"Nancy Schonhauser called," Cathryn managed to say. "Little Tad died this evening. That poor dear child."

As Charles reached out and drew his wife to him, he suddenly remembered that the Schonhausers lived on the Pawtomack River. Benzene caused aplastic anemia as well as leukemia! All the anger he had felt earlier returned in an overwhelming rush.

He broke free from Cathryn, consulted the telephone directory, and dialed a number. The connection went through. "Is this Harold Dawson?" demanded Charles.

"It is," was the reply.

"My name is Charles Martel. I was at Recycle tonight."

"I know," said Dawson. "Nat Archer called me. I'm sorry for any discourtesies you experienced. I can assure you we are not dumping anything into the river. All our toxic chemical permits have been filed with the Environmental Protection Agency and are up to date."

"Permits," scoffed Charles. "There is benzene in the river and Recycle's been dumping it. And benzene is very toxic. My daughter has come down with leukemia and a child upriver from me died today of aplastic anemia. That's no coincidence."

215

"These are wild, irresponsible accusations," said Dawson evenly. "I should tell you that Recycle, Limited, is a marginal operation for Breur Chemical. They maintain this facility because they feel they are doing the community a service. If they thought otherwise, they would close the factory themselves."

"It certainly ought to be closed," shouted Charles.

"One hundred and eighty workers in this town might disagree," answered Dawson, losing patience. "If you cause trouble, mister, I can guarantee you'll get trouble."

"I . . ." began Charles, but he realized Dawson had hung up.

He shook the receiver furiously until Cathryn took it away and replaced it in its cradle. She'd heard only Charles's side of the conversation, but it had upset her. She forced him to sit down at the kitchen table. "I think you'd better tell me about the benzene," she said.

"It's a poison," fumed Charles. "It depresses the bone marrow somehow."

"And you don't have to eat it to be poisoned?"

"No. All you have to do is inhale it. It goes directly into the bloodstream. Apparently Michelle was inhaling it all the time she was in the playhouse. Benzene causes the rare kind of leukemia she has. It's too much of a coincidence. Especially with Tad's aplastic anemia. The benzene could have caused that also."

"And you think Recycle is putting benzene into the river?"

"I know they are. That's what I found out tonight. And they're going to pay. I'll get the place shut down."

Cathryn studied Charles's face, thinking of Dr. Keitzman's and Dr. Wiley's questions. "Charles," she began, marshaling her courage. "This is probably important, but it seems to me that it's a little inappropriate at the moment. We've just learned that Michelle has leukemia. I think the primary focus should be taking care of her, not trying to get a factory shut down. There will always be time for that, but Michelle needs you now."

Charles stared at his young wife. How could he hope to make her understand that the core of the problem was that he really didn't have anything to offer Michelle except love? As a cancer researcher he knew too much about Michelle's disease; he couldn't be lured into false hope by the panoply of modern medicine. Yet he had to do something, and Recycle, Ltd., was

216

there to keep him from facing the reality of Michelle's illness.

Charles recognized that he couldn't communicate all this to Cathryn and undermine her hopes. Despite their intense love for each other, he'd have to bear his burdens alone. The thought was crushing, and he collapsed in Cathryn's arms.

"It's been a terrible day," she whispered, holding him tight. "Let's go to bed and try to sleep."

MICHELLE pushed herself into a sitting position as the morning light came into her room. The movement exacerbated the nausea that had troubled her during the interminable night. She was certain she'd not slept at all. She had pains in her joints and abdomen, and the fever, which had gone away the previous afternoon, was back. There was no way Michelle could feel any more lonely or miserable.

"Well, well." A redheaded nurse beamed as she bustled into the room. "Awake already," she said. She poked a thermometer into Michelle's mouth. "Be back in a jiffy."

After the nurse had left, Michelle pulled the thermometer out of her mouth. She did not want anyone to know she still had a fever. She held the thermometer in her right hand, so she could put it into her mouth quickly when the nurse came back.

When the next person came through the door, Michelle got the thermometer back in her mouth, but it wasn't the nurse. It was a man in white carrying a basket filled with test tubes. Michelle knew what he wanted: blood. He jabbed her arm, applied a cotton ball to the puncture, bent her arm up to hold it tight, and left without saying a single word.

"Okay," said the redheaded nurse, coming through the door. "Let's see what we've got." Michelle remembered with panic that the thermometer was still in her mouth. Deftly the nurse extracted it and noted the temperature. "Breakfast will be up in a moment," she said cheerfully as she left.

"Oh, Daddy, please come and get me," said Michelle to herself. "Please hurry."

CHARLES felt his shoulder being shaken. When he opened his eyes he saw Cathryn standing by the bed, smiling. "It's seven o'clock," she said. "You were sleeping so soundly I didn't have

217

the heart to wake you earlier. We've got a big breakfast waiting downstairs."

Breakfast was a strained affair, overshadowed by Gina's forced ebullience and Charles's reserve. When the meal finally ended, Charles and Cathryn left the house with the boys, who were going to school in the station wagon. Cathryn and Charles climbed into the Pinto. They planned to visit Michelle together, then Charles would go on to the lab.

Cathryn saw Charles wedge the jar of pond water behind his seat. After their talk the night before, she'd hoped that he would concentrate on Michelle. But now she had misgivings. She watched his profile as he drove without speaking; she was afraid to open a discussion that might trigger his temper. Finally she said, "Is there something you're not telling me, Charles?"

"No," he said, too quickly. "What makes you ask that?"

"I don't know. You seem so quiet. So far away." She watched for his reaction, but he just drove on.

"I guess I just have a lot on my mind," he said finally, and they rode in silence for the rest of the way.

They arrived at the hospital and quickly made their way to the nurses' station on Anderson 6.

"Excuse me," said Charles to the charge nurse. "I'm Dr. Martel. I was wondering if my daughter has started her chemotherapy." He purposefully kept his voice natural, emotionless.

"I believe so," said the nurse, "but let me check." She consulted Michelle's chart. "She got her daunorubicin yesterday afternoon, and her first oral dose of Thioguanine this morning. She'll start with the Cytarabine this afternoon."

Charles forced himself to smile. He knew too well the probable side effects of the chemicals. "Please, let her go into remission," he said to himself. He knew that if it was to happen, it would happen immediately. He thanked the nurse, turned, and walked with Cathryn toward Michelle's room. The closer they got, the more nervous he became.

"Here we are," said Cathryn, pushing open the door. Michelle was propped up in a sitting position with several pillows behind her back. At the sight of Charles, her face twisted and she burst into tears. Charles was shocked at her appearance. Although he had not thought it possible, she looked even paler than she had

218

the day before, and her eyes were surrounded by dark circles.

She lifted her arms to him, but Charles couldn't move. In an avalanche of horror, he suddenly knew that Michelle was not going to get better. Under the weight of this knowledge he staggered, taking a step back from the bed.

Cathryn saw what was happening and she ran to fill Michelle's outstretched arms. "It's so good to see you," she said. "How are you?"

"I'm fine," Michelle managed, checking her tears. "I just want to go home. Can I go home, Daddy?"

Charles's hands shook and he steadied them on the metal bedframe. "Maybe," he said evasively. Maybe he should just take her home and keep her comfortable; maybe that was best.

"Daddy," pleaded Michelle, "what's wrong with me?"

"I wish we knew," he said, hating himself for lying.

"Is it the same thing that my real mother had?"

"No," said Charles quickly. "Absolutely not." But that was a half-lie; although Elizabeth had lymphoma, she had died in a terminal leukemic crisis. He felt cornered. He had to get away to think. Guiltily he checked his watch. "Cathryn will keep you company. I've got to get to the lab."

Without any warning Michelle retched, her slender body heaving. Charles stepped into the corridor and yelled for a nurse. An aide came flying in to clean things up. Charles knew the medicine had caused the vomiting.

He put the back of his hand against his daughter's forehead. It was moist and hot. Michelle grabbed his hand and held it as if she stood at the edge of an abyss. She looked into the blue eyes that were mirrors of her own, but she thought she saw irritation instead of understanding. She let go of the hand and fell back onto the pillow.

"I'll be back later, Michelle." Charles started for the door, upset that the medicine was already causing side effects.

"I'll just walk your father to the elevator, Michelle," said Cathryn, seeing him leave. She caught up with him in the hall. "Charles, what is the matter with you?"

"I've got to get out of here. I can't stand to see Michelle suffer. I'm not sure she should have that medicine."

"But that's her only chance for a remission!"

Charles started to say that he was sure Michelle was not going to go into remission, but he held his tongue. "I've got to go," he said. "Call me if there is any change. I'll be at the lab."

Cathryn watched him rush down the corridor. When Dr. Wiley had told her that they were going to rely on her strength, she'd had no idea what he'd meant. Now she was beginning to comprehend.

CHARLES turned into the institute parking lot, leaped out of the car, and pulled the jar of pond water from behind the seat. In the building, he went directly to the analysis lab.

"I want this water analyzed for contaminants," he said to the technician. "I'm particularly interested in organic solvents."

The technician unscrewed the cap and took a whiff. "Whew. I hope you don't drink this stuff with your Scotch. Is it a rush job?"

"Sort of," said Charles. He hurried over to his own lab. As he opened the door, Ellen, who'd been reading the Canceran protocol, slowly put the book down. Her deliberateness bothered Charles even in his distracted state.

"What's wrong?" he demanded.

"I checked the mice who got the first dose of Canceran." She paused. "Almost all of them died last night."

His face clouded with disbelief. "Did you check the dilution?"

"I did," said Ellen. "It was very accurate."

"Any sign that they died from an infectious agent?"

"No," said Ellen. "I had the vet take a look. He hasn't autopsied any, but he thinks they died of cardiac insult."

"Drug toxicity," said Charles, shaking his head.

"I'm afraid so."

Charles picked up the original Canceran protocol and flipped through the toxicity section. Then he reached for the protocol they'd made up the day before and scanned the figures. When he had finished, he tossed both protocols onto his desk.

"That creep Brighton," he said. "He must have falsified the toxicity data, too. That means the whole study is no good. Canceran must be much more toxic than he reported."

"What are we going to do?"

"We? What are *they* going to do! The whole project has to be started over, which means an additional three years. Well, we're

220

finished with it. If Morrison and Ibanez give us trouble, we'll slap them with proof that the study is worthless."

"I don't think it's going to be that easy," said Ellen. "I think we should—"

"That's enough, Ellen!" said Charles. "I want you to start testing for immunological activity in our first batch of mice. I'll handle the administration in respect to Canceran."

Ellen angrily turned her back. She began her work, making as much noise with the glassware and instruments as she could.

The phone rang and Charles picked it up. It was the technician in the analysis lab.

"The major contaminant is benzene and it's loaded with it," said the chemist. "There are lesser amounts of toluene, trichloroethylene, and carbon tetrachloride. Vile stuff."

Charles thanked the man and hung up. He grabbed the Boston phone directory from the shelf over his desk and found a series of numbers for the Environmental Protection Agency. He dialed the general information number.

A woman answered and Charles introduced himself. He said he wanted to report the dumping of poisonous material into a river. The woman rang an extension. Another woman picked up. "You've got the wrong extension," she said when she heard his request. "You want the Toxic Chemicals Program. One moment."

Charles was put on hold. There was a click followed by a dial tone. Charles dropped the receiver and grabbed the phone directory. Checking under the EPA, he found a listing for the Toxic Chemicals Program and dialed it.

Another woman answered, and Charles repeated his request. He was told that the Toxic Chemicals Program had nothing to do with infractions and that he should call the number for Oil and Hazardous Material Spills. Annoyed, he hung up and redialed.

"Can I help you?" asked the woman who came on the line.

"I certainly hope so," said Charles. "I'm calling to report that there is a factory regularly dumping benzene—"

"Well, we don't handle that," interrupted the woman. "You'll have to call the proper state agency."

"What?" yelled Charles. "What does the EPA *do*, then?"

"We are a regulatory agency," said the woman calmly, "tasked to regulate the environment."

"I would think that dumping a poison into a river would be something that would concern you."

"It could be," agreed the woman, "but only after the state has looked into it. Do you want the number for the state agency?"

"Give it to me," said Charles wearily. As he hung up he caught Ellen staring at him. He glared at her and dialed again.

"Okay," said the woman at the state agency after hearing his problem. "What river are you talking about?"

"The Pawtomack," said Charles. "Don't tell me I'm finally talking to the right people."

"Yes, you are," the woman assured him. "And where is the factory you think is dumping?"

"The factory's in Shaftesbury," said Charles.

"Shaftesbury? That's in New Hampshire. We don't handle New Hampshire."

"But the river is mostly in Massachusetts."

"That might be," said the woman, "but the origin is in New Hampshire. You'll have to talk to them."

"Give me strength," muttered Charles as the line went dead. He called New Hampshire information and obtained the number for the state water-pollution control. Charles called the number and repeated his request.

"Where does the alleged dumping occur?" asked the woman.

"In Shaftesbury. A company called Recycle, Limited. They're discarding benzene in the Pawtomack."

"Okay," said the woman. "I'll turn this over to one of our engineers. He'll look into it."

"When?"

"I can't say for certain. It will probably be several weeks."

Several weeks wasn't what Charles wanted to hear.

"Are any of the engineers around now?"

"No. Both of them are out. Wait! Here comes one now. I'll put him on."

Charles quickly told the man why he was calling and that he'd like someone to check out the dumping immediately.

"We've got a manpower problem in this department," explained the engineer.

"But this is really serious. A lot of people live along the river. Is there anything I can do to speed things up?"

222

"You could go to the EPA and see if they're interested."

"That's who I called first. They referred me to you."

"There you go!" said the engineer. "It's hard to predict which cases they'll take on. After we do all the dirty work they usually help, but sometimes they're interested from the start."

Charles thanked the engineer and rang off. At least the man had said that the EPA might be interested after all. Charles had noticed the EPA was housed in the JFK Federal Building at government center in Boston, and he decided he'd go there in person. Restlessly he got to his feet and reached for his jacket. "I'll be right back," he said to Ellen.

Ellen didn't respond. She waited several minutes after he'd left; then she picked up the phone and dialed Dr. Morrison.

In the JFK Federal Building, Charles pushed through the revolving door and found a directory. The EPA was listed on the twenty-third floor. He scrambled into an elevator just before the door closed.

He got out on the twenty-third floor and made his way to an office marked DIRECTOR. Immediately inside the office was a large metal desk and typing stand dominated by an enormous woman whose hair was permed in tight curls.

"Excuse me," said Charles, wondering if this was one of the women he'd spoken to on the phone. "I'm here to report a recycling plant that's dumping benzene into a local river."

Patting her hair, the woman suspiciously examined Charles.

"Well, I suppose you should go down to the Water Programs Division, on the twenty-second floor."

Charles thanked her and took the elevator to the floor below.

The receptionist's desk was empty. He wandered around until he came upon a man carrying a load of federal publications. "Pardon me," said Charles. He went through his now automatic routine.

The man eased the stack of pamphlets onto a table. "This isn't the right department for reporting that kind of thing. Why don't you try the Enforcement Division, up on twenty-three?"

Charles swore under his breath as he again went to the twenty-third floor. He passed the Financial Management Branch, the Personnel Branch, and the Program Planning and Development

Branch. Just beyond the men's room was the Enforcement Division. Charles stepped inside.

A girl with purple-rimmed glasses looked up from a paperback novel. Charles told her what he wanted.

"I don't know anything about that," said the girl.

"Whom should I talk to?"

"I don't know," said the girl, going back to her book.

Charles leaned over and snatched away the paperback. He slammed it down on the desk so that the girl jumped. "Sorry I lost your place," he said. "But I'd like to speak to your supervisor."

Keeping a wary eye on Charles, the young woman got to her feet and disappeared. She reappeared with a concerned-looking woman in tow.

"I'm Mrs. Amendola. Can I help you?"

"I certainly hope so," said Charles. "I'm Dr. Charles Martel and I'm trying to report a factory that is dumping poisonous chemicals into a river. I have been sent from one department to another until someone suggested the Enforcement Division. But when I arrived here the receptionist was somewhat less than cooperative, so I demanded to speak to her supervisor."

"I told him that I didn't know anything about dumping chemicals," explained the girl.

Mrs. Amendola considered the situation for a moment, then led Charles to her office. She motioned toward a chair and sat down behind the desk. "You must understand," she began. "We don't have people walking in off the street with your kind of complaint."

"What do you people enforce if it's not laws against fouling the environment?" said Charles with hostility.

"Our main job," explained the woman, "is to make sure that factories handling hazardous waste have filed for all the proper permits and licenses. You must remember that the whole concern for the environment is relatively new. Regulations are still being formulated. The first step is registering all users of hazardous materials and informing them of the rules. Then and only then will we be in a position to go after the violators. Now, what factory are you concerned about?"

"Recycle, Limited, in Shaftesbury, New Hampshire."

"Why don't we check their paperwork?" she said, rising.

Charles followed Mrs. Amendola to the data processing room. She sat down in front of a computer terminal and typed in RECYCLE, LTD., SHAFTESBURY, N.H. When the cathode-ray tube blinked into action, all the hazardous chemicals at the plant were listed, each followed by the date its permit was granted.

"What chemicals are you interested in?" said Mrs. Amendola.

"Benzene, mostly."

"Here it is. EPA hazardous chemical number U019. Everything's in order. I guess they're not breaking any laws."

"But they're dumping the stuff directly in the river!" exclaimed Charles. "I know that's against the law."

They went back to Mrs. Amendola's office, where Charles told her the whole story: Michelle's leukemia, Tad's death, his discovery of benzene in the pond, and his visit to Recycle, Ltd.

"This is terrible," she said when Charles paused. "Can you get some documented proof?"

"I have the analysis of the pond water," said Charles.

"No, no," said Mrs. Amendola. "Something from the factory itself: a statement by a former employee, doctored records, photos of the actual dumping. Something like that."

"It's possible, I suppose," said Charles, thinking about the last suggestion. He had a Polaroid camera. . . .

"If you could supply me with some kind of proof, I think I could get our Surveillance Branch to authorize a full-scale probe. It's up to you. Otherwise it will have to wait its turn."

As CHARLES headed back to the Weinburger, he was again fighting a feeling of depression. Even with Mrs. Amendola's help, it would probably take the authorities a long time to do anything about Recycle, Ltd.

In the lab, he shed his jacket and sat down at his desk. After a few moments Ellen entered the room. "Have you noticed?" she asked with irritating nonchalance.

"Noticed what?" snapped Charles.

"All your lab books are gone," she said. "They're upstairs."

Charles leaped to his feet. "What happened?"

"After you left this morning, Dr. Morrison stopped in to check on the Canceran project. He caught me working with the mice we'd injected with the mammary cancer antigen, and needless

225

to say, he was shocked that we were doing our own work. You're supposed to go up to Dr. Ibanez's office."

"But why did Morrison take the books?"

"I think you'd better ask him and Dr. Ibanez that question. Frankly, I knew it would come to this."

Leaving his lab, Charles wearily climbed the fire stairs to the second floor and presented himself to Miss Evans for the second time in two days. She told him to wait and indicated a small leather couch. As he sat, he began to wonder if Ibanez might actually fire him. And if he got fired, he wondered if he'd still be covered by health insurance. Michelle's hospital bills were going to be astronomical.

There was a buzz on the intercom and Miss Evans said, "The director will see you now."

Dr. Ibanez stood up behind his desk as Charles entered. Directly in front of the desk were Dr. Morrison, Joshua Weinburger, Sr., and Joshua Weinburger, Jr. Although close to eighty, the senior seemed more animated than the junior. He had lively blue eyes, and he was looking at Charles with great interest.

"Come in, come in!" commanded Dr. Ibanez good-naturedly. "Sit down. I think we should get right to business. The Weinburgers, as co-chairmen of the board of directors, have graciously come to help us manage the current crisis."

Weinburger junior turned slightly in his chair. "Dr. Martel, it's not the policy of the board of directors to interfere in the creative process of research. However, there are occasionally circumstances in which we must violate this rule, and this is such a case. I think you should know that Canceran is a potentially important drug for Lesley Pharmaceuticals. To be blunt, Lesley Pharmaceuticals is in precarious financial condition. They have committed their scarce resources to developing a chemotherapy line, and Canceran is the product of that research. They must get the drug on the market. The sooner the better."

Charles studied the faces of the men. Obviously the idea was to soften him up, make him understand the financial realities, then persuade him to recommence work on Canceran. He had a glimmer of hope. Perhaps he could convince them that Canceran was a bad investment, that it was a toxic drug that should never be marketed.

"We already know what you discovered about the toxicity of Canceran," said Dr. Ibanez, lighting a cigar. "We realize that Dr. Brighton's estimates are not entirely accurate."

"That's a generous way of putting it," said Charles, realizing with dismay that his trump card had been snatched from him.

"Charles," said Dr. Morrison, "we want to ask if you could run the efficacy and toxicity studies concurrently."

Charles gazed at Morrison with contempt. "That would be reducing inductive research to pure empiricism."

"We don't care what you call it," said Ibanez with a smile. "We just want to know if it could be done."

Charles looked from face to face. His fear and panic had disappeared. His contempt remained. "Where are my lab books?" he asked tiredly.

"Safe and sound in the vault," said Ibanez. "You see, we want you to concentrate on Canceran and we feel that having your own books might be too much of a temptation."

"We can't emphasize enough the need for speed," added Joshua Weinburger, Jr. "If you can have a preliminary study done in five months, we'll give you a bonus of ten thousand dollars."

"You don't have to decide right this moment," said Dr. Ibanez. "In fact, we have agreed to give you twenty-four hours. We don't want you to feel coerced. But if you refuse, we will begin inquiries into finding a replacement for you. Until then, Dr. Martel."

With disgust, Charles whirled and headed for the door. He thundered down the stairs to his office. For the first time he felt that being part of the Weinburger Institute was a disgrace.

He looked around his laboratory, where he knew every piece of glassware, each instrument, every bottle. It didn't seem fair that he could be plucked from this environment now that he was making such progress.

His eye fell on the culture he'd set up with Michelle's leukemic cells. With great effort he went over to the incubator, peering in at the rows of carefully arranged glass tubes. The culture appeared to be progressing well, and Charles felt a sense of satisfaction. As far as he could tell, his process of isolating and augmenting a cancer antigen seemed to work as well with human cells as it did with animal cells. Since it was time for the next step, Charles rolled up his sleeves and bent to the task. After all, he had twenty-four hours before he'd have to bow to the demands of the administration. He knew that for Michelle's sake he had to give in. He really had no choice.

Chapter 5

CATHRYN felt she was being stretched to the limits of her endurance. After lunch she'd paid a brief visit to Marge Schonhauser, who had been taken to Beth Israel Hospital after Tad's death. Apparently some vital thread had snapped in her brain and now she lay in an unresponsive torpor, refusing to eat or sleep. After leaving her, Cathryn wondered if what had happened to Marge could happen to her or even to Charles. She would have thought that as a physician he'd be capable of dealing with this kind of reality, yet his behavior was far from reassuring.

When she pushed Michelle's door open, she thought at first the child was napping, because Michelle had her eyes closed. But then Cathryn noticed that her chest was heaving violently and her face had an alarmingly bluish cast.

Rushing to the bedside, Cathryn grasped her by the shoulders. "Michelle," she said. "What's wrong?"

Michelle's lids fluttered open, but only the whites showed; her eyes were rolled up in their sockets.

"Help!" cried Cathryn, running into the corridor. "Help!"

Three nurses came from behind the nurses' station. Pushing past Cathryn, they all converged on Michelle's room. One went to either side of the bed, the other to the foot.

"Call a code," barked the charge nurse.

The nurse at the foot of the bed sped over to the intercom.

Meanwhile, the charge nurse could feel a rapid, thready pulse. "Feels like V-tack," she said. "Her heart's beating so fast it's hard to feel individual beats."

The third nurse put the blood pressure cuff around Michelle's arm. "Sixty over forty but variable," she said.

Cathryn stood against the wall, afraid to move lest she be in the way. A woman resident physician ran in and went directly to the bedside, grasping Michelle's wrist for a pulse.

228

"I think she has V-tack," said the charge nurse. "She's a leukemic. Myeloblastic. Day two of attempted induction."

"Any cardiac history?" demanded the resident as she lifted Michelle's eyelids. "At least the pupils are down."

The three nurses looked at each other. "We don't think she has any cardiac history. Nothing was said at report," said the charge nurse. "Her blood pressure is sixty over forty but variable."

"V-tack," confirmed the resident. "Stand back." She made a fist and brought it down hard on Michelle's chest.

An extremely young-looking chief resident arrived, followed by two other residents pushing a cartload of electronic instruments. The nurses attached EKG leads to Michelle's extremities. Then the electronic box on the top of the cart began to spew forth a strip of narrow graph paper that bore the red squiggles of an EKG. The doctors grouped around the machine.

"V-tack all right," said the chief resident. "With the dyspnea and cyanosis she's hemodynamically compromised. We should cardiovert her immediately." He turned to one of the residents. "Let's draw up some lidocaine. Fifty milligrams. And a milligram of atropine in case she goes into bradycardia."

One resident drew up the medications while another got out the electrode paddles. One of the paddles went under Michelle's back, the second on her chest.

"All right, stand back," said the chief resident. "Here goes."

He pressed a button and in a moment Michelle's body contracted, her arms and legs jumping off the surface of the bed. Cathryn watched in horror as the doctors stayed bent over the machine, apparently ignoring Michelle's reaction. The child's eyes opened in bewilderment and she lifted her head. Her color, Cathryn noted thankfully, had reverted to normal.

"Not bad!" said the chief resident.

Dr. Keitzman arrived and went directly to Michelle. "Are you okay, chicken?" he asked, getting out his stethoscope.

Michelle nodded but didn't speak. She appeared dazed. The chief resident launched into a capsule summary of the event while Dr. Keitzman bent over Michelle, listening to her chest. Satisfied, he checked a run of EKG paper. Then, catching sight of Cathryn pressed up against the wall, he walked over and put a hand on her shoulder. "Mrs. Martel, are you all right?"

Cathryn couldn't speak, but she nodded.

"I'm sorry you had to see this. Let's go out in the hall for a moment. I'd like to talk to you."

Cathryn strained to see Michelle over his shoulder. "She'll be okay for a moment," he assured her. Then, turning to the charge nurse, he said, "I want a cardiac monitor in here, and I'd like a cardiac consult with Dr. Brubaker right away."

Dr. Keitzman led Cathryn to the chart room and held a chair for her as she gratefully sat down. He sighed. "Mrs. Martel, I feel I must talk frankly with you. Michelle is not doing well at all. And I'm not referring specifically to this latest episode."

"What was this episode?" asked Cathryn.

"It's called ventricular tachycardia. Let me explain. Usually it's the upper part of the heart that initiates the beat." He gestured with his hands to illustrate. "But for some reason, the lower part of Michelle's heart took over. Why? We don't know yet. In any case, her heart suddenly began to beat so fast that there wasn't time for it to fill properly, and it pumped inefficiently. But that seems to be under control. What worries me is that she does not seem to be responding to the chemotherapy."

"But she's just started!" exclaimed Cathryn.

"That's true," agreed Dr. Keitzman. "However, Michelle's type of leukemia usually responds in the first few days. Yesterday we gave her a very strong drug called daunorubicin. This morning when we did her blood count, I was shocked to see that there was almost no effect on the leukemic cells. So I decided to try something different. Usually we give a second dose of this medicine on the fifth day. Instead I gave her another dose today, along with the Thioguanine and Cytarabine."

"Why are you telling me this?" asked Cathryn, certain Dr. Keitzman knew she did not understand much of it.

"Because of your husband's response yesterday," he answered. "I'm afraid he'll want to stop the medicines."

"But if they're not working, maybe they should be stopped."

"Mrs. Martel, Michelle is an extremely sick child. Without chemotherapy, she has no chance at all." He stood up. "Now I want you to call your husband and have him come over. He's got to be told what's happened."

230

CHARLES CLOSED THE COVER of the tissue culture incubator. He was in the last stages of preparing a concentrated solution of a surface protein that differentiated Michelle's leukemic cells from her normal cells. This protein was foreign to Michelle's body but was not rejected because of the mysterious blocking factor that Charles was investigating. If only he knew more about its action, perhaps he could eliminate it. He was frustrated to be so close to the answer and have to stop.

He walked over to his desk and sat down, trying not to think about the recent humiliating meeting with Dr. Ibanez and the Weinburgers. Instead he recalled the visit to the EPA offices, which didn't make him feel much better. He wondered if there would be any way that he could get some sort of photographic proof of Recycle's dumping.

Perhaps if he got the evidence, he should sue Recycle directly rather than waiting for the EPA to do so. He knew very little about law, but he remembered that the Weinburger Institute kept a law firm on retainer.

In a booklet published by the institute he found the firm of Hubbert, Hubbert, Garachnik and Pearson listed under services. He dialed their number, and within minutes he was talking with Mr. Garachnik.

"I need some information," said Charles, "about suing a company dumping poisonous waste into a public river."

"It would be best," said Mr. Garachnik, "if we had one of our environmental law persons look into the matter. Is the Weinburger Institute becoming interested in environmental pursuits?"

"No," said Charles. "I'm interested in this personally."

"I see. May I ask the name of the company you are talking about?"

"It is called Recycle, Limited," said Charles. "A factory in Shaftesbury, New Hampshire."

"And it is owned by Breur Chemical of New Jersey," said Mr. Garachnik quickly.

"That's right. How did you know?"

"Because we indirectly represent Breur Chemical. You may not be aware that Breur Chemical owns the Weinburger Institute, though that is run as a nonprofit organization."

Charles was stunned.

Mr. Garachnik continued. "Breur Chemical founded the Weinburger Institute when they expanded into the drug industry by purchasing Lesley Pharmaceuticals. So you see, Dr. Martel, you essentially work for Breur Chemical."

Charles hung up the phone very slowly. He was working for a conglomerate that was ultimately responsible for dumping cancer-causing waste into a river, and at the same time running a research institute supposedly interested in curing cancer. As for Canceran, the parent company—Breur Chemical—controlled both the drug firm holding the patents and the research firm chosen to ascertain its efficiency.

The phone rang, jangling Charles's taut nerves. He snatched the receiver from the cradle.

It was Cathryn, and her voice had the same stiff quality it had had the day before.

His heart jumped into his throat. "Is everything okay?"

"Michelle is not doing so well. You'd better come over."

Charles grabbed his jacket and ran out to his car. The drive into Boston seemed endless. When he reached the hospital, he rushed up to Michelle's room and entered without knocking.

A blond-haired woman straightened up from leaning over Michelle. She'd been listening to the girl's heart. Charles gave the woman a cursory glance and looked down at his daughter. He wanted to grab her and shield her, but she seemed too fragile. His trained eyes could detect a worsening in her condition since morning. There was a greenish cast to her face, a change Charles had learned to associate with ensuing death.

Michelle looked up at her father with a weak smile

"Michelle," said Charles softly. "How do you feel?"

The child began to cry. "I want to go home, Daddy." She was reluctant to admit how bad she felt.

Charles was overwhelmed with emotion. "We'll talk about it," he said, his lips quivering.

"Excuse me," said the woman. "You must be Dr. Martel. I'm Dr. Brubaker. I'm a cardiologist. Dr. Keitzman asked me to see Michelle. She had an acute episode of ventricular tachycardia."

"What caused it?" asked Charles.

"We don't know yet. My first thoughts are either an idiosyn-

232

cratic reaction to the double dose of daunorubicin, or a manifestation of her basic problem: some kind of myopathic infiltration of her heart. But I'd like to finish my exam. Dr. Keitzman and your wife are waiting for you in the chart room."

"Don't go, Daddy," pleaded Michelle. "Stay with me."

"I won't go far," said Charles, gently smoothing her hair. She had received a double dose of daunorubicin, Dr. Brubaker had said. That sounded irregular.

When Cathryn saw Charles she leaped to her feet. "I'm so glad you're here." She put her arms around his neck. "This is too difficult for me to handle."

Holding his wife, Charles glanced around the small chart room. Dr. Wiley was leaning against the table, his eyes on the floor. Dr. Keitzman was sitting opposite him. No one spoke, but Charles could sense that something was coming. There was a painful knot in his stomach.

"About Michelle," said Dr. Keitzman finally. "She's not responding as we had hoped."

"I assumed as much," said Charles. "What's this about a double dose of daunorubicin?"

Dr. Keitzman said, "She did not respond to the first dose, so we gave her another today."

"That's not the usual protocol, is it?" snapped Charles.

"No," Dr. Keitzman replied hesitantly, "but we've got to knock down her circulatory leukemic cells."

"Well, I'm not sure your experimentation isn't lessening her chances. What about this trouble with her heart? Doesn't daunorubicin cause cardiac problems?"

"Yes, but not usually this fast. I don't know what to think about this complication. That's why I wanted a cardiac consult."

"Well, I think it's the medicine," said Charles. "I agreed to chemotherapy, but I assumed you would be using the standard doses. I'm not sure I agree with doubling them."

"If that's the case, then perhaps you should retain another oncologist," said Dr. Keitzman. "In my view, increasing the chemotherapy is the only hope for remission."

"She's not going to go into remission."

"You can't say that," said Dr. Wiley.

"Charles, the medicine is her only chance," Cathryn said.

Charles backed up, watching the others as if they were trying to force him into submission. The idea of causing Michelle additional suffering was a torture, yet the prospect of allowing her to die without a fight was equally abhorrent.

He had to get away. He turned abruptly and strode from the room. Cathryn ran after him. "Charles! Please don't leave me."

At the stairs he stopped. He gripped Cathryn's shoulders. "I can't think here. I don't know what's right. Each alternative is as bad as another. I've got to pull myself together. I'm sorry."

With a feeling of helplessness Cathryn watched him go through the door, leaving her alone in the busy corridor. Suddenly she knew that for Michelle's sake she had to handle the situation, even if Charles couldn't. She walked back to the chart room and sat down.

"We were talking while you were gone," said Dr. Keitzman. "We feel that something must be done to ensure continuity of Michelle's care. Even if the treatment were stopped for a day or two, it could mean the difference between success and failure. Your daughter deserves a chance, no matter what the odds. Don't you agree, Mrs. Martel?"

Cathryn looked at the two doctors. They were trying to suggest something, but she had no idea what it was. "Of course," she said. How could she disagree?

"There are ways of making sure that Charles cannot arbitrarily stop Michelle's treatment," said Dr. Wiley. "Let me give you an example. Suppose a child desperately needs a transfusion. If it is not given, the child will die. And suppose that one of the parents is a Jehovah's Witness. Then there is a conflict between the parents as to the treatment of the child. What do the doctors do? They ask the court to award guardianship to the consenting parent."

Cathryn stared at Dr. Wiley in consternation. "You want me to assume guardianship of Michelle behind Charles's back?"

"Only for the purpose of maintaining treatment. It might save her life. We could ask the court to appoint a guardian, but it would be simpler if you participated."

"But you're not giving Michelle standard treatment anymore," said Cathryn, remembering Charles's words.

"What we're doing is not that unusual in cases such as your

234

daughter's," said Keitzman. "Please understand, we're trying to do our best."

"I appreciate your efforts," said Cathryn, "but . . ."

"We know it sounds drastic," Keitzman said. "However, the legal guardianship doesn't have to be invoked unless the situation calls for it. But then if Charles tried to take Michelle off treatment, we'd be able to do something about it.

"You must admit he has been acting bizarrely," he continued. "The strain may be priming him for a nervous breakdown. He may be incapable of making sensible decisions."

Cathryn was swept by a turmoil of emotion. The idea of going against Charles, the man she loved, was unthinkable. And yet if he interrupted Michelle's treatment, she would be to blame for not having the courage to help the doctors. "If I were to do as you ask," she said, "what would be the procedure?"

"Hold on," said Dr. Keitzman, reaching for the phone. "I think the hospital attorney could answer that better than I."

ALMOST before Cathryn knew what was happening, she was sitting in the chambers of Judge Louis Pelligrino in the Boston courthouse. At her side was Patrick Murphy, the young hospital lawyer. Even in her distraught state, Cathryn had been charmed by his forthright manner and gentle smile. She still felt uneasy about the whole affair, but Patrick had assured her that the legal powers would not be used except in the unlikely event that Charles tried to stop Michelle's treatment.

Patrick snapped open his briefcase and took out the forms Cathryn had signed and the affidavits from the doctors. He presented them to Judge Pelligrino.

The judge peered at Patrick over his half-glasses. "Why don't you fill me in on these petitions?"

Patrick outlined the circumstances surrounding Michelle's illness and treatment, as well as Charles's behavior. Judge Pelligrino then examined the forms.

"This is the adoptive mother, I presume," he said.

"It is," said the lawyer, "and she is understandably concerned about maintaining proper treatment for her daughter."

Judge Pelligrino scrutinized Cathryn's face. "Would you like to add anything, Mrs. Martel?" he asked.

Cathryn declined in a barely audible voice.

Thoughtfully the judge arranged the papers on his desk. He cleared his throat before he spoke. "I will allow the emergency temporary guardianship for the sole purpose of maintaining the recognized and established medical treatment." With a flourish he signed the forms. "There will be a preliminary hearing in three days, and a full hearing in three weeks. I want the father notified no later than tomorrow."

Cathryn sat bolt upright. "You're going to tell Charles about this meeting?"

"Absolutely," said the judge, rising. "I hardly think it fair to deprive a parent of his guardianship rights without telling him. Now if you'll excuse me."

Patrick thanked the judge and hurried Cathryn out of his chambers. She was distraught. "You said we wouldn't use this unless Charles actually stopped treatment."

"That's correct," said Patrick.

"But Charles is going to find out what I've done," she cried. "You didn't tell me that!"

Chapter 6

AT FIVE thirty that afternoon Charles was sitting in the Pinto, which he had parked in the lee of a deserted mill building near Recycle, Ltd., to wait for complete darkness. Just after six he opened the door and got out. It had started to snow with large flakes that blew like feathers in short, swooping arcs.

Charles opened the trunk and collected his gear: a Polaroid camera, a flashlight, and a few sample jars. Then he crossed to the shadow of the empty mill building, from which he had a full view of Recycle, Ltd. Cautiously he cut across the empty parking lot to the heavy wire mesh fence. First the flashlight, then the sample jars were gently tossed over to land in the snow. With the camera slung over his shoulder, Charles grasped the mesh and began to climb. He teetered on the top, then leaped to the ground. Fearful of being seen, he gathered his things and hurried over to the factory. The going was difficult because the snow covered all sorts of trash and debris.

Charles reached the corner facing the river and looked down

at his goal: the two metal holding tanks. After a short pause, he set out to climb through the twisted remains of discarded machinery, only to find himself barred from further advance by a granite-lined sluice about ten feet across and five feet deep. The sluice emerged from beneath the building and ran toward the riverbank, where it was ineffectively dammed with wooden planks. From the opposite side of the sluice a channel led to a large lagoon. The fluid in the sluice and in the lagoon was not frozen and it had the unmistakable acrid smell of industrial chemicals.

Adjacent to the factory, Charles saw that two stout planks had been laid across the sluice. He moved carefully across this makeshift bridge, holding the sample jars under his right arm.

He reached the lagoon on the far side and bent down. Holding one of the jars, he collected a pint or so of the slowly bubbling sludge. He capped the jar and left it to be retrieved on the way back. Next he wanted to take a photo of the dam that let this chemical cesspool leak into the river below.

WALLY CRABB was spending his dinner break at Recycle playing blackjack with Angelo DeJesus and Giorgio Brezowski in the lunchroom. By six twenty he was down thirteen dollars and his luck was getting worse. Brezo dealt him a face card and the four of spades. When Wally asked him for a hit, Brezo socked him with another face card, sending him over twenty-one.

"Damn!" yelled Wally, slamming the cards down and getting to his feet. He lumbered over to the cigarette machine, put in his coins, and punched his selection. Nothing happened. He gave the machine a powerful kick that jarred it against the wall. At that moment he saw a light flash outside the dark window.

He pressed his face against the glass, and he saw the flash again. This time he caught a glimpse of its source.

"Somebody is taking pictures of the dam!" he shouted. He reached for the phone, dialed Nat Archer's office, and told the super what he'd seen.

"Must be that Martel nut," said Archer. "Why don't you go out there and teach him a lesson?"

"You got it," said Wally. Turning to his buddies and cracking his knuckles, he said, "We're going to have some fun."

AFTER PHOTOGRAPHING THE DAM, Charles worked his way over to the metal holding tanks. With the flashlight he saw that a pipe led away from the tanks and with a T connector joined the roof-drain conduit on its way to the riverbank. Using great care to keep from slipping, Charles managed to get to the edge of the embankment, which was some twenty feet above the river. The roof drain ended abruptly, spilling its contents down the embankment. The smell of benzene was intense, and below the pipe was a patch of open water. The rest of the river was solidly frozen and covered with snow. After taking several pictures of the pipe, Charles leaned out with his second jar and caught some of the fluid dripping from the end. Then he closed the jar and put it down. He was almost finished. He just wanted to photograph the T connector between the pipe from the storage tanks and the drain conduit. He stepped over the pipes, squatted down, and sighted through the viewfinder. Satisfied, he pushed the shutter release.

The flash was followed by a sudden powerful jerk as the camera was torn from Charles's fingers and tossed into the black lagoon. He looked up to see three men in hooded parkas silhouetted against the dark sky.

Charles stood up, and without words, two of the men lunged forward and grabbed his arms. The third man, the biggest one, went through his coat pockets. He found the Polaroid photographs and with a flick of his wrist sent them into the pond after the camera.

The men let Charles go and stepped back. Charles tried to run between one of the smaller men and the storage tank. The man jabbed a fist into his nose. The blow stunned Charles, bringing a slight trickle of blood down his chin.

"Nice poke, Brezo." Wally laughed.

Charles recognized the voice. Teasing him, the men cuffed his ears with open hands. Then they crowded him to the very edge of the chemical lagoon. "How about a quick dip?" Wally taunted him.

With one arm over his face, Charles drew out his flashlight and lashed at his nearest assailant. The flashlight fell and shattered. Brezo had eluded the blow, but he found himself teetering on the edge of the lagoon. To keep from falling into it, he was forced to step into the ooze to mid calf. He screamed as the corrosive chemical singed his skin. He knew he had to get his leg into water as soon as possible. Angelo DeJesus pulled Brezo's arm over his shoulder to support him, and the two men hurried back toward the entrance of Recycle, Ltd.

Charles seized his chance and bolted for the two planks over the sluice. He thundered over them, forgetting his previous nervousness at crossing. He thought about stopping to push the planks into the sluice, but Wally was too close behind him.

Charles ran as fast as possible to the fence and started to climb, but as he neared the top, Wally began shaking it violently. Charles had all he could do to hold on. Then Wally reached up and grabbed Charles's right foot. He tried to kick free, but Wally had a good hold. Charles tumbled off the fence, directly on top of him.

Desperately Charles groped beneath the snow for something with which he could defend himself, and came up with a large stick. He flung it at Wally, and although it missed its mark, it gave Charles a chance to stand and flee along the fence to the embankment. He slid down it to the river's edge, then scrambled out onto the ice and around the portion of the fence that extended out from shore. He was starting back up the embankment when Wally reached the river. Suddenly Charles's feet slid out from under him. Panic-stricken, he grasped for a hold. At the last second he caught a bush and halted his backward movement. He tried to scramble up but could not get any traction.

Wally had now rounded the fence and was starting up toward Charles. He was inches away when, slowly at first, then rapidly, he slid backward.

With renewed effort Charles inched upward and threw his body over the edge. He stood and fled toward the deserted mill building. The Pinto was parked a hundred yards behind it. But as he started for the car, he saw several flashlights swing in his direction. He had no choice. He ran for the empty building.

Dashing through a doorless opening, Charles was quickly engulfed by impenetrable darkness. He groped his way forward and encountered a wall. He stumbled along as fast as he could, using the wall as a guide. Hearing shouts behind him, he felt a surge of panic. He had to find a place to hide.

Moving quickly, he came to a door, slightly ajar. He pushed, and the door opened into a musty, foul-smelling room. Feeling ahead with his foot, he encountered a bale of material, then realized it was an old, rotting rug.

Behind him someone yelled, "We want to talk to you, Martel." Then he heard heavy footsteps. With a new surge of fear, he started across the room, hoping to find a hiding place. Almost immediately he stumbled against a low metal cabinet. Stepping around it, he discovered a pile of smelly rags, and burrowed beneath them.

Except for the luminous dial on his watch, Charles could see nothing. He waited, his breath sounding harsh in the stillness and his heart beating audibly in his ears. He was caught. There was no place else to run.

Now he could hear footsteps enter the room. A sharp ray of light was moving over every inch of the floor. With a stab of panic Charles knew he was about to be discovered.

Leaping from beneath his cover, he bolted for the door. The light silhouetted him in the doorway. "There he is!" someone shouted.

Charles started out the door and crashed into another pursuer, who grabbed him. Charles struck blindly, desperately trying to free himself. Then, even before he felt the pain, his legs buckled beneath him. The man had hit him on the back of his knees with a club.

He collapsed to the floor as the first man emerged from the room. His light played over the scene and Charles got a look at the man who'd hit him. To his astonishment he found himself looking at Frank Neilson, Shaftesbury's chief of police. The blue serge uniform had never looked so good.

"Okay, Martel, game's over!" said Neilson, slipping his billy club into its leather holster. He was a stocky man with slicked-back hair and a gut that swooped out above his belt. He grabbed Charles by the collar and hauled him to his feet.

"Cuffs?" asked the second man. He was Bernie Crawford, Neilson's deputy. In contrast to his boss, he was tall and lanky.

"Nope!" said Frank. "Let's just get him out of here."

As the trio made their way back through the deserted factory, Charles thought about Bernie's question of "cuffs." Obviously

240

Recycle had called the police and made a complaint that some-one was trespassing.

He resigned himself to a trip to the police station. No one spoke as they marched across the empty lot to the squad car. Charles was put into the back seat, behind the thick mesh guard. Frank started the car and pulled away from the curb.

Sitting back, Charles tried to calm down. His heart was still thumping in his chest, and his legs ached horribly. He glanced out the window. Instead of heading for the police station, Frank drove into Recycle's parking lot and stopped near the factory's front entrance. He blew the horn and Nat Archer came out, followed by Brezo, whose left leg was swathed in bandages.

Frank struggled out from behind the wheel and came around the car to open the door for Charles. "Out," he said. Charles complied. There was about an inch and a half of new snow, and Charles slid a little before regaining his balance.

"This the man?" asked Frank, bending a stick of gum and pushing it deep into his mouth.

Archer glared at Charles and said, "It's him, all right."

"Well, you want to press charges?"

Archer shook his head. He trudged off toward the factory. Frank, snapping his gum loudly, got back into the squad car.

Charles, confused, turned to look at Brezo, who stood smiling a toothless grin. Then, without warning, Brezo unleashed a powerful blow, catching Charles in the abdomen and doubling him up. As he crumpled to the earth, Brezo kicked a bit of snow at him and walked off, limping slightly.

Disoriented with the pain, Charles pushed himself up onto his hands and knees. He heard a car door open and felt a tug on his arm, forcing him to his feet. Frank put him back in the squad car and started the motor.

A few moments later the car stopped and the door opened. Neilson pulled him out. "I think you'd better stay away from here, buster. This town needs Recycle, and if you cause more trouble, we won't be able to guarantee your safety."

Frank got back in the driver's seat and spun his wheels, leaving Charles standing at the curb, his legs splattered with slush. The Pinto was twenty feet ahead, partially covered with a shroud of snow.

242

WHEN THE CAR SWEPT AROUND the final curve of the driveway, Cathryn ran to the kitchen window and pulled the red checkered curtains aside. Thank God, it was Charles. She hadn't heard from him since he'd fled the hospital, and she had to tell him about the guardianship proceedings before he got the court notice in the morning.

She could not see his face clearly as she swung open the door. Then he came into the light and she saw his bruised and swollen nose. There was dried blood on his upper lip. His jacket was soiled and his pants were torn. But most disturbing of all was his expression of barely controlled anger.

"Don't say anything for a moment," ordered Charles, avoiding Cathryn's touch. After removing his jacket, he headed for the phone.

Cathryn dampened a dish towel and, going over to him, tried to clean off his face.

"Cathryn! Can't you wait?" he snapped, pushing her away.

Cathryn stepped back. The man in front of her was a stranger. She watched as he angrily dialed a number.

"Dawson," he yelled into the phone. "I don't care if you've got the police and the whole damn town in your pocket. You're not going to get away with it!" Charles punctuated his statement by crashing down the receiver.

Having made the call to the head of Recycle, his tension eased a little. "I had no idea this quaint little town of ours was so corrupt," he said.

"What happened?" Cathryn asked. "Are you hurt?"

Charles looked at her, and to her surprise, he laughed. "No, I'm not hurt. Just my sense of dignity. But I need something to drink. Fruit juice. Anything."

He sank into a chair, and Cathryn brought him a glass of apple cider. She caught sight of her mother standing in the doorway and gestured for her to keep away. Cathryn sat down at the table. At least for the moment she abandoned her idea of telling him about the guardianship situation.

There was a pause while Charles drank his cider. "Are you going to tell me where you've been and what happened?" she asked finally.

"I'd rather hear about Michelle first."

Cathryn reached over and put her hand on his. "Her fever has gone up and the doctors are concerned."

"How high is it?"

"Pretty high. It was a hundred and four when I left."

"Why did you leave? Why didn't you stay?"

"I suggested it, but the doctors encouraged me to go. They said that parents with a sick child must be careful about neglecting the rest of their family. Should I have stayed?"

"Someone should be with her. A high fever at this point means infection. The medications are knocking out her normal defenses and seemingly not touching her leukemic cells." Abruptly he stood up. "I'm going back to the hospital."

"But why, Charles? What can you do now?" Cathryn felt a wave of panic, and she leaped to her feet.

"I want to be with her. Besides, I've made up my mind. The medications are going to be stopped. Or at least reduced to an orthodox dose. I'm not going to let my daughter be experimented on. Keitzman had his chance. She's not going to dissolve in front of my eyes, like Elizabeth." He pulled on his jacket and started for the door. Cathryn clutched at his sleeve. She knew she had to tell him about the guardianship right away.

"Charles," she began in a quiet tone, stepping back toward the kitchen counter, "you cannot stop Michelle's medicine."

"Of course I can," he said confidently.

"Arrangements have been made so that you cannot."

With his hand on the doorknob, Charles paused. "What are you trying to say?"

"I want you to take your jacket off and sit down," said Cathryn, as if she were talking to a recalcitrant teenager.

Charles walked directly up to her. "I think you'd better tell me about these arrangements."

Although Cathryn never would have imagined it possible, she felt a touch of fear as she gazed up at Charles. "After you left the hospital this afternoon, I had a conference with Dr. Keitzman and Dr. Wiley. They felt that you were under a severe strain and might not be in a position to make the right decisions about Michelle's care." Cathryn saw that Charles's blue eyes were cold, but she went on. "The hospital lawyer said that Michelle needed a temporary guardian and the doctors agreed."

244

"So what happened?"

"There was a hearing before a judge," Cathryn said. She was telling it poorly, but doggedly she continued. "I was appointed emergency temporary guardian. Charles, I've done this for Michelle. I'm not doing anything against you. Please believe me." She searched his face for a flicker of understanding. Seeing only rage, she broke into tears.

Gina appeared at the doorway. "Is everything all right?" she called out timidly.

Charles spoke very slowly, his eyes on Cathryn's face. "I hope to God this isn't true. I hope you're making this up."

"It's true," managed Cathryn. "You left. I did the best I could. You'll receive official notice in the morning."

Charles exploded with a violence he'd never known he possessed. The only handy object was a small stack of dishes. Snatching them off the counter, he lifted them over his head and crashed them to the floor. Cathryn cringed by the sink.

"Michelle is my daughter, my flesh and blood," Charles raged. "No one is going to take her away from me."

Overcoming her fear, Cathryn grabbed the lapels of his jacket. "Please calm down. Please," she cried desperately.

The last thing Charles wanted was to be held down. By reflex his arm shot up and knocked Cathryn's arms into the air. The side of his hand inadvertently caught her face, knocking her backward against the kitchen table.

A chair fell over and Gina screamed, running into the room and positioning herself between Charles and her dazed daughter. She began reciting a prayer. Charles shoved the woman aside and grabbed Cathryn by the shoulders. He shook her like a rag doll. "I want you to cancel those legal proceedings. Do you understand?"

Chuck heard the commotion and ran down the stairs. He took one look at the scene in front of him and sprang into the room, grabbing his father's arms from behind and pinning them to his sides. Charles released Cathryn and twisted away from his son.

He looked up to see Jean Paul in the doorway. The boy edged away when he saw his father staring at him. Looking back at the others, Charles felt an overwhelming sense of alienation. He turned and stormed out of the house.

While Gina helped Cathryn into a chair, they heard the Pinto rumble down the driveway.

"Your eye!" exclaimed Gina, tilting Cathryn's head back. "It's turning black and blue."

"I hate him! I hate him!" cried Chuck.

"No, no," soothed Cathryn. "Your father is not himself; he's under a lot of strain. Besides, he didn't mean to hit me. He was just trying to get free from my grasp."

"I think he's crazy," persisted Chuck.

"That's enough," said Cathryn. She wondered where she was going to find the strength to hold the family together.

Her first concern was safety. She had never seen Charles lose control before. Thinking it best to get some professional advice, she called Dr. Keitzman's exchange.

The doctor called back five minutes later, and Cathryn told him the entire series of events, including the fact that Charles was considering stopping Michelle's medications.

"Sounds like we petitioned for custody at the right time," said Keitzman. "Charles may be dangerous."

"I can't believe that."

"That's something that cannot be ascertained unless he's seen professionally. But believe me, it's a possibility. Maybe you should all leave the house for a day or two."

"I suppose we could go to my mother's," said Cathryn. "What are you going to do when Charles gets to the hospital?"

"I'll alert them that he's coming and tell them you have guardianship. Don't worry, everything will be all right."

Cathryn hung up, wishing she felt as optimistic as Dr. Keitzman. Half an hour later she, Gina, and the two boys trudged out into the snow with overnight bags and piled into the station wagon. They dropped Jean Paul at a friend's house, where he'd been invited to stay, and began the drive to Gina's apartment in Boston. No one spoke.

IT WAS after nine when Charles reached Pediatric Hospital. When he passed the nurses' station on Anderson 6, someone called to him, but he didn't even look in the direction of the voice. He slipped into Michelle's room through the partially open door and stood for a moment taking in the scene. The

246

cardiac monitor was visible on the other side of the bed, the signal tracing a fluorescent blip across the tiny screen. There were two intravenous lines, one running into each of Michelle's arms. The one on the left had a piggyback connector, and Charles knew it was being used as the infusion route for the chemotherapy.

He advanced silently into the room. As he got closer to his daughter he realized, to his surprise, that Michelle's eyes were not closed. She was watching him.

"Daddy?" she whispered. He went to her and tenderly lifted her in his arms. He pressed her feverish cheek to his and slowly rocked her. The emotion he felt was so powerful that he was beyond tears. "Daddy, why is your nose so swollen?" she asked, looking into his face.

Charles smiled. He made up a comic story of slipping in the snow and falling on his face. Michelle laughed, but she quickly became serious. "Daddy, am I going to get well?"

Without meaning to, Charles hesitated. The question had caught him off guard. "Of course," he said with a laugh, trying to make up for the pause. "In fact, I don't think you'll be needing any more of this medicine." He stood up, indicating the IV used for the chemotherapy. "Why don't I just take it out?" Deftly he removed the plastic catheter from Michelle's arm.

The overhead light snapped on as a nurse came in, followed by two uniformed security guards.

"Mr. Martel, I'm sorry, but you are going to have to leave." She noticed the dangling IV line and shook her head angrily.

Charles did not respond. He sat on the edge of Michelle's bed and again took her into his arms. The nurse gestured to the security men. "We can have you arrested if you don't cooperate," she said.

Michelle looked at the guards and then at her father. "Why would they arrest you?"

"I don't know," said Charles with a smile. "I guess it's not visiting hours." He stood up, bent over, and kissed his daughter. "I'll be back soon."

He waved from the doorway and Michelle waved back. Then the nurse reattached the IV and turned out the overhead light.

"I'd like to see my daughter's chart," Charles said courteously to the nurse in the hallway. When she didn't reply, he added, "It's my right. Besides, I am a physician."

She reluctantly agreed, and Charles went into the deserted chart room and pulled out Michelle's chart. There'd been a blood count that afternoon. His heart sank! Her leukemic cell count had gone up. The chemotherapy was not helping her at all.

He turned to the cardiology report. The conclusion was that the ventricular tachycardia could have been caused by either the rapid infusion of the second dose of daunorubicin or a leukemic infiltration of the heart, or perhaps a combination of the two.

Charles went back into the corridor. He thought about returning to Michelle's room, but the nurse was watching him like a hawk. He went to the elevator instead and pushed the button. As he waited, he began to outline what courses of action were open to him. He knew that now he was truly on his own.

Chapter 7

WHEN Ellen Sheldon arrived at the Weinburger the next morning, she was surprised to find Charles in the lab, hard at work. She took off her coat and struggled with a mild wave of guilt. "I didn't think you'd be here."

"I've been working a good part of the night," he said.

Ellen walked over to his desk. Charles had a new lab book in front of him and had already filled several pages. He looked terrible. His hair was matted, his eyes looked tired, and he was in need of a shave.

"I've got some good news," he added. "Our method of isolating a protein antigen from an animal cancer works just as well on human cancer. The hybridoma I made with Michelle's leukemic cells has been working overtime. I'd like you to start a new batch of mice using Michelle's leukemic antigen."

"But Charles, we're not supposed to be doing this."

Charles carefully set down the vial he held in his hands and faced Ellen. "I'm still in charge here." His voice was controlled, maybe too controlled.

Ellen nodded. She had come to be a little afraid of Charles. Without another word, she walked over to her area and began preparing to inject the mice. She thought to herself that some-

248

time after nine she'd find an excuse to contact Dr. Morrison.

Earlier that morning Charles had been served in his office with the notice concerning the guardianship. He had only glanced at the forms, noticing that his presence was required at a hearing in two days. He'd have to have legal counsel.

After checking his watch, Charles picked up the phone and called John Randolph, the Shaftesbury town manager. "I've got a complaint," he said after the usual greetings, "about the Shaftesbury police force."

"If you're talking about last night over at the factory," said Randolph, "I've heard all about it. Sounded to me like you were lucky Frank Neilson came along."

"I thought so at first," said Charles. "But not after they let some half-wit at Recycle punch me out."

"I didn't hear about that part. But I did hear you were trespassing, and pushed someone into some acid. Why in the world are you causing all this trouble?"

Charles launched into an impassioned explanation of Recycle's dumping benzene and other toxic chemicals into the river. He told the town manager that for the sake of the community he was trying to get the factory closed down.

"I don't think the community would look kindly at closing down the factory," said Randolph. "The prosperity of our town is directly related to Recycle."

"Causing diseases like leukemia and aplastic anemia in children is a high price to pay for prosperity, wouldn't you agree?"

"I don't know anything about that," said Randolph evenly.

"I don't think you want to know about it."

"Are you accusing me of something?"

"I'm accusing you of irresponsibility. Even if there were just a chance that Recycle was dumping poisonous chemicals into the river, the factory should be closed until it is investigated."

"That's easy for you to say, but those jobs are important for the town and the people who work there. Now why don't you just stay out of our business? We don't need you city folk with your Harvard degrees telling us how to live!"

Charles heard a click as the line was disconnected. So much for that approach, he thought. Then he dialed the number for the EPA and asked for Mrs. Amendola. When she came on the wire, Charles described what he had found at Recycle, Ltd.

"Did you get some photos?" she asked.

"I tried to, but I couldn't," said Charles simply, fearful that any explanation of what had happened to his camera would discourage the EPA altogether. He told her he'd appreciate it if she'd try to get some action based on the information he'd already given her. As he hung up he was not very confident anything would be done.

Returning to work, he prepared a dilution of Michelle's leukemic antigen for injection into the mice, and put the vial with the remaining antigen into the refrigerator.

Charles gave the dilution to Ellen and told her he was going out to find a lawyer; he'd be back before lunch.

After the door closed, Ellen called Dr. Morrison and told him that Charles was still working on his own research; that in fact, he was expanding it.

"That is the last straw," said Dr. Morrison. "Charles Martel is finished at the Weinburger."

In his quest for legal representation Charles headed into downtown Boston. He parked his car in the government center garage and consulted the Yellow Pages in a nearby drugstore. Avoiding fancy addresses, he looked for lawyers who were out on their own. He marked half a dozen names and began calling, asking whoever answered if they were busy or if they needed work. On the fifth try, in response to Charles's question, the lawyer said he was starving. Charles said he'd be right over. He copied down the name and address: Wayne Thomas, 13 Brattle Street, Cambridge.

The office was on a narrow alley off Harvard Square. When Charles entered, Wayne Thomas said, "Okay, sit right here and tell me what you got." Charles sat down in a straight-backed chair and studied the man.

Wayne Thomas didn't look as if he were starving. He was a solid six-foot black man in his early thirties, with a full beard. Dressed in a three-piece blue pin-striped suit, he was a commanding presence.

Handing over the temporary guardianship notice, Charles told his story. When he got to the end of his tale, Thomas asked a

250

series of probing questions. Finally he said, "I don't think there's much we can do about this temporary guardianship until the full hearing. As for Recycle, Limited, I can start right away. However, there is the question of a retainer."

"I've got a three-thousand-dollar loan coming," said Charles.

Thomas whistled. "I'm not talking about that kind of bread. How about five hundred?"

Charles agreed to send the money as soon as he got the loan. He shook hands with Thomas and went back to his car. Returning to the Weinburger, he felt a modicum of satisfaction at having at least started the legal process.

The lab and the animal room were empty. Ellen was obviously out for lunch. He went over to her work area and noticed that the dilution he'd prepared of Michelle's leukemic antigen had not been touched.

At that moment Peter Morrison walked into the lab. The two men eyed each other across the polished floor, their outward differences even more apparent than usual. Morrison seemed to have made particular effort with his appearance that day, whereas Charles had slept at the lab in his clothes.

Morrison wore a victorious smile. "You're wanted immediately in the director's office," he said.

When the two men reached Dr. Ibanez's office, the director seemed a bit uneasy. "Dr. Martel, I'm afraid you've given us no choice," he began. "As I warned you yesterday and in accordance with the wishes of the board of directors, you're being dismissed from the Weinburger Institute."

Charles felt a mixture of anger and anxiety. The nightmare of being fired had changed from fantasy to fact. Carefully hiding any sign of emotion, he nodded, then started to leave.

"Just a minute, Dr. Martel," called Dr. Ibanez, standing up behind his desk. "I understand that you have a complaint about Recycle, Limited. I think you should remember that Recycle and the Weinburger share a parent firm, Breur Chemical. Because of that, I would have hoped that you would not have made any public complaints."

"Recycle has been dumping benzene into the river that goes past my house," snapped Charles. "And as a result, my daughter has terminal leukemia."

"An accusation like that is unprovable and irresponsible," said Dr. Morrison.

Charles took a step toward Morrison, momentarily blinded by rage, but then he remembered where he was. He turned to Dr. Ibanez. "That's one reason I couldn't do the Canceran study. I had to continue my own work for the sake of my daughter."

"Did you think you could come up with a discovery in time to help her?" asked Dr. Ibanez incredulously.

"It's possible," Charles said.

"That sounds like a delusion of grandeur," said Dr. Ibanez. "Well, as I said, you leave me no choice. You'll be given two months' severance pay, and your medical insurance will continue for thirty days. You can have your lab books back, but your replacement wants the laboratory in two days."

Charles glowered at the two men. "Before I go, I'd like to say something. I think having a drug firm and a cancer research institute controlled by the same parent company is a crime, especially since executives of both companies sit on the board of the National Cancer Institute and award themselves grants. Canceran is a good example of this financial incest. The drug is so toxic that it will never be used on people unless the tests continue to be falsified. And I intend to make these facts public."

"Enough!" shouted Dr. Ibanez. He pounded his desk. "When it comes to the integrity of the Weinburger or the potential of Canceran, you'd better leave well enough alone. Now get out before I retract the benefits we have extended to you."

Charles left the office, glad to be free from the institute he now abhorred. By the time he reached his lab, a plan for action had formed in his mind. He locked the door and quickly went to work. Most of the chemicals he needed were stored in industrial quantities, so he began transferring some of each to smaller containers. He carefully labeled each container and stored it in a locked cabinet near the animal room.

While he was feverishly working, the phone rang. It was a loan officer from the bank, who told Charles that his three-thousand-dollar loan was ready. He would be glad to deposit it in his checking account. Charles told him no, he'd be over later to pick it up.

He was almost finished with his work when he heard a knock

252

at the door. He opened it to find Dr. Ibanez's secretary with his lab books. She put them on the counter and left without saying a word.

Charles returned to his work with renewed commitment. He would have to make his move that very night, before news of his dismissal spread. It took another hour to get everything he needed organized into the single cabinet. Then, donning his jacket, he left, locking the door behind him.

It was after three o'clock, and Boston traffic was building to its pre–rush-hour frenzy. His first stop was the bank. The vice-president Charles knew was not in, so he had to see a young woman he'd never met. She suspiciously eyed his soiled jacket and day-and-a-half growth of beard and took a moment to study the photo on his driver's license. Seemingly comfortable with the identification, she asked Charles if he wanted a check. He asked for the loan in cash.

"Cash?" Mildly flustered, the bank officer excused herself and disappeared into the back office. When she returned she was carrying thirty crisp hundred-dollar bills.

Charles retrieved his car and threaded his way into the tangled downtown shopping district. He double-parked and ran into a sporting goods shop. He bought a hundred rounds of twelve-gauge number two express shot for his shotgun, paying for the shells with a new hundred-dollar bill.

Back in the car, he drove to a large drugstore he had patronized when he had his private practice.

"Need to restock my black bag," he said to the pharmacist. Then he wrote out prescriptions for morphine, Demerol, Compazine, Xylocaine, Benadryl, epinephrine, prednisone, Percodan, Valium. To the list he added syringes, plastic tubing, and intravenous solutions.

The pharmacist took the scripts and whistled. "What do you carry around, a suitcase?"

Charles gave a short laugh as he paid for the items.

Once again in the Pinto, he eased into the traffic and recrossed the Charles River. Passing the Weinburger, he continued to Harvard Square, parked in a lot, and hurried to 13 Brattle Street.

Wayne Thomas' eyes lit up when Charles handed over five crisp one-hundred-dollar bills. "Man, you're going to get the

253

best service money can buy," said the young attorney. He then told Charles that he'd already filed a restraining order against Recycle, Ltd.

Charles left the lawyer's office and walked a block south to a car rental agency. He rented a large van and drove it back to the parking lot where he'd left the Pinto. After transferring the shotgun shells and the carton of medical supplies, Charles got back in the van and drove to the Weinburger. He checked his watch: four thirty p.m. It would be dark soon.

AT MICHELLE's bedside, Cathryn stood up stiffly. She stretched, then stepped silently into the bathroom, and closed the door. Flipping on the fluorescent light, she glanced into the mirror. What she saw startled her. Under the artificial light she looked frightfully pale, which only emphasized her black eye. At the corners of her mouth were lines she'd never seen before.

After running a comb through her hair a few times, Cathryn stood thinking for a moment. Fleeing to her mother's apartment in Boston had only eliminated the fear of Charles's violence; it had done nothing to relieve her agonizing uncertainty over whether she'd made the right decision about the guardianship.

As quietly as possible she reopened the bathroom door and went over to the bed. Michelle had finally drifted off into a restless sleep. The child had had a terrible day. She'd become weaker and weaker by the hour, to the point that raising her arms and head was an effort. There were raw ulcers on her lips, and her hair was coming out in thick clumps. But the worst part was her high fever.

As Cathryn watched, Michelle's eyes suddenly opened and her face twisted in pain.

"What's wrong?" asked Cathryn, anxiously leaning forward.

Michelle didn't answer, but her slender body writhed in pain.

Without a moment's hesitation Cathryn was out the door, calling for a nurse. The woman came in, took one look at Michelle, and put in a call to Dr. Keitzman.

He arrived within minutes. Skillfully he examined the child. Putting the bell of the stethoscope on Michelle's abdomen, he listened. Then he palpated her abdomen. When he straightened up, he whispered something to the nurse, who quickly disappeared.

254

"Functional intestinal cramping," explained Dr. Keitzman to Cathryn. "I've ordered a shot that will give her instant relief."

Cathryn nodded. Then she sagged into a chair.

Dr. Keitzman put a hand on her shoulder and said, "Mrs. Martel, come outside with me for a moment."

She silently followed as Keitzman led her to the chart room. "Mrs. Martel, I'm concerned about you," he said. "You're under a lot of stress, too."

Cathryn nodded. She was afraid to talk, for fear her emotions might surface and overflow.

"Unfortunately I have to tell you that Michelle is still doing very poorly. So far there is no hint of a remission. I want her two brothers to come in tomorrow for typing to see if either one's bone marrow matches Michelle's. I think we have to consider giving her a marrow transplant."

"I understand. I'll tell them."

"Good," said Dr. Keitzman, examining her face. "That's quite a shiner you've got."

"Charles didn't mean it. It was an accident," said Cathryn quickly.

"I'm concerned about him," said Dr. Keitzman. "I don't mean to frighten you, but we've seen similar cases in which the individual has become violent. If there's any way you can get him to see a psychiatrist, I think you ought to try it."

When Cathryn left the chart room, she went to the pay phone and put in a call to the institute. The Weinburger operator plugged in Charles's lab and Cathryn let it ring ten times. When the operator came back on the line, she said that Ellen was in the library, and asked if she would like to speak with her. Cathryn agreed and heard the connection put through.

"He might be just ignoring the phone," suggested Ellen. "Dr. Morrison just told me that Charles has been dismissed from the Weinburger. But I suppose you knew that."

"I had no idea!" exclaimed Cathryn. "What happened?"

"It's a long story, and I think Charles should tell you, not me."

Cathryn slowly hung up the receiver and walked back to Michelle's room. She knew that Charles was one of the Weinburger's most respected scientists. What possibly could have happened? She had only one explanation. Maybe Dr. Keitzman was right. Maybe Charles was having a nervous breakdown.

Slipping into Michelle's room, she saw that the girl's eyes were open. Cathryn went over and grasped her warm hand.

"Where's my daddy?" asked Michelle, moving her ulcerated lips as little as possible. "He told me he would come today."

"He will if he can," said Cathryn. "He will if he can."

A tear appeared on Michelle's face. "I think it would be better if I were dead."

Cathryn bent down and hugged the child, giving way to her own tears. "No, no, Michelle! Never think that for a moment."

Chapter 8

CHARLES found an ice scraper in the van and used it on the inside of the windshield. His breath had condensed and then frozen, blocking his view of the Weinburger entrance. By six fifteen everyone except Dr. Ibanez had left the institute. Then at six thirty the director appeared. Bent against the icy wind, he made his way to his Mercedes.

At twenty to seven Charles drove to the receiving dock at the back of the building. Getting out of the van, he climbed the stairs next to the platform and rang the bell.

A speaker above the bell crackled to life. "Yes?" asked a voice.

"Dr. Martel here," said Charles. "I've got to pick up some equipment."

A moment later the metal door squeaked, then slowly rose, exposing a cement receiving area. In the rear a door opened and Chester Willis, one of the evening guards, stepped out. "You workin' nights again?" he asked.

"Forced to," said Charles. "We're collaborating with a group at MIT and I've got to move over some of my equipment. I don't trust anybody else to do it."

"Don't blame you," said Chester.

Charles breathed a sigh of relief. Security did not know he'd been fired. Taking a large dolly with him, he went directly to his lab. He was pleased to find it untouched since his departure, particularly the locked cabinet with his books and chemicals. Working feverishly, he dismantled most of his equipment and loaded it onto the dolly. It took him eight trips to transport what he wanted from the lab down to receiving. Chester helped him load it into the van.

The last thing Charles brought down from the lab was the vial of Michelle's antigen that had been stored in the refrigerator. He packed it carefully in ice within an insulated box. It was after nine when everything was in the van, but he had one more task. Returning to his lab, he located a prep razor used for animal surgery. With it and a bar of soap he went to the lavatory and removed his stubble. He also combed his hair and straightened his tie. On the way back to receiving, he stepped into the coatroom and picked up a long white laboratory coat.

He drove to Pediatric Hospital and pulled into the garage. He parked within view of the attendant's booth and double-checked all the doors to be absolutely certain they were locked. Wearing the long white lab coat, he ran across to the hospital and entered through the busy emergency room.

Charles paused at the check-in desk to ask what floor radiology was on. The clerk told him it was on Anderson 2. Charles thanked him and pushed through the double doors into the hospital proper. He passed a security guard and nodded. The guard smiled back.

Radiology was practically deserted. There seemed to be only one technician on duty, and she was busy with a backlog of films. In the secretarial area, Charles obtained an X-ray request form and stationery from the department. He filled in the form: Michelle Martel, age twelve; diagnosis, leukemia; study requested, abdominal flat plate. He signed it with the name of a staff radiologist listed on the stationery's letterhead.

Back in the main corridor, Charles unlocked the wheel stops on one of the many gurneys parked along the wall. From a nearby linen closet he obtained sheets, a pillow, and a pillowcase. Working quickly, he made up the gurney, then pushed it to the patient elevator. When the elevator came, he rolled the gurney on and pressed 6.

The elevator stopped and the door opened. Taking a deep breath, he pushed the gurney out into the quiet hall. The first obstacle was the nurses' station. At that moment there was only one nurse, whose cap could just be seen over the counter top. Charles moved ahead, aware for the first time of the squeaks

257

emitted by the gurney's wheels. He passed the station and entered the long hall.

"Can I help you?" called the nurse, her voice shattering the stillness like breaking glass.

Charles felt a jolt of adrenaline shoot into his system. "Just picking up a patient for X ray," he said.

"No X rays have been ordered," said the nurse curiously.

Charles could hear her flipping the pages of a book. "An emergency film," he said, abandoning the gurney and approaching the nurse. "Here's the request. It was phoned in by Dr. Keitzman to Dr. Larainen."

She took the form and read it quickly, then shook her head as she handed it back to him. "Someone should have phoned us."

"I agree. It happens all the time, though." He walked back to the gurney. His hands were moist.

He moved down the corridor at a deliberate pace, hoping the nurse would not make a confirming call to radiology.

He reached Michelle's room and had started through the door when he saw a seated figure, head resting on the bed. It was Cathryn. Charles averted his face and backed out. As quickly as he could he pulled the gurney the length of the corridor. He had to get Cathryn out of the room. On the spur of the moment he could think of only one method.

Quietly he retraced his steps to the treatment room near the nurses' station. Luckily the nurse did not look up. He found some surgical masks and hoods by a scrub sink. He donned one of each and pocketed an extra hood. Then he crossed the corridor to the dark lounge area, where he found a public telephone. Calling the switchboard, he asked for Anderson 6, and in a moment he heard the phone ringing in the nurses' station.

When the nurse answered the phone, Charles asked for Mrs. Martel, saying that it was an emergency. The nurse told him to hold the line. Quickly he put down the receiver and moved to the doorway of the lounge. He could see the charge nurse come into the corridor and walk briskly up the hall. Once she had entered Michelle's room, Charles immediately left the lounge and scurried past his daughter's room to the end of the hall. From there he saw the nurse come out of the room with Cathryn, who was rubbing her eyes. As soon as the two women turned toward the nurses' station, Charles ran the gurney down to Michelle's room and pushed it through the half-open door.

Flipping on the wall switch, he pushed the gurney over to the bed. He could see that Michelle was perceptibly worse. Pulling down his mask, he gently shook her shoulder.

"Michelle?" he called.

Slowly Michelle's eyes opened. With great effort she lifted her arms and put them around her father's neck. "I knew you'd come," she said.

"Listen," said Charles anxiously, putting his face close to hers. "I want to ask you something. I know you are very sick and they are trying to take care of you here at the hospital. But you are not getting well here. Your sickness is stronger than their strongest medicines. I want to take you away with me, but your doctors would not like it. Do you want to go? You have to tell me."

Michelle looked into her father's eyes. There was nothing she wanted more. "Take me with you, Daddy, please!"

Charles hugged her, then set to work. He turned off the cardiac monitor and detached the leads. He pulled out her IV and turned down the covers. As gently as he could, he lifted Michelle onto the gurney and covered her. From the closet he retrieved her clothes and hid them beneath the sheet. He pulled his mask back up and put a surgical hood over Michelle's head; then he turned off the light.

As he pushed the gurney past the nurses' station, he was terrified Cathryn would appear. He had to force himself to walk at a normal pace to the elevator.

The nurse had told Cathryn she could take the call on the phone in the chart room. Cathryn had said hello three times, but no one had answered. She had waited and repeated the hellos. Then she depressed the disconnect button, and when she released it, she was talking to the hospital operator.

The operator didn't know anything about a call for Mrs. Martel. Cathryn hung up and walked out to the corridor. Just then she saw a figure in white, wearing a surgical mask and hood, push a patient across to the elevators. She felt a wave of sympathy for the poor child being taken to surgery at such a late hour.

Cathryn explained to the nurse that there wasn't anyone on the line.

"That's strange," said the nurse. "The caller said it was an emergency."

"Was it a man or a woman?"

"A man," said the nurse.

Cathryn wondered if it was Charles. What kind of an emergency could it have been? And why didn't he stay on the line?

She walked slowly back to Michelle's room. The door was completely open, and as she stepped into the room, she hoped that the light from the corridor had not bothered Michelle. She pulled the door almost closed behind her and walked carefully over to her chair in the near dark. It was then she realized that the bed was empty. She turned on the light and hurried to the bathroom. Michelle was not there either.

Cathryn ran out of the room, arriving at the nurses' station out of breath. "Nurse! My daughter's not in her room! She's gone!"

The charge nurse insisted on checking Michelle's room herself. Then she put in a call to security, telling them that a twelve-year-old girl had vanished from Anderson 6. She also flipped on a series of signal lights that called back the nurses who were on that floor. She told them of Michelle's apparent disappearance and sent them to search all the rooms.

"Martel," said the charge nurse after the others had left. "That rings a bell. I think that was the child taken down to radiology for an emergency flat plate."

Cathryn looked bewildered as the nurse picked up the phone and dialed radiology. A technician answered, and the nurse said, "You're doing an emergency flat plate on a patient from Anderson six. What is the name of the child?"

"I haven't done any emergency flat plates," said the technician. "Must have been George. He's up in the OR. He'll be back in a minute and I'll have him call." The technician hung up before the charge nurse could respond.

CHARLES wheeled Michelle into the emergency room and pushed the gurney into an examination cubicle. After closing the curtain, he took off his lab coat, hood, and mask and got out Michelle's clothes. The excitement of the caper had buoyed the girl's spirits, and despite her weakness, she tried to help her father dress her. In his hurry Charles found that he was very clumsy, and Michelle had to do all the buttons and tie her shoes.

When she was dressed, Charles found some cling bandage and wound it around Michelle's head. "We have to make it look like you were in an accident," he said. As a final touch, he put a Band-Aid over the bridge of her nose.

He picked up his daughter and carried her out of the cubicle. The emergency room was still busy, and he and Michelle passed through unnoticed.

Approaching the exit, he saw a uniformed security man jump up from a nearby chair. Charles's heart fluttered, but the man didn't challenge them; instead he scurried to open the door, saying, "Hope she's feeling better. Have a good night."

With a sense of freedom, Charles carried Michelle out of the hospital, settled her in the van, and drove off.

CATHRYN paced the lounge, becoming increasingly nervous as time passed. Checking her watch, she walked out to the nurses' station. How could a hospital lose a sick twelve-year-old child who was so weak she could barely walk?

"Any news?" she asked.

"Not yet," said the charge nurse. "I'm still waiting for a call from radiology. I'm sure Martel was the name of the child they picked up."

Cathryn turned away, wondering again about her mysterious phone call. She felt intuitively that it was from Charles. What if its purpose had been to get her out of Michelle's room? All at once the image of the man pushing the child to surgery flashed before her eyes. He was the right height, the right build. It must have been Charles! Cathryn rushed back to the nurses' station. Now she was sure that Michelle had been abducted.

"LET me get it straight," said the stocky Boston police officer. His name tag said William Kerney. "You were sleeping in here when a nurse tapped you on the shoulder."

"Yes!" snapped Cathryn, exasperated at the slow pace of the investigation. She'd hoped that calling the police would speed up the whole affair. "I've told you ten times exactly what happened. Can't you try to find the child?"

261

"We have to finish our report," explained Kerney. He licked his pencil and made a note.

The two were standing in Michelle's room. With them were a second police officer and the evening charge nurse.

Michael Grady, the other police officer, was reading the temporary guardianship papers. When he finished he said, "It's a child-snatching case. No doubt about it."

Kerney looked at Cathryn. "Suppose it was the father who took the child," he said. "Why?"

"Because he didn't agree with the treatment," she said. "That's why the temporary guardianship was granted."

Kerney whistled. "If he didn't like the treatment here," he said, "what was he interested in? Laetrile, something like that?"

"He didn't say," said Cathryn.

"We've had a few of those Laetrile cases," said Kerney. "All kinds of people seeking unorthodox treatment. I think we'd better alert the airport. They might be on their way to Mexico."

Dr. Keitzman arrived, demanding to be told everything. Cathryn was tremendously relieved to see him. "This is terrible!" he said. "It sounds like Dr. Martel has definitely had a nervous breakdown."

"How long will the girl live without treatment?" asked Kerney.

"Hard to say. Days, weeks, a month at most. We have several more drugs to try on her. There is still a chance of remission."

"Well," said Kerney, "I'll turn the report over to the detectives immediately."

As the two patrolmen walked out of the hospital, Michael Grady said to his partner, "What a story! Makes you feel terrible. Kid with leukemia and all that. Do you think the detectives will get right on it?"

"You kidding? These custody cases are a pain. Thankfully they usually solve themselves in twenty-four hours. Anyway, the detectives won't even look at it until tomorrow."

CATHRYN opened her eyes and looked around in confusion. Then she realized that she was in her old room, which her mother still compulsively maintained.

She shook her head to rid herself of the numbness remaining

from the sleeping pills Dr. Keitzman had insisted she take. Glancing at her watch, she saw that it was nine o'clock.

Slipping on an old plaid flannel robe, Cathryn hurried down to the kitchen, smelling the aroma of fresh biscuits and bacon. When she entered, her mother looked up and smiled, pleased to have her daughter home, no matter what the reason.

"Has Charles called?" asked Cathryn.

"No, but I've fixed your favorite breakfast." Gina poured her a cup of coffee.

"I'd better go and get Chuck up," said Cathryn.

"He's up, breakfasted, and gone," Gina said triumphantly. "Said he had a nine-o'clock class."

Cathryn sat down at the table. She felt useless. She'd tried so hard to be a good wife and mother and now she had the feeling she'd bungled it. Getting her adopted son up for school was hardly the criterion for being a good mother, yet the fact that she'd not done it seemed representative of her whole incompetent performance. Battling her emotions, she lifted the coffee cup to her mouth. As she took a sip, the hot fluid scalded her lips and she pulled the cup away, sloshing some of the liquid on her hand. Burned, she released the cup, which fell to the table and shattered. At that, Cathryn broke into tears.

Gina cleaned up the mess while Cathryn struggled to get control of herself. Her mother wasn't much help. "I warned you about marrying an older man with children," said Gina. "It's always trouble."

Cathryn held back the anger that only her mother was capable of causing. Then the phone rang.

Gina answered it. "It's for you," she said. "A detective named Patrick O'Sullivan."

Expecting the worst, Cathryn picked up the phone. But Patrick O'Sullivan had no information about Charles or Michelle. He said that there had been a new development in the case and asked if she would meet him at Charles's lab right away.

Fifteen minutes later she was ready to leave. She told Gina that after stopping at the Weinburger she was going to drive back to Shaftesbury. Gina tried to protest, but Cathryn was insistent, saying she needed a few hours alone. She told her mother that she'd be back in time for dinner with Chuck.

The ride across Boston was uneventful. At the institute, she saw two police cars pulled up close to the entrance. She parked, then went inside. When she arrived at Charles's lab, she noticed at once that the room had been dismantled. All the equipment was gone. The counter tops were bare.

There were six people in the lab. Ellen was talking to two uniformed policemen, who were filling out a report. Dr. Ibanez and Dr. Morrison were standing near Charles's desk, talking with a freckle-faced man in a blue sports coat. The man approached Cathryn.

"Mrs. Martel, I'm Detective Patrick O'Sullivan. I've been assigned to your case. Thanks for coming."

"What's going on?" she asked.

"It seems that your husband, after his dismissal from the institute, stole most of the equipment from his lab."

Cathryn's eyes widened. "I don't believe that."

"The evidence is pretty irrefutable. One of the evening security men apparently helped Dr. Martel load the stuff into a van. Would you have any idea why?"

Cathryn glanced around the room. "I haven't the slightest idea. It seems absurd."

The detective lifted his eyebrows. "It's absurd all right. It's also grand larceny, Mrs. Martel."

Cathryn looked back at the detective. He glanced down and shuffled his feet. "Child snatching by a parent is one thing, but theft is something else. We're going to have to put out the details and a warrant for Dr. Martel's arrest on the Teletype."

Cathryn shuddered. The nightmare kept getting worse. Charles was now a fugitive. "I don't know what to say."

"Our condolences, Mrs. Martel," said Dr. Ibanez as he and Dr. Morrison came up behind her.

She turned and saw the director's sympathetic expression.

"It's a tragedy," agreed Dr. Morrison.

There was an uncomfortable pause. Patrick O'Sullivan broke the silence. "Exactly why was Dr. Martel fired?"

"He had been acting a bit bizarrely," Ibanez said. "We began to question his mental stability." He paused. "And lately he'd become uncooperative, obsessed with his own theories about cancer research."

264

"Could Dr. Martel have taken the equipment to continue his research?" asked O'Sullivan.

"No," said Dr. Morrison. "Impossible! The key to this kind of research is the use of highly bred animals, and Charles did not take any of his mice. And as a fugitive, he'd find it difficult to get them, I think."

In the background the phone rang. Ellen answered it and called out for Detective O'Sullivan.

"This must be a very difficult time for you," said Dr. Ibanez to Cathryn. "Please let us know if we can help."

She tried to smile.

Patrick O'Sullivan came back. "Well, we've found his car. He left it in a parking lot in Harvard Square."

DRIVING along Interstate 301, Cathryn felt increasingly unhappy. She had looked forward to getting back to her own home, although she realized it would no longer be the happy refuge she once knew. When she reached their driveway, she saw that the mailbox had been knocked over and crushed. She started up the drive, moving between the rows of trees, and parked opposite the back porch.

As she got out of the car, she heard the door to the playhouse swinging in the wind, repeatedly thumping as it opened and closed. Looking more closely, she could see that most of the windows of the playhouse had been broken. She turned and walked through the snow to the back door of her house, unlocked it, and stepped into the kitchen.

In the next instant a figure came from behind the door and pushed her up against the kitchen wall. Cathryn screamed. The door shut with a crash.

Cathryn's scream trailed off in her throat. It was Charles! Speechless, she watched while he ran frantically from window to window, looking outside. In his right hand he held his old twelve-gauge shotgun. Cathryn noticed that the windows had been crudely boarded up on the outside and he had to peer out between the cracks. Before she could recover her equilibrium, he grabbed her arm and forced her into the living room. "Are you alone?" he demanded.

"Yes," she said. She was paralyzed by fear.

265

"Thank God," said Charles. His tense face visibly relaxed.

For the first time Cathryn looked around the living room. The gleaming laboratory instruments from the Weinburger stood on tables against one wall, and in the middle of the room, in a makeshift hospital bed, Michelle slept.

"Michelle!" cried Cathryn, running over and grasping the child's hand. Her eyes opened and for an instant there was a flicker of recognition, then the lids closed. Cathryn turned to her husband. "Charles, what in heaven's name are you doing?"

"I'll tell you in a moment." He adjusted Michelle's IV. Then he took Cathryn's arm and led her back to the kitchen, motioning her to a chair. "Coffee?" he asked.

She shook her head. He poured himself a cup and sat down opposite her.

"First I want to say something," he began, looking directly at his wife. "I've had a chance to think, and now I understand the position you were in on the guardianship situation. I know how doctors can bully patients and their families, and I'm sure you were trying to do the best thing for Michelle. I'm sorry that I reacted as I did. I hope you'll forgive me."

Cathryn wanted to throw her arms around him, because all at once he sounded so normal, but she couldn't move. There were still unanswered questions.

He picked up his coffee cup. His hand shook so much he had to use his left hand to steady it. "Deciding what was best for Michelle was a very difficult problem," he continued. "I hoped that orthodox medicine could give her more time. But I could see that the chemotherapy, even in experimentally high doses, was not touching her leukemic cells. Yet it was destroying normal cells, particularly her own immune system."

"But all the other doctors agreed that chemotherapy was the only way."

"They were wrong. If Michelle is to have a chance, she must have an intact immune system."

"And you have another treatment?"

Charles sighed. "I think so. I hope so!"

Cathryn wanted desperately to believe that, but under the circumstances it was difficult. "Do you mean there's a chance you can cure her?"

"I don't want to get your hopes up too high," said Charles, "but, yes, there is a chance. Maybe a small one, but a chance. And more important, my treatment won't hurt her."

"Have you been able to cure any of the laboratory animals that had cancer?"

"No, I haven't," admitted Charles. Then he added quickly, "But I was just about to try a new technique, using healthy mice as intermediaries, to cure the diseased ones."

"You don't have any animals here," said Cathryn, remembering Dr. Morrison's remarks.

"I have one large experimental animal," said Charles. "Me."

Cathryn swallowed. A red flag went up as again she had to question her husband's state of mind.

"That idea surprises you," he said. "But in the past, most medical researchers used themselves as experimental subjects. Anyway, my research has advanced to the point where I can take a cancerous cell from an organism and isolate a protein, or what is called an antigen, on its surface, which makes that cell different from all the other cells. That in itself is a major advance. My problem, then, was getting the organism's immune system to react to the antigen and therefore rid itself of the abnormal cancerous cells. This, I believe, is what happens in normal organisms. I think cancer is a fairly frequent occurrence but that the body's immune system usually takes care of it. It is when the immune system fails that a particular cancer takes root and grows. Do you understand so far?"

Cathryn nodded.

"When I tried to get the cancerous animals to respond to the antigen, I couldn't. I think there is some kind of blocking mechanism. Then I got the idea to inject the isolated surface antigen into well animals to make them immune to it, but I didn't have time to carry out the tests. Cathryn, do you remember that horses were used to make diphtheria antiserum?"

"I think so," said Cathryn.

"What I'm explaining to you is something like that. I've isolated the surface antigen of Michelle's leukemic cells, and I've been injecting the antigen into myself."

"So you will become allergic to Michelle's leukemic cells?" asked Cathryn, struggling to comprehend.

267

"Exactly," said Charles with excitement.

"Then you'll inject your antibodies into Michelle?"

"No," said Charles. "Her immune system wouldn't accept my antibodies. But there is a way to transfer immunity from one organism to another. Once my T-lymphocytes are sensitized to Michelle's leukemic antigen, I will isolate from my white cells what is called a transfer factor and inject that into Michelle. That should stimulate her own immune system to eliminate the existing leukemic cells and any new ones that evolve."

"How long will this take?" asked Cathryn, now realizing that from his point of view everything he'd done had been rational.

"I'm not sure it will even work," said Charles. "It depends on how my body reacts to the antigen. I won't know that for a couple of days. During that time I'm prepared to fight any attempts to have Michelle taken back to the hospital."

Cathryn glanced around the kitchen, noting again the boarded windows. Turning back to Charles, she said, "I guess you know the Boston police are looking for you. They think you've taken her to Mexico to get Laetrile."

He laughed. "That's absurd. And they can't be looking for me too hard, because our local police know I'm here. Did you notice the mailbox and the playhouse?" She nodded. "That's thanks to our local authorities. Last night a group came up from Recycle, Limited, bent on vandalism. I called the police and thought they hadn't shown up until I noticed a squad car parked down the road. Obviously they condoned the whole thing."

"Why?" asked Cathryn, aghast.

"I retained an aggressive young lawyer who's giving Recycle some trouble, and they want to scare me into calling him off."

"Oh, Charles!" exclaimed Cathryn, beginning to appreciate the extent of her husband's isolation.

"Where are the boys?" he asked.

"Chuck's been staying at Mother's with me. Jean Paul is in Shaftesbury, staying with a friend."

"Good," said Charles. "Things might get rough around here."

Husband and wife stared at each other across the kitchen table, and a surge of love swept over them. They stood up and fell into each other's arms, holding on desperately. "Please trust me, and love me," said Charles.

268

"I love you," she said, feeling tears on her cheeks. "That's never been a problem." She pulled away to look up into his face. "Everyone thinks you've had a nervous breakdown. I didn't know what to think, particularly with your carrying on about Recycle when the real issue was Michelle's treatment."

"The most frustrating part of her illness was that I couldn't do anything. Recycle galvanized my need for action. My anger about what they're doing is real enough, as well as my commitment to get them to stop. But obviously my main interest is Michelle. Otherwise I wouldn't be here now."

Cathryn felt freed of an enormous weight. She was now certain that Charles had never lost contact with reality. "What about Michelle's condition?" she asked.

"Not good. She's a terribly sick child. I've given her morphine because she's had awful stomach cramps."

Cathryn felt Charles tremble as he fought back his tears. She held him as tightly as she could. They stood together for another few minutes. There were no words, but the communication was total. Finally Charles pulled away. "I don't think you should stay here," he said. "Without doubt there will be trouble. It would be better if you went back to your mother's."

"If you think," she said vehemently, "that you can get rid of me now that you've convinced me what you're doing is right, you *are* crazy! I'm staying and I'm helping."

"All right, all right," he said with a smile. He kissed her gently on the lips. Then he stepped back to look at her. "You really can help," he said, checking his watch. "It's almost time to give myself another dose of Michelle's antigen. I'll explain what you can do to help after I get it prepared. Okay?"

She nodded, and Charles squeezed her hand before he walked back to the living room.

Cathryn picked up the phone and dialed her mother. Gina answered on the second ring. Cathryn kept the conversation light. She said nothing about Charles and made up an excuse for spending the night in New Hampshire. As quickly as she could without seeming to be rude, she hung up.

When she went into the living room, Charles was holding a syringe, tapping it to get rid of air bubbles. Quietly Cathryn took a seat and watched. Michelle was still sleeping, her thin hair splayed out on the white pillow. Peering between the boards on the windows, Cathryn could see it was snowing again.

"Now I'm going to inject this into my arm vein," said Charles, looking for a tourniquet. "I don't suppose you'd be willing to do it for me." He walked over and held out the syringe.

She felt her mouth go dry. "I can try," she said reluctantly.

"Would you?" he asked. "Unless you're an addict, it's incredibly hard to stick yourself in a vein. Also I want to tell you how to give me epinephrine if I need it. With the first intravenous dose of Michelle's antigen I developed an immediate allergic reaction that made breathing difficult. I've tried to cut down on that effect by altering the protein slightly. I want delayed hypersensitivity, not immediate."

Cathryn took the syringe with her fingertips, as if she expected it to injure her. Charles brought a chair over and placed it in front of hers. He put two smaller syringes within reach.

"These other syringes are the epinephrine. If I suddenly go red as a beet and can't breathe, just jam one of these into any muscle and inject. The drug should counter my allergic reaction. If there's no response in thirty seconds, use the next one."

Cathryn felt terrified. But Charles seemed blithely unconcerned. He unbuttoned his left sleeve and rolled it up above his elbow. Using his teeth to hold one end of the tourniquet, he applied the rubber tubing to his upper arm. Quickly his veins stood out. "Take off the plastic cover," he instructed.

With trembling hands Cathryn got the cover off the needle. Charles tore open an alcohol pad and swabbed the area. "Okay, do your stuff," he said, looking away.

She took a deep breath. Trying to hold the syringe steady, she put the needle on Charles's skin and gently pushed. The skin merely indented.

Charles looked down at his arm. Reaching over with his free hand, he gave the needle a forceful lunge and it broke through the skin. "Perfect," he said. "Now draw back on the plunger without disturbing the tip."

Cathryn did as he said, and Charles removed the tourniquet. "Now slowly inject," he instructed.

After the plunger completed its movement, Cathryn pulled the needle out and Charles slapped a piece of gauze over the site. "Not bad for your first time," he said. Suddenly his face began to get red. He shivered. "Damn," he managed. His voice was abnormally high. "Epinephrine," he said with difficulty.

She grabbed one of the smaller syringes. Charles, who was beginning to blotch with hives, pointed to his left upper arm. Holding her breath, Cathryn jammed the needle into the muscle. This time she used ample force. She was about to use the other syringe when Charles held up his hand.

"It's okay," he gasped. "Whew! Good thing you were here."

Cathryn put down the syringe. She was shaking.

LATER, when Cathryn had gone into the kitchen to prepare some food, Charles went to work in his makeshift lab. He took a sample of his blood, separated the cells, and isolated some T-lymphocytes. Then he incubated the T-lymphocytes with some of his microphages and Michelle's leukemic cells. He patiently looked through the phase contrast microscope. There still was no sign of a delayed hypersensitivity.

When Michelle awoke from her morphine-induced sleep, she was overjoyed to see her stepmother. Feeling somewhat better, she ate a little solid food.

"She seems stronger," whispered Cathryn as she and Charles carried the dishes back to the kitchen.

"It's more apparent than real," he said. "Her system is just recovering from the other medicines."

After Michelle went back to sleep, Charles built a fire and, struggling, brought his and Cathryn's mattress down to the living room. He wanted to be near his daughter in case she needed him.

Once Cathryn lay down, she felt a tremendous fatigue. As the wind blew snow against the front windows, she held on to Charles and let sleep overwhelm her.

A crash and a tinkle of glass awoke her. Cathryn sat up by pure reflex. Charles, who had been awake, rolled off the mattress and stood up. As he did so he hefted his shotgun and released the safety catch.

"What was that?" demanded Cathryn, her heart pounding.

"Probably our friends from Recycle." Something thudded against the front of the house. "Rocks," he said, peering between the window boards. Cathryn came up and looked over his shoul-

271

der. Standing in their driveway was a group of men carrying torches. Two cars were parked down on the road.

"They're drunk," said Charles.

"What are we going to do?"

"Nothing. Unless they try to get inside or come too close with those torches."

"Could you shoot someone?"

"I don't know," said Charles. "I really don't know."

"I'm going to call the police," said Cathryn.

"Don't bother. I'm sure they know about this."

"I'm still going to call." She made her way back to the kitchen, where she dialed the Shaftesbury police. A tired voice answered and identified himself as Bernie Crawford. Cathryn reported that their house was being attacked by a group of drunks and that they needed immediate assistance.

"Just a minute," said Bernie. "I gotta find a pencil."

She heard a yell outside, and Charles ran into the kitchen, going up to the window facing the pond.

"Okay," said Bernie. "What's the address?" Cathryn quickly gave it.

"Zip code?" asked Bernie.

"Zip code? We need help right now."

"Cathryn!" yelled Charles. "They're torching the playhouse, but it may be just a diversion. Somebody has got to watch the front door."

She shouted into the phone, "I can't talk. Just send a car." She slammed down the receiver, ran back into the living room, and turned her attention to the front lawn. The group with the torches was gone, but someone was lifting a can out of the trunk of one of the cars. "Oh, God, don't let it be gasoline," said Cathryn.

She could hear glass breaking in the back of the house. "Are you all right?" she called to Charles.

"I'm all right. The creeps are breaking your car windows."

Cathryn heard him unlock the rear door. Then she heard the boom of his shotgun. The sound reverberated through the house. The door slammed shut.

"What happened?" she yelled.

Charles came back into the living room. "I shot into the air. A

272

gun is the only thing they respect. They ran around this way."

Cathryn looked out. The group had reassembled around the man coming from the car. In the torchlight she could see that he was carrying a gallon can. He knelt down to open it.

"It looks like paint," she said. Charles came over to see.

The group began to chant the word Communist, while the man with the paint can led the way to the house. The others were carrying an assortment of clubs. Charles recognized Wally Crabb and Brezo, the man who had punched him.

The group stopped about fifty feet from the house, but the man with the paint kept walking. Charles pulled away from the window, making Cathryn stand behind him, and slipped his finger around the trigger of his gun. The footsteps stopped and he heard the sound of a paintbrush against the house. After a moment there was a clatter as the can hit the front door.

Rushing back to the window, Charles saw the men whooping with laughter as they walked down the drive and climbed into the two cars. With horns blaring, they drove off into the night.

Charles let out a long breath. He put down the shotgun and took Cathryn's hands in his. "Now that you've seen how unpleasant it is, won't you go to your mother's?"

"No way," she replied, shaking her head.

Fifteen minutes later the Shaftesbury police cruiser skidded up the driveway and came to a stop. Frank Neilson climbed out quickly, as if he were responding to an emergency.

Charles went out on the front porch. "Get the hell off my land," he snarled.

"Well, if you don't need me." Frank shrugged and then said loudly to his deputy, "Strange people this side of town," and got back into the car.

Chapter 9

MORNING crept over the frozen countryside, under a pewter-colored blanket of high clouds. Charles and Cathryn had taken turns standing watch, but the vandals had not returned.

Michelle had improved considerably. Although she was still extremely weak, she managed to sit up for her breakfast.

While Charles drew some of his blood and again tested it for signs of delayed hypersensitivity, Cathryn tried to make their topsy-turvy house more livable. With Charles's equipment in the living room, there was little she could do there, but the kitchen soon responded to her efforts.

"No sign of any appropriate reaction," said Charles, coming in for coffee. "You can give me another dose of Michelle's antigen later today. In the meantime, I must think of some way to make us more secure here."

"Vandals are one thing," said Cathryn. "But what if the police come, wanting to arrest you?"

Charles looked at her steadily. "Until I finish with what I'm doing, I have to keep everybody out of the house."

Cathryn nodded slowly. "Maybe I can stop the police from looking for you. I could go see the detective who's handling the case and tell him that I don't want to press charges."

Charles took a large gulp of coffee. "All right," he said. "Take the rental van. I don't think your car has a windshield."

Putting on their coats, they walked hand in hand through the inch of new snow to the locked barn. They both saw the charred remains of the playhouse at the pond's edge, a sharp reminder of the terror of the previous night. As Cathryn backed the van out, she felt a reluctance to leave. Despite the circumstances, she treasured her newly regained closeness with Charles. She waved good-by to him and drove slowly down the driveway.

Reaching the foot of the hill, she turned to look back. Across the front of the house, COMMUNIST was painted in large red letters. The rest of the paint had been splashed on the front door. It looked like blood.

At the Boston police headquarters on Berkeley Street, Cathryn found Patrick O'Sullivan's office without difficulty. As she entered, the detective got up and came around his desk. "May I take your coat?" he asked.

"That's okay, thank you," said Cathryn. "I'll only take a moment of your time." She sat down.

O'Sullivan returned to his chair. He tipped it back, his fingers linked over his stomach.

"Well," Cathryn said uneasily. "I came to tell you that I'm not interested in pressing charges against my husband."

274

Detective O'Sullivan's expression was blank.

"It's not that I don't care," added Cathryn quickly. "But my husband is the biological parent, and he is an M.D., so I think he's in the best position to determine the kind of treatment the child should receive."

"Where is your husband?" asked O'Sullivan.

"I don't know," said Cathryn, knowing she sounded less than convincing.

Abruptly O'Sullivan tipped forward in his chair. "Mrs. Martel, I had been led to believe that the child's life was at stake unless she got very specific treatment as soon as possible."

Cathryn didn't say anything.

"It's apparent to me that you have been talking with your husband."

"I've spoken with him," she admitted, "and the child is doing all right."

"You do remember we have a warrant for his arrest. The authorities at the institute are eager to press charges."

"They'll get every piece of their equipment back."

"You should not allow yourself to become an accessory to the crime," said O'Sullivan.

Cathryn stood up. "I think I should go. Thank you for your time," she said as she started to leave the room.

"Mrs. Martel, we know where Charles is."

Cathryn stopped at the door.

"Why don't you come back and sit down?"

For a moment she didn't move. Then reluctantly she returned to her seat.

"I should explain something else to you," O'Sullivan said. "We didn't put out the warrant for your husband's arrest on the Teletype until this morning. I kept hoping that somehow the case would solve itself, that your husband would call somebody and say, 'I'm sorry, here's all the equipment and here's the kid; I got carried away . . .' and so forth. But then we got pressure from both the Weinburger and the hospital. So your husband's warrant went out over the wires this morning and we heard back immediately. The Shaftesbury police phoned to say that they knew Charles Martel was in his house and that they'd be happy to go out and apprehend him. So I said—"

"Oh, no!" exclaimed Cathryn, her face blanching.

"What is it, Mrs. Martel?"

Cathryn described Charles's crusade against Recycle, Ltd., and the attitude of the local police.

"They did seem a bit eager," admitted O'Sullivan, remembering his conversation with Frank Neilson.

"Can you go to New Hampshire and oversee things?"

"I don't have any authority up there," said the detective. "But I'll call them." He picked up his phone and called Shaftesbury.

Bernie Crawford answered. "We got him surrounded," he said, loud enough so that Cathryn could hear. "But that Martel is crazy. He's boarded up his house like a fort. He's got a shotgun and he's got his kid as a hostage."

"Have you called in the state police?" O'Sullivan asked.

"No! We'll take care of him. We've deputized volunteers. We'll give you a call as soon as we bring him in."

O'Sullivan hung up and looked at Cathryn. The conversation with Bernie had substantiated her claims. The idea of deputizing volunteers sounded like something out of a Clint Eastwood western. "There's going to be trouble," she said, shaking her head. "And I'm afraid Charles will fight back."

O'Sullivan stood up abruptly and took his coat from a rack near the door. "Come on, I'll go up there with you, but remember, I have no authority in New Hampshire."

Cathryn drove as fast as she could in the van while O'Sullivan followed in a plain blue Chevy Nova. Once they neared Shaftesbury, Cathryn could feel her pulse quicken. Rounding the turn before the house, she saw a large crowd of people. Cars were parked on either side of Interstate 301 for fifty yards in both directions. The noisy crowd gave the scene a carnival aspect, despite the freezing temperature.

At the base of their driveway two police cruisers blocked the entrance. Cathryn parked the van as close as she could and O'Sullivan pulled up behind her. "This looks like a family outing," he said when he reached her.

"All except for the guns," she replied.

Milling around the two police cruisers were a large number of men dressed in all manner of clothing, from army fatigues to ski parkas, and each was armed with a hunting rifle. Some carried a

276

Uldis Klavins

gun in one hand, a beer in the other. In the midst of the group stood Frank Neilson, with his foot on the bumper of one of the police cars, pressing a walkie-talkie to his ear. A man atop a local TV van was filming the entire scene.

O'Sullivan left Cathryn and walked up to Neilson, introducing himself. As if it were an effort, Neilson withdrew his foot from the bumper and assumed his full height, towering a foot over O'Sullivan.

"How's it going?" asked O'Sullivan casually.

"Fine," said Neilson. "Everything's under control." He was wearing his blue police uniform, complete with massive leather-holstered service revolver. On his head was a fake fur hat with the flaps tied on top. His walkie-talkie crackled, and he excused himself and spoke into it, saying that the tomcat group should approach to one hundred yards and hold. Then he turned back to O'Sullivan. "Gotta make sure the suspect doesn't sneak out the back door."

O'Sullivan eyed the armed men. "Do you think it's advisable to have this much firepower on hand?"

"I suppose you want to tell me how to handle this?" asked Neilson sarcastically. "Listen, Detective, this is New Hampshire, not Boston. I'm in charge here and I know how to handle a hostage situation. First secure the area, then negotiate. So if you'll excuse me, I got work to do."

He turned his back on O'Sullivan and picked up a bullhorn. His husky voice thundered out over the winter landscape.

"Okay, Martel, your place is surrounded. I want you to come out with your hands up."

The crowd stayed perfectly still, and the only movement was a few snowflakes drifting down among the trees. Not a sound emanated from the white Victorian house.

"I'm going closer," said Neilson. He lumbered up the driveway to a point about fifty feet beyond the two police cruisers. It was snowing a little harder now and the top of his hat was dusted with flakes. "Martel," he boomed through the bullhorn, "I'm warning you, if you don't come out, we'll come in."

Neilson began walking closer to the house. Suddenly the front door burst open and Charles Martel emerged holding his shot-gun. There were two almost simultaneous explosions. Neilson

278

dived into the snowbank lining the drive, while the spectators took cover behind cars or trees. As Charles slammed the door, bird shot rained harmlessly down over the area.

There was a cheer from the crowd as Frank scrambled to his feet. Then he ran back to the police cars as fast as his legs would carry his overweight body. "That's it!" he shouted. "That creep is going to get what he deserves."

A young female commentator emerged from the TV van and held a microphone under the police chief's nose, asking him to give the audience an idea of what was happening.

"Well," began Frank, leaning into the mike, "we got a crazy scientist holed up here." He pointed awkwardly over his shoulder at the house. "He's got a sick kid he's keeping from the doctors."

While Neilson talked, O'Sullivan wormed his way out of the crowd, searching for Cathryn. He found her near her car, terrified by the spectacle.

"I want to get to Charles," she said.

"Are you crazy?" asked O'Sullivan. "There must be forty men with guns surrounding this place. You've got to be patient. I'll talk to Neilson again and try to convince him to call in the state police." He started back toward the police cruisers, wishing he'd stayed in Boston where he belonged. As he neared the make-shift command post, he saw three men dressed in white hooded parkas and white pants walk up to Neilson.

"Chief," he heard one of them say. "How about letting me and my buddies storm the place?"

Neilson remembered the men. They were from Recycle, Ltd. "I haven't decided what I'm going to do," he said.

The idea of storming the house horrified O'Sullivan. "Chief," he said. "What about tear gas?"

Neilson glared at the detective. "We don't have sophisticated stuff out here, and to get it I'd have to call in the state boys. I want to handle this affair locally."

There was a yell, followed by a burst of shouting. O'Sullivan and Neilson turned in unison to see Cathryn run diagonally across the area in front of the cars.

"Damn!" exclaimed Neilson. Then to the nearest group of deputies he shouted, "Don't let her get to the house!"

With a whoop of excitement, half a dozen deputies began to run up the drive. O'Sullivan found himself clenching his fists and urging Cathryn on, even though he knew her presence in the house would only complicate the situation.

Cathryn was gasping for breath. She knew her pursuers were gaining on her. Ahead she saw the red-spattered door swing open. Then there was a flash of orange light and the roar of an explosion. She stumbled up the front steps, and Charles yanked her into the house.

Cathryn collapsed on the floor, her chest heaving. Then she heard Michelle calling, and after a moment she pulled herself to her feet and went over to her.

"I missed you, Mommy," the child said, putting her arms around her. Cathryn knew she'd done the right thing.

Charles came over to the two of them and, putting his gun down, enveloped them both in his arms.

After several moments, Cathryn told them what had happened. "That Neilson is a psychopath," she concluded. "I wonder if it wouldn't be better if we gave up now. Maybe then you could continue your experiment at the hospital, if you explained it to Dr. Keitzman."

"No," said Charles. "If I lose control over Michelle now, I'll never get to touch her again. Besides, I think my body is starting to show some delayed hypersensitivity."

"Really?" said Cathryn. She tried to share Charles's enthusiasm, but knowing the evil outside, it was difficult.

BECAUSE of the falling snow, darkness came early. Cathryn made dinner while Charles devised methods to make the house more secure. He boarded up the second-story windows and constructed a trap by the kitchen door with some hundred-pound bags of potatoes he had found in the root cellar.

It was time for the next injection of Michelle's antigen. Charles had Cathryn slip a catheter into one of his veins, a technique that, to her surprise, she was able to manage after a few tries. He took the epinephrine by IV almost immediately afterward, and his allergic reaction was easily controlled.

As evening turned into night, Cathryn and Charles could see the crowd beginning to disperse. By nine thirty the thermometer outside had dipped to a chilling five degrees above zero.

Michelle was asleep, and except for the occasional sound of the oil burner kicking on, the house was silent. Charles, who was taking turns with Cathryn watching the windows, began to have difficulty staying awake. He sat down for a moment near one of the front windows, letting his head rest against the chair back, and in that moment he fell into a deep sleep.

AT EXACTLY two a.m. Bernie Crawford put his arm over the front seat of the police cruiser and woke the snoring chief, as he had been asked to do. Neilson struggled up, coughed, and lit a cigarette. After several puffs, he took out his walkie-talkie and contacted Wally Crabb. Neilson wasn't entirely happy with Wally's plan, but midway through the evening everyone had run out of patience, and Neilson had felt obligated to agree to something or lose respect. So they had decided on two a.m. as the time and had chosen Wally Crabb, Giorgio Brezowski, and Angelo DeJesus to hit the house. Now the walkie-talkies crackled as Frank gave the signal.

"We read you," Wally replied. He slipped the walkie-talkie into his parka and closed the zipper. "You guys ready?" he asked the two men huddled behind him. They nodded. The group moved cautiously up the hill toward the barn, skirting the dark, boarded-up house. Dressed in white, they were almost invisible in the light snow.

Reaching the barn, they made their way behind it until Wally was able to look around the corner at the rear of the house. From that point it was about a hundred feet to the back door.

"Check the equipment," said Wally. "Where's the shotgun?"

Angelo passed it to Wally. The gun was a two-barrel, twelve-gauge Remington, loaded with triple-zero magnum shells capable of blasting a hole through a car door. Wally flipped off the safety. Each man had also been issued a police thirty-eight.

"Everybody remember their job?" asked Wally. The plan was for Wally to lead, blast the lock on the rear door, then pull it open for Brezo and Angelo to rush inside. The two men nodded. They'd made a bet with each other. The one who got Martel would be a hundred bucks richer.

After checking the dark house once more, Wally noiselessly

crossed the hundred feet, stopping in the shadows below the back porch. The house remained quiet, so he waved to Angelo and Brezo. They joined him, holding their pistols ready.

Wally thundered up the steps and aimed the shotgun at the lock of the back door. A blast sundered the peaceful night, blowing away a section of the door. Wally yanked it open. At the same moment Brezo ran past Wally, heading into the kitchen. Angelo was right behind him.

But when Wally opened the door, he triggered Charles's trap. A cord pulled a pin from a simple mechanism that supported the several hundred-pound bags of Idaho potatoes. Charles had hung them by a stout rope from a hook directly above the door, and when the pin was pulled, the potatoes began a rapid, swinging plunge.

When Brezo saw the swaying sacks, he turned and collided with Angelo. The potatoes hit Brezo's back square on. The impact caused his finger to tighten on the trigger of his pistol. The bullet pierced Angelo's calf and both men were knocked through the door. Wally, not sure of what was happening, vaulted over the porch railing and scrambled toward the barn.

Charles and Cathryn had bolted upright at the blast. Charles reached frantically for the shotgun and ran into the kitchen. Beyond the open back door he thought he saw two white figures heading for the barn. One seemed to be supporting the other.

Pulling the door closed, Charles used some rope to secure it. Then he stuffed the hole made by the shotgun blast with a cushion from one of the kitchen chairs. With a good deal of effort he hung the potatoes above the door again.

Returning to the living room, he explained to Cathryn what had happened. Then he reached over and felt Michelle's forehead. Her fever was back with a vengeance. Gently he tried to wake her. She finally opened her eyes and smiled, but fell immediately back to sleep.

"That's not a good sign," said Charles. "Her leukemic cells might be invading her central nervous system. If that happens, she's going to need radiotherapy."

The rest of the night passed uneventfully, and when dawn broke, Cathryn looked out on six inches of new snow. Without waking Charles, she went into the kitchen and fixed coffee, bacon, and scrambled eggs. When everything was ready, she carried it into the living room and got her husband up. Michelle awoke and seemed brighter than she had been during the night, but she wasn't hungry. Her temperature was 102.

After breakfast Charles drew some of his own blood and tested the T-lymphocytes. He patiently looked for the result under the microscope. There was a reaction! Charles was elated. He told Cathryn that with the continued injections he expected his delayed sensitivity to be adequate by the following day.

By midday, though little had happened, a considerable crowd of spectators had again gathered at the bottom of the driveway. Frank Neilson had issued sniper rifles and positioned his men in various spots around the house. Then he'd tried contacting Charles with the bullhorn, asking him to come out on the front porch to talk. But Charles never responded.

Neilson was drinking a cup of coffee when he saw a long black limousine come around the bend and stop. Four men got out. Two were dressed in fancy city clothes; the other two looked like bodyguards.

After speaking to one of the deputies, the men approached Neilson. One of them said, "Chief Neilson, I am Dr. Carlos Ibanez. And this is Dr. Morrison. We're pleased to meet you."

Neilson shook hands with the two scientists, then took another sip of coffee.

Ibanez said, "We're the owners of all the expensive equipment your suspect has up there in his house. And we're very concerned about it." Frank nodded. "We rode out here to offer our help," Ibanez continued. "In fact, we brought two security men from Breur Chemical, Recycle's parent company, with us. Mr. Eliot Hoyt and Mr. Anthony Ferrullo."

Mr. Hoyt and Mr. Ferrullo smiled.

"I think I have enough manpower right now," said Neilson.

"Well, keep us in mind," Ibanez said.

After Neilson excused himself, Ibanez and Morrison went back to the limousine. "I don't like this situation one bit," said Ibanez. "All this press coverage may whip up sympathy for Charles: the quintessential American guarding his home against outside forces."

"I couldn't agree more," said Morrison. "He could very well

cause irreparable damage to the entire cancer establishment."

"And to Canceran and the Weinburger in particular. We've got to get that police chief to use our men."

"We've planted the idea in his head," said Morrison. "I don't think there's much else we can do at this point. It has to look like his decision."

JEAN Paul drifted aimlessly on the periphery of the ever in-creasing crowd. He'd never experienced derision before, and he found it extremely disquieting. People were accusing his father of being crazy. The family with whom he was staying had tried to comfort him, but it was obvious that they, too, questioned his father's behavior.

Jean Paul wanted to go up to the house, but he was afraid to ask for permission. He hovered uncertainly for a few minutes by the squad cars, then spotted Chuck at the edge of the crowd. He was dressed in a tattered army parka with a fur-tipped hood.

"Chuck!" called Jean Paul eagerly.

Chuck took one look at Jean Paul, then turned and fled into the trees. Jean Paul followed, calling out to his brother.

"For Pete's sake!" hissed Chuck when Jean Paul caught up to him in a small clearing. "Why don't you yell a little louder so everybody hears you?"

"What do you mean?" asked Jean Paul, confused.

"I'm trying to keep a low profile to find out what's going on, and you come along yelling my name!"

Jean Paul had never considered the idea of concealing him-self. "Oh," he said.

"I can't get over Dad," continued Chuck. "He's telling the whole establishment just what he thinks of it! And I think I know how we can help him!"

"How?"

Chuck told Jean Paul his plan. Then the two boys left the clearing and approached the police cars. Chuck had appointed himself spokesman, and he went up to Frank Neilson.

The chief was overjoyed to see the boys. Although he dis-missed their request to go up to the house to reason with their father, he persuaded them to use the bullhorn and, after coach-ing them on its use, handed it to Chuck.

Pushing the button, Chuck started speaking. "Dad, it's me, Chuck, and Jean Paul. Can you hear me?"

The paint-splattered door opened about six inches. "I hear you, Chuck," Charles called.

At that moment, Chuck dropped the bullhorn and bolted up the driveway. Jean Paul followed at his heels. The deputies were intent on watching the house, and this gave the boys a chance to start up the hill.

"Get them! Get them!" shouted Neilson.

A murmur went up from the crowd. Several deputies, led by Bernie Crawford, sprinted around the two squad cars.

Although younger, Jean Paul was the athlete, and he quickly overtook his older brother. About forty feet beyond the squad cars, Chuck's feet went out from under him on the slippery driveway and he hit the ground hard. As he struggled up, Bernie grabbed his parka. Chuck tried to wrench free but instead managed to yank Bernie off-balance. The policeman fell over backward, pulling the boy on top of him.

The two slid a few feet down the driveway, rolling into the next two deputies on their way up. Taking advantage of the confusion, Chuck pulled himself free, scrambled out of reach, and ran after Jean Paul.

As the boys reached the front porch, Charles opened the door wider and they dashed inside. Charles slammed the door behind them and secured it. He turned to his sons, who were standing near the door, gasping for breath. "The one thing I thought I didn't have to worry about was you two," he said sternly. "What on earth are you doing here?"

"We thought you needed help," said Chuck.

"I couldn't stand to hear what people were saying about you," said Jean Paul.

"This is our family," added Chuck. "We should be here, especially if we can help Michelle."

"How is she, Dad?" Jean Paul asked.

Charles didn't answer. His anger at the boys abruptly dissolved. Chuck was right. They were a family, and the boys should not be excluded. Besides, as far as Charles knew, it was the first unselfish thing Chuck had ever done.

Charles suddenly grinned. He hugged his sons, and Cathryn

came up and kissed them both. Then they all went over to Michelle, and Charles gently woke her. She gave them a broad grin, and Chuck bent to put his arms around her. Charles couldn't remember ever seeing that before.

AFTER the Martel boys had managed to get up to the house, Neilson had to admit the situation was deteriorating. Rather than rescuing hostages, he was adding to their number. He knew that if he didn't bring the affair to a successful conclusion soon, the state police would intervene. That was something Neilson wanted to avoid at all costs. He wanted to have the credit for resolving this affair. Maybe help from the chemical company wasn't a bad idea after all, he thought.

He went over to the limousine and got in. "Knowing how sick the little girl is, I decided to take your offer of help," he said.

"That's why we're here," said Dr. Ibanez. "Mr. Hoyt and Mr. Ferrullo have some special equipment. Mr. Hoyt, perhaps you'd like to show us."

Mr. Hoyt handed Neilson a weighty object that was shaped like a tin can with a handle protruding from one end. "This is a concussion grenade," he said. "It's what antiterrorist units use to rescue hostages. It's thrown into a room or airplane and when it detonates, instead of hurting anyone it just befuddles everyone for twenty, sometimes thirty seconds. I think you could use it to advantage in this situation."

"Yeah, we could," said Neilson. "But we got to get it into the house. And the guy's boarded up all the windows."

"Not all," said Mr. Hoyt. "An attic window is free, and accessible from the roof. And there's an aluminum ladder in the barn. It would be easy for Tony Ferrullo, who's expert at this sort of thing, to sneak in. Then we can rush the doors."

"Could we try it tonight?" asked Frank Neilson.

"You're the boss," said Mr. Hoyt. "Tonight it is."

AT TEN p.m. Charles switched off the dialyzer. Then, as carefully as if he were handling the most precious commodity on earth, he reached into the machine and withdrew the dialysate in a small vial. His fingers trembled as he put the clear solution into the sterilizer. He had no idea of the exact structure of the

286

small molecule contained in the vial, except that it was dialyzable, which had been the final step in its isolation. But the fact that the structure of the molecule was unknown was less important at this stage than knowledge of its effect. This was the mysterious transfer factor, which he hoped would transfer his delayed hypersensitivity to Michelle.

That afternoon Charles had again tested his T-lymphocyte response with Michelle's leukemic cells. The reaction had been dramatic, with the T-lymphocytes instantly destroying the leukemic cells. He had decided not to take another dose of antigen. Instead he had announced that he wanted to draw off two pints of his blood. Cathryn had turned green, but Chuck and Jean Paul had helped Charles with the task.

Before dinner Charles had separated out the white blood cells in one of the machines he had taken from the Weinburger. Next he had begun the task of extracting from the white blood cells the small molecule that he was now sterilizing.

At that point he knew he was flying blind. All he had was a theory: that in Michelle's system was a blocking mechanism that had kept her immune system from responding to her leukemic cells' antigen. Charles hoped that the transfer factor would bypass that blocking mechanism. But how much of the factor should he give her? He would have to improvise and pray.

Now he started another IV while Cathryn sat holding Michelle's hand. The two boys were upstairs, watching for any suspicious movement outside.

Although Charles had diluted the solution with sterile water, he was concerned about its side effects. After giving Michelle a minute dose, he monitored her pulse and blood pressure. He was relieved when he could detect no reaction whatsoever.

At midnight he gave her another dose of the transfer factor and she again tolerated it with no ill effects. Convinced the molecule was nontoxic, Charles added the rest of the solution to the IV, fixing it to run in over the next five hours.

Although they were all exhausted, the family decided to take two-hour watches at the windows. Chuck went upstairs for the first watch. The others fell asleep almost instantly.

The next thing Jean Paul knew, Chuck was gently nudging him, telling him it was two a.m. and time to get up.

287

Jean Paul nodded, then went upstairs. Slowly he went from room to room, gazing out at the dark. It was utterly silent except for an occasional gust of wind that rattled the storm windows. Then he heard a sound like metal against stone. Walking softly in the direction of the noise, he found himself facing the fireplace in his parents' bedroom. He heard the sound again. With no further hesitation he ran back down to the living room.

"Dad," whispered Jean Paul, "wake up. I heard a noise up in your bedroom. Sounded like it came from the fireplace."

Charles sprang up, waking Cathryn and Chuck. He gave the gun to Cathryn and sent her to the back door. He positioned the boys by the front door with Jean Paul's baseball bat. Taking a poker for himself, he climbed the stairs and went into the master bedroom. He stood by the fireplace but could hear nothing except the wind under the eaves. Wondering what Jean Paul could have heard, he walked out to the hall. Suddenly the ceiling joists above him squeaked. Freezing, Charles listened intently. The sound was repeated. Someone was in the attic!

Holding the poker and feeling the perspiration on his hands, Charles began to follow the sounds above him. Soon he'd advanced to the door leading to the attic stairs. He could just make it out in the darkness. He heard a step on the stairs and his heart began to pound. Whoever was coming down the stairs was agonizingly slow. Charles gripped the poker tightly, walked to the side of the door, and waited.

All at once, to his horror, the doorknob began to turn. He lifted the poker above his head.

Anthony Ferrullo carefully opened the door about eight inches. He could see across the short hall to the balustrade connecting to the banister of the main stairs. From there it was a straight drop to the living room. He unclipped the concussion grenade from his belt and pulled the pin from the timing fuse.

Charles could not stand the waiting another second, especially since he wasn't sure he'd be able to strike the intruder a decisive blow. He lifted his foot and kicked the attic door shut. Suddenly there was a tremendous explosion. The attic door burst open, sending Charles flying backward, his ears ringing. Scrambling on all fours, he saw Ferrullo topple from the attic stairs to the floor of the hall.

The explosion was followed by a rush of footsteps on the front and back porches. A sledgehammer crashed through the front door just inches from Chuck's head. A hand reached through the opening, groping for the doorknob. Chuck grabbed the hand, and Jean Paul leaped to his brother's aid. Their combined strength forced the arm against the splintered wood. The man yelled in pain, and the boys let go.

In the kitchen, Cathryn tightened her hold on the shotgun as two men wrestled with the back door. They pulled the rope loose and opened the door. The potatoes swung out, but this time the men were able to duck. Wally Crabb grabbed the sacks on their return swing, while Brezo headed through the door. With the gun pointed downward, Cathryn pulled the trigger. A load of birdshot roared into the linoleum, ricocheting up to spray the doorway. Brezo reversed direction and followed Wally off the porch.

As abruptly as the violence started, it was over. Jean Paul ran into the kitchen to find Cathryn immobilized, still holding the gun in her shaking hands. Chuck went upstairs to see if Charles was all right and was surprised to find his father bending over, examining a dazed stranger.

With Chuck's help Charles got the man downstairs. Together they bound him to a chair in the living room.

"Who are you?" Charles asked his prisoner.

Anthony Ferrullo sat as if carved from stone.

Charles reached into the man's jacket pockets and pulled out a wallet. He opened it and found a business card: ANTHONY L. FERRULLO, BREUR CHEMICAL, SECURITY.

Charles felt a shiver of fear pass over him. For a moment the security man was less an individual than a symbol of evil, and Charles had to keep himself from striking him in blind anger. Instead he began turning on lights, all of them. He wanted no more darkness, no more secrecy.

He gathered the family in the kitchen. "At noon today it's over," he told them. "We're going to walk out of here and give up."

The boys looked at each other in consternation. "Why?" asked Chuck.

"I've done what I wanted to do for Michelle, and she might need some radiotherapy at the hospital."

"Is she going to get better?" asked Cathryn.

"I don't know. Theoretically there's no reason why not, but there're a hundred questions I haven't answered. At this point all we can do is hope."

He walked over to the phone and called all the media people he could think of, telling them that he and his family would emerge at noon. Then he informed the Shaftesbury police. He hoped that the presence of newspaper and TV reporters would eliminate any possible violence.

At exactly twelve o'clock, Charles removed the planks securing the front door. It was a glorious day with a pale winter sun shining in a clear blue sky. At the bottom of the drive, in front of a crowd of people, were an ambulance, the two police cars, and a handful of TV news vans.

Charles looked back at his family and felt a rush of pride and love. Walking to the bed, he scooped Michelle into his arms. Her eyelids fluttered but remained closed.

"All right, Mr. Ferrullo, after you," Charles said.

The security man stepped out onto the porch. Next came the two boys, followed by Cathryn. Charles brought up the rear with Michelle.

As they started down the driveway, Charles was surprised to see Dr. Ibanez, Dr. Morrison, Dr. Keitzman, and Dr. Wiley all standing together near the ambulance. One person clapped, and that was Patrick O'Sullivan, who was immensely pleased the affair was coming to a peaceful close.

Standing in the shadow of the trees, Wally Crabb slid his right index finger onto the trigger of his favorite hunting rifle and pressed his cheek against the cold stock.

The sharp crack of a firearm shattered the stillness. The crowd strained forward as they saw Charles stumble. He sank to his knees, and as gently as if handling a baby, he laid his daughter in the snow before he fell beside her, face down. Cathryn turned and screamed, then rushed back and knelt beside him.

Patrick O'Sullivan was the first to react. Grabbing the handle of his service revolver, he charged up the driveway. Hovering over Cathryn and Charles like a hawk guarding its nest, he scanned the crowd, looking for suspicious movement.

Chapter 10

NEVER having been a hospital patient before, Charles found the experience agonizing. It had been three days since he'd been shot and then operated on. He looked up at the tangle of tubes and bottles, monitors and recorders, and was thankful that at least he had been transferred out of intensive care.

The door opened silently. Charles was afraid it was the technician who came every four hours to forcibly inflate his lungs fully, a procedure he would not do himself because of the severity of the pain. Instead it was Dr. Keitzman.

"Could you stand a short visit?" he asked.

Charles nodded. Although he didn't feel like talking, he was eager to hear about Michelle. All Cathryn had been able to tell him was that she wasn't worse.

Keitzman pulled a chair over to the bed and adjusted his glasses. "Well, I have some good news," he said, "though it might be a little premature. First, Michelle responded to the radiotherapy extremely well. A single treatment seems to have taken care of the infiltration of her central nervous system. She's alert and oriented."

Charles nodded, afraid to let his hopes rise. There was a silence. Dr. Keitzman cleared his throat self-consciously.

"The other thing I want to say is that Michelle's leukemic cells have all but disappeared. I think she's in remission."

Charles felt a warm glow suffuse his body. "That's great," he said with enthusiasm. Then a sharp twinge of pain reminded him where he was.

"It certainly is. Tell me, Charles. What did you do to Michelle while she was in your house?"

Charles had trouble containing his joy. Maybe Michelle was cured. Maybe everything would work as he had guessed. But, not wanting to go into a detailed explanation at that point, he said, "I just tried to stimulate her immune system."

"You mean by using an adjuvant like BCG?"

"Something like that," agreed Charles. He was in no shape to get into a scientific discussion.

"Well," said Dr. Keitzman, standing up. "Whatever you did

292

helped the chemotherapy she'd been given in the hospital. I
don't understand the time sequence, but we'll talk about it when
you feel stronger."

"Yes. When I'm stronger."

"Anyway, I'm sure you know the custody proceedings have
been canceled." Keitzman headed for the door. He left as a
technician came in pushing the hated respiratory machine.

Charles's elation over the news dulled the painful treatment
even better than the morphine. The procedure lasted for twenty
minutes, and when the technician finally left, Charles was exhausted. He fell into a fitful sleep.

He was roused by a sound in the room. Unsure of how long
he had slept, he turned his head, and there, next to the bed,
sat Dr. Carlos Ibanez. "I hope I'm not disturbing you," he
said softly.

Charles shook his head slightly in response.

"I'm here to negotiate, Charles," Ibanez began. "Let me be
frank. I know that you could cause us a great deal of trouble now
that you've become a celebrity of sorts. But that wouldn't be
good for anyone. I have convinced the board of directors not to
press any charges against you and to give you back your job—"

"The hell with your job," said Charles sharply, then winced
with pain.

"All right," said Ibanez consolingly. "I can understand if you
don't want to return to the Weinburger. But there are other
institutions where we can help you get the kind of job you want,
a position where you'll be able to do your research unhindered."

Charles thought about his treatment of Michelle. Had he
really hit on something? To find out, he needed laboratory
facilities. He examined Dr. Ibanez's face. "I have to warn you
that if I negotiate, I'm going to have a lot of demands."

"I'm prepared to meet your demands, provided they are reasonable. In return I ask only that you won't embarrass the
Weinburger. We've had enough scandal."

For a second Charles was not sure what Dr. Ibanez meant. He
had not realized that since he was a prominent scientist who had
risked his life to save his daughter, the press would be happy to
hear any criticism he might have of the institute.

Dimly he began to realize his negotiating strength. "Okay,"

he said slowly. "I want a research position where I'll be my own boss."

"That can be arranged. I've already been in touch with a friend in Berkeley."

"And all the existing Canceran tests have to be scrapped. The drug has to be studied as if you'd just received it."

"We've already started an entirely new toxicity study."

Charles stared in astonishment. "And there's the matter of Recycle. Dumping of chemicals into the river must stop."

Dr. Ibanez nodded. "Your lawyer got the EPA involved, and I understand the problem will be solved shortly."

Charles had begun to wonder how far he could go. "I also want Breur Chemical to make a compensatory payment to Tad Schonhauser's family. They can keep their name out of it."

"I think I can arrange that."

There was a pause. "I guess that's it," said Charles.

Dr. Ibanez stood up. "I'm sorry that we are going to lose you, Charles. I really am."

Charles watched Ibanez walk to the door and close it silently behind him.

Chapter 11

CHARLES decided if he ever drove cross-country again, it would be without kids and with air conditioning. The three children had been at each other's throats ever since they had left New Hampshire. That morning they had been relatively quiet, as if the vast expanse of the Utah desert awed them into silence. Charles glanced in the rearview mirror. Jean Paul was directly behind him, gazing out his side of the car. Michelle was next to him, bored and fidgety. Way in the back of the refurbished station wagon, Chuck was reading a chemistry text, having announced that he wanted to be a doctor after all.

As they crossed the Bonneville Salt Flats, Charles glanced at Cathryn, who was sitting next to him doing needlepoint. Sensing his stare, she looked up and smiled at him. She saw that the tension that normally tightened the skin around his eyes was gone. To her relief he was finally relaxed. "You know, Charles, there's one thing I still don't understand," she said. "Why did the Weinburger make such an about-face? They couldn't have been more helpful."

"I didn't understand it either," Charles answered, "until I remembered how clever Dr. Ibanez really is. With all those reporters milling around, he was terrified I'd be tempted to tell them my feelings about their brand of cancer research."

"If the public ever knew what really goes on!" said Cathryn.

Charles looked over his shoulder in time to see Jean Paul snatch Michelle's wig from her head and jam it haphazardly onto his own.

"Daddy," cried Michelle. "Make him give back my wig."

"You should have been a girl, Jean Paul," said Chuck. "You look a thousand times better with a wig."

"Jean Paul!" cried Cathryn. "Give your sister her wig."

"Okay, baldy." Jean Paul laughed, tossing the wig to Michelle and shielding himself from her ineffectual punches.

Charles and Cathryn exchanged glances, too pleased to see Michelle better to scold anybody. They would never know whether she had responded to the immunological injections or to the chemotherapy she had received earlier.

"It's a shame you won't get credit for her recovery," said Cathryn.

He shrugged. "No one can prove anything, including myself. Anyway, at the institute in Berkeley I may be able to show that what happened to Michelle was the first example of harnessing the body's immune system to rid itself of an established leukemia. If that—"

"Dad!" called Jean Paul. "Could you stop soon?"

In a few minutes Charles pulled onto a dusty shoulder of the road. "Okay, everybody out for R and R and whatever."

"It's hotter than an oven," said Jean Paul, searching for some sort of cover.

Charles led Cathryn up a small rise affording a view to the west. It was an arid, stark scene of desert leading up to jagged, rocky mountains that soared into the cloudless blue sky. He took a deep breath. "Smell the air. It makes Shaftesbury seem like another planet." He put his arm around his wife. "You know what scares me?"

"What?"

"I'm beginning to feel content again."

Cathryn laughed. "Wait until we get to Berkeley with no house and little money and three hungry kids."

Charles smiled. "You're right. There is still plenty of opportunity for catastrophe."

Epilogue

WHEN the snows melted in the White Mountains of New Hampshire, hundreds of swollen streams flooded the Pawtomack River. In Shaftesbury the clear water raged against the quays of the deserted mill buildings, spraying mist into the crystal air.

As the weather grew warmer, green shoots thrust up through the ground along the river, growing in areas previously too toxic for them to survive. In the shadow of Recycle, Ltd., tadpoles and rainbow trout appeared for the first time in years.

Then, as the nights became shorter and hot summer approached, a single drop of benzene appeared at the juncture of a pipe at one of the new chemical holding tanks. No one supervising the installations had fully understood the insidious propensities of benzene. From the moment the first molecules had flowed into the new system, they began dissolving the rubber gaskets used to seal the line.

It had taken about two months for the toxic fluid to eat through the rubber and drip onto the granite blocks beneath the chemical storage tanks, but soon the drops came at an increasing tempo. The poisonous molecules worked their way down into the mortarless masonry, then seeped laterally until they entered the river. The only evidence of their presence was a slightly aromatic, almost sweet smell.

First to die were the frogs, then the fish. When the river fell, as the summer sun grew stronger, the concentration of the poison soared.

Robin Cook

Every reader of *Fever* is likely to wonder about the magical-sounding "transfer factor". Is such a cure for cancer really being developed, or does it exist only in the author's imagination? Robin Cook, bestselling novelist and himself a doctor, says that the transfer factor has been established as a phenomenon but has no therapeutic uses at the present time. Though the method sounds simple as employed by *Fever*'s Dr. Charles Martel, there are many problems to be solved before it can be applied in treating human beings, and funds available for this type of research are short.

Dr. Cook feels that there are two central issues in fighting cancer: a basic understanding of its evolution, and control of the environmental factors that cause so many of its forms. "We impose speed limits for motorists," he says, "and regulations on the use of guns. It's clear that we need similar limitations on our freedom to pollute the air and water, because passive absorption of poisons is a leading cause of cancer."

After graduating from New York's Columbia University College of Physicians, Dr. Cook joined the navy. Clearly a man of enormous talent and energy, he was soon bored with his duties as a medical officer and started casting around for a new challenge. The result was the first Cook novel. "It did fairly well," he says now, "but I wasn't satisfied." So, three years later, he sat down and wrote *Coma*—a medical thriller that quickly became a hugely successful bestseller and film. *Fever* is his fifth novel.

Usually busy with his practice as an ophthalmic surgeon, the forty-one-year-old author took leave of absence to write *Fever* and to work on the screenplay of his fourth novel, *Brain*. He was married in 1979 to Barbara Mougin, and the Cooks live in Waterville Valley, New Hampshire, a lovely ski area within commuting distance of the Boston hospital where Dr. Cook will eventually resume his medical career.

FLASH
Joyce Stranger

Flash

A CONDENSATION OF THE BOOK BY
Joyce Stranger

ILLUSTRATED BY LIZ MOYES
PUBLISHED BY COLLINS & HARVILL

Geordie still had nightmares about the car crash in which his parents had died. It was hard for an eleven-year-old to get used to being an orphan, and life in the Scottish village where he went to live with his grandmother seemed strange. Mrs. Graham was kind enough, but she had no understanding of a small boy's needs.

Gradually Geordie began to make friends. The young farmer Andrew and his crusty old helper Tom both felt an affection for the lonely youngster. But it was through the sheepdog puppy, Flash, that Geordie began to live again. When a new nightmare suddenly separated him from his pet, he determined that nothing would keep them apart for long—somehow, he would find Flash again.

Author Joyce Stranger's abiding love of animals and the countryside shines out of this touching story of a boy and his dog.

CHAPTER ONE

The boy should not have been there, but Andrew Grant hadn't the heart to send him home. From milking time they had waited together in the farm kitchen; they had watched the stars come out of the dark and the moon rise high; they had sat together, watching and hoping, while Megan, the ten-year-old collie, moved her body painfully, waiting for the litter that should never have been conceived.

If only she hadn't got out. She was far too old for pups and Andrew would never forgive himself. He should have had her spayed.

He stood up to brew tea. He was a slender man in his early thirties, a lonely man, left a widower by the death of his young wife in an accident some years before. The loss had bound him to Geordie, who had come to live with his grandmother in the village when his parents both died in a multiple crash on the M1. Geordie still limped from his own injuries. He had spent six months in plaster; the lame leg was healing but the doctor would not say if it would ever be right.

Andrew pushed his thick dark hair away from his eyes and looked across at the boy. Geordie was small for an eleven-year-old, brown-eyed, brown-haired and fair-skinned. He would have been a plain child had it not been for those eyes; enormous, expressive, and just now focused on the bitch. Andrew should send the child home.

Suppose the bitch died? Another half hour at most and he would have to ring the vet. She was already overdue and the pups should have begun to come by now.

"I think she's going to need help," Andrew said. "It should have been over by now. It's high time you went home."

"Grandy's at a meeting, and I don't like being home alone," Geordie said. He had been longing all week for the puppies, especially when Andrew had said he could stay and watch so long as Megan didn't object to him. Geordie was sure she would not. He and the bitch were inseparable when he was at the farm. He stroked the soft white ruff, and the bitch licked his hand.

Andrew made the tea and poured it into the two big mugs. Sheena Graham, Geordie's grandmother, would have been horrified if she had seen how strong it was, but Geordie took it rapturously. He was only allowed milky tea at home. Andrew always treated him like an adult, not like a baby.

Andrew walked to the window and looked out at the village of Drumkinnon, nestling under the mountainside. Then he turned back to the room. Geordie was kneeling beside the bitch, holding her head as she whimpered. She stared up at her master, agonized, and Andrew cursed to himself softly and ran to the telephone.

The ringing tone showed no sign of stopping. But if Angus McGregor were out, he would have left a recorded message. "McGregor here," a voice said suddenly, loud and brusque.

"Megan's in trouble," Andrew said.

"I'm no' surprised. Bring her in, and quickly."

"Geordie's here. I'll drop him on my way."

"It's out of your way and ye'd best be quick, with the bitch almost eleven," Angus said. "Bring the lad and I'll phone Sheena."

"Can I come?" Geordie asked, and followed Andrew, ecstatic. He was worried about the bitch, but he knew Andrew would not let harm come to her, and neither would the vet. Geordie had supreme confidence in both men. Angus McGregor had operated on an in-lamb ewe last year and saved her life and Geordie had bottle-fed the lamb, now a fine young ram running on the mountain with the rest of the flock.

Andrew started the old Land-Rover's cantankerous engine and put the vehicle into gear. They were off, Megan lying in her basket in the back, with Geordie crouched beside her. The bitch whined. Geordie, holding her tightly, could feel shudders under her skin. Her nose was hot and dry and she was panting. It was a forlorn hope.

The unmade lane from the farm was pocked and rutted and the headlights failed to reveal half the pitfalls. The vehicle crashed into a pothole and heaved itself out again. Fear settled on Geordie. He had never felt safe since his parents died. One minute they were all there laughing together and the next. . . . Memory returned; the sudden scream of brakes, the crash of metal, shouts. He gripped the back of Andrew's seat. He had thought that he was no longer afraid in a car, but now he was wet with sweat, willing Andrew to slow down.

They kept off the main road, and sped up the mountain flank along a twisting narrow lane. It was a crazy short cut to take in the dark, but it saved almost five miles. Angus lived in the next village.

An owl drifted by, ghostly, and Geordie shivered. Bird of evil, bird of ill-omen; his mother had been very superstitious. But Grandy was intensely religious, and God knew best.

Geordie thought of Grandy now, walking slowly along the road home after a committee meeting of the Ladies of the Village, who planned all the fund raising for various charities. Grandy was small and nearly seventy. She sometimes had blinding headaches, and then Geordie went to see Andrew. It was very lonely being an orphan. Though Grandy was kind, she tired easily and said "no" more often than she said "yes".

The Land-Rover was running downhill to the end of the corrie. Then they were on the main road and Andrew was speeding along, covering the miles until they had left the end of the loch behind and come to the edge of Drumbeattie. They passed the straggle of homes and the brash new red-brick houses on the little estate. The last building was an old one in vast overgrown grounds, and the headlights flashed briefly on the sign: Tigh na Bhet.

The vet's house. Geordie expelled a long breath. They were there, they were safe, and Megan would be all right now. He watched as Andrew lifted the bitch gently in his arms and carried her in through the open door.

At any other time Geordie would have been fascinated all over again by the vet's house. By the immense stone-flagged hall, where spears and daggers and duelling pistols hung on the walls and a large bronze statue of Venus was decked with the children's school hats and satchels; by the stuffed pheasants and ducks in the glass case at the end of the hall near the surgery door; by the tubes on the table containing kidneys and pieces of liver, embryo fish, a tapeworm. Angus McGregor was the bane of his wife, who never quite knew what he would bring home next: an aeroplane propeller, or the engine of a vintage car that might come in handy.

A log fire burned now at the end of the hall. There was a movement on the hearthrug. A muddle of furry bodies sorted itself into a tabby cat and two kittens, a sleepy-eyed Labrador pup and Tycho, the fox cub, hissing to himself at the approach of strangers. Tab had adopted him with her kittens after a local farmer had killed his mother.

Angus was waiting for them in the doorway of his surgery, a broad-shouldered bull of a man, with the blond hair of a Viking and beard to match.

"Can I come with her?" Geordie asked.

"No, lad. Get to the kitchen and find Donald and Davina. They're making toffee apples for bonfire night. Ye can help them."

The surgery door shut. Geordie stood looking at it. Supposing Megan died? Andrew had promised him a pup for himself, a collie pup that could round up the sheep on the hill.

There were warm smells coming from the kitchen. Geordie knew his way round the place, and stopped to look at two cases filled with bright tropical butterflies. It must be exciting to have Angus for a father, he thought, missing his own parents so much that it hurt all over again.

"Geordie! What are you doing here?"

Catherine McGregor was a tiny woman, with a vivid dark-skinned face, and brilliant dark grey eyes. She reminded Geordie of a gazelle; elegant, graceful, with dainty movements.

"Megan's puppies won't get born," Geordie said.

"Angus will soon cure that," Catherine McGregor said, with absolute confidence in her husband's skill. "Come and see the twins."

The kitchen was along the passage and down three steps, and the warmth hit them as they opened the door. The giant Aga was turned up high, and the dogs, lying in their baskets, greeted them with barks. Sultan and Tartar, the two big Alsatians, came forward to sniff suspiciously at the stranger and then relaxed, and six-month-old Limbo, the latest Alsatian pup, bounded up to Geordie.

306

"I think this house should be called House of Beasts, not the vet's house," Catherine said, as she cut giant slices off a currant cake and handed one to Geordie and one each to the twins. The twins were both slender, dark-haired, like their mother, but with their father's vivid blue eyes and robust temperament. Davina was stirring a saucepan, muttering to herself as if casting spells, and Donald had picked up one of the stickiest of the toffee apples and was trying to chew it. "It's set like rock," he said.

Geordie ate his cake without tasting it. He usually loved the big kitchen with the settles against the walls, padded with patchwork cushions and littered with baskets for the animals. There was always one animal or another near to the Aga, recovering from a birth or an operation.

Then the surgery door opened and he heard the men's voices in the hall; Angus deep and gruff and Andrew answering in a lighter tone. Geordie raced to meet them.

"Is Megan all right?" he asked.

"Right as rain," Angus said. "I had to operate. The first pup was crossways and was dead. The other pups are alive, only. . ."

"Only what?" Geordie asked.

"One of them is very small, and I don't think it will survive. I'm going to put it down."

"You can't." Geordie was fierce. No animal was ever going to die while he was around.

"It's no use keeping it, lad," Andrew said gently. "The bitch has no milk and we're going to have to hand-rear. Catherine says she will do it for me, but she can't do all of them. It's for the best."

"My cat can rear it. She lost two of her kittens and she's lots of milk," Geordie said.

"The cat will never take a pup," Andrew said. "It's no use, lad. It's too small to rear, and that's the end of it."

"Can I see them?" Geordie asked.

Angus nodded, and the boy went into the room. Megan was lying under a lamp, stretched out, still unconscious. The pups were in a cardboard box under the heat of another lamp, beside the fire. They were moving restlessly. The smallest whimpered. Geordie put his finger down in front of it and at once it was seized and sucked vigorously.

"He isn't weak at all," Geordie said furiously. "He's strong; it's

307

just that he's so small. Please let me try. My dad said I could have a pup this year. I want this pup."

Andrew sighed. Children. You could never make them out. The boy could have any pup in the litter; but he had to choose the feeblest.

"You can have the pup. But don't blame us if it dies," he said.

"You're nuts," Davina said. "A sick puppy never survives."

"It isn't sick," Geordie said stubbornly.

"I'm leaving Megan here. If you bring that home you'll need a hot-water bottle to keep it very warm."

Geordie watched while Catherine filled a hot-water bottle; he fed the pup himself from the dropper when the milk was mixed, and took a carton of dried puppy food with him into the Land-Rover. The hot-water bottle was tucked inside his coat and the pup was wrapped in cotton wool, tucked in beside the bottle. He could feel it moving against his hand, could feel the small wet nose and the tiny damp mouth, and he sat in a daze of excitement cradling his hand over it all the way home.

Andrew stopped at the gate. "I wonder what your grandmother will say," he said.

The thought had never crossed Geordie's mind. Grandy hadn't been very pleased when Trippie had kittens.

"Will you come and tell her?" he asked.

Andrew shook his head. The boy had to learn to fight his own battles; but the man felt very mean as he watched the small figure trudge up the garden path, his hand held firmly over the pup.

Andrew sighed. He and Angus were both insane. They should never have agreed. The old lady would never allow the pup into the house.

SHEENA GRAHAM stared at her grandson with hostile brown eyes. It had been a bad day. The arthritis in her hands and hips had drained her of energy, and she was not yet used to the change in her way of life.

After ten years of widowhood Sheena had thought she would be alone for ever and the cottage she had retired to was small and delicately furnished. The death of her only son had been a terrible shock, but perhaps even worse had been the slow realization that there was no other relative in the world to care for Geordie. Ian had been an only child and so had his wife; Margaret had a cousin living in Manchester who had been very close to her, and she would have taken the boy, but Sheena was proud. No one would ever say she had refused to give a home to her orphaned grandson, but there were few people who knew the effort it cost her. She was sixty-eight; and felt, at night, when her bones ached from the extra work that Geordie caused, that she had earned a rest.

She looked now at the tiny pup in his hands, and she had no words at all. If she spoke she would snap at the boy and see again the forlorn bewildered look on his face, and feel that he was turning against her.

Ian had been a good father, taking him fishing and going on the long country walks that his wife had loved too, but all that had ended, snuffed out in a moment when a lorry skidded on an oil patch and its trailer jack-knifed and hit their car.

Grandy had insisted that the boy was moved to the hospital near her as soon as possible; although she did not like animals she had brought Trippie, the cat, home to live with them, knowing that one link with his past life would help the boy; but Geordie felt a stranger still in her house, afraid of breaking the fragile ornaments, afraid of dirtying the pale carpets, afraid of making too much noise.

Sheena looked down at the pup, and her thoughts raced, thinking of bottle-feeds and of the mess a puppy would make in her neat little home. How could the child have a dog? It was bad enough to have the boy here. . . .

She checked her thoughts and led Geordie indoors. The night before she had chided him for untidiness and he had exploded at her, shouting at her that he hated her and her silly little house, and the awful ornaments that broke if he only looked at them. He had stormed upstairs to fling himself on his bed, sobbing noisily. Sheena had left him alone, thinking that the outburst would do him good. But the scene had left her drained and exhausted and she could not face another.

Sheena went back into the tiny sitting room that seemed so much smaller with Geordie there, and with Trippie and her kittens. She hadn't wanted the cat, and was horrified when she realized that the cat was in kitten by the time Geordie was beginning to be about again. The kittens were now four weeks old. Mercifully Trippie was

309

beautifully clean and had trained her own kits, but they were mischievous. And now the pup.

Geordie knelt by Trippie's box and held the pup against the cat. Trippie, fluffed to three times her normal size, hissed at the intruder and her swift paw, claws outstretched, scratched the tiny head, bringing blood. The four kittens, copying their mother, arched and spat too.

It wasn't going to work.

"Geordie, you cannot make her take the pup. She'll kill it," Sheena said. "It hasn't a chance of life, lad. Ye'll have to take it back to the bitch. I cannot think what Andrew was about, letting you bring the wee thing here."

"Megan hasn't any milk. They were going to put this one down, but I wanted it," Geordie said. "My father said I could have a dog for my birthday this year, but I didn't have one. I was in hospital. You never let me have anything. I want something to play with. I want my dog."

His voice was rising and Sheena knew she couldn't stand it again. "You can feed it tonight, but in the morning it goes back to Angus, or to Andrew," she said. "Geordie, if Trippie won't take it, it will have to be fed every two hours, day and night, for over three weeks; how are we going to do that?"

"I can do the feeds; I'll set my clock," Geordie said.

"And what about school? Do you sleep all day at your lessons? And how do I clean the house and look after a wee helpless motherless pup? And do the cooking and the shopping and all there is to do about the place? You must be sensible, lad."

The pup moved its head, seeking for warmth and food. Its small blind head nuzzled against Geordie's warm woollen jersey. The tiny mouth fastened onto his finger and sucked.

"It's time for food," Geordie said. He tucked the pup carefully into his pocket, its head peeping out. Then he went and prepared the feed, measuring meticulously. Andrew had given him a dropper to use, and he would have to drip the milk down the pup's throat.

He sat back in the chair, wrapping the tiny creature in a thick wad of paper tissues, holding it delicately, every sense concentrated on what he was doing. The pup was hungry, opening its mouth greedily for the milk; each drop had to be placed accurately on the small tongue, and Geordie had to wait till the pup had swallowed.

310

There was only an inch of milk in the pipette, but even so it took nearly fifteen minutes to get it down and then the pup had to be massaged, or he wouldn't function and would die by retaining his own wastes.

There was nothing so obstinate as a boy, Sheena thought with exasperation. She went out into the kitchen and found a shoe box. She lined it with thick cotton wool and fetched a small hot-water bag that she used for her back when it was bad, and filled it, laying it carefully under the cotton wool and covering everything with a woollen square of blanket. Geordie's vivid smile was an unlooked-for reward.

"I'll feed him for you at midnight and you can get up at two. I'll do the four o'clock feed. But I'll not change my mind, so don't set your heart on keeping the pup."

Geordie put the pup in the box. Then he kissed Sheena good-night, a dutiful peck on the soft wrinkled cheek. Sheena had never been a demonstrative woman, and Geordie missed his mother's bear hugs and her warm greeting, her laughter and her blithe disregard of untidiness. He missed his friends, too. He would have loved to spend more time with Donald and Davina but there was no bus or train link between the two villages and he could only visit when someone was going over by car and willing to have a boy as passenger.

He sat on the edge of his bed, worrying about the pup. It needed something to snuggle against. He opened the trunk in which Grandy had packed all his old toys and rummaged frantically. The toy he was looking for had been the one he loved most. His mother had knitted it for him—she was a bad knitter, but the woolly donkey would be perfect for the pup; he could nestle between its soft floppy legs. Geordie grabbed Old Flop from the corner of the trunk and ran downstairs.

His grandmother was sitting in the chair, her eyes closed. She jumped as he came in.

"This will make him feel safer," Geordie said, and held the untidy woollen toy to the fire to warm it before tucking it into the box. It took up most of the space, and the pup instinctively wriggled himself between the long woolly legs and tried to nurse from the soft underbody. A moment later, warm, fed, and secure, he was asleep. Geordie stroked the soft, almost invisible fur.

"Bed, Geordie, fast," Sheena said.

The door closed behind her grandson. Then, seeing Trippie stalk the box, Sheena took the cat's basket and the kittens into the next room. It was much too cold for them, and she had to put on the electric fire. That would mean more expense.

The minutes ticked by. A coal fell, and then, startlingly, came a tap at the window. Sheena stared at the drawn curtains. No one could possibly be calling at a quarter to midnight. She drew back the curtain and then felt unreasonably angry as she recognized Tom Fazackerley, Andrew's stockman. Tom was as old as she but a sight spryer; no one would think he was nearly seventy. They had been at school together.

Tom came in. He was grizzled in hair and brows, with unnervingly bright blue eyes that stared right into her mind and read it accurately, as they always had. "So the lad won?" he said.

"Of course not. But I can't leave the creature unfed till morning," Sheena said tartly.

"I told him he was mad," Tom said. He never referred to Andrew by name. "Told him you'd never agree."

Sheena said nothing.

"Geordie's had a raw deal," Tom said. "And he's had the pup long enough to mind too much if it's taken from him. I'll come and do the night feeds if ye'll do the day feeds. I don't sleep well these days as it is. Bones complaining, and I have to walk around or I get too stiff. Let the lad keep the pup."

"And when it starts running around?" Sheena asked. "Puddles on the carpets and chewing at things; what then? Couldn't you take it till it's house-trained?"

Tom shook his head. "Geordie wants a dog. He has to know what having a dog's about. The training will teach him responsibility."

"Make yourself a drink," Sheena said, hating him. She left the room and went wearily to bed.

She woke to find Geordie standing beside her, shouting. "You didn't wake me. The pup will be dead."

"Geordie!" It was Tom's voice from downstairs.

Geordie ran out onto the landing and stared at the man.

"I fed the pup and it's fine except for that scratch on its head; Angus will do something about that. Come down and give it a feed. But go back and apologize to your grandmother first!"

312

Geordie crept meekly into his grandmother's bedroom again. "I'm sorry," he said.

"You didn't know. I'll be up soon and make your breakfast, lad."

Geordie went downstairs. Tom had the kettle on and the feed made up ready for him. Bacon sizzled in the pan and toast browned under the grill. The table was laid for two.

Geordie went into the sitting room. The skin on the pup's head was puffy; the scratch had a yellow crust on it. But the pup fed well, taking each drop and swallowing.

"I should try it on the bottle, lad. Less chance of the milk going down the wrong way," Tom said, and watched approvingly as Geordie finished giving the feed and massaged the pup, and then sat it against his hand to break the wind. The pup settled comfortably against Old Flop and within moments it was still, sleeping with its head on the round plump belly of the toy.

"That was a brainwave," Tom said. "Now come and make a tray for your grandmother and take her her breakfast in bed. Time she had a bit of fussing."

Geordie found the pretty plate and cup and saucer that she loved and laid the tray carefully. Tom made tea and paper-thin toast, and boiled an egg. He carried the tray upstairs and gave it to Geordie when he reached the landing.

Sheena stared at the tray when Geordie came into the room.

"Faceache thought you'd like your breakfast in bed," Geordie said, using Tom Fazackerley's nickname.

"That's lovely, Geordie," Sheena said gratefully. Geordie balanced the tray carefully on his grandmother's knees, gave her the soft stole that she wore when reading in bed, and switched on the electric fire.

"Tom says he'll help with the pup," Sheena said, and was rewarded by an impulsive hug that almost upset her tea in her lap.

"I won't let it be a nuisance, I promise," Geordie said.

By teatime, the skin round the pup's scratch was obviously puffy and swollen. Geordie went to find Andrew, who came home with him and bent to look at the tiny creature.

"I think we'll have to take him to Angus," Andrew said. "An infection on the head at this stage could be very dangerous."

Angus had just finished surgery when they arrived. He looked down at Geordie. "Trouble already?" he asked.

Geordie nodded forlornly. "Trippie scratched him when I tried to make her feed him."

Angus took them into the surgery. Geordie leaned against the medicine cupboard, watching Angus set the pup on its back on the table, still wrapped warmly and lying on the hot-water bag.

He bent to look at the scratch. "I'm sorry, lad," he said. "It's formed a wee abscess. This pup will never survive. Let me put it down now, before you're too fond of it."

"You can inject it," Geordie said.

Angus shook his head. "I couldn't even work out the dose for a pup as small as that. I could just as easily kill it with an injection as cure it. I've never tried to save one this age. It isn't sense."

"Then you're just a murderer," Geordie said fiercely. "I suffered in hospital but nobody put me to sleep."

Angus looked at Andrew and shook his head. "I'll try," he said.

He went to the cupboard and took out a hypodermic syringe. He measured a minute dose of antibiotic into it, took the pup and injected it. He cleaned the cut on its head and gave the wee creature back to the boy. "That's all I can do," he said.

SHEENA GRAHAM had nothing to say when they returned. Andrew Grant paused at the door, looking at her. Tom had told him off properly the night before when they were mucking out the sow, a vast, prolific creature that Tom had named Queenie. He was absurdly proud of the squealing piglets that she produced without effort at regular intervals.

Tom was staring at Queenie as Andrew approached.

"He's as daft as any creature I ever met," he told the sow, knowing well that his employer was behind him. "Giving that wee useless thing to a lad barely eleven years old with no one but an old lady to bring him up. The pup will die; the lad will be desolate and the woman will suffer."

Andrew had stopped in his tracks. He had thought that the need to look after the pup would help the boy. He had not been thinking of Sheena at all. After all, Sheena Graham was not farm-bred and she avoided animals. And she was almost seventy.

Now, he did not know how to apologize. "I am sorry, Mrs. Graham. I did not think. . . ."

Sheena looked at him and saw the unhappiness in his eyes. "It

314

will do the boy good," she said. "He has to learn about living. And he has to live with me, so I must do my share. Tom's promised to help. We'll manage."

Andrew left, reassured, and she went back into the sitting room. Geordie had re-filled the hot-water bag and put it at the bottom of the shoe box. The pup was tucked in between Old Flop's legs, sound asleep and breathing faintly. Geordie was kneeling above it, all his feelings in his eyes. Sheena could not bear to look at him.

She went out into the kitchen and prepared the pup's feed, and then busied herself with making the boy's favourite tea. "You must eat, Geordie," she told him.

Geordie looked at the plate. Two fried eggs and baked beans and chips, crisp and golden, just the way his mother had made them. He began to eat.

When he had finished Geordie lifted the pup for its evening feed. It was very sleepy and it would not suck. Geordie tried again and again, but the milk just lay on the small tongue and dripped out of the sides of the tiny mouth. Geordie was almost in tears when Tom arrived, bringing Megan with him.

"She hasn't any milk. But maybe she can mother the wee beast and make him take his food," Tom said.

Sheena, coming into the room, set her mouth when she saw the bitch.

"You needn't look like that," Tom said. "She's as clean as you are. She hasn't fleas and she might be what the pup is needing. She has to work during the day but she can come for the night. I've brought her basket."

Megan went, unerringly, to Geordie and sniffed at the pup. She took it firmly in her mouth, settled herself on the rug, and tucked the pup against her. Within seconds, his small nose was working, his head pushing against the sleek black fur, and he was trying to nurse.

"Get down on the rug beside her, Geordie, and try to feed him now."

Geordie knelt and put his hand around the pup. This time, the small mouth opened of its own accord and the pup swallowed. He took the whole feed, and then Megan rolled him on his back and licked him clean.

Tom put the basket down beside her, lined with a thick white

towel. Megan lifted the pup, and stepped in. Within seconds both bitch and pup were cuddled down, the pup's small sides lifting and sinking, lifting and sinking, in steady breathing.

"Now we just have to wait and see if that scratch will settle," Tom said.

Sheena was crocheting, sitting on the settee. Geordie could not take his eyes off the bitch and the pup; Tom was stroking his empty pipe, a slight smile on his face; the ticking clock was a soothing background to a room that suddenly seemed more complete than Sheena had ever known it. She had been without people belonging for so long that she had forgotten the happiness that came amid all the work. The place was a home again.

Geordie looked up at her, and she smiled, a sudden warm smile. "Bedtime, Geordie," she said.

The boy looked at the clock. He kissed his grandmother goodnight and said goodnight to Tom, who nodded. The door closed.

"It does not take much to please a child," Tom said. He watched the animals and Sheena worked at her shawl until it was time for the next feed, which she made, and Tom gave. There was no need to talk.

At bedtime, Sheena brought down two blankets and a pillow. "You can stretch out on the sofa," she said.

By morning, the pup was obviously stronger. Geordie was downstairs by half past five, creeping into the room where Tom was dozing. The man woke and stretched himself, and folded the blankets.

"You're an early riser," he said. "The beastie's hungry. Make its feed now."

Geordie was on his knees beside the basket. The scratch was clean; the swelling around it gone.

This time Geordie took the pup on his lap again carefully. Megan sat beside him, nosing the pup constantly, licking away dribbles of milk. The pup sucked vigorously, its paws

317

scrabbling against Geordie's hand. There was intense satisfaction in feeding the pup, in handing it back to Megan who took it delicately in her jaws and settled with it in the basket, licking it all over to wash and massage it.

The days settled into a pattern. Geordie fed the pup before he went to school; Tom left with Megan; and Sheena put the pup back with Old Flop. She had, against her will, become interested in it. She was alone when it opened one eye and stared at her, through a blue haze. Geordie was home in time to see the second eye open, some hours later.

That night it crawled to Megan across Geordie's knee, greeting her with a lifted face. It was now obviously a small sheepdog, black and white, sleekly shining from Megan's ministrations. There was a white mark down the centre of the black nose.

"A flash of white. I'm going to call him Flash," Geordie said.

Flash grew and became an imperious and demanding personality, hungry, shouting for food with shrill squeaks. By the time he was four weeks old he was a ball of black and white fluff, stumbling eagerly to greet Megan when she came at night, with a lick of the hand for Tom. He knew Geordie and he came to meet Sheena when she brought his bottle. Tom had rolled the carpet back near the fire and spread the floor with thick layers of newspaper, and Sheena found she did not care all that much about her immaculate room being turned upside down. Geordie was so much easier to live with, running home every day to feed his pup. He had woken out of his nightmare, and was taking part in lessons again.

By the time the pup had had his inoculations he was showing signs of future beauty. His coat was dense and long, the fur on back and tail and legs deep glossy black. His chest and shoulders were white; and so was the tip of his right front paw. He had a straight white line from forehead to the tip of his muzzle and one white spot below his left ear. His eyes were set wide on his head, and when he was puzzled he sat with one ear forward, one back and his forehead wrinkled.

Trippie's kittens had gone to new homes, and Trippie herself now tolerated the newcomer, though she would not yet come close. For one thing, Flash was becoming mischievous, and with each day he mastered movement, and made discoveries.

Television mystified him. He would sit, almost on top of the

318

screen, until there was a sudden movement, when he would bark, and rush under a chair. Only after some minutes had passed would he venture out again. The pup was a constant source of laughter, and Sheena found a new pleasure in the shared amusement.

Flash was nine weeks old when Geordie discovered that he was obsessed by shadows. They were walking down the garden path when Sheena switched on a light indoors. Their shadows sprang onto the ground in front of them, Geordie's long and thin and Flash's small and oddly angled. The pup leaped on his own and growled, then froze as the shadow moved. He stared up at Geordie, who was watching him, grinning. He had never thought of shadows before.

By the time the pup was fully weaned and Tom had ceased to come regularly at night, Sheena and Geordie often switched off the lights and sat in the dancing firelight, watching Flash prowl along the floor, and sit, absorbed, opposite the glass-fronted bookcase where a second fire flared and flickered and died, the dark spines of the books acting as a mirror.

Christmas came and went, a long holiday which gave Geordie time to play with his pup, wild games now, with a rope to pull at in an endless tug-of-war, or a battered old ball which Flash commandeered and raced away with, refusing to bring it back, standing carefully poised, and ready to run as soon as Geordie had almost caught up with him. Sheena bought a collar and a lead for the dog, and Tom made a box on legs so that the pup could sleep out of the draughts.

Andrew's present was a case of tinned dog food. He knew that Sheena was finding things tight: there was still no news from the lawyers about the settlement of Geordie's parents' affairs or about the compensation for the road crash. So he began to call in with gifts of potatoes and other vegetables, saying that he had a surplus he couldn't use.

Sheena knew he was helping and saving her face, and was grateful: Geordie had grown out of all his clothes and been re-fitted, using some of the money from her tiny savings. It frightened her to see her small capital vanish. Suppose the money never came? Also, the house where Geordie had lived was still unsold, and would be worth less as the months went by. Worry kept her awake at night, and she was glad to get up each morning and be greeted

by the vociferous pup racing towards her, his tail wagging frantically, his brown eyes welcoming her.

And then Flash discovered sheep.

Andrew had brought the first lambs down from the hills, as they
expected snow in the next few days. The clouds had a lowering
darkness, with a sulphurous glow between them, and they grouped
low on the flanks of the mountains.

Flash saw two ewes, and began to stalk: slow, slow, down, slow,
slow, down. Suppose the pup jumped the sheep or worried them?
Geordie was about to call the pup, but Andrew put a finger to his
lips. Geordie need not have worried. Flash was a born sheepdog;
he moved carefully, without training, and only at the last did
excitement master him so that he panicked the sheep and they
bolted to the other end of the field.

The dog returned, his mouth wide open in his greeting grin,
pride at his own achievement mastering every other feeling.

"He'll make a grand dog," Andrew said.

CHAPTER TWO

Sheena had once enjoyed singing but somewhere, during her life,
the pleasure had been mislaid. Now it was returning. Geordie
loved the songs of the Isles, and one late afternoon, when the snow
lay so deep outside that he could not visit Andrew, she sang to
him, her voice soft in the firelit room, while he sat on the hearthrug
with Flash curled against him. Flames flickered on the polished
furniture; wood flared and crackled and fell into a soft red ash.

Suddenly Sheena's voice stopped. Geordie looked up at his
grandmother. She was lying back against the cushions, fighting
for breath.

"Grandy!" Geordie switched on the light and looked at his grandmother helplessly.

Slowly, her colour returned. "I think I have flu," she said at last.
"Geordie, can you ring the doctor, lad?"

He went to the phone, but the line was down and the instrument
was dead. He opened the front door. There were no landmarks:
the mountains were giant bulks of white against the sky, the road
had vanished and the path had gone; in the far distance was the

shapeless lump that was Andrew's farmhouse, with smoke pluming from the chimney into the sky.

He went back into the room. Sheena was lying against the cushions, her eyes closed.

Fear became terror. He would have to go out into the snow to try to reach Andrew, and Tom would have to fetch the doctor. He tried to remember all that Tom had told him about snow in the past; about the dangers of lying in a drift till the thaw came; about the dangers of getting lost; of finding no landmarks; of falling through into the ditches.

He looked at his grandmother again. Her eyes were closed and she was breathing heavily: he had no choice. He fetched blankets from her bed to cover her, filled the hot-water bags and put them against her, and banked up the fire and put the guard against it.

He was desperately afraid. Suppose Grandy was dying while he was looking for help? Suppose she recovered and found him gone? He found a pen and wrote a note which he put on the table beside her.

> I have gone to tell Tom to get the doctor.
> Love,
> Geordie.
> P.S. Don't worry. I'll be all right.

He tried hard to think. Wellingtons. An extra jersey and his warm, lined anorak and his thick gloves. And food—never go out in snow without food, Tom had said. There were two bars of chocolate in the pantry, and raisins. That's what explorers took.

He picked up Flash and then took the keys from his grandmother's handbag, buttoning them up in his pocket. Now it was all up to him. The door closing behind him felt unpleasantly final. Geordie stepped into the snow.

He had forgotten that there were two steps, and both he and the pup fell sprawling. The pup, meeting snow for the first time, sniffed it, and regaining his feet, began to dig.

"Come on, Flash," Geordie said impatiently.

He lifted the dog up and set out again, step by careful step, feeling his way to the garden gate. It was impossible to open. He climbed over, nearly losing a wellington in the process.

321

Panic overtook him. He began to run, stumbling down the lane. It was bitterly cold and his ears ached and his face hurt, and the stinging wind brought with it huge clinging wet flakes. Now the farmhouse was within sight, and Geordie forgot caution, stepping to one side of the path.

The snow gave way and he fell, floundering in a drift. He could see nothing. Struggling only sent him deeper, and worst of all, he had dropped Flash. He landed with a bump in a dug-out cave in which were three sheep, huddled together, that Andrew had failed to find.

Geordie tried to fight his way out of the drift, but more snow fell in on him. He would be better off staying quite still with the sheep for warmth, and he crept between them again and nibbled at one of the bars of chocolate. He wondered how long he could live if he rationed himself carefully. No one would be looking for him—his grandmother might be dead and now he had every chance of dying too. And Flash had no chance at all, a tiny dog, alone in the snow.

Tears began to trickle down Geordie's cheeks and nothing he could do would stop them.

FLASH HAD BEEN BORN DETERMINED. He fell on hard-packed snow when Geordie dropped him, and now he stood and shook himself, bewildered by the disappearance of his master. The world was very strange and very large.

Flash nosed the snow around the drift, aware that Geordie was there, able to scent both the boy and the sheep. The pup dug, but it was futile: the drift was far too deep for his small paws.

Over at the farmhouse, Andrew was carrying hay for the sheep in the byres. He had moved the cattle into the big barn and packed the sheep into their place. The work was endless; a constant bringing in of hay, and a constant mucking out. He slipped on a patch of ice, fell headlong, and yelled in fury.

Tom called out from the top of the stack. "Are you all right?"

The familiar voice sounded along the lane, and the pup set off to find it. The snow was hard packed from the constant passage of sheep, for Tom and Andrew and Megan had been working all day. The pup plodded on, aware of the sting of cold in his eyes, and the bitter numbing cold beneath his paws.

There was a sudden crack as the sky forked into lightning, and the clouds bellowed their rage. The pup ran. He had never heard thunder before and he was terrified, whimpering loudly. Megan heard him and began to bark.

"For heaven's sake," Andrew said irritably. "What in the world is wrong with that bitch?"

She barked at them, chasing frantically between Tom and Andrew, frustrated beyond measure at their stupidity. She was telling them, as plainly as she could, that her pup was out there in the snow, crying for her, and she needed the farmyard gate open so that she could go to him.

"Maybe there's a fox out there," Tom said, walking to the gate and peering down the lane. He stared in disbelief at the tiny black

and white pup walking wearily along in the distance. "Holy Joe! It's the pup! What in the world. . .?" Tom opened the gate and Megan ran down the lane, over the hard-packed snow. Flash greeted her rapturously. Tom, reaching the two dogs, bent to lift the pup, but Flash turned and began to plod back towards the drift. When the man bent down again, the pup lifted his head and howled.

Andrew came running down the lane with his crook. "Surely the boy wouldn't have come in this snow?" he said.

Tom was looking at the wires lying on the ground. "The phone's out of action, and Sheena Graham's no kitten," he said.

He put the pup back on the ground. Flash set off again, nosing his own trail until he came to the piled-up snow, where he began to dig. Megan was digging too, barking as the snow flew behind her frantic legs.

Tom had brought his spade as he left the farmyard, in case Megan found more stranded sheep. Now he shovelled snow as if a life depended on it. He grunted when he caught a glimpse of red that was Geordie's anorak, and dug more carefully.

Geordie stared up at them, lying between the sheep.

"Lad, lad, are you all right?" Tom's face was as anxious as his voice.

"I haven't been here long," Geordie said. "Grandy's ill, very ill, and the phone's dead."

Andrew pulled the boy out. "Tom can take the Land-Rover to the village," he said. "We've cleared the path to the road on our side. The main road's clear—they've been working on it all day. We'll get back and see what we can do."

Sheena had not moved. Andrew looked at her, knowing this was more than flu; a heart attack, or a stroke maybe; she was a bad colour and breathing with difficulty. He sent Geordie to fill the hot-water bags again, while he himself added an extra blanket and stoked the fire.

Geordie came back into the room. The pup came to the fire to warm himself but the return of life to his frozen paws was painful and he whimpered unhappily.

"Move him from the heat and rub his paws," Andrew said. "Are you dry, lad?"

Geordie shook his head.

324

"Then go and have a bath and put on dry clothes." Andrew was glad to be able to think of a natural occupation that would take the boy out of the room. He was afraid Sheena would die before the doctor arrived.

Flash followed Geordie upstairs and curled up on the bathmat beside the bath. He was not letting Geordie out of his sight again. He stood up once, paws on the edge of the bath, and licked at Geordie's hair.

Geordie, feeling the water warm him, feeling the numbness leaving his hands and feet, was too worried about his grandmother to notice the pain in his fingers and toes. He was sure Grandy would have to go to hospital; and what about him? Perhaps Andrew would give him a bed and he could help on the farm; he didn't want to stay in the cottage, all alone. How did you survive with no one at all belonging to you, Geordie wondered, as he towelled himself dry. There was only his mother's cousin, Jennie Anderson, in Manchester. She was a teacher and had visited them when he was small. But he couldn't remember her.

The doorbell rang while he was combing his hair and he heard the doctor's voice. Then there was a long terrifying silence.

Was Grandy dead? He dared not go downstairs. He sat on the top stair, shivering, with the dog held tightly against him as if the pup could keep the troubles of the world at a distance.

"Geordie," Andrew called up. "Your grandmother will have to go to hospital for a little while, but you can come home with me. It will be nice to have company for a change. Pack yourself a bag, and find Trippie's carrying basket."

Geordie did not ask the question lying on his tongue: will she be all right? Andrew had given him no reassurance. He packed his case. Shirts and pants and socks and jerseys; toothbrush; his four favourite books; and lastly, hidden under all the clothes, his old teddy bear.

When he went downstairs there was an ambulance man at the gate, and a second bringing a stretcher. He watched as they wrapped Grandy up in blankets, tucking in hot-water bags on either side of her, pulling up the covers to protect her face. Was she dead?

Then her eyes opened and she saw Geordie and tried to smile. "Be a good boy," she whispered.

Andrew was making the fire safe, ensuring that the guard was in place. "I'll get Tom to come in every day and put the electric fires on for a while to keep the place warm for you to come back to," he said.

"Will I come back?" Geordie asked.

"I don't know," Andrew said at last. "We don't know how bad your grandmother is. A lot depends on how quickly she reaches the hospital."

"How will they get her there?" Geordie asked. Glasgow was a three-hour journey in the best of weather.

"By helicopter. It won't take long," Andrew answered, and squeezed the boy's shoulder, wishing he could provide more comfort, wishing the boy had some hope of a happy childhood. He was being forced into adulthood far too soon.

The snow began again that afternoon. It fell all night and all of the next day, and Tom could not get back to his own home. They shovelled desperately in the yard, keeping the path free to feed the beasts and clean them out. Geordie worked with the men, carrying and fetching hay.

There were no papers, no telephone. The radio was their only link with the world outside, and that carried stories of farms like theirs, of animals stranded on the moors, and hay dropped by helicopter for the deer and the ponies. Luckily, Andrew was well stocked. The deep freeze was full and Tom was a good bread maker; at teatime they ate hot buttered rolls by a blazing fire, while the dogs stretched out in front of the flames, and then Tom would cook mountains of ham and eggs.

Geordie could not go to school. Time seemed to stand still as day followed day; the needs of the beasts and their own needs, and the need to shovel the snow that fell nightly, were unchanging. Fields and woods and lanes and roads had vanished.

Night after night Geordie lay wondering about his grandmother. Had she died? And if not, would she be well enough to come home again? Was it his fault she was ill? Had he made too much work for her? He did not know.

The pup slept on his bed. Though Andrew disapproved of dogs in bedrooms he recognized the boy's need and allowed Flash to follow Geordie upstairs. The dog and the boy were inseparable: Flash was a shadow, always at heel, and at night he slept in the crook of Geordie's arm with his head on the boy's shoulder. It was a comfort in the night to know the little animal was there and to hear the soft breathing. It eased the loneliness, which was something that neither Tom nor Andrew could do.

By day Geordie was quiet, helping out with the air of someone twice his age. He laid the table, washed the dishes and fetched the eggs; listened quietly to the news; looked out over the white desolation. Sometimes it was hard for both men to realize he was only just eleven.

In the evenings there was peace. Geordie loved the big kitchen, the tiled floor, the rag rugs, the wicker chairs that creaked as you moved, the big dresser with plates and cups and saucers and the prize cards won at shows by the animals. The fire would blaze as Geordie lay on the rug with Megan at his feet and Flash at his side, listening to Tom's deep voice reading aloud from one of Andrew's books.

Tom took Geordie into the big barn every day to show him how to train his dog. Flash enjoyed working, moving swiftly at heel, his eyes on Geordie's face. He moved so fast at times that Geordie had to make him keep to heel, and not outpace him. Flash hated staying; he hated Geordie moving away from him, and time after time he followed.

Again and again Geordie put him back, reassuring him, making him stay still. When he called the dog to him, Flash came so fast that he almost overbalanced as he braked. "He'll do," Tom said at last after one session, as the dog came to Geordie for praise, knowing he had done well.

The pup was young for training but the boy needed distraction. Short lessons did no harm, and there was little they could do about the farm. Flash had already begun to explore the barns, staring up at the cows, who nosed him in turn, curious. He was almost four months old: it was late February and they had been snowed up for over a month.

Flash was in need of exercise. He raced into the biggest barn one morning after Chitty, the ginger cat. He misjudged his distance, shot between some stored sacks of fertiliser, and disturbed a half-grown vixen that had come in to shelter.

She leaped at him, vicious teeth raking his ear and his jaw. He yelped and bit her shoulder, but as he leaped clear she caught his paw and held on. Tom heard the din and ran. He seized the broom, slamming the handle down on the vixen's nose. She yelped and fled through the barn and across the yard and, leaping the wall, was buried in a drift.

Geordie lifted his pup. The ear was torn; the jaw had been badly bitten, a gash of open flesh where the teeth had raked his lip, but the paw was worst of all: the vixen's teeth had met and the pup could not bear any weight on the leg. Tom took him indoors, and bathed the injuries. Flash needed an injection, right now, and they had nothing at all they could give him.

That night, when Geordie went to bed, Flash did not follow him, but lay by the fire shivering. By daylight he had no desire to move, and Geordie had to force glucose and water into him. Tom knew the small animal had a high temperature; but they could only keep the pup warm, and hope that his resistance was strong enough to let him recover without veterinary help.

Eventually the torn ear and the gash on the pup's face began to heal, although he would have a twisted lip. The paw festered and Tom poulticed and lanced the wound; but the poison was deep and he feared that it would spread through Flash's whole system.

Geordie worked with the men without speaking, running back frequently to look at the pup, now very sick indeed. He would eat a very little, so long as Geordie fed him with his fingers, and at night he lay against Megan. He could not even mount the stairs.

Tom came downstairs on the second day of March and heard an unusual sound. There was a slither and a scurry. Megan barked and the pup lifted his head to listen. There was a crash and the windows darkened as there was another sliding noise.

"Listen," Tom said. "It's thawing."

He looked at the pup. Flash's small body was starvation-thin, and his eyes were dull. Perhaps, if they were lucky, they would be able to get through to the village and get help from Angus; be able to have news of Sheena.

"Snow'll be gone by morning and we'll get Flash to Angus somehow," Tom said.

THE THAW CONTINUED. By the second day the road was passable. The telephone lines were not yet repaired, but by ten o'clock the snow plough had arrived, and Tom sent an urgent message to

328

Angus, who came at lunchtime, having been able to leave his own home for the first time for days.

The vet came into the room, his face sombre, and handed a note to Andrew, who read it and put it in his pocket. Geordie, aware of a change in the atmosphere, thought it was because his pup was going to die. He knelt beside Flash, who had not even wagged his tail that morning. He was a small, sick, sorry little beast, the bite on his paw a swollen mass.

Angus examined the paw, his face revealing none of his thoughts. "I can't promise, Geordie," he said. "I'll do what I can."

Flash did not even lift his head when the needle went in. He was in a lonely world of pain, aware of little that went on around him.

"Keep him warm, and I'll be back this evening," Angus said.

Tom had been down to the village with the snow plough and come back with a large supply of fresh bones. He started to make bone broth in the pressure cooker.

Geordie would not leave the hearthrug and Andrew watched him, wishing he could reach the boy. He had little hope for the pup, and the note in his pocket burned into his mind. Somehow, he had to tell Geordie that his grandmother had died and been buried while they were snowed up, and that the boy was to go to his mother's cousin, Jennie, in Manchester. He couldn't tell him now. Wait and see what happened to the pup.

At lunchtime Geordie barely ate. Neither man knew what to say to the boy. There were some things that no amount of consolation could ease. Later, in the pigsty, where Queenie was suckling twelve little pigs, Andrew showed Tom the note.

"Better if the dog dies," Tom said. "The boy can't take it to Manchester with him. No life for a collie."

It was a thought that had not occurred to Andrew, who found himself in a dilemma. He didn't want the pup; and who would take it? An untrained dog was a danger on the farm with no one to watch over him. Worry needled him all day, so that when he came in at teatime he was surly and in no mood to break his news to Geordie.

Angus returned at six.

"I haven't told him," Andrew said. "I don't know how; not now. Is that pup going to live?"

Angus shrugged. The pup had not moved from the hearthrug;

had not even lifted its head. "I can't do much more," he said. "Another injection."

The slow evening passed. Tom had gone home. Andrew sat, trying to read the paper, one eye on the boy. Geordie said nothing when spoken to. He sat on the rug, the pup's head on his knee, stroking, stroking. Flash did not respond, not even by the faintest twitch of his tail. Twice Andrew tried to speak, to tell Geordie about Sheena's death, but the words would not come, and the time crept on. The boy should be in bed, but he would only fret. Andrew could not bear to send him upstairs.

Geordie fed the pup with bone broth every hour, dripping it into Flash's mouth from a tiny eye dropper. There was medicine too. Geordie added the medicine to the broth; it was easier to give both together. He lifted the pup's head.

The warm drops fell on the dog's tongue. There was a flicker in the brown eyes. A moment later, the pup swallowed, by himself, without the need to stroke his throat.

He swallowed a second time, and his tongue licked his chops. Geordie dripped in a third drop, almost holding his breath. Had he imagined it? Had the pup moved? Had his expression changed?

Andrew was watching. He remembered an old dodge he had used before on animals near to death. He fetched the brandy bottle and poured six drops from it into the saucer of bone broth. "Try that, lad," he said.

Geordie re-filled the pipette. He squeezed the rubber bulb, and the warm brandy-laced broth dripped into the pup's mouth. He swallowed. Geordie emptied the pipette. "Shall I give him more?" he asked.

Andrew nodded. The pup took all the broth in the saucer. Megan washed the sticky lips, and the pup nosed her, and curled against her; this time, he slept.

"He's turned the corner," Andrew said. "Bed, lad. I'll watch over him tonight." He watched the boy's smile.

"Can I have something to eat, please?" Geordie asked.

Andrew went out into the kitchen to warm milk and to make toast, and knew, as he did so, that he was going to miss the child. He did not want to part with him. If only he and Elspeth had had a child . . . but there was no point in that thought. He had never wanted to marry again; there was no time for courting, and it needed a special kind of person to take on the job of a farmer's wife. But a son. . .

Geordie ate for the first time since the pup had become ill. Flash woke and wagged his tail when Geordie spoke.

"He's getting better," Geordie said. He bent to hug the pup before going up to bed, and Andrew knew he could not break bad news tonight. The lad needed sleep, and would sleep dreamless now.

"Sleep well," he said, as Geordie went towards the door.

The boy paused and looked back. "Grandy's dead, isn't she?" he said.

Andrew stared at him, startled. "How did you know?"

"You'd have said if she'd been all right," Geordie said.

He went out of the room, leaving Andrew staring into the fire, pondering the extraordinary mentality of children. Geordie showed no emotion whatever. But perhaps he had exhausted his capacity for feeling in the past few days. He had not even asked where he was to go.

Andrew fed the pup and dosed it again at two o'clock. This time the pup cooperated, taking the broth greedily. It was definitely on the way to recovery. Andrew went up wearily to bed, yet once there he dreaded the thought of the morning. He did not want to tell Geordie he was to go and live in Manchester. He wondered if perhaps he could phone the unknown cousin and ask her to take the dog.

He woke to find he had overslept and Tom was shaking him. "One of the milkers is down," Tom said. "I rang Angus. They've repaired the line. Have you told the boy?"

"I didn't need to. He guessed," Andrew said.

"The pup's on its feet," Tom said, as he went out of the room.

Andrew dressed and went in to see Geordie. The boy was still sound asleep, and Andrew let him sleep on. The morning was bitingly cold, and Andrew shivered as he went outside and walked across the yard.

Tom was talking to Queenie at the top of his voice, always an ominous sign. "The man's daft, lass," he was saying, his back expressing all his indignation. "Sending the boy to someone he doesn't even know when he could stay here, where he gets on. He won't settle in Manchester with that fancy cousin. And it'll break him to leave the pup."

Andrew walked away. It was bad enough to have to tell Geordie; and he had enjoyed having the boy around. He grew more irritable as he began the milking. The old machine needed replacing and the pump stopped twice; the cows seemed more than usually awkward. By the time milking was done and the churns lugged outside to the tractor, Andrew's temper had risen so that he snapped at Tom, and Tom walked off, furious in his turn.

Geordie had made bacon and eggs. The pup was lapping bone broth, and when he saw Andrew his tail wagged. He stumbled on three legs to the door, asking to go out. Andrew examined the paw.

The swelling was less; and soon Angus would be here to give another injection. The pup was definitely mending. It was astonishing how quickly an animal could recover.

Tom stumped into the room.

"I'm ready for that; looks good," he said, and was rewarded by Geordie's vivid smile. Andrew stabbed his fork into a slice of bacon. He couldn't tell the boy; not today. Let him enjoy himself for a while longer. The cousin wouldn't be coming for some time, surely. He would tell the boy tomorrow.

It was a decision he was to regret.

By lunchtime the pup was hungry, and Geordie fed him with some more of the bone broth. He wondered if the pup would eat something, perhaps just a little fish, and he went into the kitchen, carrying Flash snuggled securely in his arms, just as a large new Jaguar drew up in the farmyard.

The kitchen hearth was swept, the fire burning cheerfully; the highly polished wooden overmantel reflected the flames, and Flash sat to watch his shadow, his ears pricked, the brightly interested expression back on his face. Geordie glanced up at the calendar. Twelve days since Grandy had been buried. Andrew had promised to take him to put flowers on the grave, but Geordie did not want to go. Grandy and he had visited his parents' grave and the green mound and headstone had had nothing to do with them at all. He wanted to remember them playing with him, laughing with him, not dead and buried in the ground, and he wanted to remember Grandy as she had been in life.

There had been voices outside, and now they came closer. A strange woman's voice; and a strange man. Geordie stood up. Flash, startled by strangers coming into the room, barked for the first time in his life, a high falsetto yelp that appeared to surprise him as much as it astounded Andrew and Geordie.

"He *is* better," Andrew said. "Geordie, this is your cousin Jennie from Manchester."

"I've come to take you home with me," Jennie said. Geordie stared at her. She was younger than Andrew, and pretty, with curly red hair and a pleasant face and smile. She was tall, and the smartly dressed man who stood beside her, frowning slightly, was even taller than Andrew.

Geordie did not know what to say.

"This is my fiancé, Jonathan Broome," Jennie said. "He very kindly drove me up to fetch you, as I have to be back in school tomorrow. I'm a teacher. I've made my spare room all ready for you; you'll like it, Geordie."

Geordie said nothing. He felt as if he were a parcel, to be wrapped up and taken away; never consulted as to what *he* wanted.

"Perhaps you could pack some things and send the rest later," Jennie said to Andrew. "I'm sure you don't want to be bothered with a boy about the place when you're so busy. We are very grateful to you for looking after him."

"I can pack," Geordie said. He marched out of the room, determined not to show Andrew that he cared. So Andrew didn't want him and had telephoned this beastly cousin, and he was to go off to Manchester; to live in a ghastly flat in a ghastly town in England. He had never been further south than Carlisle and even that had felt foreign, with the people talking strangely.

Andrew wished this cousin had not turned up out of the blue without warning. And now, whatever he said, Geordie would resent. Andrew had seen the sudden stillness in the boy's face.

"I was quite willing to keep the boy," he said awkwardly.

"He needs his family; and his mother and I were as close as sisters," Jennie said.

Her voice carried up the stairs. Geordie had not heard Andrew's words; only Jennie, used to making her voice heard above classroom noises, had been audible. Geordie went up wearily as if every step were a mountain. His head ached and he felt sick.

There was a nudge at his ankle. Flash had followed him. He carried the pup up, and pushed his clothes into the holdall. Then he picked up the pup and the holdall and went down.

333

"Will you stay for a meal?" Andrew asked.

"We must get back," Jennie said. "We'll stop on the motorway. Are you ready, Geordie?"

Geordie nodded, and began to walk towards the car, holding Flash tightly.

Jennie caught her fiancé's eye. "Oh Geordie, no. We can't have a dog in the flat," she said. "We're in the middle of a town. In a lovely street, with trees, but nowhere for a dog. He'll be better here and I'm sure Mr. Grant will give him a very good home."

Geordie stared at her, and then at the distance to the door. Suppose he ran past her, raced out fast and up the hills, and tracked over the pass to Angus and the twins. They'd have him, and the dog. But he knew, even as the thought entered his head, that it was impossible. Andrew and Tom would find him and send him to his cousin. They didn't want him; and he hated them both for the false faces they had shown him.

He put the pup down on the hearth and walked out to the car.

"I hope you know what you're doing," Jonathan said acidly, as they walked down the path. "He's a surly little devil."

"So would you be in his place," Jennie snapped. She had not been thinking about the boy's point of view when she made her plans; but what other choice was there? And she had never dreamed of a dog. But he'd soon get over that; he would take a day or so to settle. Boys had short memories and the novelty of living a much more interesting life would soon compensate for the loss of his pet.

Andrew wanted to grab Geordie and snatch him out of the car. The boy sat there, staring ahead, and did not reply when Andrew spoke. The farmer watched the car drive out of the farmyard, and then went indoors. The room had never been so empty. He called the pup to him, but Flash had seen Geordie go and he sat in the middle of the hearthrug and howled.

Not even Megan could soothe the pup.

CHAPTER THREE

Jonathan drove fast, overtaking ruthlessly, cutting in sharply, hooting impatiently at anyone in his way. They stayed in the outside lane, often exceeding the speed limit, twice touching a hundred

334

miles an hour. Jonathan was proud of his driving, and was showing off to Jennie. He had totally forgotten that the child's parents had died in a crash in which he also had been injured.

Geordie felt sick. The old feeling of terror snatched at his throat. He closed his eyes and leaned back.

When they stopped at the service station Jennie shook him. "Come on and eat," she said. She was feeling worried; the child looked green.

Geordie stared at her, and then began to shiver uncontrollably. "I'm not hungry," he said.

"Come on and don't be stupid," Jonathan said angrily. He had not planned this sort of weekend at all. The boy was a damned nuisance and Jennie was an idiot to try to make a home for him. There were plenty of institutions to put him in where he'd be much happier.

Geordie followed them miserably into the restaurant. He had a lump in his throat so big that he could scarcely swallow. When the meal ended he climbed back into the Jaguar, a small trapped animal.

Jonathan drove even more impatiently. Geordie flattened himself against the back of the seat, waiting for the impact, his shivering so pronounced that Jennie was worried. She wished she had not been so ready to take on this responsibility, but she had taken it on and she was renowned for her obstinacy. Geordie should have a home again, a home with her. She owed that to her aunt, Geordie's grandmother, who had rescued Jennie when she herself was left an orphan at sixteen.

The journey ended at last. Jonathan dropped them at the door, refusing to come in. He had no time for this surly shivering little wreck, he drove off as soon as he had put Geordie's holdall on the kerb, the tyres screaming.

Jennie set her lips and led the way indoors, twisting her expensive sapphire and diamond ring round her engagement finger. Geordie followed after one disgusted glance down the street. Nothing but houses; tree-lined pavements certainly, but only tiny patches of ground in front of each tall three-storey building.

From inside, the sole view from Geordie's bedroom was a small backyard, and the rear of an equally ugly house. Geordie looked round the room. Jennie had left him, intending to heat some soup, as she was worried about the shivers that racked the boy. He sat on the bed, and reached out a hand automatically for Flash.

335

There was no dog there.

Pent-up sobs choked him, and when Jennie came in with the soup she did not know what to do. Finally she brought a cold flannel and washed Geordie's face. He did not look at her, ashamed that she should have found him crying, and then he came down and sat in front of her electric fire and drank the soup. It warmed him, and the shivering eased.

Jennie began to mark a pile of exercise books. She did not know what to say. She had thought herself experienced with children, but she was beginning to realize a child in a classroom was one thing; a child in her home was something else again. She had had visions of a responsive little boy, eagerly accompanying her on expeditions to the town's museums and art galleries, helping her about the flat, chattering to her when they ate, grateful for her provision for him. She had not realized that Jonathan hated children, and she had not realized till now that Geordie himself might not fit her picture.

"When I marry Jonathan," she said, "we're going to live in a lovely house on the edge of the country; a big black and white house. There's a lovely lawn where you can play football; and a swimming pool. You'll have your own room and we'll choose the furniture together. That'll be fun, won't it?"

Her voice died away. The boy was staring at her, without expression. "Can I have Flash there?" he asked.

Jennie was exasperated. She was exhausted by the day and unhappy at Jonathan's reaction to her plan. "No," she said angrily. "I hate dogs."

There was a moment's silence. Geordie stood up. "I'll go to bed now. Thank you for the soup. Thank you for bringing me here." His voice was formal and remote.

Jennie watched him go out of the room, a small, desperately lonely little figure. She sat staring at the books, knowing she had failed the child, but not knowing how.

It was very late when she went to bed. She looked in at the boy. He was lying on his back, wide awake. He did not answer when she said goodnight.

THE WEEKS THAT followed made little difference to their relationship. Geordie was formally polite, thanking her for meals and going off to his new school, where he sat in class and stared out of the

336

window all day, pretending that out there, just out of sight, was a busy farmyard. Andrew had written once, telling him that Flash was better, although very lame, and that the twins had adopted the pup. He would have a good home at the vet's house.

Geordie's end of term report was atrocious, but when Jennie chided him he only stared at her, and said nothing. Jonathan's visits were rare now, and there was little talk of the new house or the wedding. When he did call, he sat smoking cigarette after cigarette, glowering at the boy, and Geordie, who knew perfectly well that he should have gone to his room, sat by the fire and read, refusing to be tactful. Jennie would make frantic conversation and cups of coffee, and wish she had never offered Geordie a home.

The only bright spot in Geordie's life was the weekly letter from Davina, the vet's daughter, giving news of Flash. Once she sent a photograph, but that was too painful to look at and Geordie put it at the bottom of a drawer. Otherwise, life was a routine: getting up and going to school, where he felt even more alien than at Jennie's flat. His soft Scots burr made the other children laugh and he could not always understand their flat northern vowels. They mocked him and laughed at his limp, some of the bigger boys walking behind him with exaggerated mimicry.

The only man with whom he felt at ease was the biology master, Charles Vicars, whom the boys called Chas. Chas had been born in the country and hated the town. He found out Geordie's background, having been worried by the small set face at the back of the classroom, and was interested by the drawings of sheep, cattle and horses that invariably decorated Geordie's rough notebooks.

"That horn's at the wrong angle," Chas would say, pausing by Geordie's desk. "If it's a Rough Fell, and that's what it looks like, the horns are curved more."

One day Chas took him off at break to help clean out the rabbit hutches. There was one big black and white buck that behaved like a dog, rubbing against a caressing hand, and Geordie, overcome with longing for Flash, held the rabbit against him and tried to swallow the lump in his throat. He went back to the rabbits that evening after school and helped Chas feed them, and then helped with the goldfish and the gerbils, relaxed for the first time since he had left Scotland. He found himself telling Chas about the farm; and then about his dog.

Chas listened, recognizing that here indeed was a child out of context: imprisoned as surely as any animal in a cage. He watched the boy's face close again when he suggested it was time that he went home, and wished he could wave a magic wand and transport the boy back to the hills where he belonged.

Geordie did not want to go home. He loitered, looking into shop windows. He stopped to stroke a Labrador dog lying at a gate. He knelt beside it, wishing desperately that it was Flash. And then he determined that he would ask if he could go back, back to live somewhere where he could have the dog.

The decision gave him the energy to run. He reached the house and hurried up the stairs. Jennie's flat was on the first floor.

The voices sounded through the door as he came up to the landing. "I am not tying myself to a woman who is always going to have a child at her heels." Jonathan's voice was furious. "I never see you alone. That damned boy sits there with a face as long as a yard measure, and he's going to haunt us for the rest of our lives. Get him into some home. Why on earth should you throw away your life for someone else's brat?"

"His mother was almost a sister to me, and his grandmother took me in when my parents died," Jennie said, equally furiously. "I know how he feels. Poor little devil. He's not been here a term yet, give him a chance."

"You have your choice now," Jonathan said. "Take it or leave it. You get him into an orphanage, or the wedding's off."

"Take your damned ring," Jennie shouted. "I'm glad I found out what you're like before the wedding. You're a mass of selfishness. Get out and don't ever come back."

The door opened and Geordie hastily flattened himself among the coats as Jonathan stormed out, slamming the door behind him. A few seconds later came the sound of tyres protesting as the car skidded away, the engine roaring. Geordie stayed where he was. He had not known that Jennie had been orphaned too, or that his grandmother had been her aunt and had given her a home. That explained a lot. He suddenly felt sorry that he had been so surly. She had been trying, but he hadn't helped. And now her wedding was off, and all because of him.

He went into the kitchen. Jennie was chopping onions, her eyes watering and red.

338

"Hi," she said, smiling at him. "Come and cry with me. We're going to have oodles and oodles of fried onions. They're a passion of mine, but the place smells of them for hours afterwards, so I don't often cook them. We're on our own tonight, and I don't mind the smell, do you?"

"I love fried onions," Geordie said.

Jennie cooked steak and game chips, and peas as well as the fried onions; and Geordie laid the table for the first time. They ate in silence, but Jennie, in spite of her own misery, was aware of a change in the boy. She was aware, too, of her ringless finger; aware that there was now a great gap in her life which would have to be filled; and, rather surprisingly, aware, as she ate, of a sense of relief, because she was free to choose what she would do. She would walk in the hills again; the boy would like that.

"I forgot," she said, "There's a letter for you."

Geordie took the letter, and asked the question that he had been hesitating over all evening.

"Jonathan? Our wedding's off, Geordie. We're not right for one another. He won't be coming here again. Now, off to bed with you."

She needed time alone. Time to absorb the hurt.

Geordie went off to his room and opened Davina's letter. Davina was an untidy writer, her letter full of blots and crossed-out words, sprawling across the page.

Dear Geordie,

I don't know how to tell you. Flash ran away. He went two weeks ago but we hoped we'd find him. Dad thinks he's gone to look for you as he's been seen near Andrew's.

But he's killing sheep. The farmers are looking for him, and going to shoot him. There isn't anything we can do. He won't come if we call though we've been near him twice. He just runs off. I'm sorry Geordie. We did try. Dad said I had to tell you. I hope you like it in Manchester.

Love,
Davey.

Desolation settled over Geordie as he thought of his dog alone on the moors, out in the dark night and the rain; so hungry that he was chasing the sheep and killing them to keep himself alive. He sat on his bed and stared at the lighted windows of the houses that backed onto theirs. A woman bathed a small boy in front of a fire; another woman held a baby against her, while a man sat at a table by the window, his head bent over his work. Families; with children and parents together.

Only he belonged nowhere. He had ruined Jennie's life.

He read the letter again. He knew what he had to do.

SPRING HAD BEEN MORE than a rumour when Flash had run away. There were lambs on the hills, primroses in the woods, flowers on the slopes of the mountains. Trees were blossom-laden. The twins had taken the dogs out for a long romp beyond their garden, hoping the dejected Flash might liven up. For weeks he had driven everyone mad by lying near the gate and leaping up every time he heard a car in the distance. He could not understand that Geordie was not coming back.

Flash had never been outside the garden walls. Now he sniffed at the heather; he lifted his head and smelled the air. There were scents that reminded him of home; the rank reek of sheep and the grassy breath of cattle. He recognized that somewhere beyond the mountain was a familiar place where he belonged. Flash ran up the hill. Davina and Donald chased the dog, calling, but they could not catch him.

Flash ran until he was exhausted, and then dropped to rest by a mountain burn that spilled out of the rocks. He drank briefly, and lay panting, savouring the sunshine that warmed him. Then he slept.

When he woke, the sun had slipped behind the mountains, and it was cold and dark. There were stars in a remote sky, and the world was very large and, suddenly, very frightening. An owl hooted, long and low. There was the sharp tang of a running fox; the scent of rabbit.

Rabbit. Flash had never hunted for food, had never been left hungry in his life, but now instincts were roused in him. He knew how to run without frightening the small creature that browsed unheeding; knew how to crouch; and how to make the final snaking dash and the quick neck-biting kill. He fed on warm raw meat for the first time in his life, and with the meal the memory of civilization deserted him. He found a narrow cave in the rock and crept there out of the wind, and slept.

He was still a pup, half-grown, but now age-old instinct taught him. He learned to find shelter from the rain among the craggy tumbled rocks. He learned to herd the sheep, for fun, packing them on the hill. There were no farms near, and no one saw him. On the second evening of his freedom he came upon four fox cubs. He was used to Angus's pet fox, and he watched them play. One of them, a dog fox as big as Flash, saw the collie and came forward, curious. He stood, one paw raised, then bent his front legs in invitation, and Flash flirted his tail and began to romp. They played at tag and rolled together, biting and kicking, until the vixen returned, a rabbit in her mouth. At her inquiring bark, Flash vanished, remembering the still-painful paw that caused him to limp on three legs when it began to ache. The poison had gone, but the muscles were drawn tight, shortened as the injury healed. Flash would always be lame, though he could run as swiftly as any other dog. Now he skirted the stream, making his way steadily back to Andrew's farm.

Flash's herding instinct was strong. Again that evening he herded the lambs, unable to resist the need that drove him, running round them, moving them gently, patiently, into a huddle. Then he stopped to drink at a stream, and nibbled the heather. He was hungry. He had not fed since he caught the rabbit.

He remembered men. There would be food in the village. He ran towards the houses, came to the road and watched a car speed by, and chased it hopefully for a moment, but it vanished in the distance. The dog plodded on. He was very small and he was lonely again. The car had reminded him of his master.

He came to a cottage and ran under the gate. There was food by the back door, a saucer for the old tomcat. Flash ate the bread soaked in milk, and turned just in time to dodge the old warrior who leaped at him. He barked and ran back onto the moors.

That night was wet. Flash found some protection from the rain at the back of a shelter where two horses were standing patiently. The wind was wailing with eerie persistence over the moors, cutting right through the shelter. Flash crept further in and discovered two scattered hay bales, put down for fodder. The hay was warm, and he pushed himself into its depths and slept.

The next day was a Saturday, a bright sunny day that tempted walkers onto the hills. Flash hid from the shouts and calls and the heavy thump of boots, but the warmth tempted two hardy Scouts to camp. They set up their tent under the lee of a sheer rock face and went off to find water, leaving food in polythene bags among their belongings. Flash watched their shapes disappear round a corner, and then he went hunting inside the tent, pulling aside the polythene that wrapped bread and cakes and sandwiches. He found a foil-covered parcel containing a pound of stewing meat, and fed until he was so full that he could barely walk.

He left the tent and made his way to a small cave above the burn, where he curled up and slept. The Scouts, returning, found chaos, and thought they had been visited by a fox. They grumbled as they set off down the long road to the village to replenish their stores from the village shop.

Flash slept until late on the Sunday afternoon and then he started off towards Andrew's farm again, travelling slowly over a long scree that ended in a grassy plain crowded with sheep. The dog could not resist them. He herded them expertly, unaware that he was watched by two climbers above the scree, fascinated by his expertise, who later that evening spoke to a shepherd they met on his way home. The shepherd was worried to think of a collie loose on the hill. It might turn killer. But he knew Flash was missing, and that the dog was harmless and only half-grown, and consoled himself with thinking that the stray must indeed be Flash.

He in his turn spoke of the incident the next evening in the local bar. "There's a sheepdog working alone on the hill," he said.

"It will be the pup that Angus lost, without a doubt," said old Rory MacFarlane, brushing away a rim of beer from his hang-draggle moustache. "But we will have to catch it, all the same. You never know when hunger might prompt a stray to kill."

Tom Fazackerley, who had been standing at the corner of the bar, looked up. Tom was worrying about the dog. Let it develop a taste for sheep . . . that did not bear thinking about.

FLASH HAD BEEN RUNNING wild for a week when the shepherd from the farm beyond the long corrie strode over the hills with his own dog Fly. They worked the sheep together, and Sandy Ferguson freed one five-year-old from a tangle of thorny sticks and separated two lambs that seemed sickly and that he could drive home. His dog brought the ewes to them; and then Fly growled, deep and long and low.

Sandy followed the dog's gaze. There, a few hundred yards away, a black and white collie was crouched over a dead lamb, the throat torn from it and the body part eaten.

Sandy sent Fly after the intruder, but there was no time to give chase. He had work to do and whistled his dog back, cursing. A killer loose on the hill was trouble indeed. Few people realized how wild a dog could be; even a pet dog, brought up very carefully, could wreak havoc. Poodle or terrier, all had an urge to kill that could not be denied when the hunting instinct took over. That night, in the bar, Sandy told of the killing, and faces grew grim.

"We'll have to shoot it," old Rory said, his blue eyes fierce. He loathed a collie turned killer more than any other dog; it was sheer treachery.

"Flash would not kill sheep," Tom said obstinately from his corner.

"There is no other collie straying," Sandy said. "We would have heard. And none of us has a dog that wanders."

Tom swallowed his drink without tasting it and went off to tell Andrew. There was no choice now for any of them. Every farmer on the hill would be carrying his gun; it was only a matter of time.

Andrew listened, his face set. He wished more than ever that he had fought to keep Geordie. He knew Davina wrote; and Angus had said that Geordie's answering letters contained nothing but questions about Flash. Long after Tom had gone, Andrew sat by the fire sucking an empty pipe, unable to face his bed.

FLASH WAS NOW no longer a dog that was cared for and fed: basic instincts had revived in him and taught him how to survive. He had learned that men were unpredictable. Some shouted at him and threw stones.

He learned to hate bad weather, sheltering from the high mountain snow in a tiny cave. He learned to read the wind, which told him of shepherds and sheep moving on the mountainside, and of other men about, hiking or climbing. He learned to hide, using the heather as cover, running low against the ground, freezing. And the wind brought news of food.

343

Flash was hard and lean. His small body was all muscle, and he was ranging further than any sheepdog in the course of its daily work. He wandered in an immense circle, the centre of which was Andrew's farm, in an ever present hope that one day Geordie would return. The memory never faded. Flash had given his allegiance for all time and no other man would own him. Often he lay, nose on paws, watching the farm below, waiting for the sight of a small figure running.

The days passed. The need to shelter from rain drove Flash to hunt the hillside more thoroughly, and he found an abandoned fox earth. He widened the den at the end of the tunnel and lay there, dry for the first time for days. The earth became his home.

He knew that guns could kill. He had seen rabbits die. One day, having hunted fruitlessly on the mountainside, he went across the hill among the sheep. The shepherd, seeing a stray collie, was sure that this was the killer that had already been reported, and peppered Flash with shot. The dog was almost out of range, but the pellets stung, and added yet another fear to those that had begun to master the dog.

CHAPTER FOUR

Geordie lay awake all through the night, thinking of Davina's letter. He had visions of his dog running on the hills, alone, untended. Geordie knew what that meant in farming country. There would be no second chance for Flash. And Flash would not come for the twins, nor for Angus. He would not go to Tom or to Andrew. But he would come for Geordie. Geordie knew just how the ears would lie flat against the small black and white head, the way the dog's body would race towards him. Flash would never kill again if Geordie were there to look after him, and Geordie knew he would find Flash as soon as he began to search the hill.

The church clock struck four. Geordie switched on his light and dressed himself, and then packed his small holdall. He opened his wallet, a present from Andrew, together with five pounds that Angus had sent to him as a birthday present. There was also his pocket money for the term, as there was nothing he wanted to spend it on. All he had bought was a new lead for Flash, sure that

Andrew would invite him for the summer holidays. He took it out of the drawer, and added it to his clothes.

He switched off the light and opened the door carefully, then slipped out onto the dark landing and crept down close to the wall. He unbolted the front door, opened it, and went outside. In front of him the empty street was a long desert, the tall houses dark, the only light small pools cast by the street lamps on damp pavements. Geordie drew a deep breath. He had more than ten pounds, enough, he hoped, to get him to Scotland by train.

There were no buses till six o'clock. But the bus stop was close to a house which had a high fence, and behind the fence were thick shrubs. Geordie could hide till daylight. He settled himself under a bush with his holdall acting as a cushion behind him, against the trunk of a tree.

He dozed, and woke to find there was a thin drizzle falling. He crept out, looking carefully up and down the street, but there was no one about. He walked briskly to the bus stop, arriving at the same time as the bus, which would, he knew, take him to the local station. There he could catch a train to Manchester, and from there an Inter City train to Glasgow; his station was on the Glasgow to Oban line, and he could walk from the station to Angus's house. The twins would help him.

The bus was almost empty; the conductress was half asleep and she did not even spare a second glance for him. He had packed his clothes in a bag that could have been a school bag, and he wore his school cap.

He was not yet twelve and small for his age, and the booking clerk at the station did not query the half-price ticket. Geordie sat back in a half-empty compartment and relaxed for the first time.

By the time the train reached Manchester he was very hungry. His ticket to Glasgow bought, he had nearly four pounds left over, and he had half an hour to spare. He bought a ham sandwich and sat eating, feeling sure that everyone was staring at him and knew he was running away. He had not left a message for Jennie; he had intended to write her a note, but in the excitement of packing and leaving unseen had totally forgotten to do so. Would she alert the police?

Geordie stuffed his school cap into his bag and joined the crowd on the platform. The train was on time, and he watched Manchester

slide away. Soon they were beyond streets, running across bleak moors, and then he slept.

The train stopped and he woke with a jump. A woman was sitting opposite him. She was plump, grey-haired and wore spectacles which did not hide the fact that her blue eyes were kind. She looked like a safe, serene grandmother.

"Better for your sleep, love?" she asked, with a little smile, as Geordie blinked at her.

"Yes, thank you," he said.

"I've made far too many sandwiches and you can help me eat them. Travelling makes me feel proper clemmed, and I feel a pig eating alone."

Geordie had been long enough in Manchester to know that "clemmed" meant hungry. Come to think of it, he was proper clemmed too, and he had never tasted sandwiches like hers: fresh home-baked bread, wonderful butter, and delicious fillings. The woman bought chocolate and coffee from the trolley that came round and shared it with Geordie, talking all the time, telling him of her own grandson, Stephen, and how he liked animals.

"Going visiting your gran?" she asked.

Geordie shook his head.

"Friends," he said. "They're twins. They live in Scotland."

"I'm only going as far as Carlisle," the woman said. "We'll be there any minute now. I'll leave you the rest of my sandwiches. I won't need them and you look like you could do with fattening up."

Geordie was sorry when she left, but he was glad of the food which would save his precious pence. He was not sure he had enough money to take him on to the village where the twins lived.

It was raining when the train reached Glasgow. Geordie wandered forlornly through the streets, with four hours to kill before his connection; the Oban train left at six o'clock. He discovered he had enough money for his ticket and more than a pound to spare, and he spent some of it on sandwiches from a shop round the corner from the station and on two bananas and an apple. Then he added a meat pie in case he could not contact the twins. No use going to Andrew or Faceache or Angus; they would only send him back.

The compartment was half empty. Two men sat opposite one another, discussing sheep prices, and Geordie listened with pleasure to the soft burr, so different from the Manchester accent. It was good to hear his own kind of talk again.

"There's a collie killing sheep on the hill," one of the men said suddenly. "Ten ewes in the last two weeks have been killed, and all from the one farm. We're hunting it on Friday, twelve of us— we should be able to corner it and bring it down."

The train stopped at a halt and the two men got out, without a backward glance at the boy crouched in the corner. Geordie felt sick. He had two days to find Flash. What had made the dog take to sheep killing? Hunger? Faceache had once said that no true collie would turn killer; there had to be a rogue streak. Flash had been gentle and affectionate and had herded sheep gently. He would never kill.

But it was no use running away from facts. Flash *had* killed. Geordie stared into the darkness so miserably that he almost missed his stop.

Angus's house was at the far end of the village street. Geordie did not want to be seen by anyone he knew, so he climbed the wall into the fields behind the houses and plodded through the tussocky grass.

He had been up too long and was very tired. It was hard to put one foot in front of another in the dark and he plunged ankle-deep into a rabbit hole, tripping headlong and knocking the breath out of himself as he hit the ground. He sat, leaning against the wall until the sick feeling had eased. He would have to wait for the moon to rise.

The moon was half full, and the going was easier once the sky was lit. Geordie could see the trees dark against the grey, and the bulk of Angus's house. He walked on, making his way along the grass verge beside the drive round to the front of the house. Davina would be the best contact; Donald was excitable and raised his voice easily, but she always had her wits about her.

Davina slept in the little room over the porch. Geordie threw pine cones expertly at the window, and she opened the sash after some minutes and peered out.

"Davina. It's Geordie. I've come to find Flash."

"Wait!" Davina's voice was urgent.

Geordie sat with his back against one of the big conifers and was so tired that he fell asleep. He woke, sharply aware that Davina and Donald were shaking him. "Have you run away?" Davina asked.

Geordie nodded, yawning. He wanted a bed.

"You'd better come in," Davina said. "Only creep; Mum wakes if a fly breathes."

The moonlit hall was eerie, light glinting on the spears and swords and on the antlered heads around the walls.

"Careful or the dogs will bark," Donald said, and even as he spoke a crescendo of noise broke out. A door opened on the upstairs landing.

"Who's down there?" Angus called.

"It's only me," Donald said. "I came down for a drink."

"For heaven's sake," his father said. "Hurry up and go to bed."

Donald headed for the kitchen, speaking to the dogs, while Davina led Geordie along the carpeted landing and up the second flight of stairs to the attics. She opened a door and they were inside a room in which was stored the junk of ages; more heads mounted on shields; piled trunks and boxes and some battered furniture.

"Behind that old wardrobe there's a camp bed," Davina whispered. "Donald and I play up here sometimes, but no one else ever comes. You can come down when Mum and Dad are busy, and wash. I'll bring you food when I can."

348

"They're going to hunt for Flash on Friday," said Geordie.

"We'll be out before them," Davina promised. "We're not going to school on Thursday. It's a special holiday."

The door closed behind her. Geordie moved uncertainly across the attic and dropped on the bed. He removed his outer clothes and pulled a blanket over him.

He was so exhausted that he slept till Davina crept in with food for him, just before she went off to school.

"Quick," she said. "Everyone's downstairs. Come down and wash. I've brought you Donald's clothes—he's gone outside so anyone who sees you will think it's him."

Geordie slipped like a thief behind Davina. He had never been so glad in his life to wash and clean his teeth. Then Davina hurried him swiftly up the back stairs, and he went to hide again behind the old wardrobe.

Sitting cross-legged on his bed, Geordie ate bread and butter and two sausages, a slice of cheese, a banana and a chicken leg. There were several books on the floor beside the camp bed, and he chose one of them and settled down to read. His watch had stopped, and he had never known that a day could be so long.

Geordie started at every sound, afraid that Catherine might come to the attic. Once he heard a pattering of claws in the corridor outside, and there was a long snuffling at the door. He was terrified that the dogs would give him away.

When Davina came Geordie breathed again. "I've been shopping," she whispered. "Luckily we've just had a birthday. Here's crisps and biscuits and some ham and some bread and butter, and I've pinched one of the kitchen knives. We told the post office we were having a picnic tomorrow."

Geordie sat eating, wondering just how they were going to find Flash in the morning. And what they were going to do when they had found him.

"The police are looking for you," Davina said. "It's in the paper. Mum and Dad think you're making for Andrew's farm. They said you would never settle in a town. Was it awful?"

"Yes," Geordie said. He didn't want to talk about it. Instead, he told Davina about the dogs snuffling at the door.

"You'd better hide in the old shepherd's hut tonight," she said. "They don't use it any more. Mum and Dad are out this evening.

We can leave while they're gone; and you can have a bath and some food and a hot drink."

Geordie stretched out on the bed again when Davina left; he had food and drink and something to read, but for all that he was aware of the noises in the house: a door banging, a sudden barking from the dogs, the coming and going of cars. He jumped when the door opened.

"Come on down. They've gone," Davina said.

It was good to soak in a hot bath. And it was good to walk into the warm kitchen and drink scalding hot soup and eat crusty new bread with butter and honey, and the apple pie and cream that Davina found. Donald was scrambling eggs; the twins did not bother about the order of courses but tended to discuss what they would eat next while eating what was already available. By the time they had finished Geordie was sure he would not want to eat again for several days.

For all that, Davina packed the holdall with more food.

"Mum'll just think we've been piggier than usual," she said, though Geordie was sure she would get into trouble.

Davina stayed at home as the twins had promised to answer the telephone. Donald and Geordie left the house by the back door, climbed the garden wall and set off up the hill. Geordie stared up at the mountains, black against the sky. There was so much country—and where was the dog? He could be anywhere, but if sheep were moving, then the dog would be there for certain. The telltale flocks would give Flash away.

The hut was high on the hill. It was half ruined, the roof open to the sky in several places, and the mud floor was dusty. Donald had brought two sacks which he spread for Geordie, who was wearing jerseys and an anorak and even so was cold. It was going to be a long night.

Geordie could not sleep. There were noises all around him; strange snorting noises that proved to be a sheep snoring; a stamp of a hoof from a deer. Somewhere inside the hut there were noises too, and when the moon rose Geordie found himself staring into a pair of glinting eyes. The animal came towards him and he realized it was only a sheep, and moreover a sheep that must have been hand-reared and was used to people. It settled against him and he huddled up to it, glad of the woolly fleece to keep him warm.

350

Day dawned at last. Geordie went outside. He had been conscious, all night long, of the soft chatter of a burn on the hillside. He could hear it still, but when he reached the door he saw that the world had vanished. He was enclosed by mist. There was not a trace of wind. No one could hunt the dog in this. If only the mist lasted, it would mean one day longer for Flash.

Geordie settled himself in the doorway of the hut, and ate and drank. His spirits had risen: the food was good, the thermos flask of hot coffee was warming. Geordie wrapped himself in a plastic sheet Donald had provided, stretched out on the ground again, and slept. The sheep came back and nosed him. She was an outcast from her own kind, preferring the farmyard where there were titbits to eat. Now, nosing the holdall, the ewe found food and ate until nothing was left. Full and comfortable, she settled beside Geordie and slept.

Geordie woke, hungry, at two in the afternoon. The mist still hid everything, and there was nothing to do but eat again. The torn paper and crumbs in the bag told their own story, and he looked at the culprit. It was his own fault; he should have zipped up the bag. He drank some of the coffee, and found a remnant of cheese. Sometimes mists lasted for two or three days. He could not move, no one could reach him, and

Donald and Davina would think he had enough food for several days.

He sat, watching the mist swirl away and return thicker than ever. Far away, a dog barked and sheep bleated frantically. Was it Flash? Suppose the mist was local, and that there on the other side of the hill, in brilliant sunshine, men were hunting his dog?

CHAPTER FIVE

Jennie had been frantic when she found Geordie gone. She stared, unbelieving, at the neat bed, searched his wardrobe and found clothes missing. She hunted for a note, but there was nothing.

She sat miserably on the edge of his bed. She had thought the boy was settling down; had thought she was giving her cousin's child a better chance than he would have had in the remote country village where she felt that schooling was inadequate. She had no idea of the many skills involved in farming.

She did not know where to start looking. Later that morning she rang Geordie's school to ask if he were there. When she heard he was not, she rang the police.

A constable called on her soon afterwards. He took down particulars, but Jennie could not think where Geordie would have gone. He had never talked to her about any of his real interests— she knew Davina wrote to him, but the boy had taken good care that Jennie never should know how much Flash meant to him and he had taken all Davina's letters with him. Jennie hunted through his room after school that day, but there was nothing personal there.

That evening Chas called on her. He also had been interviewed by a policeman, as he knew more about Geordie than any of the rest of the staff. He was concerned about the boy and ready to condemn the cousin who knew so little about the child that she did not even realize that his main interest lay with animals. Geordie had talked to Chas about his dog, and Chas had recognized the intensity of the boy's feelings, and knew how totally he was rejecting town life.

He soon realized that Jennie did not know because Geordie had never talked to her. She was nothing like what he had expected: Chas had thought she would be a hard woman, unable to under-

352

stand a boy's needs, and instead he found that she was bewildered and vulnerable and overcome by a sense of defeat. He knew at once that she needed help and he was prepared to give it, regardless of his own affairs.

He made Jennie laugh as he told anecdotes about the boys, and by the end of the evening Jennie felt better. She knew she had been wrong, but she knew now that she had failed through lack of knowledge, not through lack of care. Chas reassured her about that, and Jennie found it a relief to talk to him.

"Why not phone the vet in Scotland?" Chas asked. "Perhaps Geordie has gone back there. He often talked about the twins."

But Angus knew nothing and did not think of asking Donald or Davina. Andrew and Tom knew nothing either: Geordie had not been anywhere near the farm, and they were disturbed to hear that he was missing.

Jennie could only wait.

On the Thursday evening, when she was almost sick with worry, thinking of the boy out alone, heaven knew where, the doorbell rang.

"Look," Chas said, as soon as she opened the door. "It's nearly the weekend, and I have Monday off. You said your Head would give you leave of absence. Would you like to come with me to Scotland? I'm pretty sure the boy will make for the farm and for his dog. I know it's a long drive and my car's an old banger, but at least it'll be better for you than sitting here waiting for the phone to ring."

Jennie couldn't pack fast enough. She rang the police station and told them she was making for Scotland. At last she relaxed, aware that she was no longer on her own.

UP IN THE BOTHY on the far side of the mountain, Geordie waited for the twins. In the evening a breeze dispersed the mist, and they came scrambling up with a satchel loaded with food, having spent almost all their pocket money. "I'm starving," Geordie said, grinning at the twins, but not wanting to admit how pleased he was to see them both.

"You had stacks of food," said Davina.

Geordie pointed at the old ewe that was standing in the doorway of the bothy. "*She* had stacks of food," he said. "She ate it all while I was asleep."

353

The twins laughed as Geordie delved hungrily into the satchel. There were crusty fresh rolls filled with ham and cheese, and Donald poured coffee from a flask.

"They won't catch Flash," Davina said. "He's too clever. But he's gone quite wild, Geordie."

It was no longer any use saying Flash wouldn't kill sheep. Flash clearly *had* killed sheep. Donald had seen one of the lambs that had been brought to his father, the only lamb they had been able to save. It had needed eighteen stitches in its wounds.

Geordie tore at his ham roll. He wanted to shout at the injustice of the world. If they hadn't made him go away from his dog, this would never have happened. It wasn't the dog's fault. It was Tom's and it was Andrew's. It was the fault of the lorry driver that killed his parents, Jennie's fault for making him go away. Nothing was fair.

"I'm going to look for Flash now," Geordie said, totally obstinate.

The twins watched Geordie transfer the food from the satchel to his own bag. He set off, his face grim, pausing only once to look back at the twins and wave. He was going over the top of the mountain, and down towards Andrew's farm. It was a dangerous route, and sleeping in the cold and damp had made his leg ache, but if he followed the winding sheep paths he'd avoid the steepest places.

Geordie limped over the rough ground. It was growing dark, and he was coming to an area where there were precipices. He found a small dry cave, ate, and then curled up and slept.

He woke the next morning, stiff and cramped, his leg aching so much that he felt slightly sick. But he had a drink from the burn and plodded on towards the bare peak that towered above. The sun had hidden behind menacing clouds that threatened rain, and after a while Geordie felt as if he had been climbing for ever. The ground was rough and boulder-strewn, and among the boulders were flints and pebbles that would turn an ankle if he went too fast. Yet there was no time to waste. The men would be watching all the time for a small black and white dog, chasing among the sheep.

"Flash. Fl-a-a-sh. Flashie boy, come."

There was not a sound, nor a hint of movement.

The path wound towards the peak, and then rounded it. Geordie followed it, more slowly now, and then quite suddenly he was on the other side of the mountain. He looked down. There was Andrew's farm, seeming miles below him, totally dwarfed, and the village was there, dear and familiar on the other side of the loch.

Geordie stopped and sat on a boulder, staring down. The sheep were at ease, scattered; fleecy grey shapes, black-faced. He knew this hillside, every rock and shrubby bush and every grass patch, and he knew those particular sheep. If only he could go down to the farm and find Tom and Andrew—but they would be angry with him for running away.

Only then did the enormity of his action strike him. Jennie would be frantic, wondering where on earth he had gone.

There was a ewe moving along the ridge. A second joined her and then a third; now an anxious head twisted, the long pathetic nose turning towards something hidden in the heather. Something was shifting them.

"Flash," Geordie shouted, standing up and waving wildly as he glimpsed a black and white back. But the wind carried away Geordie's voice, and the dog took no notice. He was driving the sheep now, moving purposefully, his body crouched against the ground as he eyed first one and then another. Then came the long low running and the instant crouch again, almost as if a shepherd were directing him. But Geordie knew that no man was there.

Geordie looked down on the dog, which was bigger than he had expected. Flash had grown. He was far below, but near enough for Geordie to see the black and white muzzle, the white chest, and the white beneath the tail. The ears, only half lifted before, were now pricked and alert, the red tongue flopping in amusement.

Geordie began to run. If only he could head the dog off—but the sheep trail led nowhere, petering out in a cliff face. There was no way down. It would take more than an hour to make the detour down the mountain, and that would bring him out far away from the dog. In that time Flash could have killed fifty sheep.

Geordie began to retrace his steps, half running, half walking, his breath rasping in his throat. He packed food into his pockets as he went, and dropped the bag. He could return for it later and it hampered him. Then he turned and looked back.

He watched, horrified, as the dog singled out a lamb from the flock and worked it away from its fellows. The lamb was running dementedly, with the collie driving it, relentless and intent. The lamb turned to make its way back to the flock, but the dog snaked swiftly, crouched almost flat, and cut it off and headed it away, wanting it on more even ground where he could leap and kill.

Geordie picked up a stone and flung it, but it fell noiselessly into dense heather. The dog did not even notice its fall.

Geordie began to run along the path, hoping that in spite of everything he could call Flash to him, but it was no use. His leg ached too much, and he had already turned his ankle once on the uneven ground. He sat down, unable to look away from the dog below him. The collie was crouching now, having driven the lamb onto a flat area that was part grass and part rock. The dog moved so swiftly that Geordie lost sight of him for a moment, and then he saw it leap, saw the wild tear at the lamb's throat, saw the gush of blood. The lamb dropped and the collie began to rip at the flesh. Behind him, the sheep moved swiftly away.

Geordie had to believe now. He had seen for himself. He could not go down to the dog, not while he was tearing at the carcass. Flash must be mad, there could be no other reason for his behaviour, and a mad dog might bite even his own master.

Men had been watching too. Geordie saw them approaching, an army on the move, all the shepherds and farmers in the area, the gamekeeper from the forest beyond the Long Glen, the three wardens from the National Trust, all of them carrying guns; a posse hunting an outlaw. A sheepdog ran along the line. Geordie recognized Megan and saw Tom and Andrew walk purposefully into view.

A gun spoke, and on an instant the killer was gone, speeding into cover. Nothing was left except the bloodied fleece on the ground.

Geordie crouched behind a rock. He did not want to be seen. He did not want to face the men yet, or face reality. He needed time to think, time to come to terms with the knowledge that all his dreams were daydreams, the visions of a small boy, not of an adult. How did a pup grow up so bad? What went wrong? The questions were too difficult to answer.

He remembered the little hidden glen where he and Flash had once bathed in a pool below the waterfall. Perhaps the dog would go there to drink.

The glen was sanctuary; a long gully, tree-clad, that cut into the mountain. The pool welcomed him, the water deep and clear and cold, and Geordie washed his filthy hands and face. It was good to rest and ease his aching leg.

Geordie was starving. He had cut himself off from his food supply, for the twins didn't know where he was now and would probably think he had gone to Andrew. To return to the bothy was out of the question. His place was with Flash, whether he was a bad dog or not, and Geordie knew that when Flash died, he must be there to cradle his head, and hope that in those last moments the dog would remember him and know his master had not left him alone for ever.

The men had gone, having scoured the hillside. Geordie was exhausted. He ate some of the chocolate and the raisins, and then he stretched out and slept.

The sun slipped lower in the sky. He woke, startled by the touch of a soft warm tongue. He stared, not daring to move: Flash was sitting watching him, only a handsbreadth away, his tail wagging uncertainly. He was beautiful, even with his matted coat and muddy sides.

Geordie held out his hand, fist clenched. "Flash, good boy. Here then, Flashie," he whispered.

The dog inched forward, almost flat on his belly, his long tail wagging doubtfully. The warm tongue licked Geordie's hand again. Then, somewhere below, a voice shouted. Flash turned and ran, racing up the hillside, and vanished as if he had never been. Geordie rolled over. It was the end of his world.

BELOW HIM on the mountain Tom and Andrew walked back together, guns tucked beneath their arms. Megan followed them, aware that this was no time for frivolity. Today both men were extremely grim.

Andrew's thoughts were busy with Jennie's phone call. He had been shocked to find that Geordie had run away.

"Do you reckon the lad will make for here?" Andrew asked. He wanted Tom to reassure him, to remind him that they had had no choice, but Tom had his own opinions about that.

"It's his home," Tom said, ending discussion, not wanting to think of the lad on his own, so miserable that he had run away from his fancy town-bred cousin, who would never understand the boy in a year of Sundays. They should never have let him go, but no use saying so to Andrew. The man was tormenting himself as it was, and had had more bad news that morning too, as his sister's husband had died of a heart attack the day before, and she with no children and no relative other than Andrew.

As soon as the funeral was over she was coming up from Cornwall to visit, maybe to stay, and Tom was not sure he wanted a woman in the place again, not even a woman he had known as a girl. Maybe Kitty had grown into a tartar who would insist on cleaner habits and tidier behaviour than either he or Andrew had time for. They got on very well as they were, with no need for the niceties. Tom did not like changes in his life.

They turned in at the farm gate, still not speaking. Tom took the hose and the yard broom and began to clean the yard, working with savage determination. Then he called to Andrew. Together they looked at the sky.

The wind was strengthening and tonight would be a wicked night to be out on the mountain: the clouds were riding high, building up from the peaks, the great smoking anvil shapes presaging thunder roll and lightning flash, and water swirling over the falls to flood downwards over the higher pastures. Andrew whistled Megan and walked up the hill. They spent the next few hours working the sheep towards the safer fields lower down.

THE LOWERING STORM brooded all evening. Geordie, hunting for Flash on the hill above the Long Glen, where he had last seen the dog, was unaware of danger. He knew there would be rain, but he had completely forgotten that the streams would grow within

358

minutes to gushing torrents, sweeping everything near them away.

He caught sight of the dog working sheep-high on the skyline and made towards it. Then he stopped, numbed, as lightning cut the sky in two, zigzagging between the clouds. The sheep knew about the thunder rumbles, and made for shelter, working their way to overhangs of rock or the thick clusters of bushes.

Then the dog sprang and killed. Geordie sat helplessly looking on: the animal was far above him, running from one part of the hill to another, killing wherever he chose, not for food, but for the joy of satisfying a new-found blood lust. It was impossible to catch him.

Geordie thought of the draggled animal that had come to him briefly and licked his hand. There was very little time left for his collie. The men were hunting, and they would go on hunting as long as the dog killed. Tomorrow . . . the day after. . .

The rain began, slicing through the sky, battering him with hailstones. Geordie dropped flat in the heather, shielding his face as best he could. There was nowhere else to hide. He was aware of the constant lurid flashing in the sky.

The hail ceased. Geordie ran, ducking and dodging, avoiding the slippery patches of rock, knowing that a fall might mean disaster, or even death. Nobody knew where he was, and it might be too late when they did find him.

There was a deserted cottage a few hundred yards away. Most of the roof had gone but the walls were still standing, and there would be a little protection from the rain. He raced across the open ground, his lame leg dragging at him, and was soaked again in a fresh downpour.

He reached the cottage at last, climbing over fallen bricks and tiles, and settled himself under the shelter of a heavy door put roofwise across the piled bricks by some other stormbound traveller. Rain drummed above him. His teeth were chattering and he huddled in a corner, trying to sleep.

Then the night had gone and it was dawn.

The rain had stopped; Geordie realized he must have slept. He went outside and looked down to a rutted track edged with grass. Above him the bulk of the mountain was white from the hail that lay like snow in the gullies, and beyond him the burn was wild water, swelling over the fall, thundering downwards.

Geordie had to go down. He would have to face Andrew's anger.

If he stayed here, he would die from the cold. He could not stop shivering, and his hands and feet were numb.

He tracked downwards across the barren ground, boulder and flint and intermittent scree, leading to the long gradual grassy slope to the village.

The wind had died with the storm's ending, and the air was very still. Geordie heard the sound first; the familiar but still heart-stopping bleating of a harried flock, somewhere very close. He did not know that men were already there, waiting, and that the dog, racing through the heather, had been seen by a shepherd who gave the signal to Andrew's farm below by waving a white cloth. The message was phoned from farm to farm and now from each farm came a man stalking quietly, gun at the ready.

Geordie had travelled a considerable way down the mountain and was crouched behind a dry-stone wall that separated Andrew's sheep from the moors beyond; the dog was working them away from him on the far side. He could see men ranged all round the field, and he wanted to shout to them, to yell to them to stop, to scream and warn the dog, but if he did so the dog might identify the direction of the sound and run straight into the path of the guns. If he kept quiet perhaps it would sense danger and vanish in the heather.

The dog had no eye for anything but the lamb it was herding. He separated it swiftly from the flock, and it fled, terrified, straight towards Geordie, the dog at its heels.

The guns spoke.

The dog somersaulted twice, and died.

His dog! Geordie ran towards it. He bent to take the body in his arms, and then he stared. Flash had been muddy, but this dog was clean. The white mark down the centre of the head was broader than that on Flash's head, and this dog had four black paws, and a white tip to his tail.

Geordie let the body fall and, as Andrew and Tom reached him, he drummed frantically at Andrew's chest, shouting, "It isn't Flash. It isn't Flash. It isn't Flash."

Andrew examined the dog and bit back the words he had been going to say. The boy was soaked and exhausted and shivering with shock and relief. The farmer put his coat round the boy, and he and Tom carried him back to the farmhouse and rang for the doctor.

CHAPTER SIX

The doctor diagnosed exposure. Andrew travelled in the ambulance on the way to the hospital, holding the boy's hand. Geordie was doped and half asleep, half demented, talking feverishly and rapidly.

"It wasn't Flash," he kept saying.

"No," Andrew replied, soothing him. "It wasn't Flash. It was the dog belonging to the young family at the edge of the Forestry Commission land. The wife goes to work and lets the dog out every morning; she never has the least idea what it's up to all day. You can't keep a sheepdog like that. It needs training and controlling. You have to take care when you buy a collie."

The words were brief comfort.

"I want Flash," Geordie said. "He came . . . he licked me. He's up on the hill. It's cold on the hill. . . . It wasn't Jennie's fault. Jonathan wouldn't marry her with me there. I thought I'd best come. Then he'd come back. It really wasn't the twins' fault either."

Andrew was beginning to glean a story he did not like. He waited until Geordie was comfortably in bed in the hospital and then took the train home and rang Angus.

The vet questioned the twins until Davina was in tears. "You hopeless insane little nitwits," their father shouted at them. "How many times have I warned you about being alone on the mountain? How could you let Geordie go up there all alone? Why didn't you tell us?"

The twins didn't know. It had seemed a good idea at the time and they had been sure Geordie would come to no harm. He had had food and shelter, and it had been good weather when he started out.

"The weather changes fast," Angus said, despairing of his children ever growing up and gaining sense.

The twins were more concerned than they cared to admit when they went with Andrew to visit Geordie in hospital. His soaking in the storm had chilled him, he was flushed and feverish, and the doctors were anxious about his leg. He had strained the healing muscles badly on his journey and would limp worse than before.

By now Jennie and Chas had arrived and were staying in the local hotel. They visited the hospital, neither knowing quite what to say. Geordie was far too ill to be scolded.

"He'll be OK," Chas said that night, seated comfortably in Andrew's big kitchen. "But the Lord knows what you're going to do with him. He'll never settle in a town."

"It was madness to try," Tom said irritably.

"We had no choice," Andrew said. "Jennie had the right; and she had to try, or she would never have forgiven herself."

Jennie smiled at him gratefully.

"I'd like the boy to stay here," Andrew said.

"Without a woman in the house?" Jennie asked.

"My sister's coming to live. Her husband has just died, and I've offered her a home," Andrew said. "We both wanted children and we both missed out. The boy would be more than welcome here with us."

"But what sort of future is there?" Jennie asked doubtfully.

"I've no heirs," Andrew said. "He'd inherit the farm."

GEORDIE HAD ONLY one thought in his mind when Andrew visited him in hospital.

"I've got to find Flash," he said. "I saw him out on the hills."

"No, Geordie, you saw the other dog and mistook him for Flash. There's been bad weather. Flash can't have survived."

"Flash is there," Geordie insisted. "He came and licked my hand. He knew me. Only someone shouted and he ran away."

"Geordie, lad, you dreamed it," Andrew said patiently. The dog had been missing for three weeks. Unless he too were killing sheep. . . There had been enough killed to account for two dogs running wild.

"He wouldn't kill sheep," Geordie said, almost as if he were able to thought-read.

Andrew was unsure. Suppose Flash had kept himself alive by eating the other dog's kills? Suppose he were still out there, killing on his own account? But there had been no more reports of dead lambs since the killer died.

"Please, as soon as I come back, can we look for Flash? Before I go back to Jennie? It's no use anyone else looking; he's got nervous and he'll only come to me."

"All right, we'll look," Andrew promised. For the boy's sake, they would have to try. "But there's been wild weather on the hills and he may well have been swept away in the torrents. The other dog was older, and he was weather wise."

"Flash will know what to do," Geordie said obstinately. Then he reverted to his other big worry. He hadn't intended to say anything, but he couldn't help himself. "Have I got to go back with Jennie? Jonathan said he wouldn't marry her with me around. We had to have fried onions for supper so I couldn't see Jennie had been crying, but I could. Then I got Davina's letter about Flash, so I came home."

Home. One little word. He had lost everybody and everything and now he had lost his dog.

"Would you like to live with me, Geordie?" Andrew asked. "I wanted to have you before, but Jennie *is* your family and she'd never have forgiven herself if she hadn't tried; it's no one's fault it didn't work. My sister's coming to live with me, as her husband died suddenly last week. She'd like to have you there too. And the farm can be yours when you grow up, if you want it. There's nobody else."

Geordie said nothing, but the hand that gripped Andrew's so fiercely told the farmer all he wanted to know.

"We'll look for Flash, I promise," Andrew said.

That night, Geordie lay awake savouring the thought of returning to the farm. Now at last, home had some meaning.

FLASH HAD LEARNED a great deal while he was running free. He had learned to avoid the killer dog and had learned about weather and wind. But the storm on the hills was worse than anything he had ever endured in his short life.

Lightning cleft the sky. Lightning flashed continually, it forked and struck the ground. He had never known such rain.

First came the hail, savaging his small body so that he crouched soaked and helpless under the lee of a rock that gave little protection. Then the water began to rise. The bed of the burn was of boulders tumbled together, and as the surging water pounded down the mountains the boulders began to roll, echoing the thunder crash. The dog had to change his resting place. He fled, herded by the noises, not noticing where he was running. Finally he crept

364

into cover among thick shrubby bushes, digging at the ground to make a den for himself, and remained there till the storm was over.

When the long, wild night was over he dried himself in the sunshine, and then made his way towards Andrew's farm. Now fear of another storm was greater than his fear of man.

He skirted the long gash of raw earth torn by the avalanche. Beyond it was a riverbed which he had known only when it was dry, for there had been very little rain on the hills since he had run away. Now it was a seething torrent. He began to climb higher, away from the water.

The rain had made the ground so muddy that the dog slipped and fell into the water, hurtling downwards in a maelstrom of white surf. He was battered by the branches of trees as he paddled frantically, trying to keep his head above the surface. A long spur projected from the cliff face into the pool. At last he managed to haul himself out, and dropped flat, panting.

The sun, blazing now from a clear sky, dried his fur. But Flash was cut off. He was marooned on the rocky spit, penned against the wall of the cliff, and he dared not face the fierce water again. He ran to and fro on the ledge, barking, but there was no one to hear. At last he curled up and slept a deep sleep of sheer exhaustion.

When he woke, he lapped at the water, and slept again. The will to live was weakening. He was bruised, and had not fed for two days.

BEFORE CHAS AND JENNIE had driven back to Manchester, Jennie had assured Geordie that all was well with her; that she did not blame him for wanting to come back to Andrew, nor for Jonathan's defection. That would have happened in any case: they were not right for one another.

She had met Kitty, who had arrived the night before. Andrew's sister was pleased to find she would have something to distract her from her own grief. Yet Geordie could talk of nothing else but his dog, and Kitty wondered what they would do when the boy was at last convinced that his dog had died. For no one believed that Flash was still alive; it was impossible that so young a dog could survive alone on the mountain. If he had not perished before, he must surely have died in the storm. Running water was everywhere. The mountain gushed white.

Andrew did not want Geordie to go with them on the search, but Kitty recognized the pent-up tension in the boy and thought it would be better for Geordie if he went. His leg was still aching, but he was not going to admit that. No one was going to keep him at home.

Andrew and Tom were striding ahead, Megan at heel. She turned back, barking at Geordie, and the two men paused, waiting for the boy to catch up. Geordie had borrowed a pair of binoculars and was sweeping the hillside with them. Scree, and the raging waters of the little burn. He hoped that Tom and Andrew would not notice that his limp was growing worse, or hear the quick sudden suck of his breath as he stumbled on uneven ground and the aching muscles knotted in protest.

The two men were only too aware of the limp and of the whiteness of the boy's face. At lunchtime Andrew forced a long halt on a grassy patch under the lee of a rock. Kitty had made sandwiches and filled a flask with coffee. The drink was welcome, but Geordie found the food was hard to chew. There had been no sight or sound of a dog anywhere all through that morning.

Andrew, looking bleakly at the slopes, saw gully and crevasse and precipice; the sheer sides where men had once quarried stone and the deceptive potholes that delved deep into the ground at the drinking places; saw death in a hundred forms. If the dog had met a fox . . . or met the killer, a powerful dog that would fight to the death. . . .

Clouds were gathering on the hillside. The slopes were dark, the peaks hidden, and from far away came another thunder growl.

"You are not getting another wetting," Andrew said. "You're more important than any dog, lad, so it's home now. We'll come out tomorrow if the weather's fit. I'm not risking another chill."

There was no chance to argue. Geordie knew when Andrew spoke firmly there was no changing his mind.

That night thunder rumbled endlessly again and lightning flashed on the hills. Geordie lay thinking of his dog, wet, alone. He fell asleep at last, exhausted, as the clouds parted and the sun rose and the birds greeted the morning. He woke again at the clang of the milk churns, and was dressed and downstairs before Tom arrived.

"When are we going up the hill?" he asked Andrew.

The twins and Catherine McGregor came over to help. Catherine and the twins went up one side of the mountain and Geordie and Andrew took the other, while Tom quartered the lower slopes with Megan.

"The waterfall in the glen is three times its normal size," Andrew said, wanting to distract the boy. "Come and see the falls. It's a once-in-a-lifetime sight."

Geordie followed Andrew. The hunt seemed pointless and it didn't matter whether he saw the falls or not. Catherine and the twins crossed the damp ground to join them, spray blowing into their faces.

They watched the water hurling itself downwards, sunlight trapped in each drop. The noise was phenomenal, so that Tom, reaching them, had to take each one by the shoulder and point to the path, wanting them to come higher up and look down on the maelstrom in the pool.

They stared, awed, at the raging torrent. Geordie climbed higher, finding himself on a small plateau. The water here ran over the edge of a steep, but low, cliff. This was the pool he had washed in, but it was quite unrecognizable: the water swirled and foamed and frothed and the little ledge where he had sat was partly submerged, but the long spit beyond it was dry and bright with sunshine. The cliff cast a long shadow and in that shadow was something, lying. An animal that slowly lifted its head . . . a black and white head, with floppy half-pricked ears.

Geordie forgot the pain in his leg and raced down the slope, hurrying so fast that he almost passed Andrew who reached out an arm to steady him. It was no use talking in the din of the falls, but Andrew gave the boy a small shake to remind him to be more careful! A slip on the wet ground and he would fall downwards to instant death.

Geordie dragged the farmer by the sleeve up the path beside the waterfall. The dog stood in the sunshine, wagging an uncertain tail, looking up at Geordie, having recognized his master. Geordie looked at the water, and looked at Tom and Andrew. Tom shook his head.

"Impossible." His mouth formed the word, though it was barely audible above the din of the falls.

But they could drop food to the dog. Perhaps they could keep him alive till the water subsided, and rescue him then. There were more than half the sandwiches left, and the twins had some food as well.

Tom had a large neckerchief tucked into the collar of his shirt. He took it off and put the food inside, leaving a wide gap, and weighted the bundle with a stone. He dropped it over, and it fell within yards of the dog. Flash crawled uncertainly towards the bundle, and sniffed at it. A moment later he had his front paw on the cloth to hold the package steady, and was ripping it open, savaging the food. He ate every crumb.

"We can go and get more," Geordie yelled to Andrew.

Andrew nodded. He was eyeing the cliff face. It would be days before the water was low enough to rescue Flash; and the dog was constantly at risk, as he might attempt to swim the falls and would then most certainly drown. There was a faint possibility . . . if only they could call in the mountain rescue team; he knew the men and was sure they would help so long as there was not a more pressing emergency on the hills. There was nothing more they could do that day.

Flash had finished the food. He sat, watching the faces above him, knowing they had helped him and now expecting to be rescued from his predicament. Andrew touched Geordie on the shoulder and pointed down the mountain. Reluctantly Geordie followed the rest of the party.

The dog watched them go. His pricked ears dropped, his tail went down between his legs and he whined, high and thin, forlorn. He walked slowly back to his former position against the cliff, and curled up, nose to tail.

Geordie, helping with the milking, thought of his dog alone on the rock. He could think of nothing else.

"There's nothing we can do tonight," Andrew said, knowing Geordie's thoughts. "Tomorrow I'll ask the mountain rescue team to help, but they can't get here quickly and they can't work at night either."

Geordie helped Kitty lay the table. She was very like her brother, slim and dark, though there were grey hairs among the black. She moved quickly and was deft and competent.

"No one can work miracles, Geordie," she said, piling the table high with food, as the twins and Catherine were staying to tea. Tom had reluctantly decided that Kitty was an asset; she was a cook in a thousand and they had never fed so well on their own. But Geordie ignored Kitty's splendid cakes. His thoughts were exclusively on the mountain.

THREE MEN ARRIVED at dawn next morning in the mountain rescue team's Land-Rover. Andrew knew one of them, John Timmis, a big, bearded, merry man who was happier on rock faces than at ground level. He was an instructor at the Aviemore sports centre, teaching climbing and skiing. His Alsatian bitch, Nikki, had tracked and found a number of lost walkers, and also found people buried in snow avalanches; she had no part to play today, but she was never far away from John, and she sat beside him now.

Geordie was desperately worried in case they refused to rescue a dog. John would not commit himself as he wanted to see the place first before he made up his mind. If it were too dangerous, they could not risk human lives. The big man looked at Geordie, and, quick to sense other people's worries, smiled.

"If there's a chance for your dog we'll take it," he said. "We're all used to tricky places."

They drove the Land-Rover as far as possible up the hillside, and then left it and walked. John talked all the time, telling Geordie of mountain rescues in gales and storms, of helicopters hovering close to cliff faces, of men trapped on narrow ledges.

"No fear of storm today," John said as they climbed over the shoulder of the hill, turning away from the slope that led back to the village and coming onto much steeper ground. The noise of the falls was in their ears. As they topped the first small peak the full fury of the water met them.

"Where is the dog?" asked the second of the mountaineers, Dannie, a tall fair student from Glasgow University. He climbed ahead of them, dropping back at intervals to talk to Geordie and cheer him up, teasing him as he teased his own small brother.

The last member of the party, Sam, was much older than the others, a small man with grey hair, intense blue eyes and little conversation, but he turned often with a warm smile that helped Geordie as much as the teasing and the talk from the other two. Tom had stayed behind to help Kitty, who had taken up farm life as if she had never left it.

The party reached the plateau and looked down over the ledge towards the spur beyond the water where Flash had been trapped. The light was fierce on the rock, and at first Geordie thought the dog had gone. Then he saw him, lying in the deepest shade, curled nose to tail.

Geordie dropped his food parcel onto the ledge. The dog's ears pricked, he looked up and wagged his tail. The parcel had dropped against the cliff face, well away from the water. The dog went to it, tore away the paper and began to eat.

John and Dannie had gone higher up the hill to survey the ledges and to discuss their procedure. Andrew lay on the grass looking down at the dog. The water had cleaned him and there were obvious injuries, but they could soon be put right; he was in pretty good shape considering the length of time he had been running wild. He was starvation-thin, as was only to be expected, but since seeing Geordie, Flash had clearly begun to want to live again. He waited patiently for rescue, aware that these men had come to help him. He finished eating and settled himself at the edge of the shade, watching Geordie.

John came down the slope again. He had to cup his hands round his mouth and shout at the top of his voice to make himself heard. "The cliff face isn't too bad, it looks worse than it is. If we rope Geordie, would he like to go down and rescue his dog? There's more chance that Flash will trust him than one of us. There's a small cliff above we can practise on; Geordie only needs to balance himself against the face of the rock. The dog doesn't look heavy."

Geordie's face was alight with eagerness. He could do something at last, and *he* would rescue his own dog, no one else. He looked down at the cliff face and at the seething water in the falls beyond, and then wished he hadn't. But he followed John up the slope and stood while the ropes were settled safely about him, and watched as Dannie demonstrated the way he needed to lower himself.

It looked simple enough on the little cliff face, with grass beneath him. He knew it would not be so simple on the steeper cliff above the water, with the noise in his ears, and the dog in his arms. Suppose he dropped Flash? Suppose the rope broke?

Andrew cupped his hands and bellowed. "Are you sure you want to go? I'll go down if you like. The dog knows me."

Geordie shook his head vigorously. He wanted to go.

"No hurry," John shouted. "Do exactly as I told you."

370

Geordie nodded, his heart beating wildly. He lowered himself very gently over the lip of the cliff, feeling the rope tighten as Dannie and John and Sam gripped it. John had spread his anorak over the cliff edge to stop the rope from rubbing.

He swung suddenly and terrifyingly away above the spur, and had visions of himself crashing down as the rope gave way. Then he remembered what he had been told and grabbed at the cliff. The rock was rough and there were finger holds and toe holds.

He looked up and John put out his hand, thumb uppermost, and smiled. Dannie signalled with his arm, easy, easy, and the slow movements told Geordie to take care. Here the rock was slimed and green in places, and his foot slipped and he caught his breath. The sudden jar hurt his leg. He moved delicately from crack to crack.

And then he was almost down and the dog was beneath him, jumping excitedly at him, trying to reach him. He eased himself to the ground. The spit was much bigger than he had realized, but the water made him dizzy, flinging itself in perpetual movement into the boiling pool.

Flash was leaping up at him, licking face and hands, and then Geordie knelt and the dog came to his arms, wriggling in ecstasy. Geordie opened his anorak and zipped the dog inside. The lower part of the anorak was firmly bound by the rope; Flash would be quite safe.

Geordie could feel the dog's heart beating and the warm breath on his face; could feel a consuming excitement that buoyed him to face the dizzy spinning against the rock, to fend himself off with his hands so that he and the dog didn't bang against the cliff, to swallow the sickness that suddenly overcame him as he unwisely looked down into the seething water and the great tumbled boulders. He used his feet as Dannie had shown him. He used one hand to fend off the cliff, the other protecting his dog.

Then he was at the top, eight hands pulling him to safety, Dannie and John and Sam and Andrew grinning with relief. Dannie offered to take Flash but Geordie would not let the dog go. He held him tightly, covered in dust from the blown scree grit and soaked by the spray. His eyes gleamed with achievement.

John whistled to Nikki and they made their way down the hill. Geordie forgot the pain in his leg and twice he almost tripped,

never taking his eyes off Flash and unable to watch where he was going.

The twins were waiting at the farmhouse, and Angus was there, ready to examine the dog. He had obviously had a tough time, but his injuries were healing. Geordie took the dog indoors.

Flash recognized the house. He was home. He raced round the rooms, greyhound fashion, leaping on and off Geordie's bed, so pleased to be back that he could not control himself. The men laughed as the dog whirled through each room, tore up the stairs, bounded down again, and leaped at Geordie, his tail threatening to come off. At last, completely exhausted, he fell asleep, curled against his master, who had stretched out on the hearthrug. Geordie was so worn out that he fell asleep himself, his arm around the dog.

By the time Geordie woke Kitty had prepared a celebration tea. But first there was something that Tom wanted to know.

"There's facts to face, lad," he said to Geordie. "No use blinding yourself. That dog's been running wild and sheep have been killed. They may have kept him alive. He may have got a taste for mutton. We'll take him out in the field . . . and we'll watch. One go at those lambs. . ."

Geordie had thought it was over. He wanted to cry. He looked at Andrew, who nodded.

"We have to know. We can't keep a killer, Geordie. You know that."

Silently, they went outside. The dog followed them, jumping up eagerly at Geordie's hand.

Tom opened the field gate. It was only then that Geordie realized the man was carrying his gun.

"Best to get it over quick, lad, if we have to," Tom said. No use glossing facts. The boy would have to find out there was no room for softness if he was going to be a farmer.

Flash saw the sheep. Instinct took over.

He forgot Geordie. He forgot his injured paw, and forgot his bruises and bites and cuts. He began to herd. Slowly, gently, round the sheep. Geordie could not stand still and watch. He whistled, softly, remembering how he had taught Flash to work in the early days. The dog obeyed him at once, dropping at the signal. Geordie signalled again and again. The dog ran left, ran right, brought in a straggler, and at the end singled out one of the lambs. Geordie whistled again. The dog dropped, tail beating against the ground. Geordie called.

"Flashie boy, here. Good dog." The small body hurtled into his arms.

Geordie turned to face the house, where John and Dannie and Sam had returned for tea. Kitty had put on an impromptu party, and the farmhouse was full of laughter. Andrew, stretched out in the armchair, watched as Geordie limped into the room and put the dog down on the hearthrug. The dog did not stay. He followed Geordie to the table, both of them limping.

"You're both laglegs," Donald said, his mouth full of food. Davina kicked him under the table and he stared at her. "Come on and eat, Geordie," he added, suddenly guessing the reason for the kick.

Davina had noticed the expression on Geordie's face and realized that lagleg was an expression he must hate. But as Geordie watched the dog limp towards the plate that Kitty had just put down on the floor for him, he no longer cared. So what if they did limp? They could both get by. Flash could still herd sheep; and he could do everything that he could do before except perhaps play soccer, and that wasn't such a great loss.

Geordie looked out of the window at the towering peaks. He had conquered the mountain and so had Flash. He sat and watched the dog feed, and then, when Flash had finished and came to sit with him, his head on his master's knee, brown-yellow eyes watching, intent, Geordie sighed deeply, and a moment later realized, as the smell of food wafted towards him, that he had never been so hungry in his life.

Tom had gone outside to talk to Queenie. He scratched the sow's ear and she groaned in delight. "He'll do," he told her.

Joyce Stranger

Nestling on a green hillside in the tiny Anglesey village of Dwyran is Joyce Stranger's home. She and her husband converted the three-hundred-year-old house six years ago, and now her study looks out over peaceful fields where cattle graze. It's obviously the home of an animal lover: her two dogs give visitors an uproarious welcome (though the Siamese cat is a little wary), and pictures and photographs of animals decorate the walls of every room.

Brought up in Kent, Joyce Stranger took a degree in zoology at London University and took up writing after her children were born "as a distraction from nappies". She became a feature writer for the *Manchester Evening News*, and then the novels began to appear: some for adults, some for children, all with animals as their theme and all tremendously popular with young and old alike. "Just because a book is about animals doesn't mean it's only for children," she insists. "Animals are *not* for children—they are not toys, but creatures with needs of their own. What I hope to do in my books is to teach a more responsible attitude towards animals." This is a lesson that many evidently wish to learn. "I get letters from all over the country," says the author. "Now I run a sort of pet advisory service, by correspondence, for more people than I could count."

Joyce Stranger has a strictly organized day, writing from nine o'clock until lunchtime. The afternoon may be spent visiting friends, dropping in on the local RSPCA, or taking her German Shepherd, Chita, to compete in dog trials. One day a week is set aside for the local dog club, which she has been running devotedly for several years. And as if there wasn't enough to fill her day, she has recently taken up script-writing: one of her books, *The Fox at Drummer's Darkness*, is currently being filmed on Anglesey with local actors and film crew. "You might think all this doesn't leave me much time for research," she smiles, "but in a way, you could say my whole life is research for my novels. Everything I do is relevant."

Joyce Stranger's daughter and two sons are now grown-up with children of their own. We can only hope that the demands of five grandchildren will not prevent this delightful author from continuing to write the books which have been a joy and inspiration to so many readers.

COLD IS THE SEA
Edward L. Beach

COLD IS THE SEA

A CONDENSATION OF THE BOOK BY

EDWARD L. BEACH

ILLUSTRATED BY CHRISTOPHER BLOSSOM
PUBLISHED BY HODDER & STOUGHTON

To the men of the submarine service, Admiral Brighting is both a bully and a genius. This irascible perfectionist is the driving force behind the Navy's growing fleet of nuclear submarines. And to match his formidable vessels, Brighting has handpicked and vigorously trained a new breed of fighting men. Now, the latest Polaris-carrying sub, the USS *Cushing*, has been sent to the Arctic, into territory that may not be as neutral as the Navy believes. As the *Cushing* noses forward, an alien force probes the frigid waters, senses the interloper—and moves to meet it. And the scene is set for a life-or-death confrontation under an implacable ceiling of ice.

CHAPTER ONE

TO MOST OF THE outside world, the Pentagon is a huge, five-sided pile of cement, looming squat and commanding on the Virginia bank of the Potomac River across from Washington, D.C. It contains the offices of the Secretary of Defense, the Secretaries of the Army, Navy and Air Force, the Chairman of the Joint Chiefs of Staff and the military chiefs of the three services. From their windows in the impressive, four-story, two-block façade, these important personages doubtless draw inspiration from the patriotic vista spread before them. There is the mighty Potomac itself, from its confluence with the shallow Anacostia to Georgetown. On its banks, the Lincoln Memorial, the spire of the Washington Monument, and the Capitol dome all rise as if from a garden above the low screen of green bordering the river. One can visualize the high councils taking place behind those severe windows, the low-voiced briefings, the great decisions by which United States military policy is determined.

The Pentagon was built to be the world's largest office building, and it presides over the world's biggest parking lot. Some thirty thousand people are housed in it from eight to twelve hours a day. It is not one pentagon but actually five, placed one inside another.

The outermost and largest, the E-ring, is sumptuously finished, with marble columns and terrazzo floors. The innermost, the A-ring, is favored with a view of the pentagonal central court from its windows. Between these two extremes are rows upon rows of hall-ways, with rows upon rows of cubiclelike rooms, each having a view of the concrete facing of the ring opposite.

The window gracelessly lighting Captain Edward Richardson's office held the same view as all the others in his ring: the casemented window frame of the cubicle opposite. Richardson had been gazing through it more frequently of late, now that he had relatively little to do. Today it was raining gently, a warm, flower-benefitting rain. Outside the Pentagon, the 1960 presidential campaign was in its early flowering stages as well, with nominating conventions only months away, and the news was full of discussion as to who might succeed the World War II hero who had held the post for nearly eight years.

As with the real flowers which his wife, Laura, tended so lovingly at home, Rich had had little opportunity to follow the blooming of the political scene. He usually had no leisure time to follow anything else, either, including the growing needs of his thirteen-year-old son, Joseph Blunt Richardson, named after Rich's World War II squadron commander and affectionately called Jobie.

Now it was different. Jim Barnes, designated by the Bureau of Naval Personnel—BuPers—to relieve him, had been aboard for a month and was already enmeshed in the latest urgent requirement of the Navy Secretary. He had even shown some eagerness for the job. Well, he would soon learn.

Three years in the Pentagon, in the office concerned with Navy Programs and Plans, were about enough for any naval officer who would rather be at sea. Three years of responding to the sudden demands of the Secretary of Defense, of working all night while wondering if the document being prepared at such personal sacrifice would actually be read by anyone, had given Rich a jaundiced view of Washington officialdom. But all that was over now, and there was nothing for him to do but to lend a hand if his successor needed it.

He heard footsteps approach his desk, and knew without looking that it was his secretary.

"Captain, here's something from BuPers."

Rich turned from the window. "Thanks, Marie," he said. He seized the bulky envelope and extracted a thick sheaf of paper. It was immediately evident that there was but a single typed sheet, with numerous copies clipped to it.

"From: Chief BuPers," the top sheet said. "To: Captain Edward G. Richardson, USN. Subj: Orders. Herdet Prorep ComSubRon

Ten Porich USS *Proteus* . . ." There was more official gibberish, but he needed no more.

"Are those your orders?" Marie asked.

"Yes, at last," said Richardson. "I'm getting Submarine Squadron Ten in New London."

"Congratulations, Captain. That's the squadron you were hoping for, isn't it?"

"Thanks, Marie. Yes, it is, but they've left something out, I think. There was supposed to be something about nuclear training prior to reporting." He dismissed Marie with another word of thanks, reached for the telephone, and called the office of the Chief of Naval Personnel.

"Deacon," he said, "Rich Richardson. My orders to SubRon Ten finally landed here. But they don't say anything about nuclear power training. I've had my interview with Admiral Brighting, and that was all agreed. Leaving it out was a mistake, I hope."

The voice on the other end of the line sounded slightly troubled. "I'm really sorry, Rich. I thought it was all set, too. But you know old man Brighting. The list for nuclear power training he sent over last week didn't have you on it. We thought there was a mistake, too, and called them up, but they wouldn't change."

"But damn it, man, he told me he was putting me on the list for the next class. The nuclear subs are all being assigned to Squadron Ten. I made the pitch that the squadron commander should also have a nuke ticket, and he agreed!"

Deacon Jones's voice lowered perceptibly. "Rich, you know all I can do is to run this submarine assignment desk according to what is handed to me. But—off the record—there was some kind of a flap last week between Vice Admiral Scott and Vice Admiral Brighting over the nuke list. Scott was so mad we could feel the walls shaking all the way down here."

"Are you saying there was a flap over me between Brighting and the Chief of Naval Personnel?" There was a rasp in Rich's voice as he named the two most important men in the Navy. "Why did that take me out of nuclear training?"

"All I can say is, if they didn't tell you it's because they didn't want you to know. None of us can figure out how Brighting makes up that list. Anyway, there's one bit of dope you'll be glad about. Your old exec from the *Eel*, Keith Leone, is getting *William B.*

Cushing in your squadron. And another one of your old junior officers, Buck Williams, is getting the *Manta*. Both of them have orders to the next nuke school, and when they finish they'll be reporting to you in New London. That please you?"

"It's the greatest news I've heard for a year," Rich said.

Nevertheless it was a deeply troubled Richardson who maneuvered his automobile out of the Pentagon parking lot shortly thereafter and, for once, beat the rush-hour traffic home. Jobie would be delighted to bring out the baseball gloves earlier than usual, and afterward he would have a word with Laura.

"WELL, YOU'LL just have to go and see Admiral Brighting. Whatever he has against you, he should tell you, and I think he will."

It was after dinner. Jobie had gone to his room to study, and Rich and Laura were relaxing in the living room. During the fifteen years of their marriage Rich had often taken his problems home, and he had learned to value his wife's thoughtful insight.

"Brighting is a peculiar man," Rich said. "You don't get to see him just by setting up an appointment the usual way."

"I know that," Laura said. "You ought to telephone him direct, without going through any superior office, and just ask if you can see him. If you do it yourself, I think he'll say to come on over. . . ." Laura paused, then went on. "But do you know anybody in his shop who might tell him beforehand there's another side to the story?"

Rich did know somebody. He had been surprised to see her passing the admiral's office as he entered for his interview in March. They had not met since the war, when she had been in Naval Intelligence, and he had no idea she had become a WAVE officer on Brighting's staff.

"Joan!" he had muttered, when she suddenly appeared. Their hands had touched—an impersonal handshake, a friendly warmth only. But even so, as there had been something unforgettable before, there was a strange awareness now. Rich had to make a conscious effort to put the awakened memories out of his mind.

He came back to the present. "No," he said, answering Laura's question. He rationalized the lie by thinking he had no idea what Joan's status was in Brighting's group. But he was vaguely conscious of another motive.

384

Joan Lastrada had been out of his life since the war. He had made a decision then; so had she. It had been the right decision, although difficult at the time, because it was so abrupt and final. He had wondered about her sometimes since then. She had always seemed so self-contained, so undemanding. During the period of their intimacy she had avoided telling him much about her background, what she had done before, what she was doing at the time. Then the war ended, and they parted. He would have liked to maintain some sort of contact with her, despite his approaching marriage to Laura—but he could not think of anything but the wrong reasons for doing so.

Like so much that had happened during those strenuous years, Joan had receded into the never-never land. Now, fifteen years later, she was back.

For all Rich knew, Admiral Brighting had been expecting the request for a second interview. Brighting's offices were located in a separate structure behind the main Navy Building in downtown Washington. Now the sharp-featured, hawk-nosed little admiral peered across his cluttered desk. As usual, he was dressed in civilian clothes. Two months ago Richardson had come for his first interview in uniform, but today he had decided to match the admiral's habitual attire.

"Hello, Richardson. What do you want to see me about?" Admiral Brighting spoke in a low monotone. Then his eyes returned to the loose-leaf binder filled with pink flimsies, which he had been reading. Hardly an auspicious beginning.

Richardson was already disarmed. His straight-backed wooden chair was as uncomfortable as it had been the first time, and he had long known the story about its front legs having been slightly shortened. He did seem to be slipping forward.

How to begin? "I came to try to convince you to reconsider, sir," he said. "I want very much to go to nuclear power school."

"Why don't you ask your friends at BuPers? They write the orders. They can send you to any university they want."

"Your training is the only one that can qualify me in nuclear power, sir. I'm to be responsible for administration and operations of the nuclear subs in the Thames River. It's a tricky job, and that's why I want to know something about your program, sir."

"Why aren't you wearing your Medal of Honor, Richardson? Are you trying to impress me with your modesty? Or are you ashamed of it?" The admiral's eyes flickered, then once more fell to the flimsies in his hand.

Richardson nearly stuttered. "I'm not ashamed of the medal, sir," he finally said. "I just thought I'd come in civilian clothes."

"You're a hero, Richardson. We don't need heroes in nuclear power. What we need is dedication—and workers who are willing to use their brains."

"I've never been afraid of work, Admiral," said Rich, fighting the urge to raise his voice. "All I'm asking is the opportunity to do a good job in New London, and it will be better for all the nuclear boats up there if I can talk to the skippers from knowledge."

"If you're so interested in nuclear power, why don't you study some of the books on the subject?"

"Because books are all theoretical. The only way anyone can get the operational know-how is through your program."

Brighting looked up, his pale grey eyes bleak. "No squadron commander is going to tell my skippers how to run my submarines, Richardson," he said, still speaking softly. "You people have no idea of what's required, and you're not willing to learn."

"That's not true, Admiral," said Richardson. "I'm willing to give it all I'm capable of, if you'll let me have the chance. There's bound to be a lot of nuclear stuff in New London that I'll have to deal with. All I want is to be able to do a better job."

"Did the Chief of Naval Personnel send you over here to beg?"

Rich would not succumb to Brighting's famous baiting tactics. He had already decided he would beg, if necessary. "Admiral," he said, as evenly as he could, "nobody knows I'm here. I came on my own. And I *am* begging. If you'll give me a chance, I guarantee you'll be pleased with my performance."

"What makes you think your performance one way or the other means anything to me?"

Richardson would not be able to stand this much longer. "Admiral, when we first talked about this, you told me you agreed that the commander of Sub Squadron Ten should get nuclear training. Won't you at least tell me what happened to change your mind?"

"I don't have to tell you anything. But you might consider that it costs thousands of dollars to put one man through my course.

386

You have only a few more years of service before you either retire or they make an admiral out of you. Either way, you'll have no further use for anything we could teach you. After thinking it over, I decided it would be a waste of government funds."

"But Admiral—" Rich began desperately.

"Thank you for coming to see me," Brighting interrupted. He turned to another flimsy and began to read.

"I DON'T KNOW how I got out of there without saying something disrespectful," Rich told Laura. "He was so arrogant!"

Laura was lying with her arms around him, her head pillowed on his chest. "He was brutal to you," she agreed, "but there's more to it than that."

"I practically got down on my knees to him, and he turned me down flat. What I can't figure out is why."

"You don't really believe he thinks you're too old?" Imperceptibly Laura's arms tightened.

"He knows darned well I'm not too old, and so do you." He drew her face to his, kissed her full on the mouth. Her lips parted, then opened wider as she kissed him back.

Later, when he was nearly asleep, Rich heard her whisper, "I know what the problem is, darling. He's afraid of you." She tenderly kissed the back of his hand, held it to her cheek.

"RICH," DEACON JONES said, "thanks for letting me bust in on you at home like this. Don't let on I said this—you, too, Laura—but I think I know what happened between Brighting and my boss. Admiral Scott called Brighting on the telephone that afternoon to talk about increasing the number of nuclear experts. Scott wants all submariners to be nuclear-trained as soon as possible. Eventually all surface engineers, too. In a few years, he thinks, all our submarines and most of our surface combatants will be nuclear. Brighting blew up, because when that happens he won't have control over who gets appointed, and he knows damn well that's exactly what Scott had in mind." Jones, a phlegmatic individual, usually fit the characteristics of his nickname. His unhappiness had to be great, Rich knew, for him to unburden himself this way.

"I should think Brighting would want the whole Navy to go nuclear. That would be a big personal triumph!" Rich said.

"You don't know Brighting. He's been king of the roost here for years, mainly through controlling the selection of those who get nuked. Assignments are supposed to be the job of BuPers. He gets away with it because you can't have a nuke—you can't even be aboard—unless you're a nukey pooh."

"What does this all have to do with me, Deac? I'm not fighting any personnel battles. That's up to the people wearing stars. I'm just a four-striper."

"Rich . . . this is what I'm trying to show you. You could be an admiral in a couple of years, if the selection board is smart, and you're the senior person to apply for nukedom. Scott has been supporting your application for all he's worth."

"So what!"

"So you must be dumber than I thought. You've got a Congressional Medal of Honor. You're a big hotshot skipper of the war. So you're Scott's spear carrier in this fracas. And what do you think Brighting did when Scott's call let him figure this out?"

"Crossed me off his list?"

"That very minute. You think he'd miss a chance to show the Navy who's the real boss? That's why Scott was so furious."

Deacon Jones's information was comforting. But, Richardson decided afterward, Jones had told him nothing that would help further his hopes for "nukedom," as Deacon termed it.

Laura had the same reaction. "He did clear up one thing, though," she added. "None of the reasons Brighting gave for turning you down are the real ones. It was entirely Admiral Scott's call. Brighting thinks you were a full-fledged member of that scheme."

She smiled enigmatically. "If only there were someone on Brighting's staff who could get the word to him that you had nothing to do with it. You must know someone over there." The strange expression was still around her mouth. "Some man or woman from the war, maybe?"

A thought was growing in Richardson's mind. Joan Lastrada had been moving in Navy circles ever since the war. It was totally possible that she and his wife had met somewhere. Although he had never discussed it with Laura, he had often wondered if she knew of his wartime affair. It was even possible she had heard of Joan's early relationship with Jim Bledsoe, Laura's first husband. Recognizing the possibility made it harden into probability. Laura

388

must know. But, womanlike, she must have it from him. He would have to tell her something.

"I do know someone—a WAVE lieutenant, Joan Lastrada. I ran into her when I was over there. I knew her when she was in intelligence in Pearl Harbor, during the war."

Again that unfathomable ghost of a smile. "Good. Now maybe we're getting somewhere. How can we get Joan Lastrada to tell Brighting you had no part in Scott's scheme?"

"We can't, Laura. Joan's only a lieutenant in his shop. I'm not about to go to her with any such idea!"

"I know you far better than you think, husband mine, and I wouldn't love you as much if I thought you would. But she might do it anyway, if she finds out what's been going on. . . ."

"We're not going to get Joan or anybody else mixed up in this," he said again, a little too loudly. But there was a cryptic look in Laura's eyes, an attitude of listening to another tune entirely, and the conversation remained in Richardson's mind for days.

Finally there was the good-by luncheon given by his office mates and the arrival, on Friday morning, of a moving van at his house. But the tearing up of the home of three years—always a traumatic routine—seemed overshadowed by a quietness of waiting. Even Jobie sensed it. "It doesn't feel like we're moving to where we're supposed to be," he announced.

Late in the afternoon the van was about to pull away from the house when the telephone, now on the floor in an empty hall, sounded its insistent tocsin. Rich picked it up. "Just a moment for Admiral Brighting," said a female voice.

Then Richardson heard the now familiar monotone. "Richardson, there's a vacancy in the next class out in Idaho. It starts tomorrow. Do you want it?"

"Yes, *sir!*" Euphoria flooded Richardson's body. He could say nothing more.

"You're to wear civilian clothes the entire time you're on the base. There are officers and enlisted men there whom I have put into positions of responsibility, and you're to accept orders from them as though they were from me. At no time are you to use your rank for any reason. I will not have my program disrupted by the requirement of toadying to you. You will be there for one purpose only: to learn what they can teach you. Is that clear?"

"Yes, sir," said Richardson again.

"Be in Idaho Falls tomorrow morning. There is a flight you can catch tonight. I'll have someone meet the plane when it arrives."

Richardson's elation evaporated. Abandoning Laura and Jobie without warning could not be vital to any training course. "Admiral," he began, "our car is packed, and we're about to start for New London. May I have the weekend to get my family safely up there? I can be in Idaho Monday morning—" But Laura was frantically shaking her head as the flat voice cut in.

"Richardson, if you want nuclear power training, you'll be at Idaho Falls tomorrow morning. An officer as resourceful as you should have no trouble arranging his affairs." The telephone clicked dead.

Laura was hugging him, nearly crying her relief and delight. "Of course I can handle the move," she said. "Jobie and I will repack a suitcase for you right now."

There was an interval of furious activity. The car had to be partially unloaded and the two largest suitcases packed for a lengthy stay in Idaho. Deacon Jones had to be tracked down and asked to prepare new orders. Airline reservations had to be made and tickets purchased. Finally the Richardsons set off—not for New London, but for Washington National Airport.

It was only after hurried good-bys had been said and Rich was strapped in his seat in the airplane that he was able to unwind enough to admit the thoughts which had been knocking at his consciousness for the last hour. Why had Admiral Brighting changed his mind? Could Joan Lastrada have had a hand in it? He had managed to ask Laura this during a moment's breathing space. But Laura's answer was totally unsatisfactory. "What makes you think anyone had anything to do with it? Maybe old man Brighting just had a change of heart."

CHAPTER TWO

ADMIRAL BRIGHTING'S empire, carved out of an unlikely combination of Navy, industry and science, was the most complete and efficient Richardson had ever seen. A Lieutenant Commander John Rhodes met him very early Saturday morning at the Idaho Falls airport and drove him immediately to "the site", as Rhodes referred to it. The site was nearly one hundred miles away, near the town of Arco, and the station wagon hurtled along at top speed over a flat, hard-baked plain which stretched in all directions, as level as the sea. The road was two lanes wide, with hardly a curve, and during the entire trip, which took just minutes longer than an hour, they saw only two other cars.

Their destination came into view while still some twenty miles distant, a white dot poised on the horizon at the base of slate-gray mountains. "That's the prototype, or rather, the building it's in," said Rhodes. "It's six stories high, and most folks can't believe it's that far away."

At closer range the dot grew into a windowless, sand-colored cube, dominating a number of lower buildings. A tall chain link fence surrounded the complex, and a cloud of steam rose from a squat structure alongside the building housing the prototype.

"That's the cooling pond," said Rich's companion. "We've been critical for three months. There's not much heat going into it right now, though. At full power it steams up a lot more."

Rhodes, the officer in charge of the prototype, was a short, dark young man. He had not been talkative during the ride from the airport and was clearly ill at ease. "Rhodes with E. G. Richardson," he said to the guard at the gate, and instantly Rich understood the reason for his companion's discomfiture.

"Here's where you'll be staying, Mr. Richardson," Rhodes said. The car had stopped in front of one of a small group of Quonset huts. "I'll help you with your luggage, and then I'll take you over to the prototype and start you off. It's warm in there, so don't bother with a jacket or a tie."

"Fine, John," said Richardson, searching for the way to start off on the right note. "Look," he said, "I'm here for one thing only, to learn everything you fellows can teach me. So why don't we just knock off the rates for the time being. My friends call me Rich. Is your name Dusty, like all the Rhodes in the Navy?"

"Right—uh—Rich. Nobody calls me John anymore."

"Okay, Dusty." Rhodes's handshake contained considerably more warmth than it had at the airport. "That goes for everybody else here, too. . . . Is there time for me to shave before coming over?"

"I really don't think so, Rich." This time Rhodes's eyes were unflinching, and Richardson had a sense of concealed urgency.

Once in the prototype building, however, Richardson was surprised to discover only a duty section—a very small percentage of the total force—present. Rhodes had a glassed-in office suite opening directly into the cavernous interior housing Mark One, as the prototype reactor for the *Nautilus*—the first nuclear-power submarine—was known. The main room of the building occupied almost all the interior, from concrete floor to metal roof. Toolboxes, workbenches, storage lockers and bins were everywhere. Mark One was festooned with steel ladders, catwalks, wire cables, the ordered confusion and paraphernalia of many functions and many workers.

And, of course, Mark One itself was breathtaking—a dark gray horizontal section of a huge submarine's pressure hull projecting through the side of a tremendous circular steel tank which was filled with light green seawater. The purpose of the salt water, Rich knew, was to duplicate the radioactive shielding effect of the sea. The hull section, with the reactor and engine compartments, was identical to the *Nautilus'*, except that, for economy, only a single turbine and propeller shaft had been installed.

"There she is, sir—Rich. You're to be here fourteen weeks and learn all about it. Then we'll give you an examination, and if you pass it you'll be a qualified reactor operator."

Dusty Rhodes was looking with proprietary satisfaction at the surrealistic monster. It was humming softly. In a sealed compartment beneath its deck, he explained, the prototype's heart was pumping out an unceasing supply of steam, which was piped into the engine room to turn the turbine and thus the propeller shaft. Via electric turbogenerator sets, the steam also provided power for the myriad pieces of machinery that made up the complex whole. It was then cooled to form water, which was pumped back into the steam generator to repeat the cycle.

There, in the steam generator, the water was reheated to become steam, not by combustion of oil, gas or coal but by the pressurized water of the reactor primary loop—water under such great pressure that it could not flash into steam, even under the tremendous temperature of nuclear fission. Here was the secret, for the nuclear power plant needed no combustion anywhere in the power cycle, and the fuel—built into the reactor—would last for several years.

Rich listened to Rhodes's explanation, his whole attention captured. It was then that Rhodes, his guard perhaps let down by Rich's ready acceptance of his role as a student, forgot himself. "You'll have two days' head start," he said. "The class won't really begin until the other students get here Monday morning."

The moment he'd spoken, consternation showed on Rhodes's face, but the words were beyond recall. Rich now knew that Brighting had hauled him out to Idaho two days early, days when Rich had been needed at home. He struggled to conceal his anger.

The slip made little difference, he assured Rhodes. He would have known soon anyway, and he was too grateful for Admiral Brighting's change of heart, whatever the cause, to quibble over his pettiness. Rich kept a second reason for silence to himself: whatever or whoever had changed the admiral's mind—Joan maybe—was owed something, too.

But Rich's anger remained with him until it was replaced on Monday by the pleasure of welcoming his two old friends from the *Eel*, Keith Leone and Buck Williams. It had been years since the three of them had been in the same duty area. Despite occasional correspondence, their wartime closeness had begun to dim. Now, magically, it was all restored.

Rich took a long look at his newly arrived friends, fifteen years older now. Buck's hairline had receded a trifle, lines had become permanently etched around his mouth, but he was still the wiry, humorous activist. Keith's shock of brown hair was as full as ever; the wide-spaced gray eyes still gazed directly from a youthful, though more self-confident, face. Only his capable hands, slightly wrinkled, betrayed that he was nearing forty.

Richardson looked no different in his own eyes, certainly felt no different, although he was now nearly as old as Joe Blunt had been when named to be their squadron commander during the war. Rich's sandy hair was farther back over the temples; the skin under his chin a little looser. But he had kept his weight down, although it had been a battle because of Laura's cooking.

Richardson spent several hours guiding his friends through an inspection of Mark One before he realized there were no other students. Keith, Buck and he were the entire class. It must have been organized and scheduled just for them.

"You're here to participate in the actual operation of a submarine nuclear reactor," Dusty Rhodes told them that first day. "The whole function of all this machinery is to turn that propeller shaft." The four men were standing on the floor of the mammoth enclosure in which the prototype rested. "As I guess you know, we call this Mark One, and the *Nautilus* herself is Mark Two. They were building her in Groton at the same time they were building Mark One here in the desert—only Mark One was kept a few months ahead of schedule, and everything was tested and proved out before its duplicate was allowed to be installed in the ship."

There was a note of pride in Rhodes's voice. Mark One was a monument to the genius of its designers and constructors, particularly that most irascible engineer of them all, Admiral Brighting. And now he, Lieutenant Commander Dusty Rhodes, had been entrusted with its exclusive charge.

After a moment Rhodes went on. "What we do here is operate Mark One just like a submarine under way for a long cruise. We go through all the evolutions of starting, maneuvering, stopping, and coping with casualties to the machinery. The trainees stand all the watches, along with the instructors.

"We'll put you fellows right into the system. The only thing different about you guys is that normally a trainee is here for a year, sometimes longer. So he stands his watch every day and then goes home to Idaho Falls, or maybe Arco, wherever he lives. But you three are going to have to cram the whole year's program into fourteen weeks. So my orders are to have you sleep on the site and spend most of your time in Mark One." He paused.

"You won't find this the most comfortable place in the world. The Quonset huts aren't bad, but we don't have a mess hall. I'm afraid you'll have to get your meals from the vending machines they have around. I even got vetoed on having you out to my place in the Falls some weekend for a change of scenery."

"Thanks, anyway, Dusty," Rich said, knowing Rhodes's job under Brighting's difficult leadership must have its problems.

"Well, then," Dusty went on, "I'll just give you our training schedule. You're supposed to complete the entire program, exactly like the regular trainees. At the end we'll give you a comprehensive test. You'll pass it, all right, if you do everything on the schedule. You can ask any questions you want. The only rule is you've got to do all of the things, each one of you, yourself."

INSIDE THE BUILDING housing the prototype there was neither night nor day; electric lights kept the windowless cavern bathed at the same level of illumination. The passage of time became a question of how often one's wristwatch had been around all the numbers, punctuated by weekends. Not that a weekend provided relaxation, except in a very particular way. Saturdays and Sundays, when there was only a duty section at the site, were the most valuable times of all, because of greater freedom from interference.

Gradually a routine emerged. Living on the site, never leaving it, the three trainees could easily be at work in the prototype before the day shift arrived, and they always remained there until well after the second shift departed at midnight. Meals were haphazard—a hasty sandwich or can of soup from one of the many food dispensers. There was no time for relaxation, nor any diversions, not even reading—except for the engineering manuals. The best times were the nightly conversations the three shared in their Quonset hut, but after a succession of eighteen-hour days spent crawling through the cramped innards of the submarine hull, or poring over blueprints, even these were cut short.

Afterward Richardson had trouble distinguishing any chronology pertaining to his time at the site. Everything was compressed into a set of kaleidoscopic impressions. Since there were no women present during the evening and morning watches, it was possible to confirm the suspicion, after a few days, that the ladies' rest room contained a cot. Here the students could lie down between particularly interesting evolutions of Mark One. So, fortified by a few hours of fitful slumber, Keith, Buck and Rich often skipped their Quonset hut bunks entirely. Once, during a test for flux density, Keith noted with mock dismay that they had not been outside the prototype building for two days.

And then, midway through the program, Richardson got into an angry telephone exchange with Admiral Brighting.

The subject was the proposed construction of a cafeteria, so that on-site subsistence would not have to depend on the dispensing machines. The cafeteria had already been authorized, and Dusty Rhodes had circulated a request for opinions as to the most desirable location. The three trainees had all responded with suggestions. Then a building contractor had appeared, and Rich had been one of several who had talked with him.

The denouement began when Dusty Rhodes appeared suddenly, on his hands and knees, alongside the spot where Rich was lying on his back, tracing a nonconforming hydraulic supply line on Mark One's outside skin.

"You're wanted on the telephone in my office!" Rhodes shouted above the roar of the turbine in the hull overhead.

"Who is it? Tell him I can't talk now!" Richardson was out of sorts, furious at the necessity to inch his way on his back along the dirty, oil-soaked concrete.

"It's the boss, Rich, and he's mad!"

Rich wormed his way out of the corner into which he had wedged himself. "What about, Dusty? Is he mad at you or me?"

"Don't know for sure. Both of us, probably. It's something to do with the cafeteria."

Brighting's familiar voice came over the telephone as usual, not bothering with salutation. "I thought you understood you were to keep your nose out of everything but your studies. Can't you carry out a simple order, Richardson?"

"In what way have I not carried out your orders, Admiral?"

"Don't try to play innocent. I hear you want to install a cafeteria at the site for the convenience of you and your friends."

"Not so, Admiral!" Richardson was speaking rapidly. Brighting would not be listening long. "The cafeteria was approved last year. I was asked where I thought it should be located. So were others."

"I don't need any suggestions about the site from you, now or any other time! You have only one job out there, and I expect you to give it your full attention!" Richardson found himself holding a dead telephone.

Two days afterward a downcast Dusty Rhodes handed Rich an official flimsy. It was a carbon copy of a one-sentence order canceling funding for the cafeteria.

VICE ADMIRAL BRIGHTING'S arrival, several weeks later, was apparently part of a pattern long set. That is, it was unexpected. For the first time in Rich's memory, Rhodes was late driving in from Idaho Falls. The reason became clear when the passenger beside him was seen to be Brighting. Rhodes had simply received a telephone call at home the previous evening, directing him to be at the airport next morning.

All this Rich learned later. His own awareness of the admiral's arrival came when Brighting suddenly appeared in the lower level of the engine room. Rich was drawing a steam bubble in the pressurizer, a critically important function in the cold start-up procedure that allowed him only a brief, surprised nod of recognition as he concentrated on his task. When he straightened up, satisfied that the bubble had formed, the admiral was gone.

Later Rich was grateful that he had been observed carrying out an important evolution instead of monitoring some static condition. Not until that evening did it occur to him that Brighting might well have timed his trip so as to be able to make a personal evaluation of a significant part of the program.

Brighting, it developed, had the exclusive use of one of the Quonset huts on the base, and it was here that the three trainees found themselves summoned that evening. No one else was present, not even Dusty Rhodes. Never had any of the three seen their chief so relaxed. There was a puckish quality about him as he waved them to chairs and took one himself.

"Now do you see what I'm trying to do?" he asked.

"Yes, sir," said all three together. Keith and Buck glanced toward Rich, willing him to continue.

"I think we do, Admiral," Rich said. "None of us has ever been through a training period this tough, nor this satisfying."

"You admit all the training you've had before was wasted."

"Not wasted, Admiral, but clearly not on a par—"

"You know it's been wasted. You could have learned twice as much in half the time if you'd been forced to put your mind to it. That's the trouble with our Navy. People are more interested in organization charts than in what really counts!"

Richardson felt they were being baited. There was a set to Admiral Brighting's mouth that conveyed as much. But he could not be certain. He decided to try another tack. "There's one thing sure, and that is your nuclear power plants have been making records for reliability ever since the *Nautilus* went to sea—"

"They've been making records like that ever since Mark One first went critical in 1953!" Brighting interrupted. He swept on without pausing. "Before *Nautilus* was even launched, her prototype, right here, made a full-power run that was the equivalent of crossing the Atlantic Ocean. No new power plant has ever been put to this sort of a test before. If some of them had, perhaps we'd have had fewer problems with some of our ships!"

The simulated transatlantic trip was, of course, well known throughout the nuclear power program. Mark One had been relentlessly kept at full power, her single turbine screaming its high whine, the enthusiasm of her crew building to an emotional crescendo as the plotted line on their chart approached the coast of Ireland. Some of the more conservative engineers had counseled shutdown once the ability of the plant to attain its designated operating characteristics had been demonstrated. It was Brighting, monitoring the test from his Washington office, who had refused all such requests, assumed all responsibility, insisted the run be carried through to completion.

Predictably, Brighting's detractors had pointed out that such a severe test of any new machinery was not good engineering practice. A breakdown at this early stage would have delayed the entire program. Some whispered that the test run was more for the personal aggrandizement of the admiral than for any other reason. No one mentioned the fact that the nuclear reactor, the heart of the entire nuclear power effort, had flawlessly provided the energy source for the entire "trip" without difficulty of any kind. Its performance had been extraordinary.

The familiar story, now told again by Brighting, sounded a different note for Richardson. For the first time he was able to understand the vitally important view Brighting took of his tests, his refusal to accept a halfhearted trial as adequate witness of performance to be expected during the exigencies of war.

Admiral Brighting spoke for some time. No one would have guessed that this articulate man was known for his taciturnity. His face had a look of exaltation, something Richardson might have expected of a young idealist. Then, suddenly, Brighting was talking about the central question of all. "Have you figured out what you're here for?" he asked.

"Sure," said Buck. "To learn how to handle nuclear power."

"That's only part of it."

Rich began, "Nuclear power in the years ahead—"

Brighting interrupted impatiently. "You're like all the rest. You see everything as just small improvements on the stuff you're used to. This is a totally new program. Suppose we'd had the *Nautilus* in World War Two?" he asked. "What do you think you could have done with her?"

"With the *Nautilus* and good torpedoes," began Rich, "one submarine could have taken on the whole Japanese Navy. We'd not have had to worry about recharging our batteries, or evading at slow speed—" Again Brighting broke in.

"You're a piker, Richardson! Who cares about World War Two torpedoes? Did you ever think of a submarine that could stay submerged weeks or months? Or go twice around the world without coming up? What if your submarine had been the size of a cruiser, with a load of missiles that could hit any target in the world from any position in the sea?"

"We could have ended the war a lot quicker," said Keith.

"We're not talking about the last war!" A note of triumph sprang into Brighting's voice. His own inconsistency was brushed aside. "We're not even talking about the next war, either, or the one after that. We're talking about the prevention of all war by total control of the sea!"

The three submariners sat silent. Rich could feel the impact of Brighting's vision.

"The sea is the last and most limitless resource of man," Brighting went on. "It's three-dimensional, yet for all these years its surface has been the prize we were after, because it provided cheap transport. That's what navies have been built for since year one. But changes are coming fast. First mobile power, for new and wonderful ships. Then stationary power, with fantastic capability on the land or in the sea, wherever power is needed."

"You're talking about an entirely different kind of navy, aren't you, Admiral?" said Richardson.

"Not just a new navy, Richardson! A whole new type of civilization!" The puckish look was gone. In its place were the pinched nostrils, the glaring eyes of the zealot. "War, as you and I have known it, is over. Out the window," Brighting continued. "What will come next is a struggle to survive on earth. In a hundred years all the oil will be gone. That's only three generations away. In ten generations all the rest of the fossil fuels will be gone."

"What about tides, solar energy and the internal heat of the earth?" asked Buck.

The disdain in Brighting's face was palpable. "Sure!" he said.

"We've been talking about those things for years, but where are they? Nuclear power is here now. But, like anything else, it has its problems. So people are afraid of it. They lack confidence in their own ability to control it. And they're right.

"Maybe you fellows can handle diesel submarines, but they're nothing. You're worthless if you can't discipline yourself to handle a nuclear power plant. That's what you're here for. This program is a lot bigger than just submariners or the Navy. Now do you see why I have to do things the way I do?"

For a moment no one spoke. There was nothing to say. Then Brighting again seized the initiative. He simply rose to his feet in a clear gesture of dismissal.

"Good night, gentlemen," he said.

Buck Williams put the cap on the evening as the three officers thoughtfully walked back to the prototype and their interrupted study program. "No wonder the Navy hates him," he said, "and still lets him get away with it all. He's a bully and a genius at the same time. Tonight we saw the genius. We're damned lucky to have him in our Navy."

"CAPTAIN! WAKE UP, CAPTAIN!" A hand was shaking him. The voice using the unaccustomed salutation was Keith's.

Richardson rolled upright on the cot in the ladies' room. It was early Sunday evening. Tomorrow was the final exam, and Rich was snatching a few moments of sleep before going back to the prototype for some last-minute drills.

"How long have I been out?" he asked.

"Not long." Buck was standing beside Keith at the side of the bed. "Probably only fifteen minutes. We were going to let you caulk off another half an hour, but we think there's an emergency."

Richardson's mind subconsciously recorded the fact that both former subordinates were putting him into the role of years ago. Simultaneously his own habit asserted itself. "Yes, what is it?"

"Some kind of trouble in the town of Arco!" Keith answered. "There's a telephone call in Dusty's office for the senior man on the site. That's you."

The deep masculine voice on Dusty Rhodes's desk telephone spoke hurriedly, obviously unaccustomed to pleading. "Captain Richardson? I'm Dr. Danforth at Arco Municipal Hospital. We've

401

had a power failure in town. There's an emergency operation going on, and our patient will die if we can't get help!"

"I'm not in charge here, Doctor. I'm only a student," said Rich.

"I know, but you're a Navy captain, and you're the senior person around. And I know that Admiral Brighting has forbidden what I'm about to ask. I've already tried to call Commander Rhodes in Idaho Falls, but I can't reach him." The doctor's voice rose. "This woman will die if we can't get some power fed to us right away! Our emergency generator has been broken down for a month. We've had new parts on order, but they've not come. Now the whole town's gone black."

"What do you need?"

"Electricity. Right now! There's a line from our power company into your place for emergency use in case *you* need it. Now the emergency is the other way. We have three surgeons in town, and all of them are in the operating room now. If the lights and power come on soon, we may be able to save her. Otherwise, she's gone!"

Richardson could feel a quickening of his attention, a heightened awareness of the need for action. He paused only long enough to get the doctor's telephone number, then turned to Keith and Buck, who had been standing by.

"Keith!" he barked. "Find the shore power switch. Figure out how to transform our four hundred and forty volts into whatever they need in Arco. Maybe the power company can help. Take half of our electricians on watch to help you!"

"Got it, Skipper," said Keith, and went off.

"Buck, you take the rest of the electricians and start from the turbogenerator sets. Find out what's the best way to pump power into that shore line, and meet Keith halfway!"

"Right!" Like Keith, Buck dashed away.

The task of communicating with Admiral Brighting in Rhodes's absence Richardson allocated to himself. But in this he was unsuccessful. There was no answer at Brighting's Washington apartment or his office. True to form, there was no second-in-command. Between efforts to get in touch with the admiral, Richardson lost himself in the welter of reports, impediments and suggestions, interspersed with increasingly urgent calls from Dr. Danforth.

Three moments—two decisions and an instant of warm satisfaction—stood out. Wiring had to be improvised to bring the output

402

from the turbogenerators around to the transformer. This took several conferences with Keith and Buck. Then there was the decision to close the emergency power switch and build the paralleled generator sets to full power, so that current could flow into the Arco line. After this there could be no turning back.

The instant of satisfaction occurred when Rich called Dr. Danforth to let him know there was now power on the line, and heard the gratitude in the doctor's voice. The operating-room lights were functioning at last, and the operation was proceeding normally. The patient's life would be saved.

But after all the others had left, and the three friends were standing in Rhodes's office, Keith put into words the shadow lying in the back of Rich's mind. "Boss," he said in a low tone, "did you ever get in touch with Brighting?"

During the months in Idaho, Richardson had many times pondered Brighting's clear dictum that under no circumstances was power to be provided off-site. It might be brought in, but never sent the other way. Dusty Rhodes's explanation had been vague. "Far as anyone knows, he figures there'll be a temptation to count on us as an area resource if we do anything like that. Then sometime when we want to shut down for overhaul, we might not be able to without their okay. It would cut into his complete control."

But a life-or-death emergency clearly lay outside the intent of Admiral Brighting's instructions, Rich mused uncomfortably. All the same, he realized he had disobeyed not only the standing orders of the site but also the personal order about leaving his rank outside the chain link fence. And with the town of Arco and its power company involved, there was no way Brighting could fail to learn all the details almost immediately.

Dusty Rhodes was finally located and came to the phone. He was incredulous when he learned what Rich had done. "You know I'll have to tell the old man," he said. "It will be all over the papers. Arco's been trying to get us to do this for years. They've even gone to the State Power Commission to try to force us."

It was a badly shaken Rhodes who greeted Richardson Monday morning. "He chewed me out all over the Bell Telephone System," he said. "He already knew all about it. He must have spies everywhere. He said I'm in charge and should have been here, even on a Sunday. So now I've got to move into the hut alongside yours and be on board whenever the reactor is critical. To hell with family life. And the Navy calls this shore duty!"

Rhodes audibly expelled his breath. "Also, I've got to tell you you can't take the exam today. It's okay for Keith and Buck, but not you. I tried to tell him how it was, but he wouldn't listen."

"I get the message," said Richardson. "Brighting won't hear my side of the story."

Rhodes looked at him curiously. "You're awfully calm about it," he said. "I thought you'd be mad as hell."

Rich grimaced. "Well, I'm not happy about it," he said bitterly.

He had expected something like this, but the unfairness of the summary decision cut deep. The effort he and the others had made, the agonized decision to proceed without permission, the life saved—all were treated contemptuously. Fury boiled within him.

But the inner rage did not come out. It would be stupid to let Brighting goad him into doing something disrespectful.

When Buck and Keith announced they would also skip the exam, however, he was less reserved. It was almost a relief to shout at them. "Certainly not! You two fools get in there and take that exam! And you'd better get damned near perfect marks, both of you!"

As the morning wore on to noon, and the afternoon turned into evening, it became almost impossible for Rich to control his emotions. He paced restlessly outside the examination room, wishing he were anywhere except where he was and yet not able to go away for more than a moment. Occasionally he could not help seeing Keith and Buck, scribbling madly on pads of ruled paper, drinking cup after cup of coffee. In this, at least, he could participate. Frequently one or the other cast him a glance of gratitude for the coffee he brought them, of sympathy for the pain he was feeling. But for the most part they kept their eyes on their papers. Finally, still at a loss, Rich forced himself to go down to the prototype.

Keith found him there, in the reactor compartment, two hours later. "Well, we're finished," he said. "Buck's winding up his last question right now. Boy! That was some exam!"

"How did you do?"

"Oh, I'm sure I did pretty well. It was fair enough—it just asked me everything I ever knew. That's why it took all day. Dusty's crew has already started to grade my paper. But what a lousy deal this is for you!"

404

"We can't help that," said Richardson, speaking as normally as he could. "I'm just glad he didn't lay it on you and Buck for helping. You're the guys who will need the tickets with your nuke boats."

"Ships, you mean," said Keith, sensing that Rich would like to change the subject. "Some of us have been calling them ships ever since the *Triton* was commissioned—she's as big as a cruiser. I suppose we'll be heading home tomorrow—about time, too. I'm anxious to get back to Peggy and the *Cushing*, both."

"Spoken like a true sailor," Rich said, glad for the new topic.

"I don't know which needs me the most, *Manta* or Cindy." Buck Williams had come up behind them. "But I know which one I need most, and she's no damned submarine!"

"You young bucks are all the same," Richardson growled.

Someone was approaching rapidly on the other side of the reactor housing. Dusty Rhodes. "Rich," he said abruptly, "Brighting's changed his mind! Can you take the exam right away?"

"You mean right this minute? You bet! What's happened?"

"Damned if I know. He suddenly called up out of the clear blue and said to give you the test immediately."

There was neither disrespect nor lese-majesty in the blows Keith and Buck were suddenly raining on his back. Within minutes Rich found himself seated in the examination room, fortified by a cup of black coffee, and staring at his first question.

"There's no time limit, but you have to do it all at one sitting," Rhodes said. "Just work till you finish, and then lay your papers on my desk. I couldn't give you the same test as the others, though. Brighting's orders. This one's a little tougher. It's the one for reactor supervisors. I'm afraid you'll be working pretty late."

After Rhodes had left, Keith said quietly, "Buck and I will go watch-and-watch on you so there'll be one of us around for moral support and coffee. Just yell if you need anything."

The examination taken by his two friends had contained thirty questions, they had said, but Rich found forty-two in his. It had taken them nine hours to finish, he thought, so they averaged ten questions every three hours. At the same speed, this one would take more than twelve hours. He put his wristwatch on the table, picked up the first of a boxful of sharpened pencils and began.

"Sketch and describe the control rod configuration," the first question started.

405

What could have caused Brighting to reverse his decision? Or had he been hazing him the entire time? And why had he been forced to begin this special test at the end of a long and emotionally exhausting day? Maybe this, too, was part of the hazing.

No matter. He had been given his chance. He could work as long as necessary, or as long as his brain could function. It was now just seven o'clock. With luck he'd be dropping the completed exam on Dusty's desk sometime in midmorning.

IT WAS NEARLY NOON of the next day when Richardson carried into Rhodes's office ninety-two closely written sheets of ruled, legal-size paper. "Here it is, Dusty," he said.

His mind was still awhirl. He had been sixteen hours at his desk, had used up all the pencils sharpened by Keith and Buck, and had drunk many cups of coffee. He had expected to be exhausted, physically and mentally. But sometime during the night there had come on him an inner strength, a mental second wind. He felt positively ebullient. He wanted to talk, could not sit still.

"You'd better turn in, Rich," said Rhodes. "You're so wound up you'd go *boing* if I tapped you with a pencil. We'll start marking your paper. The old man will be pleased, I know. He called a few times this morning, and I told him you were hard at it."

So it was over, what Buck called the "sweatshop time." From Idaho, Rich's two friends would leave to take command of their subs and eventually bring them to SubRon Ten in New London. Rich himself would proceed directly to New London.

But before he left the site, he learned that he had achieved an almost perfect score on the exam. He also learned that Admiral Brighting had handed him a lower-grade certificate than the one awarded to his friends. Still, he supposed he was lucky to get a nuclear certificate at all.

CHAPTER THREE

"**N**O ONE'S ever figured out Admiral Brighting, Peggy. You're wasting your time." Laura Richardson had not intended to speak so sharply. Instantly she realized her impatience with Peggy Leone had shown in her voice. She tried to smooth over the momentary awkwardness. "Now that our husbands are nukes, I guess Brighting is just someone we'll have to learn to live with. Rich says he's totally dedicated."

"Keith says the same thing." The warm midmorning sun streamed through the windows as Peggy raised her coffee cup, thoughtfully sipped the hot brown liquid. "But I'm surprised you can defend him after the way he treated your husband."

"I'm just glad it's over. The big thing was to be nuked, as they say." Laura changed the subject. "When does Keith get in with the *Cushing*? Have you gotten mail from Cape Canaveral?"

"He's been so busy with those ship qualification tests, he's only written a couple of times. They'll be back next week. I thought you would know that."

There was something accusatory in the comment, some fine edge of feeling not yet out in the open. Peggy was a small, intense, very pretty woman. Her increasingly frequent arrivals at Laura's door were always preceded by a polite phone call citing an errand bringing her across the Thames River, from Groton to New London. But lately Laura had begun to realize that the increasing regularity of Peggy's visits must be more than mere happenstance.

"I guess I did know it," Laura carefully replied. "Rich says Keith's got his crews very well checked out, and the *Cushing*'s flying through her tests. But it is a pretty strenuous time for them. It ought to be easier when they finally start going on patrol."

"I don't think I'll like it any better, to tell the truth. The missile boats stay away so long."

"Come on, Peggy," Laura said. "Keith's going to be home a lot of the time, counting overhauls and such. How was it with his previous boat?"

"Just the same," said Peggy. "He was married to it, too. It's just not fair the way the Navy treats people. Especially ones like Keith, who didn't go to Annapolis!"

"That's not true, Peggy. Keith's been treated exactly the same as everyone else."

"Then why does he always get the tough jobs?"

"They're not only tough jobs. They're also very good jobs. The *Cushing* is the newest and the best of the big Polaris missile subs. Don't you think every submarine skipper around would like to take Keith's place? Why do you think Keith was picked?"

No answer from Peggy. She was staring into the distance. Laura had the feeling that nothing she could say would change Peggy's growing determination to find fault with the Navy.

PROTEUS, A FLOATING MACHINE SHOP built during the war to tend diesel submarines, had been enlarged and modified for the servicing of nuclear submarines and Polaris missiles. She seldom moved from her berth at a pier on the New London side of the Thames River, where there was always at least one and sometimes as many as four submarines alongside her. The subs' dark whaleback hulls lay very low in the water; only a tenth of their structure showed above the surface. Were it not for a prominent protuberance amidships—the "sail"—their presence would be easy to overlook.

As Commander Submarine Squadron Ten, or ComSubRon Ten, Rich had an office on the topmost promenade deck of *Proteus*, with large circular ports opening out on the forecastle two decks below. Aft of his main room Rich had a dining area, a comfortable bedroom and a bath. The suite had a twin, on the other side of the ship's centerline, which was assigned to her skipper.

Now Richardson swiveled around from his desk to face Keith Leone, who was slouched in an armchair.

"You must really have pushed your gang on the *Cushing*, Keith. All the tests down at Canaveral were perfect, and you got away three days early. What can we do for you up here?"

"The usual, I guess, Rich—I mean, Commodore. Get us ready for the next drill. My crew is tired, though, and I am, too." In what was an unusual gesture for him, Keith passed his hand wearily across his face.

"Well, I'll not keep you long, Keith. You deserve some time off. My apologies to Peggy and little Ruthie for asking you to come over this morning at all."

"What's up?"

Richardson rose, swiftly shut the door between his room and the dining area, then closed the door to his bedroom. "Keith," he said, "we've got to lay a special mission on you. It's top secret. There may be danger—in fact, we know there will be. If for any reason you'd rather not take it on, say so, and they'll send another sub. There'll be no prejudice against you or the *Cushing* if you decline."

"We'll not decline anything," said Keith. "Tell me more."

"All I know is what's in this folder." Richardson took a large manila envelope from the top drawer of his desk. "This was sent by messenger from Washington a week ago, but I thought I'd hold it until after your first night in port. Study it carefully, Keith. Then come back. Don't let it out of your possession."

"What is it?" Keith asked, eyeing the envelope eagerly.

"It's an under-ice mission. They want you to make a test deployment in the Arctic Ocean, to see if it's feasible to fire missiles through the ice. As the newest missile sub, *Cushing* is better off than the others in under-ice capability, and that's one reason Washington picked you."

"It may be possible in some areas up there at least part of the year, when the ice cover is less," Keith answered slowly.

"What we're looking for is a year-round capability. That's why they're sending you right now. Even though we're coming into spring here in Connecticut, the ice is thicker now in the Arctic Ocean than at any other time."

"But our launching system has nowhere near enough power to break through heavy ice cover."

"Well, read the operations proposal. They have a couple of things for you to try." Richardson thrust the envelope toward his old friend.

Keith's ship was alongside the *Proteus*. To reach it he had to climb down three decks, walk through *Proteus'* big machine shop, and cross a portable walkway or brow. To his surprise, there was another submarine outboard. She must have come in during the night. The number on her sail was a familiar one: Buck Williams' boat, the *Manta*. Keith felt warmed by the thought. Before he left for home he must see his friend.

Manta and *Cushing* were totally dissimilar in design, save for the nuclear power plant. The *Manta* was much smaller, lacking the raised deck over the sixteen missile tubes which were *Cushing's* reason for existence. Buck would probably have the *Manta* for only a couple of years and then shift to one of the much faster Skipjacks or Threshers, or even to one of the new ballistic missile ships like the *Cushing*. Keith toyed with the idea of surprising Buck right away. But that would have to wait. The large envelope in his hand had a magnetism he had felt before.

His own gangway watch was saluting. Keith returned the salute, then swiftly retreated belowdecks to the sanctuary of his tiny stateroom. He gently closed the door and locked it from the inside.

Each of the thirty closely typed sheets of bond paper in the manila envelope bore a stamped notation in large red letters: TOP SECRET. EYES ONLY.

> This is not an operation order. An operation order for conduct of this mission will be prepared later, after consultation. Whoever undertakes this mission must be prepared to improvise according to conditions and circumstances found. The purpose is to investigate the Arctic Ocean as a potential area for nuclear submarine strategic operations and to determine appropriate tactical and matériel adjustments. Safety of ship and crew is paramount, but certain potential hazards must be recognized from the rigorous environment and from possible interference by unfriendly powers.
>
> The most favorable entry for a submarine into the Arctic Ocean basin is via the Greenland or Barents seas. Undetected submerged entry should be possible here at any time of the year, even during spring, when the ice cover is heaviest. During summer the Arctic ice pack generally retreats north of Spitsbergen, reducing in size through surface melting and wave action. During winter it has on occasion been solid well south of Spitsbergen. The edge of the ice pack is always marked by block ice which has broken loose from the parent floe. Icebergs—of much greater size—may be encountered frozen into the ice cover. . . .

Keith had read only part of the material when his executive officer, Jim Hanson, knocked on the door to announce lunch. Carefully Keith locked the envelope in his desk. For the time being, it was best that his officers did not know something was brewing.

IT WAS A LOVELY MORNING in late February, 1961, when Richardson shook hands with Keith and crossed from the *Cushing* to the *Proteus*. The shorter walkway between the *Cushing* and the *Manta* had already been removed, and now the huge crane aboard the submarine tender lifted away the brow over which Rich had just passed. *Cushing*'s lines were cast off, and in a carefully orchestrated maneuver, one which kept steel from grinding on steel, *Cushing* backed out of the nest of ships into the Thames River.

On the upper deck of the *Proteus*, Rich glanced at his watch. It was precisely ten a.m., the agreed-on time for getting under way.

410

Watching, Richardson experienced a gut feeling of unspoken anxiety. The departing ship was going on a special mission, into danger above and beyond that usually associated with a submarine voyage. As in the war years, she might never return.

Richardson's reverie was broken by one long blast of a foghorn. The *Cushing* was turning. Water was surging gently from her single propeller. Now clear in the river, the sleek, whale-shaped form began to gather headway.

Keith waved from the departing submarine's bridge. Richardson waved back. Buck Williams, on the *Manta*, did the same.

Richardson watched until the submarine was lost to view. Disquietude still possessed him as he returned to his quarters. This was not the first time he had watched a departing ship until she was out of sight, nor the first time he had thought of the ridiculous old adage that doing so brought bad luck. Why, then, did it rest like a weight in his mind?

Three days later Buck Williams was seated facing Richardson in the commodore's office on board the *Proteus*. Williams' normal combination of jocular seriousness was totally absent.

"What I can't understand," he was saying, "are the priorities. I know you couldn't give the *Manta* priority until the *Cushing* got under way. But what's holding things up now? All we need to finish our refit is a little help from *Proteus* with some of the bigger jobs."

"I know, Buck," said Richardson.

"Yesterday the squadron engineer said he didn't know when we'd have all our work done. We're all keyed up to get into that North Atlantic barrier exercise we're scheduled for. It's the first time the Iceland-Faeroe barrier will have nukes in it!"

Richardson was looking steadily at Buck. "I've been doing a lot of thinking in the last few days, since Keith shoved off. If he runs into any kind of trouble up there under the ice"—Buck's eyes flickered—"we've got to have a way to help."

"Under the ice, eh? I guessed that was it. *Cushing* will be the first missile ship up there, won't she?"

"Yes."

"Pretty rugged for a shakedown cruise. There won't be many potential missile launch spots this time of year, if that's what he's supposed to look for."

"That's part of it, but I can't talk to you about it."

But Buck was not to be put off. "I know he has a bottom mapping rig attached to his fathometer, and that new bump on his forecastle has to be a closed-circuit TV. What do the Russians think of all this? Or do they know about it?"

Richardson's face had the faintest suggestion of a smile. "Damn you, Buck, you ask too many questions. I don't know if the Russians know or not, but that's not what's worrying me. Suppose Keith breaks down up there? What can we do to help him?"

"Keith's not in trouble, is he?"

"No trouble so far as we know. But I asked you to come up here today because I think we should send another ship on that barrier exercise in your place."

Williams stared, wordless. Finally he said, "Wait a minute. Of course I want to be ready to help Keith. But why scrub us just on the off chance something might happen?"

"We're not scrubbing you. I was sort of hoping you'd volunteer. It may all be for nothing, but if we're needed, we'll be needed badly, and in a hurry. It's true that another boat could probably do the job, but, frankly, I'd rather have you, because it's Keith we're talking about."

"Can't you tell me anything at all?"

"Not much. But maybe I can make you feel a little better about the rest of the mystery. How many nuclear submarines are fitted with stern torpedo tubes?"

"Not many—there're only five in the *Manta* class. You can't put stern tubes in a single-screw submarine. They'd have to shoot between the propeller blades, and that won't work."

"Right. None of the new single-screw boats have stern tubes. How would you take the *Cushing* under tow beneath the ice?"

This was it! Buck could feel his excitement mounting. "You mean without surfacing, without sending divers out? I don't think we could. We wouldn't have a Chinaman's chance to rig the towline, even in warm water."

"I suppose we'd need some cold-weather divers along, just in case," said Richardson, "but the way to do it, if at all possible, is to make the contact submerged, hook on and drag her out all in one motion." He rose to his feet, led Buck into his adjoining sleeping quarters, unrolled a blueprint on the bed. "You may as well see this," he said. "It's designed for one of your after torpedo

412

tubes. We're building two of them in our machine shop right now."

Buck Williams studied the blueprint in silence. There was a circular steel thing labeled ANCHOR BILLET, evidently sized to lock into the breech of the open torpedo tube. There were two lengths of chain, one with a heavy grapnel-like hook on one end, a tight coil of eight-inch cable, a strange football-shaped object with stubby wings labeled FLOATING PARAVANE, all shown in detail.

Buck turned to Richardson. "I see it fits our stern tubes, but what is it? What does this have to do with Keith?"

"It's a contraption we hope will snag his anchor chain. You take off the inner door of one of your after torpedo tubes, slide this into it, and lock the anchor billet in place of the door. When you open the outer door, the paravane streams out and upward, dragging this first chain with the hook and six hundred feet of premium nylon hawser. The other end of the cable is attached to the anchor billet via the second chain. We've set the paravane to tow off to the side, just enough so that it will stream across his anchor chain and snag it with this hook. Then the hook will slip down and engage the anchor itself."

"Anybody ever use this before?" asked Williams.

"Nope. We've only just now invented it. That's where you and your ship come in. It'll be ready for a trial in a couple of days."

"What a terrific idea!" Buck exclaimed. He looked down again at the blueprint. "But there's a weak point in the scheme. You could make a dozen passes and miss, but once you do pick up the other ship's chain you have only one shot. There'll be no way to rig a new line. If you break the line, you're dead."

"You'll have another whole rig for your other stern tube," said Richardson. "But if you break that one, too, it's the other fellow who's just found out he's dead."

Buck saw a look cross Richardson's face that could only be described as foreboding.

MONTAUK POINT was well astern when Keith climbed down from *Cushing*'s bridge into the control room. "We'll be diving in a minute," he said to the men on watch. "What's the sounding?"

"Just on the fifty-fathom curve, Captain," said one of them, his eyes close to the fathometer window through which he could see a stylus tracing an exaggerated profile of the bottom.

"Control, this is bridge! Sounding!" The control room speaker blared the order from the officer of the deck above. "Is the chief engineer ready for the dive?"

Lieutenant Curt Taylor pressed a switch, spoke into the microphone. "I'm ready, Howie!" He turned to Keith. "I have the first watch, sir. I'll relieve Howie of the conn after we're down."

Keith nodded. His executive officer, Jim Hanson, had arranged all this several days ago. The report was unnecessary, and both of them knew it; but ship's routine required it to be made.

The control room watch had gradually assumed an aura of expectancy: the men at their stations in orderly, professional readiness, apparent in the way they eyed the controls and gauges occupying every inch of space in the compartment.

There was a bustle in the hatch trunk leading to the bridge. Two men came down wearing foul-weather jackets, the hoods drawn around faces reddened from the cold wind topside. "Lookouts," one of them said through stiffened lips to Curt Taylor.

"Okay," he responded. "Get your coffee and come on back here." The two men shambled off to the crew's mess.

Again the loudspeaker blared. "Clear the bridge! Dive! Dive!" Almost simultaneously the diving alarm sounded two raucous blasts on the ship's general announcing system. The chief of the watch was standing before his diving control console, with Curt Taylor alongside him. Both kept their eyes on the hull-opening indicator panel, which showed two red circles and a series of dashes. The chief, fingering a switch on his diving panel, glanced inquiringly at Taylor.

"Shut the induction," said Taylor. The chief flipped the switch. One of the two circles vanished, was immediately replaced by another dash. The two men continued to watch the panel, relaxed slightly when the last circle changed to a dash. "Straight board, sir," said the chief to Taylor.

"Open the vents," said Taylor. The chief's practiced fingers flew across a row of switches on his console. A faint noise of rushing air could be heard.

Two more figures garbed in foul-weather parkas came down from the bridge. "Hatch secured," the officer of the deck said.

"Aye, aye," responded Taylor. "I'll take the dive, Howie."

Lieutenant Howard Trumbull, officer of the deck, turned to

Keith. "Bridge secured, Captain. All clear topside. We're still on the same course, one two five true, speed fifteen."

As Keith acknowledged the report he could feel the slight downward inclination of the submarine. Bow and stern planesmen were sitting near the forward bulkhead, facing an impressive array of dials. Extending from the floor between the legs of each was a stubby column topped with a steering wheel minus its top quadrant, patterned after the control columns in aircraft.

Keith's mind flipped back to World War II days in the *Eel*. In some ways this was so much like going to sea on a war patrol. But yet so different, and in the space of only fifteen years!

In departing from Pearl Harbor, the *Eel* had traveled almost entirely on the surface to her operating area. Except for daily drills and the necessity to dive on appearance of an enemy aircraft, she stayed on the surface in order to make more speed. The *Cushing*, by contrast, could go faster submerged. Furthermore, she could manufacture her own atmosphere from seawater, and could dispose of carbon dioxide and carbon monoxide gases overboard. She had no need for the surface, except for entering and leaving port.

"Make your depth two hundred feet," said Keith to Curt Taylor. *Cushing*'s speed stayed rock steady at fifteen knots, her angle downward at a comfortable three degrees. As her gauges neared the two-hundred-foot mark, the planesmen pulled back on their control columns, and the ship leveled out.

"Two hundred feet, Captain," Taylor reported.

With *Cushing* once more on even keel, Keith left the control room, walked forward to his stateroom. He would keep *Cushing* on course one two five until it was time to move due east. She would find her way by sound alone, probing constantly by fathometer and forward-beam sonar against the possibility of an uncharted bottom anomaly or another ship. It was another ship that worried Keith the most. No US or NATO submarine would be routed through the vicinity of *Cushing*'s plotted positions, but there was no telling what the submarine of another nation might do. Which was another way of saying that a Russian sub might conceivably blunder into *Cushing*'s path. And if the other sub happened to be at that same depth—another remote chance in the huge world ocean—the collision could be catastrophic.

Keith gave it only a second thought, shrugged his shoulders.

Peggy had given him a letter just before he left New London, and he opened it now. As he read it his forehead furrowed.

Darling,

I know how busy you've been getting ready for this trip, so I didn't want to bother you with this before you left. I know a Navy wife is not supposed to lay a problem on her husband just before he gets under way for a long cruise, and the fact is, I wanted your last days in port to be as pleasant as possible. But I want to give you the whole story, so that you can think about it, and then we need to have a long talk after you come home.

I love you very much, Keith, and when we are together everything is just swell. But you have been away for so many long absences. You couldn't even be with me when Ruthie was born, because the Navy had you out on some sort of exercise. I'm afraid this is going to be the way our whole life together will be. We have never really been able to establish a home.

I know how much the Navy means to you, but remember, it's really the only thing you have ever known. This year you'll reach twenty years' service and become eligible to retire. This is what I want you to think about. We could move anywhere in the country, have our own little place. You could easily get a good job, and with your retirement pension we'd never have to worry.

Keith turned the paper over. Peggy digressed into a discussion of the idyllic joys of a permanent home, the garden she proposed to start, and the general peace and contentment long-term permanence seemed to spell for her. The letter was four pages long, closely written. Midway through, Keith's frown deepened.

It's different with someone like Laura Richardson or Cindy Williams, you know. Their husbands are graduates of the Naval Academy, and that means that the Navy will look out for them. You're not. Someday the Navy is just going to drop you when you least expect it. I've been seeing quite a bit of Laura lately, even if she sometimes seems so smug because of her husband. I know he was your former skipper, and you think the sun rises and sets on him. So does she, even though she was married once before and she must have heard of that Joan person he had the wartime fling with.

Laura never has said much about the war. One time something nearly came up but somehow she sidestepped it. She is a pretty cool number, not like Cindy Williams. Cindy is just a sweet kid. I wonder if Laura's heard that story going the rounds about how maybe the commodore's old friend, Joe Blunt, didn't die of a tumor on board the *Eel*, after all. I know you don't believe it, but a lot of people are still talking about it. The way I hear it now is that somebody got to him in the middle of that depth charging when you all must have been half crazy anyway, and the Navy covered it up with that business about a brain tumor.

Keith clenched his fist. It was like Peggy to say nothing to him of all these thoughts, then lay them all out when he was unable to answer, unable to prevent her from doing whatever it was she had in mind. He felt trapped, his comfort and security at home suddenly endangered. Damn Peggy, anyway!

RUNNING DEEP beneath the surface, USS *William B. Cushing* effortlessly put three hundred and sixty nautical miles behind her per day. She would make a landfall near Spitsbergen—if landfall was the proper term, for the latest air reconnaissance report had placed the edge of the ice pack well to the south of that frosty land. After Spitsbergen, at the reduced speed their orders required under the ice, the North Pole would be some four days away.

The time passed swiftly. The ice pack appeared on schedule, just at noon. Keith had instructed Jim Hanson to adjust speed in order to reach it during daylight. At the proper time, Jim slowed the ship and brought it to periscope depth. Keith spent long minutes inspecting the thin white ribbon on the horizon. *Cushing*'s other periscope had been turned over to the crew.

Seen from a distance, the ice looked like a solid line between the gray of the sea and the leaden blue of the sky. As the *Cushing* drew cautiously nearer it became evident that it was not solid but a mass of broken blocks, most weighing several tons, crumbled off the solid ice behind. When Keith had approached as close as was prudent, he turned to a course parallel to the frontal edge for a more detailed inspection.

The coloration of the ice was fascinating. White on top, of course, from the snowfall built up during the years. But where the ice entered the water it assumed a greenish tinge, shading swiftly to almost black. The discoloration was the combined result of normal sea growth, and water action on tiny organisms frozen into the ice when it was formed. This growth on the undersurface made up much of the food for the seals, porpoises, whales and fish—and through them for man himself.

Cushing had been built with an ice suit; her sail, propeller, hull and control surfaces were specially strengthened. In addition, her sailplanes were designed so that they could be put on ninety degrees rise—straight up and down—to facilitate breaking through ice if necessary. She could cope with the ice, if handled intelligently, and it was Keith's duty to learn what he could of this common yet most unusual substance.

Sunlight was waning when he housed the periscopes, ordered deep submergence and set a course due north. From this time onward, except for occasional tests of missiles, *Cushing* would be confined beneath a virtually impenetrable layer of ice twenty feet thick. As she drove northward, her echo-ranging sonar probed ahead, listening for the somewhat mushy return echo which would spell danger. There was an underwater television transmitter mounted on her main deck. With two strong searchlights, synchronized in direction with the television head, Keith could see about a hundred feet in any direction. The only thing visible, however, was the *Cushing*'s rounded bow.

Next day Keith ordered *Cushing*'s speed slowed to the minimum and gently planed upward, in order to raise a periscope. There was danger in this, of course. *Cushing* could inadvertently come too close to a hummock—a downward projection of ice—and damage her periscope. But to find an open area of water, a polynya, and surface through it, use of the periscope was imperative. (Of course, even the polynyas would be frozen over now, in winter, but with thinner ice.)

By careful calculation, the top of the scope was no closer than twenty-five feet from the bottom of the ice floe. But Keith had momentarily forgotten that the scope had a magnification of one and a half times, and his first reaction was alarm as the huge menacing cover filled the delicate lens. Training the scope forward, he saw the powerful rays from the television searchlights reflecting upon the bottom of the ice, giving it an eerie surreal effect. To either side, the ice appeared like heavy green-tinged rain clouds, except much closer and more menacing.

Cushing had just entered the ice pack, but already the vista was discouraging. The ice detector had found no polynyas at all; only solid ice, fifteen or twenty feet thick, far too much to shoot a missile through. Keith motioned for the periscope to be lowered. The entire time it was up had been one of tension.

With a sense of concern, he ordered *Cushing*'s depth increased. His mission was going to be more difficult than he had imagined. There were millions of square miles of ice in the Arctic Ocean. On his side, he had a fine ship, with a magnificent, ever supplying heart—the reactor. But compared to the vast expanse of solidity under which he must maneuver, *Cushing* was only a matchstick suspended under a flat ceiling of ice.

CHAPTER FOUR

PEGGY LEONE'S almost twice-weekly visits had become a bore, but Laura had not yet shown any of the impatience she was beginning to feel. So far there had been but one subject on Peggy's mind: her desire that Keith exercise his option to retire from active duty in the Navy. His retired pay would be fifty percent of his active-duty pay and he could easily get a job paying at least that much again, Peggy reasoned. They would buy a home somewhere, have a flower and vegetable garden. Ruthie and any later brothers and sisters would grow up in a stable environment, not traveling hither and thither like gypsies. Keith had already made his contribution to the country and the Navy; now that he was a commander, he had advanced in rank about as far as the Navy would allow a nonacademy graduate to go.

Laura was bone-weary of citing the holes in Peggy's arguments. The *Cushing* was one of the best submarines in the Navy, expected to be a candidate for all sorts of special missions. It was a feather in Keith's hat to have been given command of this somewhat special ship. But none of Laura's arguments made the slightest impression on Peggy.

For the better part of a week now, Peggy had not visited. Then this morning there had come the usual telephone call. Could she stop in on the way over or back from her doctor in New London? She had never mentioned a doctor before. Until today Peggy had cited shopping as the reason for her trip across the river.

419

Instead of offering morning coffee, Laura invited Peggy to a cup of tea in the late afternoon. Rich's return would automatically put an end to the visit. Now they were sitting in the Richardsons' small living room, a pot of tea and some cookies on the low coffee table between them.

"Keith's been gone three weeks," Peggy was saying. "I don't think I'll ever get used to having him away at sea like this."

"You know the old Navy story, don't you?" Laura said lightly. "It's a fair deal if you're happy half the time. So in the Navy you get a sure thing, because your husband is at sea half the time. One way or the other, you can't miss."

"It's all right for the men," Peggy said, after a pause barely long enough to acknowledge the ancient joke. "They're so wrapped up in their boats they can't think of anything else. It's the ones who have to stay home who suffer. The wives and kids."

Laura sighed inwardly. "Nothing is perfect, Peggy. Just living in the same old place and doing the same things for years can be pretty dull, too. I've read somewhere that there are fewer divorces in the Navy than anywhere else, for example."

"But that's not the point. The point is that some people go to the Naval Academy, and then they're in. They get promoted, and when they're admirals, they're in charge. But Keith'll never be an admiral. He'll be lucky if he makes captain!"

Laura gave up. "Look, Peggy, if you want Keith to retire from the Navy, that's your business and Keith's. I can't help, either way."

That was exactly the opening Peggy had wanted. Her large, innocent eyes turned full on Laura.

"Joan. Joan Lastrada," she said. "She helped Rich. Didn't she, Laura? He knew her pretty well during the war, you know. She was in some kind of intelligence work then. Now she's with Admiral Brighting. Didn't Rich tell you he'd seen her there?"

There was a silence in Laura's mind, a full tick in time before conscious reaction was possible. Fight for control, she thought. Show nothing. Another tick and tock of time.

"Oh, sure. Joan was a wartime romance of Rich's, before we were married, but he'd lost sight of her until now. Why bring her up? She can't help Keith."

"No, but you could." There was something furtive in Peggy's

expression. Her eyes were hidden now, veiled, her hands clenched tightly in her lap.

"What do you mean, Peggy?"

"It's just—you know—Keith thinks so much of Rich. Maybe Rich could talk to Keith, explain how the Navy really works. Keith will believe it then." Peggy's eyes bored into Laura's. "We women have to stick together," she almost whispered.

The words were said with deliberation, even the hint of a threat. Suddenly Laura realized she knew nothing about the mind behind Peggy's studied demeanor. Why had she brought up Joan Lastrada so unexpectedly?

Laura had never told Rich how much she really knew, how well she actually understood the forces driving Joan, Rich, and Jim Bledsoe, her first husband, during those tense war years. Rich had never mentioned Joan until recently. Intuitively Laura knew his reticence was at least partly because of Jim, just as hers was. She would never forget how hard it had been to keep silent, early in her marriage to Rich, after that busybody wife of a senior officer had told her that Joan had been involved with both of them.

But she had managed it, and Rich had never suspected. Then a few years later she had gotten on a train in New Haven and found herself by chance sitting next to Joan Lastrada, of all people. Quickly Laura had taken in the slender figure, the heavy black hair coiffed with just the right nonchalance, the dark eyes accentuating the slightly concave cheeks. There had been some strangeness at first, but that had passed, and Laura evermore treasured that fortuitous, completely private encounter. Years of prejudices and misconceptions had fallen away, and although their paths had crossed again, she knew it sufficed for both of them for all time.

Not so with Peggy Leone. Something was wrong with her, with her thinking. What lay behind her strange words about women sticking together? How much did she know of Joan's wartime romance with Rich? Did she know there had also been an affair with Jim Bledsoe? What was she saying now?

". . .thought a lot of Captain Blunt to name his son after him— why do some people say it's because of his guilty conscience? I don't see anything for Rich to feel guilty about. People ought to be forgetting those old rumors after all these years. . . ."

Something congealed within Laura. "What are you talking about,

Peggy?" Of course she had heard the rumors about Joe Blunt's death aboard the *Eel*. Blunt had been Rich's idol during his first years of submarine service. When Rich was made skipper of the *Eel*, Blunt had been strongly supportive. Rich had told her all about it. Then, during the latter stages of the war, Blunt had inexplicably changed. As squadron commander he had behaved irrationally, endangered the *Eel* during a near disastrous depth charging, had hurt his neck, and then had suddenly died while sitting inactively in the wardroom during a furiously fought surface action. The *Eel* had brought his body back to Pearl Harbor.

An autopsy disclosed a brain tumor, aggravated by the stress of combat. The neck injury itself was ruled out as the cause of death. But there were those who said the Navy might be covering up that someone aboard the *Eel* might have done something to him, during that terrible depth charging. Perhaps even Rich.

"Of course, I don't believe a word of it, Laura. Nobody could who knows Rich. But I thought you ought to know what they're saying." Peggy's voice was barely audible.

Peggy herself might have revived that old story, Laura thought. But why? And how to stop her without risking the spread of destructive gossip?

"Don't worry yourself about that idle talk, Peggy," she said coolly. "Rich and I have heard it all, and so has the rest of the Navy. It doesn't amount to anything." That's enough, she thought. Now get off the subject. "And don't concern yourself about Joan Lastrada, either. She's a fine person, and a good friend of ours." Enough of that subject, too. "But I can't influence Rich's official Navy actions, about Keith or anything else."

"You will speak to him, though." Peggy was still looking at her intensely, trying to project something without saying it.

Decisively Laura rose to her feet. "I'll tell him what you've told me. Now I've got to get ready. He'll be here in half an hour." Just then Laura heard the car enter the driveway. "He's home early!" she said with surprise.

A moment later Rich came in, and she knew something was wrong. The slight bustle attendant upon Peggy's departure provided a respite. Laura could sense his urgency for her guest to leave. "What's the matter?" she said when they were alone.

"Nothing that we can't fix, I hope. That's why I came home early.

422

I can't do anything on the *Proteus* right now, but I'll probably have to spend the night aboard. . . . What were you and Peggy Leone talking about?" he asked.

To Laura's sensitive antennas, it seemed there was the slightest— barely the slightest—emphasis on Peggy's married name, almost as if Keith's wife were the last person he had wanted to see.

"Just girl talk," Laura said lightly. Then intuition flooded her mind. "Is something the matter with Keith and the *Cushing?*" she asked.

The look on Rich's face told her she had hit the mark.

IT WAS QUITE DARK as Richardson parked his car near the *Proteus'* forward gangway and approached the accommodation ladder. He returned the sentry's salute, and heard *Proteus'* loudspeaker announce his arrival. Slowly he climbed the twenty-seven varnished steps to the gangway.

Buck Williams, alerted by the speaker, was waiting for him.

"We'll be fully provisioned and ready to leave by day after to-morrow if you need us, Commodore."

"Good," said Richardson. The two disengaged themselves from the obligatory attentions of *Proteus'* officer of the deck and walked toward Richardson's cabin. "I'm sorry to do this to you, Buck, but there's not much choice after that message from Keith."

"Thank God we got this little invention of yours built, Commodore, and a chance to try it out. At least there's something we can do. But maybe there won't be any need."

"Maybe," said Richardson. "I don't suppose there's been any new message?"

"Not from *Cushing*. There's one from ComSubLant, but all it does is confirm what he told you on the telephone, that you're operational commander."

When the two officers reached Richardson's cabin, Rich pushed Williams inside wordlessly, shut the door, and pulled out a message flimsy from the desk safe.

It was from the Commander, Submarine Force of the US Atlantic Fleet. For a moment, reading the flimsy again, neither spoke. It was as if, by the intensity of their concentration on the paper, they could elicit some further meaning that Keith might have put there.

URGENT FOR COMSUBLANT AND COMSUBRON TEN FROM CHAR-
LIE JULIET X POSITION GOLF NOVEMBER TWO NINE X NO POSSI-
BILITY LAUNCH EXCEPT SURFACED THROUGH MINIMUM THREE
FEET ICE COVER X ONLY FOUR POLYNYAS FOUND DURING WEEK
IN OP AREA CMA ALL ICED OVER TWO DASH THREE FEET AND
SMALL X TOP SECRET X COLLISION WITH FOREIGN SUBMARINE
WHILE SURFACING X PROPELLER DAMAGED X TOP SECRET X

Williams broke the silence. "It tells us practically nothing. He's
left out everything we need to know."

"That's not quite true. The information about the collision came
at the end of the message instead of the beginning."

"You'd think that would be the first thing on his mind."

"How about an add-on," Rich said.

"Add-on?" Buck was incredulous.

"Encoding a message is the hard part. That and writing it carefully. Keith probably spent half the day getting his routine message
encoded and ready to broadcast the minute the *Cushing* got her
antenna above the ice. I think he added on that last 'top secret' bit
hurriedly. The collision could have happened only minutes before
that message got on the air!"

"You think that's why he made it so short?"

"That's my guess. It's the first thing we've gotten from him since
he went under the ice pack. He must have had more to say. I think
he scrubbed at least half of what he had there at first. And he made
it short because he didn't want to transmit for long."

"But why not, boss? The other sub must also be damaged. It's
probably trying to surface to get off a message to its headquarters,
too. What difference does that make?"

"Not so fast, Buck. Two boats have collided under the ice. It's
bound to annoy that Russian skipper a little."

"How do you know the other skipper's a Russian?"

"All I'm doing is guessing. The Arctic Ocean is bigger than the
whole United States. If the only two subs tooling around up there
have a collision, that's one hell of a big coincidence. One sure thing
is that Keith's doing a lot of guessing too. His orders were to remain
undetected at all costs—and to be alert for possible unfriendly
reaction to his presence."

"What right do the Russians or anybody else have to object to
his being there? It's international waters."

424

"Sure. But one half of it borders on their country. They certainly won't like our putting a missile sub up there."

"If that's the way Keith's thinking, it would account for his trying to be on the air as little as possible, I guess," said Buck. "At least, that would make it harder for the Russians to locate him with their direction-finding stations. Do you think he'll send another message?"

"I sure do. Another short one, and he'll send it at the best radio propagation time, when we're in darkness. That's why I'm sleeping aboard tonight." Richardson abruptly changed the subject. "Did you find out how this message was routed?"

"Radio Asmara. Relayed on landline to Washington. We got our copy from the Pentagon and had it decoded even before ComSub-Lant, down in Norfolk."

"Radio Asmara, eh?" The cadence of Richardson's speech slowed perceptibly. Asmara, in Ethiopia, was one of the main communications stations serving the US Sixth Fleet in the Mediterranean. "It's a quarter of the way around the world. Keith must have had the devil of a time getting through," Richardson mused. "If we can intercept his next transmission direct, instead of depending on some shore station to relay it, we might learn quite a bit just from the way he sends it."

Buck was silent for a short moment, then said speculatively, "Do you think we could talk to him by voice?"

Richardson hesitated. "No. At least, not for anything important. Any real information must come coded."

"But just think, Rich, what it will do for Keith and the crew if we can talk to him!" Buck was speaking rapidly. "We don't know anything at all about what kind of shape he's in. What he and his outfit want to hear is that we're right in there with them now."

"Yes, but there may be an army of unfriendly communication types monitoring everything that goes on the air in that area."

Sensing Rich's desire to be convinced, Buck pressed the argument. "I'm talking about morale, boss, not security. We don't need to say anything about what they're doing. Don't you think Keith knows us well enough to read between the lines?"

Weakening, Rich nodded. "The problem is that we'll be making him transmit a second time. If they're monitoring the area, we're making it that much easier for them to locate him. It would be wrong to make him send a lot of procedural transmissions to establish the voice contact."

Satisfied that he had won, Buck said, "That's no problem, boss. The call-up procedure, I mean. We'll use our old wolf-pack code. It'll work like a charm!"

"The wolf-pack code?"

"Sure. Don't you remember the communication procedure Keith and I worked out during the war when you had to run that wolf pack for Commodore Blunt? It cut out a lot of excess transmissions so that we could put out the important dope in a hurry. Well, before he left on this secret trip of his, Keith and I dragged it out again and we worked up a vocabulary for the barrier exercise. There's been a lot of changes in communications, but for fast passing of dope between subs the wolf-pack code is perfect."

Richardson felt his own enthusiasm beginning to match that of his junior. "How would you use it?"

"We wait for Keith to send the next message. He'll be in his own radio room, right? The minute he gets the receipt from the shore station working him, we break in and tell him what we're up to. Then we shift over to the single sideband set and talk to him. He won't have to transmit one single syllable if he doesn't want to."

"Looks like you're planning for us to break a couple of our communication rules, Buck, but it sounds good. You'd better take over one of the staterooms and get some sleep before the message comes in. Maybe you should tell Cindy you'll not be home tonight."

Buck grinned. "I did already."

THE INTERCOM PHONE buzzed on the bulkhead above Richardson's bed. He reached for it swiftly.

"Commodore, this is Radio. We're intercepting a message from *Cushing* to shore station Annapolis, coming in loud and clear."

"Call Commander Williams. I'll be right up!" Rich slammed the phone down, jammed his feet into slippers, ran out the door in his pajamas. Buck arrived in the radio room seconds after he did.

There were three crewmen there, one a supervisor. "I called you as soon as the message began, Commodore," the senior said. "We're copying it at two stations." He indicated the two radiomen seated at typewriters, earphones on their heads, clacking the keys as their eyes stared miles beyond their radio receivers.

"Have you another set of earphones?"

"Yes, sir." The radio supervisor swiftly handed Richardson a set. Rich detached one of the earphones from its clip, handed it to Buck, and put on the headpiece.

XVTMW, said the radio waves. PLTMV ZAWLN MMPTL XZBKG—the rhythm was steady, hypnotic. Glancing at one of the typewriters, Buck Williams could see the encrypted message forming, the letters coming one by one as the distant operator hammered them out. Williams had learned Morse code early in his career. He had never become good at it, but he could recognize the letters.

"Dash dot dash dot," went the faint signal. The letter C appeared on the paper as the radioman hit the typewriter key. Then a single dash, the letter T. Then three more: O. Buck could visualize the operator, far to the north, beating out the dots and dashes as rapidly as he could, yet with that steady, precise formulation vital to accurate receipt. Keith must also at that very moment be hunched next to his radio operator, following the transmission. He would hear the signals streaming out from his ship, imagine them crossing the frozen ocean, bouncing off the ionosphere. He would hear the faint notes as Annapolis responded to his call. Finally he would hear the R for receipt that indicated the shore station now assumed responsibility for the message and its delivery to the addressees. Not until a message of this importance had cleared would Keith himself leave his radio room.

"Chief," Buck said to the radio supervisor in a low voice, "is your transmitter on this frequency?"

"Yes, sir. But we don't have the power to reach the *Cushing*."

"We can hear *Cushing* okay, and we have bigger transmitters than she has. So she ought to be able to hear us."

"Sometimes it works," said the supervisor doubtfully, "but Annapolis answered her call-up, sir. All we're doing is copying her message. There's no way she could know we're on the circuit."

"I know," Buck said. "But if we can hear him, isn't right now the best chance we'll ever get for him to hear us?"

"Where is he exactly, sir?"

"Sorry, Chief. Security. Anyway, he's in about the same longitude as we are, and so is Radio Annapolis. So that means the radio conditions in this north-south line right now are at their best." Richardson had become an approving onlooker, Buck noticed.

427

It would be necessary to disregard the rule against transmitting while in port. *Proteus'* transmitter, already on the frequency, would be fine-tuned to Annapolis' transmissions. Then, as soon as Annapolis receipted to the *Cushing*, *Proteus*, acting as though she were another ship at sea waiting for the circuit to clear, would open up with the cryptic call signs of the old wolf-pack code. These would mean nothing to anyone but Keith, if he were there.

But Keith *would* be there. The problem was whether he could afford to stay on the surface long enough for more messages.

"We don't have much time. What do we send him?" Rich asked.

Buck showed him the message he had written. "He'll spot this for the wolf-pack code as soon as he hears it."

"Ke Ri Bu C5," read Richardson aloud. "But he won't have the code book with him in the radio room."

"He won't need it. That's the beauty of it. He and I spent quite a bit of time working these out for that barrier exercise. The first three groups are the first two letters of the names we use for each other—Keith, Rich, Buck;"

"But what's this C5?" Richardson asked.

"It means crystal system number five. Since single sideband is frequency-controlled by crystal, this message tells him we want to talk to him on the SSB radio, and which sets of crystals to use."

There was a drop in Richardson's voice. "Remember, Buck, voice isn't secure. Any ideas about what we can do to help him will have to go in a classified encoding message. We told him about your towing hookup rig in our answer to his first message."

"You're boss, and you'll do the talking." Buck waved the message pad. "They're nearly finished transmitting. Can I give the chief the go-ahead? We've got to break right in before the *Cushing* closes down."

Richardson nodded his assent, and Buck began talking earnestly to the radioman. A moment later he reported with a smile, "Annapolis will hear us, too, and out of curiosity they'll listen in to see what's coming off. They'll hear the chief send our little message five times and then hear him shut down. Keith will both see it on paper and hear it in his earphones."

"You're sure he won't answer and alert anyone listening that it was meant for him?"

"He won't," said Buck with a confident grin. "It's in the code

428

not to do that. If he hears our transmission, the next thing we hear from him will be his own voice on SSB."

There was a change in the smooth cadence of the incoming message. The last few letters were drawn out by the tiniest of fractions. Then the distant transmitter fell silent. The chief, seated now at a third operating station, fingered the transmitting key, looked inquiringly at Richardson.

"Go ahead," said Rich. "Open up as soon as Annapolis sends the R. I'll take responsibility."

Buck pressed the earpiece hard against one ear. Richardson did the same. They heard a prolonged, positive dot dash dot, the letter R, sent with all the finality that could be mustered in a single monosyllabic note. Instantly came a faint tap from the *Cushing*'s operator acknowledging that he had been fully serviced. His next move would be to turn off his transmitter.

Proteus' chief swung into action. One hand on his tuning dial, the other on his transmitter key, he sent a single long dash. Then, without preamble, he began to send the wolf-pack call sign, five times without pause. The radiomen at the receiving stations typed the short message. Then, as unceremoniously as it had begun, the transmission was finished. With a loud *cachunk* the transmitter power hum abruptly stopped.

AA DE NSS, the radiomen typed, and a moment later, K. "Unknown station using this net, identify yourself." There was a faintly querulous note to Radio Annapolis' normally steady tone.

Buck and the chief were smiling. So was Richardson as he said, "Don't answer. We'll worry about confessing some other time." Then to Buck, "What now, mister communications wizard?"

"We wait long enough for Keith's people to set up his SSB set, and then we start talking."

"Do you want to take it here?" the chief asked.

"Here's fine," said Rich. "We may need your help."

"Okay, sir," said the chief, handing a microphone to Richardson. "Just press this button on the mike and talk across it. You'll hear him on our speaker when you let go of the button."

Rich fingered the microphone. "Are we all ready? Has he had enough time?"

"Yes, sir. Go ahead."

Richardson pressed the button, held the microphone to his

mouth. "Keith," he said, "this is Rich. Buck is here, too. Do you read me? How are you, old man?" He released the button.

The chief radioman had his fingers on the receiver dials, sensitively moving them. There was a crackle, then there were words—faint, surrounded by static—but words nevertheless.

"—and clear," the voice, suddenly distinct, said through the speaker. "How me? Over." It was Keith.

Richardson felt a peculiar sensation on his skin. He pressed the mike button. "We hear you, Keith. Buck's here with me. There's an answer on the way, to your first dispatch, and we've just intercepted your second. Can you stay up on voice? Over."

"Negative, Rich. There's too much activity over the equator." Rich caught the sharp glance from Buck. "Our second message explains it better. It's great to hear you, though. Over." Keith spoke rapidly now, with just enough emphasis on the word great to accentuate the undercurrent of anxiety.

"Okay, Keith. We just want you to know we're with you. Anytime you want to use this circuit, we'll be here. Over."

Keith evidently had begun talking even before Rich enunciated the final word. "—help a great deal," his voice said. "There's not much time. . . ." There was a pause, someone saying something, then Keith again. "Got to go. Thanks for calling. Out."

Rich put down the mike. "He's under a lot of pressure, Buck," he said gravely. "Something's wrong up there. Let's take this message of his and decode it." He turned to the senior radioman. "Chief, call us if you hear anything else."

Proteus' coding machine was a new model, unfamiliar to both officers. An added complication was the necessity of implementing a totally new top secret code. Many false starts were necessary before the machine finally began to type out intelligible copy. Richardson and Williams, their heads nearly touching, read the words as they appeared from under the typing bar.

FROM CHARLIE JULIET X SECOND REPORT FOR COMSUBLANT COMSUBRON TEN X MAX SHAFT SPEED TWENTY RPM WITH HEAVY VIBRATION X PROPELLER STERN PLANES AND LOWER RUDDER DAMAGED COLLISION SUBMERGED OBJECT BELIEVED TO BE SOVIET SUBMARINE X SECONDARY PROPULSION MOTOR WIPED OFF X NO SERIOUS LEAKS X NO PREVIOUS SONAR CONTACT X MILITARY TYPE AIRCRAFT APPARENTLY SEARCHING AREA X UNA-

430

BLE INSPECT SCREW WITH NO RISK DETECTION X ICE COVER
FIFTEEN DASH TWENTY FEET EXCEPT POLYNYAS FEW AND FAR
BETWEEN X INSPECTION MANDATORY BEFORE PROCEEDING DUE
VERY HEAVY VIBRATION X REMAINING IN POLYNYA POSITION
GOLF NOVEMBER TWO NINE AWAITING OPPORTUNITY USE DI-
VERS X SUSPECT BENT SHAFT X WILL REPORT RESULTS ASAP X IN
VIEW APPARENT DAMAGE BELIEVE MUST ABORT MISSION BUT
UNABLE ESTIMATE ABILITY YET TO CLEAR PACK X

Richardson broke the silence. "Buck, this is a real emergency!
You said your ship could get out of here tomorrow?"

"That's right. But we're not on any emergency basis."

"Go down now and check the critical items. Be back here in an
hour. We can have a quick breakfast while we talk it over, then I'll
phone Norfolk. By that time they'll have decoded the message and
rushed it to Admiral Murphy, and he'll be anxious to talk to us."

CHAPTER FIVE

THERE HAD BEEN no warning whatever of the presence of another submarine. It must have been running silent. Nothing
else could have produced the sudden, disconcerting heave of *Cushing's* big hull, the metallic grinding sound as her propeller blades
were mangled. The initial shock had thrown the big missile submarine forward and heavily to starboard. It was followed by a series
of smaller, more scraping blows, and suddenly it was over, the
noise gone, leaving only slow-growing appreciation of disaster.

A careful inspection of the turbine mounts and the propeller-
shaft steady bearing, conducted later, confirmed that these massive
mechanisms had been displaced as much as half an inch, and had
then returned to their normal positions. *Cushing's* engineering
officer, Curt Taylor, was incredulous, but the proof was
indisputable.

Keith had been maneuvering his ship slowly, positioning her
under a promising opening in the ice. Originally it had been a long
narrow channel, or lead, in the ice floe. It was frozen over at the
surface now to a depth of three or four feet. Seen from below, it
was the shape of a ravine.

In order to break through the thin ice cover Keith first had to align the bulbous 420-foot *Cushing* between the two downward-projecting ice cliffs on either side of the lead, then bring her up exactly midway in the thin spot. He had been using both his main power and the auxiliary "outboard motor", a retractable emergency electric-propulsion motor, when the collision came. His first reaction was that they must have struck an unnoticed, disastrously deep ice pinnacle—an unseen berg embedded in the ice.

But sonar, which had continuously been reporting all clear, suddenly announced strange noises dead astern. Why sonar had not previously given some warning would bear investigation; but Keith was aware of the vagaries of underwater sound transmission.

The foreign submarine had struck the *Cushing* right aft, on a slightly divergent heading, shoving her ahead and sideways, and positioning her by chance almost exactly where Keith had wanted her. He seized the opportunity to bring her the rest of the way up to the frozen surface, then began blowing his main ballast tanks.

Cushing's specially reinforced sail broke through the ice with a great creaking and groaning, carrying a big chunk of "frosting" atop the dark, rectangular-appearing structure. But Keith stopped blowing before the entire hull had heaved through the pack. The remaining undisturbed ice would conceal the *Cushing* from surface or air observation, while the inverted crevasse into which he had brought her would shield her from sonar detection. It was almost like an underwater garage.

Keith weighed the priorities. There would be some delay while a hastily organized work party hacked away with axes and crowbars, first to clear the bridge of ice, then to clear the ship's retractable antennas for hoisting. Ten or fifteen minutes would elapse before *Cushing*'s radio could begin to transmit. A message—long overdue, anyway—had been written by him and Jim Hanson when the decision was made to surface in this lead. Encryption had been completed only an hour ago. But the few minutes before the message could be sent were long enough to make a quick change to report the collision. He had handed the quickly revised text to the radio operator and then, donning a heavy parka, wool trousers and boots, had hurried to the bridge.

The hatch trunk leading to the bridge allowed at least some transition from the temperature inside the submarine to that of the winter Arctic. Keith's lungs nevertheless felt as though he had suddenly drawn in a shaft of solid ice. He kept his head down, knotted the drawstrings of his parka hood, and shoved his mittened hands under his armpits. In the freezing wind it was much easier to look leeward, but he forced himself to survey the entire horizon.

The month of March was at midpassage, and the sun had not yet broken above the horizon. The entire Arctic was a rapidly lightening twilight zone. The temperature topside, according to a thermometer on the bridge, was minus forty degrees Fahrenheit.

Keith had lost sensation in his cheeks. Frostbite must be near. A few feet away, four men garbed as he was were demolishing the last of the ice on *Cushing's* sail. They had been topside far longer than he. The stiffness of their features and the clumsiness of their movements showed it.

There was something he could do for them, for morale in general. He pressed the button for the bridge speaker. "Control, this is the captain. The ice-chopping crew is finished and coming below. Tell the doctor to issue them a ration of medicinal spirits. Also, be sure all hands coming topside wear face masks and full cold-weather gear." He released the button, pressed it again. "I'm going out on the ice," he said. "Send me a face mask, and keep a watch on me through the periscope."

He released the button, waited for the face mask, then began to climb over the side of the bridge cockpit. Doubtless there would be little damage he could see, but it would give him solitude to consider what next to do.

KEITH WAS GRATEFUL to the supply officer who had included white paint in *Cushing's* special Arctic equipment. While he was thawing out in the engine room, watching Curt Taylor and his machinist's mates as they crawled among the heavy foundations of the propeller shaft, another half-dozen men were earning their rations of medicinal brandy by hastily daubing a coat of white paint over all visible portions of the ship.

Damage assessment was dismaying. There was a series of dents along the sub's bottom, visible from inside, and the shock to her propulsion machinery had been enormous. Her huge propeller was undoubtedly badly damaged, and the propeller shaft showed measurable travel from side to side as the electric "creep motor" rotated it slowly. When faster revolutions were attempted, under turbine power, the instantaneous vibration transmitted to the machinery was so strong that Keith ordered the shaft stopped.

"Whew!" muttered Curt Taylor, mopping sweat off his ample face. "The shaft must be really bent out of shape!"

"It looks bad," agreed Keith, in an equally low voice. "Curt . . ." He drew the chief engineer away from the others. "We've got to hope at least one blade of that screw can still give us some thrust. The emergency propulsion motor is gone! Wiped clean off."

Taylor's eyes widened. "It was rigged out. I'd forgotten!"

Cushing, like all the big missile submarines, had been designed with a retractable electric-powered outboard motor, which could be extended below the keel, for close maneuvering, or for emergency propulsion. Normally it was carried completely housed. But Keith had been using it to help position the ship under the frozen lead, and it had been sheared off. *Cushing* was now totally dependent on her main drive for any movement.

Taylor's face showed the seriousness with which he viewed the situation. "Skipper," he said, "we had the shaft up to twenty rpm, but I don't think we could even keep that up for long. It looked to me like it's definitely bent out of line."

"If it can drive the ship at all, Curt, we've got to use it. Try loosening some of the foundation bolts—"

The telephone buzzed. "For you, Captain," a crewman said, and held out the instrument.

Keith listened, put it back on its cradle with a terse thanks, and turned to Taylor. "They need me up in control, Curt. Do everything you can. We're in deep trouble."

From the after end of the engine room to the control room was a distance of over three hundred feet, the major portion devoted to the silos in the missile compartment—sixteen tremendous cylinders, extending vertically from the bottom of the submarine through all the decks between and through the hull on top.

The huge vertical tubes, painted a light coral tone, had never failed to impress Keith with their total lack of malevolence. And yet, were these sixteen silos fully loaded with war-ready missiles—at the moment they were not—they would carry within them more power than the total used by both sides in both world wars!

Keith continued his hurried trip into the cluttered open space which was the nerve center of the ship. His second-in-command,

Jim Hanson, sprouting the red beard which would come off before return to port, was standing on the raised starboard periscope station, a look of concern on his face. "I lowered the periscope, Skipper," he said. "There's an airplane on the horizon, and I figured we'd be a little harder to see with it down."

"Is it coming this way?" Keith leaped up the metal steps.

"Couldn't tell. It wasn't coming right at us. Yet, anyway."

With a decisive movement Keith shoved the hydraulic control handle, started the periscope up. "I'll have to take a look," he muttered. "Do we have anyone topside?"

"Negative," said Hanson. "All hatches are shut."

"Good," said Keith as the periscope appeared smoothly out of its well. He snapped the handles down, hooked his right elbow over one, his left hand on the other, put his face to the eyepiece. "We can't dive out of this hole we're in until we know if we have propulsion." He began to rotate the tall, thin instrument. "We'd never get back to it." Without taking his eye from the eyepiece, he leaned to his left, letting the weight of his body help spin the periscope. He stopped suddenly, manipulated the controls. Then he looked for a long instant and flipped up the handles. The periscope began to drop away.

"What do you see?" Hanson asked.

"Three planes on the horizon, circling around something."

"You think they're looking for the boat that hit us?"

"Could be, I s'pose, but that would be pretty fast work."

"Could you make out the markings?"

"No. But I'm glad we had enough white paint to cover everything that came up through the ice." Keith paused. "Listen, I don't want to use the periscope any more than we can help. But we've got to keep a watch on them. Get a lookout topside right away. He'll need heavy-weather gear, and a heater in the bridge cockpit. Also have him wrap a white sheet around himself."

"Aye, aye, sir," said Hanson.

Keith was grateful for the reversion to official language. Jim Hanson's questions had begun to be uncomfortable. For he could already feel growing within him the dread of what he might discover when at last the propeller was inspected. With the secondary propulsion system gone and the main propulsion out of commission, he and his ship and crew were trapped in the Arctic!

435

DRAFTING THE SECOND MESSAGE had taken well over an hour, because of the necessity to compress as much meaning as possible into the fewest words. As Rich and Buck had surmised, the transmission had been timed to go out while there was the best chance of reception on the east coast of the United States. And Keith was in the radio room, earphones on, while it was being sent. There had been a perceptible thrill as he recognized the interposition of a new station transmitting his own wolf-pack code.

The radioman swiftly set up the single sideband radio and made the initial transmissions. Suddenly Richardson's voice boomed over the loudspeaker. "Buck is here, too. . . .How are you, old man?" There was a certain guardedness in the words.

Keith had not thought about security. Only now, sensing Richardson's reticence at speaking out plainly, did the possibility of interception by unwanted listeners cross his mind. Thinking fast, he said into his microphone, "This is Keith. I read you loud and clear. How me? Over." It would not do to use the name of his ship over voice radio, but his own first name would be all right.

They were still talking when the ship's telephone rang. The radioman held it out to Keith. "For you, sir."

"This is the OOD on the bridge, Captain. One of those planes seems to be headed this way."

"Keep me informed," Keith said to the officer of the deck. "And be ready to submerge!" Keith dropped the handset.

Richardson's voice on the speaker was saying, "Can you stay up on the voice? Over."

"Negative, Rich. There's too much activity over the equator. . . ." Maybe he was being a little coy, but there was no point in giving away his position to a chance listener.

Suddenly Richardson's transmission was paralleled by the ship's general communication system. Hanson's voice. "Captain, this is Jim. I'm on the bridge. That plane is closer than ever before. It's on a steady bearing. I think it's headed this way!"

Rich was saying something about maintaining a watch on the voice circuit. Keith had already begun a reply. Perhaps the plane had a direction finder, was homing in on his transmissions! Hurriedly he closed out the conversation. His voice, he knew, would transmit its own sense of exigency.

The control room was a step away, through a bulkhead. Once

there, Keith picked up the periscope-station mike, called the bridge. "Jim, I'm in conn. What's it like now?"

Jim's voice filled the control room. "It's almost out of sight now, flying low. Still steady bearing, though."

An old memory clicked in Keith's mind. The pupils of his eyes dilated as the impact sank in. The plane was flying low. There was malevolent intent in that. It might be on an attack run! "Clear the bridge!" he yelled, his fingers gripping the microphone suddenly. "Take her down!" With his other hand he pushed the control of the hydraulic periscope hoist. As the bright metal tube slithered silently up from the well he could sense the bustle of the control room crew standing up to their stations, waiting for the orders that would send the powerless *Cushing* deep into the icy sea.

Jim Hanson had sounded the diving alarm from the bridge. He would be the next to last man down. Already the lookout, bulky in the heavy clothing under his white sheet, had appeared in the control room. Keith glanced quickly at the ballast control panel. Its operator was flipping the last of the switches that would open vents, let air out of tanks.

Keith grabbed the periscope handles. Just as he had thought! The plane was flying hazardously low, almost brushing the ice, trying to remain concealed. It was headed directly for the *Cushing*.

Keith turned the periscope to look aft. Yes, his sub's rudder had vanished below the ice. He could not see whether her sail was still visible. The plane was closer, although he had been looking away less than ten seconds. "What's the depth?" Keith snapped.

"Forty-six feet." Jim Hanson, now standing beside him, answered instantly. "Zero bubble. Forty-six and a half—now it's forty-seven feet. Seven feet to go!" Good man. Jim knew the *Cushing* went completely under at keel depth fifty-four feet.

The plane was close now, a two-engine, propeller-driven, high-wing monoplane, with fixed landing gear rigged with skis.

"Forty-nine feet," said Jim. The plane was clearly not a combat aircraft. But the idea that the Russians could mount a rescue effort for their submarine in such a short time simply did not wash. Perhaps—the idea struck suddenly home—the three aircraft and the submarine were part of a combined operation. Perhaps their presence and the collision were not accidental!

The plane had suddenly assumed a climbing attitude. A small

437

object detached itself from its belly, separated rapidly from it, grew swiftly in size as the plane zoomed upward.

"Sound the collision alarm! He's dropped something! Looks like a bomb!" Keith turned the periscope rapidly, keeping the plane in sight as the scream of the collision alarm and the deep thuds of slamming watertight doors reverberated in his ears.

"Fifty-one feet," said Jim. *Cushing*'s sail must be nearly out of view, buried in the snow.

Blam! The explosion came with shocking suddenness. A cloud of white—flying snow and ice—filled the periscope lens. The plane was lost to view. But, on releasing the bomb, the craft obviously had begun climbing to escape the shock wave of the detonation, which could be as hazardous to the bomber as to the target.

"Fifty-three feet." *Cushing* was dropping faster. The periscope must be lowered soon. Keith snapped up the handles but kept his face to the eyepiece. Hanson lowered it at half speed. Just before Keith had to pull his head clear, he thought he saw the plane, barely visible through the thinning smoke and debris. Afterward he could not be sure, but there was something different about it— something suddenly askew. He did not see the wing spar give way, the wing collapse upon the craft's fuselage.

Aboard the *Cushing*, only a sonarman heard the muffled crash as the disabled plane shattered itself on the ice. The sound, transmitted first through the unyielding ice and then through water, resembled nothing he had ever heard. It was much less frightening than the explosion which had blasted into his eardrums moments before.

There was no further underwater noise. The sonarman took up his logbook and began to compose a laborious description of what he had heard in that confusing and scary instant. Not until the next day, as the submarine hovered in the quiet of the frigid Arctic, unable to move, did the man call his superior's attention to the strange noise that he had heard.

CHAPTER SIX

VICE ADMIRAL MURPHY, ComSubLant, was talking long-distance from Norfolk. "Yes, they just brought me the message, Rich. I was about to call you." The uneasiness in his voice was unusual.

"This will have to go to the Chief of Naval Operations right away. He'll probably take it to the Joint Chiefs. The National Security Council and the President will have it this afternoon!"

The idea that the very highest authority would immediately become involved was a shock to Richardson.

"How long has Leone been up there?" the admiral asked.

"He's been in the operating area just nine days, sir."

"Umm—maybe we should have turned him around before."

"How's that?" Rich's voice had risen.

"Probably we should have told you. This whole business has gotten a lot hotter than we thought it would. Somehow the Russians got word of Leone's mission, and they protested even before he entered the area."

"I see, sir." Richardson paused, then went on. "We had Leone on single sideband three hours ago." He told of the attempt at voice communication and its sudden termination.

"Why didn't you report it?" There was now a tone of acerbity. "We didn't mind your fooling with the towing contraption, but you should have asked me before trying that voice caper."

"There wasn't time, Admiral! He'd have been gone in a minute." Rich was speaking swiftly now. "It's that towing rig I want to report on. It will work. We've tested it. I'm recommending we send the *Manta* to snake the *Cushing* out."

Admiral Murphy's change in attitude was instantly obvious. "Do you really think it will do the job?"

"It'll work, all right. It takes some practice, but we're pretty sure we've got the bugs out of it."

"Um. Okay, Rich. I'll report this to Washington right away."

IT WAS MIDNIGHT of the same day. Richardson's office on board the *Proteus* had been converted to a small conference room, and Rich had just finished describing his towing device to the powerful group of naval officers present. All except Rich and Buck were in civilian clothes. Admiral Donaldson, Chief of Naval Operations, a near legendary destroyer commander during World War II, had taken charge, but Rich was also conscious of the darting eyes of Vice Admiral Brighting, sitting in the second row.

"Commodore Richardson has come up with an idea to save the situation," Donaldson was saying. "It was a good enough idea to bring us up from Washington for this conference aboard his own flagship. Sending *Manta* after *Cushing*, as Richardson proposes, is one alternative. Are there others?"

"There's still a chance the *Cushing's* propeller isn't entirely gone," said Admiral Murphy. "We should be getting another message with more information anytime. Maybe Leone'll be able to get out on his own."

"When did your message to him clear, Murph?" Donaldson said.

"About noon. He ought to have answered before this."

"Maybe he can't. What do you think, Rich?"

"If he's at shallow depth," said Richardson, "he can receive messages through his underwater antenna. But he can't transmit unless he can get an antenna through the ice cover. My guess is that he can't move."

"How long can he last there?"

"His reactor must be all right, or he'd have said something. So he's got plenty of power. He can control his own atmosphere. Provisions are his limiting factor. Assuming nothing happens to his reactor, he can last three months or more."

Donaldson nodded. The set of his mouth was suddenly grim. "If Leone won't transmit, we have to assume it's because he can't. So, if we don't get something pretty soon, we'll have to take action based on not expecting to hear from him at all. The Joint Chiefs have considered ordering him to scuttle and sending Arctic-equipped planes to pick up the crew, but we don't know whether they can get out. Even so, we've directed the Air Force to get two transports ready, but preparing the aircraft will take two weeks."

"We ought not to abandon the ship." It was the monotonous, expressionless voice of Admiral Brighting. "That's our newest and best reactor. Scuttling should be our last option."

"We all agree on that, Martin," said the Chief of Naval Operations, "but saving the crew is the very bottom line. Tready, have your boys come up with any ideas? Is there a way to fix the propeller or replace the emergency propulsion motor?"

Rear Admiral Treadwell, in charge of the New London submarine flotilla, shook his head. "We've been brainstorming all day, but either one of these fixes is a dry-dock job. Up there under the ice, there's no way at all." He cleared his throat morosely.

Richardson, who had been carrying on a low-voiced discussion

440

with Buck Williams, caught Donaldson's eye. With Donaldson's nod of assent, he said, "There's really three things *Manta* can do when she gets up there. One is to try the submerged tow operation. Another is to serve as communications relay station, assuming the *Cushing* is immobilized under the ice and can't transmit—the *Manta* may be able to talk to her through her underwater voice communicating set. The third thing is that if worse comes to worst she can come alongside under the ice and take *Cushing*'s crew aboard through the escape hatches.

"The problem is though, that it will take her two weeks to get up there. About as long as to get the planes ready. But it's one string to our bow. We ought to send her now, and in the meantime get the planes ready, too."

There was a glint in Donaldson's eyes. "That's a convincing argument to me, Rich. Does anyone have anything more to add? . . . Then that's settled. Now—can anyone enlighten me on this next item?" He extracted a folded paper from an inside pocket, put on a pair of Navy-issue glasses and began to read:

"US sub shoots down Soviet research plane, claims Kremlin (Tass). In an unprecedented action, the Soviet Foreign Office today released the text of a secret report from the commander of the current Russian polar exploration expedition, claiming that an unnamed American submarine in Arctic waters had without cause opened fire on and shot down a Soviet research aircraft attached to his group. The aircraft had approached the submarine to ascertain its nationality and request it not to interfere with the research being conducted. Instead of responding to this legitimate request, the submarine, later identified as a nuclear missile-launching type belonging to the United States, opened fire with a sophisticated weapon, a single shot of which caused the plane to crash on the ice with the loss of one crew member and injury to the others.

"Clearly the fact that one of its submarines has invaded the peaceful waters of the Arctic Ocean shows the perfidy of the United States. . ."

Admiral Donaldson finished reading. No one spoke. "What do you reckon happened?" Donaldson finally said. Then, singling out Admiral Murphy, "Murph, this has got to be the *Cushing* they're talking about. You're not putting any new weapons on your boats, are you?" Although there was a light tone to his question, the look on his face had no levity.

441

"No, sir," said Murphy. "The *Cushing* has no such weapons. A couple of rapid-fire rifles, maybe. What do you think, Tready?"

"It probably was the *Cushing* all right," said Treadwell, "but I agree with Murphy. She could not have shot down an aircraft."

"Brighting?" Donaldson asked.

"It seems the Soviets are saying they've lost an aircraft."

"You're right. That's the only positive statement in the whole press release," said Donaldson. "Murph, put it all in your next message to the *Cushing*. Maybe Leone'll have an explanation, if he can use his radio. Well, I guess that's it. Oh, wait a minute—Rich, have you thought about going on this expedition yourself?"

"We had thought about it, sir, but . . ." Indeed, there was nothing he wanted so much. But to be too affirmative might suggest a lack of confidence in Buck. He remembered his own ambivalent reaction at taking his old skipper, Joe Blunt, on that second, fatal war patrol of the *Eel*. "I'm sure Buck Williams is fully able to handle this mission on his own," Rich went on. "Having a squadron commander along would just weight him down."

"Your modesty does you credit, Richardson, but the place for you is aboard the *Manta*, overseeing your brainchild. I'm sure Commander Williams will agree"—Buck was nodding his head visibly in agreement—"and besides, I want someone up there who can take special initiative on his own, if the occasion demands. You may run into a lot more up there than we expect."

The eyes that returned Richardson's puzzled look were as free of hidden meaning as a child's. Rich wanted to ask him to explain the apparently offhand comment, but could not.

MANTA'S BRIDGE was as different from *Eel's* as it could possibly be, narrow and streamlined for minimum underwater resistance, totally enclosed except for a tiny cockpit just forward of the two periscopes and retractable masts.

As the submarine proceeded down the Thames River, Richardson, out on the bridge cockpit beside Buck Williams, savored the cold morning river mist. He had become well acquainted with the bracing air during the past weeks. The only difference was that this time, instead of a short jaunt to sea for testing, *Manta* was setting out on a voyage thousands of miles to the north. At its end lay a crippled submarine, whose only chance for survival rested in the efficacy of a pair of newly designed devices loaded in *Manta*'s two stern torpedo tubes.

"Topside is secured for sea, Commodore," said Buck, "and the ship is rigged for dive. We'll be securing the maneuvering watch after we round Southwest Ledge lighthouse."

"Very well," said Rich. He and Buck had been standing above the cockpit's bulwarks on folding metal steps. Buck moved down at the same time Rich did for a little more protection from the cold wind. The move brought the two men shoulder to shoulder.

"How did you leave Laura, Skipper?" asked Williams.

"Oh, she was caught by surprise, of course, but she took it in stride. She knew something was going on, especially with that late-night session aboard the *Proteus*. Also, she'd guessed it had something to do with Keith, and that's got to be nothing but a woman's intuition."

"She couldn't be your wife all these years and not know when something big is up, Skipper."

"THERE'S AN EMERGENCY ON," Laura had said, "and it's got something to do with Keith. It's all over the base." She had been asleep when Rich came back from the conference, but had gotten out of bed to help him throw together some changes of clothing to take with him. "Peggy called here a couple of hours ago. She's hysterical."

"What about?"

"Oh, everything. She's found out about the conference you've just come from. What really set her off, though, was a telephone call from a newspaper in Washington."

"What did they want?"

"Mainly, the man asked if Keith was skipper of the *Cushing*. Then he came on about Keith being mixed up in some kind of a fracas with the Russians, and that really scared her. I promised I'd call her back when I'd had a chance to talk to you."

"There's nothing I could tell her," said Rich. "Was it the reporter who told her about the conference? They ought not to be allowed to do that kind of thing. Calling up a skipper's wife . . ." He threw some khaki shirts into his suitcase. "Well, you can't call her back."

"Come on, Rich. It's her husband. And she needs help."

"Okay. But you have to say that you don't know anything about

443

any conference. So far as you know, Keith's all right. So's the *Cushing*. The *Manta*'s going on training exercises."

"Then why are you going along, Rich? She'll ask that."

"Tell her . . . tell her I'm giving the *Manta* an Operations Readiness Inspection, an ORI. Got that? It'll take a month. And Keith's going to be all right. That's the second point."

"That sounds pretty mixed up to me," said Laura. "You're giving the *Manta* an ORI, and somehow Keith's going to be okay."

"Just tell her what I said. And keep saying that she's not to talk to any reporters. They'll just get her upset."

Laura compressed her lips, said nothing.

"Look, Laurie," he said, coming around the bed and sliding his arm around her waist, "we're getting under way tomorrow, and I'll be gone for quite a while. And I can't tell you anything, even though I know I can trust you all the way. But we don't trust Peggy, do we? Go ahead and call her. Right now, if you want to. But don't get into any long talk. Just say she should keep her faith in the Navy. Then hang up and come back here."

Laura's face was close to his, her eyes wide open. She nodded her head against his. "Aye, aye, sir, Commodore," she said.

CHAPTER SEVEN

THE TRIP NORTHWARD in the *Manta* was unlike any submarine voyage Richardson had ever experienced. It was the first time he had embarked for such a distance in a nuclear submarine. Diving was effortless. There was none of the old hurly-burly, no necessity for split-second timing. The people on the bridge were allowed to get below with some dignity. When the bridge hatch was closed, *Manta* gently nudged downward to the ordered cruising depth of five hundred feet.

Underwater, there was no feeling of motion, no feel whatever of the sea. The interior of the ship was a quiet cavern, full of controlled activity. But no one encased in that steel cylinder was unaware of the sea. It was never far away, in some cases only inches. And it needed only a single entry point to begin its deadly work.

Manta's annunciators had been placed on AHEAD FLANK, her course set on a great curve around Nantucket, the Grand Banks and Iceland before finally settling on due north. Her sonar was actively searching ahead and to both sides, her fathometer recording the depth of the water beneath. Her whole being was concentrated on but a single objective: to reach, as soon as possible, the vicinity of position Golf November two nine on the polar grid, *Cushing's* last reported position.

Once a day, however, *Manta* slowed to come to periscope depth. Since she had no apparatus for making oxygen from seawater, nor for removing carbon dioxide, she routinely conserved her supply of compressed oxygen by exchanging her internal air with the atmosphere. After a full day, oxygen depletion was noticeable, and the instant restoration of vitality when fresh air could finally be drawn in became one of the pleasures of the ship's routine.

CINDY WILLIAMS was tall and angular. There was a strength about her which belied the vulnerability of her mouth and the sympathetic set of her eyes. Her calm personality was the perfect complement to Buck's more volatile makeup. At least, so Laura had always thought. Cindy was not beautiful the way Peggy Leone was beautiful, but she was sincere, devoid of self-consciousness.

Now Cindy and Peggy sat on opposite ends of Laura's sofa, while Laura faced them across the coffee table in her living room. On the table stood the remnants of afternoon tea. A long telephone conversation with Peggy, late on the morning of *Manta's* departure, had fully discharged any duty to her, Laura believed. That and the previous, much shorter call she had made, with Rich's reluctant approval. Now Laura was determined to escape further embroilment with this fretful, tiresome woman.

Perhaps Cindy sensed Laura's feelings, for she had adroitly deflected Peggy's first attempt to steer the conversation to Keith.

"How about another of these little biscuits," Laura was saying.

"Thanks. I will," Peggy replied. "With my sweet tooth, Keith says I'm lucky I don't look like a balloon."

"All the girls in the squadron are green over you, Peggy," said Cindy. "I wish I didn't have to worry about gaining weight."

"If all your worries are only about gaining weight, you're lucky." Peggy's voice had a characteristic petulance.

Quickly Laura said, "Tell us about that school you've just put Ruthie in. What's its name—the Thames Valley Junior School?

From what I've heard, they have a very advanced curriculum."

Peggy could not resist the bait. For half an hour she expanded on the virtues of the newly formed school and its program for preschoolers. Finally, however, the teapot was empty, the contents of their cups no longer hot. Sensing that Peggy could not be further denied, Laura had the inspiration to suggest sherry. The wine might ease the strain for Peggy a little, she reasoned.

Peggy, perhaps not appreciating that Laura was quietly arranging the best atmosphere possible for a difficult discussion, chose the moment to discard all subterfuge. "I want to talk about Keith," she said bluntly, putting down her glass.

Laura caught Cindy's quick look of sympathy. Peggy was understandably upset. But what could Laura tell her? Most of what she knew was actually only surmise.

"I can't stand it anymore," Peggy was saying. "Every time Keith leaves it's worse, and this time it's worse than ever. I'm sure he's in danger!" Peggy's voice broke. "What am I going to do?"

Laura swiftly skirted the coffee table, perched on the sofa, and leaned to put her arm around her. Cindy, she saw, had started to get up also. "It's especially rough for you right now, Peggy," Laura said, "but the reporter was only guessing about Keith. He may be nowhere near where the Russian plane got shot down."

"Maybe none of it's true," said Cindy.

Peggy had her tea napkin to her eyes. "I just know it's Keith they're talking about," she sobbed. "It must be the *Cushing* up there under the ice. I'm scared. Maybe I'll never see Keith again!"

"Remember what Rich said to tell you before he and Buck got under way," said Laura. "He said to keep your faith in the Navy. Remember?" She squeezed Peggy's shoulder.

"Keep your faith in the Navy! What faith?"

"The faith all of us have."

"I have faith, all right! Faith that the Navy will never back its people up in a tough spot! That the trade-school boys will look out for themselves. They always put people like Keith in the most danger, and then they go off and leave them to face it alone! Faith in the Navy?" she almost shouted. "That's a laugh!"

"You're upset, Peggy, and what you're saying is just not true." Laura spoke quietly, though it took an effort. "Do you think the Navy will simply abandon a very valuable ship and its crew of a

446

hundred and twenty-five men? That's never been done. It's contrary to naval tradition."

"Well, why don't they tell me something, then?"

"Peggy, if the Navy makes any announcement, even to a few people, that's practically the same as telling the Russians. If things are as bad as you fear, do you think that will help Keith?"

Cindy said, "You've got to think of it from Keith's point of view, too, Peggy. What he thinks must mean something to you."

"Keith has put his trust in the Navy, Peggy," Laura offered. "If he could, he'd tell you so right now."

"No, he wouldn't! I wouldn't let him! I hate the Navy! Even when he's home I hate it, because he's always planning that next trip. It's just not fair!" The napkin was twisted into a sodden ball in her hand.

"It's true the Navy asks more of its conscientious people," said Laura. "But that's why Keith's had such important assignments. Rich says he's one of the best officers it's got."

Laura's arm was still draped over the back of the sofa. Peggy brushed it away. "That's so!" she said. "The Navy's using him for a patsy. It always has. I've seen it too many times."

"Don't be silly," Laura said, still in the quiet tone.

"You, of all people, ought to know what I'm talking about, Laura! Your first husband didn't go through the trade school, either, did he?" Peggy accentuated the words "trade school."

"Nobody cared where Jim Bledsoe's diploma came from! He was one of the best sub skippers we had!" Laura was surprised at how angrily her words came out. Memories flooded in on her. It was the first of the war years, and they had been married only five days, during which Jim worked fourteen hours a day on board the *Walrus*, getting her ready for the Pacific trip from which neither returned. It was not long enough to build a marriage.

The hurt had come slowly, the days dawning with hope, passing with growing disappointment. Jim went to sea, and she wrote two long letters a week, even when the sparse replies made continued cheerfulness a misery. He was at war, fighting. He was rarely in port long enough to answer letters. Then came the day she met the wife of the ship's engineer carrying a handbag full of thick envelopes—when she had only two thin ones. The worst was when Jim took the *Walrus* to Australia, where he was lionized as a brilliant

447

combat submariner. Friends spoke of the pride she must feel, and she had been forced to smile through her shame, for then there were no letters at all in her purse.

But that was all long ago. Now she thought of Jim with a deeper understanding. Perhaps their marriage might have survived had it not faced the insuperable handicap of the war and what war did to people. She knew, now, that her own inadequacies as a young bride were not at fault. Neither was Jim's neglectful correspondence, nor his infidelities with Joan Lastrada and with others. She had not blamed Joan. She, too, was a child of the war. But it was terribly painful, all the same. Finally it was Rich who came to seek her out after it was all over, who restored her self-respect and (it seemed at the time) her sanity. She had been astonished how quickly the world turned right again.

No, as to all this, she was now invulnerable. The pain and anguish were far in the past. Her only vulnerability was for Jim himself. She was proud of him, proud of his great sacrifice. She would protect him—and his memory.

Laura's flash of anger left her almost as quickly as it came. For a few seconds no one said anything. Then Laura broke the silence, her voice low and soft, but with a faint vibration of emotion. "He's still out there, you know," she said. "He's forever there, with his ship and his crew, and forever young. He was the oldest man aboard, and he was only twenty-nine. Once a year there's a ceremony on Pearl Harbor for the boats still on patrol. That's what they call it. 'Still on patrol.' For some, like Rich, it's a very sentimental occasion. The *Walrus* was his old boat, too, you know." Tremulously, she smiled. Cindy, she saw, understood. Her eyes blinked away the moisture that had gathered there.

But Peggy saw her chance, leaped at it. "Jim was only from Yale. So they took Rich off and gave the boat to Jim. They should have sent the *Walrus* home for an overhaul, but instead, they sent him off to the most dangerous area, and he got sunk! *Walrus* was due to come back to the States for a six-months overhaul, wasn't she? You'd have had that six months together. But instead, the Navy sent him out again, and he got sunk. That's why he's still on patrol! That's not going to happen to Keith, I can tell you!" She looked triumphant.

Cindy and Laura were both on their feet. The blow had been

448

below the belt. Cindy spoke sharply. "That's not fair, Peggy! Rich was in the hospital with a broken leg. The whole sub force knows the story of Jim Bledsoe and the great patrols he made. It also knows how Rich and the *Eel* wiped out the Japanese force that caught him!"

"That didn't help Jim much."

"It showed what Rich thought of him!"

Laura tried to exercise self-control, for Peggy was clearly in no condition to do so. "None of this concerns Keith," she said. "If there's anything Cindy or I can do to help you, we want to do it. There's no use wasting time on things we can't influence."

Cindy nodded in agreement, her eyes fixed on Peggy, almost as though she were sending her a signal. Peggy, however, paid no attention, perhaps really did not care what she was saying. "I know what I'm going to do! I told you—I'm not going to let anything like that happen to Keith!"

"Peggy, you've got to stop thinking you can have any effect on what happens to Keith! The way you're acting does no one any good." Cindy spoke warmly, but her eyes were flashing.

"Yes, it will! I'm sick of being scared to death, and sick of nobody telling me anything and sick of what the Navy puts you through! As soon as Keith gets back I'm asking him to put in his retirement papers! And if he won't see it my way, Ruthie and I are leaving!" Peggy downed the remaining half of her sherry, reached for the bottle and refilled her glass.

Laura could feel Cindy's cool eyes focused on her. "Peggy, dear," she began, "we—that is, I—we understand, believe me. This whole thing has been awfully hard on you." Peggy was crying again. What to do? How to help her? Laura had the sensation of diving headfirst into quicksand. She drew a deep breath before she went under. "Listen, there's one thing I can tell you that might help. . . ."

Another deep breath. She didn't really know anything for sure, but it was a good guess based on what she did know. "This is confidential, now, but the Navy isn't forgetting Keith up there in the Arctic. There's been all sorts of conferences on what to do." (Peggy certainly knew about the conferences. And, yes, almost certainly the *Cushing* was in the Arctic.) "They've sent Rich and Buck to join him. That's what Rich meant when he said you should keep faith in the Navy."

A smile of relief on Peggy's face, or was it gratification? Cindy gave her a startled look. But there was no turning back.

"Our three men served together during the war. That's why Rich is out with Buck right now. This is all very secret information"— God forgive her!—"but you two are married to the two skippers involved, and if anyone has a right to know, you do."

Laura could sense Cindy's disapproval. No doubt Cindy, too, had her own ideas about her husband's mission. Perhaps Buck had told her more than Rich had told Laura. But then he would also have sworn her to secrecy.

No help for it. It had had to be done.

"Peggy," Cindy was saying, "all of us have to be realistic. Our husbands have gone through a lot together. Whatever's happening, if Rich and Buck are in it, too, you can be sure Keith could have no better help."

"Realistic, you say! Realistic!" The word had triggered some wild irrationality. "I'm the one who's realistic!" Peggy rose to her feet, face flushed, hands clenched. "The Navy does anything it wants to you. Anything!" Her eyes were glaring. "I hate it, I tell you! And I hate both of you, too! You're both part of the clique that's running things. I know all about that patrol on the *Eel* when old Commodore Blunt was killed, and I know all about the Lastrada dame, too. She had a much bigger piece of Jim than you ever did, Laura, my dear. She had a piece of Rich, too, before you got him. She was with him every night for a while. There's a lot more to that story than you know!

"And Rich should never have brought old Blunt back. He should have dumped the body at sea, the way they do everybody else. The Navy tried to cover by saying he died of a brain tumor, but they never explained that broken neck he also had. . . ."

The look on Peggy's face was positively leering. Her mouth was distorted, twisted. Laura stood rigid, fighting the temptation to smash her across the face with every bit of strength she possessed. Instead, she steeled herself to speak coldly. "Peggy, that is absolutely unforgivable. There is nothing more I can do for you. You are unwelcome in my house. Please go away. Now."

Cindy hustled Peggy to the hall closet, draped Peggy's coat around her shoulders and threw on her own, and then, nervously but determinedly, led her out the door.

450

CHAPTER EIGHT

UNLIKE KEITH, Rich and Buck planned no ceremonial inspection of the edge of the ice cap. When they reached its southern boundary *Manta* simply remained deeply submerged and at high speed, aware of the cap only from ice patrol reports and, as she passed under it, from her upward-beamed fathometer. Henceforth she would depend on her stored oxygen and waste-removal capabilities. If necessary, Buck figured, they could stay submerged for thirty days. After that they might have a problem.

By this time, *Manta's* course was due north. There were less than a thousand miles to go to reach the *Cushing's* estimated position at polar grid Golf November two nine. They could only hope that Keith would be waiting for them.

Prior to *Manta's* departure from New London, a priority message had been sent to Keith in the hope that even though unable to transmit, *Cushing* was still able to receive signals. It conveyed the purpose of the *Manta's* voyage, details of the submerged hookup, and the procedures required of the *Cushing*. On the day of *Manta's* projected arrival, *Cushing* was directed to echo range on her active sonar, release an air bubble through her main ballast tanks, and blow a police whistle on her UQC, the underwater voice communication set, all in a specified time sequence. She was to keep this up until further instruction.

In the meantime *Manta* would patrol the vicinity of *Cushing's* last known position and home in on the noises. Once the two submarines were at close range, conversation was authorized over the UQC at minimum volume. Keith was to transmit to Rich, by voice, an already enciphered message stating his condition and any information he had regarding the aircraft the Russians claimed to have lost in his vicinity. Before doing anything else, the *Manta* was to seek a polynya in which she could surface and relay the message.

Not until then would *Manta* be free to begin the hookup and extraction operation. Although acting as a radio relay link had initially been Rich's suggestion, he had privately argued against the additional delay. "If the *Cushing's* in the shape we think—without propulsion but otherwise okay—there'll be a good chance of hauling both ship and crew out of there. Why waste time? If there's any

451

kind of skulduggery going on, as soon as whoever's doing it realizes we're trying to get our people out—"

But Admiral Donaldson shook his head. "I know exactly what you're saying, but I've got my orders, too. This is an affair of state now, and the Joint Chiefs want answers just as soon as they can get them. Sorry, Rich, but that's a direct order."

"Don't they see this puts Keith and his crew in even greater jeopardy?" Rich said desperately, momentarily forgetting he was speaking with the Chief of Naval Operations. He was thinking only of the possibility of the lengthy radio transmissions being overheard, and then allowing time for possible reaction. He recovered himself in confusion. "Sorry, Admiral. But look. Whatever made Keith go off the air so suddenly came right after his long second message. Direction finding is a fact of life in radio communications. They could have homed in on him. Now we're telling him to make a long transmission on the UQC, the one most easily detected by sonar! If they pick it up, they'll know there's another sub there. And then the *Manta* has to go find a thin place in the ice, break through, and repeat the same thing on the air. Even if they don't pick up the UQC, there's nothing secure about our ship-to-shore frequency. Either way, they'll be alerted. If their sub is still around, and if the collision was no accident, it will join the party for sure!"

"I know it, Rich," said Donaldson gravely. "Don't apologize for telling me what you think. If I can get the Joint Chiefs to lift the requirement, I'll get a message off to you right away, but for now this is the way it's got to be."

But no message had ever come. Without doubt, Donaldson had made the effort. He must have been turned down.

Finding the *Cushing* proved not an easy task. She was not at Golf November two nine. But Keith almost certainly had not been able to move his ship far. She must be somewhere close by.

Manta began slowly circling *Cushing's* position as last reported, listening for evidence of her presence. She made two complete circles two miles in diameter, then changed the circle into an ever enlarging spiral, at maximum submergence depth.

At long last, faint beeps on the echo-ranging sonar were heard. "He wasn't on for long, only about three pings," Jeff Norton, the ship's communicating officer, reported breathlessly. "We didn't get a good bearing, because he quit too soon."

"What's the approximate direction?" Buck asked.

"Southwest. But the three beeps were very faint."

"Maybe he's farther away than we thought," Rich muttered.

"Make your course southwest by grid," Buck said to the OOD. "Increase speed to ten knots. In half an hour we'll be five miles closer to him." He consulted his watch. "The next signal is air blowing. It's due in thirty-two minutes."

Nothing was heard at the appointed time, nor at the next, twenty-seven minutes later, when the police whistle was scheduled. "We'll continue as we are for another fifteen minutes," Buck said, "and we'll be twelve miles nearer to him, if that was Keith we heard. Then we'll circle again." Rich was nodding his approval. *Cushing's* next scheduled signal, in forty-three minutes, was to be echo ranging at long scale, five pings at maximum gain.

It had been assumed that the pings of the active echo-ranging sonar would be heard from the greatest distance. On hearing them, *Manta* would send her own ping simultaneously with the termination of *Cushing's* fifth, beamed in the other sub's direction, and start a stopwatch the instant the transmission was cut off. *Cushing* would have started a stopwatch with the cutoff of her own fifth ping, would stop it with receipt of *Manta's*, and transmit a single sixth ping to stop the *Manta's* watch. Sound travels sixteen hundred yards per second in water. Since a round trip by sound was involved, the time in seconds on their stopwatches, multiplied by eight hundred yards, would give each submarine the approximate distance to the other.

With forty-three minutes to wait, *Manta* slowly described several complete circles in the water. She was as though suspended in space. Above, below, in all directions, nothing but water. Hundreds of feet overhead, a solid sheet of ice, twenty feet thick or more. Thousands of feet below, the floor of the Arctic Ocean. *Manta*: a tiny blob of life, the size of a particle of dust, launched into an Olympic-size swimming pool in search of another dust-size particle.

When there were only five minutes left to wait, Buck, Rich, and Jeff Norton all crowded into *Manta's* cramped sonar room. Norton held a stopwatch in his hand; the sonarman, Rich noted, held another. Rich and Buck stared at their wristwatches, carefully reset to Greenwich Mean Time. Keith would also have done this, would probably start his pings on the second.

Norton made a snapping motion with his hand, precisely as the clock in the sonar room reached sixteen hours, twenty-eight minutes and zero seconds, and started his stopwatch. The second hand crawled slowly around its dial. Rich had stopped breathing. So had everyone else in the tiny compartment. The second hand was at seventeen when a spoke of light appeared on the dark red dial of the sonar receiver. Norton stopped his watch, and simultaneously, a faint ping filled the compartment.

"Seventeen seconds and a fraction," said Norton.

"Sh-h-h-h; don't talk!" whispered Buck.

The spoke had vanished, leaving a decaying fluorescence on the sonar dial. Then it reappeared, along with an amplified ping, went out again, came on again, five times. Simultaneously with the cessation of the fifth ping and its light spoke, *Manta*'s sonarman punched his hand key and started his stopwatch. A brilliant white spoke on the sonar dial dwarfed the dimmer one from the distant station as the sound signal beamed out, sixteen hundred yards per second, toward the source of the five incoming pings.

Jeff Norton had reset his watch, started it again at the same time as his sonarman, and now was figuring on a scrap of paper. "If Captain Leone sent his first ping out exactly on the dot, he's twenty-eight thousand yards away; nearly fourteen miles."

Buck smiled. "Good, Jeff. We'll be able to check it when we hear his sixth beep." Deep feelings of relief were stirring within him. It must be Keith. And he must have received the message, therefore knew they were on their way, was therefore okay.

The sixth ping came. "Thirty-six seconds," said Jeff. "That's twenty-eight thousand eight hundred yards, just under fourteen and a half miles."

Richardson was leaving the sonar room. Buck followed, then turned back. "Jeff, that was real good work. A beautiful job. We're going to close him now. I want you to have your men log everything they hear from that bearing as we go in."

"ALL STOP!" said the OOD. "All back one-third—all stop!"

The bow planesman twisted the annunciator knobs on the console in front of him. "Answered all stop, sir," the man reported.

Lieutenant Tom Clancy, *Manta*'s engineering officer, at the moment on watch as officer of the deck and diving officer, turned to face Richardson and Williams, who were watching from the periscope station behind him. "All stop, Captain," he reported. "Speed, zero. Depth, one five zero feet." There was a suggestion of professional pride in his voice. The newer attack subs and all the missile submarines were fitted with automatic hovering gear. With *Manta*, it had to be done by hand. Doing it well bespoke someone who knew his ship and his business.

"Good, Tom," answered Buck. To Rich he said, "That's it, Commodore. By plot we're within a quarter of a mile of the *Cushing*. The underwater voice set's turned all the way down. You should be able to talk with Keith now, but she shouldn't carry over a mile. I'll keep the scope up—maybe we can see her."

Richardson raised the UQC microphone, pressed the button, began to speak. "Keith, old man, this is Rich. Do you read? Over." He released the button, could hear the reverberations as his voice was carried by the sound waves. He had leaned his head against the UQC speaker, mounted on the after bulkhead of the periscope station, and was concentrating his attention on the answer he was willing it to give. Thus, when it came, the clipped voice spoke loudly, right into his ear.

"Rich! Skipper! It's so good to hear you! I read you loud and clear, how do you read me? Over." There were worlds of relief in Keith's voice.

Richardson could not see much of Buck's broad grin of happiness, for his face was covered by the rubber eye guard of the periscope as he slowly turned it around. The rest of the control room crew had glad expressions.

Soon the work of making the submerged hookup could begin, but first it would be necessary to carry out the preliminaries. "Keith," Rich said, "obviously you received the message from ComSubLant. Do you have your reply ready?"

"Affirmative, Skipper. Our message is long. Can it wait till we're out from under the ice? We've hardly been able to budge since the collision, and we're pretty itchy. Over."

"Sorry, Keith. Orders. But if you couldn't budge, how did you get so far from the reference position? Over."

"We tried some gliding. It's all in the message."

"Are you ready to pass it over?"

"That's affirmative, boss. Stand by to write."

"Standing by." Richardson flipped a small switch that had been taped to the side of the UQC speaker. The switch turned on a light near an extra speaker in the radio room. The two men on watch had been instructed to copy everything they heard on that speaker whenever the light was on.

Now a new voice took over the UQC, *Cushing*'s chief radioman reading in measured cadence the gibberish of the encoded message. Each letter and number was spoken phonetically. To guard against errors, the message was then fetched from *Manta*'s radio room and read back. The entire exchange took two hours.

"THIS IS CRAZY," grumbled Buck. "Half a day looking for a lead or polynya to break through, and all we've seen is solid ice cover, twenty feet thick. Everything is go to snake the *Cushing* out of here, but we can't because of that dumb message!"

"Ours is not to reason why," said Rich. "But it is important for Washington to know about that plane and the bomb, and that some kind of long-planned operation is going on up here."

"All the same, I'd feel better if we were on our way with her."

After spending several hours in the control room, hoping that a usable polynya would turn up quickly, Rich and Buck adjourned to Buck's stateroom, leaving a special watch on the ice detector. Two changes of watch later, they felt the ship heel suddenly. The telephone bell rang. "Captain? This is Jerry," said Buck's executive officer. "We've just passed under a possible, and we're turning to go back to it."

"We'll be right there." Buck and Rich walked swiftly to the control room.

"It's the best one I've seen." Jerry Abbott was holding a piece of paper just removed from the ice detector. "About six feet thick. At a guess, the thin spot is about an eighth of a mile long."

"What do you think, Commodore?" Buck asked Richardson.

"I'm with you. I'd like to get this message off and go back to the *Cushing* as quick as we can. Did you tell me your sail can push up through six feet of ice?"

"That's what the Electric Boat designers say."

"It's your decision, Buck. But if you're asking me, I say let's give the EB designers a test of their product."

"Good!" said Williams. "Jerry, put us right under the polynya

457

with all engines stopped. I'll take over when you're ready, and we'll bring her right on up."

"Tom Clancy asked to be called if we're going up. He wants to handle the ascent."

"Okay. Call him. Also alert radio, and have the topside crew ready with ice-clearing tools."

In a few minutes movement stopped. Then Buck, looking through the periscope, maneuvered *Manta* into the center of the thin-ice area, using her propellers sparingly. Finally ready, he spoke to his engineering officer. "Tom, bring us up flat. Remember, there's probably a layer of fresh water under the ice, so we'll be losing buoyancy. I'll drop the scope at eighty feet."

"Aye, aye, sir." Clancy turned and gave orders to the chief petty officer, who also had come on watch for the occasion. There was the sound of air blowing into tanks. The submarine had assumed half a degree down angle, but the bow now was rising faster and she was on an even keel again.

"Eighty-five feet," called out Clancy. "Rising steady. Zero bubble. Eighty-two feet. Eighty-one."

"Down scope," said Buck. He folded up the handles, and the precious instrument dropped into its well.

"Seventy-five feet," said Clancy. "She's going up a little faster."

"We'll hit the ice at around fifty feet," said Buck. "With six feet to break through, it'll be a pretty solid jolt."

Tom Clancy was calling out. "Sixty-five feet. Sixty feet."

"Bow planes rigged in," reported the chief petty officer.

"Fifty-five feet," said Clancy. "Fifty-four. Fifty-three. Fifty-two. Fifty-one. *Fifty* feet!"

Crunch! Manta's deck seemed to drop away from them, her sturdy hull twanging, the myriad gauge dials in the control room vibrating in jangled disharmony. There was squeaking and moaning of steel girders, a heavy scraping noise.

"She's going on up now," said Clancy. "Forty-nine, forty-eight, forty-seven, forty-six, forty-five. Top of the sail is through, sir."

As he hastily put on cold-weather gear, Buck ordered. "Blow all ballast! Let me know when the upper hatch is clear." He adjusted his face mask, spoke hurriedly to Jerry Abbott, and began to climb through the lower hatch.

But it was several hours before *Manta's* deck could be cleared of ice and the radio antenna raised. More time was lost trying to raise Washington. Counting the time spent looking for a thin place in the ice, Keith and Rich used up twenty hours sending off Admiral Donaldson's message. Only then could they submerge, relocate the *Cushing*, and begin what they'd come to the Arctic to do.

CHAPTER NINE

"K EITH," said Richardson over the UQC, speaking softly, "do you have our dispatch about towing procedure? Any questions? Before trying to hookup, we want to look you over through the periscope. What is your heading and exact depth?"

"Affirmative on the dispatch, and three cheers, no questions. We're against the ice. Depth seven three feet," replied Keith.

"Okay, old man. We'll pass under you with the scope up and take a look. There's enough light coming through the ice."

"Roger."

Rich lowered the microphone and turned to Buck. "What depth do we need so as not to hit him with the scope up?" he asked.

"The high scope will just graze him at one three five feet, if we go right under him. Recommend we make our first pass a few yards abeam and check for anything dangling below his keel."

"That sounds like good sense."

Slowly *Manta* positioned herself in line with the *Cushing*'s heading. With her propellers turning at creeping speed and Buck and Rich manning both periscopes, she swam toward and beneath the *Cushing*. Gradually the range shortened. The *Cushing* was nearly dead ahead. "Last range, one four oh," said Jeff Norton. "Ten degrees off the port bow."

"I wonder if sonar can hear any of his machinery noise, Buck," said Richardson, his face against the scope's eyepiece.

"Ask them, Jerry," said Buck, likewise immobilized against his own periscope. "Also ask the *Cushing* if they can hear us."

Both heard the answers to Abbott's questions directly. "Affirmative," said Jeff, using the ship's intercommunicating speaker from the sonar room. "We can hear a steady hum."

"Affirmative," said Keith over the UQC. "We can hear you very loud. You must be about to pass under us."

459

Suddenly, shockingly, a tremendous black mass swept into view dead ahead. Startled, Buck grabbed for his periscope control lever, stopped just in time. "Wow!" he exploded.

To Jerry Abbott and the other anxious watchers, it was clear that both Rich and Buck had had a scare. The huge bulk of the *Cushing* appearing so suddenly in their fields of view must have seemed about to strike them. But both men had recovered, were tugging at their scopes, adjusting their angles of sight.

"Say," said Buck Williams, "Keith's sail is painted white! It sure wasn't that color when he left New London!"

"There's a dent!" said Richardson. "A small one."

"Where?" asked Abbott, pencil poised over a clipboard.

"After end of missile compartment, port side, halfway between keel and waterline!"

"There's the emergency propulsion motor! It's dangling about fifteen feet below the keel!" said Buck. "It's really mangled, too!"

"Here's another dent! A big one! Ten feet below the waterline, I'd estimate. No doubt she was hit from the port side."

Jerry Abbott was writing rapidly. "Can you see the propeller?"

"The top rudder looks okay," said Rich. "The lower rudder is bent to starboard—but maybe it's still operable. The propeller is a mass of twisted junk. It wouldn't give him any thrust at all." He drew back from the scope.

"We ought to know whether Keith can steer or not," he said to Buck. "Towing him will be hard if he can't. While you're maneuvering around, I'll tell him what we're up to."

"Keith," Rich said a few moments later into the UQC mouthpiece, "we're dead astern of you. How do you read?"

"A little mushy, but clear enough, Rich. How does it look?"

"Not good. Several big dents, your port stern plane is folded up against the side, and the rudder is bent. The propeller is useless, I'm afraid. Can you operate your rudder?"

"Affirmative. It moves slowly, but I think it's usable."

"That's very good news. We're going to get clear now and prepare for towing. We'd like you to drop down to a hundred and fifty feet. Lower your anchor to the fifty-fathom mark and set your brake, but not too tight. We want it to slip a little to ease the initial shock. Be ready to tighten the brake as the pull begins."

"Wilco," said Keith.

"Let us know when you're ready."

"Wilco," said Keith again.

To Buck, Rich said, "His anchor will be at four hundred and fifty feet. We'll make our depth five hundred."

"Roger, Commodore. Do you want to go to towing stations?"

"Whenever you're ready."

Buck spoke into the hand microphone for the ship's general announcing system. "All hands, rig ship for towing. Port side. This is the captain," he said. "This time it's for real."

Manta had departed from New London with her two sets of towing gear stored in the after torpedo tubes. The inner doors of both tubes had been replaced by anchor billets. Getting ready to tow involved only opening the outer door of the designated tube and ejecting the contents, a large metal canister, which split open and sank, releasing the football-shaped paravane. This immediately began to rise, carrying with it the large steel hook and heavy chain. The chain was attached to a long white nylon hawser, now being dragged outward and upward from the open tube. The inboard end of the hawser was followed by another section of chain which was firmly attached to the anchor billet.

Whilst the paravane was being deployed upward and to port, Buck was maneuvering the *Manta* into position astern of the *Cushing*, waiting for the ready signal from her. When it came, Buck set the course so that *Manta* would pass parallel to and below—but not directly beneath—the disabled submarine. *Manta*'s diagonally towed hawser could not fail to intersect the hanging anchor chain.

"ONE MINUTE until abeam," said Jerry Abbott.

Rich, sitting on the stool which had been his station since the beginning of the drills, nodded agreement.

"Two minutes till we might feel the chain!" Buck announced over the mike. To Tom Clancy he said, "Remember, the chain will pull us up by the stern. Let her seek her own depth. But when she starts taking on the weight of *Cushing*'s anchor, you're going to have to pump out a lot of water. Don't let her get an up angle."

"Abeam to port! Twenty-eight yards!" announced Abbott.

Buck grabbed the mike. "We're abeam! We'll begin to feel the chain one minute from now. Silence throughout the ship."

Rich knew that the first contact of the nylon hawser against the

Cushing's anchor chain might be faint. More pronounced would be the links of the two chains rattling against each other; most noticeable of all would be when the hook finally engaged the chain, then slipped along it toward the anchor. By careful calculation and actual experience, this must happen exactly two minutes thirty-six seconds after the anchor was passed abeam. If the hook did not engage the chain at that point, it would pass it, necessitating another try.

Buck, trying to look confident, was succeeding much better than his slight, taciturn exec, Rich noticed. "Two minutes!" whispered Jerry, holding up the same number of fingers.

Rich tried to keep his emotions contained. If something had gone wrong, they would try again, passing nearer to the anchor, and there was always the other rig. . . .

"Two minutes thirty!" Jerry said. Buck was eyeing his stopwatch. At the thirty-six-second point he intended to stop, as planned, regardless of whether the chain had been engaged.

But all of Richardson's worries were forgotten in an instant as the speaker interrupted with a report from the passive sonar system. "The JT operator hears the chains!"

"All stop!" barked Buck. "Maneuvering, make turns for two knots!"

"Maneuvering, aye, aye!" said the speaker.

"Conn, this is sonar," another voice said from the speaker. "The JT reports hook slipping! We can hear the links!"

"Great!" said Buck. He flipped a toggle switch and put the mike to his lips. "Northern Lieutenant," he said, using the official voice call for the first time. "This is Flat Raider, at your service, sir. Do you feel my pull?"

Instantly the speaker came back—Keith's voice. "This is Northern Lieutenant. Affirmative your last. Thank God you've come! And thanks to whoever invented this towing idea!"

"We're going to build up to three knots for starters," said Buck over the mike. "Course, depth, and speed changes will be very gradual, and announced in advance." He glanced inquiringly at Rich, who made a cutting motion across his throat. "That's about all for now, Keith. Out."

"YOU AND YOUR CREW were marvelous, Buck. Here we are, towing the *Cushing* at four and a half knots, and we haven't a care in the world. Once we snake them out from under the ice, we can come to periscope depth and then send our message to ComSubLant."

Rich and Buck were having dinner in *Manta's* wardroom, surrounded by most of the officers. In celebration of the occasion, the cooks had prepared the best meal of which they were capable, for officers and crew, and a holiday spirit prevailed.

"I know you'd like to turn in Commodore," Buck said. "So would I; but could you go aft and say a few words to the crew first? I know they'd appreciate it."

"You bet I will, Buck."

At that moment, however, the arrival of a messenger from the OOD changed everything—and it was never the same again.

"There's a sonar contact!" the young lad said.

"THE JT PICKED it up first," said the scared-looking sonar watch stander. "He had it on sonic. Then it came in closer, and I could hear it over the big set, the BQR. It's staying on a steady bearing, a little abaft our starboard beam."

"What's it sound like to you?" asked Buck.

"Sounds like a ship, sir. JT thinks so, too."

Buck seized a pair of earphones, plugged them into a jack. His face contorted as he listened. Without a word he handed the earphones to Richardson. As soon as he adjusted them, Rich heard distinct machinery noises, a pump running, gears whining, the sibilant swish of water past a hull.

"It's louder now than when we reported it," said the sonarman.

"How does it sound on JT?" asked Rich.

Buck reached for a switch on the bulkhead. Muted machinery noise filled the tiny sonar compartment. "That's what he's hearing up forward with his sonic ears," Buck said.

"Is it only on that bearing?"

"Yessir! Everything else is all clear all around."

"I wonder if Keith has this same contact," said Richardson.

"We can ask him on the UQC."

"Can you give it to him in your wolf-pack code?"

"Yes. I'll get the book." Buck dashed forward, snatched the pamphlet from his desk safe, ran back to the sonar room.

When he returned, Richardson was looking thoughtfully at the underwater voice set. "What does Qs Ss mean?" he asked. "First he sent Ri Ke—that means Rich from Keith—then Qs Ss."

"Where did that come from?" said Buck, almost breathlessly, flipping the pages of the thin booklet.

"From *Cushing*, just now, on the UQC. He sent it in Morse."

"It means, 'Sonar contact to starboard, said to be submarine.'"

"I think it's a sub, too, Buck."

"What's it doing?"

"Nothing. Just keeping up with us."

"Could it be the same sub that rammed the *Cushing*?"

"Whoever it is, he's looking us over. That's clear."

"We're stuck, too. Towing the *Cushing* like this, we can't change speed or course. Damn it anyway! It's all because of that message we had to send! If they were monitoring the area by sonar, they heard it once on the UQC, and then later they heard us send the same message by radio. So they had to know another sub's up here, and this guy was sent to investigate."

Richardson had put down his earphones. He and Buck were hunched together in a corner. The sonarman, heavy earpieces over both ears, was at his console, oblivious of them. Rich glanced at him uneasily, then said, "I don't like this at all. Keith obviously doesn't either. That's why he used the wolf-pack code."

"I've already ordered that no one is to use the UQC."

"Good. Maybe he's only curious and will go away when he realizes we're hauling the *Cushing* out of here."

For two more hours the Russian submarine (for such it could only be) remained in the area. Then its noises grew more distant and finally faded out altogether. With almost a corporate sigh of relief, a gradual but sweeping course change was executed. As an additional precaution, silent running for both submarines was ordered. Then Rich and Buck gratefully climbed into their bunks for their first rest in nearly thirty-six hours. Still uneasy, however, Rich flopped down fully clothed, removing only his shoes.

The ventilation blowers had been turned off in the silent condition, and he was perspiring heavily when he awoke. The clock told him he had been asleep for about five hours. Something was not right. Groggily he searched for his shoes, put them on, but all the while an instinctive part of his mind was probing. An atmosphere of dread permeated the ship. It could only be one of two things: either there had been some casualty—to the *Cushing*, the towline or the *Manta*—or the Russian was back.

464

Rich stepped quickly across the passageway. Buck's room was empty. So was the wardroom. He started for the control room, had to wait for an instant because a messenger was coming through the bulkhead door.

"Commodore! I was sent to get you, sir! There's distant pinging, coming closer!" The young sailor's face was flushed.

"Thanks, son," said Richardson, demonstrating a calm he did not feel. He ducked through the door, headed for the sonar room.

Jeff Norton and Buck were already there, as was the chief sonarman, Palmer Schultz. Tom Clancy was standing in the passageway outside. He made way for Richardson, but there was not room to enter. Rich stood in the doorway, craned his neck into the darkened space. Buck nodded, acknowledging his presence.

"I heard distant pinging first," the sonarman at the console was saying. "So I reported that. Chief Schultz came running in, and then Mr. Norton. By that time the pinging was all around. I think he was searching. Then he started to beam it right at us. That's when you came in, Captain. He's pinging right on us now."

"That's right, sir," said Palmer Schultz, serious-faced. "He's got a solid contact, but he's not getting louder quite as fast as he was. So I think he's slowed down."

"Put the BQR return on the speaker, Schultz. We may as well all hear it," said Buck.

The pings transported Richardson back in time. They were exactly the same as they had been during the war.

In a few moments another noise, a high hum, began emanating from the same bearing. "We're picking up his machinery," said Schultz. He spoke into his mike. "JT, can you hear his propellers yet?" he asked.

There was no answer. Then, "Turn count, one two oh!" said the speaker suddenly. "It's a single-screw ship!"

Helplessly the crowd around the sonar shack heard the alien submarine close in. After a minute, Buck turned to Richardson. "I don't like this at all. I think we should go to battle stations."

"I think you should, Buck," said Rich. "Does your code have a signal for telling the *Cushing* to do the same?"

"We can tell Keith we're doing it. We don't have anything in the code for telling another skipper how to run his ship."

"Well, tell him we are. He'll know what to do."

In a moment the musical chimes signaling battle stations sounded through *Manta*'s general announcing system. It was the first time in sixteen years Rich had heard them except in drill.

CHAPTER TEN

"I THINK he's closing us," said Palmer Schultz from the sonar console, where he had taken over. "He sounds louder, and the decibel meter is reading a little higher."

The darkened sonar room was dominated by the console, in the center of which lay a circular glass-faced tube dimly backlighted in red. Greenish-white flashes emanated regularly from the four-o'clock sector, halfway to the edge, and each flash coincided with a piercing high-frequency ping which jumped from the three pairs of earphones listening to it. Richardson wondered why Schultz, Norton and Buck Williams were not deafened by the echo-ranging signals sent by the other submarine.

Tapping urgently on Buck's shoulder to get his attention, Rich said, "He's not being very polite. We may as well go active ourselves. I'll tell Keith to do the same. Wait one minute, then aim it right into his receiver. Keith will go off with you."

Inwardly seething and at the same time worried, Rich walked to the periscope station, picked up the UQC microphone, and spoke tersely to Keith.

Back at the sonar shack, Rich was gratified to see that both submarines blasted forth their beams at nearly the same instant. The spot on the scope occupied by the stranger was bathed in a succession of flashing pings. Schultz checked the range. "He's still closing us . . . no, the range is stabilized on thirty-two hundred."

Williams gave a coarse laugh. "That barrage slowed him down."

"Maybe," said Rich, "but don't bet on anything permanent."

Suddenly all echo ranging ceased. There was nothing on the screen. "He's stopped, too, sir," said Schultz. Then he grunted vindictively. "Serve them right if their eardrums are busted!"

"Skipper," Buck said in a low tone, "have you any guess at all why he went away and then came back the way he did?"

"How long was he gone?"

"It was five hours forty-three minutes. I had Jeff look it up."

"Then I'd guess he took about a two-hour run to a base somewhere to ask for instructions, got his orders and tore back looking for us. In the meantime we covered about twenty miles."

Rich paused for a moment, then came to a decision. "Buck, could you have your plotters assemble every scrap of info they've got on that sub, and plot it? See if we can figure out what direction he departed in, and what direction he came back from. And see if your code lets us ask Keith the bearing and distance of the spot where he was rammed, and the estimated position those planes seemed to be operating around."

"Glad to. But what good will that do us now?"

"You never know. But the more you find out about your enemies, the more you're apt to luck into something. And I don't mind telling you, I'm scared. If our friend yonder decides to play rough, there's damned little we can do. We're on a steady course, and he knows exactly what it is."

"But what could they want?"

"For one thing, our latest model Polaris missile submarine."

"Keith would never surrender his ship."

"Agreed. But what if he got into absolutely desperate straits, and only the Russians knew where he was? They claim he shot down one of their aircraft. What if the price of saving his crew was for Washington to order him to surrender and let the Russians cut a hole in the ice to get them out?"

"Couldn't Keith be the last man out and open the vents?"

"With the whole crew hostage? Buck, the Soviets had us over a barrel when there was only the *Cushing* here, and they knew it."

"So, the *Manta*. . ."

"Exactly. We're the fly in that ointment. It's *Cushing* they want. And we're snaking her out from under their nose."

"You think we're the target?"

"If they decide to play real rough, we are. If we disappear, their hardball diplomacy is strengthened."

"Then you do think the collision with the *Cushing* wasn't an accident! But their sub could just as well have been the one sunk."

"She hit from aft, and she was running silent. It wouldn't have been too hard to fix one of their boats with some kind of protection, or even a projection to ram a revolving propeller."

"But they couldn't have had that sub just hanging around up

467

here waiting for someone maybe to show up. They must have known Keith was coming pretty far in advance. He didn't know himself until a few weeks before!"

"Sure. But they could have been watching construction of the *Cushing* at Electric Boat. She's the only missile sub with an ice suit, you know. So she's the only one we could have sent."

"I see what you mean," Buck muttered, half to himself. "The *Cushing* was the boat for them to watch."

The sonar room was almost silent. Palmer Schultz, wedded to his precious sonar set, was unconscious of the low-voiced conversation two feet above his head. His concentration on the electronic instrument in front of him was total. He had already decided to call attention to the slightest deviation in the Russian submarine's movements simply by striking out with his left hand. He would not distract his attention by speaking. With perhaps his own life and those of all others aboard depending upon him, he knew this was exactly what his superiors would expect.

Buck broke the silence. "I think I'll go start Jerry on that plot we want," he said. "Back in a minute. We'll have to use the UQC to get the information we need from Keith. Okay?"

When he returned, Buck found Richardson and Schultz huddled over the sonar display. "He's echo ranging again," said Rich. "And he's moving out ahead of us. He's up to something!"

"If he shoots a torpedo, I'll have to maneuver to avoid it. The towline will break."

"I know, Buck. We'll have the other one to hook up with, if we get the chance." Then a thought struck Richardson. "Don't you have a couple of decoys up forward?"

"Yes."

"Have them get one ready for firing. Quick, man!"

Buck picked up the telephone, gave the order. Then he was silent for a long, thoughtful minute. "But where do we go after we shoot it? There's not much maneuvering we can do."

"If you stop your screws, put her in full dive and flood negative, the *Cushing* will coast overhead. If you're lucky, you might not even break the towline."

"We should warn Keith, shouldn't we?"

"We should; but that sub must be monitoring us. We'd better not take the chance. Keith will cope."

468

Buck felt an elbow in his middle. Schultz was pointing to the illuminated spot on his dial. The enemy submarine had drawn well ahead and was no longer echo ranging.

"What's he doing?" said Rich. "Getting ready to shoot?"

"Echo range, Schultz! Full power and short scale!" Buck ordered. Grabbing the phone, he said, "Tubes forward, set the decoy for short-scale pinging. Then flood the tube and shoot it!"

"Good for you, Buck," said Rich. "He's likely got a quiet, fairly slow torpedo, programmed to finish its run by homing on noise. He shut off his pinging so as not to confuse it. If he plans to shoot, he'll do it now, while we're pinging, so his fish can home on us."

Buck still held the phone to his ear. Suddenly he said sharply, "The decoy's away. Secure pinging!" Schultz flipped a switch on his console as Buck thrust past Richardson, stepped into the passageway outside the sonar room. "All stop!" he called peremptorily. "Flood negative! Twenty degrees down angle! Make your depth seven hundred feet!"

There was a clank of mechanism beneath their feet, the sound of rushing water, and *Manta* began to incline downward with an ever increasing angle, with the *Cushing* still in tow.

The depth gauge was at five hundred and fifty as Buck struggled back to the sonar room. Schultz was saying, "The decoy looks just like another submarine out ahead! It's pinging. I can even hear machinery noises."

"How about the Russian? Are we sure he fired at us?"

"We think so, Buck," said Rich. "The JT reported a faint swishing noise in the water, ahead of the Russian."

"What's he doing now?" Buck asked.

"He's just stopped. Hovering, I guess, waiting for us to catch that fish of his."

"Would you authorize shooting one at him?"

"If he's really fired at us, I'll sure think about it!"

The three men in the sonar room had to brace themselves against the steep downward inclination of the submarine. Now Buck heaved himself through the doorframe, holding to it for support. He skidded forward, hung on to the rail around the periscope stand, reached the diving station and Tom Clancy.

"Tom," he said, "we might be firing a torpedo or two forward, to make it a little less boring for you. He's already shot at us!" Buck left Clancy staring after him as he started back to the sonar room. The angle had lessened and the climb took only moments. "How's it going?" he asked Rich.

"Our decoy's out about a thousand yards ahead, still sounding like a great little old submarine, and JT reports he thinks that thing the Russian shot is about to merge with it."

"Schultz, what do you think?" Buck had to lay a hand on his shoulder to attract the sonarman's attention.

"There was something out there all right, coming closer to us, but now it's sniffing around the decoy." Suddenly Schultz ripped off his headset. "Ouch!" he said, massaging his ear. The room was filled with the reverberations of a sharp, distant explosion.

Rich and Buck stared at each other. "How long do we have before he realizes he didn't tag us?" asked Buck.

"A couple of minutes, maybe. The longer we stay in *Cushing*'s sonar shadow, the longer it will take him to figure out what's happened," said Rich.

"What about Keith?"

"He'll guess we fired the decoy."

"I'd like to shoot one of our Mark Forties at that bastard!"

"Buck, I'm in command of this force. I order you to return the fire. See that my specific order is entered in the log!" Buck Williams stared at his superior. The look on his face, the determined fury in his eyes, were clear and all too familiar.

"Aye, aye, sir!" Buck picked up the phone. "Tubes forward," he said, "the commodore has ordered us to return the fire. Load the other decoy in the empty tube. Prepare one Mark Forty for firing! This is a war shot. This is not a drill!"

Backing out of the sonar room, Buck took three steps forward and to the right, where D. D. Brown, a tall, blond lieutenant who held the anachronistic title "gunnery officer," was at his station. "Deedee, tubes forward have been ordered to prepare one Mark Forty for firing. Set your inputs accordingly!"

"Aye, aye, sir!" Brown's blue eyes were shouting the questions.

"Quartermaster! Enter in your rough log as follows: 'The intruding submarine has opened fire, and is identified as an enemy ship of war. The explosion just heard was an attempt to sink the *Manta*. The squadron commander has put this ship on a war footing and directed *Manta* to return the fire.' Got that?"

470

"Yes, sir!" said the man.

Buck went on. "We're already at general quarters. Do not sound the alarm. Have the word passed by telephone."

He turned back to Brown, who was busily manipulating the torpedo data computer. "How are you doing, Deedee?"

"Ready in a minute! We need range and depth of target."

"You'll have to use three hundred feet for depth. When you're ready to shoot, we'll get you a ping range."

Buck returned to the sonar room. A moment later Brown came to the doorway. "We're ready," he said. "Outer door's open."

"All right." Buck turned to the sonarman. "Chief, get a single-ping range and the best bearing. Feed 'em both to the TDC." A single white spoke lashed out from the center of the sonar dial, impinged directly upon the faint dot representing the enemy sub.

"Thirty-eight fifty," said Schultz. "Bearing zero three seven and a half, relative. TDC's got them both, sir!"

Buck could not remain in the sonar room. He leaped out the door again, heard Deedee call, "Set!" Rich was right behind.

"Fire!" cried Buck sharply.

Brown punched the firing key hard to the left. He stepped back, waited, eyes on the indicator lights. "She's away," he said.

In the sonar shack, Schultz watched the path of the torpedo speeding toward the spot occupied by the enemy submarine. It would slow, make a circling search, finally go back to speed, and home in on magnetic attraction. The Mark Forty was the best torpedo the US Navy had, fast, nearly silent, and deadly.

"Good shot," said Richardson. "I think he's a dead man!" But as they watched the sonar scope, suddenly the spot the Russian submarine occupied became suffused with its own white light. The speeding trace of the torpedo entered the enlarged spot and vanished. Disbelievingly, the three men in the sonar room watched for an appreciable time, but nothing happened. The large white spot died down, disappeared, leaving not even the original indication of the presence of another submarine.

"I think I saw him take off," said Schultz, by way of possible explanation.

"At least you scared him silly, Buck. Maybe now he'll leave us alone!" But the grim look on Rich's face showed he did not believe his words. "How fast do you think we can tow Keith?"

"Maybe six knots, or a fraction more," said Buck.

"Make another course change, away from the direction he went, and go as fast as you can. I'll explain it to Keith."

Resuming towing resulted in only a few bumps as the line was again stretched. Once a steady condition was achieved, Buck gradually increased speed until both ships seemed fairly flying along, close under the ice cap. After three hours Buck was contemplating ordering the crew off action stations, when Schultz, still religiously maintaining his solitary watch, brought the bad news.

"Sonar contact," he announced in a heavy voice over the speaker system. Rich and Buck crowded into the sonar shack. "It's him again!" said Schultz. "I'd know that signature anywhere!"

"We have to break the towline, Buck! We'll have to fight this guy on even terms! If he sinks us, Keith's done for, anyway."

"I've been thinking the same. Shall I do it now?"

"Yes! I'll go tell Keith!"

As Richardson picked up the UQC handset he heard Buck order, "All ahead full!"

"Keith," Rich said in the customary low tone, "that fellow is back again, and we're going to have to break the towline. After we dispose of him we'll pick you up with the other rig."

"I understand," said Keith's distorted voice. And Rich knew he did, fully. "If we get a chance, we'll try a Mark Forty on him ourselves. We still have a few options left. And, Skipper"—Keith's voice deepened—"whatever happens, we'll never give up this ship."

It was Rich's turn to say, "I understand." Then the nylon line snapped, and Buck sent *Manta* sliding down to the depths.

"IT'S US HE'S AFTER, so it's us he'll chase, Buck. We've got one decoy left, and we've no idea how many fish he's got, nor how many of those defenses against the Mark Forty."

"It didn't make any noise, at least nothing we heard. Maybe it's not a weapon he shoots at all," said the disconsolate Buck.

"You mean, some kind of a magic energy device?"

"All I mean is, he might not have to shoot a piece of hardware. So it wouldn't be something you could count, like our decoys."

"True, old man, but right now our problem is to kill him before he kills us. We have six Mark Fourteens and five Mark Forties left forward, is that right?"

472

"Plus two Mark Forties in the skids in the after torpedo room."

"So if you have one of the Forties and our remaining decoy loaded aft, you can also have a salvo of Fourteens in the other tubes forward."

"You don't expect him to get within range of an old Mark Fourteen!"

Buck's exhaustion was showing in his slowness at picking up the idea, Rich decided. "Maybe this magic energy thing can stop the electric motor in the Mark Forty, but if that's what it does, it won't faze an old straight-running steam fish," he said—and was delighted when Buck's eyes brightened and he gave the orders.

As had become virtually a necessity during the past few encounters, they were in the darkened sonar room, awaiting developments which could only be seen, and that poorly, with the sonar equipment. The enemy submarine had approached to within about a mile and had apparently stopped. She made a faint but discernible note. It was this tiny noise, which Schultz and the passive sonar operator were so strenuously keeping in their earphones, that created a spot on the sensitive scope.

The *Cushing* was not visible on the tube. She was somewhere overhead, resting against the ice with all machinery stopped. All unneeded personnel had been ordered to their bunks. Keith could remain in this condition for seventy-two hours before his battery would be too low to restart his reactor.

Buck had also stopped every piece of nonessential machinery, but had kept the reactor functional in a low-power condition. Full power could be restored in minutes. *Manta*, too, was stopped, hovering at three-hundred-foot level.

For the time being, it was a standoff. "I'll bet he can't see *Cushing*, either," said Buck. "Maybe he's even lost us, and is making up his mind whether to go active with his sonar."

"Then he'll find us both, and he'll know the one against the ice must be the *Cushing*. Also, she'll give the bigger echo."

"We could try keeping our broadside to him. Then our echo will be about as big as Keith's."

"If we ease up against the ice ourselves, it will confuse him even more," said Rich thoughtfully, "but then, sound is so funny we might lose contact on him."

"We can always come back down again, boss. Let's try it!"

And so Tom Clancy blew some air into his tanks, and the *Manta* slowly drifted upward until she bumped gently against the ice, her broadside turned toward the intruder. Minutes later the tiny spot that was the enemy lashed out with six strong pings.

Buck chortled. "He can only see us by going active!"

"Right," said Rich. "The echoes he got must have been nearly identical, and he can't tell which is which."

"Shoot our last decoy?"

Rich snapped his fingers. "Get it programmed to simulate us trying to get away. Then load two Forties. Can the wolf-pack code tell Keith to get some fish ready?"

"That's one of the things it was made for."

Preparations were going forward when the sound of inimical pings filled the compartment. "I think he's getting ready to shoot," said Schultz. "There!" He pointed to a wispy, wavering discontinuity in the smooth blankness of the sonar scope. "There's another! He's still pinging, and he's fired twice!"

There were two discontinuities on the sonar scope, emanating from the enemy submarine, one diverging across its face, the other coming in remorselessly towards its center. "He's fired at both of us!" said Buck.

"Buck!" There was a decisive snap to Richardson's voice. "Set the decoy to run in circles under us! Maybe that will attract the fish! I'll tell Keith to do the same!" Rich dashed away, returned a moment later. "He's going to try," he said. "These are pretty slow-running torpedoes, so there may be time. Also I told him to shoot his Forties with us. Is our decoy away?"

"Affirmative!"

"There'll be a minute or so more before his fish gets here. Time to shoot ours."

A quarter of a minute later, a thin streak arrowed on the scope toward the Russian, traveling much faster than the weapon he had fired, passing it close alongside. As before, a brilliant phosphorescence bloomed over the spot, and there was no explosion.

"He's still there, I think," said Schultz. "He didn't run this time. The *Cushing*'s fired, too!"

Another streak, which could only have come from the *Cushing*, moved swiftly across the scope. The Soviet sub's reaction to this second shot would show whether she could remount her anti-tor-

474

pedo protection quickly. Then a violent explosion shook the *Manta*. The resounding roar, reverberating inside the sturdy hull, threw clouds of dust and paint particles into the air. On the sonar scope there was nothing but a startled whiteout.

"All compartments report to control!" Buck shouted into the telephone. The Soviet submarine was reappearing on the scope.

"He can't keep this up!" said Rich. "That must be a whale of a lot of energy. Shoot again!"

A third swift streak raced toward the enemy submarine. Buck's executive officer appeared at the sonar-room entrance. "No damage, here, Captain," Jerry Abbott said. "It was close though. Must have gone off right under us!" A second, distant explosion filled their consciousness. "Get a report from Leone!" Richardson snapped to Abbott.

Again the halo effect enveloped the enemy. Again the speeding Mark Forty, the US Navy's best torpedo, entered the immune area and disappeared.

"*Cushing* reports she's been hit!" gasped Abbott.

"*Cushing*'s fired again!" said Schultz.

"Are you reloading forward, Buck?" asked Rich.

"Affirm. Two more Forties."

"Shoot again, as soon as ready!"

In all, six Mark Forties, from two different locations, converged on the intruder. In succession they ripped into the area where the sonar scope showed her, into that halo effect—and disappeared.

There was a cry from Schultz. "He's fired again! He's fired at us! It's coming this way!"

"You'll have to try to outrun it, Buck!"

"Maneuvering, coolant pumps in high speed!" ordered Buck on the telephone. "How much can you give me?" He listened anxiously. "Not enough!" he said. "Don't wreck the reactor, but if you can't give me more speed right now, it won't make any difference! The *Cushing*'s been torpedoed, and there's another fish headed our way!"

Turning to Rich, he said. "They'll do it!" Suddenly he grinned tightly. "Wish old Brighting could see us! Where are all those reactor safeguards now, hey?" He darted out into the passageway again, called, "Left full rudder!" Back in the sonar room, he said swiftly to Schultz, "Where's the fish now?"

"It's about half a mile away," Schultz said anxiously, beads of sweat all over his face.

"Do we have any speed estimate on it?"

"It took about three minutes from the time he fired until he hit our decoy. That's thirty knots!"

The look on his superior's face had never been grimmer. Buck picked up the telephone again. "Maneuvering? The fish chasing us can make thirty knots. How bad do you guys want to live?"

Hanging up, he said to Rich, "This old bucket's never gone that fast in her life, but she's sure going to try now!"

Strange, Rich thought, that with total and terrible dissolution perhaps only moments away, he could feel so calm, so detached, even enjoying the heightened sensation. Buck was experiencing the same emotions, Rich knew. His asides during the emergencies which flowed upon him proved it.

"The fish is pinging!" Schultz murmured.

It must be close, close enough for the last-stage, target-searching cycle. It would home in on the echoes with the full speed of its little motor until fatal contact was made.

"Twenty-six knots! Increasing slowly!" called Jerry Abbott.

"Open vents!" Buck ordered. "Blow main ballast! One minute, wide open!"

"It's still pinging astern!" Schultz said.

There was that tight smile on Buck's face. "Here we go, Skipper." He leaned out the sonar-room door, called, "Right full rudder! Leave it on! Thirty degrees down angle! Make your depth nine hundred feet! All hands stand by for steep angles!"

At twenty-seven knots, the *Manta* pitched into the curve like an aircraft doing a spiral dive. Her bow swept downward, her gyro-compass repeaters spun like so many tops. Rich could feel the centrifugal forces on his body. Hanging on to the motor-generator stand outside the sonar room, he heard Abbott say with forced calm, "Speed nineteen. Passing five hundred feet. Two complete circles." There was a roaring somewhere in the water. Rich could sense the furiously flailing screws stirring it up in a way no submarine had ever stirred it up, into a veritable column of violently disturbed water, a five-hundred-foot spiral of currents, impervious to sonar, filled with its own sound and its own echoing defiance.

"Eight hundred fifty feet! Leveling off!" said Jerry.

"Rudder amidships!"

"Rudder is amidships!" cried the helmsman, throwing his weight into the effort, yet stopping the rudder exactly on center. *Manta's* deck flattened out with a smooth snap roll. Then, relieved of the slowing effect of the hard-over rudder, she bounced forward almost as if shot from a bow, rocketing through the sea depths with a reckless abandon as her powerful heart rammed superheated pressurized water through her steam generators.

"Nine hundred feet!" called Abbott. "Speed increasing rapidly."

Blam! A loud, somewhat muffled bang. Close, but not intimately close. Buck grinned, that same tight smile. "We beat it the hard way, Skipper," he said, then grabbed the handset. "Maneuvering, you did it! Cool her down gently and treat her like the queen she is! May Martin Brighting live a thousand years!"

CHAPTER ELEVEN

"**B**UCK, THAT WAS beautiful!" said Richardson. "That vertical corkscrew you made in the ocean must have seemed like a solid wall to the little fellow's sonar. So it drove into it and set off the detonator. I never saw a submarine handled that way before!"

"Actually, we'd practiced it," said Buck. "But we never did it with that kind of speed before."

"Well, it sure saved our bacon, old man!" Richardson put his hand on Buck's shoulder. Then his smile faded. "I wonder how far we are from the *Cushing's* last position?"

"Three miles by the dead-reckoning tracer. Good thing we set the DRT on automatic when all this started," Buck said, pleased. "Do you really believe the Russian may think we're sunk?"

"I'd bet on it. The last he saw of us was when we took off with his fish in hot pursuit. And when the fish exploded you slowed down to nothing. It's not like the two times he hit our decoys. So now he's waiting. If Keith's sunk, too, we'll hear the Russian start up and go away; if not, he'll take his time nosing around."

"And we're running silent, waiting for a false move."

"We can't leave Keith till we know for sure."

"Agreed. I'm trying to think of what to do if we find our other playmate, too."

"The first thing is to find him before he knows we're still alive. The second thing is to kill him." The words were said without expression, almost as if Richardson were referring to a routine happening. But Buck knew better.

The two men still sat in the sonar room. A slight reduction in the urgency of the situation was indicated by the mugs of black coffee they held. Schultz had refused relief and was still at the sonar console. A large towel, with which he repeatedly wiped his face, lay around his shoulders. Buck had tucked the end of his own towel under his belt. Rich's was stuffed behind a wire cable.

Manta had been running for several hours with all ventilation, even the air conditioning, shut down. The atmosphere was fetid, the heat nearly unbearable. All metal which communicated to the sea outside was alive with condensation. It dripped off everything: pipes, stanchions, bulkheads. Puddles of condensed moisture on the decks made footing hazardous.

"I'm hearing something!" Schultz's simple statement brought Rich and Buck to his side.

"What's it like?"

By way of response, Schultz flipped a switch, spoke into a microphone mounted on the face of his console. "JT, do you hear pounding off the port bow?"

"Affirmative! I was just going to report it!"

"Well, don't let me beat you to it again! You're supposed to hear sonic noises before I do!" Turning to his skipper, Schultz said, "Pounding, forty port."

Buck was already clamping on the spare set of earphones. "Here!" He detached the left phone, handed it to Rich. Instantly both men heard rapid intermittent blows of steel on steel, rhythmic for a short period, then spasmodic, then hurried again. Frantic was the word that came to mind.

"I'd say that's a hammer or mallet," said Rich. "Fairly close aboard. He sounded in a hurry to get it done."

"Repairing something, maybe?"

"My guess is it's Keith."

"Why not the other?"

"Keith was damaged. He might have had to do it. If we've ever been quiet and listening, now's the time!"

Buck spoke softly into the telephone handset. "Absolute silence,

479

all hands!" To Schultz he said, "Chief, we'll make a slow circle. Search for any other noise, and check the bearing of this one."

Again the deep stillness of waiting. Slowly *Manta* described two complete circles, far below the authorized depth, as deep as Buck dared go. All her machinery was quiet. Her battery, which ran her sonars, her planes and her propellers, was totally silent.

The third circle was nearly finished when all three men heard the JT report. "More pounding. Quietlike. It's above us, I think. Sounds as if a rubber hammer's hitting something." Schultz nodded, pointed to his own earphones. He, too, had heard it.

"Keith!" said Rich. "He's okay! They're making repairs!"

And then Schultz was pressing both earphones against his head. Finally he put his finger on his scope, tapping it gently. "I hear something," he said. "About here!"

"Is it the Soviet sub?"

"I think so; but it's still faint. . . . It's him. That's the same signature we've been hearing."

"SKIPPER," SAID RICHARDSON, "I'd give my right arm to be able to see up!"

"So would I, boss," returned Buck. "We'll raise the scopes as soon as the hoists can lift them against sea pressure. They can't do it below about two hundred feet."

Plot and the dead-reckoning tracer both indicated they were under the immobile *Cushing*. Tom Clancy had been directed to bring *Manta* up slowly. The enemy submarine, estimated to be a mile away, was approaching cautiously. A Mark Fourteen torpedo salvo, judged to have the best chance of being immune to whatever exotic defense system he had was ready. But it required point-blank range and a positive depth determination.

When *Manta* had passed the two-hundred-foot mark, Jerry Abbott, at the periscope station, called, "Scopes starting up!" and Rich and Buck took their places.

Rich impatiently grasped the hoist rods, tried to force his periscope to rise faster. It did no good. Buck had the shorter periscope, as was his right, because its eyepiece would be the first out of the well. He fixed himself to it as it came above deck, slowly rose with it. Heaving it around he said, "The bottom of the ice is almost white, and translucent. But there's no black hull anywhere!"

480

Two hours later there was still nothing in sight. A thought struck Richardson. Not knowing *Manta* was there, if Keith were to get an unexpected sonar contact he might shoot a Mark Forty at it. Well, this risk would have to be accepted. Then Rich's thoughts took another tack. If *Manta* could hear the approaching enemy, the *Cushing*—with its more modern sonar—could also.

"I'm having Jerry swing us around to put our bow on that sub's noise," said Buck's voice in his ear. "Plot calls his speed at four knots. Range half a mile, Schultz figures."

Half a mile. How far could one see horizontally? Rich wondered. Not far. A ship would have to be almost directly overhead for its hull to be outlined against the dull light through the ice. Where the devil was Keith?

Another hour passed as they slowly traversed the area, keeping *Manta's* bow whenever possible on the bearing of the enemy, to reduce the possibility of detection. Then Jerry Abbott suddenly jumped onto the periscope platform. "He's pounding again!" he whispered. "Schultz says it's right overhead!"

"That will bring our playmate over here," said Rich.

"We're ready!" said Buck. "But we have to be sure which is which before we shoot!" And then Buck saw the *Cushing*. "I've got Keith in sight!" he said. "Bearing, mark! Almost straight up! As high as you can elevate!"

"Two four eight," said the quartermaster, and he helped Rich swing his heavy periscope.

There, in silhouette, surprisingly near and quite distinct in outline, was the unmistakable shape of a US missile submarine! From beneath, a fish's eye view, Rich searched the bow section, saw the thin line of the anchor chain hanging vertically down. Keith might even be under a relatively thin place in the ice pack, for there seemed to be considerable light around him. Now where's the other one? As he thought the question, he heard Buck ask it.

"Very close! On zero two three, coming in slow!" said Abbott.

"We may see him in a minute, Buck! I hope he's shallower than we are!"

"He will be, boss! He'll be looking Keith over! And you know what he'll do if he thinks it's too big a job to bring her in."

"There's no doubt what his instructions are." The thought had been growing in Rich's mind for several hours. A negative decision on the part of the foreign submarine skipper would dictate another torpedo, and one for the *Manta*, too, once her continued existence was revealed. The sea would claim two more victims, and no one would ever know what had happened under the silent white overlay which sealed the mysteries of the Arctic.

Rich and Buck saw the enemy submarine simultaneously. She was moving very slowly, with three periscopes up, at a depth roughly halfway between *Manta* and *Cushing*. She had a bulbous bow, a conical stern and a large single propeller. She was bigger than the *Manta* but considerably smaller than the *Cushing*. What instantly struck both Americans was the strange structure of her bridge and forward portion. It looked massive—deformed, even. Then Rich realized what it was: great steel beams and protective plates, built around the sleek basic form, which had been bent and twisted out of their original shape by some strong force.

"That's the damage he took when he hit Keith," said Rich. "Thank goodness we're well below him, where it's dark. There's no way he could see us."

The noise level of the enemy submarine was increasing. The skipper had his reactor running—heavy machinery of some kind, anyway—and there was a strong hum, a whine of high-speed gears, which could be heard by all hands. The eerie feeling associated with the foreign noise of the submarine, which had done its best to destroy them, affected everyone.

"The bastard's too close to shoot. When he moves off a bit Keith may try. We'd better be on *Cushing*'s other side when he does!"

"Listen!" A series of whistles came over the UQC speaker. "Keith's sending Ri Ke! He wants to know if it's us!"

"Well, we can't answer him! Not yet, anyway."

The intruder was slowly passing beyond the *Cushing* now. Soon he would turn, probably, for a pass on her other side. "All right, Buck. I think this is our chance. You know what to do!"

The *Manta* swam slowly, silently, in the opposite direction, turned. At that depth, her screws were silent.

"We're ready forward," said Deedee Brown. "Depth set, one two oh feet."

"He's turning," called Schultz from the sonar room. "He's swinging to the right! Now he's broadside to us! Shoot! Shoot now!"

"Make haste slowly," said Buck. "Make sure we don't miss.

Deedee, set in starboard ninety. He'll go ahead emergency as soon as he hears us, so spread the fish forward to cover a ten-knot speed increase. Schultz"—he raised his voice—"can you separate the *Cushing*'s echo from the target's?"

"Yes, sir! I've got them both! He's the far one!"

"Good," said Buck. "Get me a single-ping range and bearing!"

A wail from Schultz. A cry of pain. "*Cushing*'s fired!"

"He's not shooting at us!" Buck said. "Single-ping range! Now!"

The ping went out instantaneously, so loud that everyone jumped. "Set!" said Deedee Brown.

"Fire!" said Buck Williams. The word was an expletive.

Unlike the new torpedoes, which swam out of their tubes silently on their own power, the older ones had to be expelled by a blast of water. In the forward torpedo room the firing ram slammed resoundingly back and forth four times. Four water-hammer jolts shook *Manta*'s hull, ten seconds apart. Four times the compressed air snarled and snorted through its control valves and the vents at the end of the stroke. Four old Mark Fourteen torpedoes roared out of their tubes, headed for the enemy.

"He's got his halo up!" Abbott called from the sonar shack. No need for silence now. There was noise in the water, lots of it, as the steam-driven torpedoes, roaring like banshees, drove madly through the sea. "*Cushing*'s fired a Mark Forty! It's gone into the halo. . .! It's stopped! We heard the motor stop!"

"At least, now Keith knows he's not alone," said Buck.

THE ENEMY SUBMARINE'S captain had heard the single-ping range being taken and had immediately increased speed. As the whine of his propeller filled *Manta*'s sonar shack, the fan of torpedoes, covering two ship lengths, passed under the *Cushing* and kept on.

The first torpedo, aimed to hit amidships, missed astern by a large margin. The second missed by only a few feet. The fourth and last inevitably missed ahead, for the third one struck home.

Whatever their shortcomings, Mark Fourteen torpedoes packed far more explosive than the newer antisubmarine torpedoes. The Mark Fourteen's mission, after all, had been to sink big surface ships, to shatter a keel or tear off a whole side. By contrast, only a small hole, big enough to let in the sea, is needed to send a submarine to the bottom forever.

The detonation of eight hundred pounds of torpex was cataclysmic. The entire middle of the enemy submarine disintegrated, blown into thousands of pieces. The two ends, the propeller still spinning on the cone-shaped stern, upended and sank separately to the Fletcher Abyssal Plain, twelve thousand feet down.

"KEITH," said Buck softly on the UQC, "it's Buck. Do you read?"

"Affirmative, old man! What a relief to hear your voice! I'll never in my life forget that uproar when your firing ram started cycling over there behind us. I kept thinking it had to be you, but I had heart failure, anyway."

"Sorry we couldn't warn you. We had to let him think he'd sunk us. But how're you doing? The boss wants to know."

Keith's voice dropped. "Not too good, Buck. That last fish of his hit in the double hull, back aft. We're not taking water very fast, but we can't stop the leak. I've had to abandon the auxiliary machinery compartment. For now we can hold her by pumping. But I'm afraid we're done!" Keith had evidently placed his hand over his mouth so that he would not be overheard.

"What's the time, Keith? Rich is right here."

Again the muffled voice. "We can hold out for two or three hours more. But the water's gaining. We'll finally be hanging on our forward ballast tanks with an up angle, and when she gets heavy enough she'll drift away from the ice."

Richardson and Williams conferred hurriedly; then Rich said, "Keith, how many wet suits have you?"

"Four, I think—yes, four."

"We have six. And three qualified scuba divers. How many do you have?"

"Two. Some others have done it for recreation."

"All right. Stand by to transfer your men to the *Manta* through the escape hatches! Get your scuba experts suited up, and one of the amateurs. We'll do the same. Our boys will bring our extra suits and tanks over to you. Buck is bringing the *Manta* alongside right now. We'll rig a line between us, and the divers can guide your men across the line to our hatch, then cycle the gear back to you. Rig your forward escape chamber so you can use the lower hatch and keep an air bubble inside. Can you handle that?"

"Affirmative! You bet!" Keith had taken his hand away from his mouth. He was letting everyone in the control room hear. "I'll start briefing our people right away. Be ready for you as soon as you get alongside!" There was a pause, then Keith said, his voice again muffled, "You sure you can do this okay? That's taking a big risk, bringing another sub alongside submerged like this!"

"We'll worry about that, Keith. The water's still and we'll come up real slow and easy. Just get your crew lined up."

Tired as they were, *Manta*'s crew handled their submarine with professionalism. Buck positioned her exactly where he wanted her, assisted by periscope angles and Schultz on the sonar. The *Cushing*'s underwater television camera, with its lights, illuminated the entire scene as *Manta*'s diving control group caused her to rise slowly and gently. When Buck finally housed his periscopes for fear of striking the ice, the two submarines were on nearly opposite headings, bows overlapping by some fifty feet, hatches abeam twenty feet apart. As soon as the upward motion ceased, the hatches on the two submarines opened, and a black rubber-suited figure with silver tanks on his back appeared on the deck of each. Each man had a line attached to his middle, which he clipped to the safety track on the deck of his sub.

Then a heavy nylon line was brought out from the *Cushing*. One end was looped around an opened cleat in *Manta*'s forecastle, then belayed to one on *Cushing*'s bow. A *Manta* diver carried a sack of scuba equipment over to the *Cushing* and handed it into the hatch.

"Our men say two divers will be enough to monitor the transfers," said Keith. "That will give us more suits, and we'll be able to transfer more men per group."

"Maybe, but the extra scubamen can stand by, over here, and we'll shift them when they get tired. Let's start with three monitors," said Richardson. It was a conservative decision he was later to regret deeply.

Slowly, seven men at a time, the transfer began. Seven men, with their tanks, filled the *Manta*'s escape chamber nearly to capacity. Then it was necessary to close the outer door, quickly release the pressure, and open the lower door to her forward torpedo room. Aboard *Manta* there were many hands available to strip the newcomers of their scuba equipment and bundle it hurriedly into sacks for the return journey to the *Cushing*.

The water was cold, several degrees below the freezing point of fresh water, but not uncomfortable with the suits on, the *Cushing* men told Rich. Nevertheless, he ordered the divers to shift their jobs after an hour in the water, the limiting time according to the instruction manual.

Things were going well. But seven men per transfer, opening and shutting hatches and changing equipment, took time. One hundred and twenty-seven men, *Cushing's* complement, counting her skipper, would take eighteen trips, with one man left over. At ten minutes per group, the fastest time achieved, eighteen transfers would take three hours. A nineteenth transfer would be necessary for the one man still aboard the *Cushing*. Richardson knew well who that last man would be.

He would never forget the sinking feeling in his chest when one of the scubamen reported that the *Cushing* was lower in the water. Eleven transfers had been made. Rich told Keith to hurry, that he would authorize more men per trip, with only two monitors. Keith's voice as he responded told Rich what he was afraid to hear: the ship would not last longer than half an hour.

Then more disaster. Two of the scuba tanks ran out of compressed air and had to be recharged; one of the mouthpieces was dropped and damaged. Again, time was lost.

"Boss," said Keith over the UQC, "we can't hold her. Depth's increasing! We have a full outfit of escape breathing gear, with hoods. I'm going to let out a group without waiting for the wet suits!" Richardson and Williams could imagine the scantily clad men, each wearing a breathing bag with oxygen, and a yellow plexiglass-faced hood over his head, being herded out of the *Cushing's* air lock. The scubamen would help them to the now tightly stretched nylon line, and along it into *Manta's* air lock.

The men came in, nine of them, faint with cold, gasping, but alive.

"Twenty-three men left, Rich! We're putting ten of them out this time! It's all our hatch can hold! Stand by to grab them!"

The rope connecting the two submarines was extending downward at an appreciable angle now. The action of the line, stretched to its uttermost, was causing the sinking *Cushing* to drift slowly under the *Manta*. Hurriedly the divers urged the men onward and up the line. Then, near the *Cushing*, but with a snap audible inside the *Manta*, the line broke.

486

The released nylon snapped backward like a rubber band. The short end of it struck the scubaman on the *Cushing*'s foredeck, knocking him off. At that instant the two submarines touched, *Manta*'s keel scraping across the bullet-shaped bow of the *Cushing*. Pulling himself back by his safety line, the scubaman found to his horror that the line was jammed in its slot on *Cushing*'s deck, where the *Manta*'s scraping passage had crimped the recessed track. He could feel the pressure increasing in his ears. Frantically he struggled with the belt around his middle. It seemed jammed, too. He let out all his breath, tried to force the belt over his hips. It would not move. The buckle was suddenly too complicated to operate. Desperately he tried to shove it over his shoulders, but he had forgotten about the tanks on his back, and now he had lost his mouthpiece. A huge dark shadow, the *Manta*, and safety, was just above him. He could almost reach it with his hand!

He grabbed for his mouthpiece hanging on its hose, jammed it into his mouth. There was pressure on his chest. No air in his lungs. He would have to inhale water, swallow it. Then he could get air! But a violent coughing fit seized him. He lost the mouthpiece again. He could not release himself from the *Cushing*. With a last convulsive effort, he managed to yank the toggles which inflated his life jacket. The jacket lifted him to the limit of the tether connecting him to the sinking submarine. He was like a kite on the end of a string, floating above the slowly descending *Cushing*. Despairingly, he saw the *Manta* receding. He reached for it with both arms, and knew that he was doomed.

Three of the ten hooded men had gotten into the *Manta*'s rescue chamber before the line broke. The remaining scubaman got four more in, but three floated away, lifted up against the ice by the air in their hoods. Heedless of instructions, the scubaman released himself from his safety line, swam after them. Grabbing the nearest one, he motioned toward the dark submarine seventeen feet below. The man nodded, tried to paddle downward. He could not. The scubaman squeezed the hood, forced out a bubble of air, but the hood expanded again with air from the breathing bag. He tried wrenching the hood off, tried to use a buddy-breathing technique with his mouthpiece, but the man did not understand.

Anxiously the scubaman swam down, tried to enter *Manta*'s rescue chamber. It was closed. The men inside were transferring into the interior of the sub. He banged on the deck with a hammer tied there for the purpose. After an interminable wait, the door opened and he entered. Minutes later he emerged, carrying a length of line with a buoy on the end. Swiftly he knotted the line outside the outer hatch, released the buoy, followed it up. He was not far from the men in the hoods, who were floating with their heads against the underside of the ice. He reached the nearest, gripped his arm—and recoiled in horrified dismay. The man was dead.

So were the other two. Several more figures floated up from the *Cushing*. Rapidly he swam to each, dragged him to the buoyed line, started him down. Gratefully they obeyed. The next to last man got only partway down, became entangled and stopped, desperately gripping the line. The man above was forced to stop also. When the scubaman was finally able to clear the tangle, he had to pry both bodies free. Two more yellow hoods appeared from below. Helplessly, fatalistically, the scubaman let go of the stiffened body in his arms, lunged for the newcomers. He was able to get both of them started down the line.

There were five dead bodies, with yellow plexiglass-faced hoods, floating up against the ice. The scubaman swam to each one and checked it carefully. Finally he swam to the submarine. The two men he had just sent down were holding the end of the line near the closed hatch. They could not last long at this temperature. He banged on the hatch, banged again. By the time it opened, both men were unconscious. He shoved them inside and followed, yelling to the suited diver waiting to take his place, "Watch for more guys coming up! I'll be right back out!"

But when he got outside there was no one in sight except the other scubaman, and the five hooded bodies above, against the ice. In vain they searched for the diver who had been on the *Cushing*'s deck. Ten minutes, fifteen, they waited. No more yellow hoods came up from below. The five overhead had so nearly made it! Disconsolately the two scubamen returned to the *Manta*.

"RICH," SAID KEITH, speaking over the UQC in a quiet, yet tense voice, "we got everybody out but four. My exec, Jim Hanson, and our engineering officer, Curt Taylor, are with me still, and chiefs Hollister and Mirklebaum. I'm afraid we're going to have to ride her on down, boss. I hope all the others made it!"

488

"Five, Keith. You didn't count yourself!"

"That's right, five. Did you get all the rest?"

"I'm sure we did, Keith. We're still taking a muster with your list. And I have your ship's log and your unfinished report. Is there anything at all you can do, Keith?" he could not refrain from asking. "How about your anchor and chain? Could you try a big bubble in main ballast, to boost you up for one final escape? One more time would do it."

"We've done all that. We all tried to pile in the escape hatch the last time, but the ship upended, and everybody fell down against the bulkhead. So I had to slam the hatch on the two that were in already. Now we're at two hundred feet, and I'm in the control room sitting on the bulkhead to reach the UQC. It's down between my feet. We're making our last dive, and it will be a deep one."

Richardson felt something salty on his face. More than one submariner in a sinking submarine had closed the hatch over his own head, thus closing the trap upon himself as well as the shipmates trapped with him. This was precisely what Keith had done. In fact, since he had shut the hatch himself, he must have actually entered the escape chamber, taken hold of the hatch, and pulled it shut behind him as he backed out! Captain of the ship, he could not leave so long as there were men for whom he was responsible still aboard.

What to do? What to say to one's own deep, personal friend? Rich felt his eyes stinging. He gripped the mike to control himself, finally said in a voice he could not recognize, "We understand what you're saying, Keith, old friend. Buck's here, too. All that we've heard will be reported fully, and believe me, there's going to be some truth told when we get back. We're so terribly sorry, Keith. What can we do for you and the fellows with you? Tell me." Something like a vise was closing down Richardson's throat.

"Tell our wives that we love them. No, Stew Mirklebaum says he's divorced. The rest of us. Mirklebaum says to find Sarah Schnee—Schneehaulder"—Keith spelled the name. "One of the fellows you've picked up will know who she is. Tell her he's thinking of her. Jim Hanson wants you to tell Mary he loves her and little Jimmy. Larry Hollister sends love to Eleanor and says not to forget they'll meet by the first bloom of the lilac tree. Curt says Suzanne knows he's always hers. And tell Peggy and Ruthie for me"—here

Keith's steady voice broke for a moment—"tell them I love them, and would like to have gotten Peggy that little house I promised her. Tell her the Navy didn't let me down. It did all it could, and so did you and Buck. There's nothing more anyone could do. Tell her we're not suffering, and aren't going to."

The stricture in Richardson's throat threatened to suffocate him. "I've got it all, Keith. I promise, and so does Buck," he choked out. "And there'll be a full report on how you carried out the best and finest traditions of the United States Navy, and how you told that foreign submarine, by that last torpedo of yours, that you weren't about to give in to him or anyone. And we'll also tell how you stayed with your ship to the very last, giving your own life to save your crew and making sure they escaped, even though you couldn't."

"I'm not the last, Rich. There's Jim and Curt and Larry and Stew, and we're all together now. Passing three hundred feet."

Buck handed Rich a piece of paper. Richardson looked at it, frowned thoughtfully, did not speak for a full fifteen seconds.

"Rich, are you still on the line?"

"Yes, Keith. We've just gotten a report on your muster. For a minute I thought of lying to you, but I can't. All of your crew made it except five. They were in the last two groups, and didn't have the wet suits. Jim Baker, Howard McCool, Willson Everett, Abe Lincoln Smith and John Varillo. I'm sorry, Keith. They died in the water before we could get them into the chamber. Also, we lost one of our divers when the line carried away."

"I'm dreadfully sorry, Rich and Buck, too. What was the diver's name?"

"Cliff Martini."

"I'm sorry, Buck. Tell his family for me. We're going down faster, now. Just passed four hundred feet. About the five of our men who died, they were all good men. John was a fine young officer and would have been a credit—I understand he was engaged to a girl named Ellen Covina. She lives in New York. Look her up for him, will you? And also the next of kin for the other four—I don't know all the details—oh, we know. McCool's family is in Groton. So's Abe Smith's. Everett lived in Waterford. Baker was born and brought up in Norwich, Larry says. Passed five hundred while I was talking."

"Okay, Keith. Wilco on all of it, old friend."

"We're nearing six hundred. I'll try to keep giving you the depths. The designers might like to know." Keith's voice was growing fainter, and the time of transmission from the sinking submarine was lengthening. "Seven hundred, Rich!"

"Haven't been able to think of the words to say, got to try to get it in." Keith's voice had risen in pitch. "Buck knows what I'm talking about. Tell Peggy I love her, and for her to take the insurance and get that house and garden, far away from New London. But don't you talk to her, Rich. Not unless there's someone with you—Buck or Laura. Ask Buck! This is going to throw her, and sometimes she's—passing a thousand feet—sometimes she says things she doesn't really mean, or doesn't really know about but makes you think she does. Don't let her upset you, Rich. She's my wife, and you're my best friend, and I love you both. That's all I can think of to say. The others are over in the corner. They said they don't need to talk to anyone. Eleven hundred. Going fast, now. I can hear the internal bulkheads squeezing. Twelve hundred. I can smell chlorine. The battery's spilled for sure. Took a long time, though. It's a good design. Thirteen. We're off the deep gauge. Give it to you in sea pressure. Where's a sea-pressure gauge? I'm disoriented. Here's one. I can barely read it from where I'm sitting—the gauge shows seven hundred pounds. That's more than fourteen hundred feet. Now it's nearly eight hundred. I'll hold the mike button down with my foot and maybe I can stand up partway to read it—it's eight fifty. I'm shouting. Can you hear me? Don't answer. It doesn't matter, but I'll keep trying. . . ."

Rich felt Buck's arm around his shoulders, put his own arm around Buck's neck. Both of them were aware of the other members of *Manta*'s crew, many members of the *Cushing*'s crew. Rich felt Buck's quiet, shaking grief, knew his own was communicating itself to Buck. There were soft noises of anguish from others in the control room, but otherwise silence, except for many men, breathing as quietly as they could. In a far corner, someone let out a tiny wail, "Oh, God—" It was savagely shut off.

Keith had said not to answer, but Rich had to say something. He cleared his throat, swallowing the lump that was in it. "Keith," he said, willing his voice to work. "Most of your crew is here with me. They're all blessing the best submarine skipper they ever had, and

491

the best friend they ever had. Those who traveled in deep waters with you are with you still." He released the button, heard the sound of the message beaming out.

" . . . hundred pounds. That's amazing, Rich! Eleven hundred! Who could have thought—twelve hundred! Tell Peggy I love her! Tell Ruthie the last thing her dad did was to think of her. Thirteen hundred! Something's given way down aft! I think she's going! Good-by! Thanks for all! Fourteen—"

A smashing roar came over the UQC speaker—Keith had been holding the button down—and then it was silent. But everyone in the *Manta* heard the awful, crushing implosion where the pressure of the sea, at whatever depth *Cushing* had reached, burst the stout high-tensile steel into thousands of pieces, all of them driven inward with a velocity beyond comprehension. The sea followed instantly, with a voice like thunder, compressing the air and raising its temperature high into incandescence.

Keith, Jim, Curt, Larry and Stew did not suffer. Their awareness ceased instantaneously.

Great sections of curved steel fluttered down through the black water like leaves. When they came to rest they covered a wide expanse of the Fletcher Abyssal Plain. Under them, deeply buried in the ancient ooze, were the last resting places of the two halves of the Soviet nuclear submarine *Novosibirsky Komsomol*, and the *Cushing's* reactor, which sank swiftly in one piece because of the immense pressure it had been built to contain.

CHAPTER TWELVE

THERE WAS a new compulsion in the *Manta* as she raced for the edge of the ice pack to send a message. For the better part of a day Rich and Buck labored over its wording. They must report the loss of the *Cushing*, give the names of the men lost with her, tell of the battle with the intruding submarine, and describe their suspicions that there was a Soviet base not far away.

The message, encrypted in the highest classification code available on board, ended with terse naval jargon: UNODIR PROCEEDING RECON GUARDING VLF ONE HOUR NOON GREENWICH—unless otherwise directed, *Manta* would try to locate the base and discover its

492

nature and purpose. Once a day, at noon Greenwich Mean Time, she would come to as shallow a depth as possible, to listen to the very-low-frequency radio circuit for instructions. Otherwise the *Manta* would most likely be at deep submergence and unreachable.

Thirty hours were required to find an area where the ice cover was thin enough to break through. When the message was at last cleared, *Manta* went deep and headed toward the place indicated on Jerry Abbott's plot.

Buck Williams, sitting at the head of the wardroom table, was wagging his head. He and Richardson had adjourned to the wardroom to study Jerry's work, leaving the exec free to continue the complicated task of organizing sleeping and mess arrangements for an influx of nearly double the crew of the *Manta*.

Jerry had plotted backward every known movement of the enemy submarine, as Buck had instructed, but he had had to make a number of assumptions. Fortunately Keith had given an estimated position of the aircraft he had seen in his last message, the one transmitted via the *Manta*. How long ago had that been? Less than two days. A decoded copy lay on the table.

Buck tapped the copy. "This little piece of paper cost Keith his life! I hope they choke on it down in Washington! Do you really think Admiral Donaldson will get it across to the people responsible how much this has cost?"

"If I know him, he certainly will. The lives of eleven damn good men, not to mention a brand-new submarine, is a stiff price." Rich paused. "But right now we've got to figure out what's going on up here, Buck. These guys are no little exploration party!"

After several hours of study, an indicated circle of probability was decided on. It was twenty-five miles in diameter. As soon as it was reached, a methodical, crisscross search would begin, with both periscopes up. Echo ranging was ruled out.

For two days *Manta* made a fruitless search of the Arctic, not even certain what she was looking for. Then, midway on the third day, the sonarman on duty reported hearing a beacon.

Palmer Schultz, instantly on the scene, confirmed it. "It sounds like those homing beacons divers use. It's a standard intermittent buzz. You can only hear them a mile or so!"

"It's for that sub!" said Buck. "He navigates to a mile or so of this place, picks up this little thing, and homes in on it!"

"So will we, after we've made a couple of circles around it," Rich replied. "Now that we've found their base, it's up to us to find out everything we can about it!"

Moving slowly and deliberately in the dead-silent condition, *Manta* made three complete circuits around the sound source, at different depths, recording every scrap of information that could be obtained. Finally Buck ordered her periscopes raised and told Tom Clancy to gradually increase depth to a hundred and eighty-five feet.

Richardson had no idea when he first realized he was looking at something other than water through his scope. It emerged slowly, a gradual gathering together of vague nothingness in the sea until there was something, square and angular, huge and sinister. And close. Very close!

"Down scope!" he rapped out, snapping up his control handles.

Buck's "Down scope!" was almost simultaneous. "Left full rudder!" he shouted. "Take her down fast!" The whoosh of air and the rush of water into negative tank pervaded the control room. Buck made a show of wiping the sweat off his forehead. "Did you see what I saw, boss?"

"I think so," said Richardson. "Damn good thing we were going so slow! I think we'd have passed under it, but it sure scared me."

"What was it, Skipper?" asked Abbott. "An iceberg?"

"No. Too regular for that. Something straight up and down. And the bottom looked squared off."

"That's what I saw, too," said Rich. "It was man-made, all right. Let's come on around and ping on it, to get a sonar picture. We'll have to chance nobody will hear us."

Manta made several circuits of the strange object, pinging first strongly, then progressively less so. Gradually the outline of what they were looking at became clear. Rich recognized it first. "It's a cylinder, Buck! Four cylinders, rather. Fastened together and standing upright in the water!"

"How big do you make it?" said Buck.

"If the bottom really was a little above the tops of our periscopes, that would put it at a hundred and twenty feet or so. From the sonar picture, it's about two-thirds that in width."

"And the top's got to be frozen in the ice pack."

"That makes sense. But what is it?"

494

"Let's close in again, boss," begged Buck. "If anybody heard us pinging, the quicker we get this over with, the better."

"Agreed!"

The dim light filtering through the ice pack was barely sufficient to outline the structure. The control room had been darkened, leaving only red lamps glowing at the important stations. Buck and Rich kept their faces firmly pressed against the periscope eyepieces, and gradually the thing took shape. There was an impression of massive strength. The structure, four large vertical cylinders, linked by steel girders, was painted sea gray. It was relatively new, for as yet there was very little growth on the surfaces. At several places steel ladders could be distinguished. Here and there the periscope focused on black lettering with the occasional "reversed" characters of the Russian alphabet. Three sides of the complex were evidently frozen into the ice overhead. But on the fourth side there was a large opening in the ice, through which bright sunlight streamed.

"Ever see anything like this before, Buck?"

"It looks like the grain elevator in my hometown. That had six silos. *Silos!* Could these be missile silos?"

"By God, they could be! With that polynya for a resupply dock. Buck, I think you hit it. This is the headquarters of that Soviet polar expedition they were talking about in that lousy press release. It's really an intercontinental missile base! I'll bet you five there's an ice runway alongside it, too."

"We've got to report this, boss."

"Just as soon as we can. But we've got to be sure first. Maybe we can ease on up and take a careful look."

"And take a batch of pictures through the periscope to prove it! Our intelligence boys will love that!"

"Better go to battle stations, Buck. But don't sound the alarm. Pass the word quietly, in case they've got a sonar watch on."

POSITIONING THE *Manta* in the center of the large, artificial polynya was easy; the difficulty lay in bringing the submarine up slowly, using buoyancy only, and stopping her ascent at exactly the right depth. Fortunately Tom Clancy was entirely equal to the task.

With Buck at a half crouch, the tip of *Manta*'s high periscope came one inch above the mirrorlike surface of the artificial lake. Buck spun it around swiftly, dropped it two feet below the surface.

"I didn't see anyone looking," he said quickly, "but there's a lot going on. I could see cranes, a hangar and several huts, all painted white. Quite a few people wandering around."

"Can I have a look?" Rich could not hide his eagerness.

"That's what we're here for! That and the camera!"

Through the periscope, Rich was first conscious of the height of the ice around the polynya: nearly ten feet above the surface. This was not an ordinary floe. The Soviets had preempted an ice island for their missile station! Then he saw the hangar, a large, white building resembling a Quonset hut. The elevated booms of two cranes were prominent against the sky. Near the hangar he thought he could distinguish an aircraft, though the height of the ice interfered, and it would not be wise to raise the scope higher. Alongside the white structure enclosing the tops of the silos, mooring cleats—they could only be for submarines—had been built. They, too, had been painted white, but there were dark rope burns, which proved they had been used. And, as Buck had said, there were numbers of people in heavy clothing.

Rich dunked the scope several times as he made his traverse. When he finally turned it over to the camera party, he was surprised to note that he had been using it less than five minutes. The camera party itself accomplished its mission in half a minute.

Buck retrieved the periscope, spun it twice rapidly, then dropped it to the bottom of its well. "Mighty well done, Skipper," he heard Rich say. "Now let's get away from here and get off a report!"

Rich might have gone on, but all thought was abruptly reoriented by a thunderous crash! *Manta*'s deck seemed to buckle; the interior resounded like a huge steel drum. Richardson saved himself from falling by grabbing the guardrail around the periscope station, found it vibrating madly. Several men in the control room had been knocked down.

"All compartments report!" said Buck urgently to the battle stations telephone talker a few feet away. Then the second depth charge arrived—if anything, closer than the first. And then a third, and a fourth, and a fifth . . .

NIKOLAI KONSTANTINOV SHUMIKIN, commander of the First Soviet Arctic Free Missile Base, was seriously worried. For a time things had been going so well, and now, ever since he had sent Zmentsov back to prevent escape of the damaged American submarine, the sixth sense which had always served him had not been functioning. Number one, there had been a second transmission in undecipherable code from somewhere nearby, and for this last one there was no clear explanation.

Grigory Ilyich Zmentsov, skipper of the *Novosibirsky Komsomol*, had suggested that the first transmission they'd heard must have been from a US submarine sent to render assistance to the one they had so cleverly immobilized. The trapped vessel, the newest model of Polaris missile submarine, must not be permitted to escape. The Americans had no right to attempt to make the Arctic Ocean into a place from which they might shoot Polaris missiles! His own top-secret missile base was, of course, very different, more like an extension of Russia's landmass a little farther into the sea— perfectly legitimate, even if subterfuge had been necessary because of stupid treaties.

It had been an extraordinary stroke of luck to have been forewarned of the appearance of the enemy sub, and to have had Grigory Ilyich and his specially configured *Novosibirsky Komsomol* ready. Reporting the loss of one of his aircraft as due to a weapon fired from the damaged submarine had given the Kremlin an excellent pretext for taking the damaged vessel into custody. It was simply unfortunate that she had managed to surface and get those two initial messages off.

That had been the beginning of the bad luck that had dogged him ever since. The second submarine had undoubtedly come in response to the call for help, but had been stupid enough to reveal her presence by sending a long message. Shumikin had immediately ordered Grigory Ilyich to investigate. Grigory had returned with the extraordinary report that the second submarine, a smaller, older model, had actually rigged a towline to the first one and was extracting her from under his very nose! There had been no time to radio for instructions, but his decision was the only one possible: to order the second submarine destroyed.

Grigory Ilyich had departed four days ago, but he had not yet returned. It was inconceivable that anything could have gone seriously wrong. Grigory has assured him that the towing sub was helpless to defend itself. It could not have that recent triumph of Soviet technology, the new force-field anti-torpedo system which made all Soviet submarines practically immune to attack. Perhaps some other difficulty was holding him up.

Shumikin was still in this frame of mind when, late on the fourth day, a messenger came. The man was excited. "There is a submarine! But it is acting strangely!" A periscope had been sighted in the lagoon, staying very low and turning in all directions.

From the observation post Shumikin inspected the waters of the polynya through binoculars. The periscope was indeed acting strangely! It was going up and down at short intervals, never exposing itself more than an inch or two above the water. Grigory Ilyich would not behave like this. Then the full implication struck him. Savagely he turned on his officer of the watch.

"Why was I not informed of this sooner?" he demanded.

The man was unable to answer. He had been expecting the *Novosibirsky Komsomol*, had not become concerned until he had seen the periscope.

Shumikin stamped his foot in rage. "Sound the alarm, you dolt! This is an enemy! Release the depth charges!"

Twenty depth charges, ready at the far side of the polynya, could be released electrically. They had been set deep enough so that their explosions would not damage the silos, nor the ice around them; hence they could not harm an interloper at shallow depth. A far more potent weapon lay in the torpedo room, built in the base of the mooring pier.

With the sounding of the alarm, furious activity struck the missile base. Other depth charges would soon be rolled into the lagoon, and numerous small guns and two anti-aircraft rifles would be manned. Most important of all, two of the latest target-seeking torpedoes could be brought into action within three minutes.

At least a minute had elapsed since the first depth charge. The surface of the polynya was roiled, and the periscope had disappeared. Shumikin grabbed the observation post telephone. "Sonar!" he barked. "Where is that submarine?"

"It's going away, Commander! Right after the depth bombs we heard it speeding up!"

"Well, keep the contact! It was your negligence that let it come up on us without warning!"

"The error is regretted, Commander, but we did not know—"
Shumikin banged the telephone down.

He called the torpedo room. "Torpedo!" he shouted. "When will you clowns be ready with those fish?"

"About a minute, Commander! We're going as fast as we can!"

"Very well! Hurry!" He slammed the phone into its cradle, leaped out of the observation post and ran toward the hatch leading down to the torpedo room. He was almost in a frenzy. The strange submarine must be American. Having detected the silo base, the submarine commander was undoubtedly hightailing it to a place from which to inform Washington. This must be prevented at all costs!

By his presence in the torpedo room he hoped to galvanize his men into even greater effort. But, even to his nontechnical eyes, they were already working as rapidly as possible. Soon both torpedoes would be on their way, and at least one of them would certainly home in on the target.

As for Grigory Ilyich Zmentsov and his heroic ship, Shumikin would spend all day composing a fitting message describing their sacrifice in the service of their country. He would begin immediately, as soon as sonar reported the two explosions. . . .

THE DEPTH CHARGE METER in *Manta*'s control room had gone wild, but it had also indicated that the depth charges were some distance below. The ship's hull vibrated resoundingly. Pipelines, cableways, even the very bulkheads shook spasmodically with every explosion. Buck Williams took a perverse pleasure in the initiation his crew was getting. He had experienced it all before.

So had Rich. Buck had felt actual pleasure carrying out Rich's order to stay at periscope depth despite the shattering blows and the storm inside the ship. It had been his evaluation, concurred in by Richardson, that the Soviets would have to set the charges deep to avoid damage to their own installation. The guess had proved correct. When the last of twenty explosions had died its reverberating death, he seized the opportunity to order greater depth and increased power.

Buck heaved a deep sigh, and at that moment heard Schultz scream, "Torpedo!"

Buck did not wait for the sweeping motion of Richardson's hand. "All ahead emergency! Take her down!" Instantly he felt the tilt of the deck, the bite of the suddenly accelerated screws. But there was too little time. The range was much too short. Even as the air whistled from the negative tank, there was a vicious jolt, and the high-pitched sound of an explosion.

"Maneuvering says the starboard shaft is stopped!" The telephone talker stuttered in panic.

Buck snatched the nearest handset. "Maneuvering, Captain here. How bad is it?"

"That explosion must have been right on the starboard propeller, Captain! She started vibrating like crazy right after!"

"Are you taking water? How's your shaft seal?"

"The seal's been damaged, and the stern room's taking water!"

"Tom! Take the angle off the boat! Start her back up! Stern room, open your drain-pump suction! Maneuvering, get some men back aft and tighten the gland! Keep me informed about the leak!" Buck turned to Abbott, who was gripping the periscope-stand guardrail. "Jerry! Get on aft! See how bad we're flooding!"

"Torpedo! Another one!" Schultz's scream was of pure terror.

Manta was still in a headlong dive, her port engine racing. Buck did not hesitate. "Right full rudder!" he ordered. "Tom, keep the angle on!"

Manta rolled to starboard like a roller-coaster car. The noise of the whirling port propeller came clearly through the hull. Richardson's face was immobile, and his eyes had a faraway look. Buck had the impression he was not there at all.

"This is it, Skipper," said Buck softly. "Just like the last time, only we've lost half our power. It's all we can do."

"What's our depth now?" Rich asked.

"Passing six hundred feet. We'll have to take the angle off her pretty soon, even if we can contain the leak."

"Buck," said Rich somberly. "Keith did one thing for us that we didn't appreciate at the time. Do you remember the depth the *Cushing* reached?"

"Yes. He told us fourteen hundred pounds sea pressure. That's over three thousand feet!"

"If the *Cushing* could go that far below her design depth, so can we! Even with a bad leak. But that torpedo won't. It's our only chance! Tell Tom to keep the angle on and level her off at fifteen hundred feet!"

Buck nodded shortly, his eyes wide. As he gave the orders, there

502

was silence in the control room—the silence of men who realized the risk but who understood the necessity for it. If ever they were to put their faith in the men who designed and built their ship, now was the time. Fifteen hundred feet was far below *Manta's* designed depth. She was there in slightly more than a minute, and the immense pressure of the sea was already obvious. Bulkheads were bowed, sheet-metal doors were jammed shut. Even decks were curved upward or downward, where their girders were compressed. All depth gauges had reached their limits. Only a few of the sea-pressure gauges could register the six hundred and seventy pounds per square inch the depth produced.

Buck left the rudder on for one more full circle to render the disturbance of the water as nearly impenetrable as possible, then set a course away from the polynya. The real battle, as everyone was well aware, was taking place in the stern room, where water was spurting in with sufficient force to break an arm or rip off clothes. But the men must be coping with the leak somehow.

Jerry Abbott returned to the control room, leaving a trail of water behind him. He stopped, facing Buck. He was soaked through and breathing hard. "We can't hold her at this depth, sir," he said. "We've got the packing nuts as tight as they'll go, but the water is coming in so hard that two of us had to hold a piece of sheet metal to deflect it so that one man could reach the gland nuts. We'll have to pressurize the compartment."

"We've got to stay down here for a while," Buck said, "until that second torpedo runs down. Have them abandon the stern room and start putting air in it."

Abbott said, "Aye, aye, sir!" As he ran aft he heard Buck order, "Port ahead two-thirds!"

"The best thing we can do is slow down, Skipper," said Buck to Rich. "If they've got another fish ready, we're still making so much noise it might be able to follow us!"

"Right!" They could hear the hiss of air as Abbott began to follow his orders at the stern-room bulkhead.

CHIEF SONARMAN SCHULTZ finally made the report that was so anxiously awaited. "When we quieted down I could still hear the torpedo pinging astern and above us," he said. "Then it sort of petered out and stopped. I think it finally ran down!"

A silent cheer went through the control room when Buck gave the order to bring the ship up.

"It's obvious we'd not have been able to stay down much longer, Commodore," said Buck. "Jerry says there's five feet of water in the stern room, but with the shallower depth and air pressure in there, he thinks we can cope with it." Then he went on, speaking with a deliberate formality. "Commodore, this illegal base has opened fire on us without cause. The submarine based here sank the *Cushing* and caused the loss of eleven good men. I request permission to return the fire!"

Williams saw again the faraway look in the eyes of his superior. Rich spoke quietly, almost pensively. "No, Buck. We're not at war, and we'll not attack in cold blood."

"My God, boss! What do you mean, cold blood? After what they've done?"

"They can't hurt us now, Buck. Shape your course away from here. We'll let Washington handle it when they get our message!"

But at that instant Jerry Abbott came in and changed the entire complexion of the private talk between his captain and their squadron commander.

"Skipper," he said to Buck. "We've got to surface! We can't stop the water! We'll have to get the stern high and remake the seal with flax packing!"

"How long can we hold out the way we are, Jerry?"

"The seal might go any minute! A couple of hours, no more."

"How long will it take to make the change once you start?"

"About an hour. It's a big job, but we have everything we need to do it, once we stop the water from coming in."

Richardson, listening, knew that Admiral Donaldson's cryptic words aboard the *Proteus* had at last achieved their full meaning. "I want someone up there who can take special initiative on his own, if the occasion demands. You may run into a lot more up there than we expect!" Aloud, Rich said, "There's only one place here we can bring her to the surface, Buck."

"How are we—" Buck began, but Richardson interrupted him.

Speaking loudly, so as to be overhead, Rich said, "Buck, enter in your log that because there is only one place to surface, which is occupied by a hostile force that not once but several times has endeavored to destroy this ship and all on board, and has now

504

seriously damaged her so that the lives of all hands depend on her coming to the surface to make repairs, the commander of Task Group eight three point one has ordered destruction of the offensive power of the said base so that *Manta* can surface unmolested!"

"Aye, aye, sir!"

"I will sign the entries in the notebook and the official log to attest to their accuracy. And now, make ready the torpedoes!"

NIKOLAI KONSTANTINOV SHUMIKIN, finally relaxed at his desk, was pleased. No matter that the American missile submarine had gotten away, or that the *Novosibirsky Komsomol* had been unfortunately lost. The American submarine which had had the temerity to lift her periscope in the middle of his own artificial lagoon was now also resting on the bottom of the Arctic Ocean. He himself had heard the torpedo explosion which had killed her, and with her had died the possibility of premature revelation of the existence of his missile base.

Now he would compose a priority message explaining that a number of exotic weapons had been used against him, and that his own inspired crew had finally sunk the American submarine responsible for it all. Having the trapped submarine slip through his fingers had been no fault of his. And, in any case, she could know nothing about the existence of Shumikin's missile base.

Loss of the *Novosibirsky Komsomol* would be the hard thing to explain. He was beginning to grapple with the problem when suddenly the alarm bell jangled. "Torpedo fired!" shouted a hoarse voice over the intercom.

Shumikin leaped to his feet, pressed a button. "What do you mean, torpedo fired?" he snarled. "Who ordered it?"

"It's not us, Commander. It's that submarine! There's two torpedoes coming!" The voice rose in a shriek, then was cut off.

A tremendous geyser of water and explosive gas burst out of the doors of one of the silos, rose high above it and drenched everything within several hundred yards. Nearly simultaneously a racking, explosive *boom* shattered the atmosphere. A plume of gray smoke shot above the ice, then lazily drifted away in the still air. The ruined silo, instantly filled with angry water, jerked sideways, hanging from its moorings.

The second torpedo struck a silo diagonally opposite the one first hit. Its exit doors burst open. A second geyser of water, mixed with smoke and gas, shot into the air, followed by a streak of white-hot fire from the ruptured fuel section of the missile inside.

The two damaged silos, flooding with seawater, now dragged down the entire structure, and the section of the ice island into which it had been built, to within inches of the water level in the polynya.

The personnel of the undamaged silos unceremoniously started up the interior ladders to the top level and ran out. They were barely in time, for great cracks had begun appearing in the ice. Water was coming through them, collecting on the surface everywhere. The base commander, confronting the men as they ran, furiously ordered them back to their stations, but they affected not to hear him, not daring to obey.

By this time violent rocketlike flames were erupting from the exploded silo doors, reaching hundreds of feet into the air, then petering out, six hundred feet above the ice, in a plume of black smoke. The whole ice slab, with its network of steel beams, insulated conduits, pipes and cables, had been laid out with great engineering skill and frozen solidly together. It cracked in several places, but the steel links in the ice held firm, and the entire camp area began to sag. Then, with a great smashing of ice, a groaning and snapping of steel, the hangar, silos, cranes and all equipment slowly descended into the sea.

Sensing the danger from the water creeping ever farther over familiar environs, everyone in the camp began to run toward the only undamaged area, the aircraft landing strip. Nikolai Shumikin despairingly followed. The last man out of the ruined missile base, he stepped reluctantly off the sinking ice and the shattered remains of his command.

His mind was still numb as he looked into the low-lying sun and saw the hangar, with one plane inside, both cranes, the radio hut and his two big anti-aircraft guns gently dropping out of sight, following the already vanished silos.

For a long time Shumikin stood looking at the scene of his disaster. That it was a personal as well as an official one could not be doubted. And then he saw a strange periscope rising out of the waters of the much enlarged polynya. It was club-headed, with two large glass windows. And it kept rising, higher and higher, until the dark foundations underneath also broke water, and then the entire hull of a submarine.

It was a strange submarine. It seemed to surface oddly tilted, with the highest exposed portion of the hull at the point farthest away from the periscope. No one came on deck, or into the bridge area, although he could hear some noises of concealed activity, apparently from that vicinity.

The periscope itself was in nearly constant motion, although frequently it steadied for long minutes, during which he felt it was leveled exactly at him.

After about an hour, air bubbled from around the hull of the submarine, and it slowly disappeared into the water.

CHAPTER THIRTEEN

"LAURA? THIS IS Joan Lastrada. I'm in New London for a few hours. May I come over?"

Laura had recognized the infrequently heard voice instantly. Minutes later a Navy sedan had stopped in front of the Richardson house, dropped off a passenger and departed. Now Laura was looking across the living room at her visitor. Joan was still slender, her complexion still smooth. The gray suit was exactly right to set off her dark hair and eyes. Laura could feel the strength in the long, tapering fingers when they shook hands.

"It's so nice to see you, Joan," Laura began. "It's been almost a year since we've talked," she went on tentatively. "I don't think I ever told you adequately how much I appreciated what you did."

Laura motioned her visitor to a chair. "Rich mustn't ever find out, though," she said. "He was very clear that I was never to bring the subject up with you. But he couldn't forbid you to call me. I couldn't even call back to find out if you'd been able to do anything. But I knew you must have."

Joan waved aside Laura's apology. "All I did was make Admiral Brighting see that Rich wasn't involved in Scott's plan for BuPers to take over selection of nuclear trainees." She hesitated. Her eyes flickered, then steadied on Laura's. "Besides, you know I used to be very fond of Rich—long ago, during the war."

"Yes. . . .I know he thinks a great deal of you, too." Now it was

Laura's turn to try to convey that, to her, Rich's wartime relationship with this still extremely attractive woman was no longer a threat to her marriage.

"That's awfully nice of you, Laura." Was there the slightest emphasis on the conventional words? "I agree, we can't tell Rich about this. He would find that hard to take."

Laura sat silently for a moment. Enough had been said. She and Joan would never be intimate friends, but they understood each other. "What brings you to New London, Joan? You're still in Brighting's office, aren't you?"

"Yes, I'm still with him. I flew up this morning on Navy business, and I have to leave in a little while. But I wanted to see you. The car that brought me will come back to take me to the airport."

"That's a fast trip."

"I'm still in Naval Intelligence, you know."

"Still?" Laura's voice rose in surprise. "I knew you were, during the war. I thought you were a regular WAVE officer now."

"Well, I am. But I'm in intelligence, and I'm assigned to Admiral Brighting's office. I'm leaving next month, though."

"Oh, really? Where are you going? To some exotic place?"

"Oh, I'll be staying in Washington. What I meant was that I'll be leaving the service." Joan had an anticipatory look, as if she expected and even welcomed the next question.

"Leaving the service?" Laura was genuinely surprised. "But why leave it now?"

"Because Martin Brighting and I are going to be married!" Joan's face was radiant.

Impulsively Laura leaped to her feet and embraced Joan. "How marvelous! What stupendous news! Rich will be thrilled, too. Oh, I'm so happy for both of you. We all pictured the admiral as a permanent widower after Marilyn Brighting's death. Can we come to the wedding?"

"Well, no. Not actually. I mean, we're going to be married very quietly, and then take off for a honeymoon in Jamaica." There was a hint of pride in Joan's smile as she added, "It will be Martin's first vacation from the Navy in years. But the next time you're in Washington, you and Rich must visit us!"

"We will! We'd love to!" said Laura, and then stopped, bewildered. A transformation had come over her visitor. The look of

508

happiness on Joan's expressive face had changed to deep sorrow. There was the glint of moisture in the large eyes. "Why, what's the matter?" Laura asked.

"There's something else I have to tell you. I really had no right to come here and be so happy. You'll have to help all you can. No, this has nothing to do with Rich," she added quickly, as Laura stiffened with alarm.

"What is it, then?" Laura asked, almost in a whisper.

"Laura, please, don't say anything about this visit. I ought not even to be here, but Martin insisted, and Admiral Donaldson agreed. Don't ask me how I know this, but we know you've been having trouble with Peggy Leone. She's going to need your help, Laura. Lots of help and soon. You've got to do what you can!"

"Joan, I can't. Peggy would never want my help. You have no idea of the things she's said to me!"

"I know what she's like. She's said a few untrue things about me, for example. And poor old Captain Blunt, too. We know she's behaved very badly. She's alienated nearly everyone around here, you more than anyone, I'll agree. But you're the wife of Keith's squadron commander. You have a duty to her."

"Joan! You're telling me that something has happened to Keith!"

"I can't tell you anything. I'm only saying you've got to help Peggy, no matter how you feel. She's always been terrified of the Navy. Did you know she's been going to a psychiatrist? We've talked to him, and he convinced us she should not be alone even for a minute, once this thing hits her!"

"You're saying Keith's dead! Joan! I can't believe it! What happened?" Laura put her hand to her face in horror.

"I can't say anything more," said Joan uncomfortably. "Whatever you're guessing is only a guess. But you've got to be with Peggy when the news breaks. Admiral Treadwell will tell you when. Will you?"

"What dreadful news! Of course I'll be there."

The good-by handshake turned into a fond, sad embrace, and then Joan was out of the house and into the car, which had arrived unnoticed. When she was gone, Laura stood leaning against the door she had just closed. The enormity of what she had heard was shattering. Poor Keith! What could have happened?

And what about Peggy? Laura's personal dislike of her had vanished. Joan had been exactly right. She was simply terrified of the Navy. Was that wrong? Especially when her fears had proved justified in the most devastating way?

Laura began to make plans. She would need help. She would probably have to sleep at Peggy's a few nights, then Cindy could relieve her. Provision must be made for Jobie, now fourteen—that would not be hard; he was already showing his father's independence. Food would have to be organized. Someone would have to be sure Ruthie was fed, taken to school, and fetched home.

And Peggy must be allowed to cry. She would be hysterical. But she must be encouraged to do as many of the routine things as possible, simply to keep her sanity. Poor Peggy! How much could she take?

Laura pushed herself away from the door, went to the dining-room table. She took a piece of paper. She would make a list of things to do, and plan some discreet phone calls. She would know how to handle this.

She knew she would not fail.

Edward L. Beach

Edward L. Beach was born in New York in 1918, and graduated from the Naval Academy. After considerable sea duty, he was ordered to the US Submarine School in 1941, where he graduated with the highest standing in his group. He then spent the rest of the war in the Pacific, participating in the Battle of Midway and more than a dozen war patrols. He was awarded seven medals for gallantry; and when the Japanese surrendered in 1945, the submarine *Piper*, of which he was commanding officer, had the honour of being the last to return home.

Captain Beach's postwar duties included service as President Eisenhower's naval aide from 1953 to 1957. Then, the following year, he qualified in submarine nuclear propulsion on a special course administered in the tiny crossroads town of Arco, Utah. His experience there is reflected in *Cold Is the Sea*. "It was gruelling," he says now, "but this type of training works very well. Everything the trainee sees, everything he experiences, is input."

Whatever else he was doing in his career, Captain Beach was always writing—colourful patrol reports during the war, magazine articles, and books. Among the last are *Submarine!*, the bestseller *Run Silent, Run Deep*, and *Around the World Submerged*, an account of his epic 1960 circumnavigation of the globe as commander of the nuclear submarine *Triton*, then the largest submarine ever built.

Today Captain Beach is retired from the navy and lives in Washington with his wife, Ingrid. The Beaches have three grown-up children, all with widely divergent interests. Elder son Ned has completed graduate work in philosophy, second son Hubert is an anthropologist, and daughter Ingrid, the youngest, is trying her luck at a stage career.